HUGH WALPOLE

In January 1907 at the age of twenty-two, Hugh Walpole vowed that he would be a novelist, good or bad, for the remainder of his earthly days, thus finally rejecting his father's plans for a career in the Church. With the publication of his first novel in 1909 he was well set on his chosen course. In this biography Rupert Hart-Davis skilfully portrays both the man and the writer. Drawing on Walpole's voluminous diaries, journals and letters, he allows his subject to speak for himself, so that the reader is charmed and held, as Walpole's contemporaries were, by his brimming enthusiasm for life and literature, his ambition, his excitement about everything, and his naive childishness. Walpole corresponded with most of the leading writers of the day – Henry James, 'Elizabeth', Somerset Maugham, Arnold Bennett, Joseph Conrad, Virginia Woolf – and the letters are personal documents, frankly and freely reflecting Hugh Walpole's character and varying moods, not mere notes of literary chit-chat. Rupert Hart-Davis has given us an intimate and living study of a novelist at work as well as a sharp and absorbing picture of the epoch and society in which he lived.

Sir Rupert Hart-Davis was a close friend of Hugh Walpole's later years and one of his executors. He is also the author of *The Arms of Time: A Memoir*, and has edited collections of Oscar Wilde's letters, the six volumes of *The Lyttelton Hart-Davis Letters*, as well as works by Max Beerbohm, Arthur Ransome and Siegfried Sassoon.

HUGH
WALPOLE

A BIOGRAPHY

by

RUPERT HART-DAVIS

Er liebte jeden Hund, und wünschte von
jedem Hund geliebt zu sein.

JEAN PAUL
Flegeljahre

A HAMISH HAMILTON PAPERBACK
London

FOR
DOROTHY
ROBIN
AND
HAROLD

First published in Great Britain 1952
by Macmillan & Co Ltd
First published in this edition 1985
by Hamish Hamilton Ltd
Garden House 57–59 Long Acre London WC2E 9JZ

Copyright © 1952 by Rupert Hart-Davis

ISBN 0-241-11406-3

Printed and bound in Finland
by Werner Söderström Oy

BY WAY OF A PREFACE

I'm sorry you have to urge pleas and considerations about your book; one's book should be the right attempt, on the right ground, rightly carried through—should be the brave bold intended thing, or not be at all. And *if* the brave bold intended thing, then no hemming and hawing.

HENRY JAMES TO HUGH WALPOLE

12 November 1912

CONTENTS

SOURCES AND ACKNOWLEDGMENTS   **xi**

Chapter

BOOK ONE: THE ENEMY IN AMBUSH

ONE	First Beginnings (1884–1893)	3
TWO	The Valley of Humiliation (1893–1903)	12
THREE	The Great Resolve (1903–1907)	31
FOUR	From Valhalla to Epsom (1907–1908)	47

BOOK TWO: THE HUMAN MAZE

FIVE	The Threshold of Fictive Art (1909–1910)	65
SIX	Collector of People (1911–1912)	81
SEVEN	Riding to Glory (1913)	96
EIGHT	The End of the Golden Age (1914)	108

BOOK THREE: THE FIRST WAR

NINE	Russian Overture (1914–1915)	123
TEN	Death and the Hunters (1915–1916)	138
ELEVEN	Red Sky at Morning (1916–1917)	151
TWELVE	London Finale (1917–1919)	165

BOOK FOUR: THE PURSUIT OF HAPPINESS

THIRTEEN	"Apple-Cheeked Hugh" (1919–1920)	185
FOURTEEN	Melchior the Dane (1920–1921)	197
FIFTEEN	The End of a Chapter (1921–1922)	213
SIXTEEN	Moments of Discovery (1922–1924)	226

BOOK FIVE: THE PROMISED LAND

SEVENTEEN	Men Under Skiddaw (1924–1925)	247
EIGHTEEN	The Rock (1925–1927)	263
NINETEEN	The First of the Herries (1927–1929)	278
TWENTY	Quite Enough Glory (1929–1932)	306

BOOK SIX: THE YEARS OF PLENTY

TWENTY-ONE	Perpetual Circus (1932–1935)	337
TWENTY-TWO	Gilded Bondage (1935–1936)	360
TWENTY-THREE	Rise, Sir Hugh (1937)	376
TWENTY-FOUR	The Wrath to Come (1938–1939)	389

Chapter

BOOK SEVEN: THE SECOND WAR

TWENTY-FIVE   The Clue to the Exit (1939–1940)   409
TWENTY-SIX   The City Under Fire (1940–1941)   430

APPENDICES: A. The Walpole Family   446
               B. Hugh Walpole's official account of the first
                   Russian Revolution   449
               C. Catalogue of the Hugh Walpole Collection
                   at the King's School, Canterbury   470
               D. Catalogue of the Hugh Walpole Collection
                   in the Fitz Park Museum, Keswick   480

LIST OF BOOKS BY HUGH WALPOLE   481

BIBLIOGRAPHY   484

INDEX   485

ILLUSTRATIONS

Mildred Barham and Somerset Walpole

Hugh: the baby and the schoolboy

90 Piccadilly

Brackenburn

Part of the library at Brackenburn (Photograph by *The Times*)

Chalk Drawing by Augustus John. 1926 (Reproduced by
  Permission of the Syndics of the Fitzwilliam Museum,
  Cambridge)

Wastwater. 1933 (Photograph by Robin Walpole)

Brackenburn. 1935

Illustrations in the text

Sketch–map of Eastern Galicia. 1915   140

The Brackenburn book-label   334

Page of manuscript of *The Killer and the Slain*   437

SOURCES AND ACKNOWLEDGMENTS

(i)

The chief sources for this book are:

(1) The daily diary which Hugh Walpole kept from 1904 until his death. The entries vary from a whole page to half a dozen lines. They were mostly written down immediately and have proved factually reliable.

(2) The fifteen volumes of the journal which he kept intermittently from 1923 to 1941.

(3) His letters, especially those to the four members of his immediate family; those to Arnold Bennett (which he bought back after Bennett's death); and those to a host of other correspondents which have survived and which I have been able to see. Except in the schoolboy letters, spelling and punctuation have been corrected or supplied where necessary.

(4) His published books, pamphlets, articles, reviews and introductions, particularly the autobiographical volumes, *The Crystal Box* (1924), *Reading* (1926), *My Religious Experience* (1928), *The Apple Trees* (1932) and *Roman Fountain* (1940). Also the twenty-five prefaces he wrote in 1933 for the Cumberland edition of his works. As evidence of fact these sources are of unequal value.

(5) The letters of his friends. Since he knew many of the leading English writers during more than thirty years, and kept almost all the letters he received, their number is considerable. Thus seventy-eight letters from Henry James have survived, seventy-three from Arnold Bennett, sixty from Virginia Woolf, fifty from John Galsworthy, thirty-two from Joseph Conrad, and so on. Every quotation from a letter is taken directly from the original or from a photostat, except for three of which the sources are stated in footnotes.

(6) The memories, presented to me either in writing or by word of mouth, of the relations and friends whose names are given below.

(7) The books mentioned in the Bibliography on p. 484 and in the footnotes.

(8) My own friendship with Hugh, which covered the last ten years of his life.

(ii)

My greatest debt of gratitude is to Dr Dorothea and Mr Robin Walpole, for making it possible for me to write their brother's life, for entrusting me with all his diaries and papers, and for six years of patience, encouragement and forbearance.

I am also deeply indebted to Mr Harold Cheevers, for putting at my disposal his unique knowledge of my subject, for scrutinising both typescript and proof, and for answering innumerable questions.

The book has, at various stages, been read and greatly improved by the criticisms of Mr and Mrs George Blake, Mr and Mrs Alan Bott, Mr Leon Edel, Mr David Garnett, Mr Richard Garnett, Mr Daniel George, Mr Thomas Mark, Mr William Plomer, Mr Arthur Ransome, Mrs Ruth Simon, Sir Ronald Storrs, Mr Allan Wade, Mr Hugh Wheeler and Mr Edward Young.

Mr F. W. Black, Sir Duff Cooper, Sir Gerald Kelly, P.R.A., Mr Charles Marriott, Miss Elsie Moore, Miss Dorothy M. Richardson, Mr Harold Rubinstein and Mr P. G. Wodehouse have been kind enough to send me written accounts of their memories of Hugh.

I am most grateful to the following friends of Hugh's, to whom I have talked, and who have lent me his letters to them and given me permission to quote from their letters to him: Mr James Annand, Mr William Armstrong, Mr Michael Ayrton, Major-General J. H. Beith, the late Mrs Belloc Lowndes, the late Mr H. J. Bruce, Mrs Cazalet, Mrs Thelma Cazalet-Keir, the late Lady Colefax, Miss Clemence Dane, Mr Alan Dent, Mr Richard Dunn, Mr St John Ervine, Mr E. M. Forster, Mr A. S. Frere, Dr Norman Haire, Mr and Mrs Joseph Hergesheimer, Mr W. J. Ingram of Bede College, Mrs Muriel Jessiman, Sir Roderick Jones, Sir Robert Bruce Lockhart, Mrs Sylvia Lynd, Mr Compton Mackenzie, the late Sir Eric Maclagan, Mr W. S. Maugham, Mr Christopher Morley, Mr Harold Nicolson, Miss Naomi Royde-Smith, Miss Vita Sackville-West, Mr Michael Sadleir, Mr

Martin Secker, Miss Athene Seyler, Canon F. J. Shirley, Mr Frank
Singleton, Miss Marguerite Steen, Mr L. A. G. Strong, Mr Frank
Swinnerton, Susan Lady Tweedsmuir, Mr Carl Van Vechten, and Miss
Rebecca West.

For lending me books and manuscripts, as well as for help and
advice in many other directions, I am indebted to Miss Eleanor
Adlard, Mrs Barbara Back, Mrs Norma Boleslawsky, Miss Lillian
Browse, Mr James Branch Cabell, Mr John Carter, Sir Edmund
Craster, Mr W. Forster, Mrs Diana Gamble, Dr John D. Gordan of
the New York Public Library, The Countess of Iddesleigh, Professor
William A. Jackson of the Houghton Library at Harvard, Mr R. W.
Ketton-Cremer, Mrs Josephine Lee, Mr J. B. Manuell of Truro, Dr
William Maxwell, Mr Charles Morgan, Mr Percy Muir, Mrs Frederick
Niven, Mr Bertram Rota, Mr C. R. H. Taylor of the Alexander
Turnbull Library at Wellington, Sir Charles Tennyson, Mrs Margaret
H. Tweedy, Sir Stanley Unwin, and Mr J. A. White.

Permission to print unpublished letters has generously been given by
Mr Harry Agate, Mrs James Bain, Lord Beaverbrook, the owner of
the Arnold Bennett copyrights, Mrs Charlotte Besier, Mrs Corwin
Butterworth, Mr Walter de la Mare, Mrs John Galsworthy, Mr
William James, Mr George Mathew, Mr H. L. Mencken, Mr J.
Middleton Murry, Dr John Rothenstein, Dr Edith Sitwell, Sir Osbert
Sitwell, and Mr Leonard Woolf.

For permission to publish copyright material my thanks are due to
several writers already mentioned, and also to: The Master of Magdalene College, Cambridge, and Messrs John Murray for extracts
from the Diary and The Trefoil by A. C. Benson; Mrs Dorothy
Cheston Bennett and Messrs Cassell for passages from The Journals
of Arnold Bennett; Madame Karsavina and Messrs Constable for a
quotation from Theatre Street; Canon F. A. Iremonger and Mr Geoffrey
Cumberlege for an extract from The Life of William Temple; Mr
Percy Lubbock and Messrs Jonathan Cape for a passage from Portrait
of Edith Wharton; Miss Quiller-Couch and the Oxford University
Press for part of a poem by Sir Arthur Quiller-Couch; the executors
of H. G. Wells for a passage from Boon; Messrs J. M. Dent and
William Heinemann for letters from The Life and Letters of Joseph

Conrad; the Richards Press for two lines by Lord Alfred Douglas; Messrs George G. Harrap for the Walpole letter from *Ego 5*; Messrs Constable for two extracts from *The Letters of Katherine Mansfield*; Messrs Hodder & Stoughton for a quotation from *John Buchan by his Wife and Friends*; Messrs Putnam for a passage from *Memoirs of a British Agent*; Messrs Hamish Hamilton for an extract from *Nocturnes and Rhapsodies*; and Messrs Hutchinson for a sentence from *Swinnerton: an Autobiography*.

To Messrs Macmillan I owe more than can easily be recorded here; for allowing me to read the firm's correspondence with Hugh, for permission to quote extensively from his books and others, for encouragement, patience, and many favours.

To all those others who have helped me, and whose names are not recorded, I offer gratitude and from them beg forgiveness.

RUPERT HART-DAVIS

October 1951

Note to new edition

It is a great joy to welcome this paperback edition of my book, thirty-three years after it first appeared. And how delighted my dear old friend Hugh would be.

A few minor mistakes have been corrected, but otherwise the text is unaltered. If I had known that the Truro painter Henry Treffry Dunn (1838–99), who is mentioned on page 6, had been for many years the assistant and 'guardian angel' of Dante Gabriel Rossetti, I should have given him a footnote, but such embellishments are irrelevant to the life of my friend, which has now been so happily resurrected.

R.H-D.

Marske-in-Swaledale
June 1984

BOOK ONE

THE ENEMY IN AMBUSH

It is the tragedy of childhood that its catastrophes are eternal.

Now fear crept on him from every side. He was afraid because there was *no one* to turn to.

You walk forward through jungle, the enemy lying in ambush.

Hugh Walpole
Jeremy at Crale

FIRST BEGINNINGS

I

Hugh Walpole was born in New Zealand on 13 March 1884, but his story begins more exactly, and much more appropriately, with the building of an English cathedral.

For eight hundred years the see of Cornwall had been merged with the neighbouring diocese of Exeter, and it was not until the eighteen-forties that there arose a movement to restore the ancient privileges of this inaccessible outpost of Christian endeavour. During the thirty years of argument which ensued, other benefits arrived: in 1859 I. K. Brunel completed his great bridge across the river Tamar at Saltash, and later in the same year the town of Truro was for the first time connected with London by railway. Many local lines were started in the sixties, and gradually the peninsula was opened up to receive the blessings of Victorian progress.

In 1876 the reformers had their way, the Bishopric was re-established by an Order in Council, with Truro (shortly afterwards promoted to City) as its cathedral town, and a year later Edward White Benson was consecrated first Bishop. This remarkable man, who had already been the first Master of Wellington College and was later to be Archbishop of Canterbury and a great favourite with Queen Victoria, was now at the height of his powers. Ardent, active, masterful, handsome, eloquent, and a good administrator, he discerned in this new appointment a call to carry the light of the Gospel to the backward Cornishmen, hidden in their sheltered valleys, beset by Dissenters and remote from the civilising influences of Church and State. The people of Cornwall took fire from his enthusiasm:

> In dereliction by the deafening shore
> > We sought no more aloft, but sunk our eyes,
> Probing the sea for food, the earth for ore.
> > Ah, yet had one good soldier of the skies
> > > Burst through the wrack reporting news of them,
> > > How had we run and kissed his garment's hem!

Nay, but he came! Nay, but he stood and cried,
     Panting with joy and the fierce fervent race,
"Arm, arm! for Christ returns!"—and all our pride,
     Our ancient pride, answered that eager face:
          "Repair His battlements!—Your Christ is near!"
     And, half in dream, we raised the soldiers' cheer.

Far, as we flung that challenge, fled the ghosts—
     Back, as we built, the obscene foe withdrew—
High to the song of hammers sang the hosts
     Of Heaven—and lo! the daystar, and a new
          Dawn with its chalice and its wind as wine;
     And youth was hope, and life once more divine! [1]

The song of hammers was indeed soon audible, as the greater part of St Mary's Church in the centre of Truro was demolished to make room for the first Anglican cathedral to be built in England since the Reformation. The architect was J. L. Pearson, the foundation stone was laid by the Prince of Wales, and before long the huge building began to grow like a granite cuckoo in Truro's crowded nest.

2

Bishop Benson made haste to gather round him a band of colleagues as eager and energetic as himself. Among those whom he summoned to his bright new enterprise was the Rev. Arthur J. Mason, a junior Fellow of Trinity College, Cambridge. The son of a Nottinghamshire squire, Mason was a man of iron will and extraordinary charm—"steel under velvet," Benson said of him. When he first came to Truro he filled the position of Bishop's Chaplain, but he was soon sent out as Diocesan Missioner, a new post which Benson created and for which Mason was particularly suited. Now, as he prepared to leave Cambridge for Cornwall, he looked around for a likely fellow-worker to take with him, and his eye fell upon a young graduate of his own college.

George Henry Somerset Walpole had been born at Newark-on-Trent in 1854 and brought up by his father, an irascible martinet who had retired from the Army to take Holy Orders and now kept his parish in more than military submission. Somerset was educated at King's Lynn Grammar School, where, his tutor reported, he was "invariably

[1] From E.W.B., by A. T. Quiller-Couch (The Vigil of Venus, 1912).

distinguished by his studious habits, excellent conduct, good common sense, cheerful disposition, and gentlemanlike deportment." He left Trinity with first-class honours in the Theological Tripos and a determination to take Holy Orders, although his father, with all the perversity of parents, had decided that he was to be a soldier. He had neither money nor clear plans for the future, so that Mason's invitation came as an answer to prayer and was instantly accepted.

At twenty-two Somerset Walpole was a shy, serious young man, with a natural belief in God and a guilelessness of heart which were to remain with him all his life. He threw himself into all the activities of the new diocese: first he taught in the college for ordinands; in 1878 he was himself ordained, and appointed, first Priest-Vicar, and then Succentor of the Cathedral. One year he suggested to the Bishop that a Carol Service should be held on Christmas Eve, as a counter-attraction to the public-houses, and Benson drew up the "Service of the Nine Carols," which is now held all over the country. Walpole also laboured a great deal among the working people, as well as starting a Philharmonic Society and a Shakespeare Society in the city.

By degrees his shyness left him, and the young A. C. Benson found him "entirely boyish and approachable."

He was a sound theologian, but in ordinary talk he had the intensest relish for argument and ideas. The delight of his company was that he never chose or insisted upon his own topics. He would take anything that turned up, convert it into a debatable question, and argue it with ineffable good-humour, pertinacity, and deftness. He had an overpowering sense of humour, and a clear, rather shrill laugh, which sometimes rendered him wholly incapable of speech. His face, with its rather irregular features and expressive mouth, was delightful, from its rapid changes and its engaging look of comradeship, as he turned to opponent after opponent. "Come, Walpole," I can hear my father say, "you must leave *something* undecided." "Not while my breath lasts, my lord!" says the undefeated Priest-Vicar.[1]

3

The leading physician in Truro at this time was Dr Charles Barham, a connection of the author of *The Ingoldsby Legends*. He had been born in 1805, had married Caroline Carlyon, who came of an old Cornish

[1] *The Trefoil* (1923).

family, and in the fifties he had been Mayor of Truro. His portrait by H. Treffrey Dunn hangs over the stairs in the Town Hall to this day. A. C. Benson recalled him as "a cultivated man with much sweetness and charm," and went on to say:

I remember his appearance at some domestic festivity in a long claret-coloured coat, very tight about the waist, with metal buttons, which he had worn at his own wedding some fifty years before, and very well it became his handsome and serene presence.[1]

The Barhams lived in Strangways Terrace, a dignified and comfortable street with houses on one side only, leading off the long climbing Lemon Street where it reaches the top of the hill, and overlooking the main part of Truro in the valley below. There were ten children, of whom the youngest was a daughter, Mildred Helen, born in 1854. A pretty, elegant little creature, she naturally became the pet of this very happy family and of the nest of relations by which they were surrounded.

Even after the coming of the railway, Truro was still almost as cut off from the rest of the world as one of Jane Austen's villages. But there were diversions enough close at hand: the high-banked lanes thick with primroses and violets in early spring, the stir of market days, the excitement of county balls, garden-parties, and summer expeditions to the sea—to Newquay and Perranporth, The Lizard and Penzance.

And then this happy little world was shattered by a severe epidemic of scarlet fever which swept through the neighbourhood. Mildred caught the disease at school, but although her father was a doctor, nothing was done to prevent the infection from spreading. One of her brothers died of it, and she herself sustained a perforated ear-drum which left her partially deaf for life. Moreover the shock of this tragic occurrence set up in her a strain of diffidence, even of apprehension, which she was never to lose.

4

Mildred Barham and Somerset Walpole were of an age. They fell in love almost at first sight, read Browning together, pledged their troth with a sprig of honeysuckle, and he asked her father's consent to their

[1] *Ibid.*

engagement. Mrs Barham was away from home, and the Doctor at once wrote to her:

Sunday, 4 July 1880.   Strangways Terrace.

Dearest Caroline,

It may perhaps have struck you that Mildred and Mr. Walpole were getting "*rather thick*," and I could not fail to perceive a strong tendency in them both, these centenary days,[1] in the direction of ultimate matrimony,—still, I was not prepared for the *declaration* which came from him last night that all was settled as between themselves, and asking my consent to their engagement. They had been to one of the musters at Penmount and had talked over matters by the way.

I wish you had been here that we might have conferred on the subject,—but I felt assured that you would agree with me that we could not do otherwise than sanction the engagement, and indeed that we should both be inclined to give Walpole a cordial welcome into our family, being thoroughly satisfied of the goodness of his character, temper and disposition. He is about a year younger than Mildred, and they both say they will not be in any hurry to get married. As to worldly goods he is slenderly endowed. The Bishop, he says, told him he should take care of him in due time, and he would not think of settling till he has a living. Such a delay will tend no doubt to calmness and solidity of character as far as these qualities may be at all lacking.

The *family* history, which W. gave me, is not very satisfactory. His father, pretty nearly related to Lord Orford,[2] was a spoilt child. He went as a youth to Australia—lost the bulk of his fortune—came home and became a Captain in some Cavalry regiment—then took Orders—for the sake of a family living. His temper was so bad and violent—towards his wife especially (she was an Apthorpe—and, it seems, good in every way)—that the household was broken up—and she went with three sons, and I think two daughters, to Australia where they are doing well. W. has never distinctly been discarded by his father, but there is very little communication between them, and he does not know where he is at this time—he thinks on the Continent. His Aunts seem very kind, and he visits them when he goes away for his holiday. He was to have gone this week but will not *now*.

The young people would very much enjoy a few days at Veryan. Would John and Con. invite them to succeed you? I thought they might meet you at Grampound Road, and spend an hour or so with you and the Freds—and go on to Veryan under William's protection. . . . Walpole would of course take any duty required at Veryan.

[1] The centenary of the foundation of Sunday Schools, which was celebrated throughout the county during 1880.
[2] See Appendix A, p. 446.

. . . I was called out by Walpole from the tea table. Mildred is rather excited you will imagine but very happy. She has no time for visiting today of course and I daresay not much inclination.

Hoping you will not be quite *overcome* by the news and with much love to you and the Cornishes.

I am ever yours,
C. B.

5

They were married by the Bishop in Truro Cathedral on 12 September 1882; the wedding was an important social occasion, and after a brief honeymoon the young couple set out on what was then a hazardous adventure—a sea voyage to New Zealand. On the advice of Bishop Benson, Somerset had accepted the incumbency of St Mary's Church (afterwards to become the Cathedral) at Parnell, Auckland.

The voyage was long and stormy: their cabin was directly over the screw and they were both very seasick. Somerset's previous travelling had not exceeded a Channel crossing, while Mildred had never before left England, and seldom Cornwall. Her upbringing had been so secluded, and her experience of the world so trifling, that at the age of twenty-eight she had little knowledge of either the married state or conditions in the Antipodes, and though her husband's devotion sustained her, as it was to do all the rest of her life, she was a sick, bewildered, and apprehensive girl when finally she landed in New Zealand.

Their new home was a little wooden vicarage alongside the church. Parishioners, anxious to welcome and assist the newcomers, unpacked most of their china and other household goods without being asked, and this simple gesture of friendliness seemed to Mildred a gross intrusion on her privacy. The more the New Zealanders—plain pioneering folk mostly, but good-natured and helpful—tried to make friends, the deeper did she retire into herself and long for the security of home. Naturally, to begin with, her shyness was interpreted as pride, her breeding as arrogance, her gently ironical humour as conceit. In the course of years she came to understand and appreciate her neighbours, but during these first months her self-confidence was so shaken that she never again quite believed that anyone liked or wanted her, and it is not surprising that her first child should have been a difficult boy, bearing through life, as his share of this forced emigration, an innate self-distrust and a permanent instability of temperament.

On 31 March 1884 Mildred wrote home to her mother:

This is Monday, and it will be three weeks next Thursday since the 13th when baby was born, and today I am in the drawing-room for the first time. Somerset and Nurse brought me in on the sofa—it is such a pleasure to be in a fresh room—though you can imagine the state it is in, as Somerset has been using it as his study, so that baby's crying might not disturb his work. Two days I have been on the verandah outside my room, and the fresh air did me good.

Baby is a dear little fellow, he is really so good and does not often cry without a reason—he seems a very gentle little boy. At present he has grey eyes (very pretty ones) and a good nose and head and a capacious mouth. Somerset is such a good nurse and can keep him beautifully quiet. He will be called Hugh we hope, I don't know whether anything else—and we want him to be christened on Easter Sunday.

They had their wish, and the baby was christened Hugh Seymour by Bishop Cowie in St Mary's Church. The godparents were A. J. Mason (by proxy), Mrs Cowie, and Mr N. F. Giblin, a local banker. The Cowies and the Walpoles became great friends, and this companionship did much to soften the pangs of homesickness and exile. Somerset's mother came from Australia to live with them, but the experiment was not a success, and she soon went back again. A new vicarage was built for them, roomier and more convenient than the old one, and from there on 29 July 1885 Mildred wrote another letter home to Truro:

I wish you could see little Hugh. You ask me to tell you about him, but it is so difficult to write so as to make him seem different to any other baby. He has got on very decidedly since I wrote last, I am thankful to say—we think this house so much better for him. He has been cutting some of his double teeth and has seven altogether now I think, and he can walk famously—almost too fast sometimes. Today I found him sprawled over two steps in our passage, neither able to get up or down.

Sometimes he looks very delicate, and makes me anxious, but I think he is stronger than he looks. He is a very gentle little boy, though he is very determined and rather impatient. . . . He is very fond of singing to himself and with the dearest little voice . . . I don't know how he learnt what printed words meant, but if he gets hold of a card or book it is so funny to hear him reading, he quite tries to carry on a conversation in his own language, and will nod his head and gesticulate in the most absurd way. . . . Everyone admires Hugh's curls.

His mother loved him, clearly, but there was something in the re-tiring fastidiousness of her nature which prevented her from showing her love in the accepted ways. She seldom hugged, kissed, petted, or spoiled her children, and the lack of such natural endearments may well explain Hugh's lifelong anxiety that everyone should love him. The quotation from Jean Paul which he printed on the title-page of his first published book, and which occupies the same position in this one, was indeed the key to his whole life: he loved every dog, and wanted every dog to love him.

Meanwhile he learnt to talk, and by February 1886 was so far ad-vanced as to call Bishop Cowie "Bishey" to his face. A year later Hugh's sister Dorothea was born, and his solitary reign was over.

All this time his father had been battling with the usual ups and downs of parochial life. He introduced Shakespeare readings and others of those amenities which had proved so rewarding at Truro, but Parnell was altogether a tougher proposition, social life was limited and diffi-cult, and when he was offered a much more congenial living at Welling-ton he was sorely tempted to accept. A friend whom he consulted said: "If you are uncertain which of two paths to take, choose the one on which the shadow of the Cross falls." Somerset accepted this counsel and decided to stay on at Auckland. As if to test his faith still further, a severe attack of food-poisoning in 1887 laid him low and almost killed him.

There are no records of the next two years, during which the children grew happily while their parents, longing for home, gradually over-came the difficulties by which they were surrounded. And then, quite unexpectedly, Somerset was offered the Chair of Systematic Theology in the General Theological Seminary of New York City. The attendant salary, the equivalent of £1000 a year, was too good to be refused, and although this new post would mean a further period of exile, they would at any rate be nearer home than they were now. The offer was accepted, and in the late summer of 1889 the whole family sailed for England.

6

Somerset travelled straight on to New York, while Mildred took the two children to Truro. All that winter they stayed with her family in Strangways Terrace, and Hugh was taught to read and write at the nearby High School for Girls, where he sat in the bottom form, weeping copiously. His grandmother solaced him with lemon biscuits out of a round silver box and gave him a Bible for Christmas.

In 1890 the three of them journeyed on to New York, where the children were taught by a governess. From 412 West 20th Street Mildred wrote home to report that "Hugh and Dorothy are getting on so happily with Miss Burkitt. . . . We have such a nice little servant who reminds me of Phoebe—she is so cheerful and neat." Anything reminiscent of home was a comfort, since Mildred found the New York seminary, the noise and confusion of the city, and the overpowering energy of its inhabitants, little more congenial than the rigours of New Zealand. Somerset, however, enjoyed his new work, and while he was in New York he wrote and had published the first of his thirty books on religious subjects.

In 1892 the family was increased by the birth of a third child, who was christened Robert Henry but always known as Robin. The question of Hugh's education now became urgent. He would soon be nine years old: he did not get on especially well with the American children he saw, and his parents wanted him to grow up an Englishman. The only solution was to send him to a boarding school in England, and accordingly in the summer of 1893 Hugh was brought home to begin the ten unhappiest years of his life.

CHAPTER TWO

THE VALLEY OF HUMILIATION

I

IT is perhaps unfair to describe Hugh's first year of school as unhappy: certainly it was blissful in comparison with what came after,
but a sensitive and difficult child of nine is seldom happy at boarding-
school, particularly when he has no real home, and his family are three
thousand miles away. Indeed this lack of all that is commonly understood by "home" persisted with Hugh for more than thirty years, until
the first main theme of his life, his passionate desire to associate himself
with some part of England, was finally resolved by his absorption in
Cumberland.

His first school was at Newham House, Truro, where Mr and Mrs
Maddrell housed, looked after, and taught six sons of clergymen. On
22 October 1893, when Hugh had been there a month, Mr Maddrell
wrote to New York:

On the whole his conduct has been very good. Just at first he clearly
showed great dislike of being corrected in any way whatever. After a little
quiet talk and explanation in my study, and by following the example of his
fellow boarders, he has now immensely improved in this respect. He "hits
it off" very well with the others and as far as I can see tries to lord it over
them less and less. I fancy they showed him that they would not stand it!
It is really delightful having such a "happy family" in the house. A little
more than a week ago he got rather excited after a bad nightmare, and he
couldn't sleep for several hours. . . . He takes a fair amount of interest in
the lessons he likes. . . . The fretfulness and despondency when a wretched
sum won't come out are gradually disappearing, and tears now are very rare
events! Altogether I am most happy and hopeful about him. He is a manly
little fellow and would scorn to do a mean thing, and I pray God that he may
continue like this.

All his life Hugh suffered from nightmares in which he "experienced
exactly the sense of sudden death; there would be a terrific noise, a
blow in the chest, a momentary agony of surprise, and then nothing

more." [1] After his experiences in Russia, his nightmares also took the form of terror at being left alone. Often he woke screaming, and his fear lest anyone should discover this infirmity always complicated his visits to strange houses.

Hugh's first recorded letter, written about a week later, tells its own story:

My dear father, I was so glad to here that you have got my letters. My favourite lessons are reading and the Bible. I am going to have my prize [for reading] at Crismus. I dont like school so much as I thought. I am put on the bed and beaton with noted hangershifs and I get a good many slaps. I like your pictours very much. I am glad to here that evrey person has not forgotten me. I am in a great rury so you will not mind a short letter there is nothing important to say. Your loving son Hugh.

It is greatly to Mr Maddrell's credit that he forwarded this document to New York, and in his covering letter can be discerned the age-old difficulty of a good and honest man grappling with the unsuspected brutality of little boys.

To all appearance the six boys agree splendidly, and besides seeing them in the early morning when I call them and several times in the evening in their dormitory, I pay them surprise visits to see that all is right. I was astonished therefore to hear of anything like bullying, especially as they are all so much of an age. The Cartwrights told me about it yesterday. It seems that there is really no cruelty whatever. On one or two occasions they put Hugh and Clement on their beds, when they were fully dressed I ought to add, and gave them a few strokes with their knotted handkerchiefs. "Boys will be boys" you know, and I am not so sure but what Hugh provoked it a little. I can confidently assure you it is nothing in the least serious and I will be on the lookout to make it stop altogether. The Cartwrights have promised to side with their weaker brethren, so when the other two have four against them they will give it up!!

This simple ruse of shifting the balance of power proved so success-ful that a fortnight later Hugh was writing:

My dear father
I take up my pen to write this letter hopeing that it will reach you safley. On Thursday we won a mach, and yesterday I whent to the bublic rooms to a concert and I would show it you only I could not find it. I am

[1] *My Religious Experience* (1928).

very well and I am so very happy with the Cartwrights. I am going to miss fosters today. I think the Cartwrights the nicest boys I ever met, I did not think there were such nice boys. I have great fun and I like school very much. I am so glad that Robin is so well and we all laughed at that funny saying of his. I remain loving Hugh.

Two further letters, of uncertain date, complete the picture of life at Newham House. The first shows a glimpse of the romantic imagination already at work:

I have spent my ε shillings but I do not want you to spend all your pence. Truro is all upset for some robers have come and they are killing all the children they can cath. I am always going out and I am going out to aunt dorras to tea today. A boy had the cane yesterday. I like school very much. I must now end up. Your loving Hugh.

Dear Father
I am going to tell you a very amusing story, this morning me and the Cartwrights got into a row. We went out to Clement's last night and had some baloons. When I woke up this morning I saw Ted with one of these baloons. Then Charlie began playing with one. And so then I began doing the same. We were called but we dident get up because we liked the baloons so much. Well and so of course we were late and Mr. Maddrell was awfully angry and he said he was disgusted that Clergymen's sons should play baloons on Sunday. I must now say goodbye send my love to all at home.
                              Ever your loving son Hugh.

In March 1894 politics made their first, and almost their last, appearance in his writing:

I am so afraid that I shall not be able to wright a long letter as I have been doing my lessons and I think that they are a great bother. I am so glad that Mr gladstone has resigned and you are to I supposed and I think Lord Roseberry will do very well I don't think Mr gladstons worth a capital letter.

And in the same month he summed up the situation to his sister: "I am nearly ten and I feel quite old . . . I like school very much but sometimes it is nasty."

2

During his seven years in America, Dr Walpole made a practice of spending the summer vacation in England, and to help with the expense he would take his family to some country vicarage, where he acted as locum during the parson's holiday. In 1894 the choice fell upon the parish of Longbridge Deverill in Wiltshire, and this visit had happy results. Four miles away, at the rectory of Kingston Deverill, lived the Rev. William Moore with his wife and four children, who were around Hugh's age; they all played together, and a warm friendship grew up between the two families. So much so that when in September the Walpoles sent Hugh to a new school at Marlow and returned to America, it was arranged that he should spend his holidays at Kingston Deverill.

The rectory, originally a William and Mary farmhouse, was a large, rambling building, with a ghost in the attic, and plenty of stairs and passages for children to play in. It was clearly much better for the boy to be one of a large family rather than to spend his holidays, as hitherto, the guest of one or other of his aunts in Truro. Miss Elsie Moore has written a description of Hugh at this time. She scarcely saw him after 1896, so that no later images have intruded to blur her childhood memory.

Hugh was always very correct in Etons and high hat on Sundays, but at other times I always see him in very strong knickerbocker tweeds and thick worsted stockings; a sturdily built little figure, hazel eyes with long lashes, well-cut features, thick brown hair with a kink in it, a rather dissatisfied mouth and clear skin shewing up the very large freckles which I think came from New Zealand. Even as children we thought him a pretty boy, but his great charm was in his voice. It was not an ordinary boy's voice—it was low and rich and rather husky; in speaking it was pleasant and rather pathetic, but in singing it was lovely, with something of the quality of a magnolia.

The Moore children, three girls and a boy, were a happy family, and their parents were people of uncommon sympathy and wide intellectual interests. Mr Moore knew a great deal about birds and flowers, history and poetry. The rectory was full of books, and Hugh was allowed to read what he wanted. He plunged into Jane Austen, Charlotte M. Yonge, Jules Verne, *The Three Musketeers*, and raced through a novel or two by Mrs Humphry Ward, renaming his favourite doll Marcella after one of her heroines. Copies of *Guy Mannering* and *Quentin Durward* from the rectory bookshelves initiated Hugh's life-long passion for their author and all his works. At Christmas the children recited poetry together and acted plays, mostly of Hugh's composition.

The rough and tumble of a large family was strange to Hugh, but certainly beneficial. "The Walpoles," writes Miss Moore, "were very careful to 'respect' their children," while the Moores' deep affection for their father was tempered by a considerable amount of awe:

Distinguished theologian as he was, I have often seen Dr Walpole bending forward in courteous eagerness to listen to what I or someone equally young and foolish had to say; while my father did not hesitate to cut us short with a sharp "Don't jaw" if he thought we were taking too large a share of the conversation at table.

Hugh was especially fond of Mrs Moore: he called her "Mother" and wrote to her every week from Marlow; indeed he was so demonstratively affectionate towards her as to surprise his own mother when she came home, while Mrs Moore made a special pet of him, to compensate for the absence of his parents, and encouraged his reading and his writing. It is characteristic of the romantic light of unrelieved misery in which Hugh afterwards liked to view his own childhood, that when he saw Mrs Moore again some ten years later, he said to her: "All I can remember of you is your coming into my room one night and giving me a scolding." Her daughter adds with much perspicacity:

As I see it, Hugh's boyish life was just one running romance of which the hero was always the same misunderstood and lonely and unhappy little boy. I take it that the retina of his memory as it were rejected all light and only retained the dark.

One day he was banished for some reason from the fireside circle in the library, and when Elsie sought him out she found him in the disused night-nursery:

I can see him now in the winter twilight, sitting the wrong way round on the old rocking-horse, facing the tail, and rocking furiously with a countenance of Byronic gloom. And that was Hugh; quite apart from a passing cloud, he was essentially a solitary child. It only strikes me now, after all these years, that though he and his parents exchanged letters each week he never alluded to their contents. I don't believe it was lack of sympathy, but just a great protective coat of reserve, perhaps inherited from his mother.

3

Meanwhile in term-time his education was proceeding all too swiftly. The school that Hugh attended at Marlow is today an admirable institution, but fifty years ago it clearly left much to be desired, particularly in the matter of supervision. The headmaster, Canon Graves, appears to have been an excellent fellow; his wife wrote regularly and fully about Hugh to Mrs Walpole and Mrs Moore, and Hugh himself wrote of her later with affection, but these good people's ignorance of what was happening is illustrated by the fact that when once by mistake Mrs Moore sent Hugh back three weeks late for the beginning of term, no one at the school had even noticed his absence.

The sufferings physical and spiritual which Hugh endured at Marlow influenced his whole life, as man and writer, so profoundly that it seems best to allow him to describe them in his own words. Thirty years later he wrote:

When I say that it wasn't all that it should be, I mean that the food was inadequate, the morality was "twisted," and Terror—sheer, stark, unblinking Terror—stared down every one of its passages. I had two years of it, and a passionate desire to be liked, a longing for approval, and a frantic reaction to anybody's geniality have been for me some of the results of that time. I have been frightened since then. I was frightened in the war several times rather badly, but I have never, after those days, thank God, known continuous increasing terror night and day. There was a period, from half-past eight to half-past nine in the evening, when the small boys (myself with them) were dismissed to bed but, instead, spread themselves in an empty classroom that is still to me, when I think of it, damp green in retrospective colour. The bigger boys held during that hour what they called the Circus. Some of the small boys (I was always one) were made to stand on their heads, hang on to the gas and swing slowly round, fight one another with hair brushes, and jump from the top of the school lockers to the ground. Every night (owing, I suppose, to my then unrecognised short sight) was a horror to me. I would be pushed up on to the lockers, then, "One, two, three—jump!" I can feel now again, as I write, the sick dizziness at my heart as I looked down at the shining floor, bent myself to jump, pulled myself together, fell, to be caught generally by some bigger boy who would push me into the arms of someone else, thence on again, and so the round of the room. Swinging round the gas was worse than the lockers—being roasted in front of the fire (shades of *Tom Brown*!) worse than the gas. Worst of all was being forced to strip naked, to stand then on a bench before them all while some boy pointed out one's various physical deficiencies and the general company ended by sticking pins and pen-nibs into tender places to see whether one were real or no—

Worse than the hour itself was the anticipation of the hour. First thought on waking was that eight-thirty was far away! Then, slowly through the day, it grew ever closer and closer until by teatime tears of anticipatory fear would fall into one's cup and salten one's hunk of bread! [1]

Sometimes he would gain a respite by cheering on the torture of some other little wretch and so postponing his own, sometimes by telling, like an infant Scheherazade, an endless serial story of adventure, whose cessation was the signal for a fresh onslaught. Luckily his romantic imagination was already active. "Once upon a time," he would begin, "in the time of Charles I, a lonely horseman could be seen spurring across the plain on a dark and stormy night . . ." and so on until his tormentors were asleep.

His own rest was disturbed by noisy nightmares, which often culminated in his being pushed out of bed or half-strangled with a towel. Other terrors included "drill," for which his short sight rendered him so inept that "Make some excuse and come and see Tadpole on the horizontal" became a catchword in the school, and the weekly fire-escape practice, when the boys had to descend from an upper window, feet first, through a long canvas funnel to the ground. The descent lasted only a few moments, but to Hugh each second was an agony of blinding, stifling confinement.

To those who would say: "We've all been through these private schools; a little roughing it does no one any harm. You ought to have stood up for yourself," Hugh replied:

Quite so. But I did not stand up for myself then and I'm not trying to stand up for myself now. The point is exactly that I was a miserable child, and one month at [Marlow] was enough to make me sycophantic, dirty in body and mind, a prey to every conceivable terror, so that the banging of a door or the dropping of a book sent my heart into my cranium, sentimental, too, like a little dog fawning on anyone who was for a moment kind, and— worst of all these, I think—muddleheaded and confused beyond any grown human's conception. I went to [Marlow] with a very fair intelligence. Mathematics I never could begin to understand (to this day I count on my

[1] *The Crystal Box* (1924).

fingers), but history and geography and literature I was nosing into like a pony with a bundle of hay. Well, [Marlow] flung the hay about my ears all right and there it has stuck ever since.[1]

It seems a trifle unfair to blame these two years for his lifelong inability to spell, add, or correct proofs. He spent seven more years at other schools and three at Cambridge, and it is probable that these failings had a deeper origin. What is certain is that his outward misfortunes at Marlow drove him to the inward world of his imagination. Partial solace could be found by creeping away from his persecutors and reading *Eric Brighteyes* in the boxroom, but his greatest pleasure was to invent an infinite variety of romantic tales, with Mrs Graves (who was young and pretty) as heroine, and himself the knight errant. "Things were hard," said Peter Westcott in *Fortitude*, "so I made them into a story—I coloured them up." Once during the holidays at Truro Hugh and some other children went out in a pony-cart which upset. They were all thrown out but no one was hurt. When Hugh told his aunt and cousins of the accident, he took all the blame for it on to himself, saying: "I ought not to have been telling them such an interesting story."

In a dilapidated writing-case, given him by an uncle, he found an old letter. He could not decipher a word of the crabbed and yellowish writing, but he decided that the document proved his claim to the Earldom of Orford, of which he was being wrongfully defrauded, and this fiction he often discussed in an increasingly serious way with the Moore children and others. Some of his schoolfellows even believed it, and eased their molestations in hope of later favours.

In his weekly letters to New York and Kingston Deverill Hugh never once mentioned his misery, perhaps from some kind of twisted loyalty: ironically enough the only letter to survive from this period is one from Canon Graves to Dr Walpole, dated 11 February 1895 and saying: "His form-master speaks well of him and he is a general favourite amongst the boys." His report for the Easter term of 1896 ran: "Conduct excellent. 7th of 22 in class. Top in Reading (excellent), 3rd in Latin and Geography, 5th in History and Divinity, 20th in Writing. Very satisfactory term."

[1] *Ibid.*

Ten years later, in the first flush of keeping a diary at Cambridge, Hugh wrote:

Of the two years spent at M. I shall say no more. Hell is realised by me for I have shared in it. I do not know that I look back on it with real regret —it has taught me much that is bad, but I have learnt sympathy. Every man, who is a man, must have his Hyde, and M. produced mine. The excessive desire to be loved that has always played so enormous a part in my life was bred largely, I think, from the neglect I suffered there.

And there is no doubt that these two years did crystallise in his imagination the concept of Evil as an actively embodied force which must be combated, and thus supplied him with the theme of almost all his books.

That's the way romantic writers are made, by having your nose rubbed in the mud, by knowing what fear is, by loneliness, a small boy crying in his bed at night.[1]

Together with this vision of Evil was born his lifelong loathing of and preoccupation with Cruelty, his insistence on Fear. In every one of his novels there is a character who is afraid of something: "to one fear of the dark, to another of physical pain, to a third of public ridicule, to a fourth of poverty, to a fifth of loneliness—for all of us our own particular creature lurks in ambush." [2] And when Hugh came to write an account of an eight-year-old boy, he introduced into what is in detail mostly fictitious this clearly autobiographical passage:

Jeremy was possessed with a new power. It was something almost abstract in its manifestations; it was something indecent, sinister, secret, foreign to his whole nature, felt by him now for the first time, unanalysed, of course, but belonging, had he known it, to that world of which afterwards he was often to catch glimpses, that world of shining white faces in dark streets, of muffled cries from shuttered windows, of muttered exclamations, half caught, half understood. He was never again to be quite free from the neighbourhood of that half-world; he would never be quite sure of his dominance of it until he died.[3]

Nor until *he* died would Hugh ever be free of the memory of Marlow. More than forty years later he wrote:

[1] *John Cornelius* (1937).   [2] *The Old Ladies* (1924).
[3] *Jeremy* (1919).

There are times when I am sure that life is, in positive reality, a dream, and that I shall wake up any hour and find that I am back in my dormitory at [Marlow] again, waking to that swaying and sinking of my bed, aware that in a moment I shall be thrown out of it, stripped of my nightshirt and beaten with corded towels. At such moments my apprehension is exactly the same as it was forty years ago—I am defenceless and naked in a world of hostile enemies.[1]

Eventually the true state of affairs was discovered; at the end of the summer term of 1896 Hugh was removed from Marlow, and in September he was sent to the Junior School of the King's School, Canterbury.

4

He was to stay there only five terms; he was not particularly happy there, and certainly no more successful than he was at any other school, but the beauty of the cathedral and the precincts made upon him an impression that was to remain for the rest of his life. For the first time he conceived the notion that cathedrals had lives of their own and characters which could inspire love, awe, and fear. (Truro he had absorbed with the unnoticing acceptance of a child.) Later he attributed this fancy to an early reading of *Edwin Drood*, just as he traced to the two *Alice* books his habit of endowing inanimate objects with human attributes.

But apart from the beauty of the King's School's surroundings, he enjoyed belonging to an institution which had endured for thirteen hundred years, at which Christopher Marlowe and Walter Pater had been educated: it was something he could feel he belonged to, as later he could never, a mere day-boy, belong to Durham School. In after life, in reference books and elsewhere, he invariably gave Canterbury as his only school, though he spent a year at Durham for every term at the King's School.

He grew more and more attached to the place as the years passed, and when in 1935 the enterprising and energetic F. J. Shirley was appointed headmaster, opportunities arose for tangible benefactions. Hugh paid for the re-turfing of the Mint Yard, he presented valuable

[1] *Roman Fountain* (1940).

furniture to the school, his portrait by Augustus John, and finally his collection of manuscripts, which is housed in the gate-room of Prior Sellingegate over the Dark Entry.[1] One of the boarding-houses is now called Walpole House, there is a Walpole Society, and there are Walpole Prizes, to keep his memory green.

But to return to the "small easy-tear-shedding boy" of 1896. On October 24 he wrote to New York:

Dear Father,

I am so sorry I had such a bad report. I have really done my best. It is so hard though. I have such a lot of lessons to learn. I am doing scanning, Ovid, decimals and lots of things I'd never done before.

I was 6th again last week. I can't get any higher. I wish I could. But most of the boys have been in the form over a year. Yesterday evening there was a penny reading. That's a sort of concert. . . . Excuse me for writing so badly and shortly. I'm writing with a bent nib and I get smacked when I'm not looking. Please send me my crest-book. Thank you very much for 2/6. The trousers have come.

Love to all.

I remain

Your affect. son,

Hugh.

His godfather, A. J. Mason, was now a Canon of Canterbury,[2] and Hugh was able to spend much time in his house and garden. In the house was a bookcase, where Hugh discovered new delights in Thackeray, Charlotte Bronte, Macaulay, and others. In the garden was a mulberry tree, in whose loaded summer shade he examined these new treasures. He was puzzled when his godfather confiscated *Tom Jones* (luckily after Hugh had finished reading it), and his mystification was increased when *Under Two Flags*, which his godfather gave him to read in the train back to Truro, was in its turn confiscated by his aunt as soon as she saw its author's name.

But now there occurred an event which was to change the course of his schooling. Dr Walpole applied for and was appointed to the post of Principal of Bede College for the training of elementary schoolmasters at Durham, and in December the family sailed for home. All

---

[1] A catalogue of this collection will be found at Appendix C, p. 470.
[2] He was later Master of Pembroke College, Cambridge. He died in 1928.

through 1897 Hugh stayed on at Canterbury, where he moved into the Upper School in September. His letters home were full of apologies for bad reports, protestations of trying his hardest, and a description or Jubilee Day at Deal, with all the school-children singing God Save the Queen on the promenade amid flags and banners.

Canon Page-Roberts preached. He has preached already for five consecutive Sundays this term. . . . I am never at peace with Graham, but I'm learning to bear it. . . . Is it decided I'm to leave? . . . I'm longing to leave.

I went to a lecture the other night on birds. It wasn't very interesting though the slides were good. It was chiefly about ladies wearing feathers in their hats. I can't bear this place now I don't know why.

5

He left Canterbury at Easter 1898, since it was much cheaper for his parents to have him living with them and attending Durham School as a day-boy, and although Hugh welcomed the change at the time, he soon came to regret it bitterly. A day-boy is usually treated as an outcast by boarders, and when Hugh discovered that Bede College and his family were similarly despised by the snobbish "cathedral set," his cup of social bitterness was full.

At last, he had thought, he was to have the home he had always longed for, but the reality disappointed him grievously. The College of the Venerable Bede stands on a hillside overlooking the River Wear, across which may be seen the clustering houses of Durham, surmounted by the castle and the mighty cathedral. At that time the Principal's house was joined on to the main building of the college; "rather as an underpaid governess is tacked on to a large overpopulated family." To get to his bedroom Hugh had to pass through one of the students' dormitories, and though in fact he was never disturbed when he got there, the juxtaposition and the bustle of the college made him think otherwise. From the first Hugh disliked everything about the place: even the large garden stretching down to the river he peopled with imaginary terrors.

He was forced to yield to the beauty of the cathedral, "hanging high in air, perfectly proportioned, pearl-shadowed, and sky-defended," and its brooding presence certainly deepened his romantic feeling for the past. But as he trudged unwillingly to school each day along the river bank, he came to think of it as a jealous cathedral, "a disapproving, snobbish, rich relation," whose servants were puffed up with pomp and circumstance. Not Bishop Westcott—he was a saint of God—but the other dignitaries seemed unbearably superior, and when the Walpoles gave a children's party, it was plain to Hugh that all the little daughters of the Canons came to it with their noses in the air.

Mrs Walpole's persistent shyness complicated social life still further. She hated housekeeping, but did it beautifully and was too conscientious to delegate such duties to another. A big crisis she faced like a lion, but the minor vexations disturbed her terribly. When she was over seventy and knew that she was soon to die, she said to Hugh: "You don't know what a comfort it is to think that I am never going to be shy again."

The only place in Durham for which Hugh felt any affection was the old subscription library, and there, his detested lesson-books corded together under his arm, he would hasten every day directly he left school. Ignoring the central table on which reposed the newest books, and leaving the lady librarian to hand out the latest works of Barrie, Crockett, Weyman, and Mrs Humphry Ward, on that system of social priority which he afterwards described in *The Cathedral*, he would climb a ladder in a dusky corner and, when he had read all Scott and Dickens, shake the dust from long-undisturbed novels by Trollope and Eugène Sue, Miss Ferrier and Wilkie Collins, Henry Kingsley, Whyte-Melville, and G. P. R. James. His appetite was enormous, he read at a furious pace, and he must during the next five years have read almost every novel, good or bad, which the library possessed.

Now too he began to collect his own library: a sixpenny edition of *The Talisman* was the first stone in that huge edifice, and before long the new shilling World's Classics joined the collection. Among them was *The Scarlet Letter* by Nathaniel Hawthorne. Hugh read it in the garden by the river, and this reading added to his Marlow vision of Evil and realisation of Fear a new terror—the sense of Sin. Hawthorne seemed to him, then and always, to be "the supreme romantic revealer of the Devil at his simplest," and to combine in himself those opposites which Hugh claimed as his own portion—"the normal and the abnormal, the law-abiding, slightly priggish, amiable citizen, and the rebel, the necromancer, the solitary outcast." [1] It would be hard to overstate the influence of this early reading of Hawthorne on Hugh's life as a writer.

Back in school it was the same old story; carelessness, inattention, inability to learn anything, always in a class with boys younger than himself. In the Easter term of 1899 he was seventh from bottom in Latin, English, and Divinity, equal last in Greek subjects and Latin verse, and last of all in French, Science, and Maths. " I am afraid," wrote his form-master despairingly to Dr Walpole, "that on any system of marking the result must have been the same."

All the time at Durham he was a difficulty and a problem to his parents. One night he overheard them discussing the seeming impossibility of his ever becoming a clergyman, as it had always been tacitly assumed that he would. "What are we to do with Hugh?... it's these wretched novels . . . his sulkiness makes it so difficult . . . he's quite unlike other boys." Their grief and worry were communicated to him and he wept.

I grew up, through those seven years, discontented, ugly, abnormally sensitive and excessively conceited. . . . No one liked me—not masters, boys, friends of the family, nor relations who came to stay; and I do not in the least wonder at it. I was untidy, uncleanly, excessively gauche. I believed that I was profoundly misunderstood, that people took my pale and pimpled countenance for the mirror of my soul, that I had marvellous things of genius in me that would one day be discovered. [2]

Besides the subscription library, he found at this time two other consolations. One consisted in endless games of bagatelle, in which he would pit against each other as imaginary opponents, not cricketers as would most boys, but authors. One day in the middle of the family meal he burst out with the remark that Hazlitt was improving and would probably, if he played well on Friday and Saturday, beat Congreve in the month's total. When he should have been struggling through a line of Æschylus he was wondering whether, with a little cheating, he could push Walter Scott to the head of the list. No wonder his parents were at their wits' ends about him.

---

[1] From an unpublished essay on Hawthorne, written in 1936.
[2] *The Crystal Box* (1924).

His second and much more important consolation lay in the writing of endless historical novels. Half a dozen of them have survived, scrawled in a childish hand and strongly bound in brown paper. The earliest is *Colchester Manor* (1897), the first volume of a trilogy dealing with Stuart times, later completed by *True and Brave* and *For the Sake of the King*. (It is curious to reflect that in the course of time his writing life came full circle, for when he died in 1941 he was engaged in an almost identical enterprise.) Other titles were *Strafford*, *Arnado the Fearless*, *At the Sound of the Trump*, *A Baron's Daughter*, and *The Sword of Damocles*. All bear marks of his adoration of Scott and Marion Crawford: they are full of gusto, crowded with characters and incident, sometimes out of control: "I forgot to tell you that Ronald had been taken prisoner by Sir Richard as there was a warrent out against him."

He also wrote several numbers of a complete magazine, containing poems, appreciations of his favourite authors, notes on current literature and the latest serials, and would delight his brother and sister with long stories on the least provocation. This was the great time for serials, and Hugh managed to read almost every one that appeared— Stanley Weyman and A. E. W. Mason in the *Cornhill*, Conan Doyle and W. W. Jacobs in the *Strand*, Q in *Blackwood's*, Max Pemberton in *Pearson's*, William le Queux in *Cassell's*, and so on, month after month.

Outdoor occupations included tennis with friends and sports in the garden which Hugh organised, compelling Dorothy and Robin to contribute from their pocket-money towards prizes which he usually won.

6

Summer holidays during the Durham years were spent at Sower Myre Farm near Gosforth, between Wastwater and Seascale in south-west Cumberland—the home of a farming family named Armstrong, with whom Hugh always kept in touch and used afterwards to visit from his own Cumbrian home. From Seascale station the family would drive inland in a cab, bicycles and luggage piled on the back, Hugh clutching a small box which held his personal treasures. He was looking forward to "that divinest of all human feasts, High Tea," and eager to read the next chapter of Max Pemberton's latest.

I remember too how, with these my worldly possessions still clutched in my hand, I stood on the pebbly path that bordered the garden behind Sower Myre Farm and drank in the scene. That moment was my initiation. That little windy garden, smelling of cow-dung, carnations, snapdragons and—in some mysterious spiritual fashion—hens' feathers, looked straight out to sea. On clear days it was said that you could catch a vision of the Isle of Man.[1]

Behind rose the craggy summits of the Langdales, Scafell, and the rest; within a few miles lay Wastwater, the most majestic and sinister of all the lakes, into which the barren Screes fall sheer. Something of that first vision of sea and lake and mountains entered unawares into Hugh's mind, bringing intimations of the promised land. At any rate those holidays made a deep impression, and when much later he found Cumberland for himself, it was more like coming home than discovering a new country.

In 1898 Canon Mason announced his forthcoming marriage, and Hugh's letter of congratulation gives further glimpses of these summer outings:

1 September 1898.   Sower Myre,
                                                        Gosforth.
Dear Uncle Arthur,

I was very pleased and surprised to hear of your engagement. I remember Miss Blore quite well. How funny that you should have the garden full of children as I suppose you will have. I am enjoying myself very much here. I've been up Scafell (3,210) and Great Gable (2,949) and some others. I've also been over the Stye Head pass down into Borrowdale and from there to Keswick passing Derwentwater. The lakes I have seen are Wastwater, Derwentwater, Windermere and Bassenthwaite. I think Wastwater is the most awe-inspiring and Derwentwater the most beautiful. The former is made lovely by the Screes descending straight into it, though it has not got the wonderful colour of the surroundings of the latter. We enjoyed going up Scafell very much. It was pretty steep in parts and one bit was quite dangerous. The view was lovely from the top. It was a regular panorama. But I don't think it was as fine as the view from Glaramara. From there we saw almost the whole of Windermere and Derwentwater. I don't think much of Windermere, there are no mountains near to it. When we walked to Keswick I saw the famous Lodore falls. They weren't much but in the winter they must be lovely. Either this week or next we propose to go in the

[1] From an essay called "The Lake District," published in *English Country* (edited by H. J. Massingham, 1934).

train to Coniston and to bicycle from there to Windermere. I *love* bicycling and I do a great deal of it. Father hired one for the time for us. Yesterday we went to a grand garden-party and enjoyed ourselves thoroughly. Today we are going up two mountains called Seatoller and Haycock. For the purpose of getting a glimpse of Ennerdale Lake.

> I must now end up,
> I remain
> Your affect: Nephew,
> Hugh.

Many years later Hugh gave a gloomy account of his first ascent of Great Gable, describing how with his father he bicycled from the farm by moonlight, "climbed the mountain and didn't see the sun rise. Instead of that we were soaked with wet mist and my bicycle tyre punctured." [1]

The Walpole children played cricket and other games with the little Armstrongs, and in the evenings Hugh would read aloud *Nicholas Nickleby* or some other novel. (He was always a good reader aloud, both of poetry and prose.) Once he bicycled over to a tennis-party at a big house near Wastwater. After playing very badly, he stole away into the house, found the library, and was soon deep in the first of many readings of *John Inglesant*. Other pleasures sometimes palled, books never.

7

With the arrival of 1902 and his last year at school, grave doubts were felt by everybody as to Hugh's chances of getting into Cambridge. He was still bottom of the Fifth Form: "Best in the form at essays and English. The rest of his form work very poor." If only his passionate interest in history, as exemplified by the stories he was writing, could have been canalised into some academic form—but examiners demand facts, and these, except for facts about fiction, Hugh all his life found it impossible to remember. His studies cannot have been helped by his bad eyesight, but this disability remained unrecognised until in March 1902 he was taken to an oculist and provided with the spectacles which thereafter he was always to need.

At the beginning of this year John Hay Beith, later to win fame as

[1] *Ibid.*

Ian Hay, came to Durham School as a young assistant master, straight from Cambridge. He remembers Hugh as big, ungainly, obstinate, and superior, unwilling to take any trouble at all with science, which Beith tried to teach him. One day in exasperation Beith said to him in class: "Well, Walpole, one day you may be Mayor of Durham." Hugh constantly repeated this story in later years, but invariably substituted "a small town" for "Durham." Indeed his feelings about Durham were altogether so painful that he expunged all mention of the city from his records, almost from his memory. He steadfastly refused to revisit the school until the present headmaster, Canon Luce, prevailed upon him to act as Visitor at the Speech Day of 1937.

Another of Beith's tasks was to produce the school's annual play. He remembers trying to coach Hugh in the part of Dogberry, but Hugh was not amenable to production, and was hurt when he was made to pronounce "ass" with a short instead of a long "a." Perhaps he was histrionically best suited to the part of Feeble in *Henry IV, Part II*, which he played in July 1902. He also took part in a performance of *Henry V* given by the students of Bede College, while he and his brother and sister acted a number of historical plays of his own writing. A curtained recess in one of the bedrooms served as stage, and Dorothy remembers Hugh becoming hysterical with excitement there when they were performing a drama of his on the subject of Belisarius. In a gay and somewhat facetious letter to his Aunt Dora, written in March 1902, he declared: "Another mania I have got at present which I have not yet confessed to the family is wondering what notorieties are like in private." He was soon to find out.

The only other event of note during this year was the acquisition of his solitary school prize, not counting that first consolation prize for reading at Truro. This was the English Verse Prize, which he won with a poem on the set subject of "The Burning of Joan of Arc in the Market Place at Rouen." When the headmaster presented the prize he said: "Walpole's attempt of some four hundred lines would thoroughly deserve the prize if the last three hundred and ninety-eight lines were as good as the first two." All four hundred have now, perhaps providentially, perished.

Probably the only human being at Durham who in any way appreciated the possibilities of this strange boy was a teacher at Bede College called Dall. He at least met Hugh on his own ground, encouraged his reading and writing, and was thereafter gratefully enshrined as the first of a long succession of benefactors. There was also a writer living in the city at this time, the novelist John Meade Falkner. When Hugh acquired Thomas Hardy's copy of the first edition of *The Lost Stradivarius* [1] he wrote in it:

How well I remember, when a small boy in Durham, watching Falkner's heavy body lumbering up the Durham street, myself eaten up with wonder, amaze and ambition. He once spoke to me. All the Cathedral set were shocked to their skins by *The Nebuly Coat*. I love the man to this day. He was a real abnormal romantic.

Somehow this last weary year came to an end, somehow he struggled through the necessary entrance examination, and in October 1903 Hugh went up to Emmanuel College, Cambridge, as a Subsizar.

[1] Now in the library of Mr Michael Sadleir.

CHAPTER THREE

THE GREAT RESOLVE

I

His first year at Cambridge was spent in lodgings at 37 Earl Street, his second and third years in College. Sizarships and Subsizarships carry with them an annual emolument and are granted to the sons of parents who cannot afford to pay the full fees. Hugh started to read for the History Tripos, played Rugby football (to which he had taken a sudden and rather unexpected liking during his last year at Durham), did a little rowing, much talking and reading and speculating—in fact behaved like most other undergraduates, trying his wings, enjoying his freedom, and learning to call his companions men instead of boys.

In January 1904 the Archbishop of Canterbury, Dr Randall Davidson, offered Dr Walpole the position of Rector of Lambeth, and the family moved to London. The last associations with Durham were thus severed, and Hugh was able to spend his vacations in the much more congenial and exciting air of the metropolis.

In June he had to report sorrowfully to his father that he had only got a Third in the first part of the Tripos, though he had confidently expected a Second and had been working very hard: "I suppose it was inaccuracy again." In the autumn of the same year he began what was to be his lifelong habit of keeping a diary. Initially a spasmodic affair, much given to undergraduate introspection and self-exhortation, it soon turned into a regular daily account of his movements and thoughts. One of the first entries reads: "At work, at games, I am mediocre and almost worse, no looking-glass can flatter my self-esteem, and I have a wonderful liking for the wrong thing. But I have been imagining a universal popularity." There is much discussion of his new literary favourites, Conrad and Meredith, while the latest novel of his old idol Marion Crawford is judicially condemned: "The Juggernaut of Popularity is on him and he has submitted." Occasionally there is a flash forecasting the novelist to be, as when he writes: "I love a windy night chiefly, I think, because the powers of Good and Evil seem to be abroad," but mostly the entries might have been written by any first-year undergraduate, until at the end of the year the second main theme of his life is introduced.

"Meanwhile I still wait for the ideal friend. . . . I'd give a lot for the real right man." All his life this searching and waiting were to go on; often he fancied he had found the person, but the tragedy for people of his temperament is that the "ideal friend" does not exist. Hugh was always to some extent afraid of women, certainly he never made love to any, and though he was to have long and devoted friendships with women as varied in age and circumstances as Lady Colvin, Ethel McKenna, Elizabeth Russell, Athene Seyler, Virginia Woolf, Sylvia Lynd, Vita Sackville-West, Clemence Dane, and Marguerite Steen, and was once actually to advance as far as a proposal of marriage, he was always easier in the company of his own sex. As the quest for the "real right man" was intensified, the words "friend" and "friendship" occurred more and more frequently in everything he wrote, acquiring a special significance of his invention. Often in early days he would frighten off new acquaintances, who he thought might be ideal friends, by the extravagant vehemence of his immediate insistence on their friendship.

The year 1905 was illuminated by the discovery of A. C. Benson. This unusual man, son of the Archbishop, after a long career as a schoolmaster at Eton was now a Fellow of Magdalene, of which college he was later Master. He was also the author of a large number of rather spinsterish books of prose and verse, which had a great contemporary vogue. His friend and one-time pupil Percy Lubbock has described the difficulty of reconciling these "easy-going mellifluous pages, with their rather faint and solemn discourse" with their "masterful, combative, richly humoured" author, and Henry James once described him to Hugh as "big and red and rough as to surface . . . but . . . ever so refined inwardly." Apart from this strange duality, Benson was a tremendous talker and an unwearying encourager of youthful talent. Hugh fell at once under the spell of his charm, and poured forth to him all his hopes and fears, difficulties and doubts.

Among these were the first stirrings of his religious conscience.

Up to now he had accepted without a thought the orthodox background of the Church of England in which he had been bred, and with
it the assumption that he would naturally follow in his father's foot-
steps. He had been dutifully bored in church, and disgusted at what
seemed to him the worldliness and intrigue of the cathedral set at
Durham; but he had imagined that perhaps other places were different.
His conception of God had been the child's traditional one of a large
old gentleman with a beard, living in a kind of glorified extension of
the Earls Court Exhibition. Now for the first time he began timidly
to think for himself, and the result was decidedly unsettling. The more
he thought about it, the more certain he felt that what he wanted to do
was simply to write stories, though at first this project seemed recon-
cilable with a position in the Church. Benson helped him with sound,
practical, calming advice, as well as extending his literary taste by introducing him to the works of Shelley, William Morris, Rossetti, and
Edward FitzGerald. In his diary for 5 May 1905 Benson wrote:

H. W. paid me a call: a nice boy, full of anxiety and good feeling: in the
midst of *Sturm und Drang*, finding what he calls his "dearest convictions"
failing him: very pathetic in one way, and rather sadly amusing in the other.
His admiration of and confidence in my literary powers and oracularity of
speech rather embarrassing. We had a long mixed vague talk; but I knocked
a few nails in, I think. I cannot help feeling that if this boy finds the art of
expression he may be a good writer; at least he seems to me to have ten times
the *fire* I ever possessed. When I realise the intense vehemence and impulsiveness of a boy like this, his "exultations, agonies," I feel what a very *mild*
person I was.[1]

It is clear from this that, though Hugh later liked to suggest that his
potentialities as a writer were unrecognised by anyone for years, Benson
spotted them immediately.

In March Hugh had celebrated his twenty-first birthday in College:
"A lot of men in my year gave me a silver cigarette-box with the crest
and their initials. Rather ripping, wasn't it?" He made a large
number of acquaintances at Cambridge, among them Walter Duranty
the future foreign correspondent, but no close friends.

[1] *The Diary of Arthur Christopher Benson* [1926].

2

In the summer vacation came his first opportunity to discover "what notorieties are like in private." Through a Cambridge friend he received an invitation to visit a castle in Scotland and tutor for a few weeks a boy called Willie, son of Sir Archibald Edmonstone and nephew of Mrs George Keppel, one of the leading beauties of the day. He accepted, but when his parents realised the identity of his hostess, Dr Walpole wrote to say that he strongly disapproved, and would prefer Hugh to cancel the arrangement. Seeing the dazzling vision fading Hugh brought all guns to bear in his reply:

My dear Father,

I am, I must confess, extremely astonished by your letter. I thought both you and Mother knew exactly what Mrs. Keppel's reputation was. As it is known to the whole of England, I must say I hardly expected you to be so surprised. I gathered that you both knew exactly what she was, i.e. the King's mistress.

There are two reasons which, unless you absolutely forbid it, will force me to go. In the first place if I didn't go I should think it extremely dishonourable. I arranged finally with Sir Archibald the other day, with my eyes absolutely open. As far as association with Mrs. Keppel goes, I suppose I shall see but little of her. Even if I do I am afraid that neither you nor Mother realise the sort of people I have been meeting at Cambridge in the last two years. Over and over again I have come into contact with men just as bad as Mrs. K. I am now twenty-one and know as much about morality generally as there is to know. Therefore when I accepted Sir Archibald finally I was quite aware of what I was doing. It would, I think, be both dishonourable and shabby to get out of it now.

Also it seems to me that I shall be doing really wrong if I do not go. This whole business was put in my way by none of my seeking. It is obviously meant that I should go. I have the kid for two months absolutely under my own control, and judging by one's own experience one can be influenced a great deal at that age either one way or the other. Sir A. specially told me that he wanted Willie to be brought up decently and I should never forgive myself if I did not go. The house being fast seems to me only an added reason for going.

I am extremely sorry to go against your wishes in this matter. If it was a matter of personal pleasure I would of course do as you wish, but in this case I have not the slightest doubt as to the right course to take.

If the worst comes to the worst and you still absolutely forbid it, I can take no further part. But you must write to Sir A. yourself, saying exactly *why* you don't wish me to go. Surely it would be extremely dishonourable to give excuses which are not true ones.

When I had quite decided in my own mind I consulted both Canon Cooper and Mac, and had a long talk with the latter. They were both strongly of the opinion that I was now bound and must go at all costs. Mac said that the risk of temptation was nil. I am sorry about this but I must say that I am surprised you should have proposed what seems to me a most dishonourable course. Unless you absolutely forbid it I go on Wednesday.

> Ever your loving son,
> Hugh.

The casuistic imputation of dishonourable conduct, however far-fetched, was well calculated to appeal to his father's simple goodness, while today the idea of this beardless boy planning to cleanse the Augean Stables of the rich and save a soul from the muck-heap is particularly delightful. At all events Dr Walpole weakened, Hugh promised that "if anything horrid happens or I feel that it is doing me harm I shall leave at once," and the plan went through. Only one letter from the Castle of Vice has survived:

> Duntreath Castle,
> Blanefield, N.B.

My dear Father,

I meant to have written some while ago but have had no spare time. Even now it is within twenty minutes of luncheon so that this can't be long.

Things still go well here. The boy isn't everything that could be desired. He gets into dreadful states of excitement and hates his lessons, but on the whole he is all right. They say he obeys me much better than anyone else he has ever had.

All your alarm was quite needless. Mrs. K. and three others play bridge every night but for quite low points—otherwise there is nothing as you anticipated. Mrs. K. is of course very beautiful and charming. She is very nice to me but I should never rave about her. She has however a horrid friend here, Lady ——. I like Lady E. and Sir A. more and more—they are delightful. The nicest of the men are Keppel, who is one of the nicest men I've ever met, and Lord Alington who is very jolly. They have all got it into their heads that I know a tremendous amount and I am continually appealed to as final arbiter in all sorts of questions.

Loch Lomond is quite close but I haven't been there yet. There is only a

Scotch kirk in the place which we attend but which is very dreary. The nearest English place is ten miles away. I went for a long motor ride yesterday but it was very wet so I didn't enjoy it much. I'm doing a lot of work and getting on fast. Am just reading *Marius* now and think it's very fine.

Love to all,

Yr. loving son,

Hugh.

One day Mrs Keppel took him for a walk all by himself, but his pride in thus being singled out was dashed when that evening he overheard her say to one of her friends: "Even the nicest people can be bores sometimes." Ten years later Hugh wrote in his diary: "Mrs Keppel's great fun. I *do* like her. She's like a sergeant in the Guards with a sense of humour." But now she was just an awe-inspiring celebrity in private life.

3

After this unexpected excursion, the Michaelmas term passed without major incident, except that Hugh read to the Mildmay Essay Club of Emmanuel a paper on "Meredith and Henry James: a Contrast in Obscurity." The Christmas vacation was spent at Lambeth, reading at home and in the British Museum, looking at pictures, going to the theatre. All his life he went to every play he could, including revues, musical comedies, and, later on, films. Thirty years failed to dim his pristine enjoyment, and at the end of his life a visit to the theatre with him was like accompanying a child who had never been before.

Now, too, he made another literary friend in Ethel Colburn Mayne, once the friend of Henry Harland (the editor of the *Yellow Book*), short-story writer and future biographer of Lord and Lady Byron. She was considerably older than Hugh, and took an almost motherly interest in his literary upbringing.

In January 1906 he went up to Cambridge for his penultimate term, and as the time drew nearer when he must decide on his future career, the idea of the priesthood grew ever less attractive. Could he somehow postpone a decision? He suggested this to his parents, was gently but firmly chidden, and on February 17 wrote to his father:

I'm afraid you'll think me terribly indecisive and inconclusive, but it really all comes from the fear that I shall be ordained and then find my heart isn't in it. My two reasons for thinking I ought to wait were:

First: I don't care about the theological side at all. I believe the main things. All the rest seems to me absolutely unessential. Also I don't feel the necessity for many of the things you regard as necessary. For instance, going to theatres in Lent doesn't seem to me wrong. I'm also not at all Christian in my attitude to other people. I dislike many people thoroughly and have no sympathy with certain points of view. I have no interest at present in theological discussion and research.

Secondly: Literature is to me at present everything. If I had a literary post offered me I should accept it at once without any thought of the Church.

These things seemed to me insuperable obstacles. I felt I wasn't honest in saying I wished to be ordained. I felt I was going to be ordained mainly because you all wished me to be, and because it was the obvious and easiest thing to do. Arthur Benson however says that:

First: I have got the essential desire to help other people, and keenness in the direction it will be most wanted, and that the rest will come.

Secondly: that my literature will help and serve the other and is quite compatible with it. He also says that everything pointing so obviously to it is a call that I should do it, and that I must trust for the rest.

I have stated my feelings exactly. If you think with Benson that I can quite honestly go on to be ordained, feeling as I do, then I will say no more and will go on to Jesus Lane without hesitation.

P.S. It sounds ridiculous, but would you ask Mother to send me some photo of me as a baby. I have to take one to a party next week. The one with the broom is best, I think.

Dr Walpole's reply has vanished, but its contents can be guessed from Hugh's further letter of February 21:

It was what I thought you would say, but I think you have rather mis-understood me. Of course when I said I did not care for theology I did not mean I did not care for the Bible—Faith—Worship. If that had been so I should not have dreamt of going on. I meant that all the disputes about trivial details seem to me, at present, so unimportant and so unnecessary. My ignorance of all theological writing is, at present, absolute, but that, I suppose, is the case with many young men before they go to a theological college. Then as to theatres and other things, of course when I was ordained I should act according to what I conceived the Church's orders to be. If I found that they disapproved of such things I should at once give them up. But it is simply that I feel it right to continue such things at present. After I have read more and thought more deeply I daresay I shall see quite differently.

The reason why I said the other day that I must wait was, really, because I felt the literary impulse was too strong to allow of my putting anything else before it. But I have had another long talk with Arthur Benson, and he says it is probably because the literature has been so long pent up that I feel so strongly. I think if I really try to put that impulse second I can.

I felt when I was giving an address at Barnwell last Sunday a zeal and a keenness that I'd never felt before, and I think it will grow and grow as I go on. One who has been brought up in a clergyman's family sees all the little disadvantages very clearly, and it was a momentary rebellion against the thought of being bound down and, as it were, narrowed down that made me speak. But I think I see now the beauty and greatness of it as I did not see before. I have quite definitely made up my mind to go on, and I will change no longer.

Early in March, Canon Lambert, the Chaplain Superintendent of the Mersey Mission to Seamen, wrote to offer Hugh a post as Lay Missioner, to start in September at a salary of £84 a year. He consulted his father, saying: "Arthur has written to Eton for me, but I don't suppose anything will come of it. I should prefer to go abroad but I suppose that's impossible." Having no feasible alternative to suggest, he was trapped: his father diplomatically steered him towards so sensible a stepping-stone, and on his twenty-second birthday he confided to his diary: "Father says I must accept Lambert's offer, so I'm going to."

The common round of university life continued: Hugh worked some six hours a day at history; took part in a debate on Enthusiast *v*. Critic ("myself for the first of course"); invited Miss Mayne down and showed her round Cambridge ("Very interesting conversation. But her hair came down. Ques: Should I tell her? I decided not to."); wrote an editorial for the college magazine, and devoted much space in his diary to enthusiastic descriptions of nature, music, painting, the theatre, and always books. His last vacation was spent at Lambeth, reading and working on a second Mildmay essay called "Some Modern Apostles of Colour." The Apostles were Pater, Swinburne, Meredith, and Maurice Hewlett, and Hugh quickly "found there was so much more to say than I had room for. I haven't a bit learned yet what to leave out." This was a lesson he never properly mastered to the end.

His diary for his last term is devoted to tennis-playing, history-cramming, and visits to Arthur Benson. Percy Lubbock, another guest, recalls his "eager literary effervescence." Many years later Hugh wrote: "I shall never forget the awful evening when I offered to Lubbock and Arthur Benson *my* notion of the theme of *The Wings of the Dove*! Lubbock's agony was an immortal thing." [1]

On May 11 he read his Colour paper to the Mildmay: "I think a success although they didn't quite see my drift." The Tripos examination took place at the end of the month, his family came down in force for May Week, and on June 14 he went to spend his last few undergraduate days with Benson at his country house, Hinton Hall. "As to A.C.B. himself! My feeling about him is too strong to write. I'm almost afraid of my attitude."

Two days later the Tripos results were announced: "A Third by all the gods! I think it's disappointing as I certainly did better than last year and have, I think, a second-class amount of knowledge—but it's my fatal vagueness of mind that's done it." He was somewhat consoled by "a splendid walk with A.C.B. in the afternoon—a most interesting talk about literary people." Next day they visited Ely Cathedral on bicycles, and when Hugh learnt that he had won the College English Essay Prize he was quite reluctant to go down. However, after receiving his B.A. degree and taking his leave of Benson, he arrived in London on June 20, ready for a fortnight of pleasure before embarking on his next adventure. He went to Ascot and the Alhambra, Lord's and the Royal Garden Party, heard Bernard Shaw lecture, Caruso and Melba sing in *La Bohème*, saw Arthur Bourchier in Sutro's *The Fascinating Mr Vanderveldt*, and bought six volumes by Henry James at a sale.

The next two months he spent tutoring the sons of some people called Darwin, friends of his parents, in their house at Dryburn on the outskirts of Durham—a happy time of croquet on the lawn, music, and poetry-reading after dinner. Here he read *Anna Karenina* and finished writing a long short story called *The Scarlet Fool*. He sent it to Messrs Smith Elder, the publishers, who returned it with "a really nice letter." And so on August 31 with a mixture of excitement and apprehension he left Dryburn for Liverpool and the Mission to Seamen.

[1] *The Apple Trees* (1932).

4

It is characteristic that on his arrival, after fixing up lodgings with a Miss Hales at 32 Peel Street, the first places he visited were not the Mission headquarters or the Seamen's Institute, but the circulating library and the public reading room.   In after years he always referred to his "year" in Liverpool, whereas in fact his sojourn there lasted six calendar months to the day.   Doubtless the time seemed like a year to him, then and afterwards: the point is a small one, but it serves to illustrate Hugh's perennial lack of precision in all facts and dates.

From the beginning it was evident that he would never fit into the life of the Mission.   Here is the account of his duties, slightly written up for her benefit, which he sent to his mother on September 18:

My day is as follows.   The morning I get for reading and lectures at the hostel.   Directly after lunch I rush down to the docks where I have a regular bit specially belonging to me.   I visit there for about an hour and a half, then I have to rush back and look after the club-rooms.   See that the men don't steal, help to write letters, give relief tickets, set them all to playing games etc.   Then as soon as October starts there is something every night.   Monday night there's a concert at the Institute.   Every Tuesday night I shall be expected to take the chair at a concert in the Sailors' Home—an enormous place where I should think there will be an audience of a thousand at least.   On Wednesdays there's a "Happy Evening" which I'm entirely responsible for— games and songs and things.   On Thursday night I'm free.   Friday night there's a lantern lecture and I have to preach in the chapel.   The whole of Saturday I get off.   Sunday I either go on the launch or take a service in the Institute. In addition to all this I'm a kind of official at the Sailors' Home and cases of drink and distress are reported to me.   Also I'm supposed to work up the Apprentices' Club.   Then the people in the parish here want me to do various things, but I'm going to stick out strongly against that. . . .

I enjoy it all and I really think I shall do a certain amount of useful work— the "human touch" is a great thing—but I must tell you truthfully now that at this present moment I could not be ordained.   My own personal religion is, of course, a great thing to me, but the "evangelising"—the getting other people there—is second to that other literary feeling I spoke so often about. I'm afraid this may hurt you but I want to be absolutely honest about it.   I love it all, I don't think I could now lead the rest of my life without helping practically in social work,[1] but I see absolutely that if I were ordained it must come first and at present it doesn't.

[1] This idea recurred at intervals throughout his life, mingled later with feelings of guilt

Of these multifarious duties some—for instance, preaching, taking services, and playing games in the Institute—were comparatively inoffensive, but others, such as visiting ships (on a "dirty-looking" launch called the *Good Cheer*) and trying to persuade reluctant sailors and apprentices to drop in for a "Happy Evening," quickly became a burden and a dread to him. In order to win the regard, or even gain the attention, of the dockside riff-raff, it was necessary to cultivate, at least to affect, a cheery thick-skinned indifference to rough language and initial rebuffs. "Throw yourself into their lives," said Canon Lambert buoyantly, but to the sensitive Hugh the least suggestion of surliness or disapproval was enough to put him off for the day. Here are some typical extracts from his diary:

Oct. 3. Rushed back to give apprentices tea, but they never turned up. "Happy Party" at the Institute. Musical chairs etc.

Oct. 9. Spent the morning hunting for apprentices. Visited six ships but only secured about three boys.

Oct. 15. Visited one ship, but suddenly the back of my bags split and I had to rush home.

Oct. 25. Tried a new way to the hostel and got lost.

Nov. 4. Tried to nail some chaps coming out of Mason's for tea, but they fought shy of me. I hate touting.

Feb. 4. Evening at the Institute. Played ludo upstairs to any extent. The room was icy cold.

Feb. 9. Operated raffle and twopenny dip at bazaar, also sold underclothing and baby garments for two hours.

Feb. 11. Badly beaten at draughts by a cadaverous sailor.

Feb. 17. Down to service at the Institute, where I read the wrong lesson.

Some of these incidents, particularly that recorded on October 15, introduce a *leit-motif* which runs all through Hugh's life and may be described as the Mr Pooter strain in his character, since like the immortal hero of *The Diary of a Nobody* he was liable at all times, and particularly at moments of stress, to minor accidents of the most mortifying nature. It would be simple, but profoundly misleading, to base upon them a study of Hugh as a great comic character.

Every spare minute was spent in reading, writing, and going to the

---

at being so happy and successful while millions were in want. But organised social work was not his portion and he confined himself to innumerable private charities.

theatre. Those were the days of the touring actor-managers, and Hugh was able to see H. B. Irving in *The Lyons Mail*, Arthur Bourchier in *The Walls of Jericho*, Forbes-Robertson in *Hamlet* ("more sunny and lovable than Tree"), Martin Harvey in *The Corsican Brothers*, and F. R. Benson in *Coriolanus*, as well as the Christmas pantomime. In Liverpool also he heard for the first time Pachmann playing Chopin:

A great experience. His face was changing the whole time like an actor playing a great part. And then he would suddenly talk aloud as though he was just gathering us round like children to whom he was telling a fairy-story. And then he would talk to the piano itself as though telling it what to do.

For reading, there were the daily newspapers to be rushed through at the Conservative Club, and the *Academy* (which he specially enjoyed) to be bought and read every week, while bookshop and library provided such new delights as *Puck of Pook's Hill* and *The Beloved Vagabond*. When influenza kept him in bed for some days he seized the opportunity to read Lewes's *Life of Goethe*, *Emma*, and Pater's *Renaissance*. He bought secondhand books guiltily whenever he could, and salved his conscience by getting up at 6.30 for a day or two and as a penance reading Farrar's *Life of Christ* before breakfast. He went to rugger matches and concerts, and took part in an amateur production of *The Man from Blankley's*, of which he depressingly recorded: "Strongitharm poor as Tidmarsh. Myself poor."

But his chief distraction, as always, lay in writing. During his stay in Liverpool he wrote a number of short pieces and from time to time sent a batch of them to Ethel Colburn Mayne. She criticised them minutely, constructively, encouragingly; he felt he was ready to tackle something fuller, and launched out into his first attempt at a grown-up novel, *The Abbey*. He wrote twelve chapters at top speed and then stuck, bewildered by the multiplicity of characters. He was not ready for it after all.

I looked at the pile of manuscript and felt proud that I could write so much—but how to continue? I must begin again, and this time I must have a plan and only so many characters as were needed. And destroy all these beautiful pages. Yes, destroy all these beautiful pages.[1]

[1] *The Crystal Box* (1924).

But he didn't, couldn't, destroy them; indeed it is doubtful whether he ever, except once, destroyed any of his writings. In 1931, when William Plomer said he had torn up the complete manuscript of a novel he had written because he was not satisfied with it, Hugh replied: "Marvellous, marvellous! What courage! I've never had the courage to destroy anything!" Then, after a pause, "Do you know, you make me feel just like a little girl taken to see the elephants for the first time."

No, these twelve chapters were preserved: fifteen years later they supplied a foundation for *The Cathedral*, and today three of them may still be seen in Prior Sellingegate at Canterbury. Apart from anything else they helped Hugh to make up his mind that he was going to be a writer and not a clergyman.

His chief friends in Liverpool were the Watsons, the family of a Cambridge friend. The Rev. Dr John Watson, who had recently retired after twenty-five years as a Presbyterian minister in the city, had also achieved an immense popular success, under the pen-name of Ian Maclaren, with such novels of Scottish life as *Beside the Bonnie Brier Bush* and *The Days of Auld Lang Syne*. Here was a man who *had* successfully combined the two professions—a living answer to Hugh's contention that they were incompatible, though even here Hugh found support for his own theory. "Dr Watson is not very popular here," he told his mother. "It is generally felt that he ought not to have given up his clerical work yet—and it only proves that you cannot honestly combine writing and the life of a clergyman—not unless you put the first underneath." Hugh lunched or dined with the Watsons almost every Sunday, and the Doctor gave him sensible advice. Realising that the boy was, at the moment, in no way ready to be ordained, but having little evidence on which to base an opinion of Hugh's literary potentialities, he suggested a temporary job as a librarian or a journalist. Hugh could decide nothing, but matters were soon brought to a head.

On 4 January 1907 he was due for ten days' leave in London, and the day before he left, Canon Lambert sent for him and gave him a "serious jaw. Said I was not serious enough, did not give up my time enough, and had too many interests. I defended myself, but what he says is perfectly true." In some ways this talk was a relief: it certainly liberated his spirit and crystallised his intentions:

I went out and down to the Mersey, and there, looking at the river, I had one of the most important hours of my life. That foaming flood tossing in grey froth and spume out to the sea was invincibly strong and mighty. Ships of all sizes were passing; gulls were wheeling with hoarse screams above my head—the sun broke the clouds and suddenly the river was violet with silver lines and circles.

At that moment I knew. The ferry arrived from the other side; people pushed out and past me. The life and bustle and beauty of the world was everywhere about me. I loved it; I adored it; but not for me to try and change it.

Looking out to sea where a great liner slowly took the sun like a queen, I vowed that I would be a novelist, good or bad, for the remainder of my earthly days.[1]

Strengthened by this great resolve, Hugh travelled to London to convince his father, who, apprised of the situation by Lambert, proved most sympathetic. To a man of Dr Walpole's simplicity of heart and straitness of outlook, Hugh at this time presented an ever-growing problem. One could not take seriously the stories he was always writing, and yet in every other direction he seemed quite uninterested and utterly unemployable.

It was agreed that all thoughts of ordination should be dropped for the moment and that while Hugh was deciding on a profession, perhaps schoolmastering, which should keep him while he tried to write, a year abroad learning French and German would do no harm. Hugh was delighted with this plan, and spent an excited ten days in London. He read some of his latest efforts to the family, who, understandably, could see little in them; he went to tea with Miss Mayne; he was thrilled by Tree and Constance Collier in *Antony and Cleopatra*, and by Granville Barker in *The Doctor's Dilemma*; he visited Mr Gabbitas, the scholastic agent, and gave his "accomplishments which looked ridiculously small on paper;" and best of all, he spent two days at Tremans in Sussex with the Benson family:

Arthur the same dear as ever. He is sure that I must go abroad and that I

[1] *The Crystal Box* (1924).

am right about ordination. He is also more or less encouraging about the writing. He shows me various things that he is writing, but they are all too like things he has already written.

Back at Liverpool for a final six weeks, Hugh began a Berlitz course in German, and was employed by the Mission in the much more congenial work of visiting hospitals, where he was sure of a friendly welcome. He was also ordered to give a lecture at the Institute, on Mary Queen of Scots. Of this, the first of countless public lectures in England and America, he wrote at the time: "I was very nervous before, but it was wonderful how easily it came once I began. A man afterwards told me it was as exciting as a novel." One day he was summoned to the office and told by Canon Lambert that he was to write a leading article on the Mission for the *Liverpool Post*. He wrote it in half an hour and it was published the following day.

So on a note of gratitude and relief his six Liverpool months came to an end, but before his next chapter opens there is one more contemporary practice which must be mentioned. At Liverpool he contracted the habit of Writing to Authors (not to be confused with Writing to Reviewers, a later and more specialised variety of the same pastime). Letter-writing in general was a favourite occupation of his leisure, and even the most fleeting acquaintances were straightway enrolled on his list of likely correspondents. By the time he left Liverpool their number was considerable, and until the pressure of other delights grew too heavy he strove to keep up with this ever-growing commitment. He himself was rarely a good letter-writer in the literary sense, but he was an extraordinarily assiduous one, and no day of his life seemed properly ordered unless it began with the receiving and answering of a batch of letters.

The early ones written to authors were simply those naïve gestures of admiration and gratitude which today are known as "fan-letters," but two of their earliest recipients were destined to play important parts in the drama of Hugh's life and works. One was Charles Marriott, whose Cornish novels from *The Column* onwards had for some time been favourites with Hugh, and who over the next two years wrote him a series of letters full of wisdom, encouragement, and good counsel. The other was the much more formidable figure of the Gräfin

Arnim, better known as the author of *Elizabeth and her German Garden*. Her answer was more exciting than he had dared to hope:

Dear Youth,

I'm glad Frl. Schmidt [1] was beneficial, and I should certainly in your place proceed to count up my blessings instead of contemplating the size of my annoyances—it's a most profitable occupation. Your letter interested me to the extent of goading me into writing to you—as you see. I wonder what college you were at at Cambridge, why you are going to France, and what makes you think you are going to produce a masterpiece. There's no earthly reason why you shouldn't, but it's unusual to be so sure. It was nice of you to call me "Miss" Elizabeth. Have you then never heard of the Man of Wrath? I leave for London tomorrow. Would you like to come and see me at my club? I'm looking for a young man to come to us at Easter and talk English to the children, as the present one leaves then to go and coach for his degree—and perhaps you know of somebody. I prefer Cambridge to Oxford, unless it's a Balliol man, and of Cambridge Colleges someone from King's or Trinity. If you want to pour out woes to a person who thinks rather like Rose-Marie on the subject of young men's sorrows write me a line care of Messrs Smith Elder, 15 Waterloo Place, London S.W.

Your obliged, amused, and interested
"Elizabeth."

It was with this intriguing letter in his pocket that on 28 February 1907 Hugh returned once more to Lambeth.

---

[1] Her novel, *Fräulein Schmidt and Mr Anstruther*, which Hugh had been enjoying as a serial.

CHAPTER FOUR

FROM VALHALLA TO EPSOM

I

THE first meeting with Elizabeth took place at the Lyceum Club on March 5. "She is a small rather pretty woman. Very outspoken and sharp. She asked me to teach her children. Took me to a queer tea-party. Funny old ladies and everything quaint." It was arranged that he should report to the German Garden in a month or two's time. If the reader wonders why Elizabeth should have engaged this unknown young man after so brief an acquaintance, the reasons will probably be found among those same qualities of his which were soon to charm Henry James and many others—his brimming enthusiasm for life and literature, his ambition, his excitement about everything, his naïve childishness—qualities which, with the modifications of age, were to make him always the most lovable and amusing of companions. Possibly in Elizabeth's case may be added his immense potentialities as a subject for teasing.

After a flying visit to Benson at Magdalene, he crossed the Channel on March 7, on his way to the house of a certain M. Marteau in the little town of Villefranche de Rouergue in the southern department of Aveyron. This was his first grown-up visit abroad, and despite a letter full of detailed instructions from Marteau he was everywhere exploited by porters and taxi-drivers. "Marteau met me. The ordinary type of Frenchman—a little man with a black beard—awfully polite and hospitable and has declared two or three times that he will never leave me during my stay." Soon this constant attention became wearisome: also it was difficult to get a bath, there were smells everywhere, and he was disappointed to discover that while Marteau seemed to know a great deal about Shakespeare, he had apparently never heard of Anatole France. However, Hugh worked hard at his French—dictation, literature, and conversation—and in his spare time plugged on with *The Abbey*, until after a week or two he abandoned it in favour of a new story called *Troy Hanneton*.

Relations with Marteau deteriorated steadily. On March 20 "after déjeuner set out with Marteau who had a gun with which he succeeded in killing a thrush. It was very hot. Coming back had a royal row with M. He said I had behaved like a pig and was a man of bad character." It seems likely that Hugh here showed some of the obstinate superiority and pride which had made him such an impossible pupil at Durham: he certainly laughed at Marteau when the latter grew angry. On Good Friday, March 29, matters came to a head:

Things began to get a little lively at déjeuner, then after dictation I asked M. if he wouldn't give me something harder as I thought I should learn more. He lost his temper entirely. I started to pack for Paris. He came in and asked for his money which I hadn't got. So here I am a kind of prisoner. I'm going to have all my meals in here.

By next day his partial imprisonment began to worry him and he "wrote a little apology to M. in the morning, not because I had anything to apologise for, but because I hate to be fighting with anyone at Easter." Some of Marteau's written reply has survived:

However, I must tell you that *you must pay me* what you owe me, it is to say £10 before Sunday 7th day of April 6 o'clock p.m. if you do not do so I *will give you* to the policemen. Noreover do not try to leave by surprise, I did the necessary to have you watched and you will be stopped at the railway station as soon as you go there without me. Your trial to leave me yesterday without my knowing it and without paying me is the cause of my doing so.

For two more days Hugh sat in his room in splendid isolation, having his meals brought by a maidservant, reading and writing *Troy Hanneton*, but on April 2 the necessary money was telegraphed by his parents. In order to draw it out of the post-office he had to produce a witness to vouch for his identity; Marteau was the only one available, and in the course of the business a complete reconciliation was effected. But Hugh had had enough of Villefranche: he wired to Elizabeth; she answered "Come at once," and he decided to do so. After two happy days in Paris, he was in Berlin on April 6, and on the next day reached the German Garden itself, which was situated at Nassenheide in Pomerania, not far from the shores of the Baltic.

2

Mrs Belloc Lowndes has given an amusing and circumstantial account [1] of how Elizabeth met Hugh at the station, pretended to be the governess, and extracted from him various friends' true opinions of herself. The story is not out of character, and it is quite possible that she did play such a trick on one of the numerous tutors she engaged for her children, but the victim was certainly not Hugh. He had already met her in London, and his diary describes how he was met by the Graf and his three daughters, the "April, May and June babies," the first two of whom were to be Hugh's pupils.

To begin with he was greatly impressed by the clean spaciousness of the house compared with the Marteaus', and by the large staff headed by a tutor, two governesses, and a lady housekeeper. His room was "charming—white walls with a green stove, looking straight out on to a mass of green trees." There were picnics in the pine-forests and by the seashore, any amount of time for writing and reading (mostly French and German, though he enjoyed a "very remarkable novel," *The Longest Journey* by E. M. Forster, one of his predecessors at Nassenheide), and many conversations with the agreeable German tutor. From these he learned that no English tutor had ever stayed longer than six months, and soon he began to understand why.

April 15. Got badly ragged by the Countess. Submitted moderately well.
April 19. The Countess thinks me "*farouche*" and I have never felt such constraint anywhere as I do here.
April 25. Got ragged about my novel after dinner.

The Countess would wait until there was a full and high-born dinner table, and then say in a cold, clear voice: "Oh, Mr Walpole, I've had such an interesting letter from your father. Do you wear flannel next your skin?" At the end of the month he wrote to his mother:

The country is beautiful with great flat plains of intense green, with rows of silver birches and pine-forests on the horizon. I am quite settled down now and very comfortable and really get through a surprising amount of reading

[1] In *The Merry Wives of Westminster* (1946).

and writing. But I cannot say that I am quite at ease with the Countess yet. She says that I have never had any experience of women and that I'm going to learn now—she intends to educate me. The result is that every meal is a campaign. She starts "ragging" about something and I have to defend myself whilst the Fräuleins and Mademoiselles sit round. At first it was appalling, but I'm becoming accustomed to it now and I am sure that she is excellent for me. But one has to be very careful how one retorts so as to get the right border-line between being stupid and being offensive. She is, however, quite charming and one of the best women I have ever met in every sense of the word. The girls I know better now, but I am not quite at my ease with them either. Boys are so much simpler and I think fourteen is an awful age for anyone to be.

And two days later to Charles Marriott:

The garden is becoming beautiful in a wild rather uncouth kind of way, but it is a garden of trees rather than flowers. I get on excellently with the German tutor—he is a first-rate fellow and very clever. I understand the children better now, and the "April Baby," now a girl of thirteen with pigtails, is delicious. But girls are extraordinary things and seem to have no motives for doing anything. The Countess is a complete enigma. I don't see much of her but, when I do, she has three moods (1) Charming, like her books only more so (this does not appear often). (2) Ragging. Now she is unmerciful—attacks you on every side, goes at you until you are reduced to idiocy, and then drops you, limp. (3) Silence. This is most terrible of all. She sits absolutely mute and if one tries to speak one gets snubbed. She was like that at lunch today, and we all made shots in turn and got "settled." You see she is not an easy person to live with, but I'm sure there's a key somewhere which I hope to find. My novel is nearly half-finished. It is remarkably bad and I haven't the slightest hope of its ever getting anywhere. The people are so flabby that it makes one ill to look at them, and they were such splendid and interesting intimates when they were in my head—now that they are on paper they are distant and rather hostile acquaintances—isn't it sad? But it has shown me, really conclusively, that there is nothing in this whole world that I want to do so much. I'm going at it again and again until I get somewhere.

Finally, I should very much like your advice. Do you know a Literary Agency, Curtis Brown? There is a chance that they will offer me a job—somewhere about £100 a year at first. If they do I very much want to take it—it would be the first step on the ladder. But various elders and betters want me to schoolmaster. I feel as if schoolmastering is a grave out of which no man rises—they say I can slide into literature from it, but I believe it would take all the stuffing out of one—"there would be no spirit in me." I do want to start definitely soon. I don't know at all that Curtis Brown will make the offer but, if they do, I feel very inclined to take it.

Soon after this the Countess told him he was idle and sent him on a solitary walking-tour in the island of Rügen. He did not enjoy it, but an article he wrote on the expedition earned him his first literary reward —a guinea from the *Guardian*.

One day at the beginning of July, Hugh, desperately anxious to prove to the Countess both his literary powers and his sincerity of purpose, lent her his diary to read. When she gave it back to him, many of the entries were completed by postscripts in her distinctive hand. These criticisms, cruel in their penetration but described by their victim as "sufficiently true to be amusing," are here printed in italics.

May 27. Read more *En Route*, which interests me enormously. I have never understood the real spirit of the modern mystic so well before. *My French dictionary is, of course, an immense help.*

June 4. Gautier's "Balzac" in the *Portraits* a moddle of what such a thing should be. *Wish I were sure how to spell that. Rather fancy it should be on the lines of noddle and toddle. Shall write to the "Academy" and ask. They like letters about things like that in their correspondence columns. It IS a splendid paper!*

June 6. Spent a pleasant but idle evening over *The Serious Wooing*—"the tipsy cake of literature" someone says—very daintily done—but Oh! this novel-reading! *Must really give it up. My brain is mere whipped cream and jam.*

June 7. Got lost in the forest and finally appeared at Rieth where I discovered an extremely rustic inn. Nice fat landlord. *Wonder if he's going to be somebody I shall want to write to.*

June 20. Played tennis and won two sets. *See no point in mentioning the number of sets I didn't win.*

June 22. Played much tennis in the afternoon. The Countess doesn't like being beaten and I shall have to be careful. [This last sentence he carefully inked out, writing in the margin as a blind: "Silly rot. Nothing to do with Duranty." *"Nothing whatever to do with him,"* added the Countess, to whom the erased passage was as decipherable as it is today.]

June 26. Read *Madame Bovary* furiously and finished it! Oh! most wonderful! *The C. offended me by telling me she doesn't think Mdme. B. a good book for boys.*

And so the game went on, with his liking it less and less. "One is so ragged that the girls never dream of obeying if they don't want to. It has been the same with all the other tutors." But outwardly he managed to keep up a fairly good face, as witness this letter to Charles Marriott, dated June 11:

I have definitely decided to go in for schoolmastering next year unless something very tempting offers itself. The Countess is very much against the Curtis Brown idea, and the long holidays in schoolmastering are a great attraction—also I think I'd be very keen on it if only I could get out of it later on . . .

Meanwhile I'm a lucky youth, I consider, and life, at present, is rather too good to be true. The novel is now three-quarters finished, and even if it never gets anywhere I shall have learnt a lot by the writing of it. I've seen into the technique of the thing to a much larger extent than I had before. I'm not quite sure what to do when it's finished. I shall send it round a little for experience' sake. . . .

I'm getting a little disgusted with sitting in a garden and thinking; one is apt to be morbid and I think I'm falling too much under the Countess's thumb.

On July 2 he finished *Troy Hanneton*. It had become immensely long, and though he had himself little opinion of it, he decided to inflict it on the willing Arthur Benson. ("He will stagger when he sees the mass of it.") The Countess suddenly decided to take the children to England at the end of the month, and on the 22nd Hugh joyfully left Nassenheide, somewhat ashamed of feeling like a boy let out of school, and proceeded, partly by train and partly on foot, to Seeheim in Thuringia, which he reached a week later.

Hugh's relationship with Elizabeth, so inauspiciously begun, gradually developed into the longest-enduring and one of the firmest of all his friendships with women. She was forty-one when they first met, Hugh twenty-three; his subjection in the German Garden to that cruel wit, those imperious commands uttered in a shrill, piping voice, did him a great deal of good, and his fear—almost his dislike—of her quickly turned to warm and grateful affection. During the next years she wrote him many playful letters beginning "My dearest Jot" and ending "Your loving Tittle," but gradually a deeper note crept in. "I do love being with you," she wrote in 1921, "and laugh more I think with you than with anybody."

In 1926, when Hugh sent her the new edition of *The Golden Scarecrow*, she wrote to say that it had always been one of her favourites among his books, "nothing to do with being dedicated (invidiously, seeing its title) to me." She went on to say that she wished he had removed her German name from the new edition, and ended her letter: "I am for ever and ever your loving friend Elizabeth, née Beauchamp,[1] late Arnim, and now very unfortunately Russell."

"Yes, of course there's a bond between us," she wrote in 1930, "but I don't think it's either strange or mysterious—it's simply real affection." And again in 1932:

You can't think with what a maternal sort of pride I rejoice in your success—almost as though at Nassenheide I had mothered you, instead of taking you on to that garden seat and goading you like a small and impish fly. By the way, H. [her first husband] has been dead twenty-two solid years—which is more than can be said for most of us.

In 1937 Hugh wrote (in the only one of his letters which was found among her papers) to say that he felt about her exactly as he had always done, "the same affection, admiration, and consciousness of not behaving rightly in his diary." He had just been to a christening and added: "*I* should like to be *your* godson." To which Elizabeth replied:

Indeed I wish too that you were my godson, or any other sort of son. You are one of the few people I would like to be related to. And I believe you and I are two of the few people who are more often happy than unhappy, and say out loud that they are.

She died in 1941, only a few months before Hugh himself.

3

At Seeheim Hugh spent the next two months very happily, learning and reading German, often visiting the opera at Frankfurt and Mannheim and being bowled over by Wagner. "German literature fascinates me," he told Marriott; "it is so strong with such backbone—like a Cornish wind." In fact he enjoyed it all so much that he was unwilling to leave. "I feel," he told his mother, "like Ahasuerus the Wandering Jew—I never seem to stop anywhere. Could you send me some more tooth-powder?" He deliberately wrote nothing while he was there,

[1] Elizabeth was first cousin once removed to Katherine Mansfield, whose name was also Beauchamp. They both came from Australasia.

but was much encouraged by a "letter from A. C. B. re *Troy*. Very encouraging and criticism absolutely true—only not severe enough." Long afterwards he enjoyed thinking that Benson, like everyone else, had failed to appreciate him, but now he gratefully took the tactfully proffered advice, and *Troy Hanneton* was the only one of his manuscripts that he ever destroyed. In September he wrote to his parents on the occasion of their silver wedding, enclosing a somewhat lugubrious ode and a photograph of himself with a moustache. But soon his time was up, and on October 3 he arrived at Tours, the last stage of this year's pilgrimage.

He had become self-conscious about the shabbiness and inadequacy of his luggage, so to avoid the scorn of porters he sent it on by train in advance. It went by mistake to the South of France, did not reach him for a month, and eventually cost him a large sum in overweight. He was lodged in a glorified inn at Pont-Cler, some four miles from the centre of Tours, and here he lost no time in beginning a new novel about a Cornish family, then called *The House of the Trojans* but later published as *The Wooden Horse*. He arranged for two lessons a week with a professor in Tours, and in his spare time read Rousseau, Balzac, the Goncourts, Hugo, and Baudelaire. For local colour he found Henry James's *A Little Tour in France* delightful, he contributed a letter on German Literature to his beloved *Academy*, and derived some solace from discovering that William de Morgan had begun to publish novels, and successful ones too, at the age of sixty-seven.

Hugh made friends with a number of other young Englishmen, including the brothers Stanley and Harold Rubinstein, and with them engaged in fierce games of Rugby football against various local sides. "It is of course not good football," he told his mother. "They are extremely brutal, and bite and kick and pull your hair, but as a great many of them have beards one has an advantage." He reported also the presence of "a crowd of very stylish superior Etonians who refuse to have anything to do with the Englishmen." One of them was Duff Cooper, who writes:

I first met Hugh in the little house in the suburbs of Tours where he was writing his first book. There was a tennis court there. I and three other boys had come to play. We had changed into flannels. He was playing with the son of the house. They were in ordinary clothes and when he saw us Hugh had to pretend that they weren't playing but only knocking up, which considerably perplexed the poor young Frenchman, who was very keen on the score.

Despite this sartorial solecism, Hugh made friends with the Etonians, and very soon he had deserted the Rubinsteins, given up lessons and football, and moved into a *pension* in the centre of Tours. To explain this move, with its extra expense, to his mother, he had recourse to a local variant of the Truro "robers": "It was very disagreeable going back to Pont-Cler at midnight, as apaches abound and I should have had to buy a revolver. Also I shall now talk French at meals—a great advantage."

Thereafter his time at Tours was largely spent with his new friends, playing bridge, visiting châteaux, walking and talking and sitting in cafés. It is doubtful whether at this time any of his friends took his literary ambitions seriously. "The one thing our set was convinced about," writes Harold Rubinstein, "was that he would never make a novelist." But Hugh worked on steadily at *The Wooden Horse*, and when he returned to England in December three chapters were completed.

4

His first visit in London was to Mr Gabbitas, with whom he had been corresponding. All available vacancies for schoolmasters had been discussed between them and narrowed down to two, one at Epsom College, the other at Bristol Grammar School. Mr Gabbitas recommended Bristol, where Cyril Norwood was then headmaster, and it seems probable that if Hugh had taken this advice *Mr Perrin and Mr Traill* would never have been written. But Epsom had the supreme advantage of being within easy distance of London, and though Hugh pretended to prefer it because it was a Public School, its geographical position in fact tipped the scale. He visited Epsom, liked the look of it, found that a relation of his was a matron there, and wrote refusing the Bristol offer. He was to start at Epsom in January, teaching Classics and English in the lowest form, also more advanced work in one other subject, at a salary of £120 a year, rising to £150 with an ultimate pension.

The Christmas holidays were spent at Lambeth, reading, writing, going to theatres and concerts with Ethel Colburn Mayne; and on New Year's Eve he wrote to Duff Cooper one of those over-emphatic, rather pathetic letters, which so often broke off a budding friendship:

I've been thinking since we parted, and I see that you are one of the *very very* few acquaintances I possess who are going to be important to my well-being in the future. You will find, as the years pass, that we shall be essentially necessary to each other—intellectually—and therefore it irks me that we've got to pass such a long space before coming into close quarters again. This is by no means an affectionate statement, but it is so seldom that either of us will find anyone whose acquaintance is worth serious development that we must be up and doing when it does occur. Now that sounds egregiously self-satisfied—but we are both conceited, you know. All I mean is that you must correspond regularly this year and I will do the same—better letters than this is.

At the beginning of January Hugh spent a week with the Darwins at Dryburn. He read aloud the three chapters of *The Wooden Horse* to Mrs Darwin, and talked with her "about morals and literature—their relation—and whether she would still be my friend if I wrote what she thought an immoral book." This was the kind of question which all his life he loved to ask his friends. "If I were sent to prison for something disgraceful, then I should know who my real friends were," he would often say, or "If I were found to be a German spy, you wouldn't visit me in prison, would you?"

On 20 January 1908 he took up residence at Epsom. With the school itself he had at first little quarrel, though he disapproved strongly of compelling "poor little children to listen to the Litany before breakfast." Schoolmastering seemed to him an excellent profession provided one need not stay in it too long. The maintenance of discipline in class presented no problems, since, as he told his mother, "they all think I'm about fifty owing to my moustache."

"Both I myself and most of the people here," he told Duff Cooper, "are such ludicrous figures that one can't take it seriously—and then there comes a delicious hour with a golden fire and an aromatic pipe, when I can fling myself into my writing and forget altogether about boys." He had hoped to be able to devote an hour a day to *The Wooden Horse*, but this proved increasingly difficult. Even his diary becomes fragmentary hereabouts. A visit to hear *Götterdämmerung* in London only made him homesick for Germany: "I took a third-class ticket from Valhalla to Epsom."

At the beginning of March he wrote in jubilation to his mother: "I sent a part of the novel I'm writing to Marriott the other day, and he has written a most warm letter back saying that it contains the highest promise for my future success as a novelist." But soon he was longing for the end of term, since "perpetual talking gets on your nerves, and last night I was teaching in my sleep, to the considerable annoyance of the man next door." Also he had once more been disappointed in his quest for the ideal friend, thinking to have discovered him in one of the older masters and finding his hopes cruelly dashed. Besides failing to respond to Hugh's doubtless excessive protestations of friendship, his colleague thought nothing of the opening chapters of *The Wooden Horse* and told Hugh bluntly that whatever else he might be he was certainly not a novelist.

The Easter holidays were a refreshment and a delight to him. He spent almost the whole of April at St Ives in Cornwall, where Charles Marriott was then living, and he quickly became a favourite with the whole Marriott family, playing mixed hockey and romping with the children. Apart from the local colony of painters, a number of writers lived in the neighbourhood, and among those to whom Marriott introduced him were Havelock Ellis and his wife; Mrs Alfred Sidgwick the novelist; and most important of all, Samuel Jeyes, the literary editor of the morning *Standard*.

Charles Marriott's first impressions of Hugh in the flesh—this was their first meeting after more than a year's correspondence—were of "gleaming pince-nez and a chin, and the chin continues to dominate my further impressions of him, physically and psychologically." The pince-nez were replaced, some time after the first war, by horn-rimmed spectacles. Hugh's hair was brown, his complexion rosy; he was five foot ten and a half inches tall.

In the midst of so much friendliness and goodwill at St Ives he worked furiously at *The Wooden Horse*, and was soon able to write in his diary :

On the whole the best holidays that I have ever spent, because I did, I believe, more or less certainly find myself. As I said to Mrs Ellis, I believe I know exactly what it is that I want and how I mean to get it. My programme is to finish this novel, then short stories and articles, then another novel. Then as soon as I am really started, to chuck schooling. I learnt a very great deal last term. There is to be no giving of myself away, no thrusting of myself forward. My one aim is to teach decently and get the novel finished.

One other incident of the first importance took place during those Easter holidays. In London he met W. A. T. Ferris, a young Indian Army officer of about his own age, and began a friendship which was to last, although years often passed without their seeing each other, for the rest of his life. The meeting was so important for him at the time that he later tore out of his diary the four pages describing it—the only example of such discretion.

Back at Epsom for the summer term, Hugh stole every possible moment for *The Wooden Horse*, and at the end of May he wrote to tell his mother of its completion:

I am terribly depressed about it. I think it is very bad. . . . I am quite sure that it is wrong for me to go on with the schoolmastering longer than is absolutely necessary. It is not that I don't like it, but the writing gets a stronger grip on me every day and all my thoughts are centred on it—*that* isn't fair to the schoolmastering.

In fact, compared with the sprawling amateurishness of *Troy Hanneton*, *The Wooden Horse* was surprisingly shapely and competent—indeed professional. The completed manuscript was sent first to Marriott, who read it with the most painstaking care, suggested a number of improvements, and wrote: "Don't worry; the book is a lot better than you know. In all essentials it is a very good piece of work, and whatever defects there are in it are merely due to inexperience."

Ethel Colburn Mayne, its next critic, was equally kind and appreciative. At the end of a twelve-page letter full of constructive criticism she wrote: "Well, to sum up, undeniable talent it shows—quite undeniable. That construction and the variety of setting should come to you so easily is well for you. And the style will gain in beauty, as style always does. . . . For a first novel, it will very decidedly *do*."

Lastly he sent the manuscript to E. M. Forster, whom also he had got to know as a correspondent by writing him a "fan-letter." From him Hugh received five pages of sincere and searching criticism, beginning: "I can say without preamble that it's good," and proceeding: "You ought to get it taken all right—though of course one can't ever speak for certain about that."

Such reports only marshalled him the way that he was going, and on July 7 he wrote to his mother: "Anyhow I think that schoolmastering is a poor game. You can't go on your own lines, and it's all conventional tradition—obsolete and useless. I shall clear out of it at the end of the year."

Lest it be thought, however, that Hugh was a total failure as a teacher, here is a testimonial from one of his pupils, Mr F. W. Black:

I went to Epsom College in the summer term of 1908 and was placed in the second form of the Lower School. The form-master was Hugh Walpole. My memories of him are very vivid. He taught us to spell by what I maintain was one of the best methods tried—he started us at the beginning of the term on a certain page in our history-book, giving us ten lines to learn each day apart from all other work. Every morning we had ten words to write down, one wrong write out ten times, more than one the whole ten ten times. On Saturday mornings if we had behaved ourselves we had a mock battle on the large black-board—we learnt tactics and strategy thereby. Round this black-board hangs a tale. It was really a large slate board immediately behind the high chair on which Walpole sat: he had a habit of tilting his chair backwards so that the back of his head rested on this board. Now in those days Walpole greased his hair and a mark soon appeared on the board, to be known henceforth as Walpole, his Mark. It was there in 1916 when I left. Walpole was tallish, wore pince-nez and of course a mortar-board and gown, the former greasy from his smarmed down hair, the latter white with continual rubbing out of chalk.

And the unorthodox method of teaching which Hugh described in after years, while it may have been actuated by idleness or disinclination, was probably a great deal more effective than he imagined:

Rows of tousle-headed boys are waiting for a lesson in French grammar, and now I begin: "This morning I will tell you a story and you will deliver up to me next lesson a translation of this in your best French—A few years ago, on a dark and windy evening in Paris, a tall man, his face hidden in a black coat, might be observed passing swiftly down a side street——." [1]

This sort of thing came easily to the practised narrator of the Marlow dormitory, and much later in life, if one of his lectures had not lasted quite long enough, Hugh would say: "Will someone in the audience give me a word, and I will make up a story round it."

During the summer holidays he stayed with Arthur Benson, with Ferris, and with other friends. He also began a new novel. As a change from the conventional restraint of *The Wooden Horse*, he decided to indulge his romantic instinct in a daring battle between Good and Evil. And what could be more daring than to make the Devil his chief character? Such was the origin of *Maradick at Forty*. That he spelt it "Fourty" throughout was a symptom less of callow ignorance, as he was fond of asserting, than of a permanent inability to spell the commonest words. His publishers and their proof-readers became used to regulating all his spelling and punctuation, though occasionally, as happened with *The Apple Trees*, an unaccustomed publisher would let a shoal of anomalies through the net.

As soon as *Maradick* was under way, the manuscript of *The Wooden Horse*, improved by the suggestions of its three critics, was despatched to its first publisher. Anticipating a long series of refusals, Hugh determined to work steadily through the best firms, beginning at the top with the great house of Smith Elder, publishers of Thackeray and the Brontes, and to them it was accordingly sent.

All October he could settle to nothing. *Maradick* was set aside in favour of an historical novel about Napoleon; this in turn gave way to a school story on the lines of those that P. G. Wodehouse wrote for the *Captain* magazine; then *Maradick* was resumed. And all this time the debate on his future continued. Once again Dr Walpole showed himself wise and understanding, particularly when it is remembered that he had no reason to believe that Hugh would ever make good as a writer. On November 3 he wrote:

My dear Hugh,
    Mother has just sent me on your letter with A.C.B.'s. I quite agree with him and though I should have preferred your having the background

[1] *Reading : An Essay* (1926).

of teaching with its healthy life and certain income, I was beginning to feel as you have felt, that it was rather hard on the teaching to play second fiddle. This step was inevitable though it has come sooner than I expected and, I may add, hoped. I don't think I fear your not getting enough to live upon—it will be moderate at any rate, and for a time perhaps only a bare sufficiency, but I expect it will be that. My fear rather is about the effect of the racket and interest of London life on your health. You will be in danger of turning night into day, getting no regular exercise, only insufficient sleep, and perhaps not enough of the solid kind of food to keep your body going. And though you will be rested in having but the one thing to do, it will take more out of you. Do think of that side. And you won't mind your old father mentioning another. If anything is true at all, it is that the exercise of the Christian Faith keeps a man's judgment sound, wholesome and uplifting. I am quite sure you will never write anything that is not healthy, strong and stimulating, but the world is a very fascinating suitor to those engaged in literature, and so many men and women fall below the expectations that were rightly formed of them when they began, that I can't help being a bit anxious. Our kinsman Horace is a very bad example of what I mean. He knew the world very well but knew nothing else.

I do wish you with all my heart God speed and hope there may always be enough margin to prevent your being a pot-boiler.

Always your loving Father,
G. H. S. Walpole.

A week later Hugh took the plunge:

My dearest Parents,

I have just written to the Headmaster tendering my resignation, which I have no doubt he will gratefully accept. I'm afraid this has been preparing for some time, but I hadn't told you anything until I was quite sure.

I have been offered a kind of flying commission by the London Literary Agency (Curtis Brown) commencing at £2 a week. I am to suggest books, discover new authors and arrange terms. I am to be given plenty of spare time. If I stick at it the pay is to increase. I am also to review regularly for the *Literary World* and the *Bookman*. I have made a new friend, Ransome, who is one of the biggest men there are just now, and he has promised me as much critical work as I like. Also Jeyes of the *Standard* will help me. Also the Napoleon book is practically certain. Also the novel is in the last selection and the Agency have asked to take any work that I have. Also Gabbitas assures me he can get an hour or two's coaching a week if I want it. Also I shall start in the summer on the Extension Lectures.

I shall start with nearly £60 in hand and no bills. If I fail altogether I can go back to mastering. Everyone advises me to do it, and I have not the slightest doubt that the time has come. The present position is impossible, and now it seems to me unnecessary. I hope you won't feel badly about it, but it is a case in which a man must decide for himself, and I have no doubt that it is the right thing. I will try and come and see you as soon as I can—this week if possible.

I have had some wonderful little dinners this week. Marriott has been in town and we have had great times.

Write soon,
Yr loving
Hugh.

Arthur Ransome would have been amused to read this letter, since at the time he was almost as struggling and unknown as its author. The editors of the *Literary World* and the *Bookman* would have been equally astonished.

But before Hugh shook off the dust of Epsom he made another move in the game of Writing to Authors. Greatly daring, and with some introductory assistance from Arthur Benson, he sent a letter to Henry James, and from Lamb House, Rye, came an answer, the first of many, many letters in that thick black writing; tender, affectionate, cautionary, elaborate, gossipy letters that no one else could have written. Small wonder that when Hugh came home for Christmas 1908 he felt that magic casements were about to open.

BOOK TWO

THE HUMAN MAZE

Clearly *you* move still in the human maze—but I like to think of
you there; may it be long before you find the clue to the exit.

                              Henry James to Hugh Walpole
                                        14 August 1912.

CHAPTER FIVE

THE THRESHOLD OF FICTIVE ART

I

SUCCESS, which ruins many, is for others the natural food on which they thrive. Hugh was one of these. Until the day, 1 February 1909, when he set up on his own in London to be a writer, he had succeeded in nothing. School, university, the Mersey Mission, tutoring, schoolmastering, even writing itself—all these had found him wanting, had indeed at times reduced him to a figure of fun. Only the visionary gleam had persisted, the unquenchable, irrational conviction that he had been born to write a masterpiece; this alone had brought him to the edge of that literary world which he so longed to enter.

It is perhaps worth while to consider what kind of world it was, and who were its leading figures. Meredith and Swinburne were at the end of their lives; Kipling had done his best work; Hardy had just completed his masterpiece *The Dynasts*; Henry James, having wrestled with the revisions and prefaces for the great New York Edition of his works, was bemoaning the public's indifference to it. Conrad had produced no novel since *The Secret Agent* (1907); George Moore was working on his autobiographical trilogy *Hail and Farewell* (1911–14). Of the younger men, Arnold Bennett had published *The Old Wives' Tale* in 1908 and so stepped up into line with H. G. Wells, whose fantastic romances were now giving place to *Kipps* (1905) and *Tono-Bungay* (1909). John Galsworthy's first Forsyte novel *The Man of Property* had appeared in 1906; Chesterton and Belloc were in the heyday of their liberal versatility; Shaw, Granville Barker, and Barrie held the stage; Ford Madox Hueffer had just begun to edit the *English Review*. It was a time of great literary activity, the Edwardian culmination of the age of plenty.

Hugh was convinced that if only he could gain a foothold in this world, be granted some initial success however small, he would never look back. And he was right. If the year 1909 may be described as his *annus mirabilis*, the February of that year was certainly the most exciting month of his life. On the 1st he moved into a room at No. 20 Glebe Place, Chelsea, for which he paid the absurdly low rent of four shillings a week; on the same day he started part-time work with Curtis Brown at a salary of two pounds a week; on the 13th *The Wooden Horse* was accepted by Smith Elder; a week later he was given the regular job of reviewing novels for the *Standard* at a salary of three pounds a week; and on the 28th he dined alone with Henry James at the Reform Club.

On the evening when the letter announcing Smith Elder's decision arrived at Glebe Place, Hugh, wild with excitement, rushed out to a restaurant on the embankment called The Good Intent. Never before had he dared to mingle with the artists who sat there at a large central table, but now he loudly told them of his good fortune, ordered wine, and called on them to drink his health. Next morning he hurried over the river to Lambeth to break the good news to his family. It was one of his proudest moments.

The engagement with Curtis Brown was less successful, savouring more of his earlier failures with their attendant scenes of comedy. He was engaged by Curtis Brown's partner, Hughes Massie, a large, vague, kindly American "like a pale bolster," but the scope of his duties was never exactly defined, and for some time he hung about the office with little to do. Eventually in desperation Massie set him to work on the preparation of a book to be called *Careers for Young Men*. This was to be assembled partly by the collection of facts from encyclopædias, and partly by soliciting the first-hand opinions of successful people. There was certainly a gentle irony in this juxtaposition of Facts (which Hugh had never been able to master) and Careers (when his own seemed so problematical). A list of suitable celebrities was compiled, including the Bishop of London, Eugene Sandow, Arthur Collins of Drury Lane, Hall Caine, the head of Marshall & Snelgrove, and a well-known writer on cricket ("I cannot today," wrote Hugh in 1931, "hear their names without a shudder"). The last of these, perhaps as being the least intimidating, was tackled first.

I knew nothing about cricket and, I fear, cared nothing. My Celebrity had not, to do him justice, any desire to impress me. He wished only to be rid of me. When I asked him the steps that anyone should take if he wished to write about cricket he looked at me, I remember, with complete blankness.

"The steps?" he asked. "The steps?"

"Yes," I stammered. "For a Career . . . how should one begin?"

"My God!" he cried, "I don't know. It isn't a Career. It's a bloody bore." [1]

Thus ended the only interview which Hugh ever conducted, since rather than face the rest of his celebrities, he parted amicably from Massie and determined to rely on writing and reviewing for his livelihood.

The post on the *Standard* was the result of a series of lucky accidents. Charles Marriott had introduced him to Samuel Jeyes. Jeyes asked Hugh to luncheon, and out of the kindness of his heart gave him one or two novels to review. Hugh took great pains with his article, but when it was finished he knew it was no good. Happening to meet Ethel Colburn Mayne in the Reading Room of the British Museum, he asked her opinion. She took him out to a tea-shop, read what he had written, and then asked him what he really thought of the books. He told her at some length, and she advised him to tear up his stilted notice and to go home and re-write it exactly as though he were talking to her. He had the sense to take her advice, and the lesson was invaluable. Thereafter many of his early reviews contained elements of that ferocity with which the young are apt to castigate their elders, and it was this lively spirit of attack which prompted Jeyes to give the regular novel-reviewing to one who in his middle years was so often to be accused of over-kindness. Hugh reviewed novels for the *Standard* for the next four years.

But above and overshadowing all these excitements was the first meeting with Henry James. They had already exchanged several letters by which, and from what Benson had told him, the Old Master, oppressed by illness and lack of recognition, was to some extent prepared for the mixture of enthusiasm, ambition, and youthful hero-worship which he was to encounter. He had already urged Hugh to hurl himself into "the deep sea of journalism," counselled him "above all keep as tight hold as you can of the temper and the faith of your almost unbearably enviable youth," and asked for more letters: "I have been writing letters for a hundred years—while you bleat and

[1] *The Apple Trees* (1932).

jump like a white lambkin on the vast epistolary green which stretches before you co-extensive with life."

Nor did he fail to warn his young friend of the meagre rewards of the artist:

I don't want to scare you, but I've never made Letters particularly or even very conveniently "pay"—and indeed I hate to talk about that side of them. It's an excellent side in itself, but any view of it should be kept in a totally distinct compartment of the mind from the view of the loved objects in themselves.

Their first meeting is recorded only by Hugh's brief diary note:

Dined with Henry James alone at the Reform Club. He was perfectly wonderful. By far the greatest man I have ever met—and yet amazingly humble and affectionate—absolutely delightful. He talked about himself and his books a good deal and said some very interesting things. It was a wonderful evening.

Towards the end of March, Hugh spent a short holiday motoring with Arthur Benson in the Midlands. Although it rained almost incessantly, and Benson was suffering from one of his recurrent fits of depression, Hugh enjoyed it all immensely, reading and reviewing novels as he went, working on *Maradick*, and correcting the proofs of *The Wooden Horse*. But there was better to come—an invitation from James to spend an April week-end at Rye, though

. . . you'll have with me in every way much shorter commons, much sterner fare, much less purple and fine linen, and in short a much more constant reminder of your mortality than while you loll in A. C. B.'s chariot of fire. . . . I am tenderhearted enough to be capable of shedding tears of pity and sympathy over young Hugh on the threshold of fictive art—and with the long and awful vista of large production in a largely producing world before him. Ah, dear young Hugh, it will be very grim for you with your faithful and dismal friend Henry James.

As far as it concerned literary production the prophecy was not without point, yet the week-end was anything but grim. In his diary for April 26 Hugh wrote:

Spent a wonderful week-end with Henry James. Much more wonderful than I had expected. I am very lucky in my friends. The house and garden are exactly suited to him. He is beyond words. I cannot speak about him.

And in answer to Hugh's bread-and-butter letter, to which doubtless was added a modicum of jam, James sent an affectionate note in which he suggested that Hugh should address him for the present as "Très-cher Maître" or "My very dear Master." This injunction was always strictly obeyed, though in the privacy of his diary, and proudly in letters to his family, Hugh boldly made mention of "Henry."

On May 14, exactly three months after its acceptance, *The Wooden Horse* was published, with a dedication to Ferris. The agreement with Smith Elder was not a very favourable one: no royalty was paid on the first eight hundred copies, and since the first edition (a thousand copies with an additional five hundred for the colonies) was not exhausted for many years, it is not surprising that Hugh's total receipts from it just paid his typist's bill. But the book achieved other results, more precious to him just then than money—reviews and letters, talk and praise, which launched him expeditiously on his long career of authorship. One of the advance copies was sent to Henry James: his criticism has perished, but it seems that he treated the work with something less than the tenderly ruthless analysis which he meted out to its successors.

The reviews were copious and on the whole encouraging. *The Times Literary Supplement* dismissed the book in five lines with: "It is a story of some merit, but the title, with its references to Greek and Trojan, seems rather a foolish one;" the *Outlook* praised the Cornish scenes and atmosphere but declared the book inferior to J. C. Snaith's *Broke of Covenden*; qualified praise was bestowed by *Punch*, the *Morning Post*, the *Observer*, and the *Guardian*; while it was left to the pseudonymous reviewer of the *Stirling Sentinel* to declare: "If we don't hear a good deal more of Mr Hugh Walpole, then my name isn't Orion." To Hugh's delight much the longest and most appreciative notice appeared in his favourite *Academy*, whose critic "could not wish a single passage altered or a word varied."

All this provided a sufficient beach-head for his invasion of London. His engagement-book did not yet resemble the palimpsest of later years, but there was no lack of new plays, new books, new friends. "I simply worshipped men of letters and went for them direct as a kitten gocs to a saucer of milk." [1] Invitations from Henry James grew more exciting, morc elaborate. Here is one dated June 16 and written from the Reform Club:

As the case stands, are you by any chance free on *Friday p.m.*—day after tomorrow? And in that case will you dine with me in some loose wild way —less ponderously than here? I find Eustace Miles [2] very favourable to my health—will you on said Friday meet me *there* at 8 o'clock?—after which we can perhaps do something else, though I think there is nothing so friendly as perhaps for you to come back here and mildly smoke in our big cool gallery.

Hugh's diary for this period is scrappy, but there are glimpses of him in the correspondence of James, who on June 5 wrote to Arthur Benson:

It isn't only that I owe you a letter, but that I have exceedingly wanted to write it—ever since I began (too many weeks ago) to feel the value of the gift that you lately made me in the form of the acquaintance of delightful and interesting young Hugh Walpole. He has been down to see me in the country, and I have had renewed opportunities of him in town—the result of which is that, touched as I am with his beautiful candour of appreciation of my "feeble efforts," etc., I feel for him the tenderest sympathy and an absolute affection. I am in general almost—or very often—sorry for the intensely young, intensely confident and intensely ingenuous and generous— but I somehow don't pity *him*, for I think he has some gift to conciliate the Fates. I feel him at any rate an admirable young friend, of the openest mind and most attaching nature, and anything I can ever do to help or enlighten, to guard or guide or comfort him, I shall do with particular satisfaction, and with a lively sense of being indebted to you for the interesting occasion of it. [3]

And again on July 24:

You mustn't think I shall keep always "thanking" you for Hugh Walpole; but I must do so at least this once again. . . . We have become fast friends; I am infinitely touched by his sympathy and charmed by his gifts (not the least marked of his merits being his affection for you); and I wish him no end of ardent existence—feeling as I do that he can handsomely and gallantly carry it. [4]

[1] *The Crystal Box* (1924).
[2] The leading vegetarian restaurant of the day.
[3] *The Letters of Henry James* (1920), vol II, from which this text is taken.
[4] *Henry James: Letters to A. C. Benson and Auguste Monod* (1930), from which this text is taken.

At the beginning of August Hugh set out on a round of country-house visits. Among others he stayed with the Darwins at Dryburn and with Lady Lovelace (to whom James had introduced him) at Ashley Combe, near Porlock in Somerset.

Mary Caroline, Countess of Lovelace, was a lady of great wealth and some idiosyncrasy. Born a Stuart-Wortley, great-granddaughter of the first Lord Wharncliffe, she was now the childless widow of Byron's grandson, and a great hostess. Ashley Combe was used only in the summer and she lived mostly at Ockham Park in Surrey.

Ockham (which has since been burned down) had been a beautiful old house, until it was "improved" by Lady Lovelace, who was a fervent admirer of William Morris. She was a fanatical opponent of smoking, which at Ockham was permitted only in one dismal smoking-room, and not even in the garden if the hostess was in sight. She also believed that the land was being ruined by too many drains, and refused to have any at Ockham. Earth closets were the rule, and hip-baths in bedrooms, with hosts of servants to fetch and carry. Whenever she considered the weather to be fine enough, her house-party would dine on a stone-flagged terrace outside the house. Food and drink were superlatively good, but the diners were often perished with cold or beset by midges and moths.

Hugh was enchanted by Ashley Combe, "the most beautiful house I've ever stayed in, built into the forest on the side of the hill with the sea at the bottom. The gardens are laid out wonderfully." He reported his doings to Henry James, who was moved to answer:

Right you are, through the thick or the thin of it, to lead your multitudinous life and keep bounding through the hoops of your apparently perpetual circus. Great must be your glories and triumphs and rounds of applause, and I break into solitary clapping here, late in the sultry night, when I hear of your lawn tennis greatness. It all sounds awfully hot and brave and unmorbid and objective—keep it up, to my fond vision, therefore, as long as you can stand it. I can do my own alembications—*you* must do my gymnastics.

Perhaps this last phrase, more than any other, sums up the relationship between the two men.

By the middle of September Hugh was back in Chelsea, with

Maradick three-quarters finished, and immediately he plunged once more into the round of amusements—a party at Glebe Place where Henry James was introduced to Ethel Mayne, Marriott, and others of Hugh's early benefactors; luncheon-parties; many promenade concerts; and, as always, theatre-going.

With James and the American novelist W. D. Howells he went to see a detective play called *Arsène Lupin*. The Master was seldom a satisfied playgoer and would often leave at the end of the second act, announcing loudly that the play was "imbecile rot." On this occasion he "lasted to the end, indeed, but left then in a tempest of fury, the rest of us huddling behind. Only, in the foyer, Howells pressed my arm, and whispered: 'Never mind. Don't tell him—but we *did* enjoy it, didn't we?' " [1] It seems unlikely that James was any more pleased by Pinero's *Mid-Channel*, which he and Hugh saw together a few days later.

There followed a blissful week at Lamb House, whence Hugh wrote:

Dearest Mother,

A very little line so that you shouldn't think that I'd disappeared altogether into some mysterious limbo, never to emerge. H. J. wants me to stay here more or less indefinitely—but I shall have to come back to town tomorrow and perhaps will return here later.

We have had some extraordinary talks. You can imagine what it must be to hear all about Thackeray, Stevenson, Dickens, Carlyle and the rest intimately from first hand. And then all his talk about the Novel and his own things is quite amazing. It is a wonderful thing for me and will of course alter my whole life. He is, I think, a really great man. The honour is all the greater as Mrs Prothero, wife of the editor of the *Quarterly*, told me yesterday that I am now supposed to have more influence over him than anyone, and say things to him that no one else can—and so I get given messages to give *him* and act the diplomatist. He wants to come to tea at Lambeth and see all of you. I'm sure you would love him.

You'll all be interested to know that *Maradick* was finished on Monday. I feel curiously lost without it.

I'll see you soon I hope.

Love to all,
Yr. loving
Hugh.

[1] *The Apple Trees* (1932).

In London new friends and fresh experiences came thick and fast. He was captivated by the charm, wit, and kindness of Robert Ross; a dinner-party, given for him at the Reform Club, was attended by, among others, Ross, Max Beerbohm, H. G. Wells, Arthur Clutton-Brock, Thomas Seccombe, Reginald Turner, and young Harold Nicolson, just down from Oxford. No wonder Hugh was able to confide to his diary: "My good fortune continues to make me gasp with surprise—it is all like a fairy-tale. I suddenly find that I have *everything* that I want." Nor do these words seem exaggerated in the light of the obscure failure of a year before.

His engagement book also mentions Duff Cooper, Neville Lytton, Mrs W. K. Clifford, Violet Hunt, Edward Marsh, Desmond Coke, and E. F. Benson; but Robert Ross was the bright star of the moment, and this friendship even survived Hugh's reading the whole of *Maradick* aloud to his new friend, though Ross "only cared for bits" of it. Inspired by this qualified praise Hugh began a new novel called *The Crabtree*, intended to be the first book of a trilogy, "tracing a man's development under the three great formative impulses—Heredity, Love, and Ambition," but though he spent six months on its opening chapters, he gladly put it aside next summer in favour of a more compelling subject.

On December 8 he sat in a box at the Haymarket Theatre with Henry James and Maurice Maeterlinck, watching the first performance in England of *The Blue Bird*. In the interval Herbert Trench, the manager of the theatre, invited them behind the scenes. Through the open door of a dressing-room Hugh caught sight of a number of middle-aged and elderly dwarfs busily shaving. He asked who they were and Trench answered: "Oh, they're the unborn babies in the next act."

And so this incredible year of 1909 ended in a whirl of work and social occasions. For the *Standard* Hugh compiled an ample Christmas Books supplement, besides trying his hand at dramatic criticism. He was even courted by publishers, and again Henry James was present with advice:

The way the very publishers dandle you on their bloated knee, each wishing to make the rosy Babe crow and kick for *him*, is a phenomenon indeed uncanny in its sort. (Don't attempt too precipitately to feed on the arid bosom of *Heinemann*, let me interpose—with whom I've had an experience—a very long one—beggaring belief; but don't either, please, quote me as the source of that warning.)

Christmas was spent with his family at Lambeth, whither James sent fervent greetings and a cheque for five pounds, "to help you to some small convenient object." To Hugh's protestations of devotion the old man answered:

I am deeply moved by your word to the effect that you will "love me till you die"; it gives me so beautiful a guarantee of a certain measurable resistance to pure earthly extinction. Yes, I want that to happen.

And so it did.

2

At the beginning of 1910 Hugh began once again to devote to each day a whole page of his diary, so that his progress can be observed in greater detail. The year began well with "a most interesting luncheon party—Mrs Clifford, Ethel Dilke, Rhoda Broughton, Lilian Braithwaite, A. E. W. Mason, and Sidney Lee. Talked to the latter most of the time and he eventually asked me to dinner." Hugh has so often been accused of furthering his literary career by other than literary means, of choosing his friends for their usefulness to him, and of sloughing them off when they had ceased to be valuable, that it may be timely to discuss the question here, in the light of a contemporary incident. Charles Marriott writes:

Not long after we settled in London [in 1909] Hugh had engaged to dine with us but threw us over for an invitation from old Lady Lovelace, explaining quite frankly that she would be of more use to him in that stage of his career as a writer. Personally I was not scandalized; given Hugh's temperament, his determination to get on, and his uncertain position at the time, his desertion seemed to me at least logical, and what interested me most was Hugh's candour and his apparent inability to see why it should have given offence; but it upset the feminine part of my family a good deal.

All through his life Hugh retained a great deal of the child in his nature, both inwardly and on the surface. The child's impulsiveness, generosity, uninhibited lack of conversational discretion, and above all enjoyment, of beautiful things, little things, everything—all these were his: all these combined to make him the most enchanting of companions. But he possessed also many of the child's simplest faults: abnormally sensitive himself, he would frequently trample with jovial disregard on the susceptibilities of others; often, with little or no reason, he would suddenly fly into a passion of rage, which usually spent itself swiftly, to be at once dismissed from his memory: and always, always, more than anything else, he wanted everyone to love him.

Endowed with these characteristics, and bursting suddenly on to the London scene at a very young twenty-five, after a miserable adolescence, he was undoubtedly guilty of many such actions as that described by Marriott. Some of the people he dropped in this way—and ironically enough old Lady Lovelace was later one of them—were naturally very hurt and angry, but Hugh was too excited to notice. Of course he wanted to be a success: most people do. But to argue from this that the whole of his life was based on a carefully worked out plan of self-advancement, and all his literary reputation on the puffing of his friends, is nonsense. He went to parties primarily because he loved them. He lectured, partly no doubt because it was profitable and good for sales, but chiefly because he enjoyed it hugely: he was a natural speaker, and people usually like doing the things they do well. And who will seriously maintain that the tens of thousands of people, increasing steadily to hundreds of thousands, who read his books all over the world did so for any other reason save that they enjoyed them?

3

At a dinner party in January 1910 Hugh met for the first time Mrs Belloc Lowndes, the novelist sister of Hilaire Belloc. She and Hugh were alike in many ways: both were fluent and amusingly indiscreet talkers; they shared an inexhaustible appetite for life and letters; they both worked hard at their writing. They took to each other at sight, and later Hugh drew her portrait with loving accuracy as Mrs Launce in *Fortitude*.

John Buchan was another new friend who promised well, but the person who most took Hugh's fancy was an American named Arthur

Fowler whom he met staying with friends in the country. Fowler said he was travelling to Lausanne in a few days' time and Hugh impulsively decided to accompany him.

Leaving his new friend after a week, Hugh went on alone and spent a few magical days in Venice, in exploration and wonder. (The subsequent visit to Rome, so plausibly described in *Roman Fountain*, was imaginary.) Back in London, he was surprised to find himself in danger of dismissal from the *Standard*. Jeyes was extremely annoyed at his having gone abroad without warning, and a sharp rebuke brought him back to his reviewing with renewed determination.

In March the number of his friends was importantly increased. The entry in Arnold Bennett's journal reads: "Tea at Rumpelmayers. Mrs Lowndes. Met a young novelist named Walpole. Stayed there fighting against the band of music till 6.15;" while Hugh was content to describe Bennett as "quite amusing, with a funny French wife—more the author of *The Glimpse* than *The Old Wives' Tale*."

Bennett was by now an established literary figure, in a position to bestow on his young friend a great deal of friendly advice and practical help. Both he and H. G. Wells, of whom Hugh saw something at this time, always addressed him as "Hughie" and referred to him as "the child." Edmund Gosse, too, took a fatherly interest in him and suggested that he should do some regular secretarial work for Lord Stanmore [1] in the House of Lords. He visited Stanmore; it was arranged that Hugh should assist in sorting and arranging the papers of his employer's father, Lord Aberdeen, and at the end of April he started work.

That same week *Maradick at Forty* was published by Smith Elder. The edition again consisted of one thousand copies (with an extra four hundred for the colonies), but this time a second impression of six hundred copies was called for in the autumn, and a third of five hundred in 1911, though this was not exhausted for eight years. Arthur Benson

---

[1] Arthur Charles Hamilton-Gordon, first Baron Stanmore (1829-1912), youngest son of the fourth Earl of Aberdeen, had been a Liberal Member of Parliament, private secretary to two Prime Ministers (his father and Mr Gladstone), and Governor, consecutively, of New Brunswick, Trinidad, Mauritius, Fiji, New Zealand, and Ceylon. His friend Charles Kingsley stayed with him in Trinidad, and wrote a book about his visit called *At Last*, which he dedicated to his host.

wrote appreciatively of the book's "great movement of emotion and force," and claimed "a not unnatural sympathy with the heavy and chilly man [in the story] who writes pretentious essays in the *Cornhill*!" Reviews were again lengthy, and for the most part favourable. Robert Ross, writing anonymously in the *Morning Post*, declared the book to be a great advance on *The Wooden Horse*. He complained of too much scenery, "moreover it is drop scenery," but continued: "There is every indication that he is to become an interesting and delightful novelist, for he is endowed with unusual imaginative gifts, not quite so wholesome as he fancies them to be." This last remark must have particularly delighted Hugh.

The Times admitted that he "writes beautifully if a little too finely," while condemning him magisterially for having "no clear idea of the difference of the respective functions of comedy and melodrama," and doubting "whether he really knows how men think and feel at forty." The *Spectator* gave the book a whole patronising column, while his own paper, the *Standard*, in an equally long notice, maintained that "the writing, somewhat in the manner of a certain master of involved phrase, is always careful and sometimes a little laboured." The reference must be to Henry James, though today *Maradick* could not possibly be called Jamesian, and certainly it did not appear so at the time to the Master himself, who on May 13 wrote to Hugh:

I "read," in a manner, "Maradick"—but there's too much to say about it, and even my weakness doesn't alter me from the grim and battered old *critical* critic—no *other* such creature among all the "reviewers" do I meanwhile behold. Your book has a great sense and love of life—but seems to me very nearly as irreflectively juvenile as the Trojans, and to have the prime defect of your having gone into a subject—i.e. the marital, sexual, bedroom relations of M. and his wife—the literary man and his wife—since these *are* the key to the whole situation—which have to be tackled and faced to mean anything. You don't tackle and face them—you *can't*. Also the whole thing is a monument to the abuse of voluminous dialogue, the absence of a plan of composition, alternation, distribution, structure, and other phases of presentation than the dialogue—so that *line* (the only thing *I* value in a fiction etc.) is replaced by a vast formless featherbediness—billows in which one sinks and is lost. And yet it's all so loveable—though not so *written*. It isn't written *at all*, darling Hugh—by which I mean you have—or, truly, only in a few places, as in Maradick's dive—never got expression *tight* and in close quarters (of discrimination, of specification) with its subject. It remains loose and far. And you have never made out, recognised, nor stuck to, the *centre of your subject*.

Many young writers would have quailed before such devastating strictures, but for Hugh they were spurs to fresh endeavour, and almost immediately he set aside the unfortunate *Crabtree* in favour of an insistent story based upon his schoolmastering experiences at Epsom: "I never knew an impulse to do something so strong."

I was walking one afternoon towards Sloane Square, where I was going to occupy a seat in the gallery of the Court Theatre, as I did regularly once a week in order to enjoy play after play of the Barker-Vedrenne management. I was in the very middle of the King's Road when I suddenly saw Mr. Perrin staring at me. By the time that I had reached the Court Theatre, a brief five minutes, the whole of the story was outlined in my mind. It sprang into reality from the Umbrella incident which had actually occurred. . . . While the young, buoyant, vital Mr. Traill was what I would have liked to be, the tortured, half-maddened Mr. Perrin was what I thought I was. As a matter of fact, of course, I was neither.[1]

As a matter of fact he was both.

The book's title began as *The Umbrella*, quickly changed to *The Brown Hill*, then to *Green-Apple Orchard*, and finally settled as *Mr Perrin and Mr Traill*. The first three chapters were written in four days, and for a month he drove ahead at every opportunity: "Worked at the House of Lords pretty hard—mainly at *Perrin* when it ought to have been Stanmore." Then, at the end of June, his purpose wavered and he spent the month of July starting yet another abortive novel, to be called *The Edition de Luxe*, dealing with the old age and death of Henry Galleon, a great novelist.

But now there appeared in Hugh's life the next claimant to the position of ideal friend. This was Percy Anderson, artist and designer of stage costumes, then aged fifty-nine. He had dressed the original Gilbert and Sullivan operas from *The Yeomen of the Guard* onwards, and also revivals of the earlier ones, as well as many of Beerbohm Tree's Shakespearean productions and a large number of other plays, including Henry James's ill-fated *Guy Domville*. His water-colour

[1] Preface to the Everyman Library edition (1935).

portrait of Coquelin is now in the Louvre, that of Conrad in the
National Portrait Gallery. "He has all the knowledge and reminiscence
of his age," wrote Hugh, "and at the same time he doesn't seem in the
very least bit old. Anyhow he wants somebody and I want somebody,
so that's all right."

On May 12, through the kindness of Mrs W. K. Clifford, occurred
Hugh's only conversation with one of the greatest of English writers:

Tea with Thomas Hardy—a little nutcracker faded man with a wistful
smile and a soft voice. Talked about the dramatisation of his books. Nice
about *Maradick*.[1]

During the summer Hugh stayed with many friends, including
Arthur Benson, Percy Anderson, and Lady Lovelace. *Mr Perrin*, taken
up again with renewed enthusiasm at the end of July, was finished at
Ashley Combe on September 4; in writing-time it had occupied exactly
two months.

A fortnight later Hugh paid his first visit to his family's new home at
No. 1 Eglinton Crescent, Edinburgh. Dr Walpole had been elected to
the bishopric of Edinburgh in May, and Hugh had written: "I am immensely proud of being your son and I know that you will make a
splendid Bishop—it is what you ought to have been long ago." Now
he was "thrilled" to hear his father preach in St Mary's Cathedral, and
to explore with him the romantic strongholds of Holyrood and the
Castle. They also made a pious pilgrimage to Abbotsford, "talking
religion all the way there and back."

On Hugh's return to London, the second impression of *Maradick*
encouraged him to take a further room at Glebe Place, and also to
change his publisher. Messrs Mills & Boon were willing to pay an
advance of £100 on account of royalties for his next novel. The first
two had earned him almost nothing, and this handsome offer was
accepted with alacrity, though he feared his new publishers would not
care for *Mr Perrin* when they saw it.

His social life continued at a great pace. Henry James had in July
left for what was to prove his last visit to America, where the death of
his beloved brother William upset him terribly and prolonged his stay.

[1] It is amusing to compare this contemporary note with the entertaining but wholly
inaccurate account of the meeting which Hugh published in *The Apple Trees* (1932).

But there were plenty of others ready to help along the coming novelist. Mrs Belloc Lowndes increased her benefactions by introducing him to Theodore and Ethel McKenna, who were to become respectively his lawyer and one of his closest and dearest women friends. Mr Pooter, too, turned up again once or twice:

Nov. 26. Lost my bag with my dress clothes on a motor bus—most annoying.
Dec. 19. Fell down in Tottenham Court Road, nearly killed by a taxi and lost one of Stanmore's books.

Christmas was spent with his family in Edinburgh, and during the last week of the year he contracted two habits which he was to maintain almost without a break until the end of his life. One was the habit of beginning his novels, whenever possible, in Edinburgh on Christmas Eve. Even when he was not ready to start writing the book, or knew that he could not continue it for months, he would nevertheless write out the title-page, list of contents, and the first pages of Chapter One. Thirteen of his novels were started in this way, and the series began on 24 December 1910, when he wrote down: *Fortitude, being a true and faithful account of the education of an explorer, by Hugh Walpole*, and followed it with the opening words, later so often quoted with admiration or derision that he wished he had never written them: " 'Tisn't life that matters! 'Tis the courage you bring to it."

The other new habit was that of adding at the end of each year's diary a list of his leading friends in order of merit. This first one is headed "List of Worthy Persons," with Ferris, Ross, and Fowler occupying the leading places, and Henry James lying fourth. In succeeding years the names were in two groups headed "First Fifteen" and "Second Thirty," and each was followed by a figure, representing with varying inaccuracy the number of years which the particular friendship had endured. Many who fancied themselves among his favourites would have been chagrined to discover that a casual word or an ill-considered action had relegated them to the second division.[1]

---

[1] Mr Geoffrey Faber tells me that Benjamin Jowett also kept lists of his friends in his notebooks. So did Lady Tippins in *Our Mutual Friend*: "She keeps a little list of her lovers, and she is always booking a new lover, or striking out an old lover, or putting a lover in her black list, or promoting a lover to her blue list, or adding up her lovers, or otherwise posting her book."

CHAPTER SIX

COLLECTOR OF PEOPLE

I

THE arrival of the year 1911 found *Fortitude* flowing strongly from Hugh's pen: four chapters were completed by January 9, when he was surprised to discover that the passages describing his hero's schooldays were in fact a revival of some from the long-forgotten *Troy Hanneton*, which in their turn had been based on his own agonies at Marlow. There was a special pleasure in contemplating that abyss from his present pinnacle of felicity. It was also agreeable to be able to present some aspects of his adored Henry James under the guise of the famous old novelist Henry Galleon. Indeed the conversation in which the old warrior discusses the young writer's beginning and shows him the road he should follow[1] was very closely based on the Master's written and spoken injunctions to Hugh.

On January 25 *Mr Perrin and Mr Traill* was published by Mills & Boon in an edition of fifteen hundred copies. Surprising as it seems today, the reviews, though generally favourable, were on the whole less full and laudatory than those of the two previous books. His own *Standard's* description of it as "a bright piece of work" seems particularly unhappy, while the *Westminster Gazette* used a phrase which fits most of the rest of Hugh's work, but not *Mr Perrin*. "We are afraid," wrote the anonymous critic, "that Mr Walpole is writing with too great facility, and we think if he would take greater pains he might do much better." To counterbalance these ineptitudes came the sane, shrewd words of Charles Marriott: "I think the new book is *miles* ahead of anything you have done before. It is real first-hand stuff, developed with sympathy and insight." Robert Ross considered "the whole character of Perrin a masterpiece of observation, invention and imagination," but damned the book's ending: "Why did you allow Traill to live? Absurd. . . . You were writing an 'unpleasant story.' Why didn't you stick to your art and ignore popularity?"

[1] Pages 288–89 of the first edition.

Henry James's verdict was delayed by his continuance in America, but on April 15, in the course of a long letter, he wrote:

I congratulate you ever so gladly on Mr. Perrin—I think the book represents a very marked advance on its predecessors. I am an atrocious reader, as you know—with a mania for appreciation, or in other words for criticism, since the latter is the one sole gate to the former. To appreciate is to appropriate, and it is only by criticism that I can make a thing in which I find myself interested at all *my own*. But nobody that I have encountered for a long time seems to have any use for any such process—or, much rather, does almost every one (and exactly the more they "read") resent the application of it. All of which is more or less irrelevant, however, for my telling you that I really and very charmedly made your book very *much* my own. It has life and beauty and reality, and is more closely *done* than the others, with its immense advantage, clearly, of resting on the known and felt thing: in other words on depths, as it were, of experience. If I weren't afraid of seeming to you to avail myself foully of your supine state[1] to batter and bruise you at my ease (as that appears to have been for you, alas, the main result of my previous perusal of your works) I should venture, just on tiptoe—holding my breath, to say that—well, I should *like* to make, seated by your pallet and with your wrist in my good grasp and my faithful fingers—or thumb—on your young pulse, one or two affectionately discriminative little remarks. One of these is to the effect that, still, I don't quite recognise here the *centre of your subject*, that absolutely and indispensably fixed and constituted point from which one's ground must be surveyed and one's material wrought. If you say it's (that centre) in Mr. P's exasperated consciousness I can only reply that if it *might* be it yet isn't treated as such. And, further, that I don't quite understand why, positing the situation as also a part of the experience of Mr. Traill, you yet take such pains to demonstrate that Mr. Traill was, as a vessel of experience, absolutely *nil*—recognizing, feeling, knowing, understanding, appreciating, that is, absolutely nothing that happened to him. Experience—reported—is interesting, is *recorded* to us, according to some vessel (the capacity and quality of such,) that contains it, and I don't make out Mr. Traill's capacity at all. And I note this—*shall* you feel, hideously?—because the subject, your subject, *with* an operative, a felt centre, would have still more harmoniously and effectively expressed itself. Admirable, clearly, the subject that you had before you; and which, when all is said, dearest, dearest Hugh, has moved you to write a book that will give a great push to your situation.

Hugh seems to have protested mildly against some part of this judgment, for James was soon writing:

[1] Hugh was in bed with scarlet fever.

I am touched by your sweet patience under my qualificatory glance at the slightly constitutional infirmity of "Mr. Perrin." I didn't in the least mean that fools and duffers shan't figure, or be of interest, in fiction; I only meant that *their experience* can only in a very minor degree. They may be rare and rich as the experience of *others* of the sentient and the perceiving—like Shakespeare's, Thackeray's and even Miss Austen's. So P. was no experience of T's—only T. of P's (comparatively.) I don't think your *girl* was really an experience of anybody's. You must work that sort of thing—kind of relation—closer.

The old man also twitted Hugh mildly with the book's effusive dedication, part of which runs: "To Punch . . . because you have more understanding and sympathy than anyone I have ever met." Punch was in fact Percy Anderson, and there was no doubt a touch of jealousy in James's good-humoured banter. Perhaps he would have liked a dedication himself, but in view of his castigation of each successive volume, it is not surprising that Hugh fought shy. Many years after James's death his *cher élève* did dedicate two separate books to his memory.[1]

Meanwhile *Mr Perrin* was an immediate success. The sales quickly surpassed those of *Maradick*, a second edition of a thousand copies was issued, the faithful Benson approved, H. G. Wells liked the book, and Hugh's situation was given just that "push" which James had foreseen. The Century Company bought the American rights, and one of Hugh's ex-pupils wrote to say that all the boys at Epsom College were delighted with the book—as well they might be. The college authorities, however, took a different view: Mr Perrin's school may have been situated on a carefully described Cornish sea-coast, but to anybody who knew anything of Epsom and the staff there in recent years, its identity was unmistakable. All communication between the author and the college ceased until in the preface to the Everyman Library edition Hugh apologised, honour was satisfied, and in 1937 Sir Hugh Walpole, C.B.E., gave an address as Guest of Honour at the official Epsom College prize-giving.

2

The success of *Mr Perrin* and Hugh's appointment as secretary to Lord Stanmore for a year "at a large income" made him decide that

---

[1] *The Apple Trees* (1932) and *The Killer and the Slain* (1942).

the time had come to leave Chelsea and move to more fashionable quarters. He accordingly set about looking for a flat in the West End and a cottage in the country. New friends made about this time included Compton Mackenzie, Somerset Maugham, and the Derbyshire novelist Robert Murray Gilchrist. Maugham, already established as a phenomenally successful playwright, did much to encourage, help, and entertain Hugh, but it was Gilchrist who attracted him the most.

Hugh wrote him the usual "fan-letter," Gilchrist came to see Hugh in London, and Hugh paid several visits to the dark low-ceilinged Elizabethan house on the Derbyshire moors where Gilchrist lived with his mother, two sisters, and a friend. After long walks on the moors, Gilchrist, a big-limbed, broad-shouldered man dressed in rough, brightly-coloured tweeds, would gently read aloud by candlelight one of his richly fantastic stories. "He is," wrote Hugh, "the oddest mixture of simplicity and complexity, of knowledge and ignorance, poetry and muscle, music and discordance." He dedicated *The First Born* (1911) to Hugh, who in his turn dedicated *The Silver Thorn* (1928) to Gilchrist's memory, described him affectionately in *The Apple Trees*, and always maintained that his books were underrated.

On his twenty-seventh birthday Hugh wrote in his diary: "All one's hopes and ambitions seem in the act of being realised without any particular difficulty on one's own part." Four days later he went down with scarlet fever and spent a miserable month in a North London isolation hospital. When he emerged, the first nine chapters of *Fortitude* were complete. He began at this time to take frequent Turkish baths, and all his life he lost no opportunity of having one, whatever part of the world he was in. Besides satisfying his passion for cleanliness and providing informal opportunities of meeting interesting strangers, they seem to have acted as a stimulus to his writing.

At the beginning of May he discovered a suitable flat at 16 Hallam Street, hard by Portland Place, and at the end of the month he was comfortably installed. For the next eight weeks he was too busy even to keep up his diary, but during May he wrote to his mother from Lord Stanmore's house at Ascot:

I am sending with this letter a tiny piece of the *Perrin* profits—for two reasons. First because I should like you to share in them, and secondly because I am very anxious for you to have a week *on your own* in London. You must please understand me in this affair. I should be most dreadfully hurt if you did not accept it—really deeply hurt—and it is also entirely selfish, because I want you to have a week here in London so that you can see some of my friends and we can go about a little.

The visit duly took place and was a great success.

At the end of July he re-opened his diary, to say that "the Russian Ballet has moved me more than anything I've ever seen in my life. . . . Old S[tanmore] is becoming excessively tiresome. . . . *Fortitude* now at Book II Chap. VII." The month of August he spent with Percy Anderson, visiting Stockholm, Munich, and—for the first time— Bayreuth. Back in London, there was an affectionate reunion with Henry James, newly returned from America, tea with John Galsworthy who promised to read some of the manuscript of *Fortitude*, and further work with Stanmore on the Aberdeen papers. Then came a week's holiday in Cornwall with Percy Anderson, during which Hugh caught his first glimpse of the little fishing-village of Polperro, on the south coast between Looe and Fowey, and knew at once that it was "beyond any kind of question absolutely my dream place."

In October Mrs Belloc Lowndes came to tea at Hallam Street. She was an expert in the business side of her profession and, like a seasoned commander planning with a junior ally the rout of their common enemy, the two of them discussed the strategy and tactics of Hugh's writing and publishing campaign. His contract compelled him to give his next book to Mills & Boon, but *Fortitude* had all along been designed to be his *magnum opus* and for it he would prefer a younger, more fashionable firm. He had his eye on Martin Secker, whom he had met with Compton Mackenzie, and who seemed to have unusually fine literary taste,[1] besides being a man of great sympathy and charm. After much deliberation it was decided that Hugh should lay aside *Fortitude* and dash off a shorter novel for Mills & Boon. The very next day he wrote the opening words of *The Prelude to Adventure*, a story of a Cambridge undergraduate who commits a murder, and in six weeks the book was finished—an astonishing feat of virtuosity.

[1] Hugh was right about this. In a few years' time Secker's authors, besides Mackenzie and Hugh, included D. H. Lawrence, Norman Douglas, Edward Thomas, Frank Swinnerton, Arthur Ransome, Oliver Onions, and Francis Brett Young.

On October 13 appeared Henry James's novel, *The Outcry*, the last he was destined to complete. Hugh reviewed it glowingly in the *Standard*, much to its author's delight.

I am touched [he wrote], I am *melted*, by the charming gallantry and magnanimity of it—my notices of *your* compositions having been so comparatively tepid. Tit *not* for Tat! . . . I seem to myself to swim in a blaze of glory—I shall wear my thrifty old hat when I next go out like a wreath of the bay imitated in fine gold.

And here the old critical Adam crept out:

Had I known you meant to crown me I should have liked to say a thing or two for your guidance—however incorrect such a proceeding would have been as from author to reviewer. . . . Never mind—you will sell the edition for me—and no edition of mine has ever sold yet!

Four days later Hugh wrote to his mother: "I had some delightful days with Henry James last week. I am supposed, everyone tells me, to be the hero of his new novel, and certainly the physical description is something like [1]—the rest not at all."

Meanwhile James was discussing Hugh with Arthur Benson, who on November 8 wrote in his diary:

Then he [James] spoke about Hugh Walpole—he said he was charming in his zest for experience and his love of intimacies. "I often think," he went on, "if I look back at my own starved past, that I wish I had done more, reached out further, claimed more—and I should be the last to block the way. The only thing is to be there, to wait, to sympathise, to help if necessary." [2]

Hugh's own diary for the year had petered out in October, and the reason can be found in a letter written to his mother on November 16:

I don't suppose that ever, in all my hectic and excited career, have I had so much work upon my shoulders. My novel must be finished by the end of December, Stanmore has taken a house at the other end of Chelsea, has been in bed for weeks and telephones for me every minute. I am carrying out the *Standard* Xmas Sup. unaided this year and it must be done by the end of the

---

[1] Hugh Crimble, in *The Outcry*, is described as "a young man in eye-glasses" whose "strength of expression" and "directness of communication" appeared to be borrowed "from the unframed and unattached nippers unceasingly perched, by their mere ground-glass rims, on the bony bridge of his indescribably authoritative (since it was at the same time decidedly inquisitive) young nose . . . his main physiognomic mark [was] the degree to which his clean jaw was underhung and his lower lip protruded."

[2] *The Diary of Arthur Christopher Benson* [1926].

month, I have five short stories on commission and none of them even begun. I love it all. I've never been in better health, and socially I'm having the time of my life.

I've been seeing a lot of Henry James and, funnily enough, the woman I'm most with now is "Elizabeth." She has strangely mellowed since her husband's death and her escape from Germany, and we are the greatest pals.

3

By the end of January 1912 the bustle had so far subsided as to leave him time to reopen his diary with remarks on a "most successful tea-party. Henry James, Galsworthy, Mrs. Lowndes, Percy. H. J. gave Galsworthy a long oration to which we listened. Poor Galsworthy sadly embarrassed. Mrs. Lowndes dear as ever. All friends."

At the end of the month the uneasy relationship with Lord Stanmore was mercifully ended by the death of the aged nobleman. It is extremely doubtful whether the papers of Lord Aberdeen were any more orderly as a result of Hugh's attentions, and he was profoundly relieved to see the last of them.

Percy Anderson took him several times to visit Elgar, whom he found "as simple and full of fun as a boy." Recalling these occasions many years later in his journal, Hugh remembered the old man's saying: "Don't be discouraged. Life's long." "He was always to me kind and generous and even tender. Never anyone with less side."

Other old friends of Anderson's, who became friends of Hugh's, were Sir Sidney and Lady Colvin. Anderson took him to lunch at their house in the British Museum, and Lady Colvin started to mother him at once. Forty years earlier (as Mrs Sitwell) she had befriended the young Robert Louis Stevenson: now at the age of seventy-three her eye for promising young writers was just as keen, her interest undiminished. She and her husband, as Hugh wrote after their death, "were alike in their enthusiasm and generosity of heart, and their passionate mutual love gave them a beautiful unity. . . . Lady Colvin had a deep understanding of all the complexities of modern life; you could not tell Colvin everything, because to shock him was to hurt him too deeply; but there was nothing that you could not tell to her." [1]

[1] *The Colvins and their Friends* (1928).

Hugh was always attracted in others by those very qualities which made himself such a gay companion, and he recorded of Lady Colvin: "Every little pleasure was exciting to her; she was like a child going to the world for the first time over a new play, a new book, a new picture." [1] She used to send him long gossipy letters, especially when he was abroad, discussing mutual friends and their doings. Thus in 1920 she wrote of "Jack [Galsworthy], who I think is on the whole the most like Christ (the *real* Christ) of any man I have ever known, without being the least bit of a prig. Drinkwater seemed a nice person, but bordering on dullness." And two years later she recorded a "great difference of opinion about Galsworthy's new play *Loyalties*. I have not seen it—but I could not feel much interest in a hero who steals money; *any* other crime one might forgive, but not that."

Meanwhile in March 1912 luncheon with Henry James provided Hugh with some *obiter dicta* for his diary. Pinero as a dramatist James described as "a little puppet dancing inside a vast deserted machine, rattling like a pea in a pod," while Bennett's newly published *Hilda Lessways* he likened to "the slow wringing out of a dirty sponge. But observation good—*au fond* journalist." Hugh reported this remark to Lady Colvin, who was not amused. He accompanied James and Elizabeth to a fancy-dress dance at the Wells's; David Garnett, who was also there, remembers that Elizabeth went as a Dresden shepherdess and that James wore plain evening dress. Hugh saw *Milestones* with James, who "thought its simplicity incredible." "But," Hugh added, "is not his complexity more incredible?"

On March 20 he gladly took up again the suspended *Fortitude*, and a week later *The Prelude to Adventure* was published by Mills & Boon, just six months after its first word had been written. The notices were better than ever, and few of the reviewers can have suspected that it had been dashed off at top speed to work out a contract. "It is a fine theme, finely executed," wrote *The Times Literary Supplement*. "Above the tremulous high-strung note of the human *leit-motif* we hear the deep encompassing swell of a Divine overtone, inexorable, merciful." Once again likenesses to Henry James were discovered, this time by the *Academy*. May Sinclair liked the book, and so did Charles Marriott,

[1] *Ibid.*

though less than *Mr Perrin*. He felt that Hugh "had rather indulged the temptation to cayenne pepper, and I don't fancy that real force is got that way." "It's jolly good," wrote Galsworthy from America: "You have the knack of holding one's attention right along in a remarkable way;" but artistically, he considered, "the book lacks its essential finality."

At the beginning of April Hugh spent a fortnight with Percy Anderson in the South of France. They drove over to Cannes and visited Edward Knoblock and Arnold Bennett, who wrote in his journal on April 11: "I have read Walpole's new novel, *The Prelude to Adventure*; satisfactory—and am to try to arrange a contract for him [in America] with Doran." In London Hugh found awaiting him two letters which gave him particular pleasure. The first was from his father. Dr Walpole, like so many parents, was usually shy and ill at ease with his grown-up and increasingly successful son. Only in an occasional letter such as this did he succeed in transcending his natural reserve.

My dear Hugh,
I have just finished your book and have read it with breathless interest. I agree with A. C. B. in a recent letter to me that it is a great advance on your previous work, on even *Perrin & Traill*. I was much struck with *The Hound of Heaven* when I read it some weeks ago, but your *Prelude* brings out its truth in an unforgettable way. . . . Of course I am sorry that the Christian Mission service is such a weak affair. . . . The book will do good in unexpected places though you only meant it to be a story. All your stories, except *Maradick* I think which always seemed in parts rather unreal, have a tremendous stir of vitality about them as well as a striking originality, and if you go on making the same progress every year you will carry us off our feet. I daresay you will be amused at this kind of criticism. I am as you know no judge of "letters" and can only look at books as the ordinary reader does, but I do feel thankful for this one, though as I have said I should have liked a less damaging account of our part in God's Cause. Some day perhaps you will draw a good strong parson and put us a little more in heart with our difficult work.

Your affectionate Father,
G. H. S. W.

I constantly think of you, more often than you think, though I can't often write.

The other letter was from Henry James, and it must have been a relief to the pupil to find his master's critical mood so tempered with affection.

I very faithfully and affectionately welcome you—the old grizzled and blear-eyed house dog looks up, that is, and grunts and wags his tail at the damaged but still delectable Prodigal Son. Dim of vision though he be, he has mastered The Prelude—he began it a day or two after you left and then couldn't, of course, put it down, and wants you to know that he found lots of good—that is of charm—in it. It is as much of an advance on Mr. Perrin, I think, as Mr. Perrin was on *his* predecessor and is exceedingly interesting, genial and promising, besides being so very performing. I should have more to say of it (I mean many things,) were we really to go into the matter—in fact I shall if you will let me. I only want to let you have it from me now that I feel you to have written a very attaching and engaging, a very coercing and rewarding thing, which will infallibly get itself greatly read.

4

The sales of *The Prelude*, like its notices, surpassed those of its predecessors. Two thousand copies were printed of the first edition, and in all four thousand were disposed of, including five hundred to America. Thus steadily was Hugh beginning to build up the firmest of all foundations for popular literary success. The writer who opens with a runaway "best-seller" has usually an uneven road thereafter, beset by fluctuating sales and disappointments. From first to last Hugh was the publisher's ideal author, each book selling rather more than the one before it, extending gradually but surely the circle of his readers.

In May he spent three happy weeks at St Ives, walking, reading, writing *Fortitude*, visiting his relations at Truro, and enjoying Cornwall. Two writers, J. D. Beresford and Dorothy M. Richardson, were living at St Ives, and with both of them Hugh soon became close friends. "Immediately at home," writes Dorothy Richardson, "he was a genial, warmth-bringing, world-bringing presence, host and guest in one; with a pleasantly booming baritone voice." Before the first evening was out he had revealed his three current enthusiasms. These were for Dostoevsky, whose *Brothers Karamazov* he had brought with him; for Wagner, "whose motifs a sufficiently sensitive ear would hear echoing in the bathroom and one of the bedrooms of the bungalow;"

and for his new dog Jacob, "bought from a dog-shop because it had hopefully put its head on one side at him as he looked in through the window." Jacob, a mongrel and the first of a long succession of dogs, later played a leading part, under the name of Hamlet, in the three Jeremy books—the only portrait there, Hugh said, which was drawn straight from life.

Dostoevsky is not a writer to be accepted with moderation by enthusiastic youth, and Hugh was so overwhelmed with excitement at his new discovery that, without pause to consider, he dashed off a letter about it to Henry James. Nor did he afterwards regret his rashness, since it called forth this splendid rejoinder:

Your letter greatly moves and regales me. Fully do I enter into your joy of sequestration, and your bliss of removal from this scene of heated turmoil and dusty despair—which, however, re-awaits you! Never mind; sink up to your neck into the brimming basin of nature and peace, and teach yourself— by which I mean let your grandmother teach you—that with each revolving year you will need and make more piously these precious sacrifices to Pan and the Muses. . . . I rejoice in the getting on of your work—how splendidly copious your flow; and am much interested in what you tell me of your readings and your literary emotions. These latter indeed—or some of them, as you express them, I don't think I fully share. At least when you ask me if I don't feel Dostoieffsky's "mad jumble, that flings things down in a heap," nearer truth and beauty than the picking and composing that you instance in Stevenson, I reply with emphasis that I feel nothing of the sort, and that the older I grow and the more I *go* the more sacred to me do picking and composing become—though I naturally don't limit myself to Stevenson's *kind* of the same. Don't let any one persuade you—there are plenty of ignorant and fatuous duffers to try to do it—that strenuous selection and comparison are not the very essence of art, and that Form *is* [not] substance to that degree that there is absolutely no substance without it. Form alone *takes*, and holds and preserves, substance—saves it from the welter of helpless verbiage that we swim in as in a sea of tasteless tepid pudding, and that makes one ashamed of an art capable of such degradations. Tolstoi and D. are fluid pudding, though not tasteless, because the amount of their own minds and souls in solution in the broth gives it savour and flavour, thanks to the strong, rank quality of their genius and their experience. But there are all sorts of things to be said of them, and in particular that we see how great a vice is their lack of composition, their defiance of economy and architecture, directly they are emulated and imitated; *then*, as subjects of emulation, models, they quite give themselves away. There is nothing so deplorable as a work of art with a *leak* in its interest; and there is no such leak of interest as through commonness of form. Its opposite, the *found* (because the sought-for,) form is the absolute citadel and tabernacle of interest.

Well might Hugh greet this with the words: "Great letter from Henry James in the evening about the Russians and Style—booming in this lonely little place like a golden gong."

But Hugh himself did his share of booming. Miss Richardson writes:

Talk, during the whole of his stay, was incessant, usually initiated by Hugh and unquenchable even by the waves that swept, at high tide, over the studio's glass roof. Twice only do I remember silence falling; and each time when the three of us were seated, after climbing to a cliff-top blue with scylla, confronted by the Cornish sea. Hugh it was who challenged the spell, the first time to announce the impossibility of conveying in words what we saw, and the second time to proclaim the "luck" of all three in having "escaped."

For himself he was doubtless remembering the prison-house of adolescence, the shadow of the Church, the fear of failure.

In those early days [Miss Richardson goes on] he was robust, outwardly full of self-confidence (though still suffering, as a result of an unhappy upbringing, a deep-seated sense of isolation and insufficiency). In sharp contrast to Beresford, a mildly intellectual collector of new thought-systems in each of which, in turn, he would for a while feel himself possessed of steering-gear, Hugh, whose brain, though lacking in subtlety, was good, was eminently a humanist, a collector of people.

And she ends by pointing out that though a humanist, "seeing life as people, he was also a traditionalist. His recoil, for example, from religious orthodoxy did not prevent his liking to go to church and sing hymns at the top of his voice."

On his way home from Cornwall, Hugh stayed once more with Lady Lovelace at Ashley Combe. John Buchan (his wife was Lady Lovelace's niece) was a fellow-guest, and together they walked and talked prodigiously on Exmoor. Hugh announced his intention of settling down to write, but Buchan suggested that he would be a better writer if he saw a little more of life first. "John a revelation to me," wrote Hugh in his diary. "Obviously sent with very direct purpose by the Good God. Would give my boots for him not to be going tomorrow." But this sacrificial offer was unavailing; Buchan left, and Hugh returned to the racket of London. A few days later Buchan wrote saying: "This Whitsuntide will always be memorable, for I think I have made a new friend. (And I haven't many, though I have a bowing acquaintance with half the world.)" Eight years later, in a letter to Buchan, Hugh referred to his "constant memory of that Somerset week years ago."

5

Hugh had long decided to change his literary agent. Hughes Massie was too bound up with a forgotten life, Henry James strongly recommended J. B. Pinker, and Hugh took his advice. He also saw Martin Secker, arranged that he should publish *Fortitude* with an advance of £150, and then set about finishing that work. But the claims on his time in London had grown with his success and the ever-increasing list of friends. More and more he felt the need of some place in the remote countryside where he could write without interruption, in the intervals of his metropolitan merry-go-round. Cornwall naturally came into his mind, and he determined that his next visit there should be a house-hunting one.

He was encouraged in this decision by the remarks of another new friend, E. V. Lucas, whom he now visited in Sussex. After reading *Mr Perrin*, Lucas wrote: "And now I feel that what you ought to do is to cut Society and acquire many more first-hand experiences of life. Go for a voyage on a merchant ship as supercargo, for example." This was perhaps the most perceptive piece of advice that Hugh ever received, but he was constitutionally incapable of profiting from it. Only once was he ever again to recapture the fresh, clear-cut realism of *Mr Perrin*—when the war forced on him the "first-hand experiences of life" which produced *The Dark Forest*.

Another week-end with Lady Lovelace, this time at Ockham, found him in a party containing both Robert Ross and Henry James, between whom there was an imperfect sympathy. Here is Hugh's diary-entry for July 7:

Such a day! H. J. talking all the time. Described Daudet's meeting with Meredith, smashed *Mrs. Tanqueray*, argued with Robbie about the drama, long walk with me during which I told him about *Fortitude* and he approved. Final summing-up of everyone to me in the small hours of the morning.

Four days later Hugh finished *Fortitude*, staying near Basingstoke with Percy Anderson, and then set off with him for a holiday on the Dalmatian coast.

In September he spent a week-end at Lamb House, where he found "H. J. in great form. Said: 'I've had one great passion in my life—the intellectual passion. What that has been for me I cannot say. Make it your rule to encourage the impersonal interests as against the personal—but remember also that they are interdependent.' The beautiful little house fits him like a case."

After a week with his mother at Sennen Cove, near Land's End, Hugh moved into rooms at Polperro, and there, on the last day of his stay, his search for a country retreat was rewarded when he discovered The Cobbles, the cottage of his dreams. Arranging to rent it by the year and to move in the following March, he returned to London, to find Pinker and Secker delighted with *Fortitude*. He dined with Maurice Hewlett: "Great fun. Said he was a man who would never be satisfied. Much happier before prosperity, etc, etc. So say they all. I swear I won't if prosperity comes and ill-health doesn't." Hugh certainly kept this resolution, but he had not to face the same difficulties as Hewlett, who spent most of his life trying to live down his early success as an historical novelist. He tried modern novels, epic poetry, and essays, but to his dying day he was famous only as the author of *The Forest Lovers*, *The Queen's Quair*, and *Richard Yea-and-Nay*. Hugh wrote a sympathetic article on him for the *Dictionary of National Biography*.

At the end of November Hugh embarked on a new kind of literary work—a dramatisation of *The Wooden Horse* under the title of *Robin's Father*. In this, the first of several attempts to conquer the theatre, he had the expert assistance of the playwright Rudolf Besier, who had made a considerable success with *Don* (1909) and *Lady Patricia*, starring Mrs Patrick Campbell (1911). They roughed out the scenario together, but Besier did most of the subsequent work.

In December, just before Hugh left for his annual visit to Edinburgh, he "all in a second got the chuck from the *Standard*. Four years' work and not a word of thanks." His pocket had by now become less vulnerable, if not his feelings. He applied for consolation to Henry James, and on Christmas Day it was accordingly despatched:

Deeply I participate in the horrid inconvenience you must be temporarily suffering at the hands of the foredoomed Standard: foredoomed, I mean, to descend to depths to which, even should they have tried to drag you, you couldn't have consented to sink with it. But don't take it, the beastly little fortune of war, harder, a mite, than you can help: *it's one of those things that happens*, simply—I mean in the common work-a-day way, at your stage of young efflorescence; and the efflorescence itself, by another stroke of fortune and before you can turn round, will smother the base incident in flowers. By which I mean that you have too many intrinsic advantages, and are too ready and present and appreciated, are in fine too unmistakeable a young actuality, for the whirligig of time not to pounce on you and pick you up and toss you quite aloft again. Your intrinsic resources, in short, are precious, and from the quarter in which they will presently be desired for annexation, some happy proposition will issue.

In Edinburgh on Christmas Eve Hugh began his new novel, *The Duchess of Wrexe*, and he worked at it until on New Year's Eve he joined E. V. Lucas in Sussex. At midnight the party walked up the downs with torches under the stars and welcomed the New Year by dancing what they believed to be the farandole.

CHAPTER SEVEN

RIDING TO GLORY

I

ON 23 January 1913 *Fortitude* was published by Martin Secker. Hugh had put all he knew into it, determined to make it his first major work, and now he awaited its reception with some concern. The first review to appear was an "unfair and most malicious" one in the *Observer* of January 26, which declared that he was a romantic rather than the realist he believed himself to be, and described some of his favourite passages as "bad Dickens." For three days he remained sunk in apprehensive melancholy, but then the clouds were broken by a two-column review from W. L. Courtney in the *Daily Telegraph* and praise from the *Manchester Guardian*. On the same day he discussed the book with Arnold Bennett, who said "first part made him think he'd give up writing if the young men were so good, second part reassured him." Letters too began to arrive; a long appreciative one from May Sinclair, and this from his mother:

Dearest Hugh,

I have just finished the book and must tell you at once how *very* much I like it. "Like" expresses nothing of what I feel about it. . . . It is *extremely* interesting, it just carries you on. I have forgotten that it was written by you sometimes, being so carried away by the reality of it. And the kernel of it is true, and Love is at the heart of it—otherwise our lives would indeed be puzzles.

I never can express much about what I care for, but this book does give one great happiness—and makes one thankful for what you can do—it *must* tell on other people.

Ever your loving
Mother.

Galsworthy's opinion, sent from France, brought further reassurance:

The water grows in volume under you, and the wind waxes in your sails—you are stretching the wings of ambition fast. There's great vigour, fertility, and aspiration in the book; too much sentiment perhaps, and not enough austerity. But of that last I am a poor judge, demanding it as I do so incorrigibly, and to the point of thinness in my own work. I can imagine that this book of yours must be pleasing 'toute une masse' (as a young Pole here is always saying) of people. I hope it's a great success. There are a lot of weird things in it, a lot of good true scenes; and it has the merit of carrying its implicit moral idea throughout.

It's full romantic—don't let yourself be swept away by the conviction, so common to the rising generation, that the last, or, shall we say, the present generation, drinking too little port at its literary feasts, must be avenged. Don't join the new two-bottle men. Keep your head and your balance, and you will write even cleaner and stronger stuff.

I suppose you are whanging away already at your assault on London. I wish you all good luck.

Meanwhile Henry James, installed in his new flat at 21 Carlyle Mansions, Cheyne Walk, was doing his best to keep up with his young friend's output. By the end of January he could report:

I have received a massive Volume, and am taking it (as, more or less impenetrable and utterly critical brute that I am, I can only take contemporary fiction—which I can't take *at all* save when it's a favoured, or favouring, young friend's) in successive gustatory sups, or experimental go's, of a certain number of pages each. So when the pages foot up *very* high, you see, it takes me some time to work along. But I have absorbed and accumulated some 150 of you, and shall have assimilated perhaps fifty more by the time we meet. "Then we'll talk"—or rather perhaps won't so much as try to, according to the light in which my fatal necessity to appreciate (that is, I mean, *estimate*) what I read may strike you as most blandly or most portentously showing. The great thing is that I do work you down—which I can't for the life of me do anyone else—save, that is, Wells and Arnold B. So you make with them my trio. And you are not, my dear Hugh, the least "spirited" of the three, or the least sincere.

Soon after this they spent the day together, of which Hugh recorded: "Wonderful to hear him on *Fortitude*. Abuses the first part but praises the second. How all these people differ!" But as the reviews poured in from the press-cutting agency, he became conscious of a new note in them: promise was beginning to pass into achievement, and for this, his fifth novel, Hugh was promoted to that interminable formation, the "front rank of contemporary novelists." Henry James took the opportunity of dilating "with great gusto on the author's choosing between Prosperity and Posterity," but Hugh was too excited to listen.

Throughout January he worked on the play with Besier, and also began to read for Methuen. They paid what was in those days the high rate of a guinea a manuscript and during the next eighteen months he reported on over a hundred. Almost every day he was invited out to luncheon, tea, and dinner, often going to a theatre or the opera as well: *Rosenkavalier* he saw again and again. But at the end of February he escaped with Percy Anderson to lodgings at Polperro, where he happily resumed *The Duchess of Wrexe*.

2

The only interruptions were the daily visits of the postman, then and always eagerly awaited. Even when in later years his correspondence reached huge proportions, Hugh immensely enjoyed opening it, and thought nothing of writing thirty letters a day, all in his own hand. Now the faithful Henry James wrote regularly, though suffering from an attack of angina pectoris and from the ministrations of "well-meaning telephoning ladies."

I hear with all sympathy of your dealings with your cottage. I wish to God I weren't just now so stricken with non-production and non-returns . . . so that I might pick up a few household objects by the leg and send them flying through the air to you. . . . I rejoice exceedingly that your book sells —also that you've vaulted straight into another saddle. How you go it, nursling of Apollo—and of Secker!

Another exciting letter came from John Middleton Murry, asking Hugh to review novels for a periodical called *Rhythm*, which Murry and Katherine Mansfield were running. These two represented the vanguard of the literary intelligentsia, with which Hugh all his life maintained a timid flirtation—a touching relationship compounded equally of admiration, envy, and fear of ridicule. The quintessence of all these emotions, coupled with deep affection, was present years later in his friendship with Virginia Woolf.

But now his own cottage was ready, and on his twenty-ninth birth-day he and Percy Anderson moved into The Cobbles. It was a whitewashed cottage (he later caused a stir by having the shutters painted blue), built at the beginning of the cliff path, overlooking the village and its little harbour where the fishing-boats rocked at anchor, and just outside the harbour piers. It could be approached only on foot along a cobbled path, and contained two bedrooms and a sitting-room. It was like living in a ship hung over the sea, with gulls crying incessantly round the windows, so that it seemed they might fly in at any moment. There was no railway station nearer than Looe, three and a half miles away. He was admirably looked after by a fisherman called John Curtis and his wife Annie: here surely he could write in peace. But first there were the usual difficulties:

Such a turmoil of a day! The ceiling falls in, the fire smokes, the oven won't burn—such a lot to see to—of course no work done. Poured hard all day but P. and I played about in the afternoon and found a delightful valley with primroses. Really beginning to settle in.

Nevertheless he found time that day to write to his mother about another interesting project:

There's been a lot of commotion in London over Henry James's seventieth birthday celebration next month. Gosse first started it. . . . Henry is to be given a present, and his portrait is to be painted by Sargent for the National Portrait Gallery. A huge sum has been collected, people subscribing from all over the world. The trouble is that Gosse himself arranged a little committee to settle things, and the letter asking for money was sent out in their name. There were only about half a dozen—Sargent, Barrie, Gosse, Edith Wharton, Mrs Clifford and, to my own amazement, myself.[1]

He left out deliberately the Colvins and Mrs Humphry Ward who are old friends of Henry's, and they are furious. At first I was miserable because I thought they'd be furious with my being on, but apparently it's felt that someone of the younger generation ought to be there. But there's been the most awful fuss.

A few days later he was "getting on slowly with Chapter 9 [of *The Duchess*]. Wish my style were sharper. *That's* what wants improving. Ripping letter from H. J., who has sent me an old desk." Not without preamble, be it said:

[1] There were ten signatories in all, the others being Percy Lubbock, W. E. Norris, Mrs M. F. Prothero, and Howard Sturgis.

I find I can't *not* take an interest, of the tenderest and most practical, in the material equipment of the Cobbles, and I want to express it in sending down to you a very pleasant and convenient and solid old Desk, with capacious table and drawers and pigeon-holes etc, which I very fondly beg you to accept from me if you have room for it *there*. (If you haven't room for it there, or see any other adverse reason, it shall, it *must*, go to Hallam St.) I don't want to despatch it without hearing from you as to placeability first. You will find it a very agreeable working adjunct, I think. But let me *know* —on the basis of its being a certain, a decent *size* of thing; not one of the very largest of its type—but large enough, probably, even for your scale of production. (There was a larger one, which I considered—but which seems to me to put a premium on the perhaps too frequent or too corpulent volume! —though I wouldn't have you thin and rare.)

Hugh answered, accepting the gift with delight, but before it had time to "fly through the air" to him, there came another letter from its donor:

I have promptly wired to Jarvis to despatch the bureau-desk, carefully packed, to the bower of your muse and the retreat of your modesty, with every charge utterly prepaid. I hope it will start, by the G.W., at the very first hour, and if any further pence are demanded of you for "delivery" or whatever let me immediately know and I will passionately remit. I hope the thing will seem to you of an adequate shape and aspect, and that when you lean your inspired elbows on its extended table you will feel a little as if resting them on your poor old friend's still sufficiently broad and sturdy and all-patient back. I vociferously applaud in advance the leaping and bounding volume that you are already astride of for riding to glory. May the glory be great—and, incidentally, even the work. . . . Let me know when the mild offering reaches port.

And sure enough, on Easter Monday the carrier's van appeared. "Rather a misspent day, because Henry's desk arrived, and that was disturbing as the windows had to be taken out." Scarcely was all at peace before yet another letter was on its way:

Your assurance that the piece of furniture will do gives me infinite pleasure. I am only sorry you had to wait so long for it—but this I feared, as it went by goods train. (I found that "passenger" rates to far Cornwall would cost money that I would rather keep to get you something else— which I am doing, though I don't exactly know what.) Tell me, I earnestly beg you, of some other household object that you stand in real need of—so that I may supply it and you employ it, and, so employing, think, under the contact, of one so well, so remarkably well, disposed to you. This information will make up a little for the always so stinted scope of your notes, never straying as they do, beyond the fewest lines. What there was of this last was in quality of assurance all I could ask—but there was so little *of* it beyond the one assurance. . . . How indeed can you develop letters while you so prodigiously develop books? I give way to the books, and they are what the bureau was meant for.

This gentle remonstrance was fully deserved. Hugh wrote often, but seldom at what the Master considered appropriate length, and it is significant that the only letters of Hugh's which James kept were those written from Russia, where his homesickness drew from him some of the longest and best letters he ever wrote. Now at Polperro there was so much to occupy him. By the same post as James's letter, for instance, came a "splendid letter from Secker saying he'd taken over *Rhythm*, now to be called *The Blue Review* and be shed of all affectations. I to be sub-editor with Cannan and Swinnerton.[1] Then a long thing from Besier about the play, which I believe Alexander will take." [2]

Soon after this he experienced one of those crises of despair and self-doubt which visit most creative writers. *The Duchess*, now well into her second Book, suddenly seemed no good at all. Was he on the wrong tack? Should be persevere or try something else, and if so, what? In a great state of indecision he posted the manuscript to J. D. Beresford, asking for his frank opinion and agreeing to abide by his judgment. Beresford read the manuscript in three days, thought it "magnificently promising," and sent it back with a long, careful, encouraging letter; but even before this arrived the crisis was over and Hugh had himself decided to carry on with the book.

All this time the search for the next "household object" was going forward in Chelsea. Hugh had asked for a looking-glass, and its approach was heralded in the familiar style:

I have sent you (my joy that you would mention a household want was of the greatest) the nearest approach to what I conceive to be a *right* little mirror that I could after much hunting find. Small and simple ones are the devil to put one's hand on—everything so big and so florid. I conceive this

---

[1] *The Blue Review* died after three issues.
[2] It was not in fact produced until November 1918.

one intended for the chimney-piece in your chamber of inspiration—and if it's too tall to stand upright it will, I think, [do] equally well (and can be easily so placed by the village carpenter,) with its short side up—the whole reposing lengthways. So let me figure it. It's warranted a genuine old morsel—and looked so to me. Let the donor's battered old mug glimmer out of it at you in some dim benediction when the reflection of your own fresh beauty doesn't too wholly usurp the scene. And I sent you longer ago a copy of my fatuous Infant Reminiscences—which I hope will have reached you safely. . . . I thank you kindly for your mention of the few of your circumjacent facts; as above all of the "real monetary success" of Fortitude. What an abashment to my little play of the lantern of criticism over its happy constitution! But I am familiar with that irony of fate (others' fate.) Very thrilling too the prospect of the Young Review and the band of brothers spewing forth Courtney and his like. Hurry up with it—have fun with it too above all—before I sink to rest.

The Infant Reminiscences were James's newly published volume of autobiography, *A Small Boy and Others*, which Hugh found "quite glorious—so beautiful and so clear and so humorous." Despite this mention of clarity, Hugh in his letter of thanks must have admitted or implied that occasionally the writer's meaning escaped him, for James answered:

You disconcert me a little—or call it much—by saying that some passages "defeat" you—that is if I know what you mean. I take you to mean that you found them difficult, obscure or *entortillés*—and that is the pang and the proof that I am truly an uncommunicating communicator—a beastly bad thing to be . . . when you come to town again *do* let me read you over the said baffling or bewildering morsels.

3

At the end of May, after spending two nights with the Galsworthys in Devon, Hugh returned to London, where he was greeted by still another useful present, this time from Arnold Bennett and accompanied by a characteristic letter:

My dear Walpole,
. . . I send you a book which I picked up as a bargain in the catalogue of a secondhand bookseller. You will see that under the headings of the different countries it gives on each double page a complete conspectus of all important events which happened during a given period. I consider it a

work which is absolutely invaluable to the novelist who deals, however indirectly or briefly, with any past period. And I have used it constantly ever since I bought a copy of the original publication about twelve years ago. It is the basis of such works of erudition as *The Old Wives' Tale* and *Clay-hanger*. For example, if you happen to have a character who was in the United States in the year 1893, you will see on pages 424 and 425, at a glance, everything of a spectacular nature which happened in the United States in that year. In fact, I can scarcely praise too highly the usefulness of this book. . . .

Yours ever,
Arnold Bennett.

It is doubtful whether Hugh took full advantage of this gift (use of it would have saved his latter-day proof-readers a great deal of work), but his friendship with Bennett began to ripen. They saw each other frequently in London, and in July Hugh spent the first of many week-ends at Bennett's house at Thorpe-le-Soken in Essex. Here also he met Bennett's "funny old Five Towns mother. *She* obviously where he gets it all from. She sits beside him and keeps him in his place."

During his two months in London Hugh arranged the publication of *The Duchess* with Martin Secker, from whom he learned that the sales of *Fortitude* had passed five thousand, and in whose company he again met Compton Mackenzie. It was often said of Hugh that while he was always generous and helpful to young, promising, and un-successful writers, he was apt to be jealous of those novelists, usually his contemporaries, who seemed likely to challenge his own speciality and popular esteem. In the thirties this was probably true of his feelings towards Francis Brett Young, with whom on the surface he maintained a cordial friendship, and some such emotion certainly clouded his attitude to Compton Mackenzie in 1913. Later that summer he was much put out by the success of *Sinister Street: Volume One*, which he condemned as "too easily written, far too many pretty descriptions, no characters. Mackenzie, in spite of his cleverness, is no good." [1] But with these two exceptions, there is no evidence that Hugh was ever jealous of other writers: nor is the accusation easy to reconcile with that

---

[1] Later Hugh made amends by buying the manuscript and presenting it to the King's School, Canterbury.

other criticism, so often expressed—that he was far too generous in his praise of books and writers of all ages. It must also be remembered that many of his contemporaries (Brett Young, for example) took much longer than he did to reach a wide public, while some (like J. D. Beresford) never reached it at all. Assuredly neither of these two writers was ever jealous of Hugh, but there were others. Success seldom goes unenvied.

One of Hugh's later detractors was his American publisher George H. Doran, who after he had retired wrote a book of reminiscences [1] (which Hugh described as "vulgar and malicious") wherein he accused Hugh of meanness as well as jealousy. The English edition of the book was suitably expurgated in this and other respects.

Doran was a tall, imposing-looking man with a small beard and a courtly manner. He had made a success of the American edition of *The Old Wives' Tale*, and Bennett was now his chief adviser, so when Bennett told him to get hold of the American rights of a book called *Fortitude*, he obediently did so. There is no evidence that he liked Hugh's books, or even that he read them, but he continued to publish them with mounting success until his firm was absorbed by Doubleday, who remained Hugh's American publisher to the end. For all Doran's expansive courtesy and seeming friendliness, Hugh, usually the last person to see through flatterers, was never quite at his ease with him, and (rightly as it turned out) doubted his ultimate loyalty.

In London the publishers continued to "dandle Hugh on their bloated knee," and Methuen offered advances of £400, £450, and £500 for his next three novels; an offer he was compelled reluctantly to decline, in view of his commitment to Secker. The months of August and September he spent in happy tranquillity at Polperro, writing hard, reading Lamb, Lockhart, and Trollope, and entertaining his mother and sister. One evening he read aloud to them the opening chapters of *The Duchess*, and his mother fell fast asleep. Undeterred by this unspoken criticism he pursued his course until on the last day of September this difficult book was finished. From Henry James came a long letter, opening on a lyrical note:

[1] *Chronicles of Barabbas 1884–1934* (1935).

Beautiful must be your Cornish land and your Cornish sea, idyllic your Cornish setting, this flattering, this wonderful summer . . .

and going on to invite him to stay at Lamb House in November:

It will be the lowest kind of "jinks"—so halting is my pace; yet we shall somehow make it serve. Don't say to me, by the way, apropos of jinks—the "high" kind that you speak of having so wallowed in previous to leaving town—that I ever challenge you as to *why* you wallow, or splash or plunge, or dizzily and sublimely soar (into the jinks element,) or whatever you may call it: as if I ever remarked on anything but the absolute inevitability of it for you at your age and with your natural curiosities, as it were, and passions. It's good healthy exercise, when it comes but in bouts and brief convulsions, and it's always a kind of thing that it's good, and considerably final, to *have* done. We must know, as much as possible, in our beautiful art, yours and mine, what we are talking about—and the only way to know is to have lived and loved and cursed and floundered and enjoyed and suffered.—I think I don't regret a single "excess" of my responsive youth—I only regret, in my chilled age, certain occasions and possibilities I *didn't* embrace. Bad doctrine to impart to a young idiot or a duffer; but in place for a young friend (pressed to my heart,) with a fund of nobler passion, the preserving, the defying, the dedicating, of which always has the last word; the young friend who can dip and shake off and go his straight way again when it's time. But we'll talk of all this—it's abominably late. Who is D. H. Lawrence, who, you think, would interest me? Send him and his book along—by which I simply mean Inoculate me, at your convenience (don't address me the volume;) so far as I can *be* inoculated. I always *try* to let anything of the kind "take."

All through October Hugh lingered on at Polperro, meditating his next novel, which was already assuming shape and even name—*The Green Mirror*. To give him a breather, Pinker arranged a favourable short-story contract with the *Storyteller* magazine, and in due course this was fulfilled with the stories about children later collected in *The Golden Scarecrow*. Now Hugh wrote to his mother:

The satisfactory part of it is that I've now got an audience and bread and butter and can take my time towards writing a really good book. I know perfectly well that the interest that people show is because of the promise rather than anything else, and if in the next five years I don't do some definite "performance" it will all go for nothing. I've got sincerity and vitality but very little else, and I hope that going about amongst people who've nothing to do with books, and travelling, and also infinite patience, will lead to a good novel one day. Of course many people would think it absurd for a mere writer of stories to take himself so seriously, but it isn't that I take *myself* seriously; it's only one's work that needs concentration or nothing would come of it.

At the end of the month he returned to Hallam Street, was gratified to find *The Times Literary Supplement* rating *Fortitude* among the twelve most popular novels of the year,[1] fell ill with influenza and so missed his week-end at Lamb House, and thereafter became involved in the affair of the Henry James portrait.[2]

4

The seventieth birthday had occurred on April 15. James had accepted the homage of his friends, together with a golden bowl, and had graciously agreed to sit to Sargent for his portrait. This work, now completed,[3] was to be shown privately to subscribers in Sargent's studio in Tite Street on three days in December. Printed letters of invitation were prepared and were to be sent out over the names of Gosse and Hugh. James took great interest in the arrangements and was consulted by Hugh on all points. The letters were sent off, and a day or two later Hugh dined with Maurice Hewlett. "I knew, dear Hugh," said he with his usual sardonic charm, "that you were fond of me but, frankly, I had not supposed that Gosse cared for me very greatly. This letter has reassured me." Hugh's heart sank: something terrible had happened. Hewlett showed him the letter on which, as on all its fellows, Hugh had forgotten to add the name of the recipient, so that they all began: "Dear," *tout court*, and ended: "We are, Dear, Yours sincerely, Edmund Gosse, Hugh Walpole." Anticipation of Gosse's anger did much to spoil that week-end at Arnold Bennett's (where the

---

[1] The twelve, in this order, were: *The Woman Thou Gavest Me* by Hall Caine, *The Amateur Gentleman* by Jeffery Farnol, *The Mating of Lydia* by Mrs Humphry Ward, *The Devil's Garden* by W. B. Maxwell, *The Broken Halo* by Florence L. Barclay, *Stella Maris* by W. J. Locke, *Eldorado* by Baroness Orczy, *The Regent* by Arnold Bennett, *The Passionate Friends* by H. G. Wells, *The Judgment House* by Sir Gilbert Parker, *The Way of Ambition* by Robert Hichens, *Fortitude* by Hugh Walpole.

[2] Hugh published two accounts of this incident, in *The Apple Trees* (1932) and *Horizon*, vol I, no. 2 (February 1940). Where they differ in detail, the earlier version is in every verifiable instance the more accurate.

[3] Later in the year, when it was on exhibition at the Royal Academy, the portrait was slashed by a suffragette. Now, repaired, it is to be seen in the National Portrait Gallery.

French composer Maurice Ravel was the other guest), but James stood nobly by his young friend, declaring that the blame was his, and soothing Gosse's wounded vanity with a supremely diplomatic letter.[1]

Hugh spent the last ten days of the year in Edinburgh, correcting the proofs of *The Duchess* and mildly discussing the possibility of a visit to Russia next year. On Christmas Eve *The Green Mirror* was duly started, and another volume of the diary was rounded off with lists of friends made, books read, plays seen. Ahead there seemed to stretch a comfortable vista of other family reunions like this, other diaries finished, other novels begun. But Hugh's next Christmas was to be spent in very different surroundings.

[1] Printed in *The Letters of Henry James* (1920), vol II, p. 361.

CHAPTER EIGHT

THE END OF THE GOLDEN AGE

I

THE fateful year of 1914 opened just like its predecessors, with Henry James wishing him "the very decentest New Year that ever was," a new novel shortly to be published, another begun, endless vistas of work and play ahead. For Hugh and his generation the Boer War had up till now marked the division between past and present; the events of this catastrophic summer were to crash on to them like a thunderbolt from a clear sky. In this respect they were more fortunate than their successors a quarter of a century later, over whom Hitler's shadow lay heavy for years before 1939.

Hugh never cared greatly for the climate of Edinburgh, except for short visits, and the first fortnight of January was relieved only by two fine letters from James. "I'm awfully amused," he wrote, "by your 'amazement' at my being struck with C. Mackenzie's novel [*Sinister Street: Volume One*]—and can only say that I have *been* so struck. . . . I mean to read *Carnival* if I can—I have been struck enough for *that*!"

In the middle of the month Hugh left to spend a fortnight with Elizabeth at her new house, Chalet Soleil, Randogne-sur-Sierre, in the south-west corner of Switzerland, overlooking the valley of the Rhone. From here he wrote to his mother:

When I see splendour like this I know why I love Polperro so. This is absolutely apart and too grand to be friendly—like staying with Queen Mary at Windsor. . . . I have also decided to give up my flat in May. London, as a matter of fact, is very bad for me except for a month's fun every now and again. I can't do a stroke of work there and I get into the habit of staying on and on and idling. Besides, I don't want to have it on my hands if I'm abroad. . . . Elizabeth is adorable.

In London at the end of the month Hugh found a letter from James, saying that he was looking forward to "the voluminous Duchess" and declaring:

Your letter from the Chalet gave me great joy, even though almost intolerably flinging across my grey old path the cold glitter of youth and sport and the awful winter-breath of the Alps—her having immersed herself in which presents little Elizabeth to me too, on her frozen height, like some small shining quartz-crystal set in the rock to which she is kindred, and yet hard enough to break by her firm edge the most geological hammer. Which means of course that if envy, aged impotent envy, of your *joie de vivre* could kill, you would already be stretched lifeless at my feet.

On February 5 *The Duchess of Wrexe* was published by Secker. The *Morning Post* treated it lengthily as a work of importance, and most of the other papers followed suit, though one or two critical voices were raised. Allan Monkhouse wrote in the *Manchester Guardian*: "If Mr Walpole could mistrust himself and his portentous methods he might become much more interesting," and the anonymous critic of the *Nation*: "Up to a point Mr Walpole holds one by his clever planning of his situations, by his bold and energetic scene-painting, by the rapid flow of his narrative, by the energy indeed of his creative imagination . . . and yet the whole effect of the story is of something half-real, pretentious, third-rate . . . in our opinion Mr Walpole has switched his talent on to a track that, whether it leads to popularity or not, is destructive of artistic quality."

Of all the charges which in their time stupidity and ignorance have levelled against Hugh, none is further from the truth than the suggestion that, having it in him to become a great writer of the stature, and perhaps in the manner, of Henry James, he deliberately surrendered this possibility in favour of money and popular success. Every book he wrote contained all that at the time he knew how to include, and if his great facility and love of story-telling led him sometimes to carelessness and over-production, that was simply the way his nature worked.

Hugh was not unduly distressed by these criticisms of *The Duchess*, since he never himself cared very much for this novel; in any case its sales were most satisfactory, and Henry James considered it his best book. *The Duchess of Wrexe* is chiefly remarkable for two reasons: first because the war quickly put an end for ever to the London it described, so that even fifteen years later its almost contemporary scene had become distantly historical: secondly, because it was one of the books discussed by Henry James in his famous article on "The Younger Generation."

Now Hugh was caught up once more in the whirl of social London. He was elected to the Beefsteak Club; at tea with Mrs Colefax he met for the first time Frederick Macmillan, who was to be for so long his publisher; he went to the Chelsea Arts Ball hand in hand with Mr Pooter ("Saw everyone—great fun only my trousers split"); he met Hugh Lane and was taken to see his pictures. At luncheon with the Colvins he argued with old Mary Cholmondeley about Conrad's *Chance*, to which he denied a leading place in its author's *œuvre*; with Somerset Maugham he dined and visited the Alhambra. ("He perfectly charming. Absolutely unspoiled, but happy about his last success.") He was a guest at a "famous lunch" given by Lilian Braithwaite at the Savoy. Among others present were the Alexanders, Pinero, the Granville Barkers, Maugham, the du Mauriers, and the Ranee of Sarawak. Hugh talked about Moscow to Granville Barker, who assured him that it was "just like Huddersfield plus patches of colour." He saw Henry James constantly, and talked for the first time to the great Lord Northcliffe: "Strange man with his fat face and shifty eyes—rather like a wicked hippo in training."

Two new friends of this time were Edmund Gwenn the actor, and Hubert Henry Davies the playwright. The latter gained a special place in Hugh's heart and memory, although the war soon separated them, and Davies died in 1917 of neurasthenia caused by overwork at British hospitals in France. He wrote eight full-length plays, of which *Mrs Gorringe's Necklace* (1903), *The Mollusc* (1907), and *Outcast* (1914) were the most successful. Fifteen years older than Hugh, he was a fellow-member of the Garrick Club, welcomed everywhere as a gay and amusing companion. When a collected edition of his plays was published after the war,[1] Hugh contributed a long biographical and appreciative introduction. Once again, as with Lady Colvin, he was able to point out qualities in his dead friend which were part of his own character:

One of the things that made his company so perpetually refreshing was the sensation that one had with him that today was the first day and the last

[1] *The Plays of Hubert Henry Davies* (2 vols, 1921).

day, there had never been any day like it before, that there would never be any day like it again, and that therefore one must live every moment of it. He had the actual consciousness of his happiness at the instant that he was experiencing it, and that is perhaps one of the rarest gifts given to human beings.

2

In the midst of all this activity, these last days of the Golden Age, there appeared the first part of Henry James's article on the contemporary novel, entitled "The Younger Generation" and published in *The Times Literary Supplement*.[1] Hitherto that journal had been supplied free each week with *The Times*; the issue of 19 March 1914 was the first to be sold separately (for one penny), and to mark the occasion the first part of James's article appeared on the front page under his name. James, who had suggested the article to the editor, had long been bewailing the lack of intelligent criticism, but having volunteered to fill the breach he was defeated by his lack of sympathy with the novelists and their works. Only Edith Wharton, his own disciple, seemed to him to have an inkling of the writer's art: the others were undoubtedly clever, but, as he so often put it, "helpless." So he veiled his distaste in skeins of equivocation such as only he could wind, and argument concerning the article centred, not so much on what he had said, as on the selection of writers discussed. In Hugh's words, "those named by him would have been triumphant indeed had they only been certain as to whether they were praised or blamed."

The first part dealt mainly with Wells, Bennett, and Gilbert Cannan[2] (D. H. Lawrence, dismissed at the tail-end of a sentence, was said to "hang in the dusty rear"); the second, which appeared on April 2, embraced Conrad, Mrs Wharton, Compton Mackenzie, and Hugh. (The fact that these last two were personal friends of James's did not pass unnoticed by the crowd.) The first part ended, apropos of Arnold Bennett, with the words: "which strikingly enough shows how much

---

[1] James afterwards included it, amplified, revised, and renamed "The New Novel," in his *Notes on Novelists* (1914). Quotations and references here are to the original article.

[2] James, in a letter to Hugh, had described one of Cannan's novels as "very helpless as to the *doing*, but again with a certain gravity of intention and considerability of squalid *renseignement*."

complexity of interest may be simulated by mere presentation of material, mere squeezing of the orange, when the material happens to be 'handsome' or the orange to be sweet," and the second part began:

The orange of our persistent simile is in Mr. Hugh Walpole's hands very remarkably sweet—a quality we recognize in it even while reduced to observing that the squeeze pure and simple, the fond, the lingering, the reiterated squeeze, constitutes as yet his main perception of method. He enjoys in a high degree the consciousness of saturation, and is on such serene and happy terms with it as almost make of critical interference, in so bright an air, an assault on personal felicity.

Full of material is thus the author of *The Duchess of Wrexe*, and of a material which we should describe as the consciousness of youth were we not rather disposed to call it a peculiar strain of the extreme unconsciousness. Mr. Walpole offers us indeed a rare and interesting case—we see about the field none other like it; the case of a positive identity between the spirit, not to say the time of life or stage of experience, of the aspiring artist, and the field itself of his vision. *The Duchess of Wrexe* reeks with youth and the love of youth and the confidence of youth—youth taking on with a charming exuberance the fondest costume or disguise, that of an adventurous and voracious felt interest, interest in life, in London, in society, in character, in Portland-place, in the Oxford-circus, in the afternoon tea-table, in the torrid weather, in fifty other immediate things as to which its passion and its curiosity are of the sincerest. The wonderful thing is that these latter forces operate, in their way, without yet being disengaged and hand-free—disengaged, that is, from their state of *being* young, with its billowy mufflings and other soft obstructions, the state of being present, being involved and aware, close "up against" the whole mass of possibilities, being in short intoxicated with the mixed liquors of suggestion. In the fumes of this acute situation Mr. Walpole's "subject matter" is bathed; the situation being so far more his own and that of a juvenility reacting, in the presence of everything, "for all it is worth," than the devised and constructed one, however he may circle about some such cluster, that every cupful of his excited flow tastes three times as much of his temperamental freshness as it does of this, that or the other character or substance, above all of this, that or the other bunch of antecedents and references, supposed to be reflected in it. All of which does not mean, we hasten to add, that the author of *The Duchess of Wrexe* has not the gift of life; but only that he strikes us as having received it, straight from nature, with such a concussion as to have kept the boon at the stage of violence—so that, fairly pinned down by it, he is still embarrassed for passing it on. On the day he shall have worked free of this primitive predicament, the convulsion itself, there need be no doubt of his exhibiting

matter into which method may learn how to bite. The tract affects us meanwhile as more or less virgin snow, and we look with interest and suspense for
the foot-print of a process.

By the time this appeared Hugh had left Hallam Street for good and
was happily working at Polperro. Although he confessed that some of
the drift of the criticism escaped him, it was clearly inclined to the
laudatory, and moreover it occupied two thirds of a column on the
front page of the leading literary journal in the kingdom. He wrote
expressing his gratitude, and back came the answer:

I am touched by your little note about the passage in the *Times* Lit:
Supp:—greatly touched; because I don't see quite how the passage can have
given you much more pleasure than a fond ingenuity may have enabled you
to extract from it. Therefore I owe your acknowledgement of my rather
meagre garland for your brow not a little to your brave good-will; which,
dearest Hugh, I deeply appreciate. The situation was very difficult for me—
and never shall I be caught in a like again. We will some day converse further
privately upon the fruits of your labour, but not again *coram publico*. The
publicity of all those remarks, on those 2 dates, has had tiresome consequences in the way of inquiries from the Neglected Young as to *why* they
were neglected, and as to whether they are not as good as those I *didn't*
neglect—also as to whether "I only speak then of my personal friends." I
shall never speak of nobody again, and the incident—an extraordinarily
accidental one—is closed. The friends of young "Mr. Beresford" (who *is*
young Mr. B?) want to know why I haven't raved about *him*—and the
enemies of young Mr. Compton Mackenzie to know why I *have* raved, etc,
etc. It's a devil's job, really—good-bye to it! (One *Mr. George* feels particularly slighted—and has sent me *The Making of an Englishman* to show me
what I have lost by not giving my article the benefit of it. But it only seems
to show me that I can't read it. For what do they take me? It was an in-
sensate step!)

By April 17 Hugh was writing to Pinker: "Quite between you and
me I thought H. J.'s *Times* things all wrong. Anyone who prefers
Edith Wharton to *Chance*, and *Sinister Street* to *Sons and Lovers*! Also
no mention of E. M. Forster, who can put the rest of us in his pocket."

3

Although the problems of *The Green Mirror* were working themselves
out in his head, Hugh was now chiefly busy with the short stories about

children which were to make up *The Golden Scarecrow*. He also did a little reviewing for *Punch* and regular reading for Methuen. Pinker reported good prospects for articles on Russia, which Hugh told him "will be entirely social and personal—*The Path to Rome* kind of thing. I want to do them as unlike anyone else as I can. I mean to have the most original time possible." Nor was he to be disappointed.

His seclusion was broken only by a visit to the Beresfords, at whose house he met the actress Athene Seyler. She was to become one of his dearest women friends—perhaps the dearest of all—since she was possessed of all those qualities which Hugh demanded from women before he could get on with them at all. Athene was intelligent, witty, forthright, and gaily affectionate without making any demands on him. The very few other women with whom he made close friends were in their different ways similarly endowed. Through the years Hugh's diary was to be sprinkled with such phrases as: "Athene is alone among women in the quickness of her perceptions and the unselfishness of her heart," and: "After Harold, Athene is of all people in the world the one I'm the most at home with. We laugh at all the same things."

Now, back at Polperro, Hugh was happier than he had ever been. Rooms in London were all very well, but here for the first time was some semblance of that home he had always longed for, and with it the opportunity to identify himself with a corner of England and make it his own. When Percy Anderson was with him, as he often was, perhaps the perfect friendship too seemed a possibility, and thus the two main themes of his life were tenuously and for a brief while joined.

Arnold Bennett, meanwhile, had some months before written an article called "Hugh Walpole, a Familiar Sketch," which now appeared in an American paper. In the course of it he said:[1]

The number of writers who really can write is extremely small at any given moment of the world's history. And when I discover a new one I am at least as excited as an astronomer who discovers a new star. *Mr. Perrin and Mr. Traill* is a book. Anybody with a passion for literature will understand what that phrase implies. I say it is a solemn thing to discover an authentic novelist. In the author of *Mr. Perrin and Mr. Traill* I discovered one. The

[1] The text here is taken from Bennett's manuscript, which was found among Hugh's papers. It is now in the Arnold Bennett museum at Burslem, Stoke-on-Trent, together with the complete correspondence between the two men.

hand of the born and consecrated novelist is apparent in *Mr. Perrin and Mr. Traill*. You cannot read it, and then say that it isn't true. You cannot read it and then say that it isn't beautiful. You may if you choose assert that there is a strain of psychological morbidity in Mr. Walpole's powerful gift. I shall not contradict you. I shall merely say that I like it. . . . About the time of the publication of *Mr. Perrin and Mr. Traill* I made the acquaintance of Mr. Walpole, and found a man of youthful appearance, rather dark, with a spacious forehead,[1] a very highly sensitised nervous organisation, and that reassuring matter-of-factness of demeanour which one usually does find in an expert. He was then busy at his task of seeing life in London. He seems to give about one third of the year to the tasting of all the heterogeneous sensations which London can provide for the connoisseur, and two thirds to the exercise of his vocation in some withdrawn spot of Cornwall that nobody, save a postman or so and Mr. Walpole, has ever beheld. During one month it is impossible to "go out" in London without meeting Mr. Walpole,—and then for a long period he is a mere legend of dinner-tables. He returns to the dinner-tables with a novel complete. . . . *Fortitude* is a long, ambitious, audacious, sombre, and comprehensive novel with an immense subject and scope. It is the sort of novel that most men are content to attempt at forty or forty-five. Mr. Walpole published it when he was yet under thirty. He probably considers it his *magnum opus*, and he is well entitled so to consider it. I should prefer to describe it as the *magnum opus* of his first period. For indeed, though he began writing long before Mr. William de Morgan, I reckon that Mr Walpole is scarcely out of his first period. (I cannot help remembering that at his age I had published nothing whatever.) His achievement is great, but his promise ought to be greater.

For which the delighted Hugh gave thanks:

My dear Bennett,

. . . I must send you a word to thank you for the sketch in the American paper—perfectly charming and I shall be proud till I die that you thus wrote about me. The only feeling I have is one of regret (but to you only I urge this because people take one at one's own declared valuation) that my stuff is still so ["perfunctory" scratched out] damned tentative. I do believe I'll find myself one day. I'm industrious enough, ambitious enough, loving it enough, and I do want to present you with a really good thing before I die. . . . The Henry James article (in *T.L.S.*) has caused much bad blood. Especially are the D. H. Lawrence supporters insulted. But *why* all this? Everybody is doing a different thing. I don't see where jealousy comes in.

---

[1] Opinions differ as to the exact colour of Hugh's hair. His sister remembers it as dark at this time, but others describe it as a lightish brown. Certainly his forehead grew ever more spacious as his hair receded farther and farther up his brow. By the end of his life his hair was quite grey.

I

I'm looking forward immensely to Russia in September. Pinker has fixed me up some articles in America. . . .

Yours always,

H. S. W.

Returning to London for the month of June, Hugh spent the first week-end with Bennett, whom he found "rather driven by money-lust and fear of indigestion. Upset by cook spelling Hors d'Œuvres 'Ordurv' on menu." For the rest, he saw a good deal of Henry James, was staggered by the genius of Chaliapin, sat for his portrait to Gerald Kelly, watched the tennis at Wimbledon, and read aloud the Umbrella chapter from *Mr Perrin* at a charity matinée. After a week in Ireland, he arrived home at Polperro on July 21, planning to start a critical study of Joseph Conrad at the end of the month—but graver events intervened.

4

The coming war first impinged on his consciousness on July 30, when in addition to his daily diary he began in a black exercise book a special war-diary, intended to chronicle the whole course of the struggle. He kept it up dutifully each day until August 15, added one more entry on the 21st, and thereafter only a page or two each year until 1920.

Most of what he recorded concerned the problematical moves of the Great Powers, and the infinitely gentle impact of war on the little community of Polperro, but underlying it all was a substratum of those agonised heart-burnings and self-communings which two generations of young men in the twentieth century have had to endure. He loved England and wanted to do something to help, but what? He knew that, being almost completely blind without his glasses, he would certainly be refused for the armed forces. Surely his brains, his literary gifts such as they were, could be put to some useful purpose?

By August 6 he could endure the strain no longer. Early that morning he took the London train among a crowd of returning holiday-makers. A friend asked him to keep an eye on a fourteen-year-old boy called Noel Coward. Hugh stood the boy lunch on the train and tipped him half a crown when they separated in London.

Next morning, still undecided as to his best course of action, Hugh was walking aimlessly along the Strand, when he ran into Valentine Williams, who was then on the staff of the *Daily Mail*. He asked Hugh if he would care to go to the Western Front as a war correspondent. Hugh jumped at the suggestion and rushed round to the Garrick Club, where he lunched, "bubbling over to all of them with excitement." After luncheon he went straight to the *Daily Mail* office, saw the editor, and discovered that Williams had misled him; there was no job available. Much disappointed, he spent the evening with Hubert Henry Davies at a music-hall, and caught the morning train back to Cornwall.

Alas, it was no longer the source of tranquillity it had once been. Very soon the solitude and lack of news began to affect his nerves, and in desperation he attempted to join the Cornish Constabulary. A journey to Plymouth met with no success, but eventually he succeeded in running to earth a stout and sweating constable at Looe. This poor man was exhausted by his efforts to hunt out German spies, and when Hugh had proudly given his name, "Of what nationality might that name be?" he asked, with a sudden look of suspicion. Expecting to be called out every moment, but cheered and calmed by the arrival of Percy Anderson, Hugh managed somehow or other to finish the second chapter of *The Green Mirror*: "It seems to me as real as anything else at this fantastic time."

And then his hopes received another setback. On August 18 he recorded: "Bad disappointment. Constables don't want me yet. Got to sit still and twiddle my thumbs." In the event, the Constabulary never called on him, and he had to content himself with an occasional patrol as an auxiliary coastguard.

Matters were rushing to a crisis with him, and its outcome is best described in his own words:

Aug. 25. Decide to enlist.

Aug. 26. Chaos. Into Plymouth to see about eyesight. Enlisting probably impossible.

Aug. 27. Enlisting stopped by possibility of going off to Russia to write articles against Slav peril.

Aug. 31. Off by the nine o'clock bus. All the village there to see me off. All of us weeping and myself plunged into melancholy all the way to Liskeard.

The first eleven days of September are covered by one compendious entry:

Now in London, the next days must be empty [in his diary]. Spent by me rushing about getting passport etc, chatting nonsense in the Garrick, saying good-bye to my friends, a visit to the McKennas. Behind it all the War, the War, the War. Wounded soldiers, Belgian refugees, alarmist placards, the Germans daily advancing nearer Paris, then suddenly checked and beaten back, 18,000 casualties, some people silly but nearly everyone cool and sensible, London very little different except lights out at night. Everyone now has fitted themselves into the war atmosphere and is ready for anything.

In a brief note to his mother he told her not to expect articles quickly, "as they are to be long and serious. But look out in the *Saturday Review* and the middle page of the *Mail*." To Henry James he wrote:

Dearest Master,
This is a hurried little letter of farewell. I'm just off to Russia for the *Mail* and others. I would have got down to you if there had been a chance but it's all been so hurried. Think of me as I cross the North Sea. I shall think of you continually and get back to you as soon as ever I can. I'll let you know regularly where I am if it's possible but I don't know where I may get to—to Berlin with the Russians I hope.

All my love to you!
Yr. devoted
H.[1]

The Master's blessing arrived from Lamb House in time to catch him:

Dearest, dearest Hugh,
I am deeply moved by your news, and only a bit heartbroken at the thought you will have left London, I gather, by the time this gets there—though I write it but an hour after receipt of your note; so that the best I can do is to send it to the Garrick to be "forwarded." You will probably be so much forwarder than my poor pursuing missive always, that I feel the dark void shutting me out from you for a long time to come—save as I shall see your far-off light play so bravely over the public page. Your adventure is of the last magnificence of pluck, the finest strain of resolution, and I bless and

---

[1] This and all the other surviving letters from Hugh to Henry James are now in the Houghton Library at Harvard.

cheer and honour it for all I am worth. It will be of the intensest interest and of every sort of profit and glory to you—which doesn't prevent however my as intensely yearning over you, my thinking of you with all the ache of privation. But of such yearnings and such aches, such privations and such prides, is all our present consciousness made up; and I wait for you again with a confidence and courage which I try to make not too basely unworthy of your own. Feel yourself at any rate, dearest boy, wrapped round in all the affection and imagination of your devotedest old

Henry James.

Hugh's last afternoon and evening were spent with Hubert Henry Davies and Percy Anderson respectively. On the morning of September 12 Edmund Gwenn saw him off at King's Cross, and that same night he embarked at Hull for his Russian adventure.

BOOK THREE

THE FIRST WAR

Glad was I when I reached the other bank.
 Now for a better country. Vain presage!
 Who were the strugglers, what war did they wage
Whose savage trample thus could pad the dank
Soil to a plash? Toads in a poisoned tank,
 Or wild cats in a red-hot iron cage—

Robert Browning
"Childe Roland to the Dark Tower Came"

CHAPTER NINE

RUSSIAN OVERTURE

I

IF anyone had asked Hugh why he was going to Russia, he would have found it difficult to frame a convincing reply. Even supposing that the "Slav peril" existed at that time, it was unlikely that he, knowing nobody in Russia, totally ignorant of the country, and without a word of the language, would be able to contribute much to the debate. Besides, there were already competent English journalists on the spot, among them Harold Williams and Hamilton Fyfe. No, he was going for other reasons: to get away from the atmosphere of doubt and inaction; to *do* something involving movement, change—something connected with the war; to find a place where his writing could go forward, perhaps even receive fresh impetus.

His journey, by way of Christiania, Stockholm, and Raumo in Finland, was surprisingly swift and comparatively comfortable. After spending a day in Petrograd, he reached Moscow on September 24 and was moved to tears by the sight of the Kremlin in twilight. His first visit was to the British Consulate, where he at once found a new friend in the Vice-Consul, R. H. Bruce Lockhart. He and his wife entertained Hugh constantly at their flat, introduced him to the English colony, took him to the ballet, the opera, the circus, and altogether looked after him. Lockhart's impression of him was of someone "entirely unspoilt, [who] could still blush from an overwhelming self-consciousness, and impressed me more as a great, clumsy schoolboy, bubbling over with kindness and enthusiasm, than as a dignified author, whose views were to be accepted with awe and respect." [1]

Hugh quickly found rooms with a Russian family who specialised in accommodating foreigners, and here he began his long struggle with the Russian language. Despite recurring bouts of homesickness he managed also to make some headway with *The Green Mirror*, and to read with enjoyment *Du Côté de Chez Swann*. Among the resorts to

[1] *Memoirs of a British Agent* (1932).

which Lockhart introduced him was a famous night-club called The Bat, a sort of offshoot of the Moscow Art Theatre, run by Nikita Baleieff, who was later to delight the capitals of the world with his Chauve-Souris troupe. Here Hugh met such towering figures as Gorky and Chaliapin, but more immediately he was charmed by the grace and talents of Michael Lykiardopoulos. Lyki, part Greek, part Russian, part English, combined the secretaryship of the Art Theatre with the translation into Russian of the works of many of the leading English writers of the day. His gift for languages and his position at the heart of literary and artistic Moscow were a great help to the lonely young Englishman.

The morale of the people was still high. The sickening defeat of the northern Russian armies at Tannenberg had been balanced by successes in the south, where the Austrians had been driven from the Galician plain. The two main factors which were to bring the army to a standstill and hasten the Revolution—the hopeless lack of arms and ammunition, and the realisation that the war was likely to be a long one—had not yet become evident. Nor, if they had, would Hugh have been any the wiser. If few in Moscow received much information from any war front, he received less than anybody. His diary hereabouts is full of complaints of his total lack of news, as he vainly attempted to dish up from his stagnant backwater some kind of material for the *Daily Mail*. On October 2 he wrote to his mother:

I'm not writing much—an article once a fortnight for the *Daily Mail*. . . . The town is under martial law, and if you speak a word of German you are put in prison. The Vice-Consul and his wife here are very nice to me, but they are the only people I know. When I know some Russian I'm going to see if I can get off to the Front, but that won't be yet.

Three weeks later he reported to her:

I'm afraid my journalism isn't coming to much. The two things I've sent the *Mail* they've thought too literary and not enough about the war. I shall do a series of half a dozen for the *Saturday Review*. . . . I go on at my novel. I find it a kind of narcotic.

On November 11 he received a "long, not very interesting" letter from Henry James, which the old man had dictated to his secretary Theodora Bosanquet, and which called forth this spirited response:

Nov. 12th   Moscow.

My dearest Master,

Your letter has just arrived—the first word I've had from you since I heard in Cornwall.[1] If *your* face fell at the blankness of my last, so did *mine* fall at finding the heart of Miss Bosanquet (an excellent thing, I'm sure) presented to me in neat type instead of your own. Three words in your own hand and in your own voice would have been everything—as it was I got nothing. Let me, in answer to this, have just three words of your own— otherwise I shall curse the censor even more than I do. For I *did* write to you, a long letter—the note I sent just as I thought I was off to Warsaw. Moreover so many letters of mine have never got to England at all and have been, I can only suppose, stopped by the censor, that I thought I'd run no risk of that note not getting to you. Now I'm going to run risks and let the censor be damned!

Well, I had the bloodiest six weeks of my whole life first. I'd never known such homesickness. I got not a line from any living soul during the first month, although letters have come in plenty since. People were kind but it all seemed to be an inferno of rain, pasteboard, policemen and prostitutes. Moscow in the rain looked appalling, all the gilt domes tawdry, the hideous modern buildings like sham scenery at Earls Court. The streets swam in mud, I got no news of the war because I couldn't read, the food was all sweets and cabbage, and I was lonely beyond belief. I felt too that I was utterly useless. They wouldn't have me in England because I couldn't see, here in the streets they thought I was a German.

The family I live with consist of a nice woman, a melancholy man and three children. The flat is minute and an incredible number of people live in it—strangers come and go, the smells and the noise only are constant. I begin now to talk a little Russian but for weeks it seemed absolutely impossible—a language like idiots talking beautifully in an asylum—it *is* most beautiful. The melancholy man has fits of awful temper—every third morning. On Monday I am woken by hearing his voice raised in a shrill trembling scream and it goes on and on. All Monday and Tuesday husband and wife don't speak. Wednesday morning he cries at breakfast and is forgiven. Thursday morning it begins again. He's very polite to me because they've no money and I mean a living to them. He offers me cigarettes and chocolates which he keeps warm in his pockets. He's an inventor and in the last month has invented a new kind of grey sock, a new paint to be extracted from the bark of trees, a new ink and a new sort of soap. The Ink Period was awful—everything was covered with it—and when he made one of his

---

[1] Hugh was constantly accusing his friends of not having written to him, when they had, and he had not written to them. He seemed determined to cook up an epistolary grievance.

reconciliations with his wife, after their embraces they were both covered with it. However the Soap Period corrected that. The bath is used by every-one in the flat indiscriminately but it is dangerous because it is surmounted by a huge spray which no one can manage. This emits a torrent of scalding water at any moment.

In the evenings there are occasional parties; ladies come in and play cards, drink tea and talk about God. God is a topic of incessant interest, half of Russia (the lower half) being as sure of Him as they are of their own fleas, the other half (the intelligentsia) being sure that He isn't, but having the sort of interest in Him that we have now in George Eliot or Tennyson. I am very lucky in that the mistress of the house is a nice woman and an excellent teacher. I work at Russian about four hours a day and have it with my meals, asking for potatoes and then being told that I have to use the genitive. It *is* a lovely language, rich as gold brocade and full of lovely words. It's meant to be used I'm [sure] in torrents of discourse all night as they use it here. I'm making a little progress now and I don't think mastering it will be im-possible but it needs a new jaw and throat.

As to the Russians themselves, what is one to say? Every Russian in the street has the softest tenderest eyes and the hard savage mouth of a barbarian. They seem to me at present to live three skins nearer to naked emotions than I should have believed possible. They seem to have no control and yet they have allowed without a murmur the abolition of vodka, the very centre of their existence—this seems to me quite the most wonderful thing the war has yet done anywhere. They are amazingly humble, always sure that every other country does things better than themselves—but their Art Theatre so utterly outdistances anything theatrical I've ever seen that my eyes have at last been opened to a conception of what acting and the whole form and spirit of drama can be. No one who has been here a fortnight can have any doubt about their victory in this war. They are a new people; this crisis has done the thing to them that everything in history has failed to do to them before—given them self-confidence. Their modern literature seems to be very slight—short stories and poetry—hardly a novel at all—two morbid men Artzybachev and Kouprin and, of course, Andreev, who now writes bad plays.

I've given up absolutely any idea of journalism for the present. It's all far too new, too deep, too interesting for me to splash my ignorance upon. My idea now is to learn Russian as hard as I can and then after Christmas to get off on a hospital-train, as a stretcher-bearer to the front.

I find, strangely enough, that nothing makes me happier than writing a bit of a novel each day. It's like being back in England and for that very reason I do think this book may be more real, more "done" and felt than my other experiments. At any rate it consoles me. For the truth is, dear

Master, that I'm appallingly lonely. Everyone here is immensely kind, but I don't seem to want them. I don't want anyone except you and, shall I say, two others? You alone—say half a day, or even luncheon (how *dare* Mackenzie smoke those cigarettes and eat those preserved fruits and look at that view?)—and I would come back here quite contented. So please let me have at once in answer to this a word from *you* and *not* Miss B.

Send me the book of essays. Books do get here if registered. I found *The Portrait of a Lady* in a dirty Tauchnitz in a dirty French shop here. It's been a step towards you. There's lots more to tell you. That shall be later.

I do love you very much.

Yr. loving "*fils*,"

H.

All the time he was worried because he was doing so little to help on the war. To his mother he wrote on November 14: "It's a consolation to me that my eyes prevented my enlisting, so that anyhow I wouldn't be able to be in the army, but it seems such a shame when I'm so strong and yet not helping more. However it's a long business, and I'm sure, later on, my chance will come." And then one day at luncheon he met an officer who promised to take him to the Polish front. Wild with excitement Hugh finished Book I of *The Green Mirror* and wrote to tell his mother the good news.

2

There were the usual delays, the officer fell ill, Hugh began to get cold feet ("Feel I don't want to go but that it's right to do so"), but on the evening of December 1 he left Moscow in a train packed with officers, one of whom proved to be a nineteen-year-old girl in Cossack uniform. Two long days in the train were spent singing Russian songs, eating cold sausage, and reading the latest novels of Arnold Bennett, Elizabeth, and May Sinclair. The officers chaffed the girl, and occasionally for Hugh's benefit shouted at him all the English words they knew—"All right," "I love you," "How do you do," and "Tennis—Love—Deuce:" otherwise they sang or slept. At Warsaw Hugh spent a week in a hotel, writing *The Green Mirror*, reading *Crime and Punishment*, eating in cafés, watching the soldiers. He was greatly moved by the columns singing as they marched to battle, and he wrote a vivid account of his impressions of Warsaw.[1] At last his escorting officer reappeared, and next day they set off for the front.

Dec. 12. Started off about mid-day. Got to a wild-looking station and crept into an army train. Was discovered by the Commandant who finally however gave me leave to go. Was travelling till midnight. Jumped off the train at Sokachoff. Believe the Germans only five miles away. Plunged right into the heart of it. Passed through all the watchfires and arrived at the town. Found a bed in a half-ruined inn.

Dec. 13. One of the days of my life and nearly the last. Endless adventures —German aeroplanes overhead—all the Russian army firing from every side. Wonderful views from the hill—the river, the fields of horses, the riding Cossacks, the regiments crossing the bridge, the cannon getting nearer and nearer, the endless lines of carts on the horizon, the smoke of the battle and the reflection of the shrapnel, the evening with the sky all red, the black village and all the army moving about silently, the graves, the wounded riding in bleeding, the dead coming in on carts, the burnt houses.

Next morning he returned to Warsaw, where he at once retired to bed with influenza and enjoyed Saintsbury's *Nineteenth Century Literature*. A few days later he was back in Moscow.

23 December 1914.   Moscow.

My dearest Master,

. . . This is only a note now to tell you that I am returned, to thank you for your splendid letter and the book.[2] I am deep in the latter and am absorbed by it. But, truly, I am so tired that I can hardly hold my head up and I shall go to sleep for a day and a half. I had a very wonderful time and got nearly to Lodz—further than the correspondents and further than any other Englishman I believe. I was for part of the time within three miles of the Germans and just escaped being a prisoner which I should have hated. I had also one or two narrow squeaks, once especially when I was caught under two German aeroplanes and the whole Russian army began to fire on every side of me. I had a lot of ground to cover before I found a trench. That little accident and others were due to my eyesight which was my chief trouble. Whenever there was a mist I couldn't see either with my glasses or without them and blundered about in a most dangerous fashion. Nevertheless I saw a great deal—a wonderful lot. In Warsaw I saw practically the working of

[1] *Saturday Review*, 30 January 1915. Altogether Hugh contributed six articles to this paper between November 1914 and March 1915.
[2] *Notes on Novelists*.

the whole Russian army and could tell you so much that I mustn't or you'd never get this.

I've come back now for two months to go on hard at my Russian which I am beginning to get hold of. Then I shall go back to the Front for a month and, at the beginning of April, come back to England, thank God. Everyone is charming to me here but I'm as homesick as ever—so good for me, I'm sure. This is *only* to thank you and tell you that I shall think of you on Christmas Day—*if* I'm awake! I'll write a proper letter later on. Ever so much love and may the time pass quickly to Easter!

Yr. loving
H.

In due course James replied:

Your mere hints of your experiences and escapes reduce me to a sense [of] my own restriction to twaddle which fairly makes me sick. . . . *Do* be careful, however, of where you take your walks when you return to the Front. If I could lend you even *my* poor old eyes (as people lend their ears) you would tread the labyrinth in such a manner as to restore you absolutely without a flaw to your affectionate old H. J.

On the same day, December 23, Hugh wrote a long letter to Mrs Belloc Lowndes in answer to a long gossipy one from her, repeating much of what he had said to James, and continuing:

As to the future of the novel, I think that some may be killed by the war and some be created, but I'm certainly not pessimistic. I don't think people will have much sympathy with cynicism, Shavianism and the rest. The great thing will be, I believe, a rather simple reality. But big work won't be affected. I don't believe any war would affect the life of, say, *Typhoon*, *Clayhanger*, or *The Portrait of a Lady*—and certainly not work bigger than those again. I've had some novels sent out by kind friends but was badly disappointed in them all except May Sinclair's which I thought very fine. When I read anything as mechanical as *The Price of Love* [by Arnold Bennett] I thank my stars that I'm as immature and feeble as I am. There's always hope so long as you're struggling to be better, but when you've found your method and are content with it, God help you! Don't you agree? . . .

Oh! It's all so strange and higgledy-piggledy here! When I was in London I was spoilt. I shall never be spoilt again. Mind you answer this and let me have a glimpse of you! Oh, this flat! The noise of the children, the mistress of it running out in her chemise (it's eleven o'clock) to answer the telephone, the purple-green towers opposite my window next to a hideous modern villa, the dirt and friendliness, the taste and the utter lack of it!

3

On 7 January 1915 he celebrated the Russian Christmas Day by having a violent argument with Lyki, who maintained that Jack London was a better writer than Conrad, and by dining with the Lockharts, where he "won prodigiously" at vingt-et-un. A few days later his old friend Arthur Ransome arrived in Moscow. He had originally come to Russia in 1913 in search of fairy stories, but on the outbreak of war had hurried home. Now he was back with an unofficial brief from the Foreign Office to keep them informed of the trend of affairs, and his activities were to have a direct influence on Hugh's career. Meanwhile Henry James must be kept in the picture:

1 February 1915.   Moscow.

My dearest Master,

I was greatly delighted to get your letter last week. I would have answered it before but I have been for several days in bed with influenza. When a thaw comes here everyone at once goes to bed with typhoid or pneumonia or diphtheria, so I was very lucky to get off with influenza. However it left me very weak and depressed if I'd let the black devil that sits on one of my bed-posts jump off it. However he's all right there for the present. Now it's a blizzard and the snow mounts higher and higher and we seem to sink lower and lower. It may be the end of the world—I'm not sure that it isn't—no Russian would mind very much if it were.

In a day or two I start on my adventures again—this time for six weeks or two months. I go first to Petrograd and there stay with Hamilton Fyfe—the *Mail* man. I shall then go on to Warsaw which, as I write, I hear the Germans are going to make a fresh effort against. I must confess that it's so cold that I don't look forward awfully to sleeping again under hedges and in half-ruined houses, but after all it's everyone's lot now. But it *is* cold. I shan't now return until September to England. Now that I know some Russian I can do much here that is of interest and even, a little, of importance. Indeed anything may happen to me after I leave here on Friday. "I cast my bread upon the waters"—good luck to it! If I thought the war would be over this year I'd come home in April and try my luck in France, but I know it won't, so there'll be plenty of time for France in September.

I haven't got much further with the Russian character. I still regard Tchekov's *Cherry Garden* as the most perfect representation of it, but it's no use only reading it—you've got to see it acted here by the Artistic Theatre people. No English writer seems to me the least right about them, because they either idealise or curse. The truth lies simply on the basis that a Russian has all the human instincts at their simplest, strongest, most primitive—the instinct for beauty, for brotherhood, for dirt, for cruelty, for altruism, for selfishness, for everything—and he doesn't know what restraint means—*yet*. When he does he'll be terrifically important but not nearly so interesting. How they eat! How they have women! How they talk about Love and God and Brotherhood! How they distrust one another and fight in the trams! How they push the women about and eat duck with their fingers! How absorbed they are in their own psychology, how interested in themselves and how distrustful of themselves! How careless and casual and hospitable and affectionate! They seem to me the last people to carry on a successful war, and yet this war is drawing wonderful qualities out of them—it may be *the* great crisis of their history. I really shall, I think, have an interesting book to write after my year here.

My novel goes on happily and is in no way embarrassed by all the turmoil —in fact, when I write it, I find myself more concentrated in it than I have ever been before. I enjoy it and it prevents me from yielding to home-sickness. The last is an awful disease and I get no better of it. Now that I've decided to stay until September it seems almost unbearable, and yet I know it's the right thing to do. As to home things, people are very good about writing. Secker sent me a delightful prospectus of the things that he's going to do this year. I like especially his pocket edition of your shorter stories. How pleasant to be in the same catalogue with you! I have appearing some-time in the spring a book about children called *The Golden Scarecrow*. It might have been possible if I'd been at home to rewrite and so on—but as it is! . . . and I can't stop it. However, the war will put a pillow quite effectively over its fair young head!

Please write to me—all letters will be forwarded. I shall send you p.c.'s, the only things possible.

Yr. most loving

H.

Please when you write tell me how you are, whether you can write much, whether you'll go to Rye.

A week later he had finished *The Golden Scarecrow* and was installed in the Hôtel de France at Petrograd. He soon came to prefer that city to Moscow. "Of course Moscow is more interesting and beautiful as a place," he wrote to Mrs Lockhart, "but as far as living goes, there simply seems to me no comparison." He worked on at *The Green Mirror*, en-joyed the company of Hamilton Fyfe, and was introduced to Lady Georgina Buchanan, the wife of the British Ambassador. And then at the beginning of March he met the man who was to be his greatest friend in Russia. This was Konstantine Andreevich Somoff, then a man of forty-six and one of the most successful painters in the country. "Sad, charming, ugly man," wrote Hugh, "a little like Reggie Turner and Robbie Ross." And again two days later, after their second meeting: "Most attractive personality. Very quiet—one of the saddest faces I've ever seen—beautiful eyes. We got on, I think. I'm determined that we *shall*. With all Russians there seems that same strange attraction—the attraction that grown-ups feel for children."

Not pausing to decide which was grown-up, which child, Hugh dashed back to Moscow, and a few days later returned to Petrograd with his books, clothes, money, a pile of letters from England, first proofs of *The Golden Scarecrow*, and a set of Conrad's books, sent him for the purpose of his critical study.

4

One of the letters was from Henry James, and in it the Master had assumed a difficult and painful duty—that of hinting that Hugh ought to come home because of what people were saying. Mrs Belloc Lowndes, who had twice guardedly suggested in letters that Hugh was missing all the fun and should come home, has described [1] how that winter she and Henry James were both guests of an important London hostess. This lady "spoke with scorn of the fact that immediately on the outbreak of war Walpole had left his country." Mrs Lowndes pointed out that Hugh had long ago arranged to visit Russia, and that his eyesight made it impossible for him to join up, but the hostess would not withdraw. This so enraged Henry James that, seizing Mrs Lowndes's arm, he muttered: "Let you and me who are friends of Walpole leave this house." Outside in the street she could see that he was "still shaken with what seemed uncontrollable anger," and that same evening he wrote to her:

I rejoice to hear that you have written kindly and considerately to Hugh W.—he will greatly value it. I don't see how one can *not* do one's friend the

[1] In *The Merry Wives of Westminster* (1946).

justice and pay him the respect of treating him as if he is neither a baby nor a beast, and that if he is *reflectively* taking a certain course, or deciding in a certain way, there may be much more to be said for it than even *our* brilliant eyes discern.

It was not James's habit to call a spade a spade, so that his warning to his traduced disciple arrived closely wrapped in a muffler of words, very tentatively and carefully chosen:

I am sorry the black homesickness so feeds upon you amid your terrific paradoxical friends, the sport alike of their bodies and their souls, of whom your account is admirably vivid; but I well conceive your state, which has my tenderest sympathy—that nostalgic ache at its worst being the invention of the very devil of devils. Don't let it break the spell of your purpose of learning Russian, of really mastering it—though even while I say this I rather wince at your telling me that you incline not to return to England till September next. I don't put that regret on the score of my loss of the sight of you till then—that gives the sort of personal turn to the matter that we are all ashamed together of giving to any matter now. But the being and the having been in England—or in France, which is now so much the same thing —during at least a part of this unspeakable year affects me as something you are not unlikely to be sorry to have missed—there attaches to it—to the being here—something so sovereign and so initiatory in the way of a British experience. I mean that it's as if you wouldn't have had the full general British experience without it, and that this may be a pity for you as a painter of British phenomena—for I don't suppose you think of reproducing *only* Russian for the rest of your shining days. However, I hasten to add that I feel the very greatest aversion to intermeddlingly advising you—your completing your year in Russia all depends on what you *do* with the precious time. You may bring home fruits by which you will wholly be justified. Address yourself indeed to doing that and putting it absolutely through— and I will, for my part, back you up unlimitedly. Only, bring your sheaves with you, and gather in a golden bundle of the same. I detest, myself, the fine old British horror—as it has flourished at least up to now, when in respect to the great matter that's upon us, the fashion has so much changed— of doing anything consistently and seriously. So if you *should* draw out your absence I shall believe in your reasons.

Hugh took the hint immediately, being perhaps half-prepared for some such advice, but he was much too excited by new prospects to let it dismay him.

15 March 1915.   Petrograd.

My dearest, dearest Master,

After three weeks (no, five) wandering I at last got my post again, and at the heart of it, your most delightful letter. I'm settled now at the above address for six weeks or two months for reasons that I'll give you in a moment, so that this is the place to write to. Meanwhile I must first say how happy I am at the fine spirits and courage of your letter. I think of you so continually, and now until the next letter comes I shall be able to have the finest picture in my mind. There are so many things in your letter about which I should love to talk to you—meanwhile I must do what I can.

First as to myself and my answer to your urging me to return home. At last all my plans are made and my ambitions realized. I now officially belong to the "Sanitar" here. The "Sanitar" is the part of the Red Cross that does the rough work at the front, carrying men out of the trenches, helping in the base hospitals in every sort of way, doing every kind of rough job. They are an absolutely official body and I shall be one of the few (half-dozen) Englishmen in the world wearing Russian uniform. I've long had this in view but whilst I knew no Russian it was pretty hopeless. Now all is settled if I pass the doctor. I have, first, six weeks' training in first aid at the hospitals here, and then I go off to the very "frontiest of the front."

I am, as a matter of fact, in a state of extraordinary exhilaration. It is not that I don't realise all the tragedy and horror—I've seen already a considerable amount of it—but to be an actor (however tiny) in the greatest piece of history in the life of the world, to see *such* things, to be tested by the very deepest tests of all and to watch other people being tested, is to be so uplifted that one isn't a human being at all but something disembodied and quite abstract. . . . Well, I mustn't get high-falutin'——

Disease is going to be our chief enemy I fancy at the front when the snow goes. I've been vaccinated and in a fortnight's time shall be inoculated for typhoid. I'm determined to come home in September even though the sky turns blue. By then I shall have had four months' Red Cross work and ought to be useful on the other front—and there I hope to be all the winter. I think that early next year will see the end of the war.

I am greatly interested by what you say about writing. I have had rather the same experience—but the novel that I have been doing here has been the most wonderful comfort and I've enjoyed a kind of omniscience in saying to my characters: "Ah, *I* know what an upheaval's in store for you after *this* little account of your troubles is concluded. If *you* only knew you wouldn't think your present worries so important." That gives a kind of fillip to the humour of it (this is the first book with a sense of humour in it written by ME!). But I don't, on the whole, feel anything but quickened and enlivened by the volcano. I'm quite ready to take my pill with the rest, and if I peg out at the front, which is possible, I shall only be wildly annoyed at being deprived of so much existence, and disappointed at dying before I've written a decent book. However I'm not going to die—the chubby people like me *must* grow into chubby old men or what's the Garrick and the Athenæum for?

Meanwhile I'm having an amusing time here. Besides my hospital and my writing I walk in the afternoons with that pillar of Philistinism, Hamilton Fyfe of the *Daily Mail*. He is truly wonderful. He is *the* Man in the Street—exactly and absolutely. He *hates* Russia. Because his clothes are three weeks at the wash he says that Tchekov is no dramatist; because the Russians don't play football he says that they must be homosexualists (which they *never* are). Because he *can't* learn the Russian language he says that they're a "brainless lot." At the same time he is a mass of stern kindness and military sentiment. He cries in a manly way over leaders in *The Times* about patriotism—so do I —only *not* in a manly way. He is always buying his wife little presents but is furious with her if she has an original idea (she very seldom has). We go for a walk every afternoon.

My evenings are spent with quite the most interesting set in Russia just now—all the chief writers, artists and musicians—Merejkowsky, Sologub, Glazounov, Scriabine, Somoff (the latter I think you would delight in). He is, I suppose, the most famous Russian painter living—very cosmopolitan, has lived much in Paris and Berlin. They are all amazing to me—just like babies in spite of their intelligence. They cry and laugh, believe everything one minute and nothing the next, don't know what they want, kind and rough—I should like to tell you and indeed the whole of England the real relation of this country to the war. I haven't seen one word in the papers that bears the slightest relation to the real psychology of the thing. . . .

I must stop to catch the post. I'll write soon again.

Your most loving
H.

5

At the end of March Hugh was for the first time invited to luncheon at the British Embassy. The Ambassador, Sir George Buchanan, was in the great tradition of British diplomacy : handsome, courageous, modest, elegant and courteous, he possessed what Bernard Pares described as "a kind of baffling simplicity" which often caused foreigners to take him for stupid. "He kept," writes his old subordinate H. J. Bruce, "to a middle register of imperturbable serenity," and up to the time when the world he knew disappeared beneath the tidal wave of

Bolshevism, his judgment was seldom at fault. Hugh's first impression —"very nice albeit something feeble"—was a typical newcomer's misconception. "They are what one would call 'homely', aren't they?" he wrote to Mrs Lockhart. "He seems to be terrified by war correspondents and was very relieved when he found that I wasn't one."

Luckily Sir George's first impression of Hugh was more favourable, and it was arranged that he should assist at the English Hospital, where Lady Georgina had organised a band of volunteers. He began this work early in April, very happy to be doing something useful at last. He would help in the wards and the operating theatre for several hours each morning, then go home and write in his rooms. Here is a diary entry of this time:

April 14. Eventful day. In the morning at the hospital eight wounded suddenly arrived from the front. Had to bathe them, the most gruesome business—one man especially with his head split open, his leg off and one hand smashed. Came back quite worn out. . . . Surely this is the great period of my life! Finished Chapter I of the *Conrad*—not well, but how can I do it when things are like this?

Most of his evenings were spent with Somoff, to whom he was becoming deeply attached. Arthur Ransome introduced him to Harold Williams, the correspondent of the *Daily Chronicle*, who had a profound love and knowledge of Russia—attributes which were to prove useful to Hugh in years to come.

Although all his writing-time was now devoted to Conrad, ideas for novels were always working themselves out in his head. Wisely he had decided to lay aside the three-quarters-finished *Green Mirror*, and already his first Russian story was beginning to take shape. *The Dark Forest* is much the sharpest in outline of all his books, much the closest to actuality; most of its scenes were straight reporting done on the spot; yet the bones of the book—its theme and plot and even its original title, *Death and the Hunters*—were in position weeks before he left for the Galician front: only the background was lacking.

Meanwhile on May 4, after less than a month's work, "finished the *Conrad* to my huge surprise. That I really should have written a critical book, however small and however bad, is truly amazing. I think the part about Conrad's methods is fair—the rest nil."

His last few days in Petrograd were busy:

May 9. Lunched at the Embassy. Old Buchanan depressed because of the poisonous gases. Much talk about the sinking of the *Lusitania*. Evening Karsavina in *La Fille Mal Gardée*—most charming thing I've seen in Russia. Her acting and dancing quite wonderful—seemed inspired.

May 14. Great day. At eleven in the morning I became a Russian officer —one of the few Englishmen in history who have been one. Strange being saluted.

Arthur Ransome, who together with Lyki and the Fyfes helped him to pack, remembers that he had great difficulty in manipulating his sword. Nevertheless, accompanied by Somoff, he left that evening for Moscow, where he spent a few days in final preparations, and on May 22 he set off with the rest of his unit for the Carpathians. He was much upset at parting from Somoff, nor did his first glimpse of his new companions reassure him. The Otriad, or small mobile hospital, which was to be attached to the Russian Ninth Army, consisted of male surgeons, female nurses, and a few male orderlies of whom Hugh was one. His Russian, never very fluent, was at this time rudimentary: he felt lonely, homesick, and apprehensive. To cheer himself up he read Dostoevsky's *House of the Dead* in the train.

CHAPTER TEN

DEATH AND THE HUNTERS

I

THE Russians' ill-advised advance through the Carpathians into Galicia, though backed by little force and less determination, had alarmed the Germans sufficiently to induce them to mount a major counter-offensive under Mackensen and Seeckt. On May 1 their bombardment had opened, and all through the month the Russian armies had been driven back until now some fragile sort of a line had been established between the Dniester and the San.

On the 24th the Otriad reached Lvov: next day they left the train at Stanislau, and completed the journey by motor. Quartered in a small village in the heart of the country, they had little to do for some days. Hugh read a lot of Browning and began writing *Death and the Hunters*. He was missing Somoff badly, and the writing took his mind from his homesickness. Rumours of troop movements and battles began to arrive, and on the moonlit evening of June 1 they set off from Maidan in haycarts towards the front. Here is Hugh's diary entry for the next day:

June 2. The dawn was beautiful. Soon after we went off to look for the battle. The cannon were booming now in the forest. We went off in our haycarts to look for them. We got right into the forests which were lovely in the early morning, the sky red and gold, the birds singing. Although the cannon sounded so near we found nothing there and went off to another part. Here we found plenty, and soon we were settled just behind a trench with a battery banging in our ear. The soldiers had settled into the trench as though they had been born in it, and they looked at us with a kind of amiable indifference. Then came a long wait. I got a bad headache from the noise of the battery and felt lonely and miserable—not frightened, though shrapnel was singing over our heads. About five we moved down to another trench where I sat until dark. Nice old colonel here—fine old farm here with a beautiful old tree—all very merry here, beautiful hot supper, soldiers sewing, laughing, waiting. Old Colonel tells stories about lovely women when the noise pauses. At dark set off to find dead. This really rather alarming, the hedges filled with silent soldiers, the moonlight making everything unreal and

138

unsafe. We found our men, then were met by an officer with a large silent company behind him who told us that we must hurry as they were going to begin an attack. We *did* hurry, and just as we got our carts out of the position and began to climb the hill, the whole landscape behind us, which had been dead still, cracked into sound. The cannon broke out on every side of us—fires and flashes and coloured lights and a noise as though the sky, made of china, had broken into a million pieces and fallen—a magnificent unforgettable spectacle. At last, after a long ride, got back to Maidan. On the way met some of ours going to the battle—gave me my first letter from K. [Somoff.]

Next morning, after a hideously uncomfortable night, he felt utterly discouraged and longed to take the first train back to Petrograd, but he reassured himself by reflecting: "This is not so bad as it was at Marlow." [1] Somehow the day passed, and then came fresh adventure:

In the evening we started off again to the forest, and found ourselves about eleven at night in the same place as the first time. Thick stars, much cannon, and at last we found ourselves on the further side under the forest. Here happened the adventure of my life. Started off with several Sanitars to find wounded, got some way and all the Sanitars sat down and refused to go any further. I forgot all my Russian, swore at them in English, at last induced them to go with me. Had then a most perilous adventure—shrapnel bursting very close to us, all amongst the lines, creeping in and out avoiding the moon, crossing the river, stumbling over hidden soldiers who didn't cheer us by telling us to be quick as they were going to begin firing. Pathetic how we longed to find a wounded man. At last found one, then one of the Sanitars refused to return, so we had to go back three, I carrying one end of the stretcher alone. I thought that journey would never end, the thing was so heavy, the shrapnel so close and the road so difficult. At last back—in all about two hours.

For his share in this exploit Hugh was awarded the St George's Cross.

Two days later the wounded began to come back in large numbers; all ranks of the Otriad were called upon to help, and Hugh wrote with some pride: "Extracted my first bullet, assisted at my first operation." Next day he was sent out with a small party to bury the dead. After

[1] Compare this passage from Osbert Sitwell's *Laughter in the Next Room*: "Even in the depths of spirit, however, to which the monotony of the life [in the trenches in 1914] reduced me, I did not hate the routine here as I had hated it in my private school. At least Bloodsworth had done that for me. I had known worse."

an exhaustive and wearisome search they succeeded in disposing of two long-perished Austrians, but they also learnt that the key position of Przemsyl had been recaptured by the enemy, and when they returned in the evening, it was to find their camp-site deserted and the unit withdrawn. The Great Retreat had begun again.

From the reading of official histories of the campaign, diaries and memoirs of soldiers and politicians, it is difficult to understand how

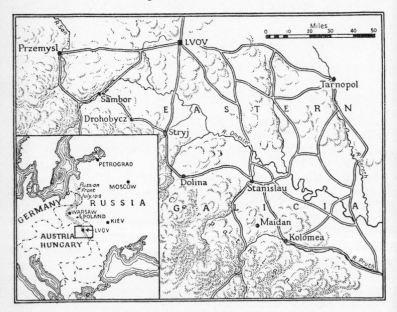

the Russian army held out as long as it did. Incompetently led, poorly clothed and inadequately armed, the soldiers displayed immense powers of courage and endurance. Their reserves of ammunition were exhausted after a few months of war, and they possessed so few rifles that many an infantryman was obliged to stand impotently by until a fallen comrade's weapon became available. The Austrians opposite them were poor fighters, but now they had been stiffened by German reinforcements, and once the Russian steam-roller was put into reverse it rumbled back a vast distance before it could be stopped.

Hugh's Otriad had not been designed for service in the forward areas, but now it was swept back by the retreating wave, together with military units of all sorts—Cossacks, gun limbers, ration waggons, haycarts—in a universal cloud of dust.

Except for the discomfort, Hugh enjoyed it all greatly. He was not only helping in the war: he was taking part in an immense human catastrophe, in which pride and a deep feeling of brotherhood with the whole Russian people carried him along. Amidst all the violent movement and frantic ministration to the wounded, the constant smell of chloroform, iodine, and garlic sausage, there were times, often whole days, when the Otriad was resting or waiting, and Hugh would lie happily in a sun-warmed orchard, writing his diary and reading Browning. "Funny how he and Dostoevsky have in this year abroad become *the* two authors who matter to me. I am, I believe, deeply religious, but led to it right through my psychological interests—*not* vice versa. And that I claim is what they also are." His diary was filled with a rich variety of *choses vues*: here indeed was the background he had been seeking, and most of the descriptive passages in *The Dark Forest* were taken verbatim from these daily pages.

Occasionally he found time to scribble a few letters and postcards, such as the following to Henry James:

June 16.   Galicia.

Letters quite impossible but I'm told there's just a chance of this p.c. getting through. Have been in the thick of things for nearly a month, under fire several times, and have decided that a dentist is much more alarming. The worst part of a battle is its invisibility and never knowing what it's going to do next. Waiting with a cart under shrapnel for wounded is depressing if it lasts long, but doing anything definite is highly inspiring, and amusing sometimes in most unexpected ways. I had the other night a race from the Austrians in a haycart that was Gilbertian, quite especially as I'd lost my braces and my glasses were crooked! Day before yesterday eight hundred wounded in twelve hours. I cut off fingers with a pair of scissors as easily as nothing!

Love,
H.

A note to Arnold Bennett, written the same day, ends:

A battle is an amazing mixture of hell and a family picnic—not as frightening as the dentist but absorbing, sometimes thrilling like football, sometimes dull like church, and sometimes simply physically sickening like bad fish. Burying dead afterwards is worst of all. I'm frightfully well and very happy. Shall return to England in September for a little at any rate.

At the end of June he developed dysentery and thereafter spent some time recuperating peacefully at Tarnopol. When he rejoined the Otriad he found it once again withdrawn from active work, and though he was grateful for a few more days of reading and writing, he soon began to grow restless. Heat and flies made eating and sleeping difficult, while his recurrent nightmares began to be peopled by the grisly corpses of the battlefield. "Our work just now," he told his mother, "is chiefly taking hot tea to the soldiers in the Position. I have really not seen a wounded man for a fortnight. . . . Although on the whole I have truly been useful, war is not my job. My imagination won't keep quiet, and nerves play a pretty strong part in this affair." Now and then he helped take food to villages where cholera was raging, "terribly tumble-down and ill-kept with the black flag outside many of the cottages." But there were gayer moments:

Wonderful sight, Cossacks swimming their horses in the lake. Hundreds of horses, hundreds of the finest men in the world flashing naked in the sun— the blue water, the little pink village with the brown church, the green reeds. Such colour and peace and happiness, the Cossacks playing with one another like babies. How to reconcile all the different sides of this amazing affair!

Back with the Otriad he read Zola's *L'Assommoir* and Charlotte M. Yonge and tried to introduce some thrills into his "Invisible Battle" chapter in *Death and the Hunters*: "If I were inventing, what an exciting thing I could make of it:" but in fact it was precisely this absence of the customary invention that gave the book its actuality and power. He decided that the two chapters he had written were "too solemn in manner—my besetting sin, which is really curious considering that I see everything too unfortunately humorously. But *The Green Mirror* is my true style, whether it prove successful or not— simple stories about clergymen and old maids and cuckoo clocks."

His tour of duty with the Otriad was nearly up, and as his departure drew nearer he vacillated between the longing to get home and a determination to see the war out on this front. Little though he knew what was happening on his part of the line or elsewhere, he could not help but realise the terrible deficiencies of the Russian army. "This war is simply a matter of ammunition," he wrote to Lockhart. "The man who's got the most bullets wins."

Aug. 8. Finished chap 4 of *D and H*. . . . Today official news of taking of Warsaw. No one seems depressed by it. Feel very strongly that I must come back here for the winter and not go to England. Believe it my duty. . . . However, we'll see.

A week later he started for Petrograd, but was obliged to spend some days at Chertkov, where he was presented with his St George's Cross by General Lechitsky. Then on by way of Kiev to Petrograd, where he was warmly welcomed by Somoff.

2

There was now nothing to prevent his immediate return to England, but two powerful forces held him back. One was the very natural desire to finish his novel while its sounds and scenes were still fresh in his mind; the other was his growing affection for Somoff. He felt that once he left he might never come back, and this splendid friendship would be brought to an end. Thus patriotism and sense of duty warred with expediency and inclination.

Staying with Somoff in a flat on the outskirts of the city, Hugh hurried on with *Death and the Hunters*, taking occasional evenings off to dine with Harold Williams or the Fyfes. He began to suffer painfully from boils, and soon this malady was aggravated by an uncalled-for but none the less tiresome attack of conscience. In fact, he had shown considerable enterprise in getting to Russia at all; he had been decorated for gallantry with the Russian armies in the firing-line; and had altogether achieved far more than, with his hopelessly defective eyesight, he could possibly have done at home. But he well knew that people, particularly women, sitting safely by comfortable London firesides, were only too ready to malign anything that seemed to them unusual in the way of war service. Since Henry James's delicate hint that he would do well to come home, no one else had attempted to advise him, and in any case Hugh had been too busy to give the matter much thought. Now Sibyl Colefax broached it directly.

Sept. 22. A critical day. At dinner received letter from Mrs. Colefax saying my friends are "bitterly criticising" my being in Russia, that I should return at once. A silly letter . . . but it stirred my conscience.

After two days of indecision he decided that he must go. Arrangements were made for him to travel as a King's Messenger in mid-October, and he set to work to finish his novel before he left. One amusing interlude interrupted this work:

Out with K. At a bookshop amused to buy a new book by Wells called *Boon*. Mad incoherent thing with much cleverness. First half about the London writing world, chiefly a furious attack on H. J. with Conrad and Shaw as good seconds. Mentions me as follows: "Mr. Thomas Hardy had a first-class ticket but travelled by choice or mistake in a second-class compartment, his deserted place being subsequently occupied by that promising young novelist Mr. Hugh Walpole, provided with a beautiful fur rug, a fitted dressing-bag, a writing slope, a gold-nibbed fountain pen, innumerable introductions, and everything that a promising young novelist can need." He's really clever about H. J. and says just half the truth. But why so fierce about Conrad? Meanwhile who is James Joyce? *Is* Crane such a good novelist, and Hueffer so good a poet? . . . tut, tut, H. G. Meanwhile you'll be a better satirist when you don't show personal irritation. The war part tommy-waffle!

The boils grew steadily more painful, and a doctor incurred Hugh's irritation by attributing them to nerves. Nevertheless *Death and the Hunters* was completed after a final spurt on October 3. In its last chapter there occurs a paragraph, ostensibly the thoughts of the story's English hero, but in fact so clearly autobiographical as to provide an adequate self-portrait of the moment:

Many scenes from my Polchester days that I had long forgotten came back to me. I was indeed startled by the clearness with which I saw that earlier figure—the very awkward, careless, ugly boy, listening lazily to other people's plans, taking shelter from life under a vague love of beauty and an idle imagination; the man, awkward and ugly, sensitive because of his own self-consciousness, wasting his hours through his own self-contempt which paralysed all effort, still trusting to his idle love of beauty to pull him through to some superior standard, complaining of life, but never trying to get the better of it; then the man who came to Russia at the beginning of the war, still self-centred, always given up to timid self-analysis, but responding now a little to the new scenes, the new temperament, the new chances. Then this man, feeling that at last he was rid of all the tiresome encumbrances of the earlier years, lets himself go, falls in love, worships, dreams for a few days a wonderful dream—then for the first time in his life, begins to fight.

This was not the first appearance of Polchester in Glebeshire, which Hugh was later to describe and people so prolifically. Mention of it was first made in a short story called *Bachelors*, and again in *The Golden Scarecrow*, which had been published in London this very week, and as the town appeared and reappeared in more of Hugh's books a vast correspondence of speculation and topographical enquiry sprang up. Enthusiastic readers drew large-scale maps of the town showing every street and building mentioned in the stories, while Hugh wrote many articles, some of them contradictory, explaining the origins of everything. Polchester was at first based almost wholly on Truro, and in the three Jeremy books there are few descriptions that do not correspond: Orange Street was taken from Lemon Street, the Pol from the Fal, and so on. In later books the town developed characteristics of its own, so that in the end it was as much Hugh's creation as a transcription from life. Except perhaps for part of the Precincts, there was only one particular, the physical domination of the town by the cathedral, for which he drew on the hated Durham.

3

Hugh left Petrograd on October 16, after a distressful parting with Somoff, and travelling by the same route as on the outward journey landed at Newcastle six days later. He went straight to the nearest bookshop and there saw his first copy of *The Golden Scarecrow*, which had been well received and was already in its third printing. In London he stayed with Percy Anderson, telephoned to Henry James at Rye, and paid early visits to Secker and Pinker, both of whom he found delightfully encouraging.

Oct. 25. I'm becoming quite a seller and I really may take today as the first date when I find myself firmly established as a novelist—not bad at thirty-one! The only thing that remains now is to write a decent novel!

By the time he reached Edinburgh he was prostrated by fatigue, boils, and insomnia. His mother immediately put him to bed, and while he was being cosseted back to health he learned that they were all very worried about his father's eyesight which was fast deteriorating: a second operation for glaucoma was soon to be tried. As soon as Hugh was well enough to travel he set off excitedly for Polperro.

Nov. 5. The most wonderful coming into Cornwall I've ever had. Most perfect November day. Almost dizzy with happiness. Eggs and bacon at Liskeard, a shave at Looe, then walked over. Sea all mists and dazzle, trees golden and *such* quiet! Just walked down the road into my cottage. Annie and John delighted. Jacob knew me at once and jumped up to the ceiling with excitement. Everyone came to their doors to shake hands with me.

He continued to feel ill, but quickly took up the abandoned *Green Mirror*, and even as he struggled to reassemble its scattered threads the theme and characters of its successor welled up into his mind. He wrote to Henry James:

My dearest Master,
I won't bother you with more than a line, but I find I can't continue to subsist on the echo of your voice through the telephone. Just send me a word as to how you are and that you still remember me.
I have come back so bewildered from Russia that I find it almost impossible to pick up the threads anywhere. You are almost the only line that I cling to still, believing it will pull me out safely somewhere.
So do let me get a touch of you soon in some way. I hear that people have been seeing you, so I hope that means that you are better.
I'm not very well—I had a great plague of boils from eating bad food but that has almost passed. My chief worry now is that I can't sleep, but that too will soon pass I hope. I am going, I expect, soon to France, but shall of course be first in London.
Here I sit, quite alone, and the peace is wonderful, incredible.
Do write me a word.

Always
Your loving
Hugh.

To which he received an immediate answer from Lamb House:

I take to my heart these blest Cornish words from you and thank you for them as articulately as my poor old impaired state permits. It will be an immense thing to see you when your own conditions permit of it, and in that fond vision I hang on. I have been having a regular hell of a summer and autumn (that is more particularly from the end of July:) through the effect of a bad—an aggravated—heart-crisis, during the first weeks of which I lost valuable time by attributing (under wrong advice,) my condition to mistaken causes; but I am in the best hands now and apparently responding very well to very helpful treatment. But the past year has made me feel 20 years older, and, frankly, as if my knell had rung. Still, I cultivate, I at least attempt, a brazen front. I shall not let that mask drop till I have heard *your* thrilling story. Do intensely believe that I respond clutchingly to your every grasp of me, every touch, and would so gratefully be a re-connecting link with you here—where I don't wonder that you're bewildered. (It will be indeed, as far as I am concerned, the bewildered leading the bewildered.) I have "seen" very few people—I see as few as possible, I can't stand them, and all their promiscuous prattle, mostly; so that those who have reported of me to you must have been peculiarly vociferous. I deplore with all my heart your plagues of boils and of insomnia; I haven't known the former, but the latter, alas, is my own actual portion. I think I shall know your rattle of the telephone as soon as ever I shall hear it. Heaven speed it, dearest Hugh, and keep me all fondestly

Yours
Henry James.

This was the last letter he ever received in the familiar handwriting, nor was he destined to see his old friend again. While Hugh was still at Polperro James had a stroke, and though he lived until the following February he was too ill to receive visitors.

Meanwhile Hugh seized the golden moment, reading and writing with great vigour. He pushed on with *The Green Mirror*, corrected proofs of *The Dark Forest* and his book on Conrad, and joined in a letter of protest against the suppression of D. H. Lawrence's novel *The Rainbow*. All this time he was "trying not to think about the war," and when such detachment proved impossible, he attempted to hold the balance between his inclination to return to Russia and what he thought was probably his duty—to get to France somehow, in the R.A.M.C. if necessary. While he was thus reflecting, he learned that the second operation on his father's eyes had failed, and that Dorothy was to accompany him to America in search of a cure. Hugh was much upset by this news, especially as it would prevent the family Christmas to which he had been looking forward.

In December he spent a fortnight in London, seeing most of his old literary friends, and making two new ones, Francis Brett Young and Frank Swinnerton, whom he liked immensely. He spent a week-end with Arnold Bennett, whom he now began to call by his Christian name. Lady Muriel Paget asked Hugh to come to Russia with a mobile hospital which she was organising: he confessed himself "most tempted."

On Christmas Eve he joined his mother and his aunt at Truro, and a few days later moved back to The Cobbles, where Mrs Walpole stayed another fortnight. The New Year was brightened by the news of Henry James's receiving the O.M., and by the completion of *The Green Mirror*. Considering the variety of circumstances which had accompanied its long parturition, and the six months' interval during which he had written two other books, it holds together astonishingly well.

In the middle of January Hugh left for London, and while he was there trying to master his fate, everything suddenly fell into place. He was summoned to the Foreign Office and told that Sir George Buchanan had cabled asking for him to be sent back to Russia in charge of British propaganda. For some time Ransome and others had been urging the creation of a modest organisation to counter the very effective German propaganda to which the Russians were ceaselessly subjected. The Foreign Office at length agreed, and the Ambassador sent for Ransome, told him that his suggestion had been approved, that it had been decided a literary man was needed to run the organisation, and that he had cabled for Hugh. This news must have been a trifle galling to Ransome, who had himself published a dozen or more books, but he made no protest, and it is doubtful whether Hugh was ever aware of the part Ransome had played in the new appointment.

Hugh was of course delighted at this stroke of good fortune. "Lord Robert Cecil said to me," he told his mother, "that I might like to feel that I couldn't be doing anything that would be more useful to my country than this. Everyone seems pleased. . . . I have a complicated business on my shoulders as regards Russia and I hope I shan't make an ass of myself."

The last weeks in London were full of incident. First he began *Maggie*, a novel which was to have a career almost as chequered as *The Green Mirror* before it was finally published as *The Captives*. Then he lunched with George Doran, whom he found "extremely effusive. It was amusing to see the difference between now and two years ago. I really seem to be a great success in America, which does me no honour as they like me for my faults not my virtues—and fickle they are!" A few days before *The Dark Forest* was due to be published, a fire broke out at the binders' and the whole edition was destroyed.[1] With astonishing speed a fresh impression was rushed through the press, and on January 31 the book was published, with a dedication to Somoff. The critics were enthusiastic. "The whole book is conceived and written at a high level of imaginative vision, and reveals capacities and powers in the author which we had hardly suspected before," wrote W. L. Courtney in the *Daily Telegraph*, while the *Westminster Gazette* declared that the "scene at the house in the dark forest where the four men draw cards for the right to remain alone to the dangerous end, is not only the most intensely realised moment of which Mr. Walpole has ever written, but is also one of the most dramatic passages in English fiction."

Arnold Bennett too joined in the chorus:

Many thanks for the inscribed *D.F.* . . . I thought the opening rather vague and lacking in direction—due no doubt to "recency" (a new word) of the impressions. However, the book gathers pace. By the time it finishes it is the best book of yours I have read since *Mr. P. and Mr. T.* This is certain. You have got hold of one of those themes that suit you, and the most important part of the story is very fine, simple, and sincere.

Then, after calling attention to a spelling mistake on page 310, he continued:

In my view you may make your mind easy about this book. You attempted an exceedingly dangerous feat,—making fiction out of a mass of violent new impressions that could not possibly have settled down into any sort of right

[1] Martin Secker's recollection is that roughly 112 copies survived the holocaust, and among them were the copies Hugh gave to his family and friends. These copies are bound in black cloth and bear at the end the imprint of the Ballantyne Press. All copies of the published edition, whether bound in black or red, carry the imprint of Spottiswoode & Co.

perspective in your mind . . . you have brought the affair very successfully off, with the help of an A.1. central idea. So God be praised, and the aged and decrepitizing hereby sing Alleluia.

Curious streaks of Conrad and H. James in the vague opening pages. They then cease.

Galsworthy's judgment was somewhat more guarded, but he kept his views to himself and contented himself with noting in his diary:

Finished Hugh Walpole's *The Dark Forest*. Very good pictures in it, and atmosphere, but incurably romantic at heart, and hampered and falsified by the form adopted. Still, an advance on the whole.

Meanwhile the delighted author spent a long week-end at Polperro, followed by a few crowded days in London, during which he visited a tax-collector and "settled him for £21"—*O si sic semper !* On February 8, proudly flaunting the silver greyhound badge of a King's Messenger, he embarked once more at Newcastle.

CHAPTER ELEVEN

RED SKY AT MORNING

I

IN the course of the year 1916 Hugh was to make the journey to Russia and back no fewer than four times. Each visit saw an apparent advance in his power and position, though in his heart he became increasingly aware of the difficulty of his task and of his unsuitability for it. When he reached Petrograd on February 14 he was quickly installed in a small office on the Morskaya with Harold Williams and Major C. J. M. Thornhill. There was no other staff and scarcely any money. Hugh's knowledge of Russian, for all his efforts, remained elementary to the end, and he would never have been able to make even a show of efficiency had it not been for the tact, experience, and kindness of Williams. This quiet, modest man was the only member of the party who ever knew what was happening anywhere, or what was likely to happen, though he never once attempted to usurp Hugh's position as titular head of the enterprise, and relations between them were unclouded.

Harold Williams was thirty-eight years old. Like Hugh he had been born in New Zealand of a Cornish mother. Now he was married to a Russian wife and had lived in Russia since before the Revolution of 1905. He was a prodigious linguist, knowing at least thirty-five languages perfectly, including an amazing number of the obscurer dialects of the Russian Empire. In 1914 he had published an authoritative work called *Russia of the Russians*, and altogether he probably knew more about the country than any other living person. Yet he remained always a working journalist. He went every afternoon to the office on the Morskaya, but without ever being in the government service or receiving any payment for his work. Nevertheless the British Embassy depended on him as its chief source of information on Russian internal politics: he was a living encyclopædia always at the Ambassador's disposal.

It is difficult to determine what exactly were the activities of the office, or whether in its early days any useful purpose was served: certainly it later developed under Hugh's influence into something grievously like a joke. In a letter to his mother Hugh referred vaguely to "very important work," "publicity," and "writing articles for the leading Petrograd paper," but his diary is more concerned with his social and literary life. He was again living comfortably in Somoff's flat, taking Russian lessons, working at *Maggie*, and lunching at the Embassy.

I spend my days [he wrote to Swinnerton on March 9] with officers and secretaries. . . . I hear of war and politics all day long and then I rush back to my flat and scribble at my novel, look at pictures and read Gissing. I'm pulled immensely two ways. On one side nothing seems to matter in comparison with Art—on the other nothing in comparison with the War—and finally one spends one's time in arranging terms between the two. It all means an absolute crisis in me who before the war had believed that Henry James and the Georgian Poets were the streets to walk in, and that to be in a London literary set was the best thing on God's earth. That's all gone utterly and for ever after last year's experiences . . . Henry James is dying, Bernard Shaw is dead, Bennett has completed his trilogy, Galsworthy is shrivelled up like a pea—no, my dear Swinnerton, the gate is slammed upon a period. They are all dead and gone.

At the Embassy he met the head of the Chancery, H. J. (Benjie) Bruce, whom he described as "a good fellow, cleverer than his good looks allow him to seem." Bruce had recently married the great dancer Tamara Karsavina, who has recorded her impressions of Hugh at this period:

I was at this time very much in foreign society. It was good then for a Russian to feel the steady optimistic spirit of our Allies. My acquaintance with Hugh Walpole, rapidly to grow into friendship, now began. He was working in Russia in the interests of allied propaganda. We could not at first converse much together; he had little Russian or French, and I absolutely no word of English. I felt at once a very real sympathy for him. He was interested in Russian life and character, not as a study in the exotic and freakish, but from a genuine love and understanding of my country. He was sharing a flat with Constantin Somoff; and, at a time when life was so troubled and one was apt to grow morbid from the constant bad news and the signs of impending catastrophe, the calm atmosphere of this circle, where art still retained preponderance, was truly soothing. Hughie was an attractive, lovable figure, with his attempts to join in the conversation. With our Russian love of Dickens, we named him Pickwick, and the parallel was even closer through an episode I remember well. During a walk to Alexander Benois's flat, Hughie fell no less than fourteen times on the snow and thin ice, always continuing his talk without comment at the point reached before the fall.[1]

2

All his life Hugh had a great love of anniversaries, but his plans to celebrate his thirty-second birthday were shattered by learning that very morning of the death of Henry James, which had occurred a fortnight earlier, on February 28. All his love and gratitude towards the old lion surged up to overwhelm him in misery and regrets. If only he had known, he could somehow have managed to pay a brief visit to Lamb House when he was last in England, but now it was too late, and he would never hear those long, affectionate, infinitely qualified sentences again. When James died, all his friends knew that the sun had set. Percy Lubbock, describing the effect on Edith Wharton, has beautifully spoken for all of them:

He was, in her life, a wide region of inexhaustible abundance, larger and richer than any other, from which there was ever more and yet more to be harvested. He was nonsuch, and while he lived there was always that big liberal genius to feast upon—a banquet spread, with laughter perpetually with him, over him, at him, all magnified by his own.[2]

"I thought of you yesterday," wrote May Sinclair on March 4, "at Chelsea in the Old Church where the Funeral Service was held. How proud he would be of you if he knew about *The Dark Forest*. It was a good time for him to die. He loved our soldiers and he has gone over with a glorious company."

Luckily Hugh was dragged from his sorrow by having to spend a week in Moscow, where he enjoyed staying with the Lockharts, and directly he returned discussions began as to the advisability of sending someone to London to obtain wider powers, greater facilities, and above all more money, for their undertaking. The Ambassador agreed to the plan, and on April 8 Hugh once more landed at Newcastle.

[1] *Theatre Street* (1930).   [2] *Portrait of Edith Wharton* (1947).

After spending two days with his family in Edinburgh, he went on to London, and the rest of his stay is chronicled in one omnibus entry in his diary:

All this week saw everyone—Edward Grey, Nicolson, Lord Newton, Benckendorff, Buchan, Masterman and many others. [Hubert] Montgomery the greatest help. Everyone absolutely approves my scheme and is ready to help it in any possible way. . . . Had long talks with Galsworthy, Wells, Chesterton. J. G. delightful, Wells degraded and decadent, Chesterton healthy and invigorating. How men are worked upon by their moral conduct, and how clearly is the victory of the soul the only thing worth tuppence!

Polperro—four days there—simply divine—that is the pivot of all the earth to me. Back in London. Interviews with Stead, Seton-Watson, etc.

3

Petrograd, when he saw it again on May 6, struck him more forcibly than ever with its barbaric beauty:

White nights, trees like green flames, cobbles, noise and dust. Above all everything huge, vast, deep ravines of darkness between the giant blocks of houses. The Neva as usual busied with its own purposes, changing every instant. Soldiers in the street more magnificent in physique than ever—a Herculean world.

But soon he confessed himself "tired and frightened by all that my war job now seems to involve"; he was worried by Russians who spoke faster than he could understand, and he wrote to his mother: "I am so tired of making up my mind on things that I don't really know enough about." It was doubtless this feeling of uncertainty which caused him to quarrel with Arthur Ransome, who was now the *Daily News* correspondent and had published in that paper an article of which Hugh disapproved. Ransome visited Hugh in his office, and Hugh told him that the article would upset Williams since it contradicted a report which he and Hugh had put in. "Very well, then," said Ransome, picking up the copy of the paper, "don't let him see it." At this Hugh completely lost control of his temper. "Put down that paper," he shrieked, while Ransome burst out laughing. The more he laughed the more hysterical Hugh became, until Ransome gave it up

and left the office. This childish outbreak has been described in detail
because it was typical of the many tantrums which all Hugh's closest
friends came to know so well. Almost always the storm subsided as
rapidly as it had arisen, to be followed by touching and humble
apology, but this time it was not so. Hugh and Ransome did not meet
or communicate for sixteen years. In 1932 Hugh wrote a warmly
appreciative review of one of Ransome's books; Ransome gladly
seized the olive branch; a reconciliation took place in Cumberland and
the two continued to meet occasionally in all friendliness until Hugh's
death.

Meanwhile two pieces of news from home helped to cheer him:

May 25. In *The Times* of somewhere about 10th I suddenly saw Henry
James had left me £100. I was immensely touched, and all the rest of the
day have been wondering whether he knew how pleased I was. I believe
he does now. I've thought of it all night, dear man.

June 2. This I call an important day because I received a letter from Pinker
saying that Macmillan had taken *The Green Mirror* for an advance of £500
on a 25% royalty! That is indeed a success, to get such an advance out of
such a firm at such a time!

Another visit to England was thought to be necessary, and he accordingly spent the month of July there, repeating almost exactly his April
programme, seeing the same people and spending four more blessed
days in Cornwall. He had hardly got back to Petrograd before he was
yet again sent home, this time with orders to obtain if possible a further
grant of money and a larger establishment of staff. This he accomplished though not without misgiving. From London he wrote to his
mother:

This all seems to me now like a nightmare in which I'm supposed to be
able to do all sorts of things I really can't, and I feel as though I were all sham
and shall soon be found out. I've had to give up all thoughts of my long
novel until the war is over. I told my agent last week that I thought I could
do another children's book now, as I could do a chapter every now and then
as there was time, and it would be easy. Two days after, the firm that published *The Scarecrow* [Cassell] came and offered £800 advance for the
stories! Isn't it wonderful! And I'm to get as much in America and do the
stories when I like. It seems so absurd that I should get £1600 for a few
stories I haven't shown them, when only three years ago they wouldn't give

me £100 for a dozen! . . . I hate the way people make up to me now simply
because I'm getting known.

By the end of September he was back in Petrograd, and within a
few weeks he was the proud occupant of large offices on the Admiralty
Quay, with a staff of twelve. His writing-paper was boldly headed
ANGLO-RUSSIAN BUREAU, and one of the first requisites of the original
scheme, that it should remain modest and under cover, had disappeared. Henceforth it was popularly known as the "British Propaganda Office," and whatever use it might have had was neutralised by
the bright light of publicity. In *The Secret City* Hugh introduced a
straight description of the place as he made it:

I went up in the lift to the Propaganda office and found it a very nice airy
place, clean and smart, with coloured advertisements by Shepperson and
others on the walls, pictures of Hampstead and St. Albans and Kew Gardens
that looked strangely satisfactory and homely to me, and rather touching
and innocent. There were several young women clicking away at type-
writers, and maps of the Western Front, and a colossal toy map of the
London Tube, and a nice English library with all the best books from Chaucer
to D. H. Lawrence and from the *Religio Medici* to E. V. Lucas's *London*.
Everything seemed clean and simple and a little deserted, as though the
heart of the Russian public had not, as yet, quite found its way there. I
think "guileless" was the adjective that came to my mind, and certainly
Burrows, the head of the place—a large, red-faced, smiling man with glasses
—seemed to me altogether too cheerful and pleased with life to penetrate the
wicked recesses of Russian pessimism.

"Our correspondence is now enormous from every part of Russia,"
Hugh told his mother, "and we had a letter yesterday from a Russian
who wished to exchange his six children (of whom he was rather tired)
for six English children!"
On October 31 the shape of things to come was briefly outlined:

Things have begun sooner than I expected. Strike of workmen on the left
bank of the river yesterday, still bigger to-day, crying "Stop the War,"
"Give us Bread." This is going to be a terrific winter, and the worst of it is
that I'm afraid things have got too much out of hand to be much improved.
The general indignation against the authorities is terrific.

Otherwise all went smoothly on its way. Each morning before he
went to the office Hugh would work for an hour or two at his children's

stories, to be called *Jeremy* ("the atmosphere partly of my early days at Strangways Terrace"), and on the evenings when there were no operas to be visited or dinner-parties at the Embassy, he read *Vanity Fair* aloud to Somoff. "I've got such magnificent novels in my head," he wrote to Pinker; "one day I suppose they'll reach birth as small misformed abortions."

Despite his misgivings, there were moments when he felt repaid for all his trouble, as when he had a "long talk with the Ambassador in bed, he asking my advice about what he is to say to the Czar on Monday concerning anti-English opinion here. Told him pro-German opinion here chiefly a matter of blood and money, neither of which things we can change."

A few days later he explained the situation to his mother:

I really *have* done the whole thing, got the money, got the men, got the furniture down to the smallest things, got Russians off military service, got the papers here in touch, got everyone in good temper. . . . A wiser man could have got it all done more quickly and better, but it is a practical business job, and I'm as proud of it as a butcher might be if he wrote a sonnet. We have now got everyone on our side, and yesterday the correspondent of *The Times* was pleased to say that it had been done on exactly the lines that he would have chosen to do it.

From November 25 he made no entry in his diary until the events of the following March cried out to be recorded, but it is known that he travelled home once more during the first week of December, presumably for further consultations with the Foreign Office, that he dined in London with Mrs Belloc Lowndes, prophesying to her the murder of Rasputin which took place a fortnight later, and that he spent Christmas with his family in Edinburgh.

For the month of January 1917 he took furnished rooms in Bury Street, St James's, and was kept busy attending meetings on a variety of Anglo-Russian affairs, besides working at the Foreign Office. He spent a week-end with Arnold Bennett and suggested that he should collect together some of the articles he had contributed pseudonymously to the *New Age*. A few days later Bennett noted in his journal: "By yesterday Walpole's scheme for me to republish Jacob Tonson articles in volume had taken shape. I read through a lot of the stuff, and found it enormously vivacious." This suggestion resulted in *Books and Persons*, published later in the year with a dedication to Hugh.

After two or three days in France, during which he was shown a section of the Somme battlefield and taken up in an aeroplane, Hugh received orders to embark at Liverpool on February 7 for what was to prove the most eventful of all his voyages to Russia.

4

His letter to his mother describing the journey is dated February 24 and headed S.S. *Czar*, Romanoff, Russia:

We were nearly a week in Liverpool, which was very trying as we had to keep to the ship all the time in case she should go off at any minute. Then we started out of harbour and were chased back by submarines and had to wait another two days, and meanwhile had the fun of hearing that two ships we had seen start out had been torpedoed.

And here, to add to the fun, Mr Pooter once more took a hand:

I complicated the matter still further by trying to drown myself. Coming on to the ship the last night in the dark, I missed my footing and tumbled over the side of the dock into forty feet of water. It was pitch dark and I was wearing my heavy fur coat which dragged me down. I sank once and then, coming up, found my head perfectly clear and collected. I stretched myself full length and so just balanced myself, my head against the ship and my feet against the side of the dock. Then I shouted for all I was worth and some men came. They let down a rope to me and I caught on to it, but that nearly finished me, as it was very slippery and my hands were frozen and my fur was dragging me down. I was quite sure I was gone then, it was exactly like someone dragging me under, and I gave all up. Then a sailor suddenly let himself down into the water, slipped the rope under my arms and supported me, and then they all hauled and so at last they landed me. You can imagine the sight I was! [1]

After that we had a perfectly marvellous voyage. . . . Our whole cargo was ammunition—fancy how we'd have gone up if we'd been touched! We got ever so far up into the Arctic and had one most wonderful day when the sea was like a glass lake and filled with marvellous colours. Then our ship got completely coated with ice and snow, like the ship of the Ancient Mariner. Finally we arrived in this harbour, which is simply the end of the

---

[1] "To fall between a ship and the quay," wrote Joseph Conrad when he learned of the occurrence, "is an abominable experience. I understand it was a very close call too and that you are en quelque sorte un 'Revenant'."

earth. There are some other vessels here, and nothing else save wolves and ptarmigans! Here we shall one day get a train to Petrograd . . . our trip may take only four days or it may be a month! I've read an enormous number of books and during these waiting days here have been writing my novel hard, so I haven't wasted my time.

The train journey, when it started, took six days, and Hugh arrived in Petrograd just as the curtain was rising on the first Revolution.

March 8. Cossacks charging down the Nevski, so suppose there have been riots.

March 9. As I supposed, trouble has broken out. All day crowds walking up and down the Nevski. On the whole they seem at present cheerful and good-tempered, singing songs and cheering the Cossacks, who are also very amiable.

March 10. Things have broken out with a vengeance. All trams and izvoshtchiks stopped. Lunched with Lintot and Brooks and on the way was caught up by surging mob in Nevski and nearly run down by Cossacks. Temper of the people quite different from yesterday, but I don't notice as yet any cry against the war—it's all for bread. Cossacks said to be friendly and determined not to shoot.

March 11. At home all day. Finished No. VI of *Jeremy* and read over *Maggie*. . . Great stories of massacres near Nikolaievsky Station; obviously a number of people killed there. After some hesitation Anna Androvna, K. and I ventured out to the French theatre. Were allowed to cross the Nevski; wonderful sight the street quite deserted under the moon save for the picket of Cossacks and their horses. Theatre nearly empty but we enjoyed ourselves.

March 12. One of the most exciting days in my life. In the morning things seemed quiet and I walked to the office easily enough. About twelve, however, on the way to Embassy heard some firing. On arriving at Embassy Lady Georgina Buchanan told me that we had taken Bagdad. Then Bruce burst in with news that four regiments had risen against their officers and seized arms. At lunch Ambassador reported Government in great state of panic. Afterwards walking back heard loud firing. Then about four a terrific noise of firing and shouting in Liteini; went to our windows and saw whole revolutionary mob pass down our street. About two thousand soldiers, many civilians armed, motor lorries with red flags. All orderly, picketing the streets as they passed. Then Garstin and I went out. Started down the Nevski; fierce battle in Morskaya so turned down Moika, but came to where dead civilian lying on snow, women screaming, etc. Had to run here for our lives, and ran straight into "Legitimist" camp, who however passed us through. Got to the Astoria, filled with wildly excited officers. Dined there with Garstin and Seale. Left for home about nine. Passed through much firing but safely. At every doorway citizens being given rifles. Got home to hear that provisional Revolutionary Government established, Rodziancko at head. Last news that Czar has given way about everything and appointed Michael Regent. Don't believe it.

March 13. Revolution developed into full size. My thirty-third birthday! A strange way of celebrating it. Left about ten and walked to office. Streets crowded with orderly and very cheerful mob, all wildly cheering soldiers who rush everywhere with red flags. First revolutionary paper published, announcing new Government, at head Rodziancko, Milyukoff etc. No signs of disorder anywhere except looting of Priestoff's houses. Arrived at office where I was joined by Dickinson. Much firing during morning, a machine-gun here. Afternoon got down with some difficulty to Embassy where I found everyone in deep depression. . . . Most unpleasant walk back with D. by Fontanka. Firing all the way and we couldn't tell where from. Our street appears to be a particularly dangerous bit. Settled down, preparing to sleep on a sofa in office when invaded by revolutionaries, who demanded to search building for police. Scene à la French Revolution, French flag, bayonets, etc. All very polite. After they left, attack on our building— machine-gun, etc. At last to sleep.

March 14. 7th Day of Revolution. Things seemed quiet in the morning, and there is obviously no question of a divided army. Another split however is occurring between the Duma Government and the red-hot revolutionaries, the former insisting on a regency, the latter on a Republic and Stop-the-War. This may be a very serious division for us. Lunch was interrupted by a lively battle in the street under our windows. Finally had to run down the street for my life, an unpleasant experience. Afternoon, much firing round us. Twice invaded by revolutionaries who insisted on searching our place as a policeman is hidden somewhere. Went down the Nevski to the France; wildly excited groups everywhere, women generally in the centre of the discussion. . . . Garstin arrived from a massacred Astoria.

March 15. Things quiet again. Posters and leaflets everywhere urging a Republic, and one persuading soldiers not to salute their officers. That way ruin lies. At the Embassy in the afternoon. Everyone very nice and cheerful again. Ambassador has asked me to write the official account of the Revolution. Harold [Williams] there rather hysterical with forebodings of a Commune. Walked home. Outside the Winter Palace watched a procession, melodramatic riders with bare sabres and high caps on caracoling horses, leading eight miserable policemen to be shot. A crowd followed but very quietly. Also saw a fine old general with a pointed white beard, very smart and aristocratic, led off to prison, his hand on a soldier's shoulder. Very glad to get back. K. glad to see me. Spent the evening looking at drawings very happily.

He began to write the official report [1] in his office on the morning of March 19, worked on at it until the small hours of the next morning, each sheet being typed, corrected, and retyped as he went along, and delivered the whole ten thousand words to the Embassy by six o'clock in the evening. "I didn't do it, I'm afraid, very well," he told his mother. "Of course all one's sympathies were with the revolutionaries, and whatever troubles there are in store, what has happened is a tremendous thing for Russia."

5

Within a few days he had settled back into much the same routine as before.

Pretty full life now, at the Bureau all day seeing to the whole place, doing the press cuttings, writing articles, interviewing, etc. Then rushing home at night, dividing my time between Russians, K., the war at home, the revolution here, the theatre, music, etc. Also, when I can, writing *Jeremy*, thinking about *Maggie* and correcting *The Green Mirror*.

New ideas for books came thronging, but there was time only to jot them down and hurry on. Little time either for letter-writing, but one event at home called for comment. Ever since Bishop Walpole had been in Edinburgh he had been working towards the completion of St Mary's Cathedral by the building of the two western spires. Contrary to general expectation he had succeeded in raising the necessary £20,000, and now Hugh could write to his mother: "I saw something about Father and the towers in *The Times*. It is splendid that they should really be finished." This letter also contained one of his more successful prognostications: "I myself think that there can be no question that the Russian Revolution is the biggest event in the war so far, and its effects on the whole of Europe must be incalculable."

But it was rapidly borne in on him that if what he had witnessed was

---

[1] It was included in Sir George Buchanan's despatch of March 20, and is here printed, with the permission of the Foreign Office, as Appendix B, p. 449.

the dawn of a new state of society, it was attended by all the portentous omens of a red sky at morning. The Provisional Government was incapable of coping with the "amiable anarchy" of the cities and the army. More and more power passed into the hands of the Workers' and Soldiers' Councils or Soviets. As is the way with most revolutions, the men who led the first rising were gradually ousted by the extremists. Stalin arrived from Siberia, Trotsky from America, Lenin in a sealed train from Switzerland. The Bolshevik Party was not to come to power for another six months, but already the days of the Anglo-Russian Bureau were numbered. The organisation had been strengthened by the enlistment of Bernard Pares and by the granting of still more money from London, but by Russians it was looked upon as the agent of a reactionary imperialistic power, and Hugh became steadily more depressed.

The first week of May saw the completion of *Jeremy* ("It has been the easiest of them all. Perhaps it would have been better if it hadn't been so easy"), and soon he was able to enjoy the beauty of the famous White Nights of Petrograd. With Somoff he went often to the circus and to wrestling matches, of which he was always fond.

May 31. So things go on, the industrial thing piling up and no one doing anything much. I bustling round, playing a part, trying to do this efficiently, that efficiently, one's inner life stirring all the time like a baby just born, needing more and more attention, and as soon as one gets lost in it everyone becomes a shadow, and the whole continuity of one's life is of another kind altogether. Like death this is, I suppose.

6

In the third week of June he was once again sent home for consultations. He was welcomed in London by John Buchan, Hubert Montgomery and others, given a room of his own at the Foreign Office, and treated there as an expert on Russia. "Dreadfully tired and jumpy," he complained, "only as I look ruddy with health no one will believe me." On July 17, while visiting his family in Edinburgh, he wrote the first words of *The Secret City*, his novel of Petrograd and the Revolution. Week-ends were spent at Polperro, with the Beresfords ("They are such a happy family that it is glorious to watch them. And yet I don't know that a happy family is the best thing for a novelist to live in"), with the Buchans, and with the Arnold Bennetts. ("We talking about changing habits, Arnold said: 'I've come to the conclusion that the moment one's born—one's done for.'")

Hugh expected to return to Russia in August, but there arose "complications at the F.O. . . . wires from Petrograd, every sort of trouble." So he made the most of his opportunity, working at his book, meeting his new publisher Frederick Macmillan, seeing his friends, and going to the theatre—in particular to the revised version of *Chu Chin Chow* with Percy Anderson, who had designed the dresses. All very entertaining, but unimportant in comparison with the arrival of a new friend—perhaps, he again thought, the ideal one at last.

This was James Annand, a large, handsome man of about Hugh's age, who had been an actor in the Benson company and was now an officer in the Canadian Highlanders ("that delightful person in kilts," Elizabeth called him). They met by chance, and Hugh was much taken by his new friend's sincerity and charm. "It is strange," he wrote in his diary, "what good company he is without being original. But he *is* original in his goodness, simplicity and strength." Annand was living with his wife and family in Surrey, and Hugh became a regular visitor. Before Hugh left for his last journey to Russia on October 2, Annand had completely succeeded Somoff as first favourite in Hugh's affections, even as Somoff had previously supplanted Percy Anderson.

7

So full of apprehension was Hugh when he had to leave his new friend and face the uncertainties of revolutionary Russia, that for the first time in his life he made a will. Sure enough, there was trouble as soon as he arrived. Hearing that Thornhill now claimed to be head of the Bureau, Hugh went to the Ambassador in a pet and offered his resignation: "Great scene, he saying he wouldn't lose me whatever happened. He in a great state." Later in the day Benjie Bruce effected a reconciliation with Thornhill and all was well. But not for long: from now on Hugh was seeking a way of escape, and on October 28 one astonishingly appeared.

In the twinkle of an eye, or rather in the picking up of a telegram, the whole world has changed. A word from Buchan, and I felt justified in asking the Ambassador whether now he didn't think I'd be better working in London than here. For myself suddenly clear that my work here is ended.

This last remark was irrefutable: the Ambassador agreed, with every appearance of reluctance, to his leaving, and it was arranged that he should start for home on November 7. The Bolsheviks had timed their *coup d'état* for the same day, though on the 2nd Hugh recorded: "I think there will be no row until people are very hungry." He said good-bye to his colleagues at the Bureau, with the realisation that it had not been a success. The rest of his farewells were a little agitated.

Nov. 6. Kahn tells me that this afternoon Kerensky has asked for full authority against Bolsheviks. He's shown such weaknesses, however, that there's not much to be hoped from him, I fear. Going home find the Nevski crowded in quite the old style. At home they beg me not to go out. However I get to the Embassy for dinner through crowded but quiet streets. There the latest news is that Kerensky has defied the Bolsheviks and arrested their committee.

Nov. 7. Alarums and excursions once again. News in the morning that Bolsheviks have the upper hand. Don't know whether to go tomorrow or not. . . . Firing in the evening. Shelling of Winter Palace. Learn as I go to bed that whole town is in hands of Bolsheviks.

Nov. 8. Up at six. K. like an angel also up. Cab arrived, drove off in pitch blackness to Astoria, where I fetched Hicks. Putting barricades up in the streets. Saw the damage shells had done to the Winter Palace. Got to the station all right and finally started. Got through Bely Ostrov without trouble. Rest of the day as usual, swooned, thought much of K. and Russia, read *Lord Jim*. Too strange to feel that this time I'm not coming back.

When he reached Christiania on the 18th he learned that the Bolsheviks were in complete control of both Petrograd and Moscow: the Dictatorship of the Proletariat had begun. He was very seasick on the voyage from Bergen, but on November 25 he landed safely and with the utmost relief at Aberdeen. His Russian adventure was over.

CHAPTER TWELVE

LONDON FINALE

I

LONDON seemed to welcome him gladly. He once more took rooms in Bury Street, started work immediately at the Foreign Office, in the Department of Information, of which John Buchan was head, and saw a great deal of Jim Annand and other friends. A dinner with Galsworthy, Lucas, and Granville-Barker was "quite fun although J. G. never sees a joke—and especially not E. V.'s." At a luncheon with Wells and Bennett, "Wells most fascinating, so that I lost all my old hatred and succumbed as I always do to him." Robin Walpole had been wounded in France, and Hugh visited him in a Plymouth hospital in company with Dorothy. Then came a fresh decision:

Dec.14. E. V. dined and suddenly, while we were at the Palace watching *Pamela* and talking about the war, I saw quite clearly, as though in a vision, that I must go into the army. Never saw anything so clearly in my life. Went home with that firm conviction. Didn't sleep.

Montgomery was against this plan, but Buchan wisely encouraged it. Three days later Hugh wrote from the Foreign Office to his mother:

The truth is I have been extremely restless and when, at the beginning of last week, I was told that I had definitely got this job here at £600 a year until the end of the war, I suddenly felt that it was much too comfortable and easy for a man of my age and health, and that it could be done by other people. So I went to the authorities and said that I must go up before the board and see whether I was liable for the army. At first they resisted this but they had no authority to refuse me. So a compromise was decided on, by which I stay here another two months and train someone in my job, and then go up to the board somewhere about February. I've no doubt the army will take me this time, as they make nothing of eyesight now.

There was a happy family reunion in Edinburgh for Christmas, with the convalescent Robin to complete the party. On Boxing Day Hugh finished the first part of *The Secret City*, and next day arrived at the Foreign Office to discover that he had been awarded the C.B.E.

in the New Year Honours. When the lists were published he was a trifle disconcerted to find that he was one of two hundred and sixty, but consoled himself by deciding that he was "the youngest and the only literary one."

On January 14 he presented himself at the Central London Recruiting Depot in Whitehall, was medically examined, graded C.3, the lowest category, and told that he must be very careful of his eyes. This result, though not unexpected, was an immense relief to him. The massed clouds of four years lifted from his spirit, and his conscience was clear again.

Four days later Macmillans published *The Green Mirror*, the first of his books to be bound in the ribbed green cloth which was to become so familiar in libraries and places where they read. The critics as usual were enthusiastic, the *New Age* hailing the book as "a masterly study of psychological terror," and Robert Lynd telling the *Daily News* readers that Walpole must now be considered as a serious writer. But some of the notices failed to please: he dismissed that of his old supporter Courtney as "imbecile," and considered that the review in *The Times*, "although long and serious, was stupid. Said my gift was for humour rather than passion. Let them wait and see!" Galsworthy made a few minor criticisms, but John Buchan liked the book, and so did Frank Swinnerton, "who objects to the mystical element, but, as I tell him, that is absolutely part of me and he'll have to put up with it."

To tell you the truth [he wrote to Swinnerton] what I miss in your books is exactly what you hate in mine—the fantasy, the "spooks," call it what you will. It's no use—it's an intrinsic part of me and it will always be there. I think the only thing that *really* absorbs me is the "spiritual" history of the human soul—the moment and the place where and when the soul and body join, and all the country in *between* this world and the other. *Don't* think this priggish or false—it isn't. It's derived I think directly from my Puritan forefathers, and I hail in my literary descent straight through Hawthorne, Shorthouse and Henry James, who after all mainly dealt with these things. I don't mean that I do this "spooky" business well—I don't—but I deeply, deeply believe in it, and I believe one day I'll do it better.

Sales too were encouraging: in five weeks the total of *The Dark Forest* was surpassed, and Hugh received from Sir Frederick Macmillan "a delightful letter, saying that they hope I'll always be with them, and wishing to make any agreement I like." For the rest of his life his relations with his publishers were of the happiest. On the one side Hugh, as has been shown, was the perfect author, in regularity of output and in the steady growth of his sales; while on the other Sir Frederick looked after him like a father. "I love him dearly," Hugh wrote in his diary a few years later. "I should like hugely to have been his son. We would have had a wonderful relation. He is the only human I know of in London of whom no one ever speaks a word of ill." In *John Cornelius* Hugh drew a brief portrait of him as Sir Donald Winchester: "the grandest old man I've ever known. He looks you straight in the eye and says what he thinks. . . . Why, any time I'm a bit low I think to myself of Sir Donald, aged eighty, sitting there in his shining white collar and black stock and white pin, and his voice with just a bit of Scotch in it and his eye as clear and sharp as a bird's."

Later Hugh became a close personal friend of Harold Macmillan, and when Thomas Mark, a member of the editorial staff and later a director of the firm, was put in charge of Hugh's work, the picture was complete. No longer need Hugh worry about spelling, punctuation, consistency, or historical fact: they were all silently dealt with in St Martin's Street. No one who has not compared manuscript with printed book will ever know what Hugh Walpole, particularly in the Herries novels, owed to Thomas Mark; but Hugh knew.

2

Meanwhile he was enormously enjoying the comparative freedom of London. He took for a year a small flat in Ryder Street, St James's, and spent happy hours settling in (he had all the true bookman's passion for *arranging* books); he lunched with Elizabeth, dined with Sir George Buchanan, and saw a lot of Frank Swinnerton. On January 30 Arnold Bennett wrote in his journal: "Turkish bath with Masterman and Walpole. Walpole very young, strong, happy and optimistic. He said he enjoyed himself all the time."

Particularly did he enjoy himself with the Annands. "I do *adore* that family," he wrote at this time. "They are what I've been wanting all my life." Often he returned to the subject ("It is my kind of Little Gidding, I suppose") and the older he grew the more he liked, the more he needed, to associate and identify himself with that sort of happy and united family which he himself could never create. His later friendships with the Priestleys, the Botts, the Blakes, the Freres, and especially the Cheevers, were particularly precious to him on this account.

Back in 1918 there were still literary giants alive. Although Hugh had published a book on Joseph Conrad, the two did not meet until Sidney Colvin arranged a luncheon-party at the Carlton Hotel.

Jan. 23. Conrad even better than I had expected—looking older, very nervous, rather fantastic and dramatic somehow—his eyes I think—"an intellectual Corsair." He talked eagerly, telling me all kinds of things about his early life. Delighted when I said I liked *Nostromo* best, although he said *The Nigger* was *the* book! Cursed the public for not distinguishing between creation and photography. His final quarrel with Wells was: "The difference between us, Wells, is fundamental. You don't care for humanity but think they are to be improved. I love humanity but know they are not!"

Conrad asked Hugh out for the evening, spoke warmly of *The Dark Forest*, and invited him to the country for a week-end in June. Opportunities for hero-worship which seemed to have died with Henry James were thus excitingly renewed.

But, as always, Hugh was acutely susceptible to the least word of derogation. An animated discussion with E. V. Lucas led to this exchange of letters with Bennett:

My dearest Arnold,
    . . . I want to ask you a question which you *must* answer truthfully. I can't ask anyone else in the world, nor am I interested in anyone else's answer—but I have been having a great argument with E.V. who says that he can't explain the difference between myself and my talk which is individual, and my writing, and he says he can only explain it by the fact that when I sit down to write I lose all individuality because I remember too much of other people's things. Now is that true to your thinking? Of course *I* don't think it true, and I believe *Perrin* and *The Dark Forest* and Henry in *The Green Mirror* to be really my own. *Do you feel or not that my writing has an individuality and character of its own?* I don't want to be too

solemn about myself and please let this be between ourselves. Moreover I don't think E.V. a good critic . . . but it has been a hot and furious argument and I *do* want your opinion. I shan't quote it to anyone. It's only for myself I want it.

Yr. affect.
H.

My dear Hughie,

. . . re Lucas, what amuses me is that *he* should make the charge, seeing that nobody could guess the realities of *his* character from *his* books. I may tell you there is nothing whatever in it. Your talk may be more dashing than your literature, in appearance, but I think that that springs from your tremendous physical "go" and youthfulness, and I attach no importance to it. In my opinion your writing is better than your talking, though less showy. For example in talking you constantly use clichés—such as "any sort *or kind*"—which would pass in a fashionable barrister such as Marshall Hall, but do not redound to the credit, as a talker, of Hugh Walpole the author of *Mr. P and Mr. T*, *The Dark F*, and *The G. Mirror*. (Has the candid E. V. L. ever told you this? I bet not.) In your writing you instinctively avoid clichés—not *always* with success; but then none of us always avoids them with success. Now the frequency or infrequency of clichés is for me a sure symptom invented by an omnipotent God to enable us to come to conclusions about style. I don't think I have concealed from you my opinion that *Fortitude* and *The Duchess* are not on a level with the other three. But this unlevelness does not worry me in the least. It is constantly found in the greatest novelists, and is natural and inevitable. No artist really knows what he is doing till long after he has done it. You can tell my views about you to anybody you like. *I* always do.

Thine,
A. B.

In a letter of gratitude for this reassurance Hugh wrote:

You told me, as always, exactly what I wanted to know. . . . You don't know to what extent I feel the value of your honesty, clear-sightedness and catholic standard. We all of us, who are your friends, appreciate those things in you, more, I am sure, than you in any way know.

3

Hugh was once more being bothered by his tired eyesight, and he also began to fear for his job. "Lloyd George has put various newspaper people in, and if things go the way I think, I and a whole lot of people will have to resign." This referred to the appointment of Lord Beaverbrook as Minister of Information, with Sir Roderick Jones, the head of Reuter's, as his chief executive and Director of Propaganda. Arnold Bennett was recruited to direct British propaganda in France, chiefly (he believed) because Beaverbrook had so much admired his recently published novel *The Pretty Lady*. Other newcomers were John Hay Beith (now famous as the author of *The First Hundred Thousand*) and the novelist Frederick Niven, with whom Hugh made great friends and corresponded for years.

The new brooms swept clean, and everything was reorganised, but Hugh's fears were unrealised, and on his thirty-fourth birthday he moved into an office in the Russian Section of the Ministry of Information in the Howard Hotel, Norfolk Street. Buchan asked him to be his private secretary, in addition to his other work, but the suggestion came to nothing.

A fortnight's holiday at Polperro was spent "working like a centipede" at *The Secret City*. Writing as much as four thousand words in a day, he finished the book with a rush early in April, and returned to London to find "things humming. Beaverbrook suddenly got on to Russia and all the Department rushing round. Went in to see him. He's of the 'One Word—Do as I tell you' type, and I should think not a very good judge of men. However there'll be some work to do now." There was, and Beaverbrook was not its only begetter, for "Roderick Jones suddenly asked for a memorandum about Russia, so I had to slave all day at the thing." Between them, his two masters kept Hugh tolerably busy for a few months, though he found time to write articles and see a good deal of his friends. Except for the German offensive in March, the war itself had by now almost completely disappeared from his diary, and April 23 was recorded not as the day of the Zeebrugge raid, but as the day on which he took up once more the half-finished manuscript of *Maggie*, abandoned now for almost two years.

A month later he chronicled a "big scene in Beaverbrook's room. B. said he wasn't satisfied about Russia, and I said if he wasn't satisfied I'd better go. Quite a rumpus. However he settled down afterwards, and I must say the more I see of him the better I like him." Two days

later the great man called Hugh in "and apologised for his temper to
me on Friday, so charmingly that I felt I'd do anything for him."
Nevertheless the work was growing more difficult and more tiresome,
and the week-end with Conrad near Ashford in Kent proved a happy
interlude.

June 2. Great and glorious day. Conrad simply superb. A child, nervous,
excitable, affectionate, confidential, doesn't give you the idea anywhere of
a strong man, but *real* genius that is absolutely *sui generis*. Said *Green Mirror*
fine—no holes to be picked—but I need more resonance. Said only thing was
to be a "glorious story-teller." Said all 'isms were rot. Said end of *Secret
Agent* an inspiration. Wrote nearly all *Romance*. Doesn't think end of
Victory anything but inevitable. Wanted to put *everything* into *Lord Jim*.

Hugh managed to attend one day of the Pemberton Billing trial,[1] and
was scandalised by the verdict of Not Guilty: "I mark it down in my
diary as the opening of the Great English Revolution." Having been
surprised by the outbreak of both revolutions in Russia, he was
determined not to be caught napping a third time, so that every strike
and industrial dispute of the next few years was announced in his diary
as the signal for revolt.

Meanwhile working for Beaverbrook became no easier, and in the
middle of June matters came to a head:

To see Beaverbrook about Poole's telegram. He very excited about it.
Gave all sorts of orders like a whirlwind. I felt in a sort of despair, my eyes
aching and I feeling that I was on the edge of a desperate breakdown. . . .
I decided to go and see Elliott [his oculist]. He said I must have six weeks'
complete rest at once. Don't know whether I was glad or sorry.

Next morning he broke the news to Jones and Beaverbrook, who
proved "both perfectly delightful. B. called me by my Christian
name and put his arm round my neck." He was sent off on six weeks'
leave, and after spending a few days of dark depression in Edinburgh
he travelled to Polperro and peace.

[1] Mr Noel Pemberton Billing M.P. was charged with libelling Maud Allan the dancer.
In a paper, the *Vigilante*, under what *The Times* called "a headline which connoted un-
natural practices," he had said that the audience at Miss Allan's private performance of
Oscar Wilde's *Salome* was drawn from the "First 47,000," whose names appeared in a
German "Black Book" as belonging to sexual perverts with weaknesses which would
render them easy victims of German agents. Billing conducted his own defence before
Mr Justice Darling.

4

He was distressed to find that Jacob the dog had just died, and to begin with he could settle to nothing. He "read a little *Heart of Mid-lothian* and actually wept, at my age too, over Jeanie's meeting with the Queen, but it's a *perfect* piece of writing." His own novel seemed hope-less, so for something to do Hugh attempted his first single-handed play, a comedy called *The Comfortable Chair*. It was never acted but it served its purpose by keeping him busy for a week and sending him back refreshed to his novel.

The trouble with his eyes, being largely nervous in origin, quickly began to clear up, though he aggravated it by writing furiously at *Maggie*: "She holds me now so that I simply live with her. It's like being married." Temporary interruptions were caused by stopping to record: "Rebecca West at me again in *Daily News*, this time classing me with [Stephen] Graham as a Russian 'Idiot-Manufacturer.' I suppose I shall survive it." Instead of letting sleeping critics lie, he made another move in the long game of Writing to Reviewers, but this time he had met his match, and his ill-considered letter called forth this crushing retort:

Dear Mr. Walpole,
    What is this about "girding at you for a lot of years"? So far as I can remember I have made but two references to you in my six years of journal-ism—one this allusion to *The Dark Forest*. The other a review of *The Golden Scarecrow*. But if I am wrong please tell me more about it.
    It was therefore not because I "thought it would be a joke to have one more dig" at you that I mentioned you in the Graham article, since I have never established the digging habit in your direction. But it was because *The Dark Forest* appeared to me—after a careful reading, for oddly enough I don't write about books I haven't read—a defence of the Russian idiot. I clearly understood that it was your thesis that the idiots (such as Trenchard) have the pick of the spiritual basket because—wasn't it your phrase?—"they cared most."
    I suggest that this talk about my "continuing for ever and ever this public scalping" is literary gossip without any basis in fact. I do not conceal my feelings when I think people are talking nonsense, and I have practised this candour over Ellen Key and Mrs. Humphry Ward and Strindberg. I also do not conceal my feelings when I think people are talking sensibly and

beautifully, and I have been equally candid over Ford Madox Hueffer and the earlier Lawrence and Archer's book on India and H. M. Tomlinson and—but you see it is a large mixed grill. If people choose to remember the far less frequent occasions of my dislike rather than the quite numerous occasions of my appreciation it is hardly my fault! Doesn't your own letter rather prove how absurd the popular attitude is? It's certainly true that I don't like your work; I think it facile and without artistic impulse. This is a sincere judgment on purely literary grounds; for I have never met you but once, at a tea-party of Mrs. Belloc Lowndes' some months ago, and you seemed, if I may say so, a pleasant person; and those of my friends who know you speak of you with liking; so there is no occasion for personal animus. I have never made any attempt to get your books to review—as a matter of fact I never ask for fiction. When one is sent to me I review it without, so far as I can remember, any remarkable paroxysm of dislike. I then never mention you again for I think about two years, when I use you to prove that a heresy is not an author's private luxury but has become a fashion. You then write to me and accuse me of having girded at you for years. And make the startling suggestion that "if you think me no good at all then leave me altogether alone"—as if it might not be the duty of a critic to point out the fallaciousness of the method and vision of a writer who was being swallowed whole by the British public, as you are! Really, Mr. Walpole! I probably shall leave you alone as I am less keen than ever on reviewing novels now—but I am appalled by the theoretical aspects of your demand. Really, Mr. Walpole!

It's sad to hear of your breakdown, and I hope you will be better soon. And I apologise for anything I've added to your discomfort by my literary offensiveness.

> Yours sincerely,
> Rebecca West.

This letter upset him sufficiently to cause him to seek consolation and encouragement from Swinnerton. Always thereafter he was more than a little frightened of Rebecca West. Now, however, his mood was lightened by another letter:

3 July 1918.   Ministry of Information.

My dear Walpole,

I was very glad to get your letter and to hear that your health is making real progress. I have no doubt that you have been feeling a postponed effect of the trials of Russia. These things often happen. However your life sounds very idyllic to anyone working in London, and I expect that the complete rest will put you right. You certainly earned it.

The novel also sounds a restful occupation as you are in no hurry with it like those unfortunate authors who turn out a given number a year. But you don't say what it is about.

Many thanks for your kind remarks about myself and the Ministry. We shall hope to deserve them. I shall hope for better news of your eyesight. Life here is very strenuous. I am just going before the Parliamentary Committee.

Yours faithfully,
Beaverbrook.

So much was typewritten, but on the back appeared the following, in his Lordship's hand:

My dear Walpole,

Give your whole heart to getting well. I want you back here when you are really restored. We have much to do and nobody is better equipped for the doing than yourself.

I value your assistance enormously and nothing will part us as long as you will stay with me and providing I don't lose my job.

Yours ever,
B.

Roderick Jones also sent a kindly note, begging him not to tire his eyes by reading or writing, and he was further cheered by visits from friends staying in the neighbourhood, among them Vita Sackville-West and Violet Keppel, the daughter of his old "celebrity"; it tickled his vanity too to learn that a shell-shocked officer in a base hospital in France believed himself to be Hugh Walpole, and was giving away copies of Hugh's books inscribed "From the Author." To Beresford, who was trying to collect money for D. H. Lawrence, Hugh sent £7 on the understanding that his name should not be mentioned. Lawrence returned to Beresford "very many thanks to you and the unknown."

5

The August Bank Holiday week-end Hugh spent with some old friends near London, and in the course of it he, for the only time in his life, made a proposal of marriage. It is clear that he approached the subject in an impersonal, almost a theoretical fashion: three months earlier he had written in his diary: "In spite of being with people all day and most of the night, one *is* lonely. Marriage really seems the only thing;" he must have pondered the matter further during his Cornish holiday, and now he thought that he had found the right person—the daughter of the house where he was staying.

From his diary one could not guess at the occasion's importance: "Had a long walk with M. in the afternoon, in which we had a pretty straight talk. She's a ripping girl and I think we understand one another;" but happily the lady's recollection of the conversation is clear. During the walk Hugh asked her what she thought of him. She answered frankly, and in return asked his opinion of her. "I've always thought of you more as a man than as a woman," he answered; "I've always talked to you as I would to a man." M., being very young, was rather flattered. When they had walked a little farther Hugh said: "Later on, say in two years' time, if you want a house and would like to settle down, I'd like to marry you."

M., although she liked him, was certain that she did not want to marry him, but she dared not tell her mother of the proposal lest she be compelled to accept it. So she told Hugh immediately that she couldn't have it hanging over her head for so long, and would rather call the whole thing off. He agreed unconcernedly and they remained devoted to each other until Hugh's death. She and her husband used to visit him in Cumberland, and on one occasion, many years later, she asked: "What would you have done if I'd said yes after the two years?" "Oh," said Hugh airily, "I should have rearranged my life accordingly. But we were really too much alike." M. believes this last remark to be true: certainly a great deal of rearrangement would have been necessary.

Meanwhile, in no way abashed by her refusal, and reassured by visits to eye and nerve specialists, he returned to the Ministry and was soon as busy as ever. The Annands were now living at Ealing, where Hugh paid them frequent visits. Another week-end with the Conrads produced its crop of sayings. The first night, after learning that his host had received "£20 for *Almayer*, £100 for *Nigger*, and £1,000 (both countries and serials) for *Nostromo*," Hugh wakened the house with his nightmares. The morrow brought compensations:

A very happy day, although Conrad is in many ways like a child about his various diseases, groaning and even crying aloud. He said some interesting things: about Gissing turning over the manuscript of *Amy Foster* and saying in a melancholy voice: "Ah! I envy you that!" About *Romance*, that it was originally written by Hueffer and called *Seraphina*. Conrad expanded it, writing the entire whole of "Casa Riego" and the "Guitar" book. That he can't read Wells, Bennett or Galsworthy—in fact, reads no one now. That it's his ambition after the war to get a yacht and sail down the Thames. That he has never studied any technique and doesn't think one should.

The following week-end Hugh spent with the Colvins in E. V. Lucas's Sussex cottage. "He [Colvin] *is* tiresome with his pedantry and narrow sympathies, but he's got a heart of gold. She's an angel but *too* sentimental and will clutch at one." However, the old lady's powers of apprehension were surpassed a week later in the course of another country-house party:

After lunch I was caught, held, made captive and finally proposed to. Spent rest of day wriggling out of it and was thoroughly miserable during process. Wretched—never knew such persistency. Evening listening to Colefax's booming voice, full of mouthings and platitudes. Bed in terror.

So determined were his aggressors to force him into this marriage that unofficial announcements of his engagement appeared in newspapers, to be promptly and emphatically denied by the terrified Hugh.

6

One day at the beginning of October he arrived at the office "to find that Bennett wants me to do the report on the work of the Ministry for the War Cabinet. A particularly hair-raising job and one for which I feel quite unfitted." But he did it, and a week later despatched it to Bennett with a letter:

This has been a beastly job—the worst I've ever attempted. When I began I hoped to make it an individual personal affair as you had suggested. But when I looked at the other chapters in the Blue Book I saw that such a method would be at once ruled out by the War Cabinet. . . . Were one writing a complete Blue Book, all by its little self, about the Ministry, one could, I think, make it both poetic and entertaining. Such an account however in this case would look like Titania sleeping with numberless Bottoms.

A fortnight later he was greatly tempted by an offer from E. W. Hornung, the author of *Raffles*, to help run a library for the troops in France, but it was clear that the war could not last much longer, and it seemed more sensible to stick to the job he knew. Also *Robin's Father*, the play he had written with Rudolf Besier before the war, was at last to be acted. Hugh travelled north with Annand and was present at the first night on November 1 at the Playhouse Theatre, Liverpool. The audience was more enthusiastic than the critics, the *Liverpool Post* declaring in artillery metaphor that the play, "though not exactly a 'mis-fire,' is quite as certainly not a 'direct hit.'" Several London managers showed interest, but nothing came of it.

Next day Hugh succumbed to the influenza epidemic, but it was a mercifully mild attack; Annand brought him back to London, and he had recovered sufficiently by the 11th to visit Hatchards' bookshop in Piccadilly, where, appropriately enough, he heard the news of the Armistice. Hopes of immediate release were dashed when Buchan, who was charged with winding up affairs at the Ministry, asked him to stay on for a few more months. He submitted with a good grace and carried on as before.

At Christmas he was granted three weeks' leave, which he spent traditionally in Edinburgh. The Walpole family always made a great affair of Christmas presents, exchanging lists of their particular "wants" well in advance. (Hugh once tried out the same plan on a family he was helping, but when their list came back headed "Grand Piano" and "Motor Bicycle" he decided that this kind of game had better begin and end at home.) On Christmas Eve he wrote the first words of his next novel, *The Cathedral*, in which the autocratic Archdeacon Brandon of Polchester was to be undone and driven to his death by the smooth and scheming Canon Ronder. Then he "pulled *Maggie* along another twelve pages" and finally brought her chequered career to an end early in the New Year. In the evenings he read *The Secret City* aloud to the family.

Before he left Edinburgh he received, through Buchan, a request to write a regular literary article in Beaverbrook's new paper, the *Sunday Express*. He managed to refuse without much effort, and was repaid by obtaining, a week later, a contract to write a fortnightly literary letter for the *New York Sun* at a salary of £700 a year.

7

In London Hugh lunched with George Doran and was persuaded by him to undertake an American lecture tour in the autumn. On January 17 *The Secret City* was published, with a dedication to Annand, and, before the reviews, came a depressing letter from Bennett:

My dear Hughie,

It appeareth to me that you have attempted the impossible in *The Secret City*. Therefore be not surprised if I think you have not achieved the same. I am of course judging the book by the highest standard. I do not see how even Joseph Conrad or Jesus Christ himself could hope to deal with recent events concerning a land and people with whom he had an acquaintance of only 2 or 3 years, and bring the thing off satisfactorily on the topmost emotional plane. These feats simply are not done. . . . You may say that you did it in *The Dark Forest*, but that book was much less ambitious and comprehensive. Further, you have deliberately added to your difficulties by thinking of a plot (the Markovitch–Semyonov idea) which is of the very highest psychological interest but also fantastically ticklish to handle convincingly. How you have come out of the affair alive I'm hanged if I know. But that you have done so is to your credit as a professional man. Of course a great deal of the material is very interesting. But I reckon that when you have run up against the impossible you have had to get clear of the problem by slanting off into something akin to conventionality. This is my view, and, dash it, you have got to know that my view exists, whether you respect it or not.

Adding insult to injury, he went on to point out instances of loose writing and grammatical error, but Hugh bore it all with a patient shrug and wrote back:

My dear Arnold,

I won't deny but that your letter was a great disappointment to me. One never can tell about one's own book, but I had felt about this one that I had got some way towards what I wanted, which was a kind of ghost story symbolizing the outbreak of the revolution. I never pretended for a moment that it was a true view of the people or the events, only that it was my view. . . . However you are to me the one absolutely honest, unprejudiced and wide-seeing critic I know . . . and therefore there must be a great truth in what you say. God bless you for your honesty, say I, and may you not be entirely right in your view! Love to Marguerite.

Your affectionate
Hugh.

Conrad was much more encouraging when Hugh arrived for the week-end.

Conrad said many wonderful things about the book: that he was astonished at its art, that it was wonderfully level, that it had true style, etc. I listened as in a dream. I was with him all day. He gave me a wonderful account about his time with the drunken captain on the *Riversdale*. He said he got only £250 for *Under Western Eyes*, £750 apiece for the next three novels by Dent. Spoke of Harold Frederic as "a gross man who lived grossly and died abominably." Said Verloc's shop [in *The Secret Agent*] was where Leicester Galleries now are; said "easier to have an intellectual friendship with a Chinaman than with an American."

When the reviews arrived they were of Conrad's opinion. "We know no other living novelist who could capture quite this lyrical fervour of the imagination, and yet keep it within the proper limits of prose narrative," "a worthy sequel to Mr. Walpole's unsurpassed best novel," "a powerful, well-constructed, beautifully written novel," "immeasurably better than its predecessors," and so on. Small wonder that he wrote in his diary: "The world is swimming round my head. The book is a success as I've never known the word success before. Everyone seems to be talking of it, and nearly everyone seems to like it. Well, I can keep my head."

One other pleasing incident occurred in connection with this book. In it he had included a brief mention of Walter de la Mare's novel *The Return*, which he described as "one of the most beautiful books in our language, whether for its spirit, its prose, or its poetry." When de la Mare came upon these words, he wrote to Hugh:

Did you know that that generous word in that fascinating place in *The Secret City* must have sold out the last remaining copies of the first edition of *The Return*? Now if I'd mentioned *The Secret City* (which time forbade or my unprophetic soul) in *The Return*, the former would still be in its first 500. What then do you owe me for refraining?

8

This chapter of Hugh's life cannot be allowed to end without some mention of his addiction to serious book-collecting and book-buying, which began during these months. He had always bought books, since he had any money of his own, whether he could afford them or not, but hitherto his purchases had been fortuitous and without plan. Now he determined to build up a library systematically. It was of course to embrace all the greatest works of literature, but he decided also to specialise in two directions. First he would attempt to collect everything written by or about Sir Walter Scott, and secondly he would seek for a first edition in its original state of every important novel in the English language. Later he enlarged his ideas to include manuscripts of the English novelists, everything published during the eighteen-nineties, "yellowbacks," American novels, books on the Lake District, and a number of other categories (at the time of his death his library contained close on thirty thousand volumes), but he never lost sight of these two original plans, both of which were carried through to virtual completion.

His passion—no lighter word will do—for the life and works of Scott went right back to the rectory bookshelves at Kingston Deverill and to his first purchase of *The Talisman* at Durham. All through his life he read and re-read the Waverley novels, the *Letters*, the *Journal*, Lockhart's *Life*, and any other contemporary accounts he could find. He even liked to imagine that in a previous incarnation he had known the great man himself:

There are times when this grey shadow over my memory seems to lift and I see myself as a bowlegged, snuff-taking, spectacled little bookseller in a little bookshop in a back Edinburgh street—and Napoleon has just gone to St. Helena, and James Hogg has just borrowed a book which, if I am not careful, he will never return; and suddenly the jingly bell rings and there is a sturdy thick-set figure in the doorway and a merry eye and a jolly voice, and someone limps across the floor and puts his hand upon my shoulder.[1]

The serious business of book-buying began on a day towards the end of 1918, when, in company with the actor Gerald du Maurier, Hugh happened to drop in at Sotheby's when books were being sold. Looking quickly round at the forthcoming lots, he decided that he wanted a first edition of that horrific novel *The Monk* by M. G. Lewis. Du Maurier explained the system of bidding, and when the book came up Hugh nodded his way to victory. Turning in triumph to his friend,

[1] *The Crystal Box* (1924).

he discovered that du Maurier too had been bidding, on Hugh's behalf, and that between them they had added a great deal to the price of the book. Soon Hugh learned to bid for himself—he certainly had plenty of practice—but he never learned to control his excitement.

As well as auctions, there were the bookshops, and in them Hugh was always happy. "I love all bookshops," he wrote at the end of his life,[1] "from the gritty, dusty, cobwebbed interior, where old crack-backed volumes of Bage and Radcliffe jostle unhappily the latest six-penny Penguins, to the smart sun-splashed West End magnificence with Mr Wilson waiting to greet you in the middle of it." His favourite bookshop was Bain's in King William Street near Charing Cross, but he bought books everywhere, from Newcastle-upon-Tyne to Penzance, from Carlisle to Los Angeles.

On his inaugural visit to Maggs's bookshop he acquired first editions of *The Ring and the Book*, Trollope's *Three Clerks*, and Coleridge's *Christabel*, as well as the corrected proof-sheets of *Redgauntlet*, but despite these excesses he still had a comfortable bank balance of some £3,500, and there were two completed books waiting to be published. He left the Ministry for good on 25 February 1919, and never again, except for illness and minor inconvenience, did he have to go anywhere or do anything unless he wanted to.

---

[1] In a Foreword to *A Bookseller Looks Back* by James S. Bain (1940).

BOOK FOUR

THE PURSUIT OF HAPPINESS

Enthusiasm's the best thing, I repeat;
Only, we can't command it.

Robert Browning
Bishop Blougram's Apology

CHAPTER THIRTEEN

"APPLE-CHEEKED HUGH"

I

AFTER a week in Edinburgh Hugh returned to London, where at first he found that release from the Ministry seemed to give him little extra leisure. He worked hard at *The Cathedral* (now temporarily renamed *The Black Bishop*) and at the revision of *The Captives*. As a rule he revised little, if at all, but this novel had been written at so many different times and places that even he could see it needed pulling together. Normally he wrote so fluently (too fluently, as he, and others, often remarked) that he seldom paused for the right word or went back to make alterations. (When a few of his manuscripts were sold after his death, people would not believe that they were not fair copies.) He had so many plots and characters boiling up in his head that he could scarcely wait to get them on paper. More than anything in the world he enjoyed inventing; he was indeed a born story-teller, and when Frank Swinnerton announced that if he made a lot of money he would retire into the country, give up novel-writing, and read Hazlitt, Hugh commented: "Strange how the thought of stopping novel-writing seems to me like dying!"

Macmillans were by now arranging to take over all the earlier novels for reissue in a uniform edition, and they further delighted Hugh by asking him to contribute the volume on Trollope to their English Men of Letters series. Regardless of fashion he had loved Trollope since he first discovered him in the dim recesses of the Durham library, and in 1918 he had written to Arthur Waugh, suggesting that Chapman & Hall should publish a new cheap edition of some of the novels. Waugh considered that the cost would be prohibitive, and it was not until some years later that the Oxford University Press filled the gap.

March was a busy month socially as well as in authorship. A Conrad week-end produced:

The usual delightful but rather tiring day, as Conrad insists on talking the *whole* day through, never reads or walks or sleeps. . . . Conrad said: "The damnation of our profession is that it has no artistic security. There's not a masterpiece in the world but you can pick thousands of holes in it if your digestion's out of order—but if a carpenter makes a good box it *is* a good box!" Also: "Journalists, like labour leaders, only shout up their professions in order to get out of them."

But many of his pleasures were simpler. He went alone to Madame Tussaud's and was "thrilled" by the Chamber of Horrors: he found a splendid old bookshop in Guildford where "they took £2 off the bill because I was I," and in general he lived up to his reputation for enjoying everything he did. For literary relief there were week-ends with the Bennetts, a "gorgeous time" with Elizabeth ("I really like her far better than any other woman alive. She has everything—brain, heart, humour, pluck"), and a lovely nostalgic evening at Gosse's, where Percy Lubbock read aloud some of Henry James's letters and they were all three much moved.

At the end of April the Annand family left for a visit to Canada, and Hugh retired to Polperro for a month's uninterrupted writing. He began by reading over his old diaries ("What a gusher I was! Everything was 'wonderful,' 'lovely,' etc.") and continued the chastening process by attempting to revise his earlier books for the uniform edition. "*Fortitude* seems to me now an incredibly childish and naïve affair. I feel as though I had taken in all the people who bought it. Such a hotch-potch of reading other people's novels."

Then he worked deep into *The Cathedral*, writing steadily each day without worry or distraction. On May 18 he reported to Bennett: "I've been working like a three-year-old and characters burst in my brain like rockets." By the beginning of June a quarter of the book was completed.

The next three months were spent in London, with numerous week-end excursions to the houses of the great. Annand, returned from Canada, was his frequent companion. Together they watched the tennis at Wimbledon, and Hugh took his friend on one of his visits to Conrad. With Bennett he saw the new ballet, *The Three-Cornered Hat*. He was compelled to interrupt *The Cathedral* in order to fulfil a contract for a book of stories promised to Messrs Hutchinson. He disliked having to switch his mind from the novel and confessed: "It's strange how I loathe writing short stories. I suppose it's because of their difficulty and my laziness." The idea of this collection was to show the effect of the war on the leisured classes and the "new poor," but Hugh tired of the plan before it was complete, and this misbegotten book eventually became *The Thirteen Travellers*.

On July 31 *Jeremy* was published by Cassell, with a dedication to Annand's young son Bruce. Hugh marked the occasion by writing in his diary: "I shall never have a distinguished style—*never*. But then neither had Trollope." The reviewers contributed their customary praise. Lady Colvin wrote appreciatively, "You *do* remember your childhood's feelings perfectly, and you have got them into *the* right words." "The best parts of it are astonishingly good—real stuff," wrote Bennett. Sales were good and for the next few years a surprising number of English boys were christened Jeremy. One of the few discordant notes was struck by Katherine Mansfield, then the regular fiction reviewer of the *Athenæum*. She poured gentle ridicule over the book, largely by means of legitimate but unkindly chosen quotations from its pages. "But for all the author's determination," she wrote, " 'the truth and nothing but the truth' does not shine through the small heart he would explore. There is, however, no doubt that he enjoyed writing his book. He positively gambols." [1] In the following year Hugh was to exchange friendly letters with his critic, but it is doubtful whether in his heart he ever forgave her. He was frightened of her, as he was of Rebecca West, and to the end of his life he maintained that Katherine Mansfield was an overrated writer.

Soon after this he collected further Conradiana:

Aug. 10. Most jolly day, although the female guest was extremely trying. How I hate most women. How conceited and egoistic and unhumorous they are! Terrifically hot and we sat under a tree in the garden all day almost without moving. Conrad in great form. Annoyed with the reviews of *The Arrow* [*of Gold*], especially Lynd's. Said I was the only younger novelist who had drive and breadth enough to be a great one. Said the only thing to be in literature was a tramp. Said his favourite books to re-read were Hudson's *Patagonia* and Wallace's *Malay Archipelago*. Scoffed at *Typee*.

[1] Her review was reprinted in *Novels & Novelists* (1930).

The great man's morose and savage humour caused Hugh to question his own felicity. "Would I be a better artist," he asked himself, "if I weren't so happy? I don't know. A decent book may suddenly spring out of me one day like a bird from the nest. On the other hand it mayn't. Tchekov makes one despondent, but I'm not a genius, so why worry?"

But if his native enjoyment occasionally troubled him, he was no less perturbed by his recurring rages and fits of ill-humour. One day in August, for instance, when he was staying with the Annands at Walton-on-Thames, he wrote: "Continued cross. We began arguing after breakfast and I had a perfectly miserable day. I don't know what these storms of misery and self-abasement are that sweep down upon me, but they are terrible while they last. They go as quickly as they come."

At the end of the month he spent a peaceful week with his family in the Isle of Mull, and when he left London for his first American lecture tour on September 20, six of the thirteen short stories were completed.

He was seen off by Ethel McKenna, accompanied by the unseen shade of Mr Pooter. Despite the most elaborate preparations going back for weeks, Hugh arrived at Waterloo without a ticket, and at Southampton it was discovered that he had failed to provide his passport with an American visa. Eventually the authorities accepted some recent snapshots as proof of identity, and without further humiliation he embarked on the *Mauretania*. The voyage was uneventful: he made friends with Lord Grey who was travelling to Washington; and he was amused by his cabin-companions, two American salesmen who pressed him to accept gifts of food and cigars. "One asked me yesterday whether I was related to the *famous* Walpoles. I modestly said yes and then found he meant the Irish Linen people!" On September 26 he landed at New York and began a new chapter of his career.

2

From the first moment he was caught up, overwhelmed, and delighted, by the torrent of American hospitality. A wealthy friend, Arthur James, carried him off for a few days in a luxurious yacht, then insisted on his accepting the loan of a suite of rooms in New York for the whole six months. Hugh was lunched and dined and fêted, particularly by George Doran, who had produced for the occasion an elegant little booklet concerning him and his works. This contained lengthy descriptions of all the books together with extracts from reviews, a portrait photograph, and a long eulogistic preface by the American novelist Joseph Hergesheimer.[1] Here was a new friend after his own heart:

Oct. 6. Great day for me because I met Hergesheimer. We took to each other almost at once. He is fat, ugly, and at first seemed egoistic and commercial, but quickly his real genius, his childishness and eagerness captivated me.

Two days later the tour, which was rapidly to become a triumphal progress, opened with a lecture at Cleveland, Ohio, where Hugh planted a maple tree in the Shakespeare garden. There followed that exhausting non-stop circus of flurry and goodwill to which generations of visiting celebrities have by now grown accustomed. Getting up at five in the morning; long train journeys with relentlessly hospitable entertainment at every stop; indigestion, interviews, autographs, photographs; "It's like being a sheet in the very middle of a printing press going at top speed," he told Swinnerton.

Luckily Hugh loved lecturing itself. He was one of those people who can think clearly on their feet, and whose voice and platform manner easily capture and hold the attention of large audiences. He spoke without notes, so that he was able to play variations on his half-dozen themes, and thus avoid exact repetition. His most popular subjects were Russia and Henry James.

Back in New York for a few days later in October, he wrote to his mother:

I'm enclosing a few of the papers I have by me. I wish I had a Chicago one headed "Apple-Cheeked Hugh"—and a really delightful leader in the *Sun* last Sunday welcoming me, headed "The Young Visiter" . . . I've been already offered the editorship of the New York *Bookman* at £2000 a year if I'd live here, and extraordinary sums for stories. Of course I refuse them all. I have neither time, ability nor inclination. Instead of making me conceited, this country makes one a midget. I never felt so small, so unimportant, so childish.

[1] *Hugh Walpole: An Appreciation.* By Joseph Hergesheimer (New York, 1919).

Still in New York, he was charmed by Frank Crowninshield, the editor of *Vanity Fair*, greatly impressed by Alfred Knopf ("a very intelligent, pushing publisher—the best in America there's no doubt") and bored to extinction by the American novelist Winston Churchill, who discoursed for a full hour and a half on spiritualism. Amid such distractions he found time to visit the seminary where he had lived as a child a quarter of a century before. "Poor Mother! My heart simply bled for her. The grim grey ugliness of it all."

Just before he resumed his lectures, Arthur Vance, the editor of the *Pictorial Review*, staggered him by agreeing to pay $1350 apiece for ten short stories. This offer arose through the good offices of Herges-heimer, to whom Hugh dedicated *The Thirteen Travellers* in gratitude. Now he just had time to agree before dashing off to the next party. "Last week," he wrote to his mother early in November, "I had a succession of receptions. Such funny things! You stand in a corner and they all file past with little speeches, and every now and then someone recites a poem to you! Individually they have so much sense of humour, in the mass *none*."

On he went, lecturing in a different town almost every day and making exciting new friendships by the way. In Philadelphia Chris-topher Morley was added to the bag, in Baltimore H. L. Mencken, in Indianapolis Dr Carleton B. McCullough. In Chicago he was guest of honour at a luncheon given by the local writers and journalists—Carl Sandburg, Sherwood Anderson, Ben Hecht, Burton Rascoe, and others.

Wherever Hugh went, now and always, he carried with him the modern counterpart of the little box he had once clutched in the cab from Seascale station. Directly he arrived in a new hotel bedroom his first action was to unpack his special treasures and arrange them in a homely and reassuring way. The treasures varied (in *Roman Fountain* he gave details of the 1939 consignment) but they generally included some photographs, a lot of books, a few small statuettes and other *bibelots*, together with one or two of the latest-bought etchings or pictures.

By the time he arrived back in New York for a brief Christmas recess he had completed thirty-five lectures, almost every town, college, and city had asked for a return visit, and his fee had risen from $200 to $400. His agent said that he had never known anything like it, and that he could easily arrange enough lectures to occupy the whole of 1920. Needless to say, the sales of the books leapt up accordingly, and *Jeremy*, so he told his mother, was "sweeping America like a prairie fire." His cup of satisfaction was filled by a newspaper announcement of the arrival of Grock, which ran: "King George and English novelist Hugh Walpole say he is funniest clown alive."

At the turn of the year he learnt from his father that their finances in Edinburgh were rocky, and responded immediately:

My dear Father,

... I'm so glad you told me exactly how things are. I feel shy of offering unless I'm told a little. I enclose a cheque for you to fill in, giving Mother all she needs for her journey, and adding to the Memorial what you would like me to give. When I get back next year I intend to have a London house and have Mother to stay at least twice a year. Do always ask me quite frankly for anything. I am well off now, but of course I am doing my best to save, as this marvellous boom may not last. I look to make about £8000 profit out of the American trip, and I want to invest that for the future. But of course all I have is yours and Mother's. The Annands and John and Annie are my only other responsibilities. Give this to Mother as though it were *my* suggestion—and *always* tell me if you want anything.

Yours affectionately,
Hugh.

The New Year opened with a rush—Louisville, Cincinnati, Cleveland, Springfield; then a brief stay with McCullough at Indianapolis, where Hugh first met Booth Tarkington, followed by visits to Iowa City, Des Moines, Salt Lake City, Portland (Oregon), and Los Angeles. From there he wrote to Swinnerton: "I'm so well, so happy, so interested, enjoying it all so hugely. . . . I feel no longer anxiety about the London cliques nor unhappiness about whether I'm immortal or no. Life is so dramatic and so big and the sun is so hot and human nature so interesting." He caught his first glimpse of the Hollywood film studios but, pressed to write scenarios, he decided he would try his hand at them later, and hurried on to San Francisco. Here he found time to visit Stevenson's house at Monterey and to purchase from a bookseller fifty-seven autograph letters of Sir Walter Scott, for which he paid the formidable price of $4000.[1]

[1] They fetched £220 at Christie's in July 1946.

After a hurried sight of the Grand Canyon, he hurtled across the plains of Texas, reading Macaulay as he went, spent a disappointing day in New Orleans, and eventually arrived breathless at Miami, Florida, where he was to spend ten days with his friend Arthur James. That same day he summed up his impressions to his mother:

As a country it doesn't seem to me to have changed one little atom since *Martin Chuzzlewit*. Everything that Dickens said sixty years ago is still true. The country is run entirely for the lower middle class, and as a mass that class is utterly ignorant, crude, vulgar, boastful and makes everything hideous that it touches. Yet there is beneath this a passionate idealism, real honesty and great courage. The Press is *awful*.

His tranquillity was somewhat disturbed by a letter from a friend telling him that his lecture-agent was on the verge of bankruptcy and would certainly not be able to pay Hugh and his other lecturers their due. In time this prophecy was fulfilled, and Hugh was some £800 the poorer, but at the moment there was nothing he could do about it, so he made the most of his holiday, finishing with much relief *The Thirteen Travellers*, and catching an enormous angel-fish in the sea.

The tour began again on March 1 with three lectures on the same day at Atlanta, Georgia. In the train from there to New York, he found himself next to a young lady from the Atlanta Library. She lent him Compton Mackenzie's newly published *Poor Relations*, "which did amuse me more than I wanted it to." In New York he met and liked James Branch Cabell, and also St John Ervine and his wife who had come over for the production of Ervine's play *Jane Clegg*. "Yesterday," he wrote to his mother, "I was offered my third editorship—this time the London editorship of *Vanity Fair* with a really amazing salary. After a little struggle I refused it of course."

And so the tour bustled to a finish, with an occasional pleasure of surprise, as when at Bronxville he was introduced from the platform by Will H. Low, the old friend of Stevenson, "now white-haired but jolly." The final lecture, at Montreal on March 30, was preceded by luncheon with Stephen Leacock, "very humorous, untidy, dirty, drinks an incredible amount of whisky and seems unaffected by it."

Before he sailed there were three weeks of holiday. In New York he complained that the Turkish baths were dirty, he spent a thousand dollars in Mr Gabriel Wells's bookshop, dined with his old friend Arthur Fowler, read with avidity the newly-published *Letters of Henry James* ("I am naturally touched by a thousand regrets and repentances"), and in company with Alfred Knopf met Willa Cather ("Liked her hugely—calm, masculine, humorous, capable").

Then came a final round of visits to the American novelists; first to Richmond, Virginia, to stay with Cabell ("a friend after my own heart, whom intellectually I can look up to and admire"). His admiration went to the length of writing about Cabell an even more glowing encomium than Hergesheimer's about himself.[1] Then he paid visits to Ellen Glasgow and Sinclair Lewis ("typical modern American, ugly, harsh-voiced, pushing, but kindly and bursting with enthusiasm"), and finally spent three happy days with the Hergesheimers at West Chester, Pennsylvania. "Joe," he confided to his diary, "helped me very much too by really seeing in me the two strands—say Hawthorne and Trollope—from which I am derived. It is delightful to have made such a friend."

Your saying [he wrote to Hergesheimer later in the year] that you think of making a man's friendship your theme interests me enormously. I could tell you many things about that. They have been the finest things in my life simply because I've never yet found the right woman, but it's a dangerous and difficult subject simply because so many people will see it only as homosexual, which is the last thing it generally is.

Altogether, as he crossed the Atlantic in the *Mauretania* during the last days of April, he could look back on the past six months with gratitude for reputation and fortune enhanced, experience gained, and new friendships sealed. As Carleton McCullough put it in a following letter, he had "left a very clear-cut and distinctly limned impression on the American mind."

3

Of the many plans he had meditated in the course of his journeyings, one had settled into a firm resolve. He was tired of living in London flats and furnished rooms: what he needed was the right little house

---

[1] *The Art of James Branch Cabell.* By Hugh Walpole (New York, 1920).

where he might spread out his treasures and entertain his friends. Accordingly his first call in London was on a firm of house agents, and after no more than two days' search he arranged to buy a twenty-one-years' lease of No. 24 York Terrace. "It is a corner house," he told his mother, "overlooking Regents Park at both ends. It has a little garden in front of it, is old Georgian and very solid, and has wonderful big rooms—one high room with a big view of the park will make a wonderful library."

This accomplished, he retired for a fortnight to Polperro. There, as he walked alone by the sea and worked at *The Cathedral*, he gave thanks for his happiness and success. Some days were so beautiful that he felt inclined to give up his fine new London house and make The Cobbles his headquarters for ever. But in his heart he knew that "it wouldn't be any good. One's got to have the other half of life too, rub one's brains up against better ones and have adventures." Still, Polperro did give him things which he could not find elsewhere: this sort of day, for instance:

May 16. One of the good old Sundays—*Guy Mannering*, Sunday dinner in the kitchen, tea party at Miss Parsons' with female scandal, evening service— "Crown Him with many Crowns" etc—supper at the L's (*cold* crab, *cold* beef, *cold* tart, sour lemonade—ugh!). However round and round the world one goes, always it comes back to this, and it's not a bad thing to come back to. Young L thinks the village is seething with Bolshevism—not *it*!

June and July were spent in rooms in London, with the usual week-end excursions. He was still seeing a lot of the Annands, staying with them at Walton, watching the tennis at Wimbledon, and so on. From a London bookshop he bought a lock of Scott's hair and the manuscript of *Count Robert of Paris*. Visits to Conrad continued, with their recorded memories:

June 6. Extremely happy day. Talking to J. C. all morning. He happier and better than last year: said of someone, "He will never know what people are like because he doesn't realise the fundamental fact about human nature, that people are not better or worse but simply different." He talked of the Napoleon novel he is about to begin.[1]

July 18. Jolly day. Conrad very cheerful. Really has started the Napoleon

[1] *Suspense*, which Conrad never finished.

novel. Showed me some of the second chapter and I was surprised to see how many foreign phrases there were in this first draft. I am thus the first person in the world, after his typist, to meet Cosmo and Henrietta. When I criticised Mrs. Travers a little, he said: "Of course, *mon cher*, it is not very good. I did my best work long ago." Cunninghame Graham and Lawrence, the Arab man, came down. The latter mild, small, modest, with fine eyes. Said the legend about him all untrue. Talked of printing and the Crusades.

July 19. More that Conrad said yesterday: That all this talk about technique was absurd, but that you must write just as well as you can and take every kind of trouble. That F. M. Hueffer belittled everything he touched because he had a *small* soul. Got very angry as usual at the mere mention of Americans or Russians, both of whom he detests. More delighted than I have ever seen him at being asked to advise some Liverpool ship men about a training ship for boys. Again at lunch spoke of *Nostromo* and one or two short stories as his best work.

Hugh also stayed with Vita Sackville-West and her husband Harold Nicolson at Long Barn, near Sevenoaks, where he found a "very happy house-party. We all talked nineteen to the dozen and Vita looked perfectly beautiful in crimson and orange. She is as lovely as she is clever, with just that touch of easiness that gives her complete distinction. Harold too is a very very nice fellow."

All this time he was working spasmodically at *The Cathedral*, and, immensely relieved to see the last of it, he delivered at Macmillan's the corrected proofs of *The Captives*, embellished by a dedication to Arnold Bennett. On the same day he signed the lease of York Terrace, agreeing to pay a premium of £2500.

The month of August he spent at Polperro, where his whole family visited him. "Physically I'm well," he told Swinnerton, "but I *must* get thin, so I'm going to take up golf savagely (a game I *loathe*) and have a rowing machine in my bedroom!" He worked furiously at *The Cathedral* now, sometimes writing as much as four thousand words a day. "Finished my chapter in the morning," he wrote on August 7. "Amy Brandon committed adultery with the least possible fuss."

In the middle of the month he dashed up to London for a couple of days' household shopping. He bought linen, a four-poster bed, a sideboard and other furniture, interviewed and engaged two servants, found for him by Ethel McKenna, and returned to Cornwall well satisfied.

Theodore McKenna had now become Hugh's solicitor, and all the arrangements concerning the acquisition of the house were made by him, while his wife helped indefatigably with all the other domestic problems. Both of them looked after Hugh as though he were their own son, and he repaid their care with deep affection; indeed he was probably, in a semi-filial way, fonder of Ethel McKenna than of any other woman he ever knew.

She had been born in 1869, the daughter of Sir Morell Mackenzie, the leading laryngologist of his day and the central actor in a drama of European importance. He was called in to advise on the case of the German Crown Prince (afterwards the Emperor Frederick III), son-in-law of Queen Victoria and father of the Kaiser, and when his patient died at Potsdam in 1888 of what was supposed, but never proved, to be cancer of the larynx, Mackenzie incurred much criticism, which now seems to have been unjust, for his treatment of the case.[1]

Ethel McKenna spent a great deal of her time looking after the old and the needy: she also had children of her own to occupy her, but she clearly felt a very special and maternal tenderness for Hugh, and she was able to demonstrate her devotion in a way which had always proved impossible for his own mother. Her letters are full of all the tiresome duties she lovingly carried out for him—engaging charwomen, finding laundresses, looking for flats for his friends—and also of her love for him. "Your affection is one of the happiest things in my life, undiluted happiness," she wrote in 1920; and again seven years later: "I don't suppose you know how much you have helped me in my life, and I want you to: by your breadth of vision, your wisdom, your sanity and your wide sympathy, which have so often helped me to realise other people's points of view and so to manage my own life better. You have helped me to learn as I could not have done without you."

Thanks to her patient and tireless efforts, No. 24 York Terrace had a warm and finished look when on September 6 Hugh proudly took possession.

[1] For a full account of this incident, see *Morell Mackenzie* by R. Scott Stevenson (1946).

CHAPTER FOURTEEN

MELCHIOR THE DANE

I

EVERY prospect pleased. The tall rooms full of light; the library with its deep blue ceiling and all the books waiting to be set in order; the drawing-room with the new pianola from the Æolian Hall; the dining-room spacious for parties. Hugh had imported an amateur butler from Polperro, and the household was completed by a cook, a housemaid, and a somewhat neurotic bulldog called Grock. All that was missing was an exciting new friend, and with almost magical precision one appeared. On September 23 Hugh went to a Promenade Concert, where "the joy of the evening was a Danish tenor, Melchior—quite superb. Just the voice for me." Just the person too, as quickly transpired. A letter, an invitation to lunch, a long talk, and one of the most important friendships of his life was under way.

Lauritz Melchior (whom Hugh always called David) was then thirty years old and beginning to make a name as a concert singer. A giant of a man, he struck Hugh at their first meeting as "a great child, but very simple, most modest, with a splendid sense of humour." Impulsively Hugh at once invited him to stay at York Terrace, "to which he readily agreed."

Meanwhile *The Captives* was published on September 28. The critics, with one or two exceptions, were enthusiastic, and Conrad most generous:

My dear Hugh,
I left the "civilities" to Jessie who has no doubt written to you already. This is only to tell you that I have read the book—which is a book—a creation—no small potatoes indeed—très chic; and if the truth must be told très fort even—considerable in purpose, successful in execution and deep in feeling—a genuine Walpole, this, with an unexpected note of maturity in design and composition; and holding the interest from page to page, which in itself is not a common quality. O! dear, no!

197

All I want to do here, really, is to shake hands with you over it in friendship and congratulation. More when we meet on Sat.

Ever yours,

J. Conrad.

No such simple verdict could be expected from Arnold Bennett:

My sweet Hughie,

It seems to me that I have to write to you in the same nagging strain as I do to Wells. In spite of my brotherly admonitions and my fatherly threats apropos of previous books there are at least as many grammatical slips in this one as in any. In particular "anybody" and "everybody" are followed by a plural verb *at least* a score times. And as regards careless writing, there are tons of it. Things like: "She had abandoned so completely any idea that he might still come that she could not now feel that it was he." Also there are some devilish shaky metaphors—e.g. on p. 313, the lines beginning: "Therefore she was building." How in hell the doors could be locked of a house of which the walls were rising, I cannot imagine. Do not suppose that I attach an exaggerated importance to these things. I don't. But I cannot understand how they could remain in a book over which you have obviously (to the seeing eye) taken such enormous pains. To my mind this is a far better book than *The Mirror*, *The City*, *The Forest*. It is more mature. It illustrates more fully than ever the extraordinary narrative gift which you undoubtedly have. Your gift in this line is Trollopian (but I am not going to accept that as an excuse for your Trollopian carelessness—I'm hanged if I do). I do not agree with all your characterisation, but your greatest enemy could not deny that these characters are immensely alive. I object to some of the stuff, which does not seem to me to have been accurately observed, but on the other hand there are lots of it with which no fault can be found. The middle of the book is the best. Round about pp 207, 208, for instance, is the *goods*, emphatically. Some of the construction I do not understand. I can't see the constructional reason, e.g. for the Kingscote Revival Meeting. But doubtless you could produce a good reason, so I shall not insist. Dealing with the book largely, and applying to it the severest standards, I am inclined to say that the excessive power of your visualising imagination has caused you to crowd it a bit, in fact a good bit. You are imaginatively very rich, but is that a reason why you should be extravagant? I doubt not you *could* make a novel out of the history of every one of the minor characters; but need you?

And lo! a certain man went forth into the streets and spake these words:

> Simplification
> Austerity
> Economy of material.

Such, imperfectly, respectfully, and fragmentarily are my views about this history which you have so affectionately dedicated to the aged one. There are lots of questions I want to ask you about it. Will you dine Thursday 21st?

Thine

A. B.

To which Hugh replied:

My dear Father in God,

Thank you for your delightful letter. I maintain and publicly maintain more and more as the years go by that you are the only critic in England worth a damn—fair, wise, proportionate and unprejudiced. More than ever do I feel that now. You have, as I learnt from Frank [Swinnerton], many other criticisms to make, but I'll go only by your written word. Anyway I distrust everything at second hand. You are of course entirely right about grammar, style etc: I am in despair on that question. No one could have sweated more over a book than I did over this. I rewrote passage after passage, but the errors tumble out of my finger-ends as I write. I shall try again, but the Devil is in me over this. Where I differ from you is over the rules of "Simplification, Austerity and Economy of Material." I'm sick of tight little right little novels done on the Flaubert model. Moreover you yourself strike me as neither austere nor simplified. *Clayhanger* is rich with spontaneity and you are being continually creative in spite of your art—which is, I believe, the right way for a novelist. However this is a tall question and I shall never be either a Flaubert or a Stendhal. They are great artists— Trollope is no artist in the austere sense at all—but I'm damned if I don't read Trollope the most often of the three. . . .

Affectionately,

Hugh.

His parents were distressed both by the ending of the story, which seemed to them immoral, and by the poor figure cut by clergymen in the book. Hugh attempted to reassure them, and at the same time to define his point of view:

My dear Father,

Thank you very much for your wise and temperate letter. I never expected you to be so patient with the book. The difficulty in all this business is that one loses oneself in one's creations. The book stands for one's personality but not always for one's opinions. I at any rate can help myself very little if a character has a certain build and direction. Paul for instance *was* like that, and then many people take him to be an indictment of the clergy. Just as when, later on, I draw (as I shall) a good and noble clergyman, everyone will think I'm upholding the Church. My main interest in life is in wondering about what lies behind it, and I would state that wonder in as many terms as I can find. For those who, like you, don't need to wonder because they are sure, I have only deep envy. But to have that wonder and to be sure that there *is* something more seems to me to be a religious point of view, and *The Captives* seems to me a deeply religious book. . . .

Your affectionate son,
Hugh.

Among a few other adverse criticisms was one by Katherine Mansfield in the *Athenæum*. It began:

If an infinite capacity for taking pains were what is needed to produce a great novel, we should have to hail Mr. Walpole's latest book as a masterpiece. But here it is—four parts, four hundred and seventy pages, packed as tight as they can hold with an assortment of strange creatures and furnishings; and we cannot, with the best will in the world, see in the result more than a task—faithfully and conscientiously performed to the best of the author's power—but a "task accomplished," and not even successfully at that. For we feel that it is determination rather than inspiration, strength of will rather than the artist's compulsion, which has produced *The Captives*. Still, while we honour the author for these qualities, is it not a lamentable fact that they can render him so little assistance at the last—can give him no hand with this whole great group of horses captured at such a cost of time and labour, and brought down to the mysterious water only that they shall drink? But, alas! they will not drink for Mr. Walpole; he has not the magic word for them; he is not their master. In a word, for all his devotion to writing, we think the critic, after an examination of *The Captives*, would find it hard to state with any conviction that Mr. Walpole is a creative artist.[1]

She went on to analyse and discuss details of plot and character. Although Rebecca West's riposte had shown him that Writing to Women Reviewers was a dangerous hobby, he could not resist the temptation once again to tackle his critic. And this time the answer was softer: from a chaise-longue at Mentone, Katherine Mansfield wrote :[2]

. . . I wish instead of writing you were here on the terrace and you'd let me talk of your book which I *far* from detested. What an impression to

---

[1] Reprinted in *Novels & Novelists* (1930).
[2] Her letter is printed in full in *The Letters of Katherine Mansfield* (1928), vol. 2, p. 62.

convey! My trouble is I never have enough space to get going—to say what I mean to say—fully. That's no excuse, really. But to be called very unfair—that hurts, awfully. And I feel that by saying so you mean I'm not as honest as I might be—I'm prejudiced. Well, I think we're all of us more or less prejudiced, but cross my heart I don't take reviewing lightly and if I appear to it's the fault of my unfortunate manner.

Now I shall be *dead frank*. And please don't answer. As one writer to another (tho' I'm only a little beginner, and *fully realise* it):

The Captives impressed me as more like a first novel than any genuine first novel I've come across. Of course there were signs enough that it wasn't one—but the movement of it was the movement of one trying his wings—finding out how they would bear him, how far he could afford to trust them. I felt you were continually risking yourself, that you had, for the first time, really committed yourself in a book. I wonder if this will seem to you extravagant impertinence—I honoured you for it. You seemed to me determined to shirk nothing. You know that strange sense of insecurity *at the last*—the feeling: "I know all this. I know more. I know down to the minutest detail and *perhaps more still*, but shall I, dare I, trust myself to tell all?" It is really why we write, as I see it, that we may arrive at this moment and yet—it is stepping into the air to yield to it—a kind of anguish and rapture. I felt that you appreciated this, and that, seen in this light, your *Captives* was almost a spiritual exercise in this kind of courage. But in fact your peculiar persistent consciousness of what you wanted to do was what seemed to me to prevent your book from being a creation. That is what I meant when I used the clumsy word "task"—perhaps "experiment" was nearer my meaning. You seemed to lose in passion what you gained in sincerity and therefore "the miracle" didn't happen. I mean the moment when the act of creation takes place—the mysterious change—when you are no longer writing the book—*it* is writing—*it* possesses you. Does that sound hopelessly vague?

But there it is. After reading *The Captives* I laid it down thinking: Having "broken with his past," as he has in this book, having "declared himself," I feel that Hugh Walpole's next novel will be the one to look for. Yes, curse me. I should have said it.

I sympathise more than I can say with your desire to escape from autobiography. Don't you feel that what English writers lack to-day is experience of Life? I don't mean that superficially. But they are self-imprisoned. I think there is a very profound distinction between any kind of *confession* and creative work—not that that rules out the first by any means. . . .

But enough. Forgive this long letter. I'll try and see more round the books. I've no doubt at all I'm a bad reviewer. Your letter makes me want to shake hands with you across the vast. . . .

Relieved and elated, Hugh replied expansively, and the correspondence was rounded off by this little note:

Dear Hugh Walpole,

Please do not praise me. But—let me say how I look forward to that talk, one of these days. The fact that you care about writing as you do, that "you are working," is such happiness that all my good wishes and my sympathy cannot repay you for letting me know.

Your from-this-time-forth "*constant reader,*"

Katherine Mansfield.

2

There were minor contretemps at York Terrace. The imported butler pined for home and was replaced by an expert so accustomed to stately homes that he stayed only a month; Grock had a fit in the park, tried to hang himself on the railings, and had to be given morphia; while the claims and distractions of London society brought the half-finished *Cathedral* to a standstill. In its place Hugh began a light-hearted novel originally called *Henry and Millicent* and eventually published as *The Young Enchanted*. But all the time his thoughts were filled by his splendid new friend. "Melchior is indeed turning my life upside down, and jolly glad I am. Two concerts after lunch at the Glentanars', and at both of them he sang Lohengrin's Narration quite marvellously. After this I'm quite sure of him, as the whole thing has restraint and dignity of the first order."

At the end of November Melchior went home to Denmark, and Hugh set about the perfecting of his house. The rest of his books were conveyed from Polperro, he bought a chalk-drawing of Walter Scott by Wilkie to hang over the drawing-room fireplace, engaged yet another butler, and secured that multiplicity of household objects which the occasion demanded. In this he was once again helped, wisely and efficiently, by Ethel McKenna.

All the time engagements increased: he stayed with the Masefields on Boars Hill and with the Asquiths at Sutton Courtney; he debated publicly for charity with Chesterton ("charming as ever") and Gosse ("spiky, old, wicked"); he watched the University rugger match with John Drinkwater ("one of the very nicest men in the world"); and gave luncheon, tea, and dinner parties at York Terrace. Just before he left to spend Christmas in Edinburgh, he learned that *The Secret City* had been awarded the James Tait Black Memorial Prize for the best work of fiction published in 1919. "This took my breath away, and the cheque was £112." It was a newly founded prize, and this the first award.

In the gladness of his heart, and sentimentally moved as he always was by the advent of Christmas, he wrote Conrad a letter of homage and affection which greatly pleased its recipient:

I was very deeply touched by your letter [he replied] and I am grateful to you for the impulse which prompted you to put your feelings (which are infinitely precious to me) into words so simple and so direct.

Your friendship is of course part of my reward for some years of honest toil which sought not the favour of men and yet without it would have been a waste of barren effort. And in so far I have perhaps deserved it. But for the warmth of your personal, for that genuine friendship which you have extended to all belonging to me thanks are due to a higher Power which having made us what we are has allowed us to come together. And this my dear Hugh I feel profoundly.

This letter was followed in January by another week-end at Bishopsbourne, during which Conrad declared "that in selling his books in America he felt exactly like a merchant selling glass beads to African natives." Hugh asked him why he didn't write more of the England he loved so much, and Conrad "said he was afraid to." The old man agreed to write a short foreword for an anthology from Hugh's work which Messrs Dent had arranged to issue in one of their series for schools. Hugh was not altogether happy about this volume, but Conrad's promise encouraged him a little. A few weeks later he wrote to Pinker:

It is really a good advertisement although I ought to be ashamed to let such middle-class stuff be collected in this way. One writes one's best and then must put a brazen front to the world. It's no use saying to everybody that one knows one's only second-rate. Besides one's young yet and sometimes the second-raters let out a first-rate thing by chance before they die. Talking of first-rate, don't let Conrad's little preface slip. I *count* on that more than anything in my little life. Only *you* can keep Dent in check until J. C. has done the thing. He need write only a few lines.

He did indeed write only a few—somewhat guarded—lines, but they served, and the small red book duly appeared later in the year.[1]

Meanwhile Hugh was in process of starting a movement which was to bring important benefits to the book trade. In November 1920 he had spoken at a dinner of the Whitefriars Club, emphasising the need for co-operation between authors, publishers, and booksellers, and urging the institution of regular meetings. His idea was eagerly accepted, and on 19 January 1921 he was able to write from York Terrace to St John Ervine:

> Last night we had here the first meeting of a little dining club that has for its purpose bringing together quite privately and informally all the different elements of book producing and distributing . . . [It] is to meet for supper in my house once a month quite informally, definitely to talk "shop" . . . I do hope you'll join.

The dinners at York Terrace prospered; Galsworthy attended one and next day wrote: "You conducted proceedings last night like a born statesman." He went on to suggest that the body be called the Fellowship Club, but in October 1921 it was given the name of The Society of Bookmen. Today it still flourishes: the membership is limited to seventy-five; there is almost always a waiting list; and the monthly dinners are attended as eagerly as ever.

One of the original publisher-members was Stanley Unwin, and it was largely his foresight and strength of character which brought about the Society's considerable achievements. The first of these was the creation of the National Book Council, out of which grew the National Book League, whose mansion in Albemarle Street is now the headquarters of books in England. Later the Society sent a delegation to study book-trade methods in Holland and Germany, and its report led to the complete reorganisation of the British book trade. When Harold Raymond hit upon the idea of Book Tokens, he first propounded it to the Society, who recommended the scheme to the booksellers and even helped to finance its launching. Indeed, it is not too much to say that all the forward movements which Unwin and others have initiated in the British book trade during the last thirty years have

---

[1] *A Hugh Walpole Anthology.* Selected by the Author with a note by Joseph Conrad (King's Treasury of Literature, [1921]).

come into being through the agency of the Society of Bookmen—
Hugh's "little dining club."

3

Later in January he sailed from Harwich to Copenhagen, where
he was to spend a month with Melchior and his wife. He was pleased
by the Danish capital, which, with its canals and boats and tufted trees,
often reminded him of Petrograd. He stayed at the Hôtel d'Angleterre,
worked every day at *The Young Enchanted*, and in his spare time listened
to Melchior singing at concerts, funerals, and for the first time in opera.
"The true quality of his voice, which is most remarkable, doesn't seem
truly understood here. I see no one who really appreciates it. However
they will one day."

Together the two friends visited Elsinore and Kronborg Castle, and
Hugh was especially delighted by a meeting with the old writer Georg
Brandes. "I liked him immensely. Over eighty but full of life and
irony, charming about Gosse and his Lords! and very pleased that old
age was his 'only disease.' Kept speaking to me as Brother. Alluded
charmingly to dear Henry James."

Nevertheless Hugh began to grow homesick; his inability to speak
or understand a word of Danish was a nuisance—he had no gift for
languages—and he was not sorry when his holiday came to an end and
he could sail home to England, taking Melchior with him.

He was greeted by his cook's giving notice. "I got splendid copy
from my hour with Mrs. B.," he told his mother, "and wrote it all
down afterwards." The good lady was quickly replaced, and Hugh
plunged once more into that whirl of lectures, concerts, theatres, and
parties, which in London he was always unable to resist. *The Young
Enchanted* (itself a replacement of the more difficult *Cathedral*) had
temporarily to be laid aside, and during the next two months he produced only a few short stories.

In March his father passed through London, and reported in a letter
to Dorothy:

I stayed with Hugh last night. . . . He was very well and full of go.
Melchior the Dane was with him and going to sing in Queen's Hall this

afternoon. Hugh was out last night so I dined in state and Robins the butler gave me his experiences with Joe Chamberlain and Viscount Grey.

4

Soon after this Hugh was taken by Dr A. S. W. Rosenbach, the American book-dealer, to see T. J. Wise, the great collector and, as has since been discovered, forger of books. Hugh was staggered by the magnificence of the Ashley Library, and described Wise as a "nice kind common little man"—Wise who was so nasty, ruthless, and extraordinary. Some time later, through Wise's agency, Hugh purchased for £400 from Mrs Joan Severn the manuscript of *The Fortunes of Nigel*, which had belonged to Ruskin. It is now at Canterbury with the rest of Hugh's collection.

Perhaps it was Wise too who implanted in Hugh the determination to acquire the thirty-two volumes of the Abbotsford Correspondence, which Scott's descendants put up for auction at Sotheby's on April 12. They contained some seven thousand letters written to Scott by hundreds of the most eminent persons of his time and preserved at Abbotsford for posterity. Hugh approached the sale in a dither of trepidation, certain that Rosenbach or another would buy these treasures for America. Afterwards he said he could remember little of the actual bidding, though he realised that miraculously the lot had been knocked down to him for £1500. In due course two volumes of extracts from the correspondence were published,[1] and the precious documents themselves, which proved of great assistance to Sir Herbert Grierson in his centenary edition of Scott's letters, now repose in the National Library of Scotland, to which Hugh bequeathed them in his will. But for his action, the collection would probably either have gone to America or been broken up and dispersed.

Another literary occasion which concerned him at this time was the eighty-first birthday of Thomas Hardy. A year earlier the Society of Authors had presented a memorial, but the subscribers were all old or elderly, and it occurred to St John Ervine that another presentation might be made, this time representing the younger writers. Hugh was

---

[1] *The Private Letter-Books of Sir Walter Scott* (1930) and *Sir Walter's Post-Bag* (1932). Both edited by Wilfred Partington.

the first Ervine consulted, the idea was after his own heart, and in April a meeting at York Terrace was attended by Siegfried Sassoon, W. J. Turner, Edmund Blunden, Ralph Hodgson, Sheila Kaye-Smith, Frank Swinnerton, Rose Macaulay, Edith Sitwell, Alec Waugh, and St John Ervine. Edith Sitwell, in a letter to Dorothy Walpole written twenty years later, recalled that "Hugh said suddenly: 'We must ask May Sinclair.' 'Oh,' said somebody, 'she's *much* over the age limit.' 'I don't care,' said Hugh. 'She must be asked. It will hurt her dreadfully from every point of view if she is not.'" Eventually more than a hundred writers signed the letter of homage, which, together with a first edition of Keats's *Lamia*, was conveyed by Ervine to the old poet at Dorchester.

5

Towards the end of April Hugh travelled down to Polperro, taking with him a new Sealyham called Mopsa, successor to the unreliable Grock. After ten days he was joined by Melchior, who caused a sensation by singing at a concert in the village. Together they drove on to Mullion, where, with the help of a friend, Charles Turley Smith, whom he had met with E. V. Lucas, Hugh had taken a furnished bungalow on the edge of the golf-course. He never liked golf nor, though he became a life member of the Sunningdale Club and once played a round with Joyce and Roger Wethered, was he ever a proficient player. But here at Mullion in the sunshine it was an agreeable, and he hoped a weight-reducing, pursuit.

Turley was a delightful opponent too, and Hugh made great friends with him. Writer of school stories, *Punch* reviewer, cricketer, close friend of J. M. Barrie, and a favourite everywhere he went, Turley lived in the little village of Cury, near Mullion.[1] Hugh once stayed with him there, but most of the rest of their friendship had for geographical reasons to be conducted through the post.

Hugh and Melchior were looked after in the bungalow by Robins the butler and their short holiday was blissful. "So happy," wrote Hugh. "Never have I had such wonderful perfect accord with any-

[1] See *Dear Turley* (edited by Eleanor Adlard, 1942), to which Hugh had promised to contribute. Turley died in October 1940.

one." Besides playing golf, they drove to Penzance and Land's End, and took part at Helston in the Floral Dance, which Hugh had already from hearsay described in *Maradick* and was to use again in *Portrait of a Man with Red Hair*. *The Young Enchanted* was finished at Mullion, and Hugh returned to London in time to watch the Derby with Melchior and some other Danish friends.

June was London in the Season—parties and theatres, Wimbledon, more golf, and always concerts. Melchior sang at Marlborough House for Queen Alexandra, "who was apparently delighted with him," Hugh told his mother, "although I don't think she heard much."

6

On June 30 *The Thirteen Travellers* was published. Hugh's own comment was: "And a rotten book too. Comes of yielding to Mammon, which I'll do no more"; yet he could not disguise his distress at a "loathsome review in *The Times*. Worst I've ever had, and in small type too, where I've never been since my first book." A favourable counterblast by Robertson Nicoll put him in better humour, and a week later he set off gaily for a two months' tour of the Continent.

First, accompanied by Melchior, he spent an exhausting fortnight in a Paris heat-wave, sight-seeing relentlessly but finding time to begin the first of the stories for *Jeremy and Hamlet*. "I have such creative impulses," he wrote to Turley, "but not the final wisdom; perhaps one day it will come."

Then came ten days at Chalet Soleil, where he found Elizabeth at her most charming, though she could not resist telling him that his work "was just misted for her like a telescope not being quite focused." He was accustomed to such remarks from her, but worse was to follow, for when the *Nation* of July 16 reached the Chalet it was found to contain a "ferocious attack" on *The Thirteen Travellers* by Middleton Murry. The best part of three columns, headed "The Case of Mr Hugh Walpole," compared Hugh with Hall Caine and Ethel M. Dell, ridiculed his style, his "romanticism," his very existence as a writer. In his diary Hugh contented himself with remarking: "I can see that I must be everything he most dislikes—but time will prove all." Then, seeking more sympathy than he was likely to receive from his astringent hostess, he wrote to Bennett:

30 July 1921.   Chalet Soleil.

My dearest Arnold,

I feel impelled to write to you chiefly because for months now I seem to have been out of touch with you, which has been partly my fault—and partly yours. I was in Paris for weeks grilling and now I'm on the top of a mountain with "Elizabeth," old Festing Jones, Middleton Murry and others. Murry lives about five minutes away and our juxtaposition is funny because as you probably saw he wrote a ferocious attack on me in the *Nation* a week or two ago. However I've no feelings about that nor has he, and if I didn't sell and found life a horrible tragedy and wrote in the Tchekov manner he'd find me a darling. He's a weird bird, his knowledge of life all from books and his solemnity amazing.

My volume of stories I didn't send you because I didn't think it would interest you. . . . Murry thinks it dreadful of me to be happy with the world as it is, but how can I help it with so much that is lovely, so much that is funny, so much that is exciting? It isn't my fault if my experience of people is that on the whole they are good sorts making the best of a difficult bargain. Well, enough of this. Please write to me here. I motor to Venice but return here soon.

Dear Arnold, my affection for you never alters nor changes nor ever will. I love you very much.

Yours,
Hugh.

Back came the answer:

5 August 1921.   Yacht Marie Marguerite
                                                              Cowes.

My dear Hughie,

Ta lettre est charmante, et j'en suis très content. I passed by Polperro in the above about 3 weeks ago, but 10 miles out to sea. However, I gazed at it through a powerful Zeiss. Murry is an ass. He writes long articles about nothing, and he has no taste of his own (except bad). I have told Massingham, who reluctantly agrees with me. I haven't seen the *Nation* for weeks. . . . Be happy, Hughie, and be damned to Murrys. . . .

Ever your elder brother,
A. B.

Meanwhile the errant Murry, wickedly invited by the Countess, came to tea at the Chalet and "was exceedingly amiable. Admitted afterwards to Elizabeth that the article was unfair. Rather late though." Later she wrote to Hugh with her usual thrust: "You know perfectly well that you yourself knew your *13 T*'s wasn't up to the mark, and knew it so well that you refused to give it to me on that ground. So why shouldn't Murry share your opinion?"

Early in August Hugh met the McKennas at Andermatt, and drove on with them through Como, Verona, and Padua, to Venice. They stayed at the Excelsior Hotel on the Lido, where a minor tragedy had soon to be recorded:

Aug. 12. Going for two minutes by tram from the hotel to the Baths my purse was stolen, all my papers, my letter of credit and 16,000 lire. Dreadfully distressed by this all the evening and feel for a moment it has entirely spoilt my trip.

The mood of self-questioning set up by this mishap caused him to ask himself for the first time whether he had been wise to entrench himself so comfortably in London. Years ago John Buchan had advised him, for his writing's sake, not to settle down too soon. Should he not sell his house, and his furniture, and his library, and be free? But these reflections served only to bring home to him the consciousness of how much he loved all these things: "One must have a centre in life, round which one revolves, and that is mine." Should he then get rid of The Cobbles? He still, perhaps more than ever, needed a country retreat to write in, but Polperro was now much more known and visited than it had been before the war, nor had he ever really experienced the longed-for feeling of "belonging" there—yes, on the whole, he thought the time had come to leave.

After the McKennas had gone, Hugh moved to rooms on the Grand Canal, whence after another week he returned to Chalet Soleil. From there he wrote:

Aug. 29. My last day here and really I'm not sorry. E. is a darling, but I'm not well here, and there *is* something of the boss about her that we all feel and want to escape from. However she is a most enchanting creature, quite unique, and amusing beyond all her sex.

From Switzerland he travelled to Brittany, where he spent ten days with his family at Camaret, near Brest. Here he corrected proofs of *The Young Enchanted* and, despite some opposition from a fair which broke out in front of the hotel, managed to read aloud the new Jeremy stories in the evenings. From Switzerland he had acquainted Bennett with his plans for a nine months' American lecture tour in the winter of 1922–23, and his consequent intention to take a year's complete rest from writing. Back came his mentor with more wise words:

31 August 1921.   Yacht Marie Marguerite,
                                                                                Fowey.

My dear Hughie,

I have yours. Many thanks. I shall reintegrate London on Oct. 1st. Thenceforward, let us much meet. When I arrived here I telegraphed to the postmaster of Polperro to know if you were at the Collywobbles. The intelligent fellow wired back that you were in Switzerland: which I deeply regretted. Still, I am cheered by your excellent news of the book. As for the lecture-tour, well, I suppose it suits you, and I know from independent witnesses that you do this stunt very well. So good. But I bet you you won't stop writing for a year. You couldn't. And it would not be a good thing if you do—believe me! . . .

My fraternal benediction is upon thee.

                                                                    Thine ever,
                                                                    A. B.

                                           7

Hugh arrived back in London on September 10. Welcomed by Melchior, he was so pleased to be home that he marked the occasion by purchasing, from the Leicester Galleries for eight hundred guineas, the complete set of twenty-three Max Beerbohm cartoons called *Rossetti and his Circle*. The glory first of the small sitting-room at York Terrace and later of the Piccadilly dining-room, they are now, by the provisions of Hugh's will, safe in the Tate Gallery.

Hardly had he arranged these treasures in their first home when Sir Frederick Macmillan delighted him by suggesting that *The Young Enchanted* should appear in a large-paper edition, signed and limited, as well as in its ordinary form. The plan proved successful, and most of Hugh's books thereafter were similarly issued.

And now came a melancholy occasion—the farewell visit to The Cobbles. For more than eight years the little cottage perched on the edge of the harbour had been for him a solace and a joy. He did not yet know what would replace it, but he felt strongly that he now needed "somewhere more open and with less village gossip and intrigue." Sadly, with lingering sentiment, he bade it farewell and returned to London. His first attempt at identifying himself with a landscape had failed—but had he perhaps found the ideal friend in the person of Melchior the Dane?

CHAPTER FIFTEEN

THE END OF A CHAPTER

I

FOR some time Hugh had wanted to write a play of his own, something more substantial than *The Comfortable Chair*, but since he lacked both a definite scheme and also the necessary technical skill, he wrote in April 1921 to his old friend and collaborator Rudolf Besier, suggesting that they should write a play together. Besier responded cordially, and it was agreed that they should meet for discussion in the autumn. But before their meeting Hugh hit upon the idea that was to produce one of the most successful plays of the next decade—the idea of a comedy based on the Browning love-letters.

Besier was enthusiastic. "I am taking the love-letters to read and digest *en voyage* and in Ireland," he wrote on September 7. "Oh my dear, if only I can rise to the height of this great argument—what a play! I wish to God my hands were utterly free and that I could start on it at once and think of nothing else."

Hugh's letters to Besier have perished, but from the other half of the correspondence it is possible to trace the play's beginnings a little further. All through September, October, and November, the two friends bombarded each other with ideas and suggestions, in conversation and by post. On September 11 Besier wrote:

Why, at the moment, without real reflection, I say I'm doubtful about dropping the first meeting between R. and E. is *pure theatre*. I'll explain when I see you. . . . Papa's scene with E. B. about the lunch "porter" is a joy. But I want to talk to you about Papa. In life he seems to have been a *pathological* problem. I seem to feel we must give him reasons and motives for his actions which he doesn't appear really to have had.

Again, on October 20:

E. B. B. says somewhere that she has some *forty* relations in London. I can see some half dozen of 'em ushered one by one with "melancholy glee" by Barrett into the darkened room to say a few words to poor dear Ba.

213

Another letter, headed simply "Sunday" but clearly written during these months, runs:

My dear Hugh:

Don't answer this. It occurs to me that we shall *have* to make our people—at any rate R. B. and E. B. B.—talk literature a little. One of the greatest English poets and the greatest English poetess—we can't avoid it. But fortunately Browning's "obscurity" will help us. "The poet whom nobody understands" is still a cliché. People who never read a line of Browning will be amused and understand talk of his obscurity. As luck would have it *Sordello* was published long before Robert and Elizabeth met. And there's a passage in *Sordello*—one of many I daresay—as impossibly cryptic as the writings of the prehistoric inhabitants of Mars. I want to make E. B. B. read it to Robert in Act I as something she can't *quite* grasp—and R. B. be as mystified as E. B. B. on hearing it.

Oh and why not grasp the nettle firmly and call the play "*BA*"? It's unique, intriguing, and the shortest title on record.

R. B.

Enough has been quoted to show that by November 1921 much of the play had taken shape in Besier's mind, but towards the end of that month, when the first act had been roughed out, the manager Vedrenne insisted on Besier's finishing some other work, long overdue, and the Brownings had to be laid aside. Three years later Besier asked whether Hugh was still interested, and in May 1925 announced that a detailed scenario would soon be ready. "Are you still game?" he asked, but by then Hugh's enthusiasm had waned, while his success as a novelist had increased, so he made Besier a present of the idea and of whatever he may have contributed to its treatment. *The Barretts of Wimpole Street*, as it was eventually produced by Sir Barry Jackson in September 1930, was entirely Besier's work, and although Hugh occasionally referred a little wistfully to the small fortune he had missed by retiring from the collaboration, he felt nothing but affection for Besier and pride in the play's success. The printed version was dedicated to Hugh, and the story can perhaps be best wound up with one more letter of Besier's, dated 5 June 1931:

My dear Hugh,

Many thanks. It's more than likely that I myself started the story! I've told innumerable people, including Barry Jackson and Guthrie McClintic, the American producer, that yours was the idea and that you very magnificently handed it on to me. I've no doubt the papers are bitterly disappointed to learn that what they hoped was a dirty piece of trickery should turn out to be a splendid piece of generosity . . .

> Always,
> R. B.[1]

2

In the autumn of 1921 Hugh spent an uncomfortable week-end with Conrad, who was suffering badly from gout.

Much odder than I've ever known before, bursting into sudden rages about such nothings as the butter being salt, and then suddenly being very quiet and sweet. Never cross with me save in a sudden tirade about publishers. . . . Too many women in this house and too many secret feelings.

It was an immense relief to get back to York Terrace and Melchior: "This is friendship in the final and absolute sense of the word, when you can hardly wait to tell your friend the tiniest details of the past day." And there were plenty of details to tell, as lectures, concerts, and parties jostled one another in Hugh's engagement book. In the middle of October he finished *Jeremy and Hamlet* in London, and on November 8 *The Young Enchanted* was published, with a dedication to Melchior. Conrad took immense pains to read and criticise it: in the course of a very long letter of elaborate analysis he wrote:

The reading of it was an absorbing experience. The meditation which came later confirmed the sense of the work's value, which I feel to be considerable. Its atmosphere is extremely fascinating (which of course means the clear atmosphere in which the author wrote), its interest very real (which means the state of mind of the reader), its detail amusing by its exactitude and manner of presentation; its ending though (perhaps on purpose) not conclusive has an episodic finality which leaves our sympathies satisfied in a way which is particularly attractive; and the whole picture, even to the framing, is very Walpolean (which means that the design, the colouring, the perspective and the very grouping have an individual quality to which I, together with a large portion of the world, am easily responsive).

It is a great tribute to your gift, dear Hugh, that when I read you it is always like a member of the public, (I suppose the more intelligent part of

---

[1] Mrs Besier tells me that her husband had conceived a similar idea as early as 1905 and that he "always realised that Hugh thought the play his own idea . . . but he was too fond of Hugh ever to wish him to be disabused."

it) but as a matter of fact reacting emotionally, that is directly to your appeal and not to any suggested reflections of my own.

Reviews were favourable, though Philip Guedalla laughed at the book in the *Daily News*, and in due course Arnold Bennett fired off a broadside:

My dear Hughie,

I don't know what you mean by "romantic." All the big realists are romantic,—no one more so than Balzac and Dostoievski and Chekov. The only sense that I can attach to the word as you use it is "sentimental"— meaning a softening of the truth in order to produce a pleasant impression on people who don't like the truth. It is quite possible to be romantic and truthful at the same time. All untruthful romance is vitiated. There is no opposition or mutual-excluding between romance and realism. Believe me.

Your novel shows once more your most genuine and even devilish gift for narrative. By God you can tell a story! Also the first half of the book is full of charming things, excellent bits of observation and fancy, new gleams of light on the world. But, also by God, I will not hide from you my conviction that the book does not improve as it goes on. The *invention* of the latter half is not good, and it gets more and more conventional. Some of the critical scenes are not really "done" . . . I am obliged to call the book "pretty"—that is as a whole. . . . I am well aware that my strictures, whether you accept them or not, will cause you pain. But I would a jolly sight sooner cause you pain than insult you by wrapping up my feelings about the book in pink paper. I do not reckon that this book has come off. At first I thought it would, but the "romantic" idea ran away with you. Don't imagine that I have any objection whatever to the "romantic" as such. But I do not accept it as an excuse for falsification, or conventionalisation, and I maintain that a process of increasing falsification and conventionalisation goes on throughout the book. The mere details of writing I think are better than in *The Captives*.

F[rank] S[winnerton] agrees with me that your skill in narrative is diabolic—hellish.

I've just had 6 days in bed—chill.

Thine
A. B.

Feeling himself on stronger ground than in earlier years, Hugh replied firmly:

My dear Arnold,

So sorry you've been ill—so have I. No, your letter didn't give me pain a bit. I never expected you to like the book and nearly didn't send it

you. Certainly no "pink paper" between *us*! I'm still rather feeble—just
got up for my party last night and went to bed again. I think you're right
about my not doing the thing well enough, but where I differ from you and
Swinny (excuse my coupling you, but you're like a pair of brothers in thought
and attitude of mind) is that I think neither of you have the capacity for
appreciating a certain side of life at all—the side that people as different as
Conrad, Masefield, May Sinclair, Clemence Dane, Rose Macaulay, Drinkwater all understand. There's a real cleavage between them and you, and
from my point of view you and Frank seem to be being left behind.
This is nothing to do with my feeling for you as artists. No one in the world
admires *Old Wives* and *Clayhanger* more than I, or *Nocturne* and *Coquette*, but
what I mean is that if I wrote with the pen of an angel about certain aspects
of life and philosophy and beauty, you and Frank would be blind to it. The
people I've named like *just* the things in my work that you two don't, and
have received this book with a chorus of praise. All the same no one is more
aware of my appalling weaknesses, carelessness, etc, than myself, although I
am going to send you the Cathedral book next year with pride. Do believe,
Arnold dear, that I *care* to do my best, that I am really not arguing that my
work is *good*, but that we, you and I, see life increasingly from different angles,
and that I don't believe in your angle *at all*.

You really *did* hurt me though when you told me you "would be abroad
and so couldn't come to my party," and now as I understand were dancing
at Devonshire House all the time!

Your loving
Hugh.

Bennett rode this accusation with "Be not hurt" and a long, fluent
explanation, continuing:

I should like to have a chat with Conrad about your theories. I should be
intensely surprised if we didn't agree. As for the rest of your list, its critical
attitude towards anything whatever in literature has no interest for me.
Get better, brother, and hurry up with that Gothic cathedral of yours.

3

The party which Bennett avoided was one of Hugh's most ambitious
at York Terrace. Melchior was the guest of honour, but others included the McKennas, Siegfried Sassoon, Lord and Lady Gerald
Wellesley, Mrs Belloc Lowndes, the Colvins, Elizabeth, the Beresfords,
the Annands, E. V. Lucas, Rose Macaulay, Naomi Royde-Smith,
Drinkwater, Sir Frederick and Lady Macmillan, the Galsworthys,

Arthur and Sibyl Colefax, the Ervines, and Victor Beigel. Beigel was a successful teacher of singing, and Hugh wanted him to give lessons to Melchior. "D. is swinging me into a perpetual sea of music," he wrote soon after this. "Thank God for it!"

In December he took Melchior to Edinburgh to stay with his family, after making due preparation: "Melchior drinks Bass's light beer," he warned his mother, "and Mopsa has Melox biscuits." The visit was a thorough success, and Melchior gave a concert in the Usher Hall. After his friend had left for Denmark, Hugh delivered a number of lectures in Scotland, replied to the toast of Literature at the Scott dinner in Edinburgh, and shortly before Christmas took up once more the half-finished manuscript of The Cathedral.

In the evenings he tried out some of its earlier chapters on his parents, and once again they were somewhat shocked at his treatment of the clergy and other aspects of religious life. In an attempt to reassure his mother, he wrote some weeks later:

I'm sure that our religious feeling comes to very much the same in the end—only I have felt for many years as though man had made a golden calf and was worshipping it instead of the Real God. Of course there will be a lot of opposition to my book, but you must not mind that. I am entirely on the side of the Angels, only I think the hatred of the Durham snobbery has been boiling in me for years, and part of it finds expression in this book.

Back in London in the New Year, Hugh resumed the sittings for his portrait by Gerald Kelly which had begun again in November. Kelly's easy conversation and civilised attitude to life endeared him to Hugh, and the two men were soon on terms of warm friendship. Many other old friends were in London, and one day "Willie Maugham came to tea and warmed my heart by speaking well of my work, especially The Captives, and actually praising my 'urbane humour,' which everyone always denies me."

At the beginning of February Hugh began to lay his plans for the campaign that was to turn Melchior into "the greatest Wagner tenor in the world." Victor Beigel agreed to give him three lessons a week in London until the autumn when, despite tempting and immediate offers from America, they decided that their protégé should join the Vienna Opera company. Two thirds of Beigel's fee were paid in advance by Hugh, the remainder by Melchior out of his subsequent earnings. Final arrangements for the second part of the plan were to be settled during a visit to Vienna in March.

But before they left, there was a lot to be done. Pinker died suddenly: Hugh wrote an obituary notice for *The Times* and consoled Conrad, who was much upset by the loss of his old friend and literary agent. A few days later, at a meeting in London, Conrad "flung his arms round me and kissed me before them all."

A slight chill caused Hugh to spend a happy day in bed, looking through the Abbotsford letters and reading Scott's *Journal*, "very nearly my favourite book in the world, I think. You can actually hear him speaking through the page." It was typical of Hugh's enjoyment of simple pleasures that on this brief rest he should comment: "Such a day as this does one as much good as a week on the Riviera."

As soon as he was well, he hurried on with the final chapters of *The Cathedral*, and after a concentrated burst of several days' writing he brought the book to a conclusion at York Terrace on March 4. More than three years had passed since he had begun the first chapter in Edinburgh, but the theme had never left his mind, even while he had interrupted his work on it to write *The Young Enchanted*. He was much affected by the death of the Archdeacon, "the thing I've been dreading all the way through, but I absolutely heard him speak and saw him move. Poor old Brandon! My companion for four years. How real he is to me, and how uninteresting he may be to everyone else." Hugh's fears were groundless, and the passage is quoted to illustrate the novelist's affection for the characters of his creation, and his unwillingness to part from them. "It is my longing to recover some of their company, I suppose," he wrote some years later,[1] "that has led me so often to drag characters by the hair of their heads from one book into another."

4

The parting from Archdeacon Brandon left him feeling empty and light-headed or, as Arnold Bennett described it, "in a hell of a state of

[1] In an article called "My First Published Book," originally published in Part Two of *The Colophon* (April 1930), and later reprinted in *Breaking Into Print*, a symposium edited by Elmer Adler (New York, 1937). A large number of the facts in Hugh's article are inaccurate.

puerperal fever," so that the trip to Vienna with Melchior became a welcome distraction. They arrived there on March 14, stayed at the Hotel Sacher, and found the whole city dull and depressing. The Opera seemed to them "riddled with Bolshevism," and in an attempt to find a less tendentious troupe they journeyed on after ten days to Munich. Here Melchior sang to Anna von Mildenburg, the great Wagnerian soprano of Hugh's youth, who prophesied that after a year with the Munich Opera Melchior would "have the world at his feet."

Naturally this judgment uplifted their spirits, and Munich seemed as friendly and delightful as Vienna had been dull and hostile. Hugh commented on the cheerfulness and industry of the Germans. He always preferred them and their literature to the French, and it was partly this perfectly legitimate preference which in 1939 built up within his mind fantasies of being arrested as a German spy.

The gaiety of Munich made him long to begin a new book. He was never content unless he had one on hand, but the imminence of his American lecture-tour kept him from starting the next novel. So he began to jot down some chapters of autobiography, to which he gave the title of *The Crystal Box*.

At the beginning of April Melchior returned to England, and Hugh travelled on alone to Florence. There, after some agreeable days spent with Reginald Turner, Norman Douglas, Pino Orioli, and Somerset Maugham, he was joined by his parents and Robin. They spent a week visiting the museums and galleries together, before Hugh went on alone to Naples, Sicily, and Rome. He enjoyed everything and had completed five of the short chapters of *The Crystal Box* by the time he arrived back in London in the middle of May.

Pausing only to make sure that Melchior was taking lessons in German as well as in singing—for Wagner could not be conquered without—Hugh travelled down to Cury, to spend a fortnight with Turley. One day a drive took him through Truro, which he found "as moving as ever. Town looking exactly the same, but I mix it up in my mind now with Polchester until I scarcely know which is which."

A recent reading of Joyce's *Ulysses* ("filthy and yet real genius") made Bennett's new novel, *Mr Prohack*, appear tame and conventional.

Yet he could not let its publication pass unnoticed; perhaps he even felt sufficiently assured to get a bit of his own back:

My dearest Arnold,

This may get to you before the day but the post is so uncertain that I dare not risk waiting. So here's *wishing* you many happy returns of the 7th.

To one human being (and I imagine to many hundreds more but I speak only of what *I've* experienced) your existence is an absolute necessity. You are the most wonderful friend, the straightest and truest; it was a lucky thing for me the day Marie Lowndes introduced me to you. . . . *Prohack* amused and disappointed me. I saw the man himself but none of his family. The episode with Lady M. admirable. But I believe you tired of the whole thing before you finished it. Have *millions* of happy returns, dear Arnold.

Yours affectionately,
Hugh.

Words so outrageously unfraternal could not go unanswered:

My dear Hughie,

Grazie, as they say at Girgenti. I can't make out your address. That's the worst of being a professional author.

re *Mr. Prohack*. How dare you differ from Mr. Forrest Reid in the *Nation*? 2 cols of *nothing* but praise, or was it 1½ cols?—I forget.

I know what *I* think about the last chapters of the book. But I'm dashed if I'm going to tell anybody.

Ever thine
A. B.

5

In London at the beginning of June Hugh was delighted to find that he had been elected a member of the Athenæum Club. His proposer and seconder were Frederick Macmillan and Sidney Colvin; his supporters included John Buchan, Arthur Pinero, Anthony Hope Hawkins, Squire Bancroft, Henry Newbolt, and E. V. Lucas. After a day or two Hugh for the first time crept fearfully into the club and consumed a solitary tea in the library. Another citadel had been peacefully penetrated.

Soon he was off on a round of country-house visits: to the Conrads, the Cazalets at Fairlawne, to Stratfield Saye and, most impressive of all, to Panshanger. A treasured newspaper cutting provides some details of the company:

Lord and Lady Desborough entertained a house party for the week-end at Panshanger, Hertford, the members of which included the Duke and Duchess of Portland, the Duke and Duchess of Sutherland, the Marquess of Londonderry, the Marquess and Marchioness of Salisbury, the Earl of Balfour, the Earl and Countess of Midleton, Lord Richard and Lady Moyra Cavendish, Viscount Farquhar, Lord and Lady Wolverton, Lord Revelstoke, the Hon. Sir John and Lady Ward, Sir Robert Horne, Sir Raymond Greene, the Hon. Evan Charteris, Colonel Baker-Carr, and Mr. Hugh Walpole.

"Had not expected so huge a place," Hugh confided to his diary. "It literally takes me nearly ten minutes to walk from my room to the dining-room." He was charmed to discover that Lord Balfour shared his love of Charlotte M. Yonge, but decided before Monday that the party was "rather too political." Much more to his taste was a dinner party he gave a few days later at York Terrace, when Melchior "sang beautifully and Ruth Draper recited masterfully."

This was the only period of his life during which Hugh entertained lavishly and often: later when he had rearranged his life there was no room for such expansiveness, and if indeed he had not expressly planned it so, he was undoubtedly relieved to be free of the strain and racket of presiding over frequent luncheon and dinner parties. His friends on the other hand may well have regretted his retirement from the position of host: certainly they appear to have enjoyed the junketings at York Terrace. As Naomi Royde-Smith wrote:

It isn't only that you have a delightful house and a gifted cook and a pretty taste in friends. It is that you have a real genius for communicating your own enjoyment of these things. I always feel more pleased with the world than I do feel naturally when I've been with you—and the feeling lasts for days at a time.

At one of his parties there occurred an incident which was to have a long sequel. St John Ervine remembers that towards the end of a hilarious and successful evening Hugh, in a moment of over-excited ebullience, claimed loudly that his house contained everything to eat and drink that his guests could possibly want. Ervine took him up on this, with impish Irish humour, and asked for some Brazil nuts. As it happened there were none in the house, and Hugh chose to regard his friend's light-hearted jest as a deliberate attempt to humiliate him before his other guests. At least so it must be supposed, for this childish incident caused an estrangement between the two men which lasted with brief interruptions for almost twenty years. Ervine could never believe that this was the sole occasion for the breach, and although Hugh had probably soon forgotten its origin, he for almost ever after thought of and referred to Ervine as his "enemy."

Enemies were an essential part of Hugh's cosmos. If life, and so he portrayed it in his novels, was one long struggle between good and evil, and if friends and their friendship exemplified the angels, it followed that the opposition must be represented by enemies. And if real enemies were scarce, what easier than to imagine them? "Once," wrote L. A. G. Strong,[1] "after he had attacked in each of a long series of lectures an editor whom he blamed for a virulent review, I told him the fact, which was that the editor in distress had greatly toned down the original script. Walpole turned pale. 'Don't tell me that, you mustn't, you mustn't. Don't take away my enemy.'"

6

There were still some six weeks before he was due to sail for America, and into them he crammed several important events. The first was his meeting with Major Douglas Chanter. For some time Hugh had been toying with the idea of engaging someone to act as secretary, chauffeur, and in part companion. His old friend Chug Ferris sent Chanter along as a possible candidate for the post. Hugh liked him at once, and when it was discovered that he was a "dab at a car," they arranged that he should report for duty on Hugh's return from the States.

Then came a hurried visit to Copenhagen, where he stayed with the Melchiors and, yielding to the never-ceasing temptation to begin another novel, composed the opening pages of *Harmer John*, the story of the arrival in Polchester of a Scandinavian gymnast, his acceptance, efforts to do good, and final rejection by the townspeople. Circumstances compelled him to lay the manuscript aside almost at once, and it was more than a year before he was free to take it up again.

[1] *Time and Tide*, 17 June 1944.

During the third week of August Melchior gave a concert in Dublin, and Hugh went with him. The Civil War was still in progress, and the sound of rifle-fire at night, the warnings to civilians to stay indoors, and the lorry-loads of armed men took his thoughts back to Petrograd.

Three days in London were quite enough, since they included a "horrible morning with the accountant over the income-tax papers, and I shall never forget it. I may have to pay thousands of pounds. The only thing to do is to Coué myself and to refuse to allow it to worry me." All through the years he carried out this policy: he kept no accounts, and as earnings from journalism, films, lectures, and serials swelled the flow of royalties from books, the precept of Dr Coué was merged into the example of the ostrich. Considering how much he allowed his periodical sessions with chartered accountants and tax-inspectors to worry him—quite unnecessarily, for his earning-power grew always greater—it is astonishing that he never took conclusive steps to clear the matter up. He enjoyed nursing the illusion that all his affairs were in perfect order, but after his death his executors were obliged to negotiate for several years before the authorities finally agreed to accept the sum of £10,000 in settlement of the *arrears* of income tax and surtax.

7

Meanwhile, casting all such thoughts from his mind, Hugh set out for a week's holiday which was to have important consequences. His family met him at Troutbeck, and together they explored the beauties of the English Lakes. This was Hugh's first visit since his childhood holidays at Gosforth, and as he viewed the lovely prospect from the summit of Helvellyn, he decided that "it's all a divine country and it has come like a new birth to me."

This glimpse of the promised land, following close upon the warning of the tax-gatherer, led to a wise decision. He was weary of London society: he needed quiet to work in: Melchior was going to Munich: there was nothing to keep him in London. "Only these things in life do I love," he told Turley; "my friends, my work, and beauty in nature and art. The first are being smothered by acquaintances, the second broken up by telephones and chatter, the third dimmed by cigar smoke." He would sell York Terrace and settle down, perhaps in Italy but more likely in Cumberland. It seemed like the end of a chapter, and he wanted every chapter to go on for ever. Nevertheless his determination was still firm when, on September 16, he once more sailed from Southampton in the *Mauretania*.

CHAPTER SIXTEEN

MOMENTS OF DISCOVERY

I

ONE successful lecture tour in the United States is very like another, and Hugh's second venture differed from its predecessor only in lasting longer and drawing even larger and more enthusiastic audiences. Knowing and secretly enjoying the procedure, Hugh slipped easily back into the routine of travelling, lecturing, shaking hands, renewing old friendships, striking up new ones, and using every moment of waiting to add another chapter to *The Crystal Box* or jot down ideas for *Harmer John*. He still felt homesick at times, missed Melchior, and welcomed letters from home, particularly those of Frank Swinnerton, full of gossip and wit. In New York he made friends with the sculptor Jo Davidson, the writer Don Marquis, and his own efficient new lecture agent, Lee Keedick.

October was spent mostly on the eastern seaboard. "In Ottawa," Hugh told Hergesheimer, "I was received as a kind of King or Barnum, three deputations at the station and the Premier giving me lunch. All the same I'm the modest little flower you've always known, and the happiest 'piece' I've had yet in the States was my day with you and Dorothy."

Encouraged by so many visible signs of a flowing income, Hugh began to reconsider his decision to dispose of York Terrace, and at the end of October he wrote to his mother:

Now that the income tax has settled itself I feel that I *cannot* leave No. 24. Especially now that I am out of England it is quite impossible to think of making my home in any other country. But I am resolved in the future to have four months of every year in absolute quiet, either in the Lakes or Cornwall or abroad. I begin on Monday a fortnight's course in New York. Many of the places kicked against my agent's high prices when I first came over, but they have all come round now and every big city in the States and all the universities are having me. Washington have taken me at last *and* at a high price.

Fresh encouragement came from the enthusiastic reception of *The Cathedral*. He had dedicated the book to the Conrads, and it was published on both sides of the Atlantic during October. When the London reviews reached Hugh through the press-cutting agency he was delighted to find that almost the only dissentient voice was, as might be expected, that of the *Church Times*. Nor was the book without its champion even there, for in the next issue appeared this letter:

Sir, We do not expect strict accuracy from those who write Romances, but when Deans write about Cathedrals they ought to know their subject. "A Dean" in his criticism of *The Cathedral* complains that Mr. Walpole makes "Canon Ryle" who is the Precentor of the Cathedral sing the services and writes: "When a Precentor sings the services he is a Minor Canon. In some Cathedrals indeed one of the Canons is Precentor, but in this case the services are sung by the Succentor." Here Mr. Walpole is right and the Dean is wrong. In Truro Cathedral the Precentor is a Residentiary Canon and yet commonly sings the service.

He is also wrong in saying that Minor Canons are not called Canons. It is incorrect and frowned upon by the Residentiaries who do not like even Honorary Canons to be called Canons, but it is very commonly done. "A Dean" also states quite definitely "The Office of Treasurer is not in the gift of the Crown." At St. Paul's Cathedral there are two Offices of Treasurer and one is in the gift of the Crown and has been so for many centuries: the other in that of the Chapter. It is pardonable that Mr. Walpole should have confused the two Offices. We must all believe that the Dean is right and Mr. Walpole wrong in their estimate of the life of the Close, and yet rumours get abroad that it is not always and everywhere so friendly a fellowship as might be desired.

Yours faithfully,
Veritas.

It was not till a month later that Hugh discovered the identity of "Veritas," and then his surprise matched his delight, for it was his own father.

My dearest Father,

I got your letter here last night and I can't tell you how deeply touched I was at your coming out in my defence.

Nothing has made me happier than the way that you and Mother have seen *The Cathedral*. It has been the one thing that has distressed me all this year. I knew that with all its faults the book was really religious, but I was afraid that you might be worried and I feared a savage attack on you as well as myself. But I could no more prevent myself writing it than I could stop breathing. However the reception has been wonderful . . . and almost everyone seems to feel that it is my best work. So that now I have had your and Mother's letters I have no more anxieties. But I was especially delighted that you should come out and help me. That's fine.

The tour is a huge success. My agent is wild with delight and will make a good deal of money, I should think. The twelve lectures in N.Y. and Brooklyn were packed. I am in splendid health and like America and the Americans far better this time. My house in London and everything in it save the books and pictures are to be sold. Next July I plan to go with an Arctic expedition into the heart of Greenland for the summer, and shall be back in England somewhere in October. I mean to be a wanderer seeing the East, etc, for some three years, then unpack my books again and have an English country house, in the Lakes I hope. I'm dead sick of publicity of every kind, being stared at, expected always to be clever and so on—less people and more quiet for me after this is over!

Love to you all.
Your loving son,
Hugh.

The decision to sell York Terrace was at last brought into effect by a telegram to his solicitor in London telling him to proceed with the sale (it produced only £600). Greenland had been suggested by a meeting with Robert J. Flaherty, the film director, who had just been there to make one of the first documentary films, *Nanook of the North*; while the idea of "a wanderer seeing the East" was the immediate result of reading Somerset Maugham's *On a Chinese Screen*. But in reality he was haunted by the beauty of the English Lakes, and as the tour progressed his determination to settle there steadily increased.

December found him in the Deep South, January in the Middle West, everywhere a success. "My Chaplain," wrote H. L. Mencken, "is instructed to pray that the intelligentsia of the cow and mining towns do not paw you to death." In St Louis "the women went quite mad, wanted to give me presents, to kiss me, quite a mad affair. I *hated* it." On his birthday the Women's Club of Cincinnati gave him a luncheon, a painting, and a cake with thirty-nine candles. And so the triumphal journey took its course: the only details worth chronicling were brief visits to Ellen Glasgow, Carl McCullough, William

Lyon Phelps of Yale University, and his old friend Arthur Fowler, now married and living in New York. Soon Fowler began to look after Hugh's American income for him; Hugh usually stayed with the Fowlers in New York, he dedicated *Portrait of a Man with Red Hair* to them, and they remained his dear friends for the rest of their lives.

A new friend was Carl Van Vechten, the American writer, whom Hugh described as possessing "a fine laughing aloofness." They exchanged a lively correspondence during this and subsequent years, and whenever Hugh's tour allowed him a breather in New York he would repair to Van Vechten's apartment, there to relax on a sofa and eat apples from a blue porcelain bowl as he exchanged news, ideas, and jokes with his friend.

Books and writers of all sorts they discussed, and Hugh introduced his new friend to the works of M. P. Shiel, whose *Lord of the Sea* was in 1924 republished in America with an introduction by Van Vechten. "What a lot you know!" Hugh wrote to him in December 1922. "How little do I—but I know more about football, curates, Charlotte Mary Yonge, Mrs Ewing and Hugh Walpole than you do." And a month later, from Waco, Texas:

> You say I absorb like a sponge, but you say that because you happen to know intimately three of the four men I care most for in America, Hergesheimer, Tom Beer, and—Carl Van Vechten . . . I like Texas—I like the plum bloom shadows on the horizon . . . The *Waco Star* had as its headline this morning "A Genius is With Us," and I looked and lo! the genius was a stout rather bald man with a finger uplifted and a heavy episcopal stare. I took a dislike to him on sight and I'm not going to hear him lecture on "Books and Friendship" tonight. A silly title anyway! *I* could tell him something on that subject that would shock his clerical soul.[1]

From Boston in February he wrote to tell Van Vechten that he was "the best, most perfect companion in America, the wittiest, the least boring, the one whose mind I like best." From Salt Lake City in April: "I often think when I am in trains and such of my affection for you and how *glad* I am that you are alive! I've thought a lot about *our* book."

This was a project for a collaboration in the form of letters ex-

[1] All the surviving correspondence between Hugh and Van Vechten is now in the Berg Collection in the New York Public Library, as also are the manuscript of Hugh's *Anthony Trollope* and most of the letters he received from leading American writers.

changed between two friends across the Atlantic, but eventually the task of reconciling their four separate publishers proved too difficult, and the idea was sadly abandoned. Van Vechten's next book, *The Tattooed Countess*, was dedicated to Hugh, and in its pages appeared the Duchess of Wrexe and others of Hugh's characters. "Don't you think," wrote Van Vechten, "that a red-haired man should know a tattooed countess?" When Hugh got home he sent "my love to my friends—Boyd, Beer, and Mrs. Van V.—the cat, the fruit in the dish, the absinthe and the sofa."

Meanwhile, during the long railway journeys, when he was not thinking of his friend, he read prodigiously: old books or new, but mostly novels. A re-reading of *Orsino* provoked the comment: "What is the secret of Crawford's perennial charm for me? All my youth seems ambered in his simple tales," and when in March the *Yale Review* asked him to write an article on Crawford [1] he felt as though he were "paying his ghost an affectionate debt of gratitude." Henry James had known Crawford, and now Hugh remembered how, at the time of Crawford's death in 1909, James "gave a magnificent picture of that splendid figure, romantic in all his gestures, so handsome and vigorous, driving his boats fearlessly into the most dangerous seas, building his palaces on the Mediterranean shore, travelling over every corner of the globe, fearless and challenging and heroic."

Apart from buying books wherever he could, Hugh now fell victim to a new craze which was eventually to lead to his large collection of modern pictures. Having a few hours to spend in Chicago, and making great friends there with an art dealer named Hugh Dunbar, he went to an exhibition of etchings, and was so captivated that he bought a large number. By April he had spent more than $3000 on etchings, and in May he added to his collection at a Forain exhibition which "took his breath away." By June he had spent at least $8000 on his new hobby.

Three extracts from letters to his mother carry on the story of the tour. The first was written at Seattle on April 16:

In places like Denver and Salt Lake City they seem to be simply hungry for literature, and it has touched me very much to see how my books

---

[1] Reprinted in part in *My Cousin, F. Marion Crawford* by Maud Howe Elliott (1934).

really do mean an immense deal in any number of obscure and lonely lives. It has given me quite a new sense of my power for good or ill.

The next from San Francisco on April 23:

In a letter I got this morning my agent says: "Without the slightest exaggeration I can say that your tour stands absolutely alone in my experience. Your success has been phenomenal. Not one word of criticism but on the contrary every letter I receive from the chairman of the committee is a eulogy of you with most fulsome praise for your lecture." This is a very level-headed unemotional man who has managed everyone—Mrs. Asquith, Conan Doyle, Belloc, etc.

And lastly from Rochester, N.Y., on May 18:

There has been great news about Melchior. He gave his first song-recital in Munich and had an overwhelming success. One of the results was that Siegfried Wagner cabled him to go to Bayreuth to sing to him, which he did, and he has now been engaged as one of the two leading tenors for the re-opening Wagner Festival at Bayreuth in 1924—the height of his ambition of course.

I am very well and very happy. This tour has been a perfectly marvellous success in every way. Last night in Syracuse everyone rose at the end and shouted "Come back! Come back!" I really don't believe that an English lecturer has ever had such a success since Dickens. This is for your private ear though.

I am really thinner and more modest since my leaving England last September!

During a visit to Hollywood, he met Charlie Chaplin and was taken to a rodeo by Mary Pickford and Douglas Fairbanks. "You should hear Chaplin doing me lecturing on America," Hugh told Van Vechten. "It's a deep and ironic betrayal of myself, America and Chaplin."

He gave his very last lecture at Oberlin, Ohio, on May 29. Altogether he had delivered almost one hundred and eighty (mostly on the English Novel), without missing or being late for a single one, and it was with profound relief that he arrived two days later in New York.

Doran met him with the welcome news that his American royalty account showed a credit of $17,500. Moreover Arthur Vance of the *Pictorial Review* had agreed to pay no less than $15,000 for the serial rights of his next novel. Hugh had intended this to be *Harmer John*, but the tour had left him so exhausted that he decided instead to write a simple thriller as a relaxation. He dashed off a synopsis for *Portrait of a Man with Red Hair*, a story of misadventure on a foggy night by the sea, with a sadistic lunatic for villain. Vance accepted it with acclamation, and on June 1 Hugh began the first chapter in New York. He had been prevented from writing for so many months that now there was no holding him. A quarter of the book was completed in ten days, and on his voyage home in the *Empress of France* he wrote at least two thousand words every day.

2

Nothing could stop the flow. A week in London, a few days in Edinburgh and a journey to Munich, all added their tributaries to the stream of words. In Munich a long discussion on Melchior's future resulted in Hugh's deciding "that he must be given another year to finish the *Ring*," for which purpose Hugh "allotted him the £800 from the English serial rights of *Red Hair*." This settled, the two friends travelled on to Bayreuth.

The Festival was not to reopen till 1924, but already there were plans for refurbishing the Festspielhaus after its years of neglect, auditions and rehearsals were in full swing, and at Wahnfried, home and mausoleum of the Wagner family, there were many visitors, musical and political. Upstairs brooded the unseen and almost legendary figure of Wagner's widow, Cosima, now nearly ninety and quite blind, while the direction of the Festival was in the hands of her only son Siegfried, whom Hugh described as "very much there, like a white heavy decaying bird."

Siegfried's wife, Winifred, an Englishwoman twenty-eight years younger than her husband, was an ardent supporter of Adolf Hitler and the embryo Nazi party, whose sinister and at the same time almost pathetic prophet, Houston Stewart Chamberlain, Hugh saw being wheeled about in an invalid chair. At a tea-party at Wahnfried he "took to Mrs Wagner hugely . . . simple sweet woman. Most plucky considering her insuperable difficulties." She showed him Wagner's grave, he watched Melchior rehearsing the part of Siegmund in *Die*

Walküre, and left Bayreuth after a stay of ten days, which with the exchange had cost him something like three shillings.

He travelled through Switzerland, writing his book as he went, and at the beginning of August joined his family at Champéry.

My dear mother asks *such* questions [he told Van Vechten], and in our *pension* there is an elderly married pair who take the bath in the evening at the same time. This puzzles Mother, or did until Father suggested that one of them soaped the back of the other. They are not having a bath this evening. It's Sunday and I heard the elderly male tell the landlady that "they'd go to church instead"!

Four days after his arrival *Portrait of a Man with Red Hair* was finished. To Swinnerton he described it as "a simple shocker which it has amused me like anything to write, and won't bore you to read. And now I have two years for the next. I've a kind of idea I shall write a splendid novel when I've come to man's estate—which will be when I'm Colvin's age." The "shocker" had taken him a few days over two months, and during that time he had crossed the Atlantic, travelled to Edinburgh and back, traversed a great deal of Europe, and gone through a few preliminary hoops with the Wagner circus.

At the end of the month he spent a week with Elizabeth at Chalet Soleil. To pass the time he wrote a short story or two and read "three very simple and beautiful books—Hudson's *A Shepherd's Life*, Dorothy Wordsworth's *Journals*, and Hardy's *Two on a Tower*. All three are pushing me still farther on the path I am going. In Cumberland I am sure I am coming for the first time straight through all the tissue paper into life. I *pray* so." A few days later he confided to his diary:

My happiness just now is wonderful. Hope for the improvement of my work, seeing myself clear of the London complications, trusting David, loving everybody and hating no one, seeing some of my faults really clearly at last, and gulping down the beauty of the world, which follows one now wherever one goes—doesn't only hang over certain places. Why shouldn't I be happy?

Back in London at the beginning of September, he took a service flat in Berkeley Street, overlooking the gardens of Devonshire House, and was relieved to discover that he did not in the least regret the lost splendours of York Terrace. He attended the first night of Maugham's

Our Betters where he saw "everyone," spent country week-ends with the McKennas and the Cazalets, bought his first car, and with Chanter at the wheel drove Melchior to Canterbury and showed him the King's School. On September 27 *Jeremy and Hamlet* was published by Cassell. More than ten thousand copies had been sold before publication, and the book quickly took its place in the long list of Hugh's successes. The dedication of the book, which reads: "To my Father and Mother from their devoted friend their son," gave immense pleasure. When his father saw it he wrote:

I have been, I am afraid, a blundering stupid father and have made lots of mistakes, but am so thankful that with it all I have not lost your affection and friendship. The pledge in the dedication of *Jeremy and Hamlet* will always be a treasure and I do thank you for it with all my heart.

3

During October there occurred another brisk exchange of letters with Arnold Bennett. The first three, thanks to the assiduity of the writers and the efficiency of the Post Office, are all dated October 7. Here are two of them:

My dearest Arnold,
You'll have a meal with me, won't you, before I go up to Scotland? I hardly dare to suggest it as I see that you are attending every conceivable function from a dinner to an American band to a luncheon to Mrs. Randolph Hearst! I watch and wonder ... I sent you *J. and H.* because you liked some of the first one. But of course don't bother with it.
                              Your loving
                                   Hugh.

My sweet Hughie,
Thank you. Dinner suits me far the best. I'll come on Wednesday 24th, if I may. You might confirm this. I haven't received *J. and H.* yet; but am looking forward to it. You won't like my *Riceyman Steps*, but you shall damn well have it.
Not a luncheon *to* Mrs. Hearst, but a luncheon *by* Mrs. Hearst. The "to" was newspaper work. My lad, I sat on her right, Hutchinson on her left, and G.K.C. far down the table level with W. L. George! Quelle vie! (P.S. She was very nice.)
Also, not a dinner *to* an American band. A dinner given by my friends the

bosses of the Savoy Hotel, at which the international (*not* American) band played for us, never having played for anybody before since time was. You must get these things right.

Ever thine
A.B.

As their meeting approached, Hugh wrote again:

My dear Arnold,

For our dinner next week whom else would you wish? Would you like to bring someone? We won't be more than four anyway, shall we?

And why do you tell conversational strangers I don't work? I work as hard as you do anyway!—and that's damned hard. Do sometimes bless my crimson head in my absence. All the world thinks you consider me the dung by the roadside. If you do tell me so.

Affectionately,
Hugh.

My sweet Hughie,

Thanks. I don't care a damn who is or isn't there on Wednesday so long as you're there. Don't listen to tattle about yourself. Most of it is necessarily untrue and all of it is reported with a malicious intent. If I took notice of a quarter of the things which you are reported to have said about me my appetite would be impaired. But I don't. I have said nothing to other people about you beyond what I have said to you, and shall probably say again.

Thine ever
A. B.

My dearest Arnold,

You are truly a pet. I never doubted your inside loyalty to me for a moment, but for years past people have seemed to wish to separate me from you more than from anyone else alive. Why I can't conceive. And apparently they've tried the same game the other end. However I love you, and although I chatter like a magpie out of sheer excitement, no one could doubt but that I *do* love you. So that's that.

However I'd like to talk to you about novel-writing one day. It's time I did again. Not especially yours or mine but in general. I think you're wrong on several points. And if you read *J. and H.* admit that the last two episodes are true.

I'm asking E. V. on Wednesday night—8.15 Garrick—no one else. Will you be bringing a copy of *Riceyman Steps* with you?

Your loving
Hugh.

4

During the brief interval before the next round of correspondence, three things happened: an end and two fresh beginnings. On October 20 Hugh went down to spend what proved to be his last week-end with Conrad. Richard Curle and G. Jean-Aubry were of the party, and Paul Valéry came to luncheon. Hugh recorded "jolly talk in the evening, mostly damning everyone, but Conrad's eyes lit over Fenimore Cooper and over Proust, who stirred him to deep excitement." On the Sunday the old man was "in great form, saying to me that I must be absolutely myself, the only thing that mattered to get myself free. Very dear he was this time and tender. Certainly happier, I think, since America, where he liked the praise. He remembers snubs like more mortal men!"

During the same week-end he met and made immediate friends with Muirhead Bone, the artist. The friendship ripened quickly and soon embraced the painter's wife and sons.

Then, at the end of October, driven by Chanter, Hugh made the first of countless motor-journeys into Cumberland. They slept the first night at Nottingham, the second at Ambleside, the third, after extensive house-hunting, at Keswick. Ten years later Hugh wrote:[1] "I have always believed that the moments of discovery are the only ones that are memorable—discovery of friendships, books, pictures, landscapes, and the true colour of the other world." The moment of one of the most important discoveries of his life came on November 1:

Day with a star indeed, because on it I bought what will I hope be the abode of my old age—Brackenburn, Manesty Park, Derwentwater. Came on it quite by chance—a stray remark from the owner of our Keswick hotel. Above Grange in Borrowdale. A little paradise on Cat Bells. Running stream, garden, lawn, daffodils, squirrels, music-room, garage, four bedrooms, bath—All! Nice people have it, the Richardsons. Entranced and excited. Slept Carlisle.

One look at the place had been enough, and Hugh had instantly agreed to pay the price asked, without benefit of surveyor or other professional advice; for which rashness he was afterwards gently re-

[1] In his Preface to an anthology called *Tales of Youth* (1933).

buked by Theodore McKenna. But for once his impetuosity was justified, and next day he hastened on to Edinburgh to tell the family of his good fortune. Then he was ready to despatch his next salvo to Bennett:

My dearest Arnold,

I've been a long while writing about *Riceyman* because I took four days motoring up here and very heavenly days they were.

The book is absorbing—your best to me since *The Pretty Lady*. You have had such fine reviews (I was delighted to see, although James Douglas always makes me sick) that I won't emphasise the virtues. Of the detail you are a master. Elsie is A.1. and her young man still better. Two criticisms. I think in the miser you have drawn two men and you haven't combined them. 1. The miser. 2. A kindly mild little R[iceyman] S[teps] bookseller. Now I am *sure* that the miser vice is so devastating to its victim that it makes him *bloody*. Your little man is never bloody. In truth he would have squeezed Elsie's throat and wrung his wife's neck. He would have been horrible, terrible, thirstily cruel (*not* Grandet but of Grandet's family).

Secondly (and this is so charmingly quid pro quo that I adore to write it) I think you have written rather carelessly. Your passion for emphatic adjectives knows no check (I saw that Squire said it did. I don't care a twopenny cuss for Squire). Open where I will I find "blazing," "extravagant," "fatal combination," "thundered," "stupid," "misguided," "heedless,"—all on p. 166. Or again at random—"thunderingly," "rarest," "deceitful," "blazing," "celestial," "wonderful," "potent." To give small things big adjectives has been long your habit, but surely here you overdo it.

I can say this the more confidently in that you at once murmur "Poor old Hughie" and with that affectionate contemptuous patronage that is your gift to me you will pass on unperturbed.

And I wouldn't have you perturbed. I love you dearly. You are one of the finest artists of our time and this is a damned good book.

I have bought a cottage in the Lakes.

Your loving
Hugh.

Two days later he began the drive to London, sleeping the first night at Durham. "What memories it awakened. Very few pleasant ones: I walked the streets under the stars and was grateful to God." Next day the car broke down at Doncaster, and the journey was completed by train. Hugh went to stay with the McKennas in Bryanston Square, where Bennett's reply was awaiting him:

My dear Hughie,

I thank thee. No. You are probably wrong and Jack Squire probably right. He does know *something* about style; you know nothing; or at any rate you write as if you know nothing. I see you believe rather in Edith Wharton, and assert that at her worst she has never descended as low as Wells and me in certain books. Innocence, you ought to see a doctor; the case is urgent. The excellent Edith is nobody at all, and she has deceived you. She never *began* to write. And what I have charged you with is not violent writing but slipshod writing. Have you ever *known* a miser, personally and well? I have, and I am in a position to tell you that you are quite wrong. In fact your idea is stagey, pseudo-romantic and beautiful absurd. My miser is a real miser.

Why the Lakes, my misguided friend? You will get wet through, and it is a hell of a way from London. Your touching sentimentality has led you to the Lakes. You wanted to get "into contact with Nature," didn't you? I bet you did, and of course the Lakes are the spiritual home of Nature. Never mind, my dear Hughie, I am entirely yours,

A. B.

To which Hugh replied:

Darling Arnold,

What an insulting letter! But you've got nearly twenty years more cocksureness in your bundle than I have, so I'll say no more. I know that I am sentimental, romantic and slipshod—that's *my* "pattern in the carpet." And you're shrewd, mathematical, and know far more about a certain section of real life than I do of any. But yours *is* only a section, and even though I'm Mrs. Henry Wood (with whom I have many affinities) that's ME. I never said or thought that the Wharton approached you as an artist, nor do I think she amounts to much, but she *has* kept her level better than you. As to "going back to Nature," haven't I lived in the depths of Cornwall all my life? I went to the Lakes eight years running during my youth, so it's no new thing to me. And it *don't* rain all the time, and it's only seven hours from Keswick to London.

Meanwhile I'm in the happy position of differing from most of your opinions and caring for you more and more. Is *that* sentimental? Surely not, because I have excellent sound honest-to-God reasons for my affection. I'm not such a fool as you think, nor is my style so bad as you say, and I believe that when I'm between fifty and sixty I shall produce a slipshod sentimental novel that will have real people in a world of its own. Let me be myself, damn you. . . .

Your loving
Hugh.

5

Harmer John was waiting to be finished, and Hugh took it up again directly he arrived in London. He carried it with him when he spent a happy week-end with the Bones at their home near Petersfield, but next day something happened to make him change his plans. Vance, who had approved the synopsis for *Portrait of a Man with Red Hair*, was horrified by the final script, which he described as "distinctly gruesome and unpleasant." He had not bargained for the sadistic "queerness" of the story; he was certain it would deeply shock his large female public, and he accordingly repudiated the book entirely. Apart from the loss of the $15,000, this decision deeply wounded Hugh's self-esteem. Seeking the cause of, if not an excuse for, the disaster, he decided that he had been led astray by the lust for gold. This was the only time he had ever written a book in response to an offer of money—there lay his fault. "I think I shall not publish *The Red-Haired Man* as a book," he told his mother. "I am at present dissatisfied with it. I shall lose a good deal of money if I don't, but that is better than publishing a poor thing." And in his diary he swore: "Never will I write anything for money again."

Wiser counsels, however, soon prevailed, and through the good offices of Doran the *Cosmopolitan* magazine was induced to serialise the book in America, though for a slightly lower fee. Still, Hugh's plans had been thrown out. Even if he consented to bring out his rejected work later on, he did not want it to be his next publication. But he had no other book ready for 1924, and he doubted whether he could finish *Harmer John* in time. There was nothing for it but to dash off something else at great speed, so back on to the shelf went poor *Harmer John*, and on November 14 Hugh wrote the first words of *The Old Ladies*.

Its theme had been in his head ever since, in the *pension* at Champéry that summer, he had seen the original of Agatha Payne gazing enviously at a fine amber necklace belonging to another female; and now the story of the three old women in the Polchester lodging-house came pouring out, as fast as, if not faster than, its ill-fated predecessor a few months ago. After a fortnight he had completed four chapters (a third of the whole) and to clear his mind he jotted down an immediate programme of work:

> Decided to publish O.L. in 1924, H. J. 1925, R.H.M. 1926, then a London novel, then *The Mountain*—also short stories, *Trollope*, and *Jeremy at Crale*.

Except that *The Mountain* failed to materialise, and that the order was not exactly followed, this list did in fact accurately forecast his output for the next five years. From now on, he was constantly making such lists for his own encouragement, sometimes for as much as ten years ahead—so overflowing was his mind with plots and themes—and it is astonishing to see how faithfully most of his plans were carried out.

Meanwhile in November he had attended a "*very* highbrow lunch" at Sibyl Colefax's, at which the company included Desmond Mac-Carthy, Virginia Woolf, and Lytton Strachey. "All very mild," commented Hugh. "Strachey in especial looked at me in the most affectionate manner, and Virginia W. said the greatest English novelist was Walter Scott, which of course I loved her for." This was his first meeting with Mrs Woolf, whose friendship was later to be so important to him.

By Christmas he was in Edinburgh, hard at work on *The Old Ladies*. At the end of the year he compiled in his diary the usual list of friends, with Melchior at the head of the First Fifteen. On the same page, less as a reflection on the assembled company than as an admonition to himself, he wrote the words: "Temper, Selfishness, Pride, Meanness."

Pausing only for a convivial evening with William Roughead ("really a man after my own heart, Scott, Conrad and all"), Hugh hurried on with *The Old Ladies*, which he brought to a triumphant conclusion on January 9. It had taken him less than two months, and since June he had written two complete novels, as well as a chapter or two of *Harmer John*.

In London he decided to look for an unfurnished flat which should be his permanent counterpart to Brackenburn. He was always abnormally lucky in house-hunting, and after Chanter and he had been searching for only four days they came upon the real right thing—another great moment of discovery. It was a Bachelor Flat on the first floor of No. 90 Piccadilly, at the corner of Half Moon Street. It was more expensive than he had intended, but he was captivated by the outlook and immediately decided to take it. The dining-room and drawing-room both looked out across Piccadilly, down the Green Park avenue which leads to Buckingham Palace, and the bedroom was situated in comparative quiet at the back. None of the rooms was big, and by the time Hugh had filled them with furniture, books and pictures, T'ang horses, Epstein bronzes, and a piano, there was space for no more than four people in either of the living-rooms. But the flat suited him perfectly. He liked living in the heart of London and yet remaining comparatively inaccessible to strangers. His number was never printed in the telephone book, and the first rush of unwanted callers could be stopped downstairs by the excellent valet John Jones and the rest of the permanent staff.

The lease was signed with jubilation on January 19, and the occasion celebrated by a visit with the Bones to the current Epstein exhibition, where Hugh purchased the first object for the new flat—"a gold baby at £130." Afterwards they all lunched with the sculptor, who invited them back to his studio.

6

A few days later Hugh set off for two months' foreign travel. After spending a week with Melchior in Munich, he retraced his steps to Paris, where he found a quantity of mail awaiting him. Among it was a letter from T. S. Eliot asking him to contribute to the *Criterion*. To be thus courted by the intelligentsia was most gratifying: he arranged for a typescript of *The Old Ladies* to be submitted, and its first two chapters were published in the April and July issues respectively.

On February 5 Hugh sailed from Marseilles to Tunis, whence he made expeditions to Sousse, Constantine, and the ruins of Carthage. The weather was so cold that he wore a heavy overcoat the whole time, while the ugliness of most of the country made him homesick for Derwentwater. Two days on the edge of the desert near Biskra were more agreeable, but on the whole he was delighted to return again to Paris, where he spent his fortieth birthday. Needless to say, this landmark, which had seemed so formidable when he was writing *Maradick*, now appeared to be life's beginning.

Back in London he stayed once more with the McKennas, and on March 20 he delivered the Annual Oration in the University of London, described in his diary as "a thumping success." But there was a cloud in the sky. Letters from his father and Dorothy warned him that his mother's health was failing. The doctors considered that a visit to Italy might improve her condition, and Hugh straightway volunteered to take her there.

They set off immediately after Hugh's lecture, travelling by train to Rome, where Chanter met them with Hugh's car. In it they visited Assisi, Orvieto, Siena, and Florence. Hugh was much occupied with *Harmer John*, but he naturally saw more of his mother than he had for many years. She, perhaps sensing that death was not far away, succeeded at last in putting aside her habitual shyness and reserve. For the first time in their lives mother and son were able to talk together without any barriers. Gradually, during those brief weeks, they came to know each other and to realise the hidden stores of their mutual love. She confessed to him that she felt she should never have married, since her nature made it impossible for her to manifest those outward signs of tenderness which husband and children need and deserve. It was as though she was begging Hugh's forgiveness for his childhood's lack of demonstrative affection. He in his turn asked forgiveness for the reticences and intransigences of his own adolescence, and, as he wrote years later, "we had a moment of perfect, felicitous communion, bringing us close together, warm in one another's company, loving and knowing one another now and for all time."[1]

In mid-April they reached Venice, where Melchior joined them bearing great news. He had been engaged to sing Siegmund at Covent Garden in May. Lotte Lehmann was to be the Sieglinde, with Bruno Walter as conductor. It seemed that Hugh's faith in his friend's talents was to be justified, and together they rejoiced.

After a happy week in Venice, Hugh took his mother back to England, and before she travelled on to Edinburgh they went together to a performance of Shaw's *St Joan*, which she appreciated with all Hugh's boyish enthusiasm: "Oh, I have enjoyed that! I *have* enjoyed that!"

[1] *Roman Fountain* (1940).

7

The next weeks were full of activity. There was much furnishing and arranging of the new flat, and a "terrible shock at the bank, finding I had seven hundred pounds less than I supposed." Such disappointments were constantly recurring, since part of Hugh's illusion that his affairs were in order took the form of always believing that the rough balance worked out on the stubs of his cheque-book was backed by the same amount in the bank. Perhaps the fault lay with his arithmetic: at all events each discrepancy was a fresh shock, particularly since they were seldom in his favour. His income at this time was between £3500 and £4500 a year, and thereafter steadily increased.

At the end of April he spent two nights in Keswick, seeing to the final arrangements at Brackenburn, and before leaving he wrote:

Have had no experience like this since my first visit to Polperro with Percy years ago. I *know* this is where I am meant to come and work. It is like a divine call, if that's not being too egoistic, and I pray God I may do my very best here.

After a few days in Edinburgh, he spent his first night at 90 Piccadilly on May 6, and thereafter prepared for Melchior's début at Covent Garden. Whatever the singer's feelings may have been, his friend died a thousand deaths before and during the performance. First Melchior discovered that he was to have no rehearsal and was not even to see his Sieglinde (she was not, after all, Lotte Lehmann) before they met on the stage. Despite this the first act "went magnificently," and in the interval Hugh hurried behind to congratulate Melchior, only to find him in despair because "they'd changed all the stage directions at the last moment to suit the new Brünnhilde and he didn't know where he would be." Hugh crept back to his seat in an agony of apprehension, but Melchior "pulled through" somehow, and when he repeated the rôle ten days later in a fine new costume designed for him by Charles Ricketts, Hugh found his performance "superb."

Worn out by this exhausting incursion into the perils of Grand Opera, Hugh had never felt more drawn towards solitude and quiet. Brackenburn was now ready for him, and on May 29 he spent his first night in the house that was to be his refuge for the rest of his life.

BOOK FIVE

THE PROMISED LAND

Derwent is distinguished from all the other Lakes by being *surrounded* with sublimity: the fantastic mountains of Borrowdale to the south, the solitary majesty of Skiddaw to the north, the bold steeps of Wallow-crag and Lodore to the east, and to the west the clustering mountains of Newlands.

William Wordsworth
Guide to the Lakes

CHAPTER SEVENTEEN

MEN UNDER SKIDDAW

I

THE first main theme of his life was resolving itself. Here in Cumberland he found what he had sought so long—a landscape with which he could identify himself, to which he could belong as he had never belonged anywhere before. To his delight he soon ceased to be regarded as a "foreigner." His neighbours—gentry, shop-keepers, and labouring men alike—made him feel that he was one of them, a man firmly rooted in this lovely cluster of hills and lakes. And as the blessed feeling of certainty filled his heart, into his mind there at once came surging a passionate desire to accomplish some great romantic work which should both express his gratitude to the country that had accepted him, and make him part of the place for ever. Not for some time were the chronicles of the Herries family to take definite shape, but already their vaguest outlines were now and then perceptible through the mists that shrouded the summits of Blencathra and Skiddaw. These next years were filled and guided by love of his new home and the determination to give that love a literary shape.

Brackenburn is some six miles by road from Keswick. The house stands on the south-western shore of Lake Derwentwater, on a tiny plateau cut into the steep hillside of Cat Bells, some two hundred and fifty feet above lake level. Behind, the ground climbs steeply through grass and bracken to the bare "tops" of the fells. In front there is a small terraced garden sloping down to a narrow road, beyond which the Manesty Woods fall sharply to the lake. On each side tall pine trees grow thick and close. The house, built in 1909 by the Richard-sons from whom Hugh bought it, is made of Cumberland stone, which Hugh described as "one of the loveliest stones in the world, having a shade of green like a tulip leaf, a purple depth like a bishop's ring, and a dove-shadowed grey over all."[1] Generally the grey predominates, but in the sunshine after rain, out flash the other colours and the whole

[1] From "The Lake District" in *English Country* (1934).

building sparkles freshly. "The rain here comes down heartily," wrote Wordsworth in his *Guide*, "and is frequently succeeded by clear, bright weather, when every brook is vocal, and every torrent sonorous." One of these brooks runs down the Brackenburn garden: Hugh caused it to flow through two little fountain-statues into a pool and he loved to lie in bed and listen to its gentle music.

When Hugh bought the house it was all on one floor, except for a tiny bedroom upstairs in which he slept. Later he enlarged the upper floor into two good bedrooms and a second bathroom. On the ground floor there were, in front overlooking the lake, a sitting-room, a minute hall, and a spare bedroom; at the back, a dining-room, another spare bedroom lined with books, a kitchen, and a bathroom. The married couple, Jack and Edith Elliot, who looked after him faithfully there from his first arrival until the day he died, slept in a small bungalow behind the house.

Outside the French windows of the sitting-room there was a little lawn, to the side of the house and on the same level. Beyond it the Richardsons had built a garage at road-level below, with a large music-room on top. This Hugh made into his library and writing-room, later adding a third storey, to provide a more extensive view over the trees. He also installed central heating and bought a petrol engine to generate electric light in both buildings.

Each morning after breakfast when he crossed the lawn, sat down at his desk in the big library, and picked up his pen, all doubts and shadows fled away: he was completely, blissfully content, doing the work he had been born for—the telling of stories.

Across the lawn, looking over the wood—now fresh with spring green leaves—to the faint blue waters of the lake, I push back the door, go up the stairs to the room that levels the tree-tops, sit down, fuss with my paper and pen, look about me, and then, suddenly, my vision is filled once again with that other world where I know every little street, the look of every hill, can hear the sound of sea crashing on the shore; figures move, first as shadows, then as it were seen from behind a window, then close to me—I hear their voices, know that they are living and true, and that I am one with them, and I begin once again to scribble on to paper what I see and hear: their vitality, their truth, these things are truly real to me while I write. Only when the last word has been written and a strange foreign thing between cloth covers appears on my table do I realise that I have once again been tricked, but already a new vision is opening up.[1]

Yet the happiness and peace which he always found at Brackenburn satisfied only one part of his sharply divided personality, and after a few weeks the other part—the social, neurotic, uncertain part—began to nag, and before long drove him back to the world. (In all his seventeen years at Brackenburn he was never there for longer than five weeks at a stretch, and very seldom for more than two or three.) His London engagement-book was now as crowded with appointments as his Piccadilly flat was soon to be with works of art. Terrified of missing anything, he was incapable of refusing an invitation. Hating to be laughed at, he rushed excitedly into friendships and situations which might easily have that conclusion. For all his jaunty air of self-confidence, his outward geniality, his tilted bowler hat, and his buttonhole, the jovial *boulevardier* never knew the single-minded contentment of the story-teller high above Derwentwater.

"The real truth," he had written years before to Mrs Annand, "is that I don't know how to manage London. I am bombarded by so many things that I can't deal with them. *This* [he was writing of Polperro, but the remark was even more applicable to Brackenburn] is my right spot. Here I am happy and good and natural, and I ought really never to live in London at all." He was unable to write anything there except short articles; after a while the tempo began to affect his nerves, and he would escape up the Great North Road to the mountains, the peace, and the next chapter of the current novel. When this cycle of events had repeated itself for several years, he began to be able to gauge in advance how long he could endure both solitude and society, and to lay his plans accordingly.

2

Meanwhile this first month at Brackenburn—June 1924—was pure pleasure: "I've found my real life at last," he told Turley. In the car with Chanter and on foot he explored the Lakes with loving thoroughness. He climbed Great Gable in pouring rain, came upon the hamlet

[1] From an article published in *John o'London's Weekly*, 8 October 1937, and reprinted in *Titles to Fame* (edited by Denys Kilham Roberts, 1937).

of Watendlath hidden in a hollow of the hills, agreed with Dorothy Wordsworth's description of it as "a heavenly scene," and found fresh beauties everywhere.

Going up above Seathwaite on the pass to Buttermere, it was like suddenly bathing in a divine pool. The stream that runs down that hill is clearer, fresher, more assured of itself and happy than any stream in the world. Sitting beside it for half an hour, I reached perfect peace and tranquillity, a blessed pause and remoteness rather like death I fancy, but infinitely reassuring and comforting.

The people of Keswick quickly became his friends, and he was soon buying silver from Mr Telford, books from Mr Chaplin, providing furniture and money for the local Toc H, and taking a close interest in St John's Library.[1]

Then came the discovery that the outlook from Brackenburn provided a sense of space which he had never known before, even at Polperro with the open sea beneath his windows; and that the light and the cloud-reflections on his own lake, on Skiddaw and Saddleback and the other surrounding hills, were seldom the same for many minutes on end. This endlessly fleeting variety of shadow, light, and colour never ceased to amaze and delight him, nor did he tire of describing it in his novels and his journal.

This (by Hugh originally entitled *The Brackenburn Book*, but here referred to simply as his journal) was one of the first results of the fresh literary, one might almost say lyrical, impulse which his arrival in Cumberland brought about. Almost all the entries in its fifteen volumes were written at Brackenburn, many of them on the eve of departure to the outside world, when the beauty of his surroundings always especially moved him.

He had been reading Woodforde's *Diary of a Country Parson*, and "realising the interest of his small details now, one hundred and fifty years later, I thought I would like to record the same." But this plan was soon abandoned: Woodforde's record was mainly of eating and drinking, and in comparison Hugh's own meals seemed meagre and uninteresting. Anyhow, he cheerfully decided, there would probably

[1] Hugh's collection of books on the Lakes and their writers (some three hundred volumes) is now part of this library.

be no posterity to read his journal—bombs and poison gas would see to that—so he might as well write simply for his own pleasure. His daily diary had space only for bare facts: the journal would be "a real attempt at honesty without any of that screwing round of the right eye to see whether anyone is watching me." Despite these protestations, the journal, particularly in its earlier volumes, bears all the marks of having been written for the enjoyment of any posterity that might escape the next round of Armageddon.

The first entry, dated June 19, is most illuminating. After a brief introductory passage come the "rules for every honest diarist":

1. No self-consciousness.
2. No sense of shame.
3. No false modesty.
4. No sham bravery.
5. No fine writing.
6. No fear of indecencies.
7. No scorn of trivialities.
8. No self-disgust.

There are others but these will do.

Then follows this astonishingly accurate self-portrait. The italic passages within square brackets represent notes made in the margin at later dates.

Well, for a start: I am forty years of age, have published seventeen volumes of more or less merit (cf. rule 3), am single and shall always be so, in excellent health save for toothache and neuralgia, never constipated, always sleep well, owe some five hundred pounds, am owed four thousand, have four thousand invested in America and two thousand here, have a library of seven thousand volumes, two thousand prints, and some water colours, own this cottage of Brackenburn, Manesty Park, and an acre of ground, and have on lease a little flat, 90 Piccadilly.

My principal friends are:
First by himself—Lauritz Melchior (alluded to in this diary as David).

Then   Don Marquis
       Muirhead Bone
       Douglas Chanter
       James Annand   *by themselves.*

Then Ethel McKenna, Lady Russell (Elizabeth), Carl Van Vechten, Hugh Dunbar, Arthur and Ethel Fowler, Carl McCulloch, Mervyn Eager, Tom Reeves, the Toyes, Gertrude Bone, Jessie Conrad, Hergesheimer, and the Cazalets.

Now as to my character:

I am kind-hearted, but have to rouse myself to take trouble. I am very sensual, but pious and pure if that sensuality is gratified. I am very non-condemnatory unless I am attacked, when I at once accuse the attacker of every crime. I am very generous about large sums and inclined to be mean about small ones. I adore to be in love but am bored if someone is much in love with me. I am superficially both conceited and vain but at heart consider myself with a good deal of contempt. [*6 Jan. 1926. Question this!*] I am greatly interested in the question of a future life but until it is settled the thought of it influences my conduct but little. [*28 Oct. 1932. It occupies me more and more.*] I adore beauty in all its forms and were I not so hurried and careless would be a good artist, but my hatred of revision and my twist towards abnormality spoil much of my work. I hate to see others suffer. I am a great coward but can be roused to endurance. I have a sense of humour which I get only too little into my work.

3

At the end of June Hugh started out once more on his travels. Stopping in London only long enough to spend a day at Wimbledon, another at Lord's watching Hobbs score a double century against South Africa, and to buy a Gauguin landscape for £145, he dashed over to Paris, attended the opening of the Olympic Games with Douglas Fairbanks, and sped on to Bayreuth. This, his second, visit lasted six weeks—six restless weeks of strain, vexation, and argument, which made him sigh more than once for the solitude of Brackenburn. He had asked Elizabeth to meet him at Bayreuth for Melchior's début, but she had declined, saying she was finally and forever sick of *Parsifal* and agreed with George Moore that it was "like a sadist preaching chastity to choirboys. Don't tell the Wagners!" Her letter went on: "Think of me sometimes in the middle of it, for my first courted me at Bayreuth, and there's not a tree anywhere within five miles that I haven't been kissed under!"

The Festival was reopening after its ten-year eclipse, and so were the jealousies, intrigues, and displays of temperament which usually accompany such enterprises. Hugh tried to work at *Harmer John*, but rehearsals by day and performances at night broke up his time disturbingly. Winnie Wagner seemed much attached to him, but her attentions became a trifle overpowering. One night after the opera he supped with Ludendorff and the King of Bulgaria, "which gave my patriotism some twinges."

But the chief cause of Hugh's distress was that Melchior had brought with him the young lady who was later to become his second wife. Hugh was jealous and attacked his friend with bitter reproaches: "We had our main row in the very middle of the *Meistersinger* rehearsal." Matters did not improve, and July 16 was written down as "one of the most critical days of my life. In the morning D. came to see me, and in the garden at the bottom of this house there was the most desperate struggle of our friendship. It ended in his victory and my resolve to pull myself round and adopt the young woman." Next day they all three drank to one another, and as Hugh began to carry out his resolve he found unexpected qualities in the lady, of whom he soon became genuinely fond. Immediate harmony had already been restored by July 23, when Melchior made his début as Parsifal. "Never have I heard such singing," wrote Hugh. "Everyone in the boxes near me was crying." Melchior was the success of the Festival, and Hugh's self-esteem was somewhat restored, if only as a spotter of talent.

Nevertheless, the emotional strain was beginning to affect his nerves, and early in August the news of the death, within a few days of each other, of Conrad and Lady Colvin added to his depression. On his last day at Bayreuth he was invited once more to Wahnfried, "where for the first time, and I expect the last, I caught a glimpse of Cosima in the upper gallery—a bent, white-haired old woman in a yellow bed-gown talking in a most vigorous voice, and about David too. Long talk with Winnie and Siegfried. They mean D. to do *Siegfried* next year."

Yes, Melchior would sing at Bayreuth next year and Hugh would be there to hear: Melchior and his new wife Kleinchen would be his dear friends for the rest of his life; but now as he travelled back to London he knew in his heart that another attempt at the perfect friendship had failed.

4

A week spent with his family in Cornwall made him surer than ever that Cumberland was his promised land, but before he returned there he filled in a bustling week in London. He took his mother to the Wembley Exhibition, and lunched in the City with T. S. Eliot, who was then working in a bank: "Enjoyed it very much. He is a very quiet man and of course I'm a little afraid of him, but he was awfully kind and seemed quite genuinely to have enjoyed *The Old Ladies.*"

By the middle of September Hugh was back at Brackenburn, happily arranging his books and reading his old diaries ("What a life I led in those days! How restless! Like a young puppy"). The Bone family came to stay at a neighbouring inn, and Muirhead made a sketch of Brackenburn. On the last day of the month the much-enduring *Harmer John* was finished, and the occasion called forth the second entry in the journal. He was as usual suffering from an acute sense of loss at being parted from his characters, but this time it was especially strong, since the character of Harmer John himself had, at any rate in its initial stages, been intimately connected in his mind with Melchior. He fell to wondering whether his fellow novelists suffered from this same divorce at the end of each book, but decided that if they did they took themselves too seriously to admit it.

The theory nowadays is that a novel *must* be "A Work of Art" and that it's very much less a "W of A" if you have enjoyed writing it or have felt excited by it or known intimacy with the characters. There is something in this, because the two of my books most successful as "W of A" are the two books whose characters were least intimate with myself, *Perrin* and *The Dark Forest*. In both I was filled with my subjects—Schoolmastering and War—but the characters in both were puppets to me.

On October 7 *The Old Ladies* was published, with a dedication to Ethel McKenna. Reviews were uniformly laudatory except in the highbrow weeklies. The *Nation*, which seldom had a good word for Hugh's works, now accused him "of all things in the world of being too much of a craftsman! Did I ever dream that that would be one day brought up against me?" While the *New Statesman* mounted "a great onslaught by someone who must be very young indeed, saying that 'there is no love in me.' Dear, dear! There is a little too much, but it isn't Lawrence's sort."

As compensation for these flutterings, letters of praise arrived from Masefield, Swinnerton, M. P. Shiel, May Sinclair, Virginia Woolf, Elizabeth, and E. M. Forster. Also *The Crystal Box* was produced in a privately printed edition of a hundred and fifty copies, *Harmer John* was accepted for serialisation in America at a fee of £4000, and Hugh was invited by the Vice-Chancellor to deliver the Rede Lecture at Cambridge in 1925. All this was very pleasant and encouraging, but there were days of discouragement and self-dislike, as towards the end of October when he wrote in his journal:

I am thoroughly ashamed of myself for losing my temper this morning, but there is no doubt that I cannot *bear* to be told of my faults. And it is not because I think myself perfect that I cannot bear it. It is for the very opposite reason. I am so conscious of a number of my faults that when someone else discovers them too I am like Adam and Eve discovered by God in the garden. It is as though *now* there was no hope of escape from them. And what is also very maddening is that they are always the same faults returning, as though two or three especially were loaded round your neck for the rest of your days. And so I suppose they are.

One of the worst of mine is my pleasure in telling other people *theirs*. I seem to myself to see my own faults even more clearly than I do other people's, and I tell myself mine and then other people (if I know them well) theirs. It is almost a sign of affection and intimacy. But I forget that other people are in the same state of suspicion about themselves that I am about myself and want reassuring not frightening.

I can't think of anyone who takes fault-finding quietly, and yet everyone is always expecting everyone else to be patient under correction. But I do undoubtedly boss others too much. There's plenty of work for me to do in that direction.

A week later he was in Piccadilly, writing to congratulate Arnold Bennett on being awarded the James Tait Black Prize for *Riceyman Steps*:

Heartiest congratulations on winning a prize. I'm sure it will be disappointing to you that I also have won it. But never mind—you have now wiped out that disgrace.

To which his agile correspondent replied the same day:

Very many thanks. The fact is, I never heard of the prize before.[1]

In the middle of November Hugh travelled to Berlin, to spend a fortnight with Melchior who was singing in the Opera there. The topsy-turvy life—staying up till four and sleeping till noon—which had got on his nerves at Bayreuth was amusing for a few days and in other surroundings. Berlin he described to his mother as "dirty and exceedingly wicked." While he was there he received from some American friends called McCormick an invitation to go up the Nile with them the following spring, and gladly accepted.

On Christmas Eve in Edinburgh he wrote the first pages of *Janet Grandison*, which he later renamed *Wintersmoon*. This was to be his "first attempt at a full-length love story," and he hoped it would occupy him for three years. In fact it was soon flowing along like its predecessors, and was completed in fourteen months. Early in the new year he recorded its progress in his journal:

How strange is the way that a novel steps out to meet you! I began this new one *Janet Grandison* with but little in my mind, determining to have a woman as its centre and a nice woman too, and for theme the English Aristocracy 1920–25, the quiet unjazzy ones who live respectably in large houses on small means, and for fable a man and woman who do not love one another marrying and love gradually coming to them through intimacy and trouble. No more than that!

And now the book is leaping out at me, tumbling into shape, arranging the characters for me, driving life into everyone without my agency. Where does this come from? [*Oct. 28. It comes from the damned pro writer's drawer.*]

Christmas was a happy one—the last the Walpoles were to spend as a complete family—and the only way Hugh could find a flaw was by writing down the names of all who had sent him presents or Christmas letters, and noting the absentees. "The only two Christmas delinquents now are the Fowlers and Van Vechten, and really I can't understand either of them forgetting me."

---

[1] Previous winners had been *The Secret City* (1919), *The Lost Girl* by D. H. Lawrence 1920), *Memoirs of a Midget* by Walter de la Mare (1921), and *Lady into Fox* by David Garnett (1922).

5

January he spent in London, seeing his friends and enjoying his flat. Now that he had given up the attempt to write in London, he found the place a little easier to cope with. After dining with Doran at the Savoy, he recorded: "Superb food. Much sentiment mixed with the champagne, but business always peeping through." At the end of the month he went up to Brackenburn, and added another page or two to his journal:

Having come up here for two nights only, to settle some things before going to Egypt, have found it enchanting. The weather has been wild and stormy but what delights me is the silence that enables one to think connectedly for hours at a time, and space and view, the uninterrupted reading and the dogs.

But, given this opportunity, *do* I think connectedly? I never seem to go very far. After ten minutes I look at a mountain or want something to eat or contemplate my novel or indulge a lascivious recollection. I am not able to sink into a train of thought so deeply that my material life vanishes. If I think of my writing, my thought soon becomes a defence of my work against some possible attack, or a prophecy of some future success, or a comparison of myself with some contemporary writer. If I think of religion I lose myself very quickly. I am frightened if I contemplate absolute non-existence, and I am not confident enough about the survival of personal identity to be truly reassured.

So then I relapse into *feeling*. I seem then to be enfolded by loving arms and protected, but if I felt *truly* would it not be more likely that I should hear an angry voice from over the hill blaming me for my many misdeeds and failings and warning me?

On February 4 he left for Egypt, reading Proust ("He is just my sort: I understand all that he feels") all day in the train to Trieste, and thence in the steamer to Alexandria. He embarked in a Nile steamer with his friends the McCormicks, and was ecstatically pleased with the sun and the scenery. At Luxor they visited the tomb of Tutankhamen, discovered just over two years earlier. The party was "ushered in four at a time, down some steps and straight into the room . . . very small . . . stood on a wooden platform and looked over on to this glittering golden figure in the shell-pink coffin, a little wreath of withered leaves on his head, the angels guarding at four corners—this gold in the heart of the dust." At Assuan they were joined by J. H. Breasted, the American Egyptologist, with whom Hugh immediately struck up a warm friendship. Somewhere on the journey Hugh acquired the green-and-white scarab ring which he ever after wore on the little finger of his left hand.

On the way home he stayed for ten days with the Brett Youngs on the island of Capri. He found them "exceedingly kind and I like greatly being with them," but despite its beauty he disliked the island and most of the other foreign inhabitants he saw. "No one here has a shred of reputation," he told his sister, "except the Brett Youngs, and they are unpopular because they are so moral!" None the less he wrote away at *Wintersmoon* and avowed himself "very happy, but thinking always of Brackenburn."

He arrived back there early in April, to find distressing news of his mother. He had suggested that she should stay at Brackenburn with a nurse while he was away, but the doctors preferred the South of France, and Dorothy had accordingly taken her to Sospel, near Mentone. Now Dorothy wrote to say that the patient was definitely worse, with a high temperature and a recurrence of phlebitis. Realising that help was needed, Hugh wired some money to his sister and wrote to say that he would join her in a few days. Before he left he wrote a short story called *Mr Oddy*, which he later selected as his best, and for which he drew in part on his memories of Henry James.

He arrived at Mentone on April 25. A friend had lent an empty villa, and his mother had been moved there from Sospel, so as to be closer to the English doctor. Although she was spending some part of each day downstairs, her temperature remained high and she seemed to be wasting away. This was the first time Hugh had met serious illness in anyone near to him; his plans were put out and his longing to help inevitably ended in frustration. He managed, however, to make a start with his Rede Lecture on *The English Novel*, and "felt pride when the French lady in the bookshop, writing down Mother's name, said: '*Comme l'écrivain*'." After a fortnight the whole business had become a burden:

I'm getting to loathe this place, especially since work hasn't been possible. Mother's illness seems to cloud everything, and I'm beginning to realise the

Mildred Barham

Somerset Walpole

The baby

Hugh

The schoolboy

London. 1909

90 Piccadilly

Derwentwater from Brackenburn.

Brackenburn

Part of the library at Brackenburn

Chalk drawing by Augustus John. 1926

Wastwater, 1933

Dorothy   Hugh   Bingo   Harold

Brackenburn. 1935

kind of exasperation that clouds sickrooms when patients *will* not get better —poor dear Mother.

Next day the doctor, realising there was little hope, advised them to take Mrs Walpole home to Edinburgh, since Mentone had done her no good, and on March 13 they all three set out for England. Leaving Dorothy to take their mother home from London, Hugh hastened to Brackenburn to finish his lecture: "Luckily I know my subject through and through," he told his mother, to whom he now wrote almost every day—letters full of tenderness, love, and sweet encouragement.

6

On May 22 he delivered the lecture at Cambridge. The Senate House was packed, and Hugh spoke for over an hour without a note. "Q told me that it was 'magnificent,'" he wrote to his mother, "and A. C. B. said it was 'an astonishing performance.' Everyone was very kind. The Vice-Chancellor had a dinner and reception for me, Quiller-Couch gave me a lunch, and the Master of Emmanuel a lunch." All of which, he confided to his journal, was "flattering to my vanity when I remember my shabby furtive career at Emmanuel with no honour and much timidity." And there was another incident to recall:

The most interesting moment was my visit to Arthur Benson. A sinister affair! How fat and red and heavy now, with a belly like an ox. How dark and fusty his rooms, a labyrinth of them, his acquisitiveness leading him to add one room to another, pulling down neighbouring shops and pubs in order to give him more, all to no real purpose and for no real use. Dark with old wallpaper, heavy lumps of furniture, old pictures, praying-stools, and organs.

In the middle of this he lies back in his deep chair like a sea-monster and in his husky charming voice dispenses kindnesses (so long as they're easy) and recalls little grudges. Tiny things (Lubbock's not writing, his treatment by the Literary Society, somebody's offensive letter) stir his petulance just as they did twenty years ago, and tiny things rouse his complacency, all minnows in the midst of whom he floats a great bloated whale.

And here, ye gods, was my romance of twenty years ago, a man at the touch of whose hand I trembled, of whom I dreamt of nights, whose splendour and beauty I worshipped. Well, he was good to me—immensely kind and really caring so long at any rate as I continued to worship. And he feels that he is as charming as ever; he has his idea of himself, thinking that he sees all his faults, condones them, but remains magnificently conscious of them. Whereas he sees none of his real faults, and only chooses virtues which he calls faults in order to show how self-critical he is.

Benson died less than a month later, on June 17. In due course Hugh's earliest letters to him were returned, and in September 1937, after reading them through (and presumably destroying them, since they were not found among his papers), Hugh wrote in his journal:

There's no doubt that I fell idealistically in love with Benson. Most purely, let it be said, but I suppose Benson saw more in it than met my innocent eye. It is amusing and pathetic to see how paternally he holds me off from throwing myself into his arms. Many of my letters are extremely silly and I now at my age would be exceedingly embarrassed if any young man wrote *me* such letters . . . I was far too crude, ignorant and, above all, egoistic to understand in the slightest *his* side of the case, and I here and now make my humble apologies to his shade and wish to tell him how deeply I recognise, when it is too late, all his great goodness to me.

7

All through these days the thought of his mother lay heavy on his heart. The Edinburgh doctors had now diagnosed cancer, and in his journal Hugh sought to find words for his feelings:

Life has been given an entirely new turn by Mother's illness. The shock of suddenly realising as an actual fact that she can and actually will very shortly die has had an extraordinary effect on me. It has made her another person and someone to be treated with infinite tenderness, not so much because she is suffering or unhappy but exactly as you feel for some friend who is going on a long journey—as you feel when they are taking the night boat and are having a last meal with you in your warm house.

Then at Mentone where everything was hateful—the empty villa with the naked floors, the pictures done up in *Le Matin* and a strange unwholesome odour of decay everywhere, and outside the roses and lemons and lilac and iris growing with an indecent, a lustful luxuriance, but always dying the moment you picked them—the house scattered with rose-petals and doors banging everywhere. The little doctor coming, knowing so little, and Mother sitting up in bed with her thin, peaked, flushed face, in her pink silk bed-gown, so weak, so eager to live, so disappointed, that tears were always trembling in her eyes. And behind it all, and the wind and dust and glaring

sea, the constant fear that one might return at any moment and find her gone.
—And then life will be different, quite different, ever afterwards. That is, as
I know from Henry James and Hubert Henry [Davies], what death does.
When someone you love goes your life isn't ruined, it can be only very rarely
that you are broken-hearted, but life *afterwards* is different. You can never
quite replace those friends. There are others but they are not *those*. How
marvellous the absolute distinctness of every human being—this *surely the
most incredible* thing in life.

Melchior's first visit to Brackenburn was overshadowed by the news
from Edinburgh, and directly his friend had left Hugh hurried back
there. Twice he returned to Brackenburn, each time to be recalled
urgently by telegram. On June 13 he found his mother "as courageous
as she can be, although she knows now, I think, that she is going to die.
. . . I read poetry to her in the afternoon, which I think she liked."

On the 19th he found her much worse and insisted on telephoning
for his brother Robin.

In the afternoon I had what I suppose I must look on as my farewell talk.
Very moving. She said that our coming together during the last years was
the happiest thing that had ever happened to her, and just what she wanted
to complete her life. That she hoped to be more with me after her death than
she had been before, and that she would have me remember Mrs Benson's
motto: "Trust God and be gentle to others." Went out very miserable.
Walked about. In desperation into a musical comedy where I stayed
wretched.

The end came on June 23:

On going up to my bath saw through the open door Father sitting by
Mother's bed, and knew the end was near. Went in and kissed her and she
just said "Good Morning," but didn't, I think, recognise me. Then sat in my
room reading Newbolt's anthology and Lucas's *Lamb*. At about a quarter
to one, called by Nurse for the end. All of us there. A blazing summer day.
Dorothy behaved superbly. Mother died about 1.20, quite quietly without
any struggle. I think she knew we were all there.

Two days later the funeral service in St Mary's Cathedral was
followed by burial at Dalmahoy. "Charming service, birds singing,
old horse swishing his tail, stream murmuring. Came back happier.
Dorothy so especially splendid." All through these days of anxiety

and grief Hugh was immensely strengthened by the indomitable fortitude of his sister.

His mother's last illness and death have been described at some length because their effect on Hugh was both great and lasting: indeed it is perhaps not too much to suggest that the emotional shock he then sustained hastened the appearance of the disease that was first discovered some six months later, from which he was always thereafter to suffer, and which was to kill him in the end.

CHAPTER EIGHTEEN

THE ROCK

I

LIFE went on; the family came to Brackenburn for a few days, and then fortunately it was time for Hugh to pay his annual visit to Bayreuth. He arrived there on July 10 and was immediately swept up into the old round of music, conversation, and intrigue. His friendship with Melchior had passed its climax: moreover Hugh decided that Kleinchen was "certainly all heart, love, and unselfishness to those she cares for," and together the three of them evolved a tolerable design for living. "She is a little darling," he told Dorothy, "and he is recognised by everyone now as the greatest *Heldentenor* in the world."

This year the storm-centre was Winnie Wagner, and into Hugh's somewhat unwilling ear she would pour out her anxieties. The Rhinemaidens were giving a lot of trouble; the *Parsifal* scenery had a nasty habit of sticking on its way up and down; she was worried about her husband's health and about the future of the Festival if he were to die; but above all she was concerned for the present and future fate of Adolf Hitler. He had been released from gaol the previous December, after a year's imprisonment for his part in the abortive Munich *Putsch* of 1923, and had hastened to Bayreuth for succour and asylum. Before his imprisonment he had been dismissed by Siegfried Wagner and his friends as "one of Winnie's lame ducks," but now his reappearance at Wahnfried as a convicted revolutionary and ex-gaolbird might bring discredit on the Royal Family of Bayreuth, so the future ruler of half Europe was compelled to dodge in and out, appearing only after dark, popping up in the Wagner box at the Festspielhaus, and generally behaving like a stage conspirator. He did not then seem important enough to warrant more than a passing reference in Hugh's diary, and it was not until fifteen years later that these meetings were mentioned at any length in print.[1]   Then Hugh described how they sat together in a box

---

[1] In *Roman Fountain* (1940), and more fully in an article (here quoted) entitled "Why

to hear Melchior in *Parsifal* and how "the tears poured down Hitler's cheeks." The account continues:

I was with Hitler on many occasions, talked, walked and ate with him. I think he rather liked me. I liked him and despised him, both emotions which time has proved I was wrong to indulge. I liked him because he seemed to me a poor fish quite certain to be shortly killed. He was shabby, unkempt, very feminine, very excitable. . . . There was something pathetic about him, I felt. I felt rather maternal to him! He spoke a great deal about his admiration of England and the need of her alliance with Germany.

I thought him fearfully ill-educated and quite tenth-rate. When Winnie Wagner said he would be the saviour of the world I just laughed. I was wrong about one thing—his evil. I didn't detect it then. I thought him silly, brave, and shabby—rather like a necromantic stump orator.

What with the embryo Führer and his prophetess, the singers and the late hours, a month's visit seemed quite long enough, and Hugh gratefully withdrew on August 8. He never went to Bayreuth again.

2

His mother's death, which the hurly-burly of the last weeks had driven from the forefront of his mind, was brought home to him with renewed force when he got back to Brackenburn. His family came to stay at a neighbouring hotel, and though he took them to the Grasmere Sports, walked and talked with his father, and did his best to make their holiday a happy one, he realised that he missed his mother most when the rest of the family were all together. "She gave us all a sparkle—even if of irritation sometimes. We are only half-alive without her."

There remained the solace of work, into which he plunged deep. Long mornings of *Wintersmoon* were interrupted only by the writing of an article for a symposium in the *Daily Express* called *What I Believe*, and by the first conscious stirrings of the Herries family. On August 28, for example, he wrote in his diary: "I'm now pinning all my hopes to two or three Lakes novels, which will at least do something for this

---

didn't I put Poison in his Coffee?" (*John o'London's Weekly*, 11 October 1940). Although the article abounds in minor inaccuracies, its substance, in so far as it concerns Hitler, is undoubtedly based on fact.

adorable place. I feel a longing desire to pay it back for some of its goodness to me."

And then out of the blue appeared another friend. One day there arrived a letter signed J. B. Priestley (a name unknown to Hugh), asking him to contribute a small volume to a series called "These Diversions" which Priestley was editing for Messrs Jarrold. Priestley at this time had published only essays and literary criticism, and was working as a journalist and publisher's reader in London. Hugh was impressed by the letter and asked Priestley to stay at Brackenburn so that they could talk over the proposed book. The impact of his visit may be judged by some extracts from Hugh's diary:

Sept. 24. Arrived Priestley—a North Country, no-nonsense-about-me, I-know-my-mind kind of little man. But I think I shall like and respect him.

Sept. 25. I find Priestley very agreeable. He is cocksure and determined but has a great sense of humour about himself, and his views on literature most strangely coincide with mine.

A two-day walk on the fells only increased Hugh's respect for his visitor:

Sept. 30. Priestley is certainly a very clever man. Like all of us he is not perhaps as aware of his own lacks as he is of others', but he is young yet and is fighting a battle. He will certainly go very far.

Needless to say, Hugh promised to write the book, and it was decided that his subject should be the pleasures of reading. He was as good as his word: *Reading: an Essay* was begun at Brackenburn on October 14, continued at the rate of three thousand words a day, and completed on October 20. Few editors can have inspired such overwhelming alacrity.

Meanwhile *Portrait of a Man with Red Hair* had been published on October 14. Hugh had been alarmed about the book ever since Vance's rejection of what he now called "my penny dreadful," and when the first review he saw proved somewhat critical, he was prepared for annihilation: "I'm going to be banged on the head over this book and quite rightly—it's a fake." But his fears were not realised. Most of the other reviewers praised the book, Clemence Dane "raved over it" at a luncheon party given by Ethel McKenna, and Benn Levy the play-wright asked permission to dramatise it.

At the end of November Hugh travelled to Berlin and stayed for ten days with Melchior, who had now scored successes at the Opera there in *Siegfried* and *Tannhäuser*, "so he seems to have sailed pretty well over the rocks. But more and more clearly I see he is lost to me as companion for ever. He will for the rest of his life never rest, always journeys, engagements, no time for any human. Well, I've done my part."

He arrived back in time to watch the University match at Twicken-ham. Finding that he had £450 less than he expected in the bank, he bought a prancing T'ang horse and decided to take out a life assurance policy which would mature when he was fifty-five. On December 16 he was examined by two doctors from the insurance company, and next day they reported an excess of sugar in the urine—an "awful blow." In *Wintersmoon* he introduced the scene and his own reactions to it:

He had thought himself at that time in the very perfection of physical health, but they had discovered something wrong with him and had refused the policy.[1] Most vividly he could recall his astonishment, sense of personal affront, hurt vanity, but above all a sudden precipitate looking down into a black, cavernous space, he insecure, helpless above it.

That same night he travelled to Edinburgh, saw his sister receive her final medical degree at the University next day, and afterwards told her his news. A specialist confirmed the diagnosis of diabetes and ordered a strict diet. The family Christmas that year was clouded by bereavement and worry.

3

On 1 January 1926 Hugh drove home to Brackenburn, and as he approached his beloved cottage he made a New Year resolution which was put into effect without further ado:

My dearest Dorothy,

I have been thinking over things this morning and have decided that you must have a little more *personal* help financially. So I am going to make

[1] Hugh's policy was not refused, but its premiums were naturally increased.

my regular £50 into £150. This extra hundred will be paid to you quarterly, not in a lump sum like the £50, and I shall instruct my bank.

Now this hundred is to be *pocket-money* for you. If I find that a penny of it has gone in housekeeping I shall at once withdraw it. If the housekeeping becomes difficult you are at once to tell me. Please keep these conditions as well as I keep my diet!

> Heaps of love to you both.
> Your loving Hugh.

Hugh had also for five years contributed to the cost of Dorothy's medical training. His belief in her capabilities was amply borne out by her subsequent career as a doctor.

Wintersmoon was now nearing completion, and Hugh read over the manuscript as far as he had gone, trying to consider it from the point of view of a critic in the American *Nation* who had recently condemned all his work for "sentimentality, preaching, and monotony." In his journal he wrote:

> Do I feel those charges to be true? I think not. The critic quotes *Jeremy* as a sentimental work. It certainly is not. I believe in the inherent goodness of many people. I believe that many people have impulses of love and generosity, but I don't think that in the main I deal with these things sentimentally. On the other hand there *is* a certain romantic colour behind all my work, and there is always a fight to improve character, and this the modern realistic critic considers preaching, because he maintains that in the novel there should only be statement of *fact*, no moral bias. I believe this will change. As to monotony, the charge is surely false when I have written books as various as *Perrin*, *The Dark Forest*, *The Cathedral*, and *Jeremy*.

Having thus happily convinced himself that all was well, he galloped on with *Wintersmoon*, becoming so immersed in it that when on February 19 the last chapter ("this has been for so long in my head that I know every syllable of it") was finished, he experienced once more that same feeling of emptiness and loss. "You write a sentence and in a moment everyone—Janet, Wildherne, Rosalind, the Duke—has fled into space." Two days later, to solace his forlornness, he began to write the third and last Jeremy book, which became *Jeremy at Crale*.

All this time he had, every fortnight or so, been making brief visits to London, in the course of which he bought a Fourth Folio Shakespeare, lunched with Sir Frederick Macmillan ("who thinks *Harmer*

John wonderful. Indeed spoke of it with tears in his eyes"), and entertained the Melchiors. An example of Hugh's readiness to point out in others faults which were very much his own is provided by his diary-entry for March 1:

Leicester Galleries. Saw [C. R. W.] Nevinson there hanging his pictures and was surprised at his agonised nervousness about the critics. As though it mattered! But he trembled all over as he talked of conspiracies, cliques, etc. Funny in so stocky, resolute-looking a man.

At this time too the Cazalets introduced him to P. G. Wodehouse, "a large, simple, kindly fellow." After their second meeting Hugh wrote: "Took to him like anything. Is that a friendship? Can't be sure yet." Together they watched the rugger at Twickenham, and Wodehouse took him to the House of Commons to lunch with Winston Churchill.

4

At the end of March Hugh started for a fortnight's holiday in Majorca, but before he left a most important decision was made. The mightiest moments pass uncalendared, and over a year ago, towards the end of 1924, Hugh had experienced, although he did not realise it at the time, the greatest single stroke of good fortune of his whole life. He had encountered the person who was to be his friend and companion for the rest of his days, who was to be the rock against which the waves of his nervous temperament and excitability were to break in vain, who was to come nearer than any other human being to the long-sought conception of the perfect friend.

Harold Cheevers, a Cornishman born in 1893, was at this time a constable in the Metropolitan Police. He was married and had two little boys. During the war he had served in the Navy. Once police revolver champion of the British Isles, he had also won the championship of the All England Police three years in succession. He was a fine swimmer and had won prizes for races over distances varying between two hundred yards and five miles.

In appearance he was large—not tall or fat but sturdy and massive—

with fair hair and blue eyes. Here is Hugh's description of him, from a short story called *The Whistle*:

He was a very large man, very fair in colouring, plainly of great strength. His expression was absolutely English in its complete absence of curiosity, its certainty that it knew the best about everything, its suspicion, its determination not to be taken in by anybody, and its latent kindliness. He had very blue eyes and was clean-shaven . . . his hair, which was fair almost to whiteness, lay roughly across his forehead. He was not especially neat but of a quite shining cleanliness.[1]

The outstanding traits of his character were shrewd common sense, unswerving integrity, deep loyalty, and an imperturbability of demeanour which was only increased by the excitable enthusiasms of others. Chance brought him and Hugh together, but though Hugh liked him from the first, their friendship developed slowly, and Harold did not enter Hugh's service for almost two years. In the light of what was to come, it is amusing to read Hugh's comment after Harold's first visit to 90 Piccadilly: "Cheevers came in and I found him a good quiet trustworthy fellow."

Trustworthiness, in the fullest sense of the word, was one of the chief qualities Hugh needed: trustworthiness embodied in someone who would modify his whims and impulses with solid common sense. By Christmas 1925 Harold had become "a jewel beyond price," and in 1933 Hugh was able to write to a lady who had been confiding her troubles to him by letter:

I understand many of your own dreads and lonelinesses—I have had them myself. In fact I should still know them were it not for one person—my secretary-chauffeur-friend and ROCK! He and his wife have for years now been behind me in everything. My life has been strengthened and sweetened in every way by them. They are simple people but marvellous in fidelity, humour and patience.

Now in March 1926 he had a long talk with Harold and they provisionally arranged that he should enter Hugh's service as chauffeur in a year's time, directly Hugh returned from his projected American

---

[1] In *John Cornelius* Hugh presented a fuller portrait in the character called Charlie Christian, and the relationship between Adam Paris and Will Leathwaite in *The Fortress* and *Vanessa* was based on Hugh's friendship with Harold.

lecture tour. Hugh would arrange for Harold to be taught all about the driving and maintenance of cars, and the loss of his police pension would be covered by a bequest in Hugh's will.

5

The Majorcan trip was spent sitting in the sun, bathing in the sea, touring the island, writing *Jeremy at Crale*, and correcting the proofs of *Harmer John*, which he dedicated to Melchior. "I've cut some sentimental bits. I can do no more—I'm too much inside it. It will seem dull and naïve to some, but to me it is the most real of all my books." He read a book about the Lake District and longed for Brackenburn. On almost every holiday thereafter this feeling of nostalgia quickly bore down on him, and he wondered why on earth he had ever come away. Indeed, the only cause seems to have been that same demon which was forever whistling him up to London, that restlessness which never for long gave him pause.

Back in London, he learned that Doran had offered an advance of £2500 for his next five novels, and commented: "What a romantic life mine is nowadays—and the best of it is that I never felt the creative impulse beating in me so strongly."

He had been a week at Brackenburn when on May 3 the General Strike began. Full of the direst imaginings of civil war he drove to London next day, and vainly tried to find something useful to do. Eventually on May 10 he visited the Guildhall and was promised a job starting on the 12th. On the 11th he drove to Dover to meet the Melchiors, who were arriving from the Continent. They were cheered by the sight of undergraduates working in the docks, and started for London in high spirits. An hour out of Dover the back-axle broke, and with great difficulty they secured a lift for themselves and the Melchiors' luggage. Then came May 12:

Got to the Guildhall by nine. Found the voluntary labour bureau in full swing. I was to be Information Officer. Went a round in the car with Woodruffe and Robins. Went to all the danger-spots—Poplar, Bethnal Green, Stepney, Islington. Saw the mayors, clerks, etc. All nervous and apprehensive of great riots end of week. General [Woodruffe] and I coming back say over and over we don't see how this can end without fearful riots, when we look up and see a scribbled placard *Strike Over*. Find this actually true. T.U.C. have unconditionally surrendered. So we are all photoed and disbanded.

He stayed on in London for a fortnight, heard Melchior sing Siegfried at Covent Garden, and once again sat for his portrait to Gerald Kelly. Altogether between 1914 and 1926 Kelly painted three portraits of Hugh.[1] At the end of May Hugh took the Melchiors up to Brackenburn for the week-end, and as though to make them feel at home the back-axle broke again.

6

The next few weeks were remarkable for Hugh's adventures among pictures. Almost certainly it was a visit to an exhibition of Augustus John's latest work at the Chenil Gallery which started him off on his collection of modern art. He "fell utterly in love" with three pictures—a portrait of the artist's son Romilly, a flower piece, and a large portrait of a Japanese. Deciding to sell his etchings and buy Johns with the money, he snapped up the three pictures for £900 and sent almost his whole collection of etchings to Christie's, where they fetched over £700 at auction. For good measure he also bought pictures by Alfred Stevens and James Pryde.

But that was not all. He decided that "John and Sickert are to me simply worlds ahead of everyone else in England." Whether this decision was solely the result of the John show, or whether the notion came into his mind from somebody else's, it is impossible to say. But having arrived at it, he felt that he had outgrown some of his earlier artistic enthusiasms, including that for the work of his old friend Gerald Kelly, to whom he had been sitting, off and on, for years, and of whom he was very fond. "Somehow, somewhere," writes Kelly, "Hugh learned that I was a photographic painter, academic in the worst sense of that word, and surely no man of sensibility could tolerate my pompous productions. So Hugh was in a fix, and, bless him, how clumsy he was!" He managed to let Kelly know that his opinions had changed, and at the same time asked Kelly to approach Augustus John and ask

[1] Two of them are still in the possession of the artist. The third belongs to Mr Lauritz Melchior.

him if he would paint Hugh's portrait. This Kelly very graciously did, John agreed, and the first sitting was arranged:

June 17. This morning the John picture was really begun, and begun, so it seemed to me, very excitingly. He worked furiously for four hours and got a remarkably vivid impression. The picture is to be red-brown in colour.

June 18. Picture progressing finely. He almost stopped altogether this morning, thinking he'd done enough. A strange, shy, most fascinating man. Said that the ambition of his life was to paint a great nude, that a legend had grown about him quite undeserved.

June 22. Portrait leapt ahead today. Going to be really fine *and* a likeness. John pleased with it. We moved several steps towards one another today. He talked of his shyness. When a boy his terror at walking up the church aisle.

June 30. Sat for picture in morning; and he seems now to me to have destroyed it all. Very disappointing. Took him out to Wimbledon. Must say it wasn't a great success. Think he was bored with me—anyhow he was very silent.

July 2. Sat this morning—most depressing. The picture seems to me to have changed for the worse, making me look old and strange, and he was in a temper with it all the morning, not talking and looking like Satan after the Fall.

July 3. All well again this morning. The picture has righted itself, and John in his most angelic mood, sweet and kind. I'm sure he has no human heart, but is "fey," a real genius from another planet than ours.

Aug. 2. (Bank Holiday) Mostly John. Went in the morning and he tried oil, pen-and-ink, pencil, chalk—all failures. After lunch he tried again, was almost in despair, and suddenly brought off a beautiful chalk head—really a stunner. He was a dear today.

7

Meanwhile at Brackenburn in July Hugh finished *Jeremy at Crale*, and thus having arrived at the astonishing position of having four completed books ready for publication, he resolved to write no more for a year. (His engagements in America enabled or perhaps enforced him to abide by this determination for nine months.) One day, in a long attempt at honest introspection in his journal, he wrote:

A serious trouble is the way that I disappoint people. Not my deep and close friends—if I disappoint *them*, as we all disappoint one another, neverthe-less they *know* that I love them—but the more casual people whom one likes when one meets and forgets afterwards. I like almost everyone when I meet them, and give them an impression apparently that they mean a lot to me. So they do when I'm with them, but there are so many of them—I like human beings so much—that their places are being perpetually filled. Then they complain that I don't meet them or write to them. . . . I must not be so apparently excited at meeting people. But how can I help it? I'm excited at everything.

At the beginning of August he visited the Cheevers family at Saltash in Cornwall, took Harold and showed him Truro, and after seeing him off wrote in his diary: "These days have been marvellous, showing me that at last after so many searchings I have found a human being I can utterly trust and believe in." This trust and belief proved to be so well founded that they grew ever stronger with each passing year.

After leaving Harold, Hugh joined his own family at Mullion, where the faithful Turley had found rooms for them all. Cornwall nowadays, he decided, did not move him as once it had, but left him "tranquilly happy as when visiting old relations," and as always he enjoyed Turley's company. He had intended to stay a fortnight, but after five days the news of the Fifth Test Match against the Australians at the Oval excited him so much that he decided he must see the rest of it. On the Sunday he travelled to London, and at eight o'clock next morning lined up in a queue in Kennington. He "got a fine seat just in front of the gaso-meter" and repeated this exploit for the next two days. By winning this match, in which the great Wilfred Rhodes made his last appear-ance in a Test Match, England regained the Ashes. Here is Hugh's description of the final day's play:

The day of my life and one of the great days in English cricket. Better seat than ever. . . . Wickets fell quickly but Tate batted finely, hitting fiercely. All out for 436. Then the rain came, soaking me through and through, as my umbrella was stolen last night. But at 3.30 the Aussies came out and the miracle occurred. First Woodfull's wicket for one run. Then the rest like ninepins to Rhodes's and Larwood's bowling. We couldn't believe our eyes, got mad with excitement. All out for 125. 30,000 people in mad rush across ground!

Next day, filled with vicarious triumph, he rejoined his family at Mullion, but by the end of the month he was back in London, buying a secondhand Rolls-Royce for £325. In this stately vehicle, driven by a temporary chauffeur and followed by Chanter in the Daimler, Hugh arrived at Brackenburn for a week's peace before the American merry-go-round.

There followed a fortnight in London, which included an evening with Priestley ("both of us talking furiously. He really seems to think me a pretty good novelist, which is refreshing, considering"), another with James Agate ("to whom I rather reluctantly lent £200"), and "a wonderful morning with old Kipling in the Athenæum. He was sitting surrounded by the reviews of his new book, beaming like a baby. He talked to me delightfully about America, and when I said it was nice the eagerness with which they greeted one, he said: 'Of course they are a marooned people'!"

On September 25 Hugh sailed from Liverpool in the *Carinthia*.

8

The voyage was uneventful. In New York he was welcomed by old friends: the Fowlers, Somerset Maugham ("charming about *Harmer John*. Don't know how sincere he was"), and George Doran ("so kind and good. Will he be when my books don't sell? We'll see"). *Harmer John* was published in both London and New York on October 15, and two days later Hugh started out on his travels. Once he was in the train, he felt as though this third tour were merging with its two predecessors into one endless journey, familiar as a dream. The first lecture was at Rome, Georgia, where the evening was "made memorable because of an embalmer, who took me for a ride under the moon—fantastic country!" In Virginia he stayed with Ellen Glasgow and James Branch Cabell; in Washington with Sinclair Lewis; then on to city after city—Syracuse, Rochester, Cleveland, Akron, Buffalo—just time for the lecture before catching the train. At Akron he managed to attend a football game, Wooster v. Akron, in the middle of which his "name was shouted through a megaphone and everyone got up and cheered."

Frank Swinnerton was also lecturing in the States at this time, and malicious gossip brought about a cooling of the friendship between him and Hugh. The details are obscure, but Hugh certainly wrote a hurt and angry letter accusing Swinnerton of making fun of him privately and publicly. Swinnerton defended himself strongly, but the harm was done, and though he and Hugh remained always on outward terms of affectionate friendship, they seldom in future met or corresponded.

In December there came a welcome breather in New York, where Hugh stayed some of the time with the Fowlers and some with the Melchiors in their apartment on Riverside Drive. "She," he told his sister, "is simply the most miraculously *good* character I have ever known, living only for others," while he was delighted to be able to report that Melchior had not been at all spoilt by success, but was "sweeter than ever." The P.E.N. Club gave a dinner to Osbert Sitwell, Ford Madox Hueffer (who now called himself Ford Madox Ford), and Hugh. He wrote a short story called *The Tiger*, longed to start a new novel, and fought against homesickness: "Marvellous how the thought of H. C., stolid, strong, unchanging, carries me on through this." Christmas with the Melchiors was a great success. On Christmas Eve "we all put on evening dress, had supper at seven, sang carols, looked at the Tree which was splendid, then our presents. Nearly a hundred between us. I heard from everyone . . . very happy." In the First Fifteen friends listed at the end of the year the leaders were, in this order, Melchior, Chanter, Kleinchen Melchior, and Harold.

9

In the New Year the tour reopened at Columbus, Ohio, and as it whirled relentlessly on its way even Hugh's capacity for enjoyment began to wilt a trifle beneath the weight of entertainments and receptions, though in his diary he complained bitterly on the rare occasions when he was not met at the station and made an immediate fuss of. At Minneapolis he was momentarily put out by the local dramatic society who performed a scene from Barrie's *Little Minister* as a curtain-raiser to his lecture, but "finally it went all right." In Detroit he was introduced to "a painter called Paul Honoré who looks like a wild animal, but I took to him immediately." In Indianapolis he saw his old friends Carl McCullough and Booth Tarkington, and at Toronto stayed with the Annands, who had now settled there.

Passing through New York at the end of January he learned that *Harmer John* had sold forty thousand copies in America and eighteen thousand in England: figures which brought with them the realisation that the book was "not going to be the great success I had privately hoped." The next lecture was in Washington, where he saw the film of *Beau Geste* for the second time but "was as much moved as the first, and my tears spoiled my collar." In Dallas, Texas, he ran into a Shoe Retailers' Convention, and anyone who has shared a hotel with such will know what that means. San Antonio pleased him so much that, having a few free days, he lingered there and one morning "sat to have my picture drawn while a lady sang to me." In the train from Phoenix, Arizona, he met a "young extremely handsome Hawaian, that day out of jail where he'd been for a year for hitting a man on the head with a spade. He was frank and honest and I gave him his fare to San Francisco."

At Los Angeles he was welcomed by Douglas Fairbanks, who took him over a film studio and asked him to come out again in a year or two as adviser on historical films. At Santa Barbara he met Stevenson's stepdaughter Isobel Strong, whom he described as a "nice, kind, wild savage." At San Francisco he was greeted by a letter from Chanter saying that by the time he got home he would "have nothing in the bank instead of the £2000 I thought I should have," but the news did not unduly depress him, and he reflected: "So long as I keep the cottage, Harold, and my health, I defy the world!" He was encouraged too by the large amount of publicity he was receiving in the San Francisco newspapers, which chronicled his every word and movement at immense length, and delighted to meet for the first time another English writer whose work he admired:

Feb. 22. Tea with Stella Benson, who is a shy, honest, funny little thing, the image of Jane Eyre—but I fancy she's married no Rochester. We liked one another I think.

Feb. 23. Stella B. takes me out to the sea. It is raining, and we go in the tram. The tram is interminable but at last we have five minutes' walk on the shore and there is a lovely silver light on the horizon. The seals sleepily balance themselves on the slippery rocks. We talk about literature—rather scornfully.

Next day he was off again and "crossing in the ferry thought of my soul, as I always do crossing in ferries." At Portland, Oregon, he met and liked Gene Tunney, the champion heavyweight boxer of the world, and took an immense fancy to Nelson Collins, the local Professor of English. Crossing the Rockies on the way from Vancouver to Calgary, he decided that "very high mountains never appeal to me as much as they should. The egotism in me, I suppose." At Winnipeg he began a lifelong friendship with Stanley Long, an Englishman who had lived for many years in Canada, where he was well known as a banker and trust company executive.[1]

Hugh spent his forty-third birthday in Chicago with "no reflections except that I'm well and happy and find life absolutely thrilling . . . *Wintersmoon* sold to *Express* for £800." Three days later came an entry underlined and marked with three stars: "*On this day does Harold come to me for good and all. A great event.*" At the end of the month he heard from Harold, who was now under instruction at the Rolls-Royce works, and on April 2 Hugh gave his seventieth and last lecture at Ames, Iowa.

There followed a brief stay as the guest of Henry Ford at the Dearborn Country Club, near Detroit. Hugh's longing to begin a new novel would brook no further delay, and he wrote the first pages of *Scarlatt: A Winter's Tale* at Dearborn. From there he was taken to dine with Robert Frost the poet, whom he "liked hugely," and also on an extensive tour of the prisons, police courts, and morgues of Detroit and Cincinnati, among which he noted "nothing anyway as bad as Marlow used to be."

During a final week in New York he decided that *Scarlatt*, of which he had written only part of the first chapter, was too gloomy and tragic for his present mood, but luckily he had in his head clear ideas for no fewer than three other novels. Of these he felt most immediately drawn to the story of an old writer called Hans Frost. So *Scarlatt* was abandoned,[2] Hugh embarked for home at St John's, Newfoundland, and began *Hans Frost* on the first day out.

[1] After Hugh's death Stanley Long bought Brackenburn and made it his home.
[2] The whole fragment was published in *The Legion Book* (1929), and in 1937 Hugh took up again both the book's central idea and the name Scarlatt, and used them in *The Sea Tower.*

CHAPTER NINETEEN

THE FIRST OF THE HERRIES

I

AFTER a few days at Brackenburn, rejoicing in his freedom and admiring the newly installed electric light, Hugh drove to London where he spent the rest of the month. Once again he found that a week or two of the usual social round exhausted him as no lecture tour had ever done, but there were compensations—"tea with old Gosse, when he talked of the chestnut-haired Gissing and the malevolent snarling Carlyle;" a gay luncheon party with Elizabeth ("always bewitching. She is getting rather like a witch now to look at"), where George Moore talked entertainingly, "abusing all English novelists other than himself for lack of freedom;" and another luncheon with Victor Cazalet at the House of Commons, "which was nice because of having a talk with John Buchan again, and nasty because of Maud Cunard, whom I really detest but might like better if she were nice to me."

One old breach was at any rate temporarily mended, for on May 18, after attending the memorial service for his old friend Sidney Colvin, Hugh lunched with the Ervines ("Great fun. St John always stimulates me"). He sold both his cars and bought a new Daimler, with which Harold was delighted. More surprisingly he also sold his copy of the privately printed edition of *Seven Pillars of Wisdom*. In 1924 he had written to T. E. Lawrence to ask whether he might be a subscriber, and had received a characteristic answer, beginning "Dear Walpole, Of course I remember . . . you are a celebrity," and going on to advise him not to waste £30 on the book.[1] Hugh nevertheless had persisted, but in all probability had never read a word of it. If he had, it is unthinkable that he who liked almost every book, good, bad, and impossible, should have parted with it now. He was not short of money, and in the whole of his life there is no other recorded instance of his

[1] This letter is now in the Fitz Park Museum, Keswick. A complete list of the Hugh Walpole collection there will be found at Appendix D, p. 480.

selling a book of any kind. But sell it he did, to Bumpus for £330, and bought two T'ang figures with the money. "No loss, I'm sure," he wrote in his diary, but later he regretfully came to think otherwise.

When he got back to Brackenburn at the end of May, the outline of the four Lake novels began slowly and insistently to emerge from the mist. The first was already in his mind, entitled *Rogue Herries*,[1] set in the eighteenth century and intended as a "fine queer book in the big manner. These four books shall *clinch* my reputation or I'll die in the attempt. It makes a wonderful difference having H. C. in the background. I love his kindly gravity, care of me, utter honesty." But the time for the beginning of the four novels was not yet ripe, and in the meantime he pegged on steadily with *Hans Frost*. "This will be a simple mild book but not imbecile . . . writing, I fear, rather in V. Woolf's manner. How can I help it when she is such a darling and *To the Lighthouse* the best of all the works yet?" And a few days later, "I like this book. It's in a new vein for me, the vein of humour I ought to have tried long ago. Virginia Woolf has perhaps liberated me."

In June he drove to Edinburgh, whence he and his sister visited their father, who was on holiday at North Berwick. They found him "old, shabby, jolly and red-faced, wearing an old suit green with age, but minding no reproofs. Blind, with a bad heart, but determined as ever to run all over the country." Hugh's diabetes was unquestionably worse, and his sister made him promise to return to his diet, which he had abandoned as soon as it had begun to do him good. On the way home he was struck once again by the beauty of Cumberland in the early June sunshine:

One is afraid to lose the sense of this weather—the miraculous otherworldliness which perhaps never will return again. And when I am driving alone with Harold through it, seeing and smelling it as I always hoped but never thought I would, I want to put out my hand and catch something that I can have always.

The Priestleys arrived for a short stay, and the two writers agreed that they would collaborate in a novel. It was to be in the form of letters exchanged between two friends and was to be called *Farthing*

---

[1] He left no record of how the name Herries first came into his head, but it may well have been absorbed during one of his many readings of *Redgauntlet*.

Hall. The object of the enterprise was to provide Priestley (whose share of the advance royalties, thanks to Hugh's name, would be substantial) with enough freedom and leisure to write the long novel he was planning. The project succeeded, and *The Good Companions*, which was dedicated to Hugh, was the result.

A brief visit to London provided some Wimbledon tennis, a car smash in Gloucester Place, from which Hugh and Harold emerged unscathed though the Daimler was badly damaged, and a rush of picture-buying:

July 19. Dorothy Warren showed me works by her new young genius Henry Moore and I bought a serpent. But *the* purchase was a Forain [1]—a little lady in a hat with yellow feather sitting on a crimson sofa. Lovely! The only woman I shall ever marry.

July 20. Still the picture fever. Changed my Sickert for three lovely drawings—absolute masterpieces. Also bought a very fine Duncan Grant for £50. This is the end. I've spent about £700 in all.

He travelled down to Sussex to spend a night with the Galsworthys at Bury, where "J. G. and I had a most interesting talk, mainly as to whether one can only find first-rate work out of actual experience—how far imagination can go. He said that after finishing the Forsyte book he thought he was done and would never write another line." Many critics have agreed with what Galsworthy then thought, though he afterwards wrote many more lines.

August was to be spent abroad, but before he left Hugh found time to write an article on how he would bring up the boy king of Roumania, and to attend several spiritualistic meetings at the Grotrian Hall. For some years he took a deep if sporadic interest in Spiritualism, but though he attended séances at Conan Doyle's and elsewhere, he never became what may be termed a believer, and gradually the subject drifted away into the background.

2

By the beginning of August he was travelling across France by train and reading Thomas Mann's *The Magic Mountain*, "a mad, morbid, decadent, smelly, pestiferous, long-drawn-out, boring affair, but

[1] Now in the possession of Dr Dorothea and Mr Robin Walpole.

catching one up and holding one absolutely—a smell of genius in it somewhere." He spent a week with his family at Diablerets in Switzerland, trying to teach them bridge and writing a short story called *The Little Donkeys with the Crimson Saddles*. Then a week with Elizabeth at Chalet Soleil, where he got in "a great day at *Hans Frost*, which Elizabeth says ought to be called *Chilblains*," and found the assembled company "very gay and merry together. . . . All the same I shan't be sorry to get home. I hate being cut off by earthquakes, torrents, Saints' Days, train smashes, from one's post—and all one's friends. How anyone can live abroad I can't conceive." His hostess he found somewhat querulous, and he judged her to be unhappy and ill, suffering from loneliness and "a fierce clutching of her literary reputation, as I saw in Ellen Glasgow. These literary women don't seem to be able to stand the pace—May Sinclair, Mrs Ward, Elizabeth Robins, J. O. Hobbes, Ethel Mayne—they can't last out."

It was therefore not without some measure of relief that he left the Chalet and journeyed by way of Geneva to Portofino on the Italian Riviera. Here he stayed with the music critic Francis Toye and his wife, bathing, loving the sunshine, and working furiously at *Hans Frost*: "I'm enjoying it, but my great impulse is to get everything off my back so as to be free for *Herries*! What fun and what work that will be!" A week later he moved on to Montreux and stayed there very enjoyably as the guest of Robert Hichens, who drove him up to Caux to have tea with Lucas Malet, the novelist daughter of Charles Kingsley. He found her "much as I expected her, bearing her seventy-three years boldly. A huge nose heavily powdered. Not very easy to talk to. Spoke enthusiastically of my books."

3

By the beginning of September Hugh was back at Brackenburn, ready to begin the formidable task of reading straight through Trollope, for the long-promised study of him must be delivered before he could embark on the immense Herries voyage. *Hans Frost* was finished on September 10, and in the course of the next nine days Hugh read all six of the Barchester novels and wrote the chapter on them for his book. "Don't think I ever felt so glad at finishing anything. . . . What

a business this book is! The hardest piece of work I've ever had to do."
And indeed it was, for his novels were more like fun than work to him,
and he had never before tackled anything which required so much
reading, selection, and arrangement. As relaxation one evening he read
his own diaries for 1918–19 and commented: "Poor Jim! What an
uncontrolled egoist I was—still am, I dare say, but at least not so uncomfortable to be with as I was."

The arrival of Priestley made a welcome break in the reading of
Trollope, and next day *Farthing Hall* was begun. Its immediate progress may be watched in Hugh's diary:

Sept. 21. Now the Priestley book is obsessing me. How caught up and
excited I get over these books one after the other, and all the time *Herries* is
lying waiting at the back. . . . It is delightful having Jack here—a friendship that does me all the good in the world because I respect so immensely
his intelligence.

Sept. 22. The book with Priestley moves. I have as I expected a burning
desire to get on with it and do it all, but I mustn't be impatient. That would
be silly.

Sept. 23. I certainly find Priestley an enchanting companion. I've never had
a writing man for a friend before who has been so close a companion. Henry
James was too old, Conrad too mysterious, Swinnerton too untrustworthy,
Bennett too egoistic—all *good* friends, but none of them with this humour
and sweetness that Priestley has. A most lovable man.

Sept. 26. Jack and I now moving at breakneck speed.

The diabetes tests had not been satisfactory of late, and Hugh consulted his dentist and his oculist in London to see whether they could
explain his recurrent attacks of neuralgia. Then back to Brackenburn
to wrestle with his two commitments. On October 11 he continued to
write some *Farthing Hall* as well as a thousand words of *Trollope*.
"Nor you nor I nor Eugène Sue," he wrote to Arnold Bennett,
"have written so many novels as that damned man." And again
to Bennett, who had sent him Hornibrook's book *The Culture of
the Abdomen* containing directions for reducing the waistline by
exercises, "Many thanks for Hornibrook. I'm going to start, but
God alone knows whether I'll keep it up . . . I'm buried beneath
Trollops (as I saw him spelt in U.S.A.), an ironic position for ME!"

On October 12 he read *The Eustace Diamonds*, "which is very nearly the best of all the Trollopes;" next day wrote three thousand words of the political chapter, and so on, day after day. Gradually, however, his attitude towards the old story-teller began to soften; after groaning at the monotony of the stories ("the eternal triangle of lovers looms at the fiftieth time over one like a nightmare"), he could admit only a few days later: "It is wonderful how well the old boy lasts. Even now after all this reading I'm not tired of him." By the end of October the last novel had been read, and all the book written but for one final chapter of general appreciation, which could be finished off at any time before the end of the year.

Meanwhile *Jeremy at Crale* had been published on October 20, and William Roughead had written to say that he considered it the best school story since *Stalky & Co*, in which judgment its author was inclined modestly to concur.

In London at the beginning of November his specialist advised the removal of most of his teeth. This was a blow, and Kipling, when Hugh sat next to him at luncheon in the Beefsteak Club, depressed him still further by prophesying that he would carry his false ones in his pocket for the first year. To cheer himself up Hugh bought a Renoir still-life, and spent an enjoyable afternoon with Montague Shearman, looking at his remarkable collection of modern pictures. The teeth were removed at Lady Carnarvon's nursing home in Portland Place, Hugh's recovery was rapid, and four days later he was recuperating at 90 Piccadilly. Many friends visited him during his convalescence, among them Clemence Dane, whom he "liked better than I ever have. Her volubility and excitement are largely shyness. She talked much of the book she is going to do about me." [1] Other visitors included J. C. Squire ("I always hit a tenderness in Squire which is very appealing to me. He is full of fine things, loyalties and honours") and the actor Charles Laughton, who Benn Levy was hoping would play the leading part in the dramatised version of *Portrait of a Man with Red Hair*.

As soon as Hugh was well again, and his new teeth installed, he went out to tea with Arnold Bennett. The only other guest was Lion Feuchtwanger, the author of the immensely successful novel *Jew Süss* which Bennett had done much to popularise in England—"a little man

[1] *Tradition and Hugh Walpole* (1930).

like a marmoset. Talked incessantly about his great novel. . . . Arnold kind and bored, his eternal attitude these days." In December Hugh attended a dinner for George Doran at which were assembled "thirty famous writers! The waiters looked so much more distinguished. Feuchtwanger between Gosse and Gibbs who both neglected him. I made it up with Rebecca."

After this little burst of social activity Hugh drove to Edinburgh, where he was distressed to find his father suffering from a severe heart attack. Hugh read *Little Dorrit* aloud to him most solicitously, and this treatment proved beneficial, since the Bishop rallied promptly and was able to take part in the Christmas festivities.

Suddenly, all in one day, Hugh polished off his book on Trollope: "rather unexpectedly, the last chapter suddenly finished itself." This left him free to correct the proofs of *Wintersmoon* and to lunch with William Roughead, "a fine, amusing, generous, clever old Scotchman." Then on Christmas Eve came the moment he had been so eagerly awaiting. As he wrote the first words of *Rogue Herries*, his elation was tinged with misgiving lest the task should prove too much for him. Would he ever manage this first eighteenth-century volume, let alone the whole four? He had never before strayed outside his own period, nor attempted anything on so grandiose a scale.

I've a lot of apprehension about *Herries*. I'm not so delighted with the opening of it. Perhaps I feel this especially after *Inglesant*, which has struck me on this reading more than ever before. How strong old Shorthouse's sense of evil, and I suppose he never slept out of his marital bed once in his life!

But as he drove home to Brackenburn through the snow, his resolve was strengthened, and at the turn of the year he was eating his meals on a tray by the fire and reading deeply in the literature of the eighteenth century.

4

January 1928 began with the installation of the Cheevers family in their new house in Hampstead Garden Suburb. Hugh took it for them on a long lease and furnished a room in it for himself. This he came to occupy more and more, for odd nights and at week-ends when he was in London. For the rest of his life it was a haven of friendliness and seclusion to which he could hasten whenever the winds of circumstance seemed likely to blow him off his course. There always he was one of the family, and as he grew older such a position became more and more necessary to him. On the first day he spent in the house, marked in the diary with a star, he wrote: "I have never been in the heart of a family as I am in this one—not even the Annands. . . . All these I have taken absolutely to my heart." To add to his good fortune, Ethel Cheevers turned out to be a woman of uncommon character, shrewdness, and savoir-faire. Quick-witted, efficient, charming, and entirely at home in every sort of company, she always succeeded in making Hugh comfortable and putting him at his ease. He also became very attached to the two boys, helping with their education and rejoicing in their successes.

In January too he spent a week with the Priestleys at Church Hanborough, near Oxford, in "a rather cold bare stone house strangely like Conrad's, but how much happier [is the atmosphere] here than there! Jane and Jack suit me exactly both in character and mind—splendid acquisitions for me. We talked a million to the clock." One day George Gordon, then Merton Professor of Poetry at Oxford and shortly to be elected President of Magdalen, came over for the day with his wife, and Hugh was immensely taken with that charming, witty, and most unprofessorial of professors. For the rest, *Farthing Hall* was continued each day until it was finished. "Greatly relieved," wrote Hugh, "as now I have nothing ahead of me but *Herries*." Nothing ahead, certainly, but an almost incredible amount behind, for at this moment he had beaten his previous record, having no fewer than *five* completed volumes awaiting publication—*Wintersmoon*, *Hans Frost*, *Anthony Trollope*, *Farthing Hall*, and a collection of his short stories old and new which he had assembled under the title of *The Silver Thorn*. "How splendidly copious your flow," Henry James had said to him years ago, and surely his old Master must now be applauding from the Shades.

Almost as if to test the truth of this supposition, Hugh attempted a little later in the year to call up that mighty spirit from the vasty deep. Of this, his most interesting and exciting venture into Spiritualism, he recorded:

Most remarkable day. Down in the morning with Ethel [McKenna] to Mrs. Leonard's. An ordinary little suburban house, ordinary little woman like a housemaid. No humbug. If it was not H. J. who spoke to me, and it was out of my consciousness, still I had great happiness from it. Remarkable about the ink-bottle. Still of an open mind but greatly touched.

Back at the end of January, Hugh met with a stroke of good fortune. Since the arrival of Harold, the position of Douglas Chanter in the household had become a little difficult: Harold had taken over some of his duties, and there was not room for two chauffeur-companions. On the other hand Hugh was fond of Chanter and unwilling to send him away. Now happily they heard of a job in the Society of Authors, which Chanter took over soon afterwards. Thereafter Harold was in sole charge. "I'm afraid of nothing when he's there," Hugh told his sister.

During the first half of February he undertook a brief lecture tour in Scotland and the North of England. After the Liverpool lecture he "walked down to the Mersey and thought of twenty years ago when I was a trembling miserable oaf in the Mission to Seamen." A break of two days at Brackenburn inspired him to add a few pages to the journal. After mentioning the recent death of Thomas Hardy and giving a somewhat fanciful account of his own meeting with him, Hugh proceeded to dismiss Hardy as a *talker* and went on:

Of all the literary men I've known Jack Priestley is by far the best talker— and he only when he's in the mood. Henry James took too long to say everything, although there were splendid things when they came, like his remark to me about Schuster and Claude Phillips, when they'd been gassing for hours, that "they spread a continent of talk around them—a perfect Holy Land."

Conrad never said anything very interesting in his last years; he was too preoccupied with money and gout. He was only thrilling when he lost his temper and chattered and screamed like a monkey. George Moore talks more *nonsense* than anyone I know, as when he told me that "Anne Bronte was the only genius in that family." But it's interesting nonsense. Beerbohm Tree at the Garrick at supper was a magnificent talker, improvising like a great artist. But men like old Birrell, for instance, greatly reputed, are in their old age terrible bores. People are unexpected. I overheard Aldous Huxley talking to Beresford once about why he wrote the novels he did, and it was like a schoolgirl enthusing about her pet rabbit. Arthur Benson used to be good when he was thoroughly malicious. He picked out his friends' weaknesses like plums out of a pudding and ate them greedily one by one.

By far the best now is Gosse, who when he talks of Tennyson, Browning, Gissing, etc, is thrilling. His imitation of Gissing's proud shyness, of Browning dining out thirty nights running and proposing to any girl who happened to be around—all very splendid. But why is it the good things are always the shabby mean ones? An old question with no answer.

As soon as the tour was over he hurried back to London to watch the final rehearsals of *A Man with Red Hair* at the Little Theatre. It was the first time he had heard his own dialogue spoken aloud in public— for *Robin's Father* in its acted form had been much more Besier than Walpole—and he found it both gratifying and exciting to see the creations of his brain given three-dimensional life on the stage, and to hear, after so many years, the names of Maradick and Treliss brought back so vividly to life. Benn Levy had made a first-rate job of the dramatisation, the cast was excellent, and Charles Laughton presented Hugh's "exact conception of Crispin." The dress rehearsal took place before an audience on February 26 and "went perhaps pretty well, but I was miserable. An old man next me snoring throughout the evening." However, the first night passed off smoothly, the critics were impressed, and though the play only ran for two months it achieved a considerable *succès d'estime*, if not *de scandale*.

In March there occurred a tiny incident which illustrates sharply how insensitive Hugh, himself hypersensitive to every word and deed, could be to the feelings of others. In his diary it is described as an "evening with Cazalets and Wodehouses. Such a silly play that Ethel W. and I laughed, which irritated Plum." While P. G. Wodehouse writes:

He had a curious blind spot about other people's feelings, due, I have always thought, to a super-selfconsciousness. I remember him taking a party of us to a theatre, where we had seats in the front row of the stalls. The play turned out to be pretty bad, and I can remember still my agony as Hugh suddenly started to apologize to us for bringing us to such a rotten show—at what seemed to me the top of his voice. He appeared quite oblivious to the fact that the actors could hear all he was saying.

On his forty-fourth birthday *Wintersmoon* was published and he recorded the Piccadilly flat "so full of flowers that it's like an actress's boudoir." This was by no means unusual, since Hugh loved always to have his rooms filled with flowers. Carnations were his favourites and for years, summer and winter, he had a weekly box sent from the growers.

Reviews of the book were all he could wish, and he would have been extremely pleased if he had known that a few days later William Temple, the future Archbishop of Canterbury, was to write to his wife:

Yesterday I finished *Wintersmoon*—it is immensely interesting. As far as it has a moral, it is in favour of the old-fashioned virtues; but I suppose the author would hate the notion that he had one at all. I have enjoyed it enormously.[1]

A month at Brackenburn devoted to *Rogue Herries* did much to restore his confidence in that immense work. "I must remember too that no one knows very much about the eighteenth century really, or only a few do. I can be venturous." By mid-April he was astonished to find he had written forty thousand words ("they seem to have come out of nowhere") and was also encouraged by the news that *Wintersmoon* had sold twenty thousand copies in its first month, not to mention forty-five thousand in America.

The volume of his daily correspondence began to worry him; "there is simply no end to it and I never get clear. So many of the letters are about nothing." The trouble was that he always insisted on answering every letter in his own hand: only in moments of illness or extreme crisis would he consent to use a stenographer. With mounting success his mail grew in proportion: at this period it was quite usual for him to receive forty letters by the first post, and it was his custom to answer most if not all of them before he began his morning's work on the novel. He had always looked forward to the postman's arrival, yet now he could write: "How little I once thought that the time would ever come when I should pray for no letters."

5

He was in no mood for London when he returned there at the end of the month, and soon he succumbed to one of those occasional bursts

[1] *William Temple, Archbishop of Canterbury, His Life and Letters*, by F. A. Iremonger (1948).

of nervous irritability which, amounting sometimes almost to brain-storms, continued to dismay and prostrate him all through his life. Usually they were occasioned by someone's chance remark, as had happened with Arthur Ransome and Jim Annand, but sometimes, as now, it was simply that he became "increasingly nervous all day, and by the evening I was really in despair, feeling that I couldn't stand either the flat or London, and that I must break everything to pieces." Years later he described the symptoms of these experiences:

I was suddenly submerged with one of those waves of passionate anger that are altogether childish, absurd and futile. I am fifty-five years of age and I have not yet outgrown them ... there is a chance word, a movement, a smile, and the blood has burst in my head like fireworks on the Fifth of November. I see nothing, hear nothing, feel nothing but a passionate flaming desire to destroy my enemy. Words pour from me. I say anything, lies, curses, accusations, insinuations, anything, anything, however rash and scandalous. A moment later it is all over and I am nothing but a fool, regretting a thousand things. Surely, surely, at *my* age? If only they were not so sudden, so unexpected, if they would but give me a little warning.[1]

He was still in the grip of his demon when, during the first week of May, he "gave the Femina Prize to Virginia Woolf. A *frightful* occasion. Rows of old female novelists glaring at me. I made a rotten speech. Everyone desperately nervous. Drinkwater went with me."

But out of this miserable occasion grew one of the happiest of all his friendships. After the ceremony Virginia Woolf asked him to dinner at her house in Tavistock Square, and a few days later he wrote: "Evening enchanting—with the Woolfs and Lopokova. It had a kind of fairy quality about it. I was diffident but Virginia encouraged me, talking about writing as though we were on a level!"

These are assuredly the accents of an essentially diffident man, and since Hugh has so often been accused of complacency and conceit, they may perhaps here be underlined. Running through all his friendship with Virginia Woolf was this note of genuine humility in face of her artistic genius. When *Orlando* was published later that year, Hugh declared in his journal that "it lights up all the cottage with its crystal shine. What a book! So English literature still lives." And in the mar-

[1] *Roman Fountain* (1940).

gin he added: "This marks the difference between genius and talent. *Orlando* is *all* genius. I have only a good talent."

So much for his opinion of her as a writer. As a woman he regarded her with a deep affection and with an awe which was almost reverential, as though she were a goddess or an oracle. Whenever he was going to visit her, or she was coming to tea with him, he would behave like a boy going to a party, taking immense pains with his appearance and bubbling over with excitement. He was immensely and genuinely flattered at being accepted even as an occasional visitor in the heart of the "Bloomsbury" intelligentsia, though always in a corner of his mind was the lurking dread that perhaps behind his back he was being laughed at.[1]

And Virginia Woolf, what did she on her side feel towards him? First, clearly, affection—the same kind of emotion which Henry James and Conrad and his other friends had felt in their time—for, as must by now have become apparent, Hugh was an intensely lovable person, who could, when he was in the mood, be enchanting company. And when he was with Virginia Woolf he was always in the mood. Then too she, who loved to look into and learn everything about the lives of every kind of person, immensely enjoyed probing for the minutest details of his life past and present, and as a talker Hugh was at his best in descriptive reminiscence. She was one of the few people who accepted him at his own valuation as a "real abnormal romantic" and he gratefully and delightedly responded.

On her death, which occurred only a few weeks before his own, he wrote in his journal:

I shall miss her all my life. There never has been, there never will be, anyone in the least like her. She was so distinguished that you felt she was made of some precious, shining, rare metal. She had immense dignity, reserve, aloofness, and yet was human, living, inquisitive. . . . I told her incidents of my life I have never told to anybody, not even Harold. Odd how I feel, with all my regret and indeed *anger* at her going, a faint relief because now I am safe again. No one shall ever know the things I told Virginia. I wonder how many others of her friends are in the same box? She had a genius for making one tell her things!

[1] Vita Sackville-West remembers that Hugh was "tried out" at a Bloomsbury party of Vanessa Bell's. He immediately realised what was happening and was liked for taking it in good part.

6

On May 15 *Anthony Trollope* was published, and Hugh was so encouraged by the favourable opinions of Priestley, and indeed of most
people, that he decided to carry out another idea which for some time
he had cherished—of making an anthology of his favourite passages in
the Waverley novels and prefacing them with a long critical introduction—"if I ever have time! But *what* fun life is!" Time was found
at last, and the book appeared four years later.

Two American visitors brought good news. George Doran reported
that the American sales of *Wintersmoon* had reached the impressive total
of seventy thousand copies, and Lee Keedick offered a fee of £1000
(which Hugh accepted) for twenty lectures to be delivered in the
States at the beginning of 1930. Encouraged by this intelligence, Hugh
travelled to Hamburg, where he spent ten days with the Melchiors and
attended his friend's début in *Otello*. "I am truly rewarded for my early
troubles," he decided, and to mark the occasion he purchased a Renoir
landscape for two hundred guineas and brought it proudly home.

When he reached Brackenburn, *Rogue Herries* "came flooding back
all day, and by evening had driven everything else of every sort from
my mind." But, alas, he had already arranged another foreign visit,
and by the end of June he was on a train bound for Reval in Esthonia,
once more deep in Proust, whom he so often chose as a travelling
companion. "I cannot ever tire of the wit and delicacy and beauty.
This seems to me the supreme achievement of the *feminine* mind in
writing. It is the other end of Tolstoy, who is completely masculine."

His week as the guest of the Esthonian Government at their National
Festival bored him profoundly, and less than ever could he understand
why he had left home. "Why do I do it? But these foreign trips give
furniture to my mind, I suppose." He had hardly got back to Brackenburn ("it smoothes me down like a bird's wing") and begun Part II of
Rogue Herries, when who should arrive but Sinclair Lewis and his new
wife Dorothy Thompson. Hugh had attended their wedding in the
Savoy Chapel in May, and now they were exploring England in a
caravan and gathering impressions which were later used in *Dodsworth*.
By the time Hugh had shown them the beauties of the neighbourhood

it was August and time for him to set off in the car with Harold for a month in the south.

Harold was by now a first-class driver, but even his massive imperturbability was shattered when he once, on Hugh's orders, attempted to teach him to drive. There is a degree of anxiety by which even the most resolute of nervous systems is prostrated, and when Harold had with some difficulty regained the wheel, they agreed that Hugh was temperamentally unsuited for driving, and the subject was not mentioned again.

Now they drove first to Clemence Dane's house at Hunthay near Axminster in South Devon, where they stayed a week, and Hugh wrote "the best bit of my life . . . describing the killing of the witch." Of his hostess he wrote in his diary: "What a fine generous creature she is, how genuine and sincere! I should never have known her if I hadn't come here." She was indeed all he claimed for her, and much more besides. In many ways she and Hugh were very similar in character and interests: both were warm-hearted, generous, and full of creative energy; both were immensely industrious and cared fervently for their writing. Reading was a common passion, and it is only questionable which was the more appreciative or the faster reader. Later, when the Book Society was in full swing, and the Selection Committee deluged with proofs of forthcoming books, guests in their respective houses reported that it was a common occurrence for either of them to take half a dozen proofs up to bed, and to come down to breakfast next morning having mastered the lot and prepared to be examined on details of all six plots: nor did either of them suffer from insomnia. Indeed, the enthusiasm of these two fervid and catholic advocates of literary talent might well have brought the deliberations of the committee to a standstill, had it not been for the steadying influence of its remaining members.

From Hunthay Hugh and Harold drove on to Cornwall, where they spent a happy sunny holiday at Penberth near Land's End. Worry about his diabetes (he had again forsaken his diet) and his eyes, which had been troubling him, disappeared in the laziness of sun-bathing and attempting to swim. Harold, who it will be recalled was an expert swimmer, for years taught, or attempted to teach, the elements of the business to Hugh, but it proved almost as unsuited to his temperament as driving a car, and though he often believed he had mastered the technique and claimed to have proceeded some distance out of his depth, it seemed to others that, unless Harold was close beside him, a few rather frantic strokes marked the limit of his achievement.

And all the time his appreciation of and affection for Harold grew steadily: "This afternoon he was perfect, with a sweetness and tenderness through his imperturbability which no one else alive has"; and again: "Sometimes I feel that things are *more* than I can manage. The general unfairness and the weakness of my own character. Then H. C. comes along and sees me through. . . . No question but this has been the best week of my life. . . . I really know now beyond any discussion what are the best things in life." More and more indispensable did Harold become, so that quite soon Hugh disliked being separated from him even for a few days.

7

The McKennas came to stay at Brackenburn during September, but neither their agreeable presence nor anything else could stay the advance of *Rogue Herries,* "buzzing like a bee in my head. If only the outside world would leave me alone for a bit! How can I contrive this? What can I do to escape letters and people?" But, except at moments of high creative pressure such as this, he did not truly want to escape them, would indeed have soon turned melancholy had he succeeded (as he so easily could) in doing so. So he compromised by deciding that, visitors or no, he would keep strictly to his working hours, as Elizabeth did at Chalet Soleil.

After breakfast at 8.30 he wrote letters for an hour and then worked uninterruptedly at his novel. After luncheon he would read or walk, or talk to his visitors, or go for a drive in the car. He never worked after luncheon except when the excitement of finishing a book drove him on, but so quickly did his pen cover the paper, without pause or hesitation, that in those few morning hours he accomplished more than most writers could achieve in a whole day. His stories had usually been working themselves out in his head for a long time before he began to

write them down, and the only notes he made were in the form of a
fairly full synopsis of each novel in a notebook, giving chapter-titles
(which were often changed when he came to write them) embellished
with red initial-letters and countless drawings of rabbits—the height of
Hugh's accomplishment as a draughtsman.

The manuscripts of his books were usually adorned in the same way,
and when they returned from the typist he would have them richly
bound, each in several morocco volumes. One or two he gave away—
Mr Perrin to the Fitzwilliam, *The Old Ladies* to the Bodleian—and one,
The Duchess of Wrexe, he sold to an American collector for £150. The
rest stayed at Brackenburn and in Piccadilly, where they stood round
him in brightly-coloured rows, to remind him of the countless hours
of bliss he had devoted to their composition.

At times he would worry about his inability to revise what he had
written, but cheered himself by remembering that Scott had often
written almost as fluently. In 1931 he said in an interview he gave to
Louise Morgan:[1]

> I don't revise much. In fact, I don't revise at all. It goes down, and there
> it stays. I was rather alarmed about this at one time. Galsworthy showed me
> a manuscript of his that was just black . . . I went home and scratched out
> masses of sentences, and rewrote them no better than they were before. Then
> I gave it up . . . I have the manuscript of *The Fortunes of Nigel*, with not one
> word changed in it. And I have a James Payn manuscript covered with
> revisions.

Just now he could scarcely spare time to correct the proofs of *Farthing
Hall*, so closely did *Rogue Herries* grip him. One day he "got absolutely
caught into the episode of the Prince, so that when I had to break off to
go into Carlisle it was like waking physically from a dream." He became so interested in the lesser actors in his drama, especially one called
Deborah, that he felt he "could write a novel about her easily, or indeed
about any of the other minor characters in this book. . . . It fills out like
a balloon and is rich like a plum cake." By the end of September, after
nine months' work, half the book was finished.

While Hugh was writing, Harold would tinker with the car, and in

[1] Published in *Everyman*, 4 June 1931.

the evenings cut out and stick into large scrapbooks any articles, reviews, or photographs which had caught Hugh's fancy in the newspapers. These scrapbooks make fascinating reading today, besides
providing illuminating sidelights on Hugh's tastes and interests. The
latter were at this time enlarged to include a man whom he believed
to be a local genius, an uneducated Cumbrian with literary inclinations
called J. M. Denwood. He had been a poacher and was famous for his
knowledge of local verse and ballads, which he purveyed at fairs and
other bucolic gatherings. Encouraged by Hugh he launched out into
prose fiction, and his first novel, a tale of a Cumberland poacher called
Red Ike, was later (when it had been knocked into shape by S. Fowler
Wright) foisted by Hugh on to the Book Society, with discouraging
results on the membership. Now Denwood paid his first visit to
Brackenburn, and Hugh thus described him:

Genius + Idiot + Peasant. The Genius showed me the stars, the Idiot said
he was a Necessitarian over and over again, and the Peasant locked his bedroom door. Altogether rather disappointed, and understand why the
Labour Party don't move faster.

Later and less difficult visitors were the Brett Youngs and Priestley.
As always Hugh rejoiced in Priestley's company, and together they
read aloud some more of Hugh's early diaries, laughing "to burst,
rather cruelly, at that earnest young man." When Hugh recorded this
episode in his journal he added: "But as a matter of fact this diary of
twenty years later is just as priggish. It's the devil of a period this to be
self-conscious in, and the only way to escape is to see oneself as an
absurd anxious-eyed chimpanzee wondering which way the next nut
will fall." On October 16 *The Silver Thorn* was published, and reading
through its stories, which covered most of his writing life, Hugh noted
in his journal that "some of the bits about other people are amusing,
but *all* the bits about myself are priggish and silly."

8

In October he spent a week-end with the Cazalets, and the accident
of talking on the same day with two of the most remarkable English-

men alive prompted him to attempt one of the more elaborate and successful set pieces in his journal:

KIPLING AND WINSTON

Seeing them both on the same day—a nice autumn Sunday down at the Cazalets', Fairlawne—and having a chance of being alone with them gives them a good opportunity of contrast.

Kipling at Fairlawne is like a little gnome. All sorts of people about. The Athlones—she with her funny old German governess who says not a word but suddenly breaks out once with "Ach, Thomas Mann—he's a splendid writer" and looks across the table scornfully at Kipling as though she'd like to tell him how inferior she thinks *he* is. And J. H. Thomas suddenly putting his arm confidentially through mine after lunch, although he scarcely knows me, and chuckling: "You're a novelist. Well, keep your eye on me, my boy, for I'm your next P.M. 'Ow's that for a prophecy?" And then catching Kipling's arm and chuckling in *his* ear some rather dirty joke about Labour Gentlemen of the Bedchamber. Not that Kipling cares in the least about any of them. He is kindly, genial, ready apparently to be friends with anyone but keeping all the time his own guard.

I asked him at luncheon whether he approved of censorship (a propos of this tiresome stupid *Well of Loneliness*). No, he doesn't approve of the book. Too much of the abnormal in all of us to play about with it. Hates opening up reserves. All the same he'd had friends once and again he'd done more for than for any woman. Luckily Ma Kipling doesn't hear this—but she's had her ear at *his* keyhole for so long that, without hearing anything, she nevertheless suspects and turns her dull eye on to me as much as to say: "Now the moment you're tiresome you *go*, so if you want to stay with him you'd better behave." Nor do I blame her. She's a good strong-minded woman, who has played watch-dog to him so long that she knows now just how to save him any kind of disturbance, mental, physical or spiritual. That's *her* job and she does it superbly.

All the same he manages to tell me all about my short stories [*The Silver Thorn*]. He's read them, he really has. Likes especially *The Tarn*. "By Jove you *are* hard on parsons," he says and manages to leave a pleasant tingle in my cheeks.

He does this, I fancy, with everyone. He's endlessly kind and endlessly reserved. His black eyebrows, which today jut out like furry rocks over his eyes, keep guard. When I tell him later that we were all amused about his mistake over Jane Austen and Scott,[1] he jokingly defends it, but she doesn't like my telling him of it and gives me another warning look.

[1] In his poem *Jane's Marriage* Kipling made Sir Walter welcome Jane in Paradise, whereas in fact she died fifteen years before he did. Kipling later revised the poem.

He really, I think, has no vanity. He's a zealous propagandist who, having discovered that the things for which he must propagand are now all out of fashion, guards them jealously and lovingly in his heart, but won't any more trail them about in public.

He walks about the garden, his eyebrows all that are really visible of him. His body is nothing but his eyes terrific, lambent, kindly, gentle and exceedingly proud. Good to us all and we are all shadows to him.

"Carrie," he says turning to Mrs. K, and at once you see that she is the only real person here to him—so she takes him, wraps him up in her bosom and conveys him back to their uncomfortable hard-chaired home. He is quite content.

Winston is quite another matter. "Tiny" [Victor] Cazalet took me over in the afternoon to his country mansion. I went in some tremor because the times that we've met he has been anything but amiable—grumpy, hunched and silent.

We found him building a wall of a garage at the bottom of the garden. He was in a dirty shirt and brown workman's trousers. He grunted at us and patted his bricks and mortar. Then as he walked up the garden Cazalet told him about Rothermere's labour views. Winston grunted again, muttered: "Well, what does he *mean* . . . etc, etc." More of R's views on taxation: "Yes, we might take it off *beer*. On the other hand . . ." Then suddenly, bringing us opposite a bright pink wall most of which he's built himself, rises to real animation—"Now *there's* a wall. Beautiful. And it's going to spread as far as this. Nice colour, isn't it? All that I built myself!" Then, his eyes sulky again, grunts once more: "We might take it off *beer* of course."

He takes us round the garden and we come to the little lake on which there are some wild-fowl and two black swans majestically floating. Very beautiful, the little lake in the evening faintly green under the shelving lawn, and then ebony black, small pink clouds floating over the wood. He's hugely proud of the two black swans. He calls to them and they, seeing he has no food, move away from him disdainfully. They are as egoistic as he and understand him perfectly. He enjoys their egotism, is fond of them for it.

We move up to the house. I say a few things but he doesn't listen at all, sulky again because he is thinking of Rothermere. Inside the house, which is very pleasant, smells nice, old panelling, dark passages, up in his room he gives me a stiff whisky and soda.

Over his writing-table there is Sargent's drawing of his mother. "There's a fine thing! She was like that! Wasn't she grand?" He is entirely changed. All the sulkiness is gone. I ask to see his paintings. He's like a schoolboy, shy

and stiff. Says they are all away, at the bottom of the garden. But they aren't.
They are all here stacked behind a bureau. So he drags them out, secretly
pleased. And they are alive and interesting, especially some chalk heads.
Lots of colour in the skies, Riviera scenes mostly. I praise some and he is
entirely modest, saying he's never had time to learn and never will have.
And I wonder to myself, would I have seen anything in these if they'd been
painted by Mr Snooks of Clapham? Yes, I would. They have vigour,
energy, personality. He's like a friendly schoolboy now, not because he
likes me but because I've turned his mind to things he's happy about.

He picks up Morley's war apologia and breaks into a flaming account of
the war—August 4th incidents. How Morley and Burns, had they waited a
day or two, would have been all right, but they wouldn't wait. How Lloyd
George nearly waited but just caught the last bus. How he had the Turkish
ship confiscated and, if war had been averted, would have certainly been
imprisoned for doing so.

Not that he would have cared for prison, you can hear him thinking. He's
the real adventurer now and ought to have a cutlass at his belt and a red cap
on his head. I like him greatly thus, but he's not very reassuring as a Minister
of our dear country. He's the king of the schoolboys and loves to be.

He takes us downstairs to the dining-room where, over the sideboard, he
has painted a picture of bottles, glasses and cigar-boxes—a very vibrating
lively picture. The bottles greet him as friends.

Then we go. He gives me a friendly goodbye but before I'm in the road
he's back into his piratical schemes again.

"Yo ho, Yo ho, and a Bottle of Rum!"

8

In London Hugh lunched with Granville Barker, bought two
Epstein drawings, spoke at a literary luncheon, and entertained to
dinner his old friend M., the lady to whom he had once proposed, and
her husband. Recording the occasion in his diary he wrote: "She's the
woman for me!" His old friend Percy Anderson was dying in King's
College Hospital, and Hugh paid him several visits, though he doubted
whether the old man recognised him. It had been arranged that Sickert
should paint Hugh's portrait,[1] but before the day of the first sitting
another meeting took place which was to have far-reaching results.

The American Book-of-the-Month Club was already a flourishing

[1] The artist had agreed by telegram: YES OF COURSE I WILL DO WALPOLES PORTRAIT I AM
GRATEFUL TO HIM FOR RECOGNISING THAT MY PAINTING IS ILLUSTRATION SICKERT.

concern, and Arnold Bennett thought it would be a good plan to start something of the kind in England. He enlisted the support of A. S. Frere (then Frere-Reeves), a recently appointed director of William Heinemann Ltd, the publishers: he in his turn enrolled Alan Bott, editor of the *Graphic*, and later Arthur Barker. They obtained financial backing and then set about looking for a Selection Committee to choose the books for them. Bennett favoured a committee of one at a salary which they could not afford, so he regretfully withdrew.

Frere had met Hugh at Elizabeth's as long ago as 1921, and they had met and corresponded at intervals in the years between. Now, in May 1928, Hugh replied to a letter from Frere: "I think the Book of the Month Club suggestion is most interesting and I would of course love to have a finger in it if it comes to anything; also I am proud to be asked to be Chairman . . . I hope though that you will get names on the committee that will reassure the public, people who are not cranks nor like to drive always in the direction of a special clique." By October plans were well advanced, and on the 26th Hugh attended a meeting in London at which he formally accepted the Chairmanship of the Selection Committee of the Book Society, as the concern was then named. The remainder of the committee, chosen by Hugh in consultation with the others, were Priestley, George Gordon, Clemence Dane, and Sylvia Lynd. The first Book Society choice was published in April 1929.

Meanwhile the Sickert portrait was begun.

Oct. 28. To Sickert to be painted. The old man very charming, beautiful eyes, soft voice, very gentle with sudden irascible obscenities. Lunched at his funny house without carpets, sitting-room with a roughcast wall, a Greek head and Tintoretto drawings. He most amiable, sweet, clever. She a little quiet mousy Frenchwoman.

Oct. 29. To Sickert again. He did nothing whatever, complaining of the light. It's no use my being fussed by this. He's apparently going to take weeks and weeks and I must just endure it.

When the portrait [1] was finished Hugh elaborated his impressions of the painter in his journal:

---

[1] There are two portraits of Hugh by Sickert: this one, which Hugh bought and bequeathed to the Fitzwilliam Museum at Cambridge; and another, also an oil-painting but dated 1929. This was presumably painted entirely from photographs and memory, and is now in the Glasgow Art Gallery.

Thinking of Sickert . . . he isolates himself utterly from everybody, even his little Oriental-faced wife.

It is not at all that he is hermit-like or scornful of life. Far from it; he is eager to hear anything about life at all—morals, furniture, personal habits, colours, games—but his personality is so entirely of its own and so distinctive that he makes a *world* of his own. A world that has all its own laws. For instance he tells me every day that he prefers Gene Stratton-Porter's *Freckles* to *Madame Bovary*—a more important book he thinks. It tells you about a little girl having her hair cut and about butterflies, things he doesn't know so much about, whereas he knows *all* about the Bovary woman.

He makes some things clear to me about portrait-painting at which I've always wondered. Why, for instance, portrait-painters should be such copyists. Why must Kelly, Orpen, etc, spend endless hours in making their sitters hang on distressfully to get the buttons, sleeves, etc, correct? Having got the spirit of the sitter in a drawing or two, surely they've got everything and can paint the rest as they please *when* they please. So Sickert does his little drawings, takes a photograph, and then the rest is *"his"* affair," not at all the sitter's.

Wandering about his studio (which is dirty, tumble-down Camden Town, Charlie Peace, pubs and cabbage) with his little grey peaked beard (grown since his illness), his most beautiful eyes (his eyes blue and affectionate, his forehead of a fine, noble, unstained whiteness), without a collar, an old grey suit with sometimes a black cap on his head, he walks like a sick man (he will not, I think, live much longer) and chuckles and laughs at almost everything. He is most affectionate, always wanting to give one something, takes nothing seriously, is French in his lightness, German in his love of food, Camden Town in his love for his boxing cabman, Regency in his love of Bath, the old London streets, and artist unselfconsciously all the time.

His complaint is that English contemporary artists know nothing about anything, and you feel it to be true when in a quarter of an hour he makes a drawing that is full of drama, irony, suggestion—a novelist's drawing. He sees all life in an iron bedstead or a jerry or a tea-pot. When the photographer comes in he is sharp and autocratic, impatient, obviously will stand no nonsense from anyone. He has some of the charming, unfeeling courtesy of Conrad. He is courteous by tradition rather than feeling. His house has bare boards on passages and stairs. The drawing-room is charming with walls as the painters left them before they put on the paper, covered with white blotches, a black pedestal with a carved head and (he says) some Tintoretto drawings the only wall adornment, on the mantelpiece a Greek marble head with a broken nose and some silver-tinsel ornaments. His study is a howling wilderness.

He trots about, his black cap on the side of his head, his body bent like a becoming-old man, courteous, ironical, gentle, interested. He talks of his work because he *must* make money, very grateful to Wilson [1] who he says "has saved his old age." Life obviously has no point at all for him except as giving opportunity for the artist of putting it into terms of art. He forgets everything else. If he likes you (and he likes me—feels me serene and tranquillising) there's no end to his kindness and generosity. But it's only so long as you have some relation to art that he remembers you.

8

In November Hugh made a new friend, who seemed a likely provider of that intellectual companionship which he still lacked, for Harold who gave him so much often lamented his own lack of higher education. This was Baron Erik Palmstierna, then Swedish Ambassador at the Court of St James's, and Hugh found him "very intelligent, very honest, very good-hearted." Now too at a luncheon party he met A. E. Housman: "Quiet little man with an apparent sneer due to his moustache, but I liked him greatly and could get on with him I think. Not at all alarming. Great sense of ironic humour." Then came a dinner at the Woolfs' and "on to Vanessa Bell's—Clive Bell, Duncan Grant, Francis Birrell, all most amiable. They denounced Hardy and Lawrence and we discussed perversion." After the *Well of Loneliness* case this was a favourite subject, and a few days later at dinner Arnold Bennett "ardently defended the liberty of the abnormal." Hugh had been one of many leading writers who attended the court to give evidence of the book's literary merit, but the magistrate, Sir Chartres Biron, condemned it without allowing them to speak.

After a week-end with the Galsworthys, Hugh drove to Canterbury to attend the enthronement of the new Archbishop. He sat with Buchan, Masefield, Holst, Newbolt, Vaughan Williams, and William Nicholson, and enjoyed it immensely. There followed a week-end with Vita Sackville-West, during which they paid a visit to the poet Dorothy Wellesley at her lovely house Penns-in-the-Rocks and "talked all the afternoon in a manner to give any worthy magistrate a fit! Happy evening before the fire. I am very fond of Vita. There is something beautiful in her personality." With her next day Hugh broadcast for the first time—a debate on "The Position of Women Today."

[1] R. E. A. Wilson of the Savile Gallery.

Brackenburn and *Rogue Herries* were waiting for him, and directly he arrived the book began to "flow like milk and honey. Ought it to or not? I can't help it." On the eve of his departure for Edinburgh he "wrote to Macmillan outlining my plans for the next seven years' writing. Never felt so full of bursting energy."

But as soon as he arrived in Edinburgh diabetic symptoms returned and he felt "ninety years old with an ache everywhere." Nevertheless he spent "a most happy Christmas Day. In the morning Father preached a really remarkable sermon, clear, concise and vigorous. Wonderful old man!" On January 4, his diabetes persisting, Hugh was for the first time injected with insulin, and although he believed this to be only a temporary measure, it soon became his daily portion.

Back to Brackenburn for the final burst of *Rogue Herries*. Once again the last chapter "wrote itself and decided just how much it should be and I had nothing to do with it." The end came on the evening of January 11. "The moment I'd finished I rushed up to the house and gave Harold a dig in the stomach." Then they celebrated in the kitchen on Oxo and brussels sprouts—all the diet permitted—and Hugh confessed to a "strange feeling of thrilling excitement." The usual emptiness and depression did not follow the completion of this book. For one thing, he now knew he could carry out his four-book scheme without its overweighting him. Indeed his mind immediately leapt still further, and beyond the four he glimpsed yet another quartet of novels, which should carry the history of the Herries family from the sixteenth century to the point where *Rogue Herries* began. But first, before even he tackled the next volume, now tentatively called *Lovers under Skiddaw* but later renamed *Judith Paris*, another story came "lustily kicking about in my mind, all Piccadilly, crowds, and corpses, with a *jolly* villain this time and no sadism!" This was *Above the Dark Circus*, originally called *Death Above the Circus*, which he began a couple of months later.

Now he was ready for a holiday, but before he left Brackenburn he took down his journal again and wrote:

I don't want to be confident, and certainly not complacent, but I think Virginia has shewn me—especially in *To the Lighthouse* and *Orlando*—how to get over a little of my sententiousness and sentimentality. I think both

Hans Frost and *Herries* show the beginning of this change and I must develop it farther without surrendering too *much* to her influence. Oh, I'll be a writer yet if I keep on at it! Anyway God be praised for giving me so thrilling an occupation! I might have been a bank clerk! No, that never, having no talent for sums. But something equally monotonous. However, I suppose nothing is monotonous if you're made for it not to be. And equally everything is if, etc.

A propos, I've just been re-reading Hewlett's *Letters* for my little notice in the D.N.B. and *there* was a man who was always asserting that he was something which just at the moment he wasn't. I remember how upset he was because he thought I'd plagiarized him in *The Duchess of Wrexe*—I don't remember how or why. How I looked up to and envied him at that time and was bewildered that so great a man should consider me for a moment. So I felt when Kipling talked to me of *The Silver Thorn* the other day. And yet I'm not exactly a modest man. But I felt then I could never come near *The Queen's Quair*. I don't feel that any more, but I do feel that I could *never* touch *Kim* or *My Lord the Elephant*. How futile though these comparisons are! All you must do is to squeeze your personality out to the very last drop. Never mind the kind of personality it is. Be thankful if you have any to squeeze.

9

At the end of January Hugh took Harold for a holiday in Spain. At Barcelona they found the Melchiors, and soon Hugh was "back in my old opera life—up all night, jealousies among the singers, general confusion at the Opera House and so on." However, he enjoyed Melchior's début in *Tristan*, despite the behaviour of the audience who talked and laughed all through the performance.

When they reached Madrid, Hugh went straight to the Prado, where "the central Velasquez room sent me to my knees. I was so excited I was trembling all over." And so on to Granada, Seville, Cordova, Toledo, and Segovia. During the trip he wrote two short stories, *The Last Trump* and *A Carnation for an Old Man*, to which he gave a Spanish background. Whenever the hotel had a wireless set he refreshed himself by listening to the cricket news from Australia.

The flat was "looking lovely" when they arrived back at the end of February, and London seemed to Hugh "like an old family nurse welcoming one home." *Farthing Hall* had just been published and was receiving what to Hugh were surprisingly good notices, there were the proofs of *Hans Frost* to correct, and as he read the book again he was charmed by it. Altogether everything was at its happiest when, on the evening of March 4, he received a telegram to say his father had died suddenly earlier in the day. The Bishop had been very lively at luncheon, had done some visiting afterwards and received some callers. Dorothy came in to find him struggling for breath, and after only an hour's illness he died. In much distress Hugh caught the night train to Edinburgh.

Next day he wrote:

Dorothy of course perfectly splendid, and the kindness and sympathy of everyone wonderful. It is marvellous to think that the old man has not left one enemy behind him, or even an approach to it ... D. and I rather desolate. When the last parent goes it is a lonely business. Consoled myself with *Quixote* and began my melodrama, *Death Above the Circus*.

He was much pleased by the *Daily Mail's* obituary notice, which was headed "The Kindest Person in Scotland." March 7 was "the most lovely day I ever remember in Edinburgh," and as Hugh saw his father buried beside his mother at Dalmahoy, "the rooks flew cawing over our heads, the ground was covered with snowdrops. A perfect end to a perfect life."

Hugh took Dorothy back to Brackenburn with him for a few days, and later in the month wrote a little about his father in his journal:

One of the most remarkable things about him was his patience under suffering. After his eyes went wrong in 1915 he must have had not only the constant fear lest he should go blind but perpetual daily irritations from limited vision, but no one ever heard him utter a word of complaint or impatience. Then last year when he had to lie in bed for six weeks he was marvellous, always cheerful, never thinking of himself.

Another outstanding thing in him was his "guilelessness." This exasperated practical people who had to work with him, especially Scotchmen, but he literally couldn't believe evil of anyone, thought everyone meant all they said and had an invincible optimism about everyone and everything. This developed in him after my mother's death and her "gentle irony" was removed.

He was quite unpractical. He had for instance no anxiety about Dorothy, although he knew that he would leave her practically penniless. He never once spoke to me of her future.

His religious faith was complete. He was as sure of heaven as though he'd been there, which I sometimes thought he had.

He had no æsthetic sense whatever. He enjoyed a good novel but otherwise art was nothing to him, morality everything.

He understood good simple people like himself—anything at all twisted, abnormal, confused, in personality was altogether outside his ken. He was obstinate as a child would be, sometimes very obstinate. But he was a saint with a child's capacity for enjoyment, trust in people, and belief in fairy tales.

CHAPTER TWENTY

QUITE ENOUGH GLORY

I

BACK to London went Hugh for most of April and May. He had quite given up trying to write his novels in the Piccadilly flat, but he found that the Cheevers's home at Hampstead provided sufficient peace, and there he now continued *Above the Dark Circus*. The Melchiors were in London, and he saw a good deal of them, and of his new friend Palmstierna. He made his first solo broadcast, saw his first talking film, and had "an entrancing tea with Virginia Woolf—simply delightful. She at her very sweetest, worried as to why Bennett and Squire thought her 'not a good writer.' How everyone worries!"

Soon the strain of continuous social activity began, as always, to get on his nerves, and it was a relief to go down to the country for a visit which gave occasion for another set piece in the journal:

I had a very amusing Whitsun at Galsworthy's—Bury near Pulborough, Sussex. A really lovely house, pearl-grey stone fronting lawns that run straight to the open fields. The house inside clean and shining like the inside of a nut, with the colour of his nephew's pictures which are all over the house. Everything artistic, Liberty fashion and a little beyond it. Very like a special edition of one of John's own books.

Delightful time—only other guests Arnold Bennett and his lady. Amusing to see John and Bennett together. They really have nothing whatever in common except their good hearts. Whatever else may be said about them this remains—that they are absolutely good-hearted men, as Kipling and Shaw are but Wells and Moore are not. I don't mean that Wells wouldn't do a kind act—he continually does many—but malevolence lurks there, just as impotence checks Moore.

The two dramatic moments were when Arnold stammering (not through modesty) related to Ada Galsworthy how for his journalism he had first 1/- a word, then 1/6, then two bob, and now half-a-crown—this "hymn of praise" rising higher and higher in his shrill uncouth voice, ending in a scream—"*And*—I *like* it—journalism—I *like* it!" While Ada grew paler and paler with horror at this commercial triumph and tried hard not to mind.

The other was when J. G. was beaten at croquet, which he couldn't bear. He has no sense of fun about games. They are battles for Galsworthian justice, and when he was beaten it was as though we had acted *Justice* all over again, there on the lawn in front of his eyes.

But he is a *dear*—gentle, honest, just, trying not to be self-conscious about his terrific present success. It was hard for Arnold to hear at dinner that a first *Man of Property* had just fetched £138 at Hodgson's, but he bore it well—only made a brief allusion to *The Old Wives' Tale* and told me my tie was the wrong colour for my suit.

We were all very happy together. They are two fine, generous, warm-hearted men, but all the time I saw Arnold a guttersnipe cocking snooks from the street at J. G. magnificently dining inside his elegant country-house. I love them both.

2

June was the month for Brackenburn. Hugh had promised the Woolfs to write a volume on "The Historical Novel" for the series of literary monographs which they were publishing through their own Hogarth Press. But after ten pages he decided that he "couldn't and wouldn't do it." This decision was an immense relief to his mind, and when he learned that the Woolfs were not angry he began joyfully to correct the proofs of *Rogue Herries*, "which I'm racing through far faster than I ought to be. I never see things in proof as I ought to see them." This was true enough, but luckily his publishers and their printers had learned to be on the alert.

When the proofs were finished, Hugh spent the "evening quietly with H. C., writing dedication for *Herries*, he knows to whom." It reads "For a Trusted Friend and in love of Cumberland." Then he returned with renewed vigour to his melodrama.

After a day in Edinburgh hunting with his sister for a house for her to live in, and some days in London, where he bought a new Alvis, Hugh set off with Harold for Cornwall. Ten days at St Buryan were filled with writing and bathing, and while Harold fished, Hugh sat on the rocks, "read an old Anthony Hope and was back in my child-hood—or back in any case in Polperro, where I used to watch the water seethe over the rocks just like this." *Above the Dark Circus* was finished in Cornwall, leaving its author free to "let *Judith Paris* go ahead now and fill my brain as much as she pleases." He also wrote a short story called *Tarnhelm*, and with Harold paid a brief visit to the Scilly Isles. He was sick on both journeys, but he saw enough of the archipelago to make him decide to return one day.

3

In August Hugh travelled to Sweden. After being fêted in Stockholm by reporters and others, he went on to stay with the Palmstiernas at Rättvik, but although he was fond of his hosts and partly occupied in writing a play called *The Limping Man*, he was soon "longing for home. Nothing can prevent it—and I was peevish with Erik on an afternoon walk. What *is* ever to cure me of these irritable outbursts? Shall I *never* learn? All my friends have to suffer from them, but none suffer so much as I myself do."

The homeward journey was pure pleasure. London found him "too happy for words," and Brackenburn "too excited almost to eat." Once he got home there was no restraining *Judith Paris*, of which the first words were written on September 5. With his brother and sister he picnicked at Watendlath, and was once again so enchanted by the tarn and its cluster of houses tucked away in a hollow of the hills, that he decided to set part of his new story in its romantic seclusion.

The publication of *Hans Frost* was marred for Hugh by the death in France of Ethel McKenna. She had been like a second mother to him and had helped him so much, particularly after the war when he had badly needed it. She had loved him dearly, and he who so desperately wanted everyone to love him had lost a great ally. "I feel this terribly," he wrote. "No one will ever be to me again what she was. I felt quite lost all the evening." He remembered too how, in his impulsive way, he had begged the McKennas to come to Brackenburn whenever they liked, and how, only a few months ago, they had proposed themselves and he, not wanting to be disturbed, had told Harold to send a telegram saying he was ill and they couldn't come. Harold had refused point-blank, and now Hugh's grief was tinged with gratitude that his waywardness had not been allowed to prevent this final meeting. It was probably meditation on his loss which caused him shortly afterwards to write to Frere:

I *know* that some sort of education is going on in my non-material self, and that that education is for a purpose. I know too that the more I lose myself in other people the happier and freer I am. A fine thing for an egoist like myself to say, but I *detest* that grubby, selfish, greedy personality of mine ... I'm as greedy, as vain, as sensual, as ever I was, but I do perceive more clearly than I did that there is a much finer, wiser, freer personality waiting to shake its mean friend off. And love *does* last—both love and friendship. Of course every relationship with every person has its own separate history—but one or two get finer and finer, I discover.

The reviews of *Hans Frost* were the best since *The Cathedral*, but more exciting than any of them was the news that Virginia Woolf had read the book. It was, she wrote,

a book I've enjoyed and read through so quick there was no holding me. We had visitors and I had an article to write and books to read, and there I sat reading on and on and on, pretending that I would only read one more chapter and then stop; and then arguing that as there were only five more chapters I might as well finish. . . . I made all sorts of notes in my mind as I went along. There's a magnificent passage on friendship. There are odd peeps and all sorts of queer vistas. There's a general radiancy and Christmas tree lustre that I find adorable. Of course, I don't think it's *my* world. I feel rather like the wife of a Pre-Raphaelite painter who has blundered in among Rubens and Matisse and cocktails and champagne and sits in a simple grey dress looking very odd and causing some alarm to her hostess. Poor woman! She is a little out of place I agree, but enjoys herself hugely, and trots off home to tell her husband, in their rather austere flat, all about it. Many, many thanks; I did enjoy myself hugely, she says.

4

In London for a week, Hugh met his new American publisher Nelson Doubleday, who had now absorbed Doran's firm, and whom Hugh described as "a big very handsome fellow, kindly, good I should think." At a party given by Doubleday at the Savoy Hugh met and talked with Edgar Wallace, whose daughter Pat was later to marry A. S. Frere and become one of Hugh's few women friends.

Almost immediately after this he spent a week-end with the Brett Youngs at Esthwaite. For his daily work at *Judith Paris* they gave him a room with a view, and he found it so stimulating that he determined to provide himself with one at home. Another room built on top of the library seemed to be the solution, since this would give him a prospect of the lake and the hills beyond, above the trees which now obscured so much beauty from his eyes.

Athene Seyler and Nicholas Hannen were welcome and favourite guests at Brackenburn. "I should like them to stay for ever," wrote Hugh with more feeling than truth. He worked every day at his novel: "Today I killed David. I was quite sad and unhappy about it. He had been my friend for so long. I felt quite done up after writing of his death." And the same day, to his sister: "I am sure no one gets so much pleasure in the actual writing of novels as I do!" Perhaps it was partly his constant change of scene in London and elsewhere which brought him back each time with a fresh zest for writing and prevented his ever tiring of this most enjoyable and rewarding of pastimes.

5

There followed six weeks in London—the usual frantic mixture of engagements, so exciting and wearing to live through, so difficult to chronicle smoothly. Twice he saw the Italian heavyweight boxer Carnera: "Marvellous sight. Grandest human being I've ever seen. Will never till I die forget Carnera rising after being downed, like a wild beast, and rushing on Stribling. A terrific scene." He visited Mrs Belloc Lowndes and later had "tea with Virginia, Vita, young Rylands. Heavenly! Virginia discussed whether she was real or no. Decided no. James Stephens at the Lynds'. Said he believed only in cocktails and God." Hugh sat for a bust by his old friend Jo Davidson, and at a luncheon party met Lloyd George: "Such a genial and charming old rogue. Characteristically talked about my books as though they were his only reading. In great spirits, mouth and eyes twinkling, hair shining."

It was almost time for Hugh's American lecture tour, but he managed to fit in two days at Brackenburn and a night in Edinburgh, where his sister was moving into her new house in Corstorphine. They both spent their first night there, Hugh in the room which he furnished and thereafter occupied on his Christmas and other visits.

Before he sailed on the *Berengaria* on Christmas Eve he took out a power of attorney in Harold's name: in later days Harold was to hold

Hugh's cheque-book and manage many of his financial affairs for him, but now the plan was something of an experiment. The voyage was remarkable only in that during it Hugh read straight through all the historical plays of Shakespeare. They docked on New Year's Eve: there was a crowd of friends on the quay to welcome him, headed by Gene Tunney who "received me with open arms amidst loud cheers of the populace." Another year was over, and when Hugh came to compile the list of his First Fifteen friends, the Melchiors held second and third places. Above them, in the position he was never afterwards to lose, stood Harold Cheevers.

6

The lecture tour followed the accustomed pattern, but twenty lectures seemed nothing after the seventy of his last visit, and Hugh bustled through them with his usual bouts of homesickness. Old friends he saw in plenty—Hergesheimer at West Chester, Jo Davidson in Brooklyn, Jim Annand in Toronto, and Robert Frost at Amherst, Massachusetts. "What a gentle, quiet and beautiful man. We seem to fit exactly and talk with the greatest ease. . . . Frost dominates everything. We are friends."

He made friends too with Thomas Wolfe, the new literary genius, and with Thornton Wilder when they conducted two public debates in Washington and New York. "I was oratorical and Wilder said some lovely things. Found him a charming companion. He is a real student, loving erudition, culture, quiet backgrounds. In the middle of his kindliness there is a little core of sharp malicious humour. He watches everything." At Dearborn, Michigan, Hugh watched a cæsarean operation and made a flight in an aeroplane provided by Henry Ford. But before long he was once again on board the *Berengaria*, and on March 14 he reached London.

7

Four days later came the publication of *Rogue Herries*, "the most important book of my life so far." The advance sales were good, but it seemed unlikely that the book would ever overtake Priestley's *Good Companions*, of which more than seventy thousand copies had already been sold. Priestley was one of the novelists of whose success Hugh might well have been jealous—as at different times he was jealous of Compton Mackenzie and Brett Young—but his affection for Priestley remained always too deep and too genuine for the intrusion of baser sentiments.

By the time Hugh reached Brackenburn a week later scarcely any reviews of his book had appeared and he began to worry dreadfully. If this book failed, would he ever have the courage and the energy to persevere with its three sequels? As he awaited the verdict of the critics, the situation assumed in his mind the stature of a crisis, nor was his anxiety allayed by "an atrocious review" by St John Ervine in the *Daily Express*. "He dismisses it with contempt. A review like this is irritating because one feels that there is personal feeling behind it, as there is always with him. In the last two years he has been irritated by me—some personal vanity." This fresh fuel cast on the still-smouldering embers of his memories of that incident long ago at York Terrace caused Hugh's indignation to flare up again. Anyone who could dismiss his masterpiece with contempt must be actuated by personal malice. From now on he had no doubt that St John Ervine was his enemy.

On the larger issue he was soon reassured. Reviews all spoke of "magnificence," "the grand tradition," "excellent descriptive writing," "thunderingly alive," "the pure stuff of romance, never old, never worn, never tarnished," "Mr Walpole's great achievement." Particularly acceptable were the closing words of Gerald Gould's notice in the *Observer*: "Even as a pageant, without these episodes which are in fact exquisitely moving, the thing would both impress and dazzle; but what most endears it is the recurrent poetry, the voice of romance calling again and again, and murmuring from Glaramara's inmost caves." And to swell the chorus of praise came a letter from John Buchan saying: "It is my clear conviction that it is the best novel published in English since *Jude the Obscure*."

All this sent him back to *Judith Paris* with a renewed faith in his ability to carry out the whole gigantic project, though in his diary he still sometimes censured himself: "There is undoubtedly too much of the schoolboy in my writing. I sometimes think that all my novels are written by 'Jeremy,' " while to Turley he admitted that in the Herries books "I've been for the first time in my life what I really am—a little boy telling stories in dormitory."

8

A week in Edinburgh produced a new friend in William Maxwell, head of the printing firm of R. & R. Clark, who printed all Hugh's books for Macmillan. He took an immediate liking to Maxwell's kindliness, literary interests, and conversational charm, declaring "he is just my man."

May in London was always an exhausting time, and once more Hugh felt "like a man who is trying to keep twelve glittering balls in the air at once." The Book Society committee now met regularly at the Piccadilly flat and waded with much friendly discussion through the multitudinous seas of forthcoming books. Hugh and Clemence Dane, with their wide sympathies and ready appreciation, could find good reasons for choosing most books, while Priestley and Gordon kept the balance by favouring no choice at all, and Sylvia Lynd, serene and witty, steered a middle course. When Hugh failed completely to get his own way he would ease his feelings by deciding in his diary that "women seem to me to have no critical opinions at all. They are all a flux of personal feelings and prejudices"—a judgment which only too often could be applied to himself, presumably when the feminine element in his nature was predominant.

Week-ends with the Galsworthys and the Cazalets made pleasant breaks in the London round. For the rest, with Frere he watched the Australians' first match at Lord's, with Palmstierna he attended the first night of Paul Robeson's *Othello*, he took tea with the Woolfs, and with E. M. Forster, where he met Forrest Reid. By the middle of June *Judith Paris* was half-finished at Brackenburn, and the new rooms above the library were almost completed.

There followed a fortnight's lecture tour in the principal cities of Germany, with a visit to the Oberammergau Passion Play ("not very impressed") on the way. In Berlin he lunched with the pianist Artur Schnabel, and in Munich:

Had lunch with Thomas Mann at his house. His wife, a translator, and a lady there. He was very friendly but speaks almost no English. Is rather the Prussian officer to look at and gives the appearance of reserve. But he laughed a lot. At the end he became still more friendly, asked about my lecture and said that what we really wanted was a New Humanism in letters. He is a man, I should think, imbedded in his own mental world.

The tour ended with a brief visit to Switzerland and a lecture at Zürich. Hugh was delighted to find the room packed and among the audience the great psychologist C. G. Jung. "He's like a large genial English cricketer! We sat together at supper after and he delighted me with his hatred of hysterics." Hugh gave him some of his books to read and was justifiably pleased when Jung wrote: "I think *The Prelude* [*to Adventure*] is a psychological masterpiece."

As Hugh travelled home he hailed the Allied evacuation of the Rhineland as the end of the last war, whereas in fact the occasion might more accurately have been signalled as the beginning of the next one. In questions of political prophecy, which filled so much of his journal in later years, he was usually wide of the mark.

9

At Brackenburn the new rooms were ready, and Hugh spent happy hours arranging and rearranging them: "Few pleasures in the world," he wrote, "are greater than this." The last great organisation of his books took place. They were disposed, according to authors and subjects, between Piccadilly, the main building of Brackenburn, and the three rooms across the lawn—the main library, a little half-landing, and the big new writing-room above. For a year or two all went well, new acquisitions filled up gaps in the right shelves, and Hugh could lay his hand on almost any volume he required. But towards the middle of the thirties all the shelves were full, and the pace of his book-buying increased. Books began to lie along the tops of other books, or were piled in heaps on the floor, or bulged over into the lavatories. By the time of his death, when the collection numbered something like thirty thousand volumes, no one (not even Hugh) knew exactly what he had got or where any particular book was to be found. Often

two or three copies of identical books—sometimes rare and costly ones
—were discovered in different places.

In the intervals of book-sorting and furniture-moving Hugh read
Rogue Herries again, in order to "bring the two books together. I see
now clearly that it is a 'ghostly' book. All the characters are shadows,
but it has a strange and original atmosphere of its own—after Hawthorne a bit. I could review that book!" Priestley came to stay and
was "at his most enchanting, a boy with a man's wit and observation."

Now cricket, which as a schoolboy he had abhorred, began to interest
him more and more—the watching of it, that is—and the presence of
the Australian touring team increased his enthusiasm. At the end of
July he watched the Manchester Test Match until the game was rained
off, and he was determined to see the final match at the Oval, though
this would mean curtailing his already brief holiday with his brother
and sister. "The Oval match doesn't *start* till the 16th," he wrote to
Dorothy; "I'm sorry I'm cracked on this cricket, but so it is, and if I
gave it up and went off with you, I'd be so restless that I wouldn't be
much fun. I can restrain most of my vices, but not apparently this one."
And sure enough, August 16 saw him at the Oval, although he was
compelled to go on crutches, having twisted his ankle a few days before
—"not," he told Turley, "that I write with my ankle as many think!"

10

Towards the end of August Hugh took Harold for another holiday
in France and Spain. They spent a fortnight bathing and lazing at
Sardiniero near Santander, but they found it hot and noisy, with too
many flies, fleas, barking dogs, and radio sets. Nevertheless Hugh wrote
a short story—"not bad, but how much better all my things would be
if I wrote them six times over—but alas I can't."

Re-entering France, they visited Biarritz, Périgueux, Tours, and the
Châteaux of the Loire, reaching London again in the third week of
September. There they found an immense pile of correspondence,
with which Hugh dealt in a single day at Hampstead, claiming to have
written almost eighty letters with his own hand. "This correspondence
is becoming rather silly. It means that I never write a decent letter and
hardly have time to think one out!"

II

One evening soon after their return Hugh went to a theatre, "then home and, half-undressed sitting on my bed, picked up idly Maugham's *Cakes and Ale*. Read on with increasing horror. Unmistakable portrait of myself. Never slept."

The character in the book called Alroy Kear is a novelist and lecturer, a time-serving eupeptic careerist, a literary and social snob, determined at all costs to build himself up into a grand old man of letters. Next day, still "dreadfully upset" about the book, Hugh rang up Priestley, "and he says that Maugham absolutely denies that it is me. But how can he, when there are in one conversation the very accents of my voice?" For days he could think and speak of nothing else. "Still fussed over the book," he wrote two days later, "although less than before. I think the thing will be a scandal, and I cannot imagine what Maugham was about in publishing it. It will amuse my enemies though."

As always he would have found it difficult to say exactly who these famous enemies were. There was of course the benighted Ervine, who had mocked at his masterpiece, and perhaps one or two other reviewers whose ideas had not always been his. All successful writers are the envy of less successful ones, and although Hugh had never deliberately wronged anyone, there must be some whom he had slighted, as in the old days he had in turn offended Mrs Charles Marriott and Lady Lovelace. From among such groups a likely set of enemies could speedily be conjured up. And now this cruel caricature of Maugham's had placed a dagger in their hands.

No wonder he was worried. As he drove up to Brackenburn he was "still brooding over the Maugham book. It is the stab in the back that hurts me so. He has used so many little friendly things and twisted them round. Anyway it's a caddish book." Not even *Judith Paris* could hold his attention, though he struggled on with it each day. A letter of protest to Maugham produced this answer:

My dear Hugh,

I am really very unlucky. As you may have seen I have been attacked in the papers because they think my old man is intended to be a portrait of Hardy. It is absurd. The only grounds are that both died old, received the O.M. and were married twice. *You* know that for my story I needed this and that there is nothing of Hardy in my character. Now I have your letter. I cannot say I was surprised to receive it because I had heard from Charlie Evans [1] that Priestley and Clemence Dane had talked to him about it. He told them that it had never occurred to him that there was any resemblance between the Alroy Kear of my novel and you; and when he spoke to me about it I was able very honestly to assure him that nothing had been further from my thoughts than to describe you. I can only repeat this. I do not see any likeness. My man is an athlete and a sportsman, who tries to be as little like a man of letters as he can. Can you really recognise yourself in this? Surely no one is the more complete man of letters than you are and really you cannot think of yourself as a famous golfer and a fervid fox-hunter. Nor is the appearance described anything like yours. Nor so far as I have ever seen do you frequent smart society. Frankau or E. F. Benson might just as well think themselves aimed at and Stephen McKenna much more. The only thing that you can go on is the fact that you also are a lecturer. I admit that if I had thought twice of it I would have omitted this. But after all you are not the only English man of letters who lectures, but only the best known; and it is hard to expect a writer, describing such a character as I have, to leave out such a telling detail. The loud laugh is nothing. All big men with the sort of heartiness I have described have a loud laugh. The conversation you mention in California has entirely slipped my memory and I cannot place it in the book. I certainly was not conscious of repeating it. Really I should not have been such a fool. I certainly never intended Alroy Kear to be a portrait of you. He is made up of a dozen people and the greater part of him is myself. There is more of me in him than of any writer I know. I suggest that if there is anything in him that you recognise it is because to a greater or less extent we are all the same. Certain characteristics we all have and I gave them to Alroy Kear because I found them in myself. They do not seem to me less absurd because I have them.

I do not think for an instant that there will be any reference to this business in the papers, but if there is I promise you that I will immediately write, protest and vehemently deny that there has ever been in my mind any thought of portraying you.

> Yours always,
> W. S. Maugham. [2]

Hugh wrote a short answer, signed himself "Alroy Maugham Walpole" and commented: "That's that." But it was not, for next day he

[1] Managing Director of William Heinemann Ltd, the publishers of *Cakes and Ale*.

[2] In a new introduction to the Modern Library edition of *Cakes and Ale* (New York, 1950) Maugham admitted that he had Hugh in mind when he devised the character called Alroy Kear, but, not wishing to hurt Hugh's feelings, did all he could to cover up his tracks.

was upset all over again by a very favourable review of the book in *The Times Literary Supplement*. "People really do like malice and cruelty in their literature these days. I cannot see that it is a good book, or in any way convincing, but I, of all people, am in this case prejudiced!"

Gradually his distress became submerged in the pleasure of finishing *Judith Paris*, but when at the end of October he took up his journal, which had lain idle for almost a year, his reflection turned immediately towards the same unhappy occurrence:

My self-consciousness this year has leapt up like the damned trees that hide the lake from my window, and then has suddenly jumped down again. My publicity has incredibly increased. It may be the Book Society; it may be that the men above me are growing older; it may be simply the result of pegging along steadily for twenty-five years, but there it is. One result is that the jealousy from which I've always suffered has increased. My power through the Book Society has undoubtedly increased it. My detractors are certainly delighted to proclaim that it is the result of deliberate self-advertisement. There they are altogether wrong, for I have never all my life long sought for a single piece of self-advertisement and have avoided many that I might have had. But the opposition comes in the main from irritation at my exuberance. This is quite natural. I should feel the same at the like in someone else.

But here comes the great consolation to myself; that there is nothing at all to be done about it. I may curb my various excitements or disguise them, but out they will come! My zest is something quite independent of myself. It is roused before I know it—by a cloudy sky, a book, a picture, a theatre, a friend, food, anything you please. It grows stronger in me as I grow older.

However all this reached a climax for myself when this summer I read Maugham's *Cakes and Ale*. The shock of that for a day or two was tremendous. It was far clearer to myself than it could be to anyone else that Maugham had taken the portrait from myself. (All the same it was *very* clear to a lot of my friends!) There were countless little points that were known especially between us, that he had chaffed me on in the past. He wrote me a letter of strong denial saying that he had never had me in mind, and I've no doubt that the picture was composite. But there it was. Of course it was unpleasant for a while to think of all sorts of people going gleefully about laughing at me and it, but that soon wore off. Nor apparently has there been so much of that as I expected, and in any case the habit of writers to put people into their books has now become so general that it is little thought of.

But the real crux of the matter was my examination of myself. Was there real justification for that point of view? After real examination I could clear myself on most of the criticism, although I can quite clearly see that I might appear just such a figure to a cynic and an uneasy unhappy man like Willie. It is his nature to be deeply sentimental and to be revolted by his sentimentality, so that he turns on anyone he thinks sentimental. He said himself that he had taken much of the figure from himself, and I think that is true.

The great result of all this year's criticism and comment has been, however, to make me very much less self-conscious than ever before. I see that both my work and personality create two exactly opposite reactions in others and that they will always do so. I have no business therefore with anything except my own conscience, my own effort to do my work as well as I can, and the opinion of my dozen close friends. So let it rest.

12

Meanwhile *Judith Paris* plunged on; "as though on a galloping horse I am borne on to the conclusion." William Maxwell came for a short visit, but Hugh wrote on, helped by pouring rain which kept him indoors, and on October 17 the book was finished. Half his great project was accomplished, and immediately the outline and the title, *The Fortress*, of the next volume fell into his mind. He had resolved not to begin it until Christmas Eve, so to keep his hand in he spent two days writing what is by common consent his most successful short story, *The Silver Mask*, "which I dreamt entirely, title and all, from the first word to the last." [1]

A month in London, during which he saw H. G. Wells, Osbert Sitwell, and other friends, and "took Palmstierna to *my* play, *The Barretts*. What an excellent thing Besier has made of it," was followed by a fortnight's lecturing all over England, and then by another ten days in London. He made friends with the painter Keith Baynes, decided to publish *Above the Dark Circus* in 1931, lunched with Karsavina and Benjie Bruce ("two of the staunchest and firmest friends I have if only I would recognise it") and with the novelist G. B. Stern, "whom I like better and better. I think she is a really good sort and my kind of writer."

In Edinburgh he corrected proofs of *The Circus*, and rewrote its culminating chapters. On Christmas Eve he duly began *The Fortress*, the first book to be started in his sister's house, and as he compiled the

---

[1] A dramatisation of this story by Edward Chodorov and George Haight called *Kind Lady* was produced in London at the Lyric Theatre in June 1936 with Sybil Thorndike in the leading rôle.

list of friends and finished off his diary for the year, his mind turned
back to the old worry:

The hardest business of the year was *Cakes and Ale*. That for a while was
unpleasant, but I am sure that Maugham did not do it deliberately, and it
can only do me harm if my character is like that. And if it is like that,
then the sooner I pass out the better.

13

On the first day of 1931 Hugh drove home to Brackenburn, and
some words written in his diary that evening illustrate perfectly both
his childishly mercurial temperament and the endless pleasure he
obtained from a thousand tiny details. "C. B. Purdom in *Everyman*
says that *Herries* is one of the twelve permanent books of 1930. Bed
happy."

He needed an exact site for the house from which *The Fortress* was to
take its name, and with his friend and neighbour Helen Fox he drove
out to seek one. After an "enchanting" drive they came to High Ireby
up beyond Bassenthwaite, and there to his amazement, in exactly the
position he wanted, stood the decaying wreck of just such a house as
his imagination had already pictured. He could scarcely believe that he
was looking at it for the first time, but there it was, "uncurtained, hens
roosting on the windows, and Uldale all befrosted in the valley below,
while the sun on Blencathra's snow was fiercely blazing." Some time
later, when Marguerite Steen came to stay, Hugh took her over to
see the place. It was dusk when they arrived, and as they stole a little
way into the overgrown garden they heard mysterious noises. It only
needed a ghost to complete Hugh's romantic picture, but as he and
Marguerite began to embroider the theme, Harold pointed out that
the noises came from a horse, which was wandering loose in the
undergrowth. "It's no use, Hugh," said Marguerite. "We shall never
see a ghost while Harold's around."

At the end of January Hugh set out on a six weeks' cruise to the West
Indies. He did not enjoy it very much: the sea was rough, and he
missed Harold badly. However, he read his way solidly through
Monypenny and Buckle's *Life of Disraeli* and wrote the whole of his
own dramatic version of *The Cathedral*. He arrived back to find *Above*

the Dark Circus just published,[1] and although he had been worrying about its probable reception, even as he had worried about that of *Portrait of a Man with Red Hair*, his fears once more proved baseless and the reviews excellent. Moreover Macmillan reported that *Rogue Herries* was still selling "hundreds a week" a year after its first appearance. In celebration Hugh bought his fourth Epstein bronze. Money spent on himself always brought feelings of guilt, and he generally excused himself by thinking up some event or anniversary which called for "celebration."

When he got back to Brackenburn he started work again on *The Fortress*. The history of the Herries family had now reached the 1830's, and as background-reading Hugh chose Greville's Memoirs and *Nicholas Nickleby*. This last particularly delighted him and he decided part of its author's secret lay in the fact that "Dickens never grew up. I believe the best authors never do." It was a comforting belief.

14

On March 28 Hugh was distressed to learn that Arnold Bennett had died the night before. "I like to think that he was especially sweet and friendly the last time I saw him at the Reform. He was, however, very jealous and critical of me the last years." Hugh travelled to London next day to attend the memorial service at St Clement Danes: "Everyone there—Beaverbrook, Barrie, Wells, Pinero, Ervine, Drinkwater and so on. No young people. Saw Virginia Woolf." Memories of his old friend and former patron continued to fill his thoughts, and when he got home to Brackenburn he attempted a brief character sketch in his journal:

The death of Arnold Bennett was followed by a torrent of comment. That was natural, for he knew every journalist in London, liked them, and was liked by them. But there was hardly a worth-remembering notice among the lot. The best one of course Rebecca West's rather catty one. Her physical description of him—the stiff body (I read that he had a double

---

[1] Hugh had originally called the book *Death above the Circus*, but now he was furious with young Pinker for allowing it to be serialised in the *Evening Standard* as *Death Above Piccadilly*. To add to the confusion, the American edition was called *Above the Dark Tumult*.

rupture), the tuft of hair, the receding chin, bright inquiring eyes, the really awful stammer, the frown—all were there.

The commentators made him out to be a very happy man ("a boy delighted with his success" was their favourite description of him). Here I am sure they were wrong. He had of course his happy moments—he had a great capacity for realising at the moment that he was enjoying himself. One of the memories of him I like the best was when with Mrs Pat Campbell I attended a rehearsal of his Russian Count Pahlen play [1] (the first time I spoke to Charles Laughton). We went into Sloane Square for a cup of coffee and Arnold did a *pas seul* with his billycock on one side while Mrs C. (huge in black) chaffed the coffee-stall men.

But the right picture of him (Edward Shanks was the only man to spot it) s in the first hundred pages of *The Glimpse*—absolute autobiography as he was after his first success. He was, I think, immensely sensitive, a victim for years of insomnia and in some ways obsessed with material success. But he knew these weaknesses in his armour, fought them continually and didn't thank you if you reminded him of them. He had his picture of himself as he *wanted* to be, and you had to play up to that. He was very kind, very generous, so long as you didn't pierce that armour or damage that picture. He for instance never forgave Priestley (whom he thoroughly disliked), Frank Harris and Rebecca West (whom he loathed), Virginia Woolf, and some of the young, and I myself undoubtedly said something on one of my American tours (faithfully reported by Swinnerton) which he never quite got over. (Probably we're all alike in this same sensitiveness. The only difference is that some of us remember the gadfly, some forget.)

He could be charming, delightful. He could be frightfully bored and fearfully boring. He was always the provincial in London, just as his clothes, made at the best tailors' and very expensive, were always provincial. Last of all and first of all he had a certain fine nobility of character—one never forgot it even when he was most aggravating. All the critics are agreed that he will live by *The Old Wives' Tale*. Indeed it is interesting to reflect that if you took *Old Wives*, *Clayhanger* and possibly *Riceyman Steps* away he would be a novelist only of the third class. Nevertheless *Hilda Lessways*, *Anna of the Five Towns*, *The Card*, *The Glimpse* and *The Pretty Lady* are worth remembering.

As a writer and critic he was invalidated by having no glamour. He could not perceive it in others, which was why he saw nothing in Virginia Woolf. He had no sense of any world beyond this one. Everything in his view was bounded by bricks and mortar.

---

[1] *Paul I*, by Dmitri Merejkovsky, produced at the Court Theatre in October 1927 and financed partly by Bennett.

15

Back to *The Fortress* went Hugh. "I sit enchanted in the middle of it, like an old witch trying to keep my cobwebs in order. . . . Described a fox-hunt on the fells this morning and hope it was right. It felt vivid to me. . . . Whatever faults these Herries have, they can't be accused of thinness! And yet I have twice as much that I want to put in."

But the literary world would not leave him alone. A month or two earlier there had been published in America an anonymous book called *Gin and Bitters*, which was in fact a vicious and scarcely-veiled attack on Somerset Maugham. Gossips were quick to whisper that Hugh had written it in revenge for *Cakes and Ale*, and he had sent off an immediate disclaimer to Maugham, who had answered reassuringly.

Now the question of English publication began to loom, and the firm of Heinemann, as Maugham's publishers, sought to prevent the book's appearance on this side of the Atlantic. For this they needed Maugham's co-operation, which was not immediately forthcoming. So Frere sent Hugh a copy of the book to read and asked him to do his best to persuade Maugham to see reason. The irony of this situation was not lost on Hugh, and it is greatly to his credit that he made no capital out of it whatever. He read *Gin and Bitters*, which he thought "vile" though "very ably written," and he added: "The book simply bristles with hate. I figure as Mr. Polehue! When will all this end?" Then he sat down on April 20 and wrote this letter to Maugham—and it must be remembered that only six months before Hugh had been, as he believed, publicly pilloried by his friend:

My dear Willie,

    I do hope you won't think me impertinent in writing you this line. I've just read *Gin and Bitters* and I do most earnestly beg you to injunct its publication in England. It is a *foul* book (I have no idea who wrote it save that it's a woman). If there were any doubt for whom it is intended that would be different, but already there have been paragraphs in the press here making it quite clear. It will undoubtedly make a sensation and although you may not care what anyone says, it is a disgrace that people who don't know you should have that impression of you. Heinemann (even if they publish it, which I hope they won't) can't prevent the general odiousness that will follow the publication. I am sure you can obtain an injunction. I'm willing to give evidence on your behalf to any extent and I'm sure many others would. The book is *foul* and you ought to stop it. I'm not writing this from hysteria or any motive but one of real and true affection for yourself. I do beg you to stop the thing as I'm *sure* you can.

> Yours affectionately,
> Hugh Walpole.

In the end all was well and the book was not published in England. Hugh's action in writing as he did to Maugham may have been influenced by various motives—wanting to prove that he bore no ill-will for *Cakes and Ale*, that his distress had been exaggerated or was at any rate over; thinking perhaps that if he spoke out publicly on Maugham's behalf he would tend in future to be less certainly identified with Alroy Kear—but these are conjectures. The simplest explanation, and the most overwhelmingly probable, is that the letter was written without any *arrière-pensée* and meant exactly what it said. With Hugh, as with a child, passion was violent but short-lived. He was more quickly moved to enthusiasm, rage, despair, hysteria, than are most grown-up people, but once the fit, the mood, the moment was past, the sun shone brightly again and, all passion spent, Hugh's natural goodness shone out with it.

16

May in London was much as usual. Hugh found Virginia Woolf "full of curiosity and wit. Heard her praise *Sons and Lovers* more than I ever heard her praise anything." She introduced him to William Plomer, whom he "liked immensely. So unlike what one would expect. Strong, virile, manly, and sensible. He should be one of the fine new figures in English Letters."

Hearing that his Aunt Dora was in financial difficulty at Truro, he arranged to make her a small regular allowance, and at the same time offered to educate the son of a friend for three years at a public school. It is not known how many sons of how many friends were educated, without word said, at Hugh's expense, but it is safe to estimate that from now on there were never less than three at any one time, and often more. In addition to this he did immense good by stealth— helping people with gifts of money, with long letters of advice and encouragement, with introductions, and in countless other ways. For ten years he corresponded with Miss Mary Sparkes, a lonely old lady who liked his books. Occasionally he would drive to Kensington and take tea with her, while she in gratitude wrote him a quantity of long, wise, amusing, affectionate letters. Though the complete story of his benefactions will never be told, since none but he ever knew their full extent, there is ample evidence to prove that they were widespread and ever increasing.

The encouragement and assistance which he gave to writers young and old are easier to assess. "He has done more, I think, than any man alive," wrote Frank Swinnerton,[1] "to make modern English writers, some of them struggling, some active and unsparing rivals of his own, familiar to a wider public, both in the United States and in England." Letters of introduction to editors and publishers, advice of all sorts, countless prefaces and reviews—all these he gave freely and for many years. He was laughed at for it of course, but this kind of laughter never upset him. Perhaps he did praise too many books, but he preferred to risk that, rather than allow what seemed to him literary merit to pass unnoticed. Nothing was too modern or too old-fashioned to find favour with him. After his death Edith Sitwell wrote to his sister:

We are only three (my brothers and myself) of the many, many people to whom he has shown endless kindness, practical sympathy and help—and such a wide and generous understanding of motives, of aims, pioneer work, of everything that came under his eyes.

While Osbert Sitwell went so far as to write:

I don't think there was any younger writer of any worth who has not at one time or another received kindness of an active kind, and at a crucial moment, from Hugh.

In case these claims appear too sweeping, here is a selected list of writers from whom letters of gratitude were found among Hugh's papers: H. E. Bates, John Betjeman, Elizabeth Bowen, Louis Bromfield, Gerald Bullett, Joyce Cary, John Collier, A. J. Cronin, Cecil Day Lewis, Mazo de la Roche, Geoffrey Dennis, T. S. Eliot, C. S. Forester, Graham Greene, Neil Gunn, Christopher Hassall, Ernest

[1] *Swinnerton: an Autobiography* (1937).

Hemingway, Claude Houghton, Richard Hughes, R. C. Hutchinson, Christopher Isherwood, Rosamond Lehmann, William McFee, Dmitri Merejkovsky, Charles Morgan, Frederick Niven, William Plomer, J. B. Priestley, V. S. Pritchett, Frederic Prokosch, Vita Sackville-West, Ethel Sidgwick, Marguerite Steen, L. A. G. Strong, Dylan Thomas, Romer Wilson, Thomas Wolfe, Francis Yeats-Brown. The catalogue could be extended to fill several pages of this book. Ford Madox Ford, for instance, was so touched by the nice things Hugh had said about his books in America, that he dedicated the English edition of his essay *The English Novel* to him in a long introductory letter—but perhaps enough has been said to show Hugh's practical appreciation of his fellow-writers.

17

June was shared between Cumberland and London. *The Fortress* absorbed him in the north, his friends in the south. He bought three paintings by Duncan Grant, saw more of William Plomer, and presided with gusto at the Book Society meetings. It transpired that the author of *Gin and Bitters* was Mrs Elinor Mordaunt, and now Hugh recorded that she had been "making a fuss. Shall I ever be free of the *Cakes and Ale* controversy? I may certainly with my hand on my heart wish that W. M. had never been born."

At the beginning of July he unveiled a plaque to Arnold Bennett at Thorpe-le-Soken. This must have revived many memories, and even more were brought back three days later, when with Harold he drove to Polperro. There he stayed with his old friends and retainers, John and Annie, "sat in the sun by the lighthouse, read *Armadale*, and felt a young man again with everything before me." After a few days they drove on to Penzance, where Hugh spent £250 in Mr Bridger's bookshop, including among his haul Ackermann's *Oxford* and first editions of Pepys and *Paradise Regained*. Then they crossed to St Mary's, Scilly, where they spent a glorious fortnight of sun and sea-bathing. Harold became the "hero of the islands" when he "swam the pool under Piper's Hole, which no one has swum in man's memory." [1]

---

[1] William Plomer, himself a fine swimmer, used this incident as the basis for a scene in his novel *The Case is Altered* (1932).

In Scilly Hugh wrote the whole of the fifteen-thousand-word preface
to his anthology of Scott's novels, which was published as part of the
centenary celebrations in 1932, under the title of *The Waverley Pageant*.[1]
When he returned from his holiday he spent a week at the Malvern
Festival as the guest of Sir Barry Jackson. One night in the theatre he
"sat next G.B.S. who talked of Henry James."

On August 28 *Judith Paris* was published, with a dedication to
Priestley, and this time not even Hugh could find anything wrong
with the reviews—"all splendid. Not one unfavourable one." John
Buchan wrote:

What I love about the book is its richness, your enthusiasm for your
characters, and your passion for that beautiful countryside. We have so
many barren rascals writing today that it is a delightful thing to get God's
plenty from you. Judith seems to me to be as real and as fully realised a
character as my beloved Natasha in *War and Peace*.

Virginia Woolf was a trifle less enthusiastic:

I'm very much interested about unreality and *The Waves*. We must discuss it. I mean why do you think *The Waves* unreal, and why was that the
very word I was using of *Judith Paris*—"These people aren't *real* to me"—
though I do think, and you won't believe it, it has all kinds of qualities I
admire and envy. But unreality does take the colour out of a book of course;
at the same time, I don't see that it's a final judgment on either of us. You're
real to some—I to others. Who's to decide what reality is? . . . Lord—how
tired I am of being caged with Aldous, Joyce and Lawrence! Can't we exchange cages for a lark? How horrified all the professors would be!

Judith's first printing of twenty thousand copies was exhausted
within a fortnight, and Hugh was able to return to *The Fortress* with a
light heart. He made one of his chief characters, Adam Paris, come and
live in a cottage on Cat Bells, so that much of the scenery could be
described straight from his window. But he had been doing too much
all round, and one morning he "woke wretched—nervous, overstrung,
overtired. Felt like murder. This was complicated by masses of Book
Society proofs. So tired and bothered that when I sat at the writing-
table I couldn't remember my own name! However, as usual work
restored me to my senses."

[1] Its dedication reads "For Virginia Woolf who does not scorn Sir Walter."

Twice he went to London for a few days, but each time his book called him back to Brackenburn. On October 26 he "wrote nearly four thousand words of young Benjie's adventures in London. Whether good or ill I know not, for I wrote like a drunken man," and on November 1 the last chapter was finished after an almost uninterrupted burst of eight hours' writing. "Now I feel lost, empty and lonely," he wrote in his diary, "but thank heaven it won't be long before I can begin *Vanessa*. Then—after that—what *shall* I feel? It will be the beginning of my downhill in writing perhaps!"

A month in London, with all its movement, could not drive the Herries family from his mind, although he found time to buy quantities of books, to lecture here and there, entertain his new friend Marguerite Steen to lunch ("she is very feminine and as usual I got nervous"), and to attend a literary cocktail party given by a publisher, where he found "two hundred authors pressed together. Not a pretty sight!"

In Edinburgh on Christmas Eve he wrote the first words of *Vanessa*, and such was his absorption in the subject and his delight in its execution, that in the next fifty-six days he wrote no fewer than seventy thousand words.

Christmas Day was the occasion of a delightful gesture. As a surprise for his sister, apart from the expected present from her "wants" list, Hugh had bought her a new bright red motor-car, and after the midday meal a garage-man drove it up to the front door. Dorothy's delight was only equalled by Hugh's, and the day was a very happy one.

As the end of the year approached, Hugh decided, neither for the first nor for the last time, that it had been the happiest of his life, and added in his journal:

My only trouble in my writing is that, wriggle as I may, I'm definitely old-fashioned. Now I'd *like* to be modern. I'd rather be a male Hugh Walpole to a female Virginia Woolf than anything else on earth. How nice if they said: "This new novel of Hugh Walpole's *may* be very beautiful, but we can't be sure because we don't understand a word of it. However, we liked the passage about the silver snails and the moonlight effects on the water-beetles." I'd truly *love* that, and again and again I'm tempted to do a little book anonymously just like that. I believe I could.

Meanwhile I've read the *Rogue*, *Judith* and the *Fortress* straight on end, and old-fashioned they certainly are—verbose, over-emphasised, unreal in many places, sometimes very dull. But they *are* something—they have caught something definite out of both this place and me, and I think that people who come up here will read one or another of them for a while to come—which is quite enough glory for me. Who cares about glory anyway? Well, I do. I want to *prove* that my life's been justified. It has if there's a secret life as well. But is there? I increasingly believe there is, and from that all my happiness comes. And *if* there is that secret happiness, it is based on Love—no doubt of it. I love people more and more.

18

1932 was the centenary year of Walter Scott's death, and Hugh was forever being asked to write articles and make speeches—which he did with an almost religious fervour, though the successive celebrations grew wearisome before they were over, and he soon felt he had "done enough on Scott for a lifetime!"

Priestley left the Book Society committee and was succeeded by Edmund Blunden, who quickly won Hugh's heart with his modest charm. The change also caused a loosening of the brakes on Hugh's enthusiasms, for Blunden was neither so great a novel-reader as Priestley had been, nor so blunt and outspoken in committee.

Early in March Hugh left for another of his unsatisfactory foreign holidays. In the train to Marseilles he read Arnold Bennett's *Journals* and found them "most disappointing. Some amusing things but material, cocksure, and plebeian. Diaries and letters are dangerous things to leave behind one! . . . Touched by Arnold's childlikeness. I have the same thing, only mine is English Vicarage not Five Towns."

Tunis was his base for a week or so. He read and wrote and went on little expeditions. The ruins of Carthage provided an atmosphere where history, if little else, might reasonably bloom, and there on his forty-eighth birthday Hugh began the first of the four reminiscences which were later published as *The Apple Trees*. During these days he also wrote the whole of the pamphlet called *A Letter to a Modern Novelist* for the Hogarth Press. His homeward route was by way of Gabes, Palermo, Naples, Rome, and he reached London again early in April. Every time he re-entered No. 90 Piccadilly after having been abroad he was prepared for the worst news, whatever that may have been, and invariably remarked on its absence in his diary: "To the flat, where there was no ill news."

He bought three Sickerts in London, spent three happy weeks with *Vanessa* at Brackenburn, and then came south again to see his doctors. After making every sort of test, they decided that the diabetes could only be controlled by regular injections of insulin, and on May 15 Hugh began the routine which was to be continued for the rest of his life. Every day, morning and evening, he injected himself with a hypodermic in the thigh. At first he managed the affair clumsily and hurt himself, but before long he grew so skilful and accustomed to the procedure that it came to worry him no more than the twice-daily swallowing of a pill. Gradually he began to vary the prescribed dose according to his own idea of what was necessary. After eating or drinking something sugary and forbidden, he would take slightly more insulin than usual, and though this empirical method worked well enough for a time, its practice grew ever more erratic and in the end may well have affected his heart.

June was a busy month during which, as Hugh wrote to Frere, he "moved on from thing to thing and person to person like a blind man's collecting-box," and he was soon longing for his promised holiday in the Channel Islands. With the success of the Herries novels, even the solitude of Brackenburn began to be invaded by charabancs and admirers. "If I don't have my three weeks by myself in Sark I shall go mad," he wrote to a friend. "I am being pestered here by visitors who peer into my windows, invade my garage, discuss my looks loudly, and so on."

Hugh and Harold enjoyed their fortnight in Sark, but they decided that it was too "shut in and shut off" and that they preferred the bare, sandy beaches of the Scillies. Hugh wrote three more reminiscences for *The Apple Trees*, particularly enjoying the one about Henry James. Then after dashing off yet another article on Scott, he gladly went on with *Vanessa*. One day he was enjoying the proofs of a "John Buchanish" novel by George Blake, and on the morrow he ran into its author on the beach. George and Ellie Blake immediately became close friends: indeed their friendship was one of the happiest of Hugh's last years.

In Sark too he read James Agate's "ferocious attack on me in the

Express over the Hogarth Letter," but without great surprise, since the Letter itself contained a fairly ferocious attack on James Agate. Still, the old habit of Writing to Reviewers died hard, and Hugh could never believe that an unfavourable notice of one of his books was based on anything but personal dislike. To the protestations of critics that they didn't know him, let alone dislike him, and simply hadn't thought his book good, he replied with bland disbelief.

Now, in answer to Hugh's letter of protest, Agate wrote: "I wonder you can do that, attack me in *a book*—a tiny one but a permanent thing —and expect Puss not to scratch back." There were times when Agate was classed with Ervine as an enemy, but he was far too clever to allow this unsatisfactory state of affairs to continue. It is difficult to borrow money from someone who considers you an enemy, and at various times Hugh lent Agate a great deal of money.

It gave Hugh extravagant pleasure to know that his juniors liked his books, particularly the Herries ones, and to such a young friend he wrote from Sark:

I really was enchanted that you enjoyed *Judith*. I thought you probably too modern. But I have had a lot of letters from the young generation lately and it seems the tide is turning. The truth is that I have all my life been a cause of battle. My books have been either too wildly praised or too contemptuously condemned, and it is pleasant now to see, about some of the old books anyway, a much more temperate judgment. If I'd been able to keep my mouth shut all my life and lived under a beech tree in the New Forest cracking nuts at the birds, I'd be thought quite a pleasant old gentleman. I think when you've read all four Herries (if you ever do) you'll see how they hang together. They have every sort of fault—more humour badly needed, for instance—but they do, in the end, make one real romantic book of English social history.

There followed a few days in Cornwall with his brother and sister, the annual visit to the Malvern Festival, and then a week in rural Germany, whence he wrote to a friend: "Here I am with Melchior and his wife in his hunting lodge miles from anywhere. It is very quiet and peaceful and is just what I want. I am very well and it is all opera scandal and frogs in the pond and *Wiener Schnitzel*." That same evening they celebrated the publication of *The Fortress* by a Fest with lanterns hung in the garden, and when Hugh got back to London he was encouraged to find that most of the reviewers hailed the book as better than its two predecessors.

19

On the way to Brackenburn, they stopped at Doncaster to watch the St Leger. Harold backed the winner, and Hugh had his pocket picked—"£20 and precious papers. I didn't mind much." Doncaster was also the scene of a mortifying incident on one of their southward drives. Hugh, eager for reviews of his latest book, told Harold to stop at the railway station so that he could buy all the newspapers. When they got there Hugh rushed into the station while Harold sat placidly smoking in the car. Time passed but Hugh did not come back. Harold began to worry a little, but he knew better than to move. Eventually after two hours Hugh reappeared in a frenzy of rage. "Where the devil have you been?" Harold insisted that he had not budged an inch. Hugh refused to believe it, but when he had calmed down a little he realised that he had crossed to a bookstall on another platform, forgotten he'd done so, gone out on the other side of the station, and then searched for Harold and the car all over the town.

Now he went back to long days of work at *Vanessa* and evening games of backgammon, at which Harold began to win so regularly that Hugh decided they had better move on to chess. In September he ploughed through a stiff crop of Scott celebrations, culminating in the centenary itself—a dinner at Stirling, a service at Dryburgh, and a procession in Edinburgh where "I was the only one in a bowler." He met George Blake again and liked him better than ever: "He is no ordinary fellow—is kind, severe, honest, very business-like, and terrifically Scotch."

Marguerite Steen came to Brackenburn for the week-end, and so did another new friend Owen Turville, who lived in the West Indies but whom Hugh had recently met in London at a Promenade Concert. Of Marguerite Hugh became very fond: she was his type of woman—intelligent, uninhibited, amusing, and undemanding. He was able also to help her a great deal with her writing: once when she despairingly committed the manuscript of a complete novel to the flames, Hugh rescued it with his own hands and persuaded her to allow it to be published: she said afterwards that this was the turning-point of her literary career. He also persuaded her to come to London, and once when she had no suitable clothes for what he considered an important party, he gave her £25 to buy an evening dress. In 1933 she published *Hugh Walpole: A Study*, in which she treated him as a great romantic, and the Herries books as his finest achievement. The book gave considerable pleasure to Hugh and to his host of readers.

Now, as soon as he was alone again, Hugh settled down to finish *Vanessa*, and with it the last quarter of his *magnum opus*. It absorbed him utterly, and as his pen hurried over the paper he was probably happier than he had ever been before, more completely and consciously identified with his life's work. Three letters to a friend illustrate his shifting moods. On October 4, "I'm so in love with Vanessa's daughter who has suddenly appeared on the Herries scene that I can't bear to part with her, which I shall do in five chapters' time. What *am* I to do? There mustn't be a *fifth* Herries. I shall have to write a private book all for myself."

During the writing of these five chapters there occurred a minor crisis, and on October 21 he wrote: "I'm in a frantic state and have been all the week, for I suddenly saw that the Herries thing properly closed in 1914, and that the whole post-war business refuses to fit the mood and colour of the rest—so I've destroyed 50,000 words! Pity me!" The need for compassion, however, was short-lived, for by the 25th he was "sunk morning noon and night in *Vanessa*, and this week she'll be finished, the 50,000 words restored. I think the end will be rather pretty—like a blue ribbon and bell round an eighteenth-century lamb's neck."

Finished she was, the very next day, when the whole five thousand words of the last chapter were written between breakfast and supper. And so the great enterprise, which he had expected to take ten years and which had actually occupied almost five, was brought to a fitting end. He had to the utmost of his ability repaid his debt to the countryside which had taken him to its heart. He had done his best to fulfil "the only ambition I truly have—to be connected for some time to come with Cumberland," which he had declared was quite enough glory for him. And if the four books failed to satisfy him completely, he was at least not ashamed of them: he had put into them everything he had to bestow. The verdict must lie with posterity.

THE BRACKENBURN BOOK-LABEL
(*Gold on claret*)

BOOK SIX

THE YEARS OF PLENTY

What a life mine has been!—half educated, almost wholly neglected or left to myself, stuffing my head with most nonsensical trash, and undervalued in society for a time by most of my companions—getting forward and held a bold and clever fellow contrary to the opinion of all who thought me a mere dreamer.

Sir Walter Scott's Journal
18 December 1825

CHAPTER TWENTY-ONE

PERPETUAL CIRCUS

I

M OST writers would have taken a long holiday after so exhausting a burst of sustained work, but such was the vigour of Hugh's imagination, so insistent the stories piling up in his mind, that as he drove to London at the beginning of November he was already planning the new novel which he would start on Christmas Eve. There was plenty to distract him in the south; indeed he complained if there was not; "spent evening alone, which I never like doing in London. I'm only happy here when I'm busy every moment."

And soon he was, for in a few days rehearsals began for his own dramatic version of *The Cathedral*. The play was tried out at the Embassy Theatre, Swiss Cottage, where it opened on November 21 with Baliol Holloway as the Archdeacon and Francis L. Sullivan as Canon Ronder. All that day Hugh felt ill with nervous anticipation, just as in the old days he had suffered before Melchior's first nights. In the evening he sat in the theatre with Harold and his wife, and up to the end of the second act he made sure the play was a failure. But at the final curtain the reception was "immense," Hugh made a speech, the Press was unanimous in its approval, and the play was soon transferred to the New Theatre.

The year was not to die without a few final obeisances at the shrine of Walter Scott. At the end of November Hugh spoke in Edinburgh and then spent a night and a day at Abbotsford itself. "Deeply thrilled," he wrote in his diary. "I am to sleep in Scott's own bed. Writing this in room where Lockhart died. Dined in room where Scott died." All next day he was "haunted by W. S." Of all the festivities this was the one which moved and pleased him most. Certainly when it was over he could claim to have honoured in full the writer he had all his life loved and read the most.

The Apple Trees was published in a limited edition by the Golden Cockerel Press in time for Christmas, and to a friend who wrote appreciatively of it Hugh replied: "Agate does a marvellous notice of it in the *Express* today, and Ervine praised *The Cathedral* on Sunday. What shall I do now without my two enemies? I shall be as naked as Lady Godiva." Virginia Woolf also wrote appreciatively:

Of all literature (yes, I think this is more or less true) I love autobiography most. In fact I sometimes think only autobiography is literature—novels are what we peel off, and come at last to the core, which is only you or me. And I think this little book—why so small?—peels off all the things I don't like in fiction and leaves the thing I do like—you. Seriously, soberly . . . I do think this is a very charming, attractive book.

On Christmas Eve in Edinburgh he began the new novel, first called *The Spring Evening* and finally *Captain Nicholas*, and when in his diary he reckoned up his gross income for 1932 he found that it amounted to the best part of £10,000.

2

In January 1933 Hugh set forth on another cruise to the West Indies. While he was at sea he learnt of the death of George Moore, on which his sole comment was: "Very few English novelists senior to me now —Wells, Galsworthy, Kipling." Ten days later, still at sea, he heard that the number had been still further reduced by the death of Galsworthy, and this news moved him personally. He had always liked and got on with Galsworthy, who "has been always so very good to me." Later he wrote a short essay on his friend:[1] now he mourned his loss sincerely, though his immediate comment on this double blow to literature, as contained in a letter home, ran: "Poor Heinemann! Their two chief authors gone in a month. I can see Brett Young buying a new suit!"

The whole of February was spent blissfully in Jamaica. He was put up and looked after by Owen Turville and his wife: scenery and climate seemed to him paradisal: "This realises my childhood's dreams of the South Seas. I'm sure they can offer nothing finer."

---

[1] In a symposium called *The Post Victorians* (1933).

3

He was back in England by the middle of March, in time to open the Walpole Hall, which had been built in memory of his father, in the Precincts of St Mary's Cathedral, Edinburgh.[1] The publication of another collection of his stories called *All Souls' Night* caused Hugh little concern. This volume, which included *The Silver Mask*, was well received, but he was never greatly interested in his own short stories, even when he was writing them. They were useful means of filling up gaps between novels and of adding to his income, but little else. He was more interested now in reading "Marguerite Steen's book on me which has some brilliant bits," and in correcting the proofs of *Vanessa*—"a colossal business. The whole Herries are painted in water-colours. I try oils but it always turns out water-colour."

The first half of May he spent in London, seeing the Melchiors, supporting a young friend through the divorce court, buying a new Alvis and a new Epstein. A new friend appeared in Robert Gibbings the artist, who had published *The Apple Trees*. "He is like the reincarnation of William Morris, huge and burly with bright blue eyes and a beard. He is a great nudist, very charming, honest."

Hugh arrived back at Brackenburn "to feel throttled by the superabundance of everything." The sky was heavy with rain, the garden ablaze with azaleas and rhododendrons, the house full of parcels, the library bulging with pictures and books. He took up his journal, neglected for more than a year, and recorded these impressions, adding:

It will all settle down in another twenty-four hours, but *what* a lot of books I have, *what* a lot of books I've written, how much nonsense I've talked, how noisy I've been and am, how good on the whole are my intentions, how muddled the performance! Have most people the sense, I wonder, of being someone's unfinished knitting? And isn't it *very* wrong to have so many things when millions of people are unemployed and wretched? I give a lot away but seem to do no good with it when I do. I really don't *clutch* my possessions, and although I love them would not be broken-hearted at losing them. What *would* I be broken-hearted at losing, except some of my friends and my love of work and my enjoyment of small things? But the

[1] His mother also has her memorial, since Bishop Walpole caused St Mildred's Church, Linlithgow, to be built and named after her.

centre of the whole affair is missing, although I dimly perceive where it ought to be.

Through the summer days at Brackenburn he worked effortlessly at *Captain Nicholas*, though in June he took time off to write a Dickensian short story called *Mr Huffam*—"one of my best, I think." In June too he spoke at an immense dinner at Blackpool, given by the Dickens Fellowship, at which most of the participants were disguised as characters from the novels. Hugh, in full evening dress, gave them an eloquent and impassioned speech on Dickens, Literature, Life, and God. It was on occasions like this that his flowing gift of oratory came into its own, and his hearers had an opportunity of imagining the preacher that had been swallowed up in the novelist.

Chess had now supplanted backgammon at Brackenburn, and when Stephen Bone arrived to paint Hugh's portrait, he preserved for posterity one of these evening games, in a pencil drawing which catches brilliantly both the outward likeness and much of the character of both the players.

4

July was spent in the Highlands, at Malvern, and in a visit to the Brett Youngs. In August Ethel Cheevers fell ill with pleurisy following an operation, and while Harold looked after her Hugh went off to Brighton by himself to finish his book. He stayed in a hotel, and there after the usual last-chapter gallop *Captain Nicholas* was completed. Then Hugh visited the Priestleys at their new home in the Isle of Wight, and with them went to see Tennyson's old house at Farringford. One day he was stricken with lumbago after a game of tennis, which may perhaps partly account for this nightmare, later recorded in his journal:

I was in the market-place of a town. It was filled with people, talking, buying and selling, all very happy and busy. Suddenly, as though a cloud came over the sun, the air was cold and the noise died down to the twittering of birds. Men and women looked about them. Everyone was silent. I my-self felt a trembling expectant fear. I looked about me, wondering why I was so apprehensive, and found that the place was emptied like a bowl of water. It was dark and cold. Not a sound. Something told me to run for my life but I could not move. Then, from a side street, a little procession came into the square. A woman was carried on a kind of stretcher that also resembled a barrow. Two men in black carried it. They were followed by a small group of quite silent persons. And in front of the stretcher was a tall, thin man with a sallow face. But what was especially horrible about him was that his head was twisted to one side as though his neck was broken.

They advanced without a sound, their feet making no apparent contact with the pavement. There was a cold silence everywhere and great but crowded emptiness as though somewhere hundreds of people were holding their breath.

I was exactly in the path of the little procession. I knew that if the yellow-faced man touched me something appalling would follow. But I could not move.

The man and the stretcher and the followers advanced nearer and nearer. I was in an agony of terror. I woke and my pyjamas were soaked with sweat. I have never had a more horrible dream.

5

He was back in London in time for the publication of *Vanessa* on September 5. To "celebrate" this important day he bought a Sickert, a Wilson Steer, a Kelmscott *Chaucer*, and Trollope's copy of the first edition of *The Cloister and the Hearth*.[1] Within a few days *Vanessa* had received "nearly sixty reviews now, and not one spiteful one;" and to round off Hugh's pleasure came word that Metro-Goldwyn-Mayer had bought the film rights for $12,500. With a joyful heart he began to work out the details of his next novel.

6

One afternoon at Brackenburn when he was out walking on the slopes of Cat Bells with his dog, he came for the first time on a jutting promontory of grass and rock high above his cottage, and as he sat there absorbing the wide panorama of lake and mountains, "the whole of my real life was stretched in front of me." He often returned to this spot, and after his death Harold, in fulfilment of a promise, caused a stone seat to be built there so that others might share his friend's delight.

That same September evening, after describing his discovery in the journal, Hugh continued:

---

[1] Hugh paid £100 for this, and it fetched £150 at Christie's in 1945.

I never can decide whether I'm stupid or clever—compared with others, I mean. On the whole stupid—that is, I have an ingenuous brain. I am baffled by the simplest riddles, utterly by bridge and crossword puzzles. Chess, which I adore so, I sometimes play well by a sudden flash of imagination—but on the whole awfully.

However, I ask this question because I am sometimes startled by the astounding stupidity of people whom I consider so much cleverer than myself. Julian Huxley's letter in *The Times* yesterday, for instance, about asking God's guidance—this arising from the row now going on about the Buchman movement. He says that to ask God's guidance is a sort of "witch" superstition belonging to Central Africans. Moreover that we abdicate all our own mental independence by doing so.

He plainly knows nothing about Prayer at all—that Prayer is not *asking* for anything, it is rather putting yourself into contact with a world—as you may pick up a telephone and speak to Persia—a world waiting to be visited. Your spirit is longing to go there. It is like a dog on the leash. But for the most part we are too busy, too tired, too egoistic to take the trouble. But the *more* we do, the easier, the more natural it becomes.

This is what Prayer is—moving from one country into another. What it is to me anyway. But how does Huxley not know that many of the grandest things in history have come through it? How can so clever a man shut himself up so tightly in his own experience?

Towards the end of October Hugh began to write the prefaces for a new edition of his collected works, called the Cumberland Edition, which Macmillan were to issue at a popular price. This entailed reading, or at least looking through, twenty-five books, but the task was accomplished and all twenty-five prefaces written in twelve days. On the eve of his departure for London at the beginning of November he wrote in the journal:

Early tomorrow morning in the half-dark Harold and I will come out. The chrysanthemums will be faintly smelling in the cold light, Bingo will be running forward eagerly, thinking that he too is coming south, the last things will be put into the car, and the last sounds I shall hear, as I step into the car, will be the water trickling into the pool, an early rustle among the leaves of the silver birch, one bird inquiringly awake—and so south to Bedlam!

A Prayer before London

Oh God,
    Help me in these coming months to be ready for guidance without weakly abandoning my independence. Help me to realise what are the unimportant

things so that I am not perturbed by them. Increase in me love of my fellow men and a humorous regard both of them and myself. Help me to sink my persistent egotism in nobler interests than my own history.

Permit me to grow with every day nearer to the country of the spirit without losing enjoyment in the country of the body.

Let me be increasingly patient, tolerant, obedient and courageous—and have a humorous sense in all things.

7

On November 15 in London he began sitting to Jacob Epstein for a portrait bust, and continued intermittently for the best part of a month. In his journal he attempted a sketch of the artist at work:

Epstein as he models throws himself into it with all his soul. His method is to squeeze his clay into little snakes, and these he throws on to the work, murmuring anxiously to the little snake: "Stay! Stay!" and the snake stays. He rushes all round one and gasps, splutters, grunts and spits. He gets fearfully hot and takes off most of his clothing. He doesn't like to talk, he is too excited, but at eleven there is a cup of coffee and then he lets himself go. He is amusing, cynical, intelligent. He says he has no man friend because he likes to be selfish, which men don't like. Women, if they like you, though, want you to be selfish. They prefer it. His house is untidy. His bedroom is crowded with the most hideous, obscene and magnificent African gods, and these leer sardonically on to a double bed with stockings and dirty collars scattered on it, a writing-desk piled (I should imagine) with unpaid bills. His writing-sitting room has some lovely busts of his own and some good Matthew Smiths. As he works his trousers are almost slipping down, he has only one tooth visible in his upper jaw, but his eyes, forehead, grey hair, very fine. "The caricaturists *will* make me too semitic," he complains . . . He is a kindly, warm-hearted child if treated right. Otherwise, I should imagine, a bit of a devil. I like him extremely.

8

During this time Hugh was more and more bothered by begging letters, which began to make him "suspicious that people are only nice to me because they want something." He consoled himself by reflecting there were some—his sister, Harold, Athene Seyler, among them—"about whom there can be no question." In this connection he had written some years before to L. A. G. Strong:

I'm getting on and have got three or four friends so excellent that I complacently hug my comforts. It isn't that one can have too many friends, but rather that every new friendship means to me a definite extra giving out of myself. And even as it is I go hopping about, half flea, half elephant, from one excitement to another!

Hugh's friendship with Strong, though mostly conducted by post, lasted for more than ten years of unbroken harmony and understanding. Apart from admiring and encouraging Strong's writing, Hugh gratefully realised that his friend was one of the few practising critics who approached his books with a truly sympathetic comprehension.

To occupy himself he wrote a short story called *The German*, and then in Edinburgh on Christmas Eve the first words of *The Inquisitor*. "The book has been in my head for years, but during the last six months since I finished *Captain Nicholas* in August it has obsessed me." He realised when he was beginning it that "as one grows older the things one *can* do get monotonous with repetition; creation of character is the only thing that can save one at my stage." He had come to believe that his great gift was for creating characters, and was faintly annoyed whenever his talent for story-telling was singled out for praise.

On Christmas morning he "went to Early Service, the first time for many years. I liked it greatly." This was the beginning of his return to regular church-going. Thereafter when he was at Brackenburn he usually attended either Matins or Holy Communion every Sunday, sometimes at St John's, Keswick, sometimes at the village church of Grange. Coming out of St John's, one early February morning a few years later, he stood enraptured by the beauty of the scene. "The view from the churchyard was superb, the hills ranged like battlements. All is so quiet then. In front, the hills, just touched with rose; behind, the little grey street, quite silent, thin spirals of smoke coming from the chimneys. The churchyard scattered with snowdrops." He would like to be buried here when his time came, he decided; and he arranged that it should be so.

9

1934 opened with another cruise to Jamaica, another stay with the Turvilles. Hugh worked on at *The Inquisitor*, but nothing seemed quite

as nice as it had been a year ago. The heat and humidity were greater
than he remembered: there was something macabre about the place,
caused by "the intensity of the sun, the shortness of life, the absence of
morality, the minority of the Whites." All right for a holiday, but he
missed Brackenburn and Harold. His journal had been brought along,
and in the silence of one oppressive night he drew up yet another, most
accurate, list of his "defects and virtues. My sincere and simple camara-
derie, my humour touched with malice, my sensitiveness to being
liked, my resentment if I'm not, my pleasure over tiny things, my joy
in the colour and movement of the sea, my delight in being alive when
things go well, my apprehension when the atmosphere changes, my
determination to get what I want, my tendency to boss." Anyone who
knew him will recognise the truth of these attributes.

That same night he jotted down in his journal a forecast of his next
ten years' literary production. It is here reproduced in full, since it was
the last reasonable example of many such prognostications, and in-
cludes ideas which he did not live to carry out. The titles and dates
of published books have been added in brackets.

1934 *Captain Nicholas.*
1935 *The Inquisitor.*
1936 Short Stories. [*Head in Green Bronze,* 1938.]
     Hans Andersen novel. [*John Cornelius,* 1937.]
1937 Cumberland Novel. Modern. Laid in Newlands. Theme—Mother
     and Son. [*A Prayer for My Son,* 1936.]
1938 *Manuscripts for Love.* Personal, free book about the collection of
     manuscripts I've made for King's School, Canterbury. Half auto-
     biography. Also literary criticism and *some* humour. A *very* personal
     book.
     Short novel. Possibly sequel to *Young Enchanted.*
1939 *Knights of the Queen.* My Elizabethan Herries novel. This will be in
     the world of *Gösta Berling.* I should like to get some of Lagerlöf's
     atmosphere, poetic, mystical, exciting. [*The Bright Pavilions,* 1940.]
1940 *The Eighteen Nineties.* Diary of a young poet. This would be an
     attempt to catch the spirit of the 1890 writers as it hasn't yet been
     done. I would try and get some of the humour as well as the
     pathos. I should be entirely frank about Wilde and the psychology
     of homosexuality. I hope Alfred Douglas will be dead by then!
1941 My novel about modern Venice—the history of an old woman who

comes here to die. A young English boy is fascinated by her and she gradually causes him to live and be a man again by her scorn and even hatred of him. A rather short novel.

1942 *Herries Moon*. My Civil War–Charles I Herries, following directly on *Knights of the Queen*. [*Katherine Christian*, 1944.]

1943 *Men under Skiddaw*. My James II and William III Herries.

1944 *Death of Queen Anne's Men*. My Queen Anne Herries, its last page leading directly to beginning of *Rogue Herries*.

Shall I do anything of this? Shall I be alive in 1944? Shall I have the energy? Anyway here is ten years' work.

Returning by way of New York, he reached Brackenburn on March 7, in good time for the opening of what may perhaps be termed the Fiasco of the Fiftieth Birthday.

10

Just as Hugh's first comment on returning home from abroad was "No bad news or anything," so was he always watching for, guarding against, dreading, the worst news of all—intimations of his own mortality. The time would perhaps come when he would welcome death as the ultimate friend bringing surcease of cares, but not just yet, not while there were still so many exciting things to be done, so many books demanding to be written. And in this long shadow-fight against an unseen adversary, his fiftieth birthday had for some years loomed ahead, a landmark and a testing-point, which on his bad days he was certain he would never reach. Even as men in immediate peril of their lives often vow that they will perform some act of praise and gratitude if they are spared, so did Hugh vow that this to him symbolical birthday should be fittingly acclaimed. He would give an immense dinner to his friends—not to the First Fifteen only, but to the First Fifty—and after the banquet each guest would be presented with a beautiful privately-printed volume. The book appeared,[1] but the dinner never took place. First it was to be held in May, then in June. The number of guests dropped from fifty to fifteen; then Hugh's Hollywood plans caused it to be postponed until the autumn. But by

---

[1] *Extracts from a Diary* (100 copies, 1934). It contains passages from Hugh's Polperro war-diary, together with extracts from the later journals. It is dedicated "To my Friends on my Fiftieth Birthday."

then he was in a nursing home with arthritis, the books were distributed by post with typewritten letters which Hugh was too ill to sign, and the banquet was cancelled. Perhaps it was just as well: once the birthday was safely in the past its importance diminished; moreover imagination boggles at the difficulty of merging harmoniously so large a body of widely differing friends. The whole enterprise was typical of Hugh in its grandeur, warmth, generosity, and folly.

II

The great day itself was spent quietly at Brackenburn with Harold, opening letters and telegrams, writing an essay on the Lake District for a symposium on the English countryside,[1] and on Easter Day he reflected once more in his journal on the birthday obstacle safely negotiated:

Now that I've passed it I feel a sort of defiant triumph, as though I'd done a particularly nasty mean sort of enemy (whom I envisage in my mind as a beef-streaked Agate) out of a trick. Even Agate I don't *really* dislike If he came tomorrow up the garden holding out his hand, I'd take it and be delighted. This is a real weakness in me and comes from some sort of fear of ostracism or exile. Shades of Marlow, I suppose! But I can never believe that good fortune will stay. Is everyone apprehensive of the future? I suppose so—but as a sense of God grows in one, so I think we become more indifferent to our personal fate.

During April he was visited by the young poet W. H. Auden, "and very jolly, simple, honest, clear-headed he is. We got on beautifully and he didn't make me feel a silly worn-out old man." The Blakes came for a week-end, but for the most part Hugh's days were devoted to *The Inquisitor*, his evenings to chess:

I have been wondering about the emotional stress that chess throws me into. My heart begins to hammer, my hand to shake, and I can't sleep after a game. This is a new mania. Indeed it has every sign of a vice! Against everyone the same thing happens—I am well on the way to victory, perhaps two pieces up, and then lose the game. This is so exactly my character. I cannot keep cool and collected for long at a time, nor will my impetuosity be checked. I regard my pieces with passionate affection. The

[1] *English Country* (edited by H. J. Massingham, 1934).

queen is my bride, the bishops my brothers, the rooks my henchmen, the pawns my children. The result of this is that when they begin to be successful I feel them flushing with pleasure and I rise in my seat and cheer them on. And the result of *that* is that I lose my head *and* the game! Shall I ever learn cool collected wisdom? That is why chess is certainly the game for me. It should teach me if nothing else will—but I shall all my life lose the game against quieter players!

12

At the end of April he drove to London, where he was soon busy buying pictures and books. He had decided to form a special collection of books published during the eighteen-nineties, and its nucleus was now arranged in the Piccadilly dining-room. But soon the bustle of what Henry James had called his "apparently perpetual circus" began to weigh him down, and he confided to his journal:

At first London is a relief after working so hard at the cottage. Then, after a week or so, the other kind of exhaustion creeps in. One is not working with one's brain at all, but working at *people* becomes just as tiring. All one's friends are so kind and affectionate. Behind them there is a background of all those who are not one's friends—not necessarily enemies, but all who do not know one as one is. This second figure of oneself as one is *not* accompanies one everywhere. "Oh, *that* is Walpole," one can hear the background murmuring. One knows that it is not! One learns not to be self-conscious about this and also perhaps to pick up from this mysterious *false* figure what may be in it not altogether false. There are things of course that one *is* that one doesn't recognise at all. One is in fact only real at certain moments, and in certain relationships, and it is this reality that one must always increase. . . . The most unchangeable relationships are made between people who either very rarely meet or who are always together. That is why a successful marriage is the finest relationship of all.

A few days later he was rung up in the early morning and asked whether he would travel immediately to Hollywood to write the scenario for the film of *David Copperfield* for Metro-Goldwyn-Mayer. He was offered a salary of £200 a week besides all travelling expenses, and assured that the job would only take him a few weeks. He accepted at once, and lightheartedly set about cancelling or postponing his other engagements, including the great birthday dinner.

There was time for only five days at Brackenburn, but during them

Hugh completed the purchase of a little house in the village of Grange, some two miles away. He named it Copperfield and made arrangements for his gardener and wife to be installed there during his absence. Later the house became an overflow for books and pictures, and one of its bedrooms was furnished as an additional guest-room for Brackenburn.

In London Hugh was horrified to discover that the bookseller whom he had commissioned to buy for him at auction the original manuscript of Anstey's *Vice Versa* had been obliged to go up to £520 to secure it. But there was little time in which to repine: shopping, farewells, and a day watching the Australians at the Oval, kept him busy until on June 6 he sailed from Plymouth in the *Île de France*.

He travelled with George Cukor and David Selznick, two important film executives who were soon to become his firm friends, and the journey proved most agreeable. From New York, where he stayed long enough to see the Baer–Carnera fight in Madison Square Garden, he wrote to tell his sister that he was being "treated like a travelling monarch and spoilt to death." On their westward journey the party stopped a day in Chicago to visit the World's Fair, and on June 19 Hugh, an eager captive, entered the gilded prison of Hollywood.

13

The boasted Californian climate soon showed its darker side. Within a week he caught a bad cold, which infected first his eyes and then his sinuses. He was hurried into hospital, and an immediate operation was prevented only by the personal intervention of David Selznick. As it was, the restraints of hospital and the twice-daily draining of the sinuses irked him considerably, and he was greatly relieved when he was allowed to return to his Santa Barbara hotel. He was further cheered by the news that *Captain Nicholas* had been chosen by the Literary Guild and was thus assured of a large sale in America.

A few days later, while the scenario and casting of *David Copperfield* were still in their earliest stages, Hugh accepted a fresh proposal and reported the news in one of his weekly letters to his sister:

Yesterday I signed a contract to stay out here till November 1.... It is very interesting but most exasperating, as you have to write every scene over and

over again, and at the fifth time it is no better than the first. . . . I work without ceasing from ten to six, and everyone is too tired by the evening to want
to be gay. Harold will come out to me at the end of August. I'd have him
earlier if it weren't for his August holiday with the boys. Everyone asks
me out—Charles Laughton, Katherine Hepburn, Wallace Beery, Charlie
Chaplin—but you have little time to make real friends with anyone. . . .
You can't imagine how shut off one is!

His expenses quickly mounted. He was obliged to hire a car and
chauffeur of his own, and at the end of July he moved into a furnished
house in Beverly Hills, for which he engaged two coloured servants.
At the studio all was apparent confusion, order and counter-order,
temperament and tears. Steerforth was time and again removed from
the film, only to be reinstated at next day's conference. Charles
Laughton was engaged for the part of Micawber, but eventually gave
way to W. C. Fields. One day "after lunch the whole of the second
half of the script was pulled to pieces, and hysterical requests were made
for me to make something interesting out of Agnes. I in my turn got
hysterical and said 'I tank I go home.' They were very sweet to me and
calmed me down." But there were moments of peace:

Some of the homes of the film stars—Norma Shearer and Ann Harding
for instance—are exquisitely beautiful, and it is lovely to sit under the moon
at midnight and watch these beautiful creatures with practically nothing on
play tennis under artificial light. But I think why I am really happy is that
here I am free for the first time from all the English jealousy that I've suffered
from for years. No one here cares a hang about the relative merits of English
writers!

From these crowds of acquaintances there emerged a few major
friends, among them the Danish actor Jean Hersholt, who shared
Hugh's passion for rare and beautiful books, and the Polish producer
Richard Boleslawsky, a large handsome man who had served with the
crack Polish Lancers during the war, and had written an excellent and
most moving account of his regiment's adventures during the first
Russian revolution.[1] Hugh was also much taken with the charm and
talents of Katherine Hepburn. After seeing her in the film of *Little
Women*, he wrote in his diary: "She is divine—no other word for it."

[1] *The Way of the Lancer* (1932).

One day he drove with her in a Ford truck to a film preview, and much enjoyed the mobbing of the crowds in the streets.

All through August and well into September the script of *David Copperfield* dragged on. Seven times did Hugh gladly announce in his diary that it was officially finished, but six of these decisions were cancelled by demands for further revision. "Again and again," he told his sister, "we go back over every sentence, even over every word, and it is no easy thing for me, who have for so long done *what* I liked *how* I liked, to fit in with all these different people."

He took a day off to visit the great Huntington Library at San Marino, and his own library was forever being enlarged by the purchase of many thousand dollars' worth of books in Los Angeles and elsewhere. When his books were sold at auction after his death,[1] most of them fetched appreciably more than he had paid for them, but not his American purchases.

Early in September his spirits were raised by the arrival of Harold, who found Hollywood much to his liking and quickly became a general favourite. With him Hugh paid his first visit to the Mount Wilson observatory, where he made friends with the astronomer Edwin Hubble and his wife Grace.

Soon after this Hugh did his first, and last, piece of film-acting. He took the part of the Vicar of Blunderstone in the scene where the boy David falls asleep in church. It had to be retaken eight times, and on each occasion Hugh preached a different and wholly impromptu sermon, "standing in a pulpit, my face rosy with pompous platitudes," as he described it to Frere. Harold afterwards learned that Selznick and the others had deliberately prolonged the shooting of this scene, in a playful attempt to dry Hugh up, but they little knew their man. Next day he started work on the scenario of his own *Vanessa*, in collaboration with Lenore Coffee.

Meanwhile *Captain Nicholas* had been published in September, and at every opportunity Hugh pressed on with *The Inquisitor*. He felt quite sad when he killed off old Canon Ronder, whom he had first invented twelve years ago, but the moment the book was finished, its successor, *A Prayer for My Son*, came floating into his head. "I'm crazy

[1] Altogether they realised just under £20,000.

to begin the novel after next," he wrote to Frere. "Boy! *That* will be a book." For the rest of his life he was nearly always in this same state of mind. He was so many books ahead of his publisher that when a new novel of his appeared and his friends expressed their appreciation, Hugh sometimes seemed almost to have forgotten which book they were discussing, and would break into their praise with some such remark as this one to Frere.

Lectures too had to be given occasionally. Once he arrived at the Hollywood Women's Club to find that he had been billed to speak, not as he thought on Dickens, but on "Life begins at Fifty." He "got through somehow with many platitudes." Every Friday evening Hugh and Harold had season tickets for the local boxing, and on other evenings they played game after game of chess. Hugh suffered a series of crushing defeats, which he attributed to a surfeit of insulin.

The script of *Vanessa* was finished during the first week of November, and Harold was given a tiny part in the film called *Clive of India*. Clemence Dane arrived and Hugh was delighted to see her. So far he had enjoyed most of his stay, and he had clearly made a success of his job, for, as he wrote to his sister:

On Saturday I was summoned to the offices of Louis B. Mayer, head of this company and one of the Three Kings of Hollywood. He made me a speech saying I combined the qualities of fine character and great ability! I felt like a schoolboy of ten—but the result is that I have signed a contract for next year for six months at a fabulously high salary. No less than Two Hundred and Fifty Pounds per week! . . . This climate suits my diabetes to perfection.

A few days later he drove out with Harold for a week-end at Palm Springs. One morning there he got up early, went for a walk in the hotel garden and fell asleep on a seat which was still saturated with dew. When Harold found him he had been there an hour, and it seems probable that this caused the acute arthritis in the right wrist which attacked him almost immediately. He suffered much pain, was unable to write or do any work (his diary had to be abandoned for two months), and his stay in Hollywood, in any case almost over, was brought to a sudden end. Harold moved him by air to New York, and after a few days in the Doctors' Hospital there, they sailed for home early in December in the *Berengaria*.

14

On board ship they found the Priestleys, the Buchans, and Beverley Nichols. Hugh was kept in bed in his cabin for the whole voyage, and his friends would sit round his bed and entertain him with conversation. Lady Tweedsmuir writes:

I remember Hugh saying to John, "Do you realise that if this ship goes down tonight four of Great Britain's best-selling writers will be lost, and that all the non-best-selling writers will probably have a party to celebrate the event?" John looked surprised and a little mystified.[1]

When they reached London, Alan Bott met them, took Hugh to Piccadilly, and next day in an ambulance to a nursing home, where he passed a miserable Christmas. The specialists considered that the source of the infection might be his remaining teeth, and on New Year's Eve these were duly removed under an anæsthetic. A day or two later he was allowed to move to 90 Piccadilly, with his wrist immobilised in plaster of Paris. He managed to get up and dress, even to dictate the first two chapters of *A Prayer for My Son* to a stenographer, but the arthritis showed little sign of clearing up until Harold by great good fortune procured a bottle of a new medicine which had been invented by an Irish doctor. Hugh took it more in desperation than in hope, but his condition immediately began to improve, and after a few bottles of this magic draught [2] he was well enough to drive to Brackenburn on January 28. He stayed for a few days only, but the sight of his beloved home and all its treasures did much to complete his cure.

Back in London, the urge to buy pictures, so long frustrated by his illness, burst out again. One afternoon as he was leaving the flat to visit a dealer, Harold came in with a bill for a few pounds, which he was anxious that Hugh should pay, for some necessary electric equipment for Brackenburn which Harold had secured at a bargain price. Hugh exploded into one of his childish tantrums, refused to pay the bill, said it was much too high, and abused Harold roundly. Before he had had time to cool down, he strode off to the picture-dealer's and

---

[1] *John Buchan by his Wife and Friends* (1947).
[2] Later a company, of which Harold was one of the directors, placed the medicine on the market under the name Ru-Mari.

paid £1100 for an unfinished Renoir oil-painting.[1] By the time he got home he was thoroughly ashamed of himself, and unwilling to admit his extravagant inconsistency to Harold, who was by now too accustomed to such waywardness to show any surprise.

For the first time they saw the films of *David Copperfield* and *Vanessa* right through. Hugh experienced a "funny, rather moving intimacy" as he watched, and was on the whole very well pleased, though he considered it ridiculous to allow Judith Paris to live to the age of a hundred and thirty. He spent a week-end in the country with the Buchans, dined with Virginia Woolf and Elizabeth Bowen, and made an exciting new friend in John Collier, the novelist, whom he helped towards Hollywood with introductions. A dramatisation of *The Old Ladies* had been made by Rodney Ackland: Hugh went to a rehearsal but "slept all the time and shall leave them to it."

Most of March he stayed in Cumberland, writing his novel and recovering from his illness. While he had been in Hollywood he had lent Brackenburn, together with food, service, and run of the library, for a summer holiday to a young newly-married friend, to whom he now wrote: "I was really worried by your tiredness the other day. Domestic happiness, I've always heard, is much more wearing than debauchery! All the same I envy you."

His birthday provided a good occasion for resuming his long-neglected journal, and in it he confessed to a "curious unreasoning apprehension. Not an unhappy one exactly, but only as though someone had been whispering in my ear that I must watch my step." Perhaps it was just the after-affects of arthritis, but for safety's sake he decided that he must be prepared for his novels to decline in popularity, and also possibly for continual ill-health.

During a fortnight in London he lunched with the Archbishop of Canterbury at Lambeth Palace. He had not been there since the days of his young manhood, and sure enough his memory preserved a picture of "sombre rooms." Now, by contrast, he found everything light and sunny; "all the portraits of the Archbishops are cleaned, their faces shining. Lang says: 'Yes, very depressing to their successor, for there they all are and not a soul alive knows anything about them.

---

[1] It fetched £1800 when Hugh's pictures were sold at the Leicester Galleries in 1945.

Only about Laud, and he is remembered because he had his head cut off.' "

A few days later Hugh attended the successful first night of *The Old Ladies*. Rodney Ackland had made a fine play out of the novel, John Gielgud produced it beautifully in a set which showed the three old ladies' rooms simultaneously, while the acting of Mary Jerrold, Jean Cadell, and especially Edith Evans in the part of Agatha Payne, was superb.

15

During those years Sir Henry Lunn used to organise cruises to Greece and the Ægean Islands. Each trip would last some two or three weeks, and among the passengers there was usually to be found a quota of eminent writers and scholars. These travelled free, and if they avoided actually singing for their supper, were nevertheless expected now and again to beguile the tedium of their fellow-passengers with lectures on some suitably relevant topic. Hugh had been pleased to be invited, and when he embarked at Marseilles at the beginning of April, he discovered that his travelling-companions were to include Vita Sackville-West, Harold Nicolson, Sir Richard Livingstone and Professor H. W. Garrod of Oxford, Lady Ravensdale, and Dr Cyril Norwood, under whom he had once so nearly worked. The first days of the voyage were uneventful, but at breakfast-time on the fourth day the ship was found to be stuck fast on a sandbank at the entrance to the Gulf of Corinth. At midday all the passengers—there were almost four hundred of them—were asked to proceed to the stern of the vessel and there to jump in unison. Obediently and conscientiously, all of them, professors and old ladies, archæologists and society hostesses, carried out these indecorous instructions to the best of their agility. Time and again, at a given signal, they jumped with all their weight, but the sand held them fast and they retired breathless to luncheon.

All next day the ship was stranded, despite the efforts of tugs summoned from all quarters. London newspapers, hearing of their plight, cabled to Hugh, Harold Nicolson, and others, for first-hand accounts of the mishap, but these were forbidden at a meeting at which Sir Henry Lunn "ordered us not to be naughty children!" Compulsory leisure was no nuisance to Hugh, who dashed on happily with *A Prayer for My Son* and played "magnificent chess, beating Garrod twice and Vita twice." Eventually the combined tractive power of a flotilla of tugs refloated the ship, and in due course the party arrived at Delphi.

When he got home Hugh wrote some account of the whole voyage in his journal and compiled a list of the twenty-one loveliest things he had seen or experienced. First of all delights, he said, was the afternoon he spent on the Acropolis at Athens. He had lunched with Sir Sydney Waterlow, the British Minister and nephew of his old friend Elizabeth. Most of his fellow-travellers were down in Athens, and Hugh sat alone, glorying in the warm sunshine and contemplating the Parthenon, with its "honey-coloured pillars sailing into world upon world of light."

But there were other pleasures almost as exciting. On the morning of Good Friday he "woke to see Rhodes like all the novels Walter Scott ever wrote," at midday he ate fresh mullet on the quay, and in the evening Sir Henry Lunn delivered an appropriate sermon. Then there was the Church dignitary, whom all the old ladies adored and who, "lecturing always everywhere, was just a *little* suggestive in his stories about the gods and goddesses." There were Hugh's own lectures, which he always enjoyed. And finally the cruise ended with the singing of Easter hymns, a fancy-dress ball off Taormina (Hugh went disguised as a judge), disembarking at Naples, and home by train through Paris. Harold was waiting on the platform at Victoria, and, wrote Hugh, "Wasn't I glad!"

16

Straight up to Brackenburn they drove, for a week of quiet before the Jubilee celebrations in London. Hugh's last dog Bingo had taken to killing chickens and had been disposed of. Now his friends and neighbours the Zanazzis presented him with the last of his long succession of pets. This was a black retriever called Ranter, a gentle, quiet, affectionate beast to which Hugh became very attached. One day, accompanied by Ranter, he set out for a walk, carrying a long shepherd's crook which he had brought home from Greece. Along the road he became entangled with a flock of sheep, and an irate motorist yelled out at him: "Why the hell can't you keep your bloody sheep on the fell?" It was the only time he was ever taken for a native Cumbrian, and he used to tell this story locally with pride.

On May 6 he was ensconced on his Piccadilly balcony, directly overlooking the route of the main Jubilee procession. With him were his brother Robin, Mrs Thomas Hardy, Lady Ravensdale, Francis Yeats-Brown, Edward Knoblock, Keith Baynes, and the complete Cheevers family. The sun shone, and Hugh shared the swelling pride of all beholders. Later he voiced it too:

> The Queen looked quite perfect. Her colours—grey, silver, mauve, white— were exactly right, but more than that she was *regal*. . . . I realised the extravagant devotion that such an emblem of one's country's history can provoke. The value of these two is that they are symbols of all one's patriotism without doing anything to disillusion one.

He was impressed too by the good humour of the people in the streets, recording that when he walked home that night in full evening dress, through the packed and dancing crowds in Trafalgar Square, "not a soul said a rude word to me or tried to knock off my hat!" To Hugh crowds were always potential removers of hats, if not of heads.

Another peaceful fortnight at Brackenburn was spent working at *A Prayer for My Son* and brooding on friendship. Harold had upset him by declaring that he had scarcely a friend who didn't want something of him, and indeed there was some truth in this contention. Hugh had now much to give, in money and influence; he was incapable of refusing a request, and suppliants were many. In his calmer moments he acknowledged that Harold was right, but then some new friend would appear and Harold would prophesy a request for help. "Nonsense," Hugh would answer; "I bet you a pound he doesn't ask me for anything." When Harold won the bet, as he usually did, for he was a shrewd judge of character, Hugh would pay up ruefully, swear never to yield again, and fall to musing once more on the pitfalls of friendship and the perils of wealth.

He was still feeling some slight after-effects of his arthritis. Francis Yeats-Brown recommended a course of orange-juice and colonic irrigation in Stanley Lief's sanatorium at Champneys, near Tring, and there Hugh reported early in June. The morrow he described as a "very melancholy day . . . nothing to eat except some salad." Then came a "miserable day," but then "all my aches and pains went after an electric towel." Yeats-Brown and Alan Bott arrived to keep him company, and he announced: "I'm extremely well, never felt better in the whole of my life." He finished *A Prayer for My Son*, and after a fortnight's stay left Champneys in fine health and spirits.

Ten days of London were enough. The weather was stuffily hot and the Piccadilly flat felt like an overcrowded oven, into which poured petrol-fumes from the interminable traffic-blocks outside. Everything got on Hugh's nerves, and it was with even more than his usual relief that he set out for Brackenburn. On the way he stopped at Worksop and met for the first time F. J. Shirley, the headmaster designate of the King's School, Canterbury: "Extraordinary man. Has marvellous plans for Canterbury, but will have terrific rows there, I'm sure."

A few days of enchanted peace among the Lakes, a trip to Edinburgh to see his sister, a visit from George Blake, four days at the Leeds Test Match, and he was back in London again, getting ready for his second Hollywood adventure. The Book Society gave him a farewell dinner: he was resigning from the committee, but remained honorary chairman and later returned to his old position.

As usual before departures, Hugh was filled with vague foreboding. "Pray for me," he wrote to Clemence Dane, "against the army of germs and the shining speckles of sand-dust that settle in one's spiritual eye above Beverly." And to the friends who saw him off at Waterloo on July 31 he jovially remarked: "Take a good look at me. You probably won't see me again." But when the *Île de France* had been at sea for two days, he regained his equanimity as he wrote the first words of *The Life and Adventures of John Cornelius*. "I look forward to this book hugely," runs his diary entry, "for I feel that I may be free and personal and spontaneous in it, and Cornelius himself is already as real to me as myself." Well he might be, for much of his hero's character was taken from himself. He had begun with the idea of a novel based on the life of Hans Andersen, but by the time he was ready to start writing, the scene had shifted in his mind from Denmark to England, and Andersen's life was merging with his own. This book always held a very special place in Hugh's affections, alongside *Harmer John*. Both were to him intensely personal books, into which he felt he had put more of himself than he had bestowed on any of his others, and in both cases he was disappointed. They received good notices and sold in large numbers, but the critics treated them as good average Walpole novels, instead of hailing them as the masterpieces their author fondly believed them to be.

Now, at any rate, Hugh was happy as he started *John Cornelius*. To his sister he wrote from the boat: "Everyone is charming to me and as I get a portly old gentleman I am more and more a sort of Father Christmas with a hint of the Devil in my red cheeks!" Nursing this pleasing conceit he travelled on, and in the second week of August arrived once more in Hollywood.

CHAPTER TWENTY-TWO

GILDED BONDAGE

I

AFTER staying a few days with George Cukor, Hugh moved into a house he had rented, number 1681 Benedict Canyon, Beverly Hills. Here, except for one short week-end, he lived uninterruptedly for more than nine months: not since he was a little boy had he stayed so long in one place, without change, variety, or movement. It was "a pleasant little house, Spanish style with a homely little garden at the back." This time he bought a car of his own, and engaged a chauffeur, together with a negro manservant to look after the house. His friendships with Hersholt and Boleslawsky were "triumphantly reaffirmed," John Collier was delightfully present, but he missed the vitality of Selznick and Cukor, who were no longer working with him. He had brought along his journal, and in it he now set down some first—or more properly second—impressions of the place:

The studio, where happily I have my old office, seems at present like the grave. This may liven up later. I have slipped back without any sound—no publicity this time whatever. It is all most pleasant, kindly, agreeable, but, more than last year, completely unreal. There is more actual positive reality in one square inch of the beach at Scarborough than in the whole extent of Hollywood.

This is partly the unreality of the pictures, which simply get more unreal, rather than less. It seems to me that they have gone back rather than forward since last year. At Grauman's yesterday there was a huge preview of M.G.M.'s latest musical, *Broadway Melody*. This was exceedingly adroit, amusing, entertaining. At moments the dancing was beautiful. Hundreds and thousands of pounds, months and months of frenzy, agony, melodrama, miles and miles of brain-stuff had been spent on this. And yet two steps down the street and everyone, outside Hollywood, will have completely forgotten. It will get its money back, and there will be no other result whatever.

In Hollywood itself, however, nothing else is talked about, morning and night, but this and similar efforts. No wars, no politics, no deaths, make any effect here. We are all on a raft together in the middle of the cinema sea!

The unreality is partly from this, but also from America itself. America (where I am always very happy) has a hollow inside itself. Go a little way down and you find nothing. Death itself is quite unreal. On Friday as reported in the paper there were, in Los Angeles alone, three suicides, six deaths from motor crashes, two murders. Nobody cares. The nice Chief of Police at M.G.M. of last year, Ellinger, was murdered just outside M.G.M. gates last December by a jealous lover of his girl. No one cares. Will Rogers's death roused a tempest of sentiment, fine speeches, regrets, all genuine. In a week he will be completely forgotten. Nothing is real here but salaries.

The Inquisitor had just been published in London, and while Hugh waited for the American edition to appear he discussed the book a little in his journal, finally deciding:

I have undoubtedly considerable gifts as a novelist but I *cannot* learn the reality of *The Old Wives' Tale*, *Of Human Bondage*, *Esther Waters*, nor have I anything new in technique or style to offer. . . . None of this matters. One does one's best, but as each book appears I realise once more that the essential thing has escaped me.

The first American review he saw, by William Soskin in the *Examiner*, ended: "These are the brayings of an intolerable ass," while *Time* dismissed the book as "readable but pretentious melodrama." A letter arrived from Priestley saying that he didn't like the book, and a gastric chill rounded off a few miserable days. Then he received the first batch of London reviews. They were "the best ever in my life," and he was happy once more.

2

Nobody had so far been able to decide what film he was to work on. While he was still in London there had been frantic cables about *Kim* and *Oliver Twist*, but by the time he reached Hollywood they had given place to Mark Twain's *The Prince and the Pauper*. After a week's half-hearted work on this, he was switched back to *Kim*, but the very next morning plans were changed yet again and Hugh was told that he was to spend a month on a story called *Burn, Witch, Burn*. He flatly refused, and was fobbed off with the promise that he should do a film about Oxford instead. In the event he did nothing at all until October 10, when David Selznick asked him to do *Little Lord Fauntleroy* for United Artists, and thus in eight weeks he had been paid something like £2000 and filled in his time as best he could—buying books and pictures, writing a short story called *The White Cat*, visiting a lion-farm, spending a day at the San Diego fair, attending a huge party given by William Randolph Hearst in an artificial forest of coloured trees, and occasionally brooding over Mussolini's invasion of Abyssinia and the probable wrath to come. He made friends with the actor Edward G. Robinson, who introduced him to an institution rather like Lief's at Tring, and he went there sometimes for treatment.

Steadily too he worked away at *John Cornelius*, which by the middle of October had grown to thirty-five thousand words. After recording this fact in his journal, he launched out once more into speculation:

Shall I have any lasting reputation? Like every author in history who has seriously tried to be an artist, I sometimes consider the question. Fifty years from now I think the Lake stories will still be read locally—otherwise I shall be mentioned in a small footnote to my period in literary history. There remains always the likelihood that some investigation in minor authors will one distant day rediscover me in a book, pamphlet, article, or the Polchester novels may survive a little. In this same way Gissing, Henry Kingsley, Hewlett, Shiel, to name a few at random, will always remain. This will be quite enough immortality for the boy who once wondered whether he would ever be published at all.

The next two months were happy. Harold had arrived at the end of September, Hugh felt well, and he had something to do. *Little Lord Fauntleroy* was the first scenario he had attempted entirely on his own, and he enjoyed the feeling that he was *making* something. Selznick and the director John Cromwell helped him with advice and were well satisfied with his work, which he finished in a month. When the film was shown early in the following year, press and public endorsed their approval.

Apart from concerts and the weekly boxing, Hugh also watched a certain amount of wrestling. And here once again he was shadowed by the persistent Mr Pooter. One evening an enormous combatant called Wee Willie Davis was hurled right out of the ring into the lap of the luckless Hugh who was sitting in the front row. His glasses were smashed, for a moment he was knocked unconscious, and they took him to hospital to be treated for shock before he was allowed to go home. But he soon recovered, and two days later he was spending $1200 at a Chinese shop on "lovely amethyst, jade, ivory, amber, and two gorgeous T'ang horses." "As good as the bank anyway," he commented, and when the objects were delivered at his house he "went almost mad with excitement . . . Am I wicked? The pleasure at least is sensual!"

His love for objects of this sort, like his love for pictures, was three-fold. First there was the fun of finding them—the "moment of discovery"—and, as James Bain said of him, "his obvious delight in a new acquisition is ever a joy to behold." Then there was the fun of having them always in sight, "scraps of beauty scattered up and down my little house." And lastly the fun of trying to immortalise them by giving them an important part in a story of his own. The piece of amber in *The Old Ladies*, the five volumes of Lockhart's *Don Quixote* in *Above the Dark Circus*, a Utrillo in one story, the Chinese horses in another—all these and many more were beloved possessions of his own.

At odd moments in the studio he wrote another short story called *Having No Hearts*, but decided that "after this I really must give up short stories about dogs, old ladies, and rare possessions." *John Cornelius* too went steadily ahead. "How I enjoy it! But then I enjoy every novel I write, so that means nothing." And again, after finishing a passage which gave him special pleasure: "I have no genius, but by God I am a novelist! Also this book will be hellishly long and will provoke the usual squawks."

As for reading, his great experience during these months was the discovery of Herman Melville. He had read *Moby Dick* long ago, but only now did he attempt the other novels, and their impact was tremendous. With the assistance of Jean Hersholt he succeeded in buying first editions of almost all of them, he read them again and again, and fell so deeply under Melville's enchantment that "it is as though he has been living in the house."

Typee shines in my mind like the sun shining through the water in one of his own wonderful waterfalls. It is his uniqueness that makes him so important. Two lines of *Lear*, one sentence of Sancho Panza's, Mr. Collins's letter to Elizabeth Bennet, Hawthorne's picture of the "Seven Gables"—

these and such as these are all that is wanted. So with the opening to *Moby Dick*, Franklin in *Israel Potter*, the escape in *Typee*. Can I claim for myself anything first-hand? Perhaps the umbrella in *Perrin*, the first battle in *The Dark Forest*, the amber in *The Old Ladies*. I don't know. It doesn't matter.

3

Harold left in December to spend Christmas at home with his family and to supervise the improvements at Brackenburn. His departure caused Hugh some disconsolation, but luckily H. G. Wells had just arrived in Hollywood and round him entertainment gathered. First Charlie Chaplin gave a dinner in his honour, at which H. G. chucked Hugh under the chin, looking "very well and delighted with the pretty women." Then Hugh accompanied him and the actress Paulette Goddard on a visit to Hearst's fantastic ranch.

What a place! A huge imitation stucco building like a German health resort, planted on a hill between the mountains and the sea. Magnificent tapestries and everywhere marble statues, sham Italian gilt, and a deserted library where the books absolutely weep for neglect. In the grounds there is a zoo with some superb lions and tigers, but the cages are too small. Water buffalo and zebra look in at your bedroom window.

Wells gave a great oration at dinner, saying in his whispering squeaky voice that the past hundred years in American history were nothing for Americans to be proud of, and that since 1920 Americans had behaved like idiots. They had the chance to rule the world, but because of greed and pusillanimity had lost all their chances. The Americans at table looked blue and were very polite.

Hugh was encouraged by excellent news of *The Inquisitor* at home, where the book was being listed as the most popular novel of the season. He was also pleased when he was once more entrusted with the scenario of *Kim*, for which another writer had prepared a first draft. As Christmas approached, his thoughts went back to the other Christmases he had spent in America: few of them had come up to his expectations, but this one he felt sure would be different. He was right. The attractive American custom of setting up in the streets large Christmas trees covered with brightly-coloured lights was, as might be expected, in Hollywood carried to extremes. The whole brittle artificial city glittered gaily every night, and Hugh had to confess that he loved it. To drive down Hollywood Boulevard, he said, took one's breath away.

He stayed at Jean Hersholt's Christmas Eve party until three o'clock on Christmas morning, and as he drove home the stars were competing with the Christmas trees. Later he went to church and "found it gay with poinsettias and a lady choir in red caps looking like Roman senators." The midday party was at the Boleslawskys', where Hugh received any amount of presents and admired the new baby, the latest in his long string of godchildren. An evening party at George Cukor's brought to an end the happiest Christmas he had ever spent away from home, and when he came to wind up his diary for the year he could write himself down as "very happy, quieter, less nervous, everyone more friendly. God be thanked!"

4

John Masefield and his wife arrived in January, and for a week or two Hugh spent a great part of his time with them. He was best man at John Collier's wedding, and he took the chair at a dinner of the Food and Wine Society. It was an English meal excellently cooked, and it made Hugh homesick for "an English breakfast—kippers, fat sausages bursting their skins, fishcakes, kedgeree. For lunch trout and marmalade pudding. For dinner roast chicken and Stilton. The only possible American foods are steaks and some soups—everything tasteless, over-sauced, greasy."

Although he was not in any sense a greedy man, Hugh enjoyed his food, particularly his breakfast (a legacy, he said, of the miserable ones at Marlow), and later all the sweet things which his diabetes forbade him to eat. Out to tea, he would gleefully eat half a dozen macaroons like a guilty schoolboy. He drank very little alcohol, and rarely smoked cigarettes. He kept cigars for his friends and occasionally smoked one himself. When he was working, and sometimes while he was talking by the fire, he would smoke a pipe, but he always experienced great difficulty in keeping it alight.

The month of January was overshadowed by the death in quick succession of King George V and Rudyard Kipling. It was surprising to discover how much the King's death concerned ordinary Americans: Hugh played his part in the obsequies by reading the lessons at the memorial service in St John's Episcopal Church. Kipling's death touched him more closely, and he remembered how kindly, alert, and unaffected the older man had always been at their meetings. He recalled too a conversation at the Cazalets' between P. G. Wodehouse and Kipling, during which Kipling said: "But tell me, Wodehouse, how do you finish your stories? I can never think how to end mine."

By the beginning of February Hugh was ticking off the days on his calendar like a schoolboy, and his nostalgia grew so unbearable that he decided he could not endure another four months without Harold; so it was arranged that he should travel back to Hollywood about the end of March. Meanwhile Hugh was getting on with *Kim*, but in the middle of February he put aside *John Cornelius*, of which a hundred thousand words were now completed, so that the last eleven chapters might be reserved for the peace of Brackenburn. He had no sooner arrived at this decision than he began yet another short story, called *The Train*, followed it with one called *The Exile*, and began work on a book of critical essays, called *Six Romantic Novelists*, which was never finished.[1]

A week-end in San Francisco—the only break in nine months—helped to restore his perspective, but also increased his sense of imprisonment. One day the English actress Constance Collier voiced his own thoughts when she said to him: "Hugh, this place is just like Donington Hall. When the German prisoners first went there they were amazed by its splendour and beauty. 'Aren't the English fools!' they said. 'Why, it's better to be a prisoner than free.' Then after walking in the grounds for a few days they discovered the barbed wire. A month later all they did was to walk on the same track up to the barbed wire and back again."

Reflecting on this, Hugh came to three conclusions: "That I'm beginning to think of *money* more than at any time in my life before, that I'm wasting my time and I haven't got so much left to me, and that I

---

[1] The six were to have been Nathaniel Hawthorne, Charlotte Bronte, Herman Melville, Robert Louis Stevenson, Henry James, and Virginia Woolf. Only the introduction and the first two essays were completed.

love England more passionately even than I knew." And he concluded: "This isn't life at all—it's shadow upon shadow upon shadow."

On his fifty-second birthday he treated himself to first editions of four Surtees novels in their original parts, and indulged in an outpouring of literary forecast in his journal. He named and dated no fewer than twenty books, all of which he declared existed in his mind, and which would occupy him up to his seventieth birthday. These included, besides the four additional Herries novels already planned, no fewer than *six* later ones designed to carry the history of the family forward from the end of *Vanessa* up to the year 1950. It is possible that if he had lived he would have carried out some such enormous scheme, but for the most part this forecast, unlike its predecessors, was born of present discontent rather than future aspiration.

5

During the whole of his stay in Hollywood he wrote every week to his sister, and in March his letters were full of notes and queries. He had received a "marvellous lecture offer" from a Chicago agency for a six weeks' tour in November and December, and had accepted it, much to the disgust of his old impresario Lee Keedick. With Selznick he had arranged to write a film scenario in England in 1937.

I expect you were pleased at my being elected President of the Edinburgh [Associated] Societies. They asked me some four months ago to stand and at first I refused. They asked me again and I accepted, but then forgot all about it until I saw it in a paper yesterday. I was amused at my beating Ramsay MacDonald of all people!

Towards the end of March he confessed in his journal that most of his film earnings had been spent (without, although he omitted this vital fact, any allowance for income tax) on pictures and books. He was loth to admit, even to himself, the full extent of his extravagance, but from his list of purchases and a number of later admissions in the margin, it is clear that during the previous six months he had acquired three Cézannes, three Renoirs, two Picassos, a Gauguin, a Braque, and a Derain, besides a large number of drawings and lithographs, by Beardsley, Toulouse-Lautrec, Marie Laurencin, and other artists. The list of books bought is also impressive, and after chronicling its peaks Hugh explained: "If I don't *see* a thing I'm all right," but by now the booksellers and picture-dealers had got his measure. They "bring things to my door, saying: 'We only want to see you for a moment. You needn't buy anything.' And then of course I fall." The London dealers also successfully exploited this weakness of his for years. Indeed, his favourite London bookseller, James Bain, delightfully justified his intentions. "I will endeavour," he wrote to Hugh, "to put every temptation in your way, as experience shows that it invariably doubles the pleasure of buying books when the act of doing so entails the breaking of a resolution." There was no reason why Hugh should not buy whatever he fancied. He had earned the money, he was supporting goodness knows how many people, his income was ever increasing. But always there lurked in his mind the instinct of guilt, the feeling that he had no right to own so much while others were starving. "I love possessions and am at the same time ashamed of them, feeling in my bones that a man ought to be like St. Francis of Assisi, owning nothing. That kind of freedom I long for, but am too weak and greedy to secure."

And as he sat there in Benedict Canyon, longing for Harold's return and filling page after page of the journal, one image began to oust all others from his imagination. "I am *possessed* these days by the moment when at Brackenburn I cross the lawn after breakfast to the library. In this are the scent of kedgeree, Ranter's tongue licking my hand, the sparkling dew on the lawn, the smell of the books as I enter the library, H. C.'s quiet, mildly blue eyes."

Harold's arrival at the end of March, and the knowledge that there remained only two more months of this gilded bondage, sufficed to keep him going. When *Kim* was almost ready, they asked him to rewrite someone else's version of *Captains Courageous*. He refused, and it was a good thing that he did, for the last quarter of *Kim* had to be written four times, in four different ways, and his labours on it were brought to an end only by his departure from Hollywood. To a friend he wrote early in April:

This place is making me lazier and lazier. It isn't a good sort of laziness in which you recuperate, but a bad sort in which your character becomes weaker and weaker and you care less and less whether you do anything properly or not. I've just been telling John Collier that he'll be completely and utterly damned, body and soul, if he stays here much longer, but he tells me that he wants to be damned and is longing to know what it's like.

At Jean Hersholt's he met for the first time, and took a great liking to, D. H. Lawrence's widow, Frieda. He went to tea with her in a furnished house which she had decorated with Lawrence's much-discussed paintings of moonshiny nudes. The two of them agreed surprisingly in their opinions of mutual friends, and Hugh refused with some reluctance an invitation to stay with her at Taos in New Mexico.

As the time of departure drew near, he became daily more nervous and wrought up. Not without cause, for two days before he was due to leave, *Kim* was still unfinished, his American income tax was unsettled, and while Harold and the coloured servant struggled with the packing, a lady came and read aloud to him a play she had made from *Captain Nicholas*.

Eventually everything was settled—or, as in the matter of the income tax, shelved—and on June 5 Hugh, with Harold at his side, took his last farewell of Hollywood. He was sad to say goodbye to Hersholt, the Boleslawskys, Cukor, and a few others, but his predominant feeling was that of a convict released after a long sentence. As a result of his experiences he was perhaps a little wiser, though in money certainly no richer. All the same, the thought of those many packing-cases filled with books and pictures was decidedly comforting.

They sailed home in the *Aquitania*, and on June 22 they reached Brackenburn. "What rapture!" wrote Hugh in his diary. "So happy I couldn't speak."

Next morning he was still nervously excited, overwhelmed by the beauty and wonder of everything. Then he picked up his beloved *John Cornelius* at the point where it had been abandoned four months ago, and immediately everything swung once more into order. He was home again.

6

After a brief visit to his sister in Edinburgh, he divided the month of July between Cumberland and London. George Blake and the actor

Leslie Howard came to stay at Brackenburn; in London Hugh rejoined the Book Society committee, went on the same day to the Surrealist Exhibition and the Royal Academy and hated them both, watched some cricket at the Oval, and wrote a short story called *The Haircut*. A week-end at the King's School, Canterbury, impressed him because of the immense progress the new headmaster had made in his first year, and he was naturally delighted to find that one of the boarding-houses had been renamed Walpole House in his honour.

At the Malvern Festival he lectured to a large audience which included George Bernard Shaw. They were fellow-guests at Barry Jackson's, and later in the year Hugh wrote of Shaw in his journal:

He seemed to me incredibly antiseptic, light and clean like a sea-washed shell. His beard is like that spidery silver stuff you have on birthday cakes, and his skin so freshly pink that Barry Jackson says he rouges. As always he is extremely patient, courteous, alert, humorous. He is indifferent too—if one fell dead at his feet he would be most kind and helpful and wouldn't give a damn. But if he himself fell dead he'd be just the same!

And old Charlotte potters along with him—seventy-nine she is—and climbs the hill above Barry's house and looks at the view, and is courteously polite to everyone because it's all charming. What does interest me though is that these two old dears—up to their chins in money—won't have maid or valet and travel the world without either. As they left Barry's, Charlotte said to G.B.S.: "Now remember, dear, you have to do your packing when you get home." And he defiantly: "I shall put it off as long as ever I can!"

A few days later Hugh joined his brother and sister for ten days' holiday at Roundstone in Connemara. He was staggered by the brilliance of colour everywhere—"emerald sea, blood-red seaweed, white cottages, dazzling green turf"—and this proved one of their most successful family holidays. *A Prayer for My Son* was published on August 26, and when Hugh arrived in London he reported to his sister that all but two of the reviews were excellent. A few days later the film rights were sold to Hollywood for £2750, and a Hull fishing company asked permission to name a new steam trawler the *Hugh Walpole*.

The first three weeks of September were occupied at Brackenburn with the final chapters of *John Cornelius*, and it is easy to see why Hugh had postponed their composition until he had left his Californian madhouse. As has been said before, this book, which had started out to be a story based on the life of Hans Andersen, had become more and more personal to Hugh himself. Although he preferred to identify himself with Cornelius-Andersen the genius, with his "simultaneous self-distrust and self-confidence," he introduced another of his percipient self-portraits in the character of the novelist Simeon Rose:

Outwardly he is plump, cherubic, rosy-faced, and with his genial smile, urbanity, and a certain mild pomposity would make an admirable Canon of any Cathedral. To meet him you would say that he was completely self-assured and very definitely pleased with himself and his success. This self-satisfaction can be irritating even to his friends. He is cheery and complimentary to everyone, so modest about his own works that no one believes in his modesty; he rushes from place to place, smiling, laughing, his voice booming, clapping everyone on the back. I myself have long suspected, however, that Rose is in reality a man compacted of misgivings and suspicions of his fellow-creatures. A lonely man, too, I daresay. A man loyal to his friends and passionately desirous of their affection but morbidly suspicious of those same friends and restlessly suspicious of himself. The keynote to his character is, I think, apprehension. This makes his work, which is garrulous, long-winded, often platitudinous, sentimental and unreal (often also readable, for he has an excellent narrative gift), surprisingly interesting to me.

In contrast to this is another novelist, Archie Bertrand (clearly based on Somerset Maugham), who is described as "Rose's exact opposite":

He is, both in his outward self and in his books, a cynic, a pessimist, and above all (what he most wishes to be) a realist, a man who sees things exactly as they are. He is apparently a modest man who writes as he can a simple English style and tells the truth about the little bit of life that he has seen. But within, Bertrand is, I think, self-assured, rather arrogant and deeply sentimental. He is, in fact, the man whom Rose tries to be in his writings, while Bertrand's writings have the cynicism that is in reality deeply embedded in Rose's character.

For the character called Charlie Christian, Harold was the model, and when Hugh had to kill him off as the story demanded, he "felt depressed all evening." A few days later: "Worked hard. Only two chapters left now. Feel quite sick at thought of leaving it. I care for this most of all my books."

His emotion prevented his sleeping properly, so that in the mornings he was edgy and inclined to be hysterical. "Am all pulled to pieces by this book. I never remember such an experience before. After I finished writing this morning I was completely exhausted. *Hate* to leave Johnny who is so real to me." On September 19, after another bad night, he wrote all day and finished the book in a state of near-prostration. John Cornelius had by now come to be so closely associated in his mind with himself that to compose the scene of his death was almost like killing himself. And by some freak of prescience, clairvoyance, or simple imagination, Hugh in that scene forecast almost exactly the manner of his own death.

Later that same evening he found the strength to write in his journal:

This is a day because on it, at eight in the evening, I finished what *I* think is, up to now, my best book. Not artistically perhaps: *The Dark Forest* is that. And not romantically: *Rogue Herries* is that. Nor the best story: *The Cathedral* is that. Nor the truest: *Mr. Perrin* is that. But the best for myself, because there is more of myself in it than in any other—it is truer to *me*, and Johnny is a real creation, consistent from first to last. He owes, of course, a lot to Hans Andersen, but I meant him to be *more* in Andersen's skin. After a while he gets quite away from him.

He slept well that night, and next morning confided to his diary: "I feel beautifully empty, like Mrs. Dionne after quintuplets." But as usual another story sprang immediately into the forefront of his brain— "the story about the girl by the sea who nearly loses her husband because his family grabs him." It had its origin in the fragment of *Scarlatt* which he had abandoned nine years before, and was later to appear as *The Sea Tower*. But now, just as the plot "was beginning to swell out like a balloon, sea, rocks, papa, everyone," he went to lecture in Manchester. There his host for the evening, J. D. Hughes the local bookseller, said as he was leaving: "You know, Mr Walpole, what everyone is wanting is a *happy* book, a happy book by an intelligent writer. They're hungering for it." "How scornful I wanted to feel!" wrote Hugh. But instead of that,

. . . standing there in the Hughes's hall with Harold waiting in the car, there flashed up and through me *The Joyful Delaneys*. I knew no more than Osric at that moment what that meant. But before we were at Brackenburn it was flooding me like the sea in Connemara. All the odds and ends of the last five years were joining together—the play about the swell boarders, the novel about the old bachelors, the novel about Shepherd Market. And the subject —found by me years ago when with Hergesheimer—the English aristocracy in their new poverty. *Exactly* the subject for me. But a *happy* book? Have I ever written one outside *Jeremy*? But the Delaneys *are* happy; they can't help themselves. They are telling me now: "If you don't portray us truly as we are, by God we'll torture you for ever." And, God helping me, so I will!

7

Another entry in his journal of this same period gives an accurate summary of one side of his perennial reading:

We were talking the other night about—to which writer do we really return, no humbug? I gave my list and it was absolutely honest. For instance, I think of Dante, Goethe, Stendhal, Blake with joy, but I don't read them.

I read *all* the time the Bible, Shakespeare, Scott. After them I return and return to Jane Austen, Wordsworth, Browning, Keats (Poems *and* Letters), Lamb (Letters), FitzGerald (Letters), *Don Quixote*, Dickens, Hardy, Proust, Dostoevsky, Macaulay's *History*.

I think this is as honest as honest—except that I still love my boyhood story-tellers—Marion Crawford, Weyman, Conan Doyle. These are the only three who have really survived for me, but Crawford for instance is ever so much better than he is thought to be—he isn't in fact in this year of grace 1936 thought about at all.

He was indeed faithful to these old friends. Back in 1924 he had written a letter to *The Times Literary Supplement* in praise of the aged Stanley Weyman, who wrote in gratitude: "I was more moved than I can say by the generosity and quixotry of it—more moved than I have been by anything of this nature since Stevenson wrote to me about the *Gentleman of France* thirty years ago." Outside Hugh's bedroom at Brackenburn stood a bookcase stuffed with these loves of his childhood, including the complete works of Charlotte M. Yonge.

Inside the room, alongside his bed which faced the lake, there was a little white bookcase of two shelves only, in which were cheap pocket-editions of the books he read constantly. Over in the library he had first editions of most of them, but these battered little copies were his familiars, for which he could reach out, night or morning.

What did he remember from all this mass of reading, to which the Book Society proofs added hundreds of new books a year? Except for the plots of novels, impressions only and very little that was accurate. Although he read poetry constantly, he had no memory for quotations, and the lines of verse or prose which he used as epigraphs for his novels, and sometimes introduced into the narrative, were almost always taken from whatever he was at that moment reading—which often explains their irrelevance. If no convenient lines came to hand, he would invent some and attribute them to his own Henry Galleon, or later to Hans Frost.

For the plots and characters of novels, on the other hand, his memory was astonishing. No matter how obscure the novel, or how long ago he had read it, the whole picture remained fresh in his mind. Right at the end of his life, in April 1941, L. A. G. Strong wrote to say that he had been asked to compile an anthology of scenes from English fiction to illustrate domestic life during the past two hundred years, and could Hugh make any suggestions. Hugh was a sick man, alone in London without any books, but he sat down immediately and wrote out from memory a list of sixty scenes from the works of forty novelists, beginning with Fielding and Fanny Burney and ending with R. C. Hutchinson, Graham Greene, and Elizabeth Bowen. Prose fiction was his *métier*.

8

But soon he set out on yet another voyage to the United States of America—"one more departure and with the usual tremors." But this time he would be back in a very few weeks, in time for a family Christmas in Edinburgh. He sailed in the *Queen Mary*, read *Gone with the Wind* all the way and wished "that the voyage might continue for weeks." In thirty-five days he lectured thirty-three times in as many different places, from South Carolina to Kansas City to Chicago—the usual circus-ring. The lectures seemed to him the best he had ever given, their audiences the largest and most appreciative. Wherever possible he stayed with friends, and he succeeded in speaking to Richard Boles-lawsky on the long-distance telephone.

When he arrived at the beginning of November, he found Americans talking of nothing but Mrs Simpson and King Edward VIII. Eagerly they seized on Hugh for the latest gossip, but he could tell them nothing; the English Press had so far preserved its organised silence: few Englishmen even knew of Mrs Simpson's existence. But while he was travelling and lecturing, the Abdication crisis rushed to its climax, and just before the end of the tour Hugh heard in Toronto the King's farewell speech. He was staying with Jim Annand, and together the two old friends sat by the wireless, listening to and grieving over the drama of those brave, tragic, momentous words.

This was Hugh's last visit to America, and it ended on December 16, when he sailed for home in the *Queen Mary*. There was just time to reach Edinburgh by Christmas Eve, and to begin *The Joyful Delaneys* on that accustomed day.

CHAPTER TWENTY-THREE

RISE, SIR HUGH

I

THE year 1937 opened with a restful week at Brackenburn. *The Joyful Delaneys*—"who are money for jam"—in the morning, some sort of a walk or expedition every afternoon, then chess and reading by the evening fire. Moments of introspection were recorded in the journal:

I can't bear anyone to tell me, until the book has been out a week or two and the reviews have come in, that it's bad work. I grow despondent about it so easily and then I'm cross in a kind of self-defence. This isn't vanity, I think, but my true self jumping up inside me and saying: "Well, you know you're not a writer of the first rank—and how you would have liked to be!"

*　　　*　　　*　　　*　　　*

Is this an awareness of God or merely common sense? I only know that when now I am about to be irritable or mean I hear quite distinctly within myself: "Reject this. It isn't worth your while." I'm irritable when I'm tired, when I've written too long, when I've lost at chess, when there's a request for money from someone. I'm mean about people when I gossip. I'm led on especially by cheerful kindly women who destroy reputations in cartloads. As I hear them crashing around me I say to myself: "One or two more can't matter in the general mêlée."

But here this companionable voice is especially constant. The minute I mention a name it begins a warning. This will make me soon *very* dull to my friends. But I'm still mean enough to be amusing. Or is it meanness? I prefer to think that we are all comic creatures and that a laugh or two are allowed. But would I like it if, from behind a screen, I heard myself scoffed at? Undoubtedly no. It has happened to me once or twice, and they are frightful, ineradicable, unforgettable crises to me. And so, perhaps, if I'm becoming a little less catty it's a good thing.

Then came ten days of London, during which he "broke his oath" by purchasing another Braque for £325, lunched with Clemence Dane, and journeyed to Twickenham to see England beat Wales. Back at Brackenburn his repose was shattered by the cabled news that

Richard Boleslawsky had died suddenly of heart failure in Hollywood. Of all the friends he had made there Boleslawsky was the dearest, and his death was a heavy blow. "I shall miss him horribly," Hugh told his sister, "but everyone dies one way or another in Hollywood." A few days later he poured into the journal his sorrow and memories of his dead friend:

In this life he was never happy for long, being more full of apprehensions than any human being I've ever known. I think his time in the White Army, his escape from Russia, and his year of almost-starvation with Norma in Hollywood, made him permanently frightened. I'm sure Hollywood killed him. He was quite unfitted to make pictures, although he put all his poetry and theatrical genius into them. He couldn't endure the tyranny of the studio bosses (who hated him) or the commercial greed. But especially what killed him was the unsatisfactory nature of the pictures themselves. The beauties he put into them were *so* ephemeral, and he was heart-broken with disappointment again and again. He had exactly the same Polish morbidity and anticipation of the worst that Conrad had. He had also, like Conrad, times of enchanting boyish gaiety and jokes. There was something of the peasant in him, in his huge frame and lumbering movements. He was utterly tender-hearted, and dogs, flowers and children absolutely knew it. But he was a stranger on this earth, always and always.

Hugh wrote a little *vers libre* poem about him for the dedication page of *John Cornelius*.

2

The end of January was further darkened by another of his unending struggles with the income-tax authorities. As has been seen, Hugh kept no regular accounts, his memory of such matters was faulty, his arithmetic and his carelessness appalling (once he accidentally made out a cheque for more than a million pounds), and his income arrived at odd intervals from so many different sources that his advisers were always struggling to keep pace. Until his second long sojourn in Hollywood all had gone comparatively smoothly, but during those nine months his tax position became entangled in a heart-breaking snarl which was not finally unravelled until some years after his death. Periodical discussions with chartered accountants became regular annoyances to him, and almost every year he was obliged to sell some shares in order to satisfy the Inland Revenue. At one particularly black moment he rallied himself by reflecting that "my big income tax does mean I'm helping the country a bit."

In February he gave his Presidential Address to the Associated Societies in Edinburgh. George Blake came to stay at Brackenburn and was pronounced the "perfect guest. Could live with him for ever." The manuscript of *The Joyful Delaneys* piled up speedily, and when the first third of the book was finished, Hugh wrote in his journal:

It has gone very easily and I think should be a nice typical book of mine. Typical! That is beginning to be the danger now. There are no new tricks for me any more. Everything I write will be Walpole—Walpole—Walpole. On the one side that is good, because no other man or woman on earth can supply Walpole but me. It may not be a very remarkable creation, this little Walpole, with its rather green eyes, large heart and impetuous twisted muddled stomach, but anyway it's unique. I think it ranges about third-class goods in the shop;

First Class: Tolstoy, Dostoevsky, Jane Austen, Balzac, Proust, etc.

Second Class: Gogol, Anatole France, George Eliot, Arnold Bennett.

Third Class: Henry Kingsley, Gaskell, Gissing, Maugham, etc.

Do I put the goods too high? The real danger begins when I myself begin to be too conscious of Walpole. When a character appears I look at it resentfully and say: "But I've seen you before!" At a phrase or scene I turn a little sick, it all seems so familiar. Thank God, that state hasn't come yet, but I *am* aware now of skirting round too-familiar devices. For instance the Thunder Storm in *Delaneys is* like the Green Cloud in *The Cathedral* which has been so much parodied. But after *The Delaneys* I won't do a London novel again for a long time.

3

The next six weeks were mostly spent at Brackenburn, with one short stay in London, a night with the Blakes at Helensburgh, and a drive to Edinburgh which ended in a snowdrift at Moffat and a slow train-journey on. Although Hugh never felt well in Edinburgh, and consequently seldom enjoyed staying there for long, he was drawn to it by his deep affection for his sister and brother, and the memory of their parents. In his diary he always referred to his sister's house as "home."

Late in March Hugh and Harold walked up to Watendlath to settle a dispute which had arisen in that tiny hamlet between rival claimants to the honour (and profit) of living in "Judith Paris's house." When Hugh told the unlucky farmer that Judith Paris never lived in *his* house, indeed never lived anywhere, he replied: "Aye, I know 'tis all bunkum." The tarn was frozen, with snow lying on the ice. "I seem as I get older," Hugh wrote that evening to his sister, "to love this peace more and more, interspersed with the bustle of life. Pieces of peace are what *you* should have, as Father had his quiet days."

4

Two days later the news of John Drinkwater's sudden death produced another brief character-sketch in the journal:

My friendship with him goes back twenty-five years. I first stayed with him and his first wife (whose name was Walpole) in a little house in the Cotswolds then. I shall never forget the night when he burst into the Regents Park house and begged to stay with me because Daisy was at that moment bearing his child in a nursing home. He cried and was in a dreadful state, but through his tears produced, as usual, a manuscript from his pocket and asked if he might read me his last poem.

He was one of the noblest men I ever knew—of absolute integrity, fidelity, much sweetness. He had humour, as *Bird in Hand* showed, but he was very solemn, even pompous, about himself. He was therefore much mocked at by the frivolous. Maugham always said he meant Drinkwater by the figure in *Cakes and Ale*, but I must honestly confess I think it was much more like me!

When he was in public the actor came out. He had a fine voice for reading poetry, and a fine presence until he got too fat. He had, I think, a very small talent, one or two good lyrics. In *Abraham Lincoln* he hit on a good recipe, but it was scissors and paste stuff. I don't think he'll be remembered at all except as one of the young Georgians with Rupert Brooke and Gibson at the beginning of the War.

Poor John! He suffered, I think, many disappointments. He was, I know, dreadfully disappointed at not being made Poet Laureate when Bridges died. He could never be very kindly about Masefield after, try as he might.

His only fault was his pomposity about himself and his works—a small one compared with his honesty, good heart, kindness, gentleness.

5

The end of March found Hugh in London, negotiating with Charles Laughton and the director Erich Pommer, concerning his first English film. After some days of discussion he agreed to write a scenario based on Daphne du Maurier's novel *Jamaica Inn* for a salary of £350 a week. Work was not due to start on it immediately, so he drove back to Brackenburn for a few more days of peace.

He arrived in time to witness the final victory in a long campaign. The trees between Brackenburn and the shore of the lake are the property of the National Trust, and although the ground on which they stand shelves sharply down to the water, they had by this time grown tall enough to shut out the view of the lake from all but Brackenburn's upper windows. For almost fourteen years Hugh had been urging and entreating the National Trust to fell enough trees to give him a glimpse of the water, but so far only a few had been removed from in front of the library. Curbing his natural impatience with difficulty, he persevered, and his efforts were rewarded when the new chairman of the local committee finally agreed to his proposals. Hugh was to remove and pay for the felled trees, and to plant flowering shrubs in their place. Now the last offending spruce crashed down, the waters of the lake sparkled through the gap, and Hugh gave thanks for the additional beauty which enriched the prospect.

6

When he drove to London three days later he knew he had a heavy programme before him. There was the film script to be written, a speech to be delivered at Stratford on Shakespeare's birthday; he had agreed to "cover" the Coronation ceremony for the *Daily Mail*; further discussions were due on the great income-tax imbroglio. But he forgot all vexations in the excitement of a new and unexpected pleasure. On the afternoon of April 22, as he was setting out for Stratford, there arrived at 90 Piccadilly a letter from 10 Downing Street, "asking me whether I'd like a knighthood! Accepted at once!"

The next few days passed in a blur of happiness. The Stratford speech, the beginning of the film, the moving of the best of his pictures and bronzes to the French Gallery in Berkeley Square, where his collection was to be exhibited—all these events shot past him, and it was only when he had contrived another few days at Brackenburn before the Coronation itself and the announcement of his honour, that he found time to reflect in his journal:

On the morning of Tuesday the 11th, I shall be lying in bed at 90 Piccadilly, and at 8 a.m. John will bring me the papers with my tea, and I shall read, I suppose, that I am a knight. This is a dangerous proceeding and there will be no doubt some mockery—"Just what he's always wanted"—"The sort of writer they *would* make a knight of!"

The point is that I've often laughed at knighthoods myself, but when I got Baldwin's letter I was childishly pleased and had no thought of refusing. Even if I'd wanted to, I am far too keen about this new King and Queen to refuse their gracious offer! Anyway it won't matter in the least if I do decent work in the future, which I mean to. I must confess that since Scott I can't think of a good novelist who accepted a knighthood. Kipling, Hardy, Galsworthy, all refused.[1] But I'm not of their class, and range with Doyle, Anthony Hope, and such. . . . Besides I shall like being a knight.

The morning of Tuesday May 11 began as he had imagined it, and soon afterwards the telephone and the front door bell started to ring. Congratulations poured in from all over the world (the bundle which survived among Hugh's papers contains ninety-five telegrams and more than two hundred letters) and they were all answered by hand within a few days. Two notes of congratulation must have specially pleased him, each in its particular way. Compton Mackenzie wrote:

I daresay that I shall have as much sentimental pleasure out of this as anybody, for, though we have taken different roads, we were bred in the same stable and started our two-year-old races together.

And Sir William Rothenstein:

My felicitations! It is pleasant to know such as you singled out for recognition. You have always stood for the gallant things—and people. And there is always a sense of relief—selfish perhaps, but a satisfaction—when decent people join the circle of knighthood!

[1] Scott accepted a baronetcy, and I know of no evidence that Hardy was ever offered a knighthood.

7

But now there was time only for the Coronation. Hugh had already attended the main rehearsal, and all was set for the great occasion.

George Blake, who was to broadcast a description of part of the procession, spent the night with Hugh at 90 Piccadilly, and they were both called at half-past four on the morning of the 12th. By six o'clock Hugh, with two of Ethel Cheevers's Cornish pasties and a bar of chocolate in his pockets, was perched high up in the Triforium, among the other journalists, with the Members of Parliament below him, the peers, peeresses, and diplomats opposite. There were five hours of waiting to be filled in before the arrival of the royal party at eleven, but for Hugh, munching his chocolate and watching the gaily coloured throng assemble, there was not a moment's tedium.

The ceremony itself held him spellbound, and in his excitement he dropped his precious invitation card over the edge of the Triforium. Later he vainly tried to recover it from among the tightly packed M.P.s. At a quarter past two the journalists were allowed to leave the Abbey, and Hugh had to make his way as quickly as possible to the *Daily Mail* office. His article was to be syndicated in America and elsewhere for publication in next morning's papers, and there was no time to be lost. The only way he could move eastward from Westminster was by crossing Lambeth Bridge, walking along the south side of the river, recrossing over Westminster Bridge, and then along the Embankment to Fleet Street.

As he left the Abbey it began to rain, and by the time he reached New Scotland Yard the drizzle had become a deluge. The Embankment was blocked by some thousands of school-children who, soaked but enthusiastic, were stepping eastward in unison. Hugh realised that his only hope was to march with them, which he did, holding aloft his now useless umbrella. Eventually he reached the *Daily Mail* office, thoroughly drenched, at half-past four.

They gave him a room and some whisky, and took his clothes away to be dried. For two hours Hugh sat there in his underclothes, drinking whisky, eating his Cornish pasties, and writing his article. As he finished each sheet of handwritten manuscript, it was removed and sent down to the compositors, without one word having to be corrected. By half-past six all three thousand words were written, and his clothes were dry. "When I had finished," he wrote in his journal, "the Editor sent for me, said it was a miracle, none of his own men could have done it, and that they and America were delighted with it." Next day Hugh's account of the Coronation was generally deemed "the best of the lot," and the Archbishop of Canterbury wrote him a charming letter of appreciation. "To all of which I can only say that journalism is the easiest job in the world, which I have always suspected." In all Hugh received about £150 for this article, which he would gladly have written for no other reward than the pleasure of being in the Abbey.

8

The rest of May and half June were occupied with the film scenario and its resultant conferences, revisions and temperamental outbursts.

I did two scripts of *Jamaica Inn* for Pommer and Laughton and both were bad. They paid me two thousand pounds for that little bit of work, so I'm afraid they're losers, but I did work as hard as I knew how. But that means as hard as I ever work at anything that isn't a novel. I can see now that the only thing in life I've ever done whole-heartedly is novel-writing. Looking back I can see that from schoolmastering through work in the war to films my heart's never been in any of them.

His only breaks were week-end visits to friends, and it was now that he first stayed with the Botts in their house on Ham Common. Josephine Bott delighted him with her warm-hearted frankness, her wit, and her gift for turning everything into gaiety and fun. (She liked Hugh's dog Ranter, and Hugh would write her skittish, affectionate letters signed in the dog's name.) She made no demands on him, she was fond of him, always pleased to see him, and she made him laugh. No wonder he quickly added her to the short list of his favourite women.

Other visits were to the Freres at Dymchurch, to Canterbury where he addressed the boys of Walpole House, and to some friends who motored him over to Penshurst, the ancient home of the Sidneys.

"We sat down to tea, a hideous collection of moderns. Ah, my brave Sir Philip all in blue and silver, what do you say to US?"

9

On June 11 at Buckingham Palace Hugh received the accolade of knighthood from His Majesty King George VI. For days Harold had polished the car, and now smart in a new blue suit he proudly drove Hugh through the Palace gates. Here is the scene as it was afterwards recorded in the journal:

I hadn't had the decency to buy gloves so, after I'd given my hat up to the cloakroom attendant, I felt very naked. Upstairs in the long picture gallery we were all put into pens, one O.B.E., two C.B.E.'s, and us Knights. I was joined by Muirhead Bone, Plum Warner, Arnold Bax, and D'Arcy Thompson. We were not a distinguished looking lot as we were all ranged up according to alphabet, and told by a court official what to do. "Mind you all stick out your left leg when you kneel. It's easier to get up." I implored Bone to lend me his left-hand glove so that I might be more decent. This he did, but then came back to say that as he began with B and I with W he would be gone before I would be free—so I gave him his glove back.

After an interval in which to admire the Rembrandts, Vermeers, and other masterpieces which surrounded the "pens":

We moved like a theatre-queue into the other room. The King in morning dress looked exactly like Robin. We were a little disappointed that he didn't speak. I kneeled, he touched me on both shoulders. I got up, shook his hand most cordially, he grinned, I thought he was going to speak. Old Sam Hoare read out my name and *that* was over.

10

On June 19, twenty-six years after the publication of *Mr Perrin*, Hugh gave away the prizes at Epsom College. He made a speech, watched the cricket, and thought of his young ambitions—so many of them now fulfilled. At last, he felt, he was free. No more film engagements, no more lecture tours, nothing but his novel to finish, and beyond it a whole row of other exciting stories waiting to be written.

July he spent with Harold in Venice and on the Dalmatian coast. They revelled in the heat, the bathing, and Hugh in the Venetian pictures, though Harold cared less for this part of the holiday, and "his only comment on the Giorgione *Tempest* was that the baby couldn't possibly suck the breast, the position it was in!"

II

Back in England, Hugh paid his annual visit to the Malvern Festival, and then enjoyed a fortnight of fine weather at Brackenburn. His brother and sister came to stay, and together the three of them explored the Lakes more thoroughly than ever before. One day they visited the house of their childhood holidays, Sower Myre Farm, and renewed their friendship with the Armstrong family. The high lights of their expeditions were recorded in Hugh's journal, and one of them runs:

Enjoying Edith's sponge cake sitting beside Ennerdale, the wind blowing the water into little waves, Ranter gazing at me hungrily, D. and R. both reading *Cornelius* uncomfortably.

The book was to be published at the end of the month, and Hugh was experiencing more than his customary apprehension. *John Cornelius* had become so personal to him, so much his beloved ewe lamb, that he dreaded its exposure to what might well prove the cold blasts of indifference or incomprehension. So he tried it out first on his family, and the result was discouraging: "D. seems completely bewildered by *Cornelius*, and her honesty is only too uncompromising." Indeed poor Dorothy wept at her inability to grasp the book's importance, but since "Harold couldn't 'get' it either, nor my brother," Hugh decided that perhaps the fault lay partly with the book itself.

On the other hand the two reviews this morning—*Times* and *Telegraph*—are excellent and there are many things in the novel to attract people. Also I *am* a good story-teller, although I say it as shouldn't. But this book is in line with *Fortitude*, *The Captives*, *Harmer John*. You might call the four my autobiography. And one day if I live I'll write one about myself as an old man. That should be pretty grim!

On September 4 from London he wrote to his sister:

I was delighted to get your letter—the nicest you've ever written me, I think. I'm sure that we three got closer to one another in the week at Brackenburn than ever before. We are very lucky, I think, to be so fond of one another, being all three rather isolated people, so to speak. As one gets older, though, one's devotion to people who are good and fine gets stronger and stronger. It seems one of the really important things.

I admired very much your conduct over the book. I was upset for a moment because I saw at once that *Cornelius* would seem difficult and queer to many people, just as *The Captives* and *Harmer John* did. That night at dinner I saw in a flash the fate of the book—and so it will prove. The reviews on the whole have been excellent but completely non-understanding. Not *one* review has alluded to the Baupon chapter, not one paid any attention to the book's mystical side, and one of the two really hostile reviews has been the *Church Times*.

On the other hand certain people, Clemence Dane, L. A. G. Strong, etc, simply love it. But it's very clear to me now that my *naked* view of life is understood by very few, and so it will always be. However I'm perfectly happy and content. I am what I am, and must write honestly as I see.

12

A few days later, still in London, he wrote out in his journal a very full synopsis of the book which was later to become *The Killer and The Slain*, explaining that "for three years and more" the theme—that of a murderer who gradually turns, physically and morally, into the man he has killed—"has obsessed me, as no idea for a book ever has before. . . . It will undoubtedly write itself, and should be *my* best macabre and one of the best ever *if* it comes out right. . . . I shall have, I think, against my will, to begin it at Christmas." In fact almost three more years were to pass before the first words were written, but the incident provides a striking proof of Hugh's claim that most of his novels waited in his brain, shaped and sometimes even divided into chapters, for years before he was ready to let them out.

The London fortnight was as usual filled with jostling engagements —a party at the Ivy to celebrate the sixtieth birthday of his intermittent "enemy" James Agate, a week-end with the Botts, and a luncheon at the Ritz where he met the famous American radio-priest Father Coughlin. Hugh was prejudiced against him by his reputation, but soon began to change his views. In the journal he described him as:

A quiet, stocky, gentle and beautiful-eyed man with whom I felt instantly a strong bond. I think he felt it for me. Our eyes constantly met during lunch. He said nothing remarkable then, except that he was very free in his talk about sex and was simple about American politics, wanting apparently some very *un*-Bolshevik Communism . . .

Afterwards I spent two hours with Coughlin. We went to Howes and bought silver for his little peach farm in Canada. I gave him a little silver mustard pot that had belonged to Rothschild. Then we went to Harrods and bought a table and sideboard. Then we went to my flat and I began to tell him some of my difficulties but pulled up. He said enough, however, to show me that he understood. Through all this he was very quiet, kind and affectionate. It's a good thing he's going to America today because his influence on me was quite extraordinary. Intellectually he is naïf and childlike, but I am sure that he is sincere, brave and kind. He has an audience of 20,000,000, a church that holds 3000, and gets 100,000 letters a week. I gave him a copy of *Cornelius*. I shall never forget him.

A week at Brackenburn gave Hugh time to finish *The Joyful Delaneys*. It had been a happy book to write, nor did its completion affect him as that of *John Cornelius* had done a year ago. He was cheered too by the letters he was receiving about *Cornelius*, and declared that "L. A. G. Strong's article on me in the *Teacher's World* is one of the most understanding I've ever had."

From September 21 to 25 Hugh stayed at Holker Hall, Lancashire, the home of Lord Richard and Lady Moyra Cavendish. Queen Mary was the guest of honour, and when he sat next to her at table and drove with her through the cheering crowds, Hugh spoke to her of ghosts and Sir Walter Scott and the Russian Revolution, and admired her regal bearing, her charm, her energy, her curiosity. After dinner on the last evening he was asked to read aloud to the assembled house-party. The piece chosen, Lady Ribblesdale's account of staying with the Gladstones at Hawarden, was a general success and greatly amused the Queen. When she said goodnight, she added: "Thank you, Sir Hugh. You read beautifully."

13

Now that the Delaneys had run their course, three or four ideas for novels were competing in his mind. Should he begin immediately on the macabre thriller he had so recently outlined in his journal? Or make a start on his Elizabethan Herries? Or get rid of that story of a marriage by the sea which he had begun to write, so many years ago, as *Scarlatt*, and which would not let him rest? He could not decide, and as if to fill up the interval, a three-act play called *The Haxtons* began to stir in his head. He let it grow there for a week or two, began to write it in October, found his Hollywood experience a great help, and finished it before the end of November.

Meanwhile throughout October he was as busy as ever, opening an exhibition at Bath, making a speech at Liverpool, buying pictures, entertaining George Blake, and agreeing to write another English film, this time an adaptation for Victor Savile of Vaughan Wilkins's novel *And So—Victoria*.

On the last day of October, when two acts of *The Haxtons* were completed, the Elizabethan Herries would no longer be denied, and although Hugh had already decided that *The Sea Tower* must be written first, he so far indulged his Herries-hunger as to jot down in his journal the rough outline of what later became *The Bright Pavilions*. After working out dates and giving indications of the plot, he added: "The theme will be God against Devil, as in all my books and especially the Herries books, and I don't care how often I do it."

November and December were divided between Brackenburn and Piccadilly, with one excursion to Scotland. In Edinburgh on Christmas Eve he duly began *The Sea Tower: a Love Story*; next day with Dorothy and Robin he visited their parents' graves at Dalmahoy; and for the New Year his journal carried forward two resolutions:

One—that in 1938 I will really *not* be so acquisitive. I have all the possessions in the world I can possibly want—I have enough books and pictures to last me for ever and ever. To give is really better than to receive and well I know it—but Oh! how I like receiving.

Two—I will strengthen loving-kindness all in my power. With Mussolini and the Japs running around there is twice the need there was for personal decency. Was I not right about the battle between good and evil? So I must watch myself or I'll be deserting to the wrong side.

CHAPTER TWENTY-FOUR

THE WRATH TO COME

I

THE year of Munich opened vexatiously. Victor Savile was away in America, and until his return Hugh's work on the scenario had to be suspended. After spending a week-end with his kinsman Lord Walpole at Wolterton, he hurried back to Bracken-burn. One evening he read in W. B. Maxwell's new book of reminiscences [1] a reference to Arnold Bennett's old habit of referring to him as "the child," and commented in his journal:

Well, you can be called worse things. But I think we all three, Dorothy, Robin and I, have a certain childishness because Mother and Father had it too. We believe what people tell us, never think people are *really* evil. And surely they are so very seldom. But *stupid*—oh Lord how stupid! Including your humble servant.

In February Hugh drove down to Canterbury for the formal presentation of his collection of manuscripts and books [2] to the King's School. Some months earlier, the Dean and Chapter had handed over Prior Sellingegate to the School, and *The Times* had devoted a column to the occasion. Then with an "odd sentimental emotion" Hugh had seen the precious collection packed up and driven off to Canterbury in a van. He himself had helped to arrange his treasures in their lasting home, and now with two eloquent speeches he formally gave them away.

The immediate applause was gratifying. A sermon in Canterbury Cathedral, several references on the wireless, another long article in *The Times*—all these pleased him greatly, but in his journal he had confessed to a further purpose, a grateful requital:

This is really a little scrap of immortality and, with my seat on Cat Bells, is certainly all that I shall have. But Canterbury and Borrowdale are the double centre of my being, with lamplit half-befogged London and the

---

[1] *Time Gathered* (1938).
[2] See Appendix C, p. 470.

Cornish sea dawdling or roaring or shouting or whispering as the other two winged influences.

From these there comes all my writing—and speaking literary you might say from *The Prelude*, from Lady Dedlock slipping down the stairs after doing in Mr Tulkinghorn,[1] and from Charles Marriott's *The Column* and *Genevra*. The sea, the mountains and the city—and, by far most of all, those weeks at Gosforth with the dung-carnation-rose smell of the farm, and the cows plunging down the hill, and the thin line of sea across the fields.

2

Later in February Hugh "broke his word" and bought a Renoir still-life for £250. "What *is* to happen to me? It's worse than drink." And indeed there seemed no end to his craving; the dealers grew warmer and warmer in their welcome, and on the least provocation or none at all would bring along a tempting canvas to Piccadilly. Few other customers could be expected to buy a Tissot and a Dufy on the same occasion, as Hugh once did, and the problem of where to hang the pictures was no worry of theirs. Harold had long given up his cautionary remarks, which Hugh remembered and put into the mouth of the old maidservant in his short story, *The Faithful Servant*:

"You know, sir, he's got far more already than the house can hold, and, as I tell him again and again, he doesn't know what he *has* got in the top rooms, all piled up against the wall they are. Why doesn't he sell some of them? I ask him that and he says he can't bear to part with them, which seems to me pure foolish as he never looks at them."

This was exactly the situation at Brackenburn, but each time they drove up from London there was always a consignment of new pictures in the back of the car. Immediately they arrived, before Harold had a moment to recover from the three-hundred-mile drive, put the car away, or enter the house, Hugh always insisted on getting out these latest favourites and hanging them at once in the writing-room over the library. This meant taking down others to make room—for the walls were thickly covered—and then it was Harold's job to find somewhere to put the fallen idols. By the time of Hugh's death, when all

[1] Hugh very seldom made mistakes about the plots of novels. Mr Tulkinghorn was murdered by the French maid Hortense (*Bleak House*, ch. LIV).

the Piccadilly pictures were crammed in with the others, those few rooms at Brackenburn held more than a thousand pictures, drawings, etchings, and pieces of sculpture.

But they were not all destined to be sold. One day, soon after this, John Rothenstein, the new Director of the Tate Gallery, came to lunch with Hugh in Piccadilly. Suddenly during the meal, as if on a sudden impulse, Hugh said that after his death Rothenstein could have anything he wanted for the Tate, and after some discussion they settled on fourteen pictures as being a suitable number. Rothenstein asked what they were to do about the twenty-three Max Beerbohm cartoons which were already on loan to the Gallery. "Oh, count them as one item," said Hugh. Rothenstein then selected the other thirteen pictures [1] with Hugh, whom his guest remembers as being "radiant with cheerfulness, generosity and health."

3

Back at Brackenburn *The Sea Tower* claimed him, but an old preoccupation intervened. Although his long "enmity" with St John Ervine was again beginning to wear thin, and only a few weeks earlier he had described it as "a very mild dislike really on my part, which I keep up because I'm sure he would snub me if I didn't," he could not resist writing to Athene Seyler:

I see by the papers that you and Beau are at once starting rehearsals for Ervine's play. It's an awful position for me because *now* I shall want the beastly man's play to be a success! My one good solid *hate* to which I cling like a mariner drowning in a sea of good-will.... I've sent you my new book of short stories. You can read one or two under Ervine's frightful nose.

The book of short stories was *Head in Green Bronze*, the last collection he was to publish, which appeared on February 25. A few days in London sufficed for the acquisition of another "tiny" Renoir to "celebrate" his fifty-fourth birthday, and on March 17 he left for his second Ægean cruise.

[1] Oil paintings by Renoir, Forain, Steer (2), Sickert, John, Tissot, and Ford Madox Brown; drawings by Blake and John (3); and a water-colour by Cézanne.

4

It was the day after Hitler's annexation of Austria, and Hugh could "remember no time since August 1914 when people were so really frightened." But as the *Letitia* steamed farther and farther into the sunshine, war's alarms receded, and when, with Lionel Curtis, he sat under the Parthenon, "watching it fly through the starry sky floodlit," and Curtis said: "One aeroplane, one bomb, would be enough," it was all too quiet for the words to be disturbing.

Hugh's chief companion this time was Sir Ronald Storrs, with whom he had made friends some years earlier, when Storrs had retired from public service and come home to live in England. During all the years of his colonial governorships he had been starved of intellectual companionship, which he much enjoyed, and being out of touch with the latest books had fallen back on the greatest books of all. Every year he made it his custom to read through the whole of Homer and Dante in their original languages, the whole of the Bible, and almost all Shakespeare. This habit delighted Hugh, and he asked Storrs to annotate his *Oxford Book of Greek Verse in Translation* and Butcher and Lang's *Odyssey*, so that he could share some of his friend's pleasure. But above all the literary interests they had in common, what made the two men especially enjoy each other's company was a common sense of humour and of the ridiculous. They found the same things funny, and they worked up between them a number of private jokes which enriched their talk and their correspondence.

On this cruise they enjoyed together the beauties of the changing scene, and its amusements, as when they found the quay at Malta plastered with posters bearing as their sole device the words SIR HUGH WALPOLE. Later Hugh summed up in his journal:

I felt a kind of extravagant happiness. I roared and sang and was ebullient, and many people must have disliked me very much indeed. But no one *appeared* to, which is all I care about. I love the blue sparkling water, the smooth passage of the ship, kippers at breakfast, sitting with your feet up reading *The Golden Bowl*, writing the novel a little, endless jokes with Ronald—always light and water and space and brilliant *new* air down the nostrils.

Intoxicated with sun, sea, and beauty, Hugh regained London early in April and almost immediately: "Oh dear, oh dear! £1200 for a Bellini *Pietà*. I'm mad. But perhaps not. Banks, etc, may all disappear! Excited and frightened all day by this purchase." That night he couldn't sleep for thinking of the picture, and next day he spent two hours in the National Gallery, "looking at my other Bellinis!" The dealer who sold it to him congratulated Hugh on his purchase and assured him that it was worth all his other pictures put together,[1] but his doubts lingered long.

5

Home again at Brackenburn he was quickly absorbed in *The Sea Tower*, despite the intrusion of other work: *The Haxtons* needed lengthening, the film was about to begin again, all sorts of newspapers pestered him for articles and stories. At the end of April, on his way to London, he spent a week-end with the Brett Youngs near Pershore, and with them watched Bradman score his customary double century in the opening match of the Australian tour on the lovely Worcester ground. Next day his old friend J. D. Beresford visited the house: the two men had not met for almost twenty years, nor had their earlier friendship survived Hugh's success and Beresford's failure. Yet they were pleased to see each other, and Hugh wrote Beresford down as "nicer, I think, than ever."

As soon as possible he hurried back to Cumberland and finished *The Sea Tower*. Three days sufficed for the alterations and additions to *The Haxtons*, and now there was nothing to hold up the flow of the Elizabethan Herries. Could he possibly hold off its beginning until Christmas Eve?

June and half July were spent in London, where Hugh bustled from one engagement to another—much cricket-watching at Lord's and the Oval, work on the film at Denham, several visits to the Glyndebourne Opera, speaking at an anti-Fascist meeting at Queen's Hall and to Dominion representatives at 10 Downing Street, week-ends with the

---

[1] Æsthetically he may have been right, though not financially. After substantia bequests to the Tate Gallery, Fitzwilliam Museum, etc, Hugh's pictures fetched close on £30,000; the " Bellini " only one hundred guineas.

Botts, bowling out Beatrice Lillie in the Authors v. Actresses cricket match, mourning the death of E. V. Lucas, making friends with the dramatic critic Alan Dent, lunching with Duff and Diana Cooper at Admiralty House, writing a short story called *The Perfect Close*, buying pictures and bronzes without end.

Hugh's part in the script of *And So—Victoria* was finished just in time to prevent his collapsing from nervous strain, and on July 15, the day *The Joyful Delaneys* was published, he escaped in the car with Harold. They reached Cornwall in two days, and when they came to Penzance, Hugh felt "all my youth returned." He had forgotten that the south could be so fair, so prodigal of cornfields and of roses. A lazy, happy week at Perranporth was broken into by an exchange of letters with James Agate, who wrote:

> I hear from the *Daily Express* that Macmillan have had orders from you not to send it your new novel.
>
> But why should a great writer like you be so afraid of a little critic like me? Isn't this rather as though an all-England batsman should accept an invitation to play in a Test Match only on condition that Neville Cardus was not allowed to write about it?
>
> You shall have anything up to ten pages of *Ego 4*, in which to justify what on the face of it looks like pusillanimity! I will even promise not to answer back except to correct any possible misstatements of fact.
>
> Come, you old badger, let me draw you!

To which Hugh replied:[1]

> I don't want you to review my books and for two reasons:
>
> 1. I don't want you to review them because you don't read them. What you do is to open my new book, find a piece of English that isn't *your* English, pick it out, pillory it under your fat caricature in your paper, make a mock or two, and so leave it.
>
> Now, you are a first-class journalist and I always read you with joy, but I can never reconcile your serious, devoted attitude to the theatre and your flippant, casual patronage of current literature.
>
> I *doubt* if you've ever read a *whole* book by anyone right through in your life! Have you? If so, what?
>
> Now, you may be right in your attitude to current literature, but, as *you* know, a book *is* a book to the author of it. One has been a year or more living with it, caring for it, cursing it. Why should one deliver it over to

[1] The text of this letter is taken from Agate's *Ego 5* (1942).

someone who will certainly mock it without reading it? All the same it *would* be so delivered over were it not for the second reason.

2. I have a great regard for our friendship. It has had some ups and downs, but by now I value it for its entertainment value and because I like you. Now, I know that a contemptuous review by you who have *not* read my book will only make me, for a time at least, think you a patronising, job-shirking bastard. Of course you are *not* that, but I, in company with others whom you have mockingly patronised, would for the moment think so. As you are not that, I don't want to think you are.

After all this you will think me super-sensitive and cowardly perhaps. I'm *not* cowardly, but I am sensitive where you are concerned.

And Agate answered:

The difference between us is that you have an immense talent for story-telling and not very much feeling for the words in which you tell your story. With me the boot is on the other leg. Since I can't tell a story, probably because I can't think of one to tell, I am forced back on to words, about which I have thought so much that I disapprove of "my" style more than plenty. . . . Have you ever in your life re-written a sentence? If so, which?

But by the time this arrived Hugh had escaped to Malvern where, in the Abbey Hotel, he surrendered to his longing and began the Elizabethan Herries. At first he called it *The Trumpet and Alarm*, from a line in Christopher Smart's *Song to David*, but this quickly gave place to *The Bright Pavilions*. Once he had begun it there was no further holding back: he read book after book on Elizabethan life and literature, worked the story over and over in his mind, and wrote it down at every opportunity. The last week of August he spent with his brother and sister at Ballymore, County Donegal, where the almost incessant rain became his ally, so that by the time he left ten thousand words were on paper.

6

September, that month of mounting international crisis, was spent at Brackenburn. A conference of journalists, held in Keswick during the first half of the month, provided additional distraction and made many claims on his time. In the intervals he pressed forward with *The Bright Pavilions*, which he described to Marguerite Steen as "a cross between *Westward Ho!* and the Marquis de Sade."

But writing grew harder as Europe hurtled towards war. Every few hours there was a radio news-bulletin to be listened to: emergency plans must be made. By the time Neville Chamberlain flew to Berchtesgaden on the 15th, everything was mapped out: they would bring the pictures up to Cumberland for safety, Harold would probably return to the police, and Hugh could surely be useful in some kind of propaganda work. Indeed, Hugh's journal for the second half of September, although it was written up only spasmodically, presents a faithful picture of the average Englishman's feelings during those dramatic days. Surprise, indignation, fear, relief, shame, succeeded each other in every heart. On the 22nd, the day of the Godesberg meeting, Hugh confessed that he had "got the jitters"; next day he regained control of himself; and so it went on. The Storrs and the Botts came to stay for a few days each, and their company was a solace amid news of gas-masks, trench-digging, and Air-Raid Precautions. This was Storrs's first visit to Brackenburn, and in his bread-and-butter letter he wrote:

It is not only the perfection of the house and library and the beauty of the setting, but the individuality of the atmosphere diffused even in the gloomiest physical and political weather: the golden radiance of a Cuyp late afternoon.

Harold alone preserved his habitual calm. When they heard the news of the hysterical scenes in the House of Commons which greeted Chamberlain's invitation to Munich, Harold commented: "What a pity the Botts left!"

For the next two days Hugh could do nothing but listen to music— and news-bulletins—on the wireless. Writing was out of the question, chess demanded too much concentration, and even reading failed him until he tried his old favourite, Marjorie Bowen's youthful best-seller, *The Viper of Milan*, and found that it held his attention. He slept badly too, and it was an immense relief when on the morning of the 30th Harold brought his breakfast up to him in bed, and with it the news of the Munich Agreement. "Peace," said Harold laconically, and added: "I hope you're not tired of fishcakes."

The wisdom of Neville Chamberlain's policy of those days is still debated, but the respite it earned for his countrymen, if only so that they might have time to gird themselves for the battle, was seized with gratitude, and by none more thankfully than Hugh.

7

As soon as the immediate crisis was past, Hugh's life resumed its customary ambience. A busy fortnight in London, during which he sat for three days on a jury at the Old Bailey, was followed by a restful one at Brackenburn. He agreed to write a "literary page" every other week for the *Daily Sketch*, and this article, which soon became a weekly affair, he contributed regularly for the rest of his life.

George Blake came to stay and as usual his company delighted Hugh. The first part of *The Bright Pavilions* was completed, and then he dreamed a dream which caused him next day to write to Mrs Lynd:

Dearest Sylvia,

I probably never had a sillier reason for writing to you than this. Last night I dreamt of you, and you were flying along in a nightdress with an Elizabethan ruff. You called to me: "Come along! Come along!" and I flew with you clumsily, and you called out over your ruff: "If you saw better you'd fly better"—which somehow seemed to explain the Universe to me! And then suddenly—Oh Lor! your left wing broke—you fell, round and round like a top—and I woke up!

So I just want a line from you to say that all is well with you and Robert.

Affectionately,
Hugh.

On Sunday October 23 he jotted down his time-table for the day, and it is given here as typical of many Brackenburn days. Reflections on the contents of the Sunday papers, on his own book, and on the scenery, have been omitted.

7. Rise.
8. Communion. Keswick.
9. Breakfast. Sausages. Egg. Bacon. Cherry jam. Read Sunday papers.
10.30–11.30. Write letters, this diary. Consider the first part of *Bright Pavilions*.
11.30–12. Read *National Observer*—which I *adore*.
12–1. Read *Legend of Montrose*, Yeats, Ben Jonson.

1–1.30. Lunch. Roast beef. Fruit. Water.
1.30–2.30. Nap. Sunday allowed.
2.30–3.30. Walk with H. C.
Tea with Foxes.
5.20. Kipnis singing Schumann *Dichterliebe* on wireless. Grand.
6.30–7.30. Reading my play.
7.45. Insulin.
8. Supper. Cold meat pie. Fruit. Water.
8.15. *Cloister and Hearth* on wireless.
8.45. News.
9.30. Chess.
11. Bed.

The play was again *The Haxtons*, in which he now made some further alterations. He also wrote a short story called *Service for the Blind*, and became so absorbed in the theme of blindness that he determined to build his next novel round it.

At the beginning of November he spoke on the opening day of the *Sunday Times* Book Fair at Earls Court. His subject was Book Collecting, and his audience numbered some eight hundred. Next he attended one of his exciting tea parties at Virginia Woolf's, where was Elizabeth Bowen, "dressed very smartly with a hat like an inverted coal-scuttle. She and Virginia sat together like two goddesses from a frightfully intellectual Olympus. Thank God I'm no longer frightened of them. In fact I even pull Virginia's leg. But she is very like my mother and my aunts—only she *observes* more sharply."

8

Two weeks of rain and wind at Brackenburn were relieved by a happy visit to the Blakes, and on December 1, the eve of another departure to London, Hugh took up his journal. After discussing the international situation and the probability of war, he continued:

Personally I'm getting older and much more tranquil. No one and nothing can take from me the grand life I've had, and, all things considered, I think I've done well with the very second-rate brain I've got.

It is second-rate partly because of the simply rotten education I had. At school from nine to nineteen, at Cambridge three years, and I learnt *nothing* except to read and write—the latter I still do abominably. I can't add or

subtract. I know no foreign language decently, my geography is appalling.
I have taught myself history, but I am inaccurate and confused about everything.

Between myself it is miraculous that I'm not found out more often. But
perhaps most people are desperately ignorant except in their own job.
Priestley told me the other day that I was a teetotaler because I didn't need
liquor, getting drunk with excitement or enthusiasm every day over trifles!
Perhaps there I'm lucky, because *if* I cared for liquor *what* a drunk I'd be!
Today, for instance, I have found *very* good.

1. Mutton at lunch.
2. Orloff playing a Scriabin concerto.
3. The carnations sent me by Allwoods.
4. Ogden Nash's poem on the Japs.
5. The cosiness of the library when the rain was peltering down outside.
6. Ordering some Firsts from Arthur Rogers.

And I don't doubt that I shall enjoy tonight the heavyweight fight on the
wireless between Len Harvey and Eddie Phillips.

On December 15 in London he bought a Quentin Matsys for £400,
and swore a solemn oath not to buy another picture for six months.
Two days later he was the principal guest at the annual dinner given by
the directors of Macmillan's to their staff, and was delighted to learn
that he was the first author to be so honoured. Christmas was spent as
usual in Edinburgh, and on New Year's Eve he drove home to Brackenburn.

9

1939 was not a year which many people welcomed with hope,
"jitterbugs" were vocal everywhere, and Hugh's journal hereabouts is
full of gloomy political foreboding. Still, cheerfulness broke in now
and again. His brother and sister spent a few days with him at Brackenburn, while he laboured away rewriting the all-important last chapter
of *The Sea Tower*. Both he and his publishers knew that the original
version was not right, but he so seldom rewrote a page of his work, let
alone a complete chapter, that he found the task a hard one. But after a
week or so, and Harold's timely suggestion of the introduction of a
red-hot poker into the scene, the job was done to his satisfaction.

He was cheered by a letter from an old lady asking him to buy some hairs from the tail of the horse that Wellington rode at Waterloo, and still more by the production of *The Haxtons* at the Liverpool Repertory Theatre. He drove there and spent most of the week watching rehearsals under the direction of his old friend William Armstrong. In some ways the chief pleasure of playwriting to Hugh lay in this part of the business, "to see one's characters move away from the paper into free life." The first night was on January 19: to Hugh's delight the play held the audience, and when he came on the stage to make a curtain-speech he was greeted with shouts and cheers.

There followed a fortnight in London, during which he broadcast, and paid visits to Vita Sackville-West at Sissinghurst and the Cazalets at Fairlawne. On February 3 he drove north, bent on seclusion and *The Bright Pavilions*, but events took another turn.

10

In the early morning of the 10th Pope Pius XI died, and next day Hugh was "excited when Ralph Pinker rang me and asked whether I'd go to the Pope's funeral for Hearst. £500 and expenses. So I accepted." On the 11th the long-distance telephone was busy. "First Hearst wouldn't pay expenses, so I wouldn't go." Then he would pay expenses, but the day and hour of the funeral were still unknown. Finally, that evening, while Hugh was in Keswick watching an amateur performance of *The Passing of the Third Floor Back*, he received word that the Pope's body was corrupting, the funeral was fixed for the 14th, and arrangements were being made for him to fly to Rome immediately.

All through the night Harold drove him southward. They reached Piccadilly at half-past five on the morning of the 12th, Hugh caught the plane that day and, flying by way of Berlin, reached Rome on the afternoon of the 13th. That evening he saw the lying-in-state, next day the funeral. When he had written his descriptions of these scenes, there was nothing to do but wait about for the election of the new Pope, and each day he must conjure out of nothing an article which was syndicated in almost a hundred American papers. However there were the beauties of Rome to admire, and congenial companions among the

other journalists. He particularly enjoyed the company of Tom
Driberg, Alfred Noyes, and Hilaire Belloc.

On the anniversary of Keats's death, Hugh and Noyes made a pilgrimage to his grave in the Protestant Cemetery, and Hugh picked a
violet-leaf which he folded away in the pages of his diary. Soon the
urge to write overcame him, and he began the first pages of the book
that was to become *Roman Fountain*. In it he combined vivid reporting
of the Papal ceremonies and Roman scenes with passages of garbled
autobiography and others of pure fiction. Despite its mixture of inaccurate fact and symbolical invention, it is of all his books the most
revealing of himself and his character. It made him smile when people
told him the best things in the book were the quest for the fountain and
the character of Mr Montmorency, since both were wholly imaginary.
"You forget that I'm a professional novelist," he would beam delightedly.

The English journalists had procured a hiding-place opposite St
Peter's, a room in a priests' lodging-house, whence on March 2 they
saw with relief the column of white smoke that announced the election
of a new Pope. Hugh's account of this moment, and of the scenes
which followed it, was declared by Hearst to be a "masterpiece" and
later made one of the most effective chapters in his book.

The coronation of Pope Pius XII took place on the 12th, and next
day, Hugh's fifty-fifth birthday, he travelled to Florence. After a few
days he moved south to Naples, where Harold joined him. Together
they visited Amalfi and Sorrento, where Hugh "walked through
Marion Crawford's garden and stood on his terrace." At Capri he
lunched with Axel Munthe, now eighty-one years old, "half blind, very
charming, sarcastic and tender." By the end of March Hugh and
Harold were back in London, and Hugh's last journey to the Continent
was over.

II

He stayed in London a few days, had tea with Virginia Woolf,
accompanied by "the frankest sex talk on both sides," and was charmed
by Stefan Zweig, to whom John Brophy introduced him. Then up to
Brackenburn and *The Bright Pavilions*, into which he once more

plunged with delight. He had just reached the scene of Campion's execution,[1] and though *Roman Fountain* was urgently insisting on being written, he could not wholly set aside his old love. So the two books grew side by side, and Hugh would spend the day on whichever seemed immediately more attractive. George Blake came to stay, but Hugh wrote on.

At the end of April he drove south for three weeks in London, during which he saw Storrs, Zweig, Compton Mackenzie, and Frank Swinnerton. One day at luncheon Harold Macmillan proposed a new edition of the first four Herries novels in one volume to be called *The Herries Chronicle*. Nothing could have pleased Hugh more than to see his bid for immortality thus compactly presented, and he welcomed the proposal with joy.

Another fortnight of sunshine and hard work in Cumberland, mostly on *Roman Fountain*, but with occasional returns to Mary Queen of Scots, ended with this entry written in his journal at the end of May, before his next departure for London:

> I have told a great whacking lie and have been miserable about it for days. The worst of it is that the lie came from my issuing in an article an anonymous criticism of a book. That was in itself bad enough, and then I could only cover up the harm I had done by a whacking lie.
>
> I find that I tell downright whacking preconsidered lies practically never, and that it is a real shock to me when I do. I have been dreadfully ashamed, and this self-shame is very bad for me, I find, because it makes me distrust myself in many other respects.

12

Back to the whirligig he went—to luncheons with Sibyl Colefax, week-ends at Canterbury and with the Freres, dinner with the Lynds. He bought a Manet drawing, watched the West Indies skittle Middlesex at Lord's, sat for his portrait to R. G. Eves, and was televised at Alexandra Palace. In June he made a speech in the Bodleian Library at Oxford, spending the night with George Gordon at Magdalen. Among the other guests was P. G. Wodehouse, who on the morrow

[1] When the book was published, Father D'Arcy, S.J., wrote from Campion Hall, Oxford, to thank Hugh for his "very sympathetic and vivid account" of Campion's character and martyrdom.

was to receive an honorary degree from the University. "Same old Plum" was Hugh's only comment in his diary, but Wodehouse has an amusing memory of the occasion:

It was just after Hilaire Belloc had said on the radio something to the effect that the greatest of all writers today was P. G. Wodehouse—purely, presumably, as a gag, to get a rise out of serious-minded authors whom he disliked—and Hugh couldn't leave this alone. He asked me if I had seen it in the papers, and I said yes, and he said "I wonder why he said that," and I said I couldn't think, and the subject was dropped for a while. But it was not long before he was muttering again "I wonder *why* Belloc said that." Eventually a plausible solution occurred to him. "Ah, well," he said, "the old man's getting very old."

Next day Hugh lunched with the Muirhead Bones, and soon after with the Prime Minister in Downing Street. "Chamberlain charming," he noted, "but looking worried and rather wistful. He seemed a bit bewildered!" A few days later, when he chronicled the meeting in his journal, a schoolboyish note, almost one of hero-worship, crept into his words:

He was most friendly, calling me "Walpole," putting his hand on my shoulder. I talked to him about Alfred Douglas getting a Civil List Pension. He was the other end of the table, but he talked with me afterwards about the Hamlets he'd seen, the best Forbes-Robertson. He seemed tired, worn, anxious. He said once with deep bitterness: "Ah, our dear friend Ribbentrop!"—but I noticed a different rather wistful accent when he spoke of Hitler. I believe Hitler letting him down was the greatest blow of his life.

13

At the end of the month Hugh paid his first official visit to Durham since he had left, a disgruntled schoolboy, thirty-six years before. He spent a "thrilling morning" at Bede College, re-discovering all the old places—the corner of the dining-room where he used to read novel after novel and play his interminable games of literary bagatelle, his bedroom between the college and the Principal's quarters, the garden running down to the river. Later, at the Durham School prize-giving, Hugh and Dr C. A. Alington, the Dean of Durham, were the chief speakers, and in the evening there was a "delightful O.D. dinner," at which, as if to bring the wheel full circle, Hugh talked and laughed with his old teacher John Hay Beith.

Next day he attended a service in the cathedral, lunched with Mrs Darwin at Dryburn, and drove home to Brackenburn rejoicing in his lot. So stimulated was he by this visit that in his diary he described his next day's work—the description of the execution of Mary Queen of Scots—as "the best chapter I've ever written in my life."

His old friend Jim Annand, on holiday from Canada, came to stay for a few days. Ten years earlier Hugh had written to him: "I've really only had three friends, you and David and my present Harold," and this declaration held good to the end. When Annand left, Hugh wrote in his diary: "I love him as much as ever." They were not to meet again.

In London at the beginning of July, Hugh bought a Tintoretto drawing, a small Constable, and a Cézanne nude, and attended the first night of a dramatisation of *Captain Nicholas* at Richmond. He enjoyed the performance more than the critics did, and the play's run was short. There followed a blissful fortnight with Harold in Scilly, and by the beginning of August he was back in London, lunching with H. G. Wells, whom he found "puckishly, gleefully pessimistic."

14

This was a nervous month of expectancy and apprehension, and until he could get back to real writing Hugh filled in time with a short story called *Miss Thom*. He was invited by Ernest Brown, the Minister of Labour, to be a member of the tribunal which, under the new Military Training Act, was to hear the cases of conscientious objectors in Cumberland and Westmorland.

The tribunal was to sit in Carlisle, and if Hugh had accepted this offer he might well have lived longer, since his duties would have kept him in the north, far from the bombs and the nervous strain which hastened his end. But he believed that if war came there would be more important tasks for him, and perhaps he knew his own temperament too well to tie himself down in this way. Anyhow he refused the offer, and went off to stay with Alfred Noyes in the Isle of Wight.

The first three days of his visit passed agreeably, with bathing and tennis, but on the third evening, just as the party was breaking up for the night, the talk turned upon modern literature. In all innocence, and without knowledge of his host's strong views on the subject, Hugh spoke in praise of James Joyce's *Ulysses*. Suddenly he found himself blackguarded, and believed that but for the lateness of the hour he would have been turned out of the house. As it was he spent a miserable night and left early in the morning, when he drove over to the Priestleys and "it was like coming home."

15

When he had recovered from this unexpected reverse, he travelled back to London. The few days he spent there were expensive ones, for he paid £750 for a Utrillo—"but *what* a Utrillo. There can be no finer in the world anywhere." This picture, with its "deep, rich, almost eatable white walls," shone over the mantelpiece in the sitting-room at Brackenburn and remained for him to the end the brightest jewel in his now vast collection.

But first it remained for a while at 90 Piccadilly, and before the war comes to change everything, here is a last glimpse of the flat in the height of its glory, preserved in the loving exactitude of Sylvia Lynd's memory:

His rooms were so crowded with beautiful things that they gave the impression of a rich background rather than a collection demanding detailed attention. A typical moment in my remembrance of him is finding him one hot summer's day sitting at the pianola in his shirt sleeves playing himself a Beethoven sonata; the purple Persian rug that coloured so much of his writing dominating the room; Gaudier-Brzeska's lovely little green stone fawn snoozing beside him; T'ang horses stepping grandly on the chimney-piece; the white Utrillo, a new possession, propped on the arms of an armchair; all sorts of trifles in jade and rose-quartz and amber giving back the light; the window filled with his big Epstein bronzes, the Green Park for their background; the whole concourse of London's prosperity going by outside; and Hugh himself, pearl pin in tie, about to put on his coat and set out for the Royal Garden Party across the way.[1]

He enjoyed a happy week-end with the Botts at Richmond, though he could sometimes be a difficult guest. He had recently

[1] The *Book Society News*, July 1941.

developed the habit of rearranging the furniture in other people's houses to suit his own taste—a trick of which his hostesses seldom approved. He would also practically commandeer any small object which took his fancy; Alan Bott once in this way lost a whole set of books, which were recovered only after Hugh's death.

To the Botts' on Sunday came Nicholas Hannen and Athene Seyler. Hugh presented Athene with an advance copy of *The Sea Tower*, and "when she saw it was dedicated to her she nearly fainted." Later, after she had read the book, she wrote to him about it, and he answered: "Reading between the lines I gathered from your letter that you didn't like it much. Sad. But at least it will tell people all the world over that I love you." On which Athene Seyler comments: "I wrote and thanked him enthusiastically—in a letter which would have deceived anyone who was not so sensitive and who had not such delicate perceptions where his friends were concerned—for indeed I had not liked the book very much."

In August Hugh joined his brother and sister at Rockcliffe on the Solway Firth for their annual holiday. They made several expeditions, including one to Burns's grave in Dumfries, and Hugh finished *Roman Fountain*. But the international crisis impinged more and more on everyone's thoughts. On the 21st the Russo-German pact was announced, and when Hugh had finished his book the holiday was abandoned and he hurried back to London.

He was impressed by the calm in his Scottish hotel and by the cheerfulness of the people everywhere, the relief at tension ended—so different from the panic of the previous September. But as he sat in his Piccadilly flat, waiting for the war to begin, he felt lonely and not a little apprehensive. Looking round lovingly at his books, pictures, and other treasures, he wondered ruefully whether they and he would survive the wrath to come. "So God help us all," he wrote in his journal. "Make us brave, quiet, humorous, unselfish. Let us face death calmly, and comfort and cheer our friends."

BOOK SEVEN

THE SECOND WAR

My God! it is a melancholy thing
For such a man, who would full fain preserve
His soul in calmness, yet perforce must feel
For all his human brethren—O my God!
It weighs upon the heart, that he must think
What uproar and what strife may now be stirring
This way or that way o'er these silent hills—
Invasion, and the thunder and the shout,
And all the crash of onset; fear and rage,
And undetermined conflict—even now,
Even now, perchance, and in his native isle:
Carnage and groans beneath this blessed sun!
We have offended, Oh! my countrymen!

S. T. Coleridge
Fears in Solitude

written in April 1798, during
the alarm of an invasion.

CHAPTER TWENTY-FIVE

THE CLUE TO THE EXIT

I

WHEN the Prime Minister's wireless announcement on the morning of Sunday September 3 was followed almost immediately by the sirens' first blast of war, Hugh was at 90 Piccadilly, supervising the packing of his most precious pictures for their journey north. He spent that night with the Cheevers at Hampstead: there was a second air-raid warning in the small hours, and at five in the morning Hugh and Harold set off for Cumberland in the car laden with pictures, through the streets with their boarded, sandbagged windows, under the silver barrage-balloons which floated "like great boxing-gloves" in the sky.

They reached Brackenburn by lunch-time and found it bathed in a peace and tranquillity which it was never to lose through all the years of war. They hung the pictures in place of others, enjoyed two quiet nights and one day of "marvellous hot weather, as there always seems to be at the beginning of these wars," and then drove back to London. There was nothing to take Hugh back, then or later, except the vague possibility of a wartime job and the restless spirit which drove him always to return to the centre, to know what was going on, never to miss anything if he could help it. Time and again his friends begged him to settle down at Brackenburn and write his books: once or twice he tried to follow their advice, but it was no good. Even if the nervous strain killed him—and in truth it did kill him—he must be there at the heart of things, where he could experience the worst and no one could accuse him of skulking in his tent.

His first action when he got back to Piccadilly was to take up his journal: for the next fortnight he wrote in it each day, and seven of its fifteen volumes deal with the twenty-one months of war he was to know. Where he confined himself to observation and reported gossip, the record maintains its interest today, but more often he launched out into wild, repetitious and often contradictory prognostications. He was not a good strategist or war-prophet, and the chief value of this part of the journal lay in the release which its writing afforded to his immediate hopes and fears. On September 7, in an attempt to rational-ise his dread of air-raids, he wrote down in detail his plans for moving, first to the basement, then to a shelter, to Hampstead, and to the country only if the West End of London became uninhabitable. Then, at the end of the paragraph, as if to quiet himself still further, he added these prophetic words and underlined them: "*It is not my fate to die yet, and I shall die in my bedroom in Brackenburn.*"

He wrote to the Ministry of Information offering his services, and to his indignation received back a letter asking him to state his quali-fications. A further lorry-load of pictures was despatched to Bracken-burn, others to the Botts' Richmond home, and the flat was re-hung with old favourites rescued from cupboards, together with one or two of the latest acquisitions from which he refused to be separated.

Hugh was fascinated by the blackout, and at the same time a little afraid of it, since even with his glasses he found difficulty in getting about. "I bump into lamp-posts, fall over kerbs, dare not cross the street." Describing it in his journal, he wrote:

For the first time one notices the London night-sky. More *velvety* than any sky I've seen. The houses in Piccadilly are like cliffs, and the tiny lights of the cars like cats' eyes. Prostitutes everywhere. Whispers everywhere through the dark. "Please, dearie—one moment." People carry their gas-masks in their little cardboard boxes gaily as though they were doing some-thing for their country.

For the first time in more than fifteen years he was compelled to spend his London evenings at his own fireside, and to his surprise found that he enjoyed them immensely. He would feel his way down Half Moon Street to the hotel where he dined, and then back to the flat, the cosy fire, his books, pictures, wireless. He read much of Froude's *History*, and even began to toy again with the final section of *The Bright Pavilions*. Walter Scott's *Journal* too helped to sustain him and to rekindle his old love for its author: "He came as close to me as a piece of white heather, whispering me good luck"; but the war naturally dominated his journal and his thoughts. Now was the time to revive the old fantasy of being arrested as a German spy. He had always preferred the Germans to the French, he had been a friend of Winnie Wagner the Nazi, had even sat and talked with Hitler himself—so did his romantic habit lead him into imaginings ridiculous but fearful. His dreams too grew more and more bizarre. One night in early September, "in my sleep I had tea with the King and Queen, and the Queen said: 'We rely on *you*, Sir Hugh,' and I answered: 'Billingsgate is the answer, Ma'am.' "

The friends he met in the daytime swung him to and fro with their prophecies. One believed the war would be over in three weeks, another that it would last for twenty years. All opinions were recorded in the journal, together with a few crumbs of comfort, or as Hugh called them, "nice war sops for little vanities": the trawler *Hugh Walpole* had been detailed for special war service,[1] the *Sunday Dispatch* reprinted his short story *Mr Oddy* with the comment: "These are the days to enjoy Hugh Walpole," the Bishop of London "in a solemn article in the *Express* makes my old ''Tisn't Life that Matters . . .' the basis of his sermon."

There were major consolations too. "Am I mad?" he wrote on September 14. "About pictures I think so." If he bought new ones now, they must either be sent away for safety or remain as an added anxiety in Piccadilly. He decided to buy no more during 1939.

Nevertheless this afternoon I go into the Leicester Galleries and in admiration for Phillips's pluck in keeping open (so I kid myself) buy, of all things, a Watts nude, an Alfred Stevens chalk drawing and a *lovely* Rossetti drawing. And a marble torso by Leonardi. Rush back with them in a taxi, to find the Watts quite impossible with my other things (it looked lovely in Phillips's shop), so dash back with it in a taxi again and exchange for a superb Despiau drawing, a Degas, and a little James Pryde. With these I rush back to the flat again and sit in an ecstasy all evening contemplating them!

2

The Sea Tower, which had been delayed by the outbreak of war, was published next day. Hugh now described the book as "sophisticated melodrama—easy to read," and when *The Times* re-

[1] The vessel survived, and in October 1950 was detained for eight days by the Russian authorities and fined three hundred roubles for fishing in the closed waters of the White Sea.

viewer described him as a creator, but not from life, he commented: "All the same I *have* my world!" And as if to add another island to his cosmos, he sketched out in his journal a rough synopsis of the novel about a blind man which he would write next. Its early title, *The Hawthorn Window*, was soon changed to *The Blind Man's House*, but its theme, Generosity of Heart, remained constant.

On the 20th he drove north for a week, relishing the journey as seldom before, since the rationing of petrol might make it the last. Brackenburn, crowded with the Piccadilly pictures, seemed "a well of peace and quietness," and directly he sat down in his library to begin the torture chapter of *The Bright Pavilions*, the war fell away from him and he was once again his happiest self. "So it has always been," he wrote, "and so I hope it always will be." Priestley came to stay, and Hugh found him "at his very nicest and sweetest."

Strange man! . . . so sensitive and vain, so sure of his uniqueness, his power, his wisdom—yet with a marvellous control of his real nature (he is peevish and complaining, but I have never known him once in all these years lose his temper), so pessimistic, but with a gorgeous sense of humour. So penurious about little things and yet so generous-minded. He is so gruff, ill-mannered, and yet how sweet he was to Mrs Brown on Sunday. He can be an admirable critic. But through all and everything there is a deep sweetness that pervades his whole nature—which is why I love him.

3

On the 28th London whistled him up again, though he was well embarked on the final stage of his novel and there was nothing important to call him south. As Harold drove him back along the roads from which the traffic had now largely disappeared, he saw the war as the true Armageddon, ending with a Communist revolution in England "and myself finally shot by a Workers' Committee in Keswick for a bourgeois Christian."

A week-end at the house of Marie Stopes in Surrey provided splendid material for his journal. Of his hostess he wrote: "She has real honest goodness and incredible pluck. There is something so honest in her that you feel warm in her defence." And of his fellow-guest, Lord Alfred Douglas:

How astonished was I when this rather bent, crooked-bodied, hideous old man came into the room. How could he ever have been beautiful, for he has a nose as ugly as Cyrano's, with a dead-white bulbous end?

He talks ceaselessly on a shrill almost-broken note, agitated, trembling. He is so obviously a gentleman, full of little courtesies, delicacies, that, as gentlemen are now as rare as dodos, he seems remarkable. He loves to talk of his ancestors fighting in border raids, of Oscar whom now he always defends. When someone he hates like Wells is mentioned, he gets so angry that all his crooked features light up and his nose achieves a sort of sombre glow. In the afternoon he had before all of us a first-class row with young Briant of the *Sunday Chronicle* about the Russians, listening to no argument, screaming like a parrot, repeating phrases again and again. At last he shrieked: "Oh go to Hell!" Upon which the young man went.

He *is* a real poet—witness "the ribs of Time," one of the finest lines in all English poetry [1]—but has a streak of craziness running through his charm and talent. When I went to bed on Sunday evening not very well, he came in to see me with most tender solicitude.

He and Marie make a strange pair in this ugly eighteenth-century house, dark and wall-peeling.

Hugh made another overture to the Ministry of Information, but with little more success than before. He managed to visit some friends of his who were working there, and to discuss with them his idea of forming, as a kind of appendage to the Ministry, a committee of authors who would be useful for cultural and other propaganda. His friends listened to him sympathetically, but he quickly realised that they were too unsure of their own position to put forward any project that might be considered costly or unpractical. So he left them in their distracted honeycomb and hurried back to his new pictures and "*The Hawthorn Window* opening slowly ahead of me."

He spent the next week-end with the Botts at Richmond, and it was well that he did so, since Alan was able to prevent his accepting a tempting proposal which he had just received. Walter Hutchinson had asked him to write the history of the war quarter by quarter, volume by volume, for a handsome fee. As always he found it difficult to refuse, but his friend's counsel was wise, for Hugh's inability to remember or assemble facts, together with his disinclination to leave the

---

[1] To clutch Life's hair, and thrust one naked phrase
Like a lean knife between the ribs of Time.

(*The City of the Soul*, Sonnet iv)

current novel, would surely have brought the scheme to grief. The moment he had decided to refuse, his previous enthusiasm seemed madness, and it was with a profound feeling of gratitude that, in the middle of October and accompanied by Harold, he took train for the north.

4

He had allowed himself a fortnight in which to finish *The Bright Pavilions*, but the final chapters of his books always got themselves written sooner than he expected. Now, with golden autumn sunshine flooding the lake and the mountains outside, he wrote away at a furious pace. In the evenings he rediscovered, after thirty years and more, the novels of Rhoda Broughton, and decided that, despite her addiction to the historic present, she was "the *wittiest* woman novelist between Jane Austen and Elizabeth." "How well," he wrote, "I remember lunching with her and Henry James and Howard Sturgis—in 1910 was it? How well I remember her sharp sparkling eyes. She leant on a stick. She said (it must have been her pet remark—she repeated it so often): 'I began as Charlotte Bronte and ended as Charlotte Yonge.'" [1]

Presently there arrived an advance copy of *The Herries Chronicle*, a massive volume of almost fifteen hundred pages. In high spirits Hugh wrote in his journal:

For so many years to see such a work has been my urgent desire, almost from the days of writing the first chapter of *Rogue Herries*. How well I remember writing a specimen page just to see whether I could get at all the proper requisite style (for I had never tried writing anything of the kind before) and he [Priestley] approving it. He was even at that moment meditating *The Good Companions* and gave me, as I well observed, only half his attention. Still it was enough.

And now I receive this handsome volume, with its excellent type and paper—nearly a million words for 8/6—and do believe that for many years to come visitors to the Lakes will look at some part of it, if only because there are here the real names of local places. It carries the English novel no whit further but it *sustains* the tradition and has vitality.

[1] C. K. Scott Moncrieff, reviewing *The Green Mirror* in the *New Witness* of 12 April 1918, had written: "The art of Mr. Hugh Walpole might be defined as that of a person who means to write like Charlotte Bronte, having only lived like Charlotte Yonge."

This was surely the best possible omen for *The Bright Pavilions*, which now rushed to its conclusion. The final words were written on the evening of October 23, three days before Hugh's self-appointed deadline, and immediately, "as soon as one novel is pushed out of my brain and heart another skips in!" *The Hawthorn Window* became daily clearer, and behind it beckoned the large if still nebulous shape of the next Herries volume, which was to deal with the period of the Civil War.

But again London called, and when he arrived there at the end of the month he found everyone settling down to what became known as "the phoney war." Quickly he fell back into his previous routine— reading and writing in the mornings, lunch with a friend or at the club, a Turkish bath or cinema in the afternoon, quiet evenings in the flat. A new pleasure was provided by the daily concerts which Myra Hess had organised in the emptied National Gallery. Almost every day Hugh attended the lunchtime session, and often the afternoon one as well, making great friends with Myra Hess in the process. "Meanwhile," as he noted in his journal, "all is hushed, as though one lived in a magic wood outside whose boundaries lurk the wolves!"

5

The last two months of 1939 were spent in London. Early in November there was a "great meeting at M. of I. about my committee. Had things all my own way. Everyone charming." But the scheme was never heard of again, and Hugh's desire to help on the war received no encouragement until later in the month he was invited by the Lord Mayor to be Chairman of the Books and Manuscripts Committee for the big sale which the Red Cross were organising for 1940. Immediately he hurled himself gratefully into this congenial work, and quickly asked so many important people to join the committee that the provision of a room large enough for its meetings would have proved difficult had a plenary session ever been called. Gradually also he wrote to every friend, writer, collector, he could think of, asking for contributions, and they responded nobly.

A new interest came into his life when in the middle of November he spent a week-end with the Anglican monks of the House of St Francis at Cerne Abbas in Dorset. He spent the time reading, writing, walking and talking with the brothers. Father Algy Robertson became his dear friend: he paid another visit to them in April 1940, and something of the quietude and dedicated simplicity which he found there remained with him during these last months of his life and helped to sustain him amid the terrors of the London blitz. "I am sure," he wrote in his journal, "that this is not the *only* life for men to lead, and that it is not *my* life because the starving of sex and creative impulse would turn me silly at my age. I'm equally sure it is the *best* life, and it has got under my skin so that I shall never lose it again."

In London Priestley came to luncheon:

I think I am fonder of him every time I see him. His growls and pessimism all come from liver. He must have one of the worst in the animal kingdom. He says we will be ruined financially, politically, every way. Admits reluctantly we are the finest people in the world and can't ever be beaten. To say this is for him like having a tooth out, and inside he bursts with pride like a frog. I tell him he is not a novelist and never will be. He admits it and says he loathes to write novels, loves to write plays.

Other events were Macmillan's announcement that sixty thousand copies of the one-volume *Herries Chronicle* had been sold before publication, and that they hoped to dispose of a further forty thousand before Christmas; Hugh's lecture to the Literary Society at Eton; week-ends with the Botts and at Canterbury; more sittings to R. G. Eves; occasional visits to theatre or opera; constant purchases of pictures and more pictures. Harold, who disapproved of this indiscriminate buying—chiefly on the perfectly reasonable ground that there was nowhere to hang new acquisitions, had by now given up all attempts to restrain him. "Has Sir Hugh been buying any pictures lately?" asked a friend. "He's been nibbling," answered Harold resignedly.

At the beginning of December the play of *The Old Ladies* was revived at Kew in what Hugh described as a "grand performance." Even the egregious Agate was moved to write: "I thought the piece as effective as ever, and a very fine adaptation of a rattling good book. How very good you are when you are not fell-bound."

Next day Hugh travelled down to Gloucestershire and spent a happy week-end with Will Rothenstein and his family. Rothenstein, who had been commissioned to do so by Macmillan, made a chalk drawing [1] of Hugh, who decided that the artist had "a grand generous heart. This family is a new friend."

A few days before Christmas he travelled by train to Edinburgh, where he found the blackout even more stringent than in London. One night, after attending evensong in St Mary's Cathedral with William Roughead, he set off for his sister's house in the Corstorphine tram, missed his stopping-point in the darkness, was carried on to the terminus, took another tram back, overshot the mark again, then "felt quite *panicky* lost. A hateful feeling, very strange and sinister. Got home icy cold."

Christmas itself was the usual happy family affair, with any amount of presents and cards, and on Christmas Eve Hugh wrote the first words of *The Blind Man's House*, the last of the long succession of books to be so begun. The annual list of friends now bore an added significance. How precious they all were to him in this world of bloodshed and hate! He held on to the thought of them, and on Boxing Day wrote to Alan Bott:

The cigar-cutter is really magnificent. I hope to have it all my life long, and with it I like to realise that our affection for one another grows stronger and stronger. You don't know how much it means to me. I'm not *really* sentimental, but am thirsty for affection, and even love, from one or two people, being never really sure that I may not be thrust back into the old abyss, which I once knew, again.

6

As the war slowly progressed and impending events cast ever blacker shadows, Hugh found it less and less possible to sit writing peacefully in Cumberland. For the first fortnight of January 1940 he worked happily enough at *The Blind Man's House*, while outside the great frost spread and hardened until for the first time he saw Derwentwater frozen over from end to end. But he soon became restless: not even thoughts of Oliver Cromwell and the next Herries novel could hold

[1] It now hangs in Messrs Macmillan's boardroom.

him; and in the middle of the month he travelled to London, bearing with him at considerable inconvenience his "White Wall" Utrillo, from which he refused to be parted. "Harold says this is imbecile, but I can't live without it. If there is an air-raid I shall take it into the shelter with me!"

A heavy cold, threatening the pneumonia so dreaded by diabetics, kept him miserably in bed for a week; nor was his recovery helped on by a visit from his income-tax adviser, who had just discovered a further £4000 of untaxed income dating back to 1938. Still, there were compensations: a "completely delightful" dinner with Virginia Woolf, a new picture by Matthew Smith, a new friend in Frank Singleton. Breaking his habit of writing only in Cumberland, he quietly pursued *The Blind Man's House* and agreed to write a war pamphlet for Macmillan. His old friend John Buchan, Lord Tweedsmuir, died in February, and Hugh mourned him as "a *very* good friend to me. I really loved him although I saw him so little."

Hugh presided at his first Red Cross committee meeting, snatched a week-end at Canterbury, saw his portrait by Eves ready for the Academy,[1] and noted that "personally, now at the beginning of the seventh month of the war, I have suffered no slightest inconvenience. I am now on a strict diet anyway. I seem to buy books no longer. On the other hand I have in the last week bought an Ethel Walker seascape, a Piper oil (very fine) and a magnificent Rowlandson watercolour *very* [much] after Rubens!" These were almost immediately joined by two Turners costing £250. "Alas, alas! But they *are* so beautiful."

7

He was back at Brackenburn in time for his fifty-sixth birthday, and two days later *Roman Fountain* was published, with a dedication to Harold. As he received the enthusiasm of his friends and waited for the verdict of the critics, he decided that he would "never write a more honest or sincere book." Desmond MacCarthy's review in the *Sunday Times* could "scarcely be called favourable, but it is the most interesting

---

[1] Now hanging in the library of the National Book League in Albemarle Street. A second portrait is in the possession of Mrs Eves.

I have had for a long time. What literary times we live in, when I can look forward to scarcely another review of importance." And he went on to wonder whether his "romanticism and religion" were intrinsically bad, or whether they only seemed so to some because of the period of history in which he was writing. "How happy would I have been," he exclaimed, "had I been writing from 1890 to 1910, when romanticism was *all* the wear. I suppose it is the influences I imbibed then that make me the writer I am. In any case it doesn't matter. Only I *have* been swimming against the stream for thirty years—which is perhaps why I am still robust!"

The weather in Cumberland was lovely, and as Hugh prepared for his next journey to London, whose bombardment must surely soon begin, the possibility of his own death came forcibly into his mind. Amid the tranquil beauty of the lakes and mountains he felt he could face the prospect manfully, but first he must make peace with his enemies—his peace with God was already, he hoped, accomplished. Who were these famous adversaries? Maugham, he had once thought, had ridiculed him in public, but that business had long since been explained and forgiven. The childish breach with Ransome was happily healed these many years. Agate's attacks were too much mixed with friendliness and requests for money to be taken seriously now. Most of his other traducers were men of straw, or dead, or forgotten. Had he then imagined *all* his enemies?

No, for there still remained St John Ervine, whose supposed enmity Hugh had nourished all these years. The origins of this famous feud had long been forgotten, but feud there undoubtedly was, and he did not want to die with it on his conscience. So on Easter morning, after receiving Holy Communion in Borrowdale, he sat down at Brackenburn and wrote this letter:

Dear St John,
  This isn't an easy letter to write but it has to be written. I have for a long time cherished a grudge against you and have said a number of rude things. That you have also said, I believe, a number of rude things is only natural. I fancied some long time ago that I had a grievance, and this resentment was added to by various odds and ends brought to me by others. But it would none of it have happened at all had I not been, at that time,

desperately sensitive and unsure of myself. I am not making excuses. I am not apologising either. I am only saying that I have been greatly in the wrong, am ashamed of my conduct and must tell you so. You must feel that it's a bit late in the day for me to say this. I am afraid it is. You will of course continue to resent me or put me clean out of your mind as you please.

I can only say that I have done wrong and am very sorry for it.

Yours sincerely,
Hugh Walpole.

To which Ervine replied:

My dear Hugh,

I'm very glad we're friends again and I'll do my best to see that we never fall out. I still don't know how the quarrel began, and I wish sometime you'd tell me; but don't bother if the telling is burdensome. The main thing is that it is over. Nora, who has hated our ill-will, bids me send you her regards, and we both hope you are well and will long remain so.

Yours very sincerely,
St John Ervine.

And so, with the last hatchet (as he thought) buried, Hugh could travel south with a quiet mind. But he did not know that one anonymous foe still lurked in ambush, ready to pounce only when he could no longer reply. The obituary columns of *The Times* are famous for honey rather than gall, yet the day after Hugh's death they contained a venomous and belittling account of his life, full of subtle half-truths and *suggestiones falsi*, stressing his ambition, industry and sensitiveness to adverse criticism, omitting all mention of his passion for literature and his endless generosities to and encouragement of writers young and old, describing him as a "sentimental egotist" and openly claiming that he was "not popular among his fellow-writers."

The old game of Writing to Reviewers was over, but in its place rose a chorus of the voices of his friends—always the sweetest music in Hugh's ears—protesting at this travesty of truth. *The Times* printed cogently indignant letters from Priestley, Kenneth Clark, T. S. Eliot, Athene Seyler, and Alan Bott, each of whom rebutted some part of the anonymous aspersion.[1] Summing up the incident a few years later,

---

[1] Even his old "enemies" joined in the chorus. Ervine wrote a long and very fair obituary in the *Belfast Telegraph*, and Agate quoted: "Now cracks a noble heart."

Charles Morgan wrote of Hugh: "May posterity reward his strange, complicated and yet childlike spirit. So good a story-teller is likely at any rate to live longer than many a *petit-maître* who sneered at him as soon as he was dead." [1]

8

But to return to 1940. On April 9 the Germans overran Denmark and invaded Norway: the war was coming nearer, but all Hugh could do was to carry on with his Red Cross sale and with the committee (of which he was chairman) for supplying games and books to prisoners of war. Week-ends with the Botts, the Freres, the Franciscans at Cerne Abbas, made quiet breaks in the routine of blacked-out, strained, rumour-swept London. The golden bowl might be broken at any moment, but meanwhile life must go on. New friends included Michael Ayrton, a nineteen-year-old artist of great precocity and promise. Hugh bought a number of his pictures and was responsible for his designing the scenery and costumes for John Gielgud's production of *Macbeth* in 1942. "There is something in your macabre," Hugh told him, "that responds to my macabre—the best part of my writing." Unlike so many of his protégés, Ayrton remained his grateful friend and after Hugh's death wrote appreciatively of him as patron and picture-collector.

But Hugh's chief opiate, now as always, was simple story-telling. To blot out the worry of the Norwegian campaign he plugged on at *The Blind Man's House*, and wrote in his journal:

The odd thing about me is that so long as the creative animal is alive within me I am happy. Let wars rumble, rheumatism snarl, my money be all taken by the Government. Dear little animal, how I love to see you poke your little head out and begin to scratch in the soil! The pictures as you scribble them seem to me lovely and fresh. Later a wind comes along and obliterates it all—or only vague fragments remain. But so long as you live and are lusty I am happy, busy, excited.

On April 30 Hugh had his last sight of Virginia Woolf. At any rate no later meeting is recorded, and this occasion was so lucent and happy

[1] *The House of Macmillan* (1943).

that there could have been no more perfect close to their friendship. Here is Hugh's brief account:

Virginia Woolf had tea alone with me yesterday. She looked like a beautiful Victorian lady of fifty years ago. She had been lecturing at Brighton on the novel and had said that I and my contemporaries with our roots in the old pre-1914 world had been like men on a tower firmly placed. Since 1920 the younger novelists had been perched on a leaning tower, and their proletarian novels had been very wobbly!

I said that I had loved her always. She asked why. I gave her my reasons and she seemed pleased.

A friend who joined them after tea remembers the evening with especial pleasure. The long aristocratic lines of Virginia Woolf's face were always beautiful, but the general effect of her presence varied astonishingly. If she was ill, or tired, or unwilling to be observed, she had the gift of putting out the light and of taking upon herself the protective drabness of a neutral background. At other times, and this evening in Hugh's flat was one of them, the lights were blazing, her witty conversation sparkled in their glow, and the beauty of her physical presence dazzled and enchanted the beholder. They sat either side of the fire, she and Hugh, talking and laughing, exchanging stories, jokes and opinions: both for the moment completely happy, the war shut out, their affection for each other triumphantly asserted. Within little more than a year they were both dead, and for the friend who shared some of this magical evening with them, its memory, though being atmospheric it cannot easily be regained in words, shines still as a moment of civilised delight among the gloom and terror of those years of war.

On May 10, the day of the German invasion of Holland and Belgium, and of Winston Churchill's appointment as Prime Minister, Hugh travelled up to Brackenburn. He worked away at his novel and comforted himself by reflecting that the mountains around him would outlive Hitler, but after a week he could stand the isolation no longer and returned to London. He was greeted by the first news of the German break-through and the disruption of the French armies: momentarily he was seized by panic almost as overwhelming as that of September 1938. The fall of France would be the end of the world;

civilisation was finished. But he soon managed to pull himself together. It was the time of the great parachutist scare, of imminent invasion, of the inauguration of the Home Guard, of wondering agonisedly whether the B.E.F. would escape from the Continent. On the 23rd "the Government proclaimed itself Dictator and everyone was delighted." Hugh drew £200 in notes from the bank and acquired sufficient petrol to get him and the Cheevers family out of London in an emergency. There was little else he could do.

On the 24th Boulogne fell, and the old bogy of the Germans across the Channel was realised. The strain began to oppress the strongest: its effect on Hugh's excitable nerves can be imagined. "Physically I'm bearing up all right," he wrote on the 25th, "except that, like everyone else, I'm sleeping badly. All day long, though, my heart beats twice as hard as usual and I have a hot head. It is, to compare small things with big, exactly as I feel when I play chess, or wait for the result of a Test Match—only this goes on and on and on."

Despite these symptoms he still managed to buy more pictures—a Matisse, a Boudin, and a Modigliani, all from Montague Shearman's collection. "I believe," he wrote, "I shall be creeping up Bond Street to look at pictures even while Hitler is making his triumphant entry into London." He also conceived the notion of a volume of stories, in some sort a companion series to his *Thirteen Travellers*, to be called *The City under Fire*, and designed to show the reactions of a group of people, including Maradick, Meg Delaney, and others of his old characters, to this new kind of warfare in the heart of London. An introductory sketch and one of the stories were found among his papers.

On June 1, as the full magnitude of the Dunkirk evacuation was becoming known, Hugh travelled down to take part in the celebration of the hundredth anniversary of the birth of Thomas Hardy. He spent the week-end with the Bishop of Salisbury, and on Sunday drove over for the service in the little church at Stinsford (the Mellstock of the novels) where Hardy's heart lies buried. The exquisite weather, the armed soldiers at roadside barriers, the tiny church "glowing like the soft heart of a flower," all combined for Hugh to make the day "one of the loveliest and most poignant of my life." The village orchestra played century-old tunes as in *Under the Greenwood Tree*, and Hugh read the lessons, which moved him so powerfully that he almost broke down in the middle of the eighth chapter of St Paul's Epistle to the Romans. In the afternoon Lord Baldwin addressed the public from the Hardy Memorial in Dorchester. The Chief Constable expressed to Hugh his concern lest there might be a demonstration against the old statesman, but all proceeded smoothly. Hugh described Baldwin as having "death in his face—leaning on a stick, trembling. . . . He spoke platitudes about Hardy, but in a beautiful voice and fine English."

9

After lunching with Priestley ("a changed creature, optimistic, buoyant, happy") and staying a day or two with the Botts, Hugh went up to Brackenburn on June 11 to try and finish his novel before France's final dissolution and the invasion of England which must surely follow. But this time he could not last out even a week. Rest and writing were alike impossible, and on the 16th, deciding to return to London, he wrote in his journal:

I have a strange detached sense that I must be "in" at the bombing, destruction, occupation of London as it may be—to write of it an immortal account. I say to myself: "I'll write down all the little things. It shall be like the de Goncourt Journal."

This is detached, cold and inhuman and mingled with stomach-fear and a really terrible love for Harold and a few more. Why wish to be immortal at such a cost? The vanity of us poor human beings. But it isn't only vanity. It's a real burning desire to be a truthful observer of one of the turning-points of the world's history.

I look at my White Wall Utrillo, my Bellini, my Manet drawing, my Cézanne water-colours, with a burning protective love. "Nothing must destroy you," I cry. "No matter if I go—you must remain."

They are certainly more important than I, but I would sacrifice the whole lot for Harold's little finger. Painters will paint plenty more.

He arrived at Hampstead just in time to hear of Pétain's request for an armistice. For the next few days the news was scrappy and confused: there was nothing spectacular to record in London: he was there ready, and in the absence of anything else to do he took up his pen and polished off *The Blind Man's House*.

As soon as it was done, and arrangements made for a copy of the typescript to be sent to the United States for safety, his mind was flooded, not with thoughts of bombing and invasion, but, such was the strength of his vocation, with the next novel, that same macabre story which had first come to him three years ago. On June 30, exactly a week after he had completed its predecessor, Hugh wrote the first words of *The Killer and the Slain*.

He was still at Hampstead, and it would not be extravagant to say that just now he clung to the Cheevers as never before: "That little family is the centre of my life, and how lucky I am to have it!" Harold was an Air-Raid Warden, and Hugh would walk with him to the local Post, through the soft scented twilight of the Garden Suburb, giving thanks for every peaceful moment that remained. On Harold's off-duty evenings they would all go to a cinema or to the theatre at Golders Green. A £70 shelter was erected in the garden, and like every other family in England they lived from day to day, waiting for the invasion that never came.

Hugh made a number of further attempts to get some kind of a war job, but nobody seemed to want him. He had long since finished collecting the books and manuscripts for the Red Cross sale, and now the only useful work he could find was to conduct some New Zealanders round London in buses, and to give an occasional broadcast for the B.B.C., who promised him more. He also took the chair at a meeting called by writers, publishers, and others, to organise a deputation to the Government petitioning that books should be exempted from the impending Purchase Tax. Priestley, Geoffrey Faber, and the Master of Balliol spoke at the meeting, which eventually achieved its object.

10

But writing was still Hugh's main preoccupation, and in the first thirteen days of July he wrote and sent to his typist the first eleven thousand words of the new book. Then he journeyed down to Carlyon Bay in Cornwall, where the King's School had been evacuated from Canterbury. He stayed with Canon and Mrs Shirley and was at once "blissfully happy."

The moment I got here in pouring rain my spirit was tranquillised. This old stone Cornish house such as all my relations have lived in for centuries and I lived in as a child—high untidy rooms, with old worn carpet, and watercolours in dull gold frames, and bookshelves filled with Marion Crawford and Seton Merriman in Tauchnitz, the sloping lawn bordered with rhododendrons, crooked and deeply green, the sea, grey and wrinkled, the smell of gorse, blackberry and gull, the post and papers *still* not in until afternoon. Heavenly. I feel that I could stay here for months and the war far, far away.

But after a week he was obliged to come back for the Red Cross sale. This took place at Christie's on July 24 and 25, when the books and manuscripts realised more than £7,000. Hugh himself bought nearly fifty lots at a cost of £250. The manuscript of *The Cathedral*, which he had presented, fetched £36.

A week-end with his brother at Stratford-on-Avon included a visit to the house of Marie Corelli:

An old servant, exactly like the old Scotch one we used to have at Eglinton Crescent, showed us round. Small, white-haired, bespectacled, in a black silk dress and apron. "I hope you were a friend of Miss Corelli's and never spoke or wrote harm of her," she said, her eyes flashing ... "She was a sweet little lady," she repeated many times, and had obviously adored her, as had all her servants.

She took us over everything—all as it had been in M. C.'s lifetime. All dead or dying. The harp, the faded photographs, paper roses, cracked looking-glasses, a spinning-wheel from which a moth flew out, faded books ... Above all the famous gondola, and the Christmas card her gondolier had sent her just before he was killed in France. The ink she had used corroded in the ink-bottle. Rows of hideous china ornaments in her bedroom. The paddock thick with grass, and her old pony over forty! The garden with no flowers, only weeds ... Death and decay over everything. Only the old servant enormously alive, repeating again and again: "She was a sweet little lady. We all loved her."

She is not to be laughed at any more, for the love she created in those around her is still alive. But a warning never to leave collected things behind you. Distribute them all, so that they may live with live people again. I left feeling very sorry that I had ever laughed at her. She seemed to be there, alive and affectionate among all the decayed material things.

II

Hugh came back to London and a "skull and crossbones day. Letter from bank saying I'm £441 overdrawn, when I thought I was £1300 to the good. I *am* in a mess. Wandered about feeling ruined all day." This customary financial miscalculation so aggravated his already strained nerves that he quarrelled that day with Alan Bott, whom he had invited to lunch at the Athenæum. They had scarcely begun their meal when Hugh began nagging his friend in a loud voice. After enduring a little of this, Bott said that if Hugh didn't stop he would leave the club. Hugh continued to storm, and Bott withdrew hungry. No sooner had he gone than Hugh, overcome with remorse, sat down and wrote:

14 August 1940.   The Athenæum.

Dear Alan,

I'm terribly sorry—and just before I go north!

It makes me quite miserable. As always with these things I think we are both annoyed at times by one another and that we are both to blame. It *is* true that in the last three or four years I have been quiet and tranquil (even with Noyes I wasn't excited) save only with yourself.

Your kindness in *acts* to me has been quite marvellous, but again and again I feel that you really dislike me, and above all deeply criticise me. It is this that so often upsets me. God knows I have every fault in the world. I think most meanly of myself at heart, which is why perhaps your cynicism about me rouses me inwardly to rebel.

In any case I am miserable about today which was all my fault. I will try to behave better and not allow myself to be so conscious of, and hurt by, your criticism. I really love you very much. Let me have a line to Brackenburn.

Yours,
H.

Alan Bott responded warmly; the incident was forgotten; and as a peace-offering Hugh asked permission to dedicate to Bott the war-pamphlet which he was about to write.

The nervous crisis was over; as the train carried him northwards to Cumberland his senses were calmed, and at Brackenburn on August 16, although *The Killer* was in full career, he wrote the first words of the next Herries novel, *Katherine Christian*, which he was never to finish. During a week in Scotland (visiting George Blake and listening with his sister to the Polish Choir in the Usher Hall) he wrote the whole of his war-pamphlet, which was published in March 1941 as *Open Letter of an Optimist*.

Brackenburn again, with its "wonderful peace and quiet" and the new story demanding to be written. "Writing a Herries novel is to me like bathing in milk! How I adore it. This one really does promise *riches*. And so do the two that follow. How I ache to get at Sedgemoor and the Monmouth rebellion! Shall I live to get there?"

The ever-growing genealogical tree of the Herries family, which had accompanied each volume of their history, had been tended by Thomas Mark, who had peopled its furthermost branches with wives, great-aunts, and cousins of the appropriate age and sex. Now Hugh once again consulted his able collaborator.

My dear Mark,

Beginning a new Herries I am attacked by a nightmare that we haven't put right my "Sylvia" mistake. Whom did we make marry Tobias Garland and become the mother of Rashleigh etc? Did you insert an extra Barbara and make *her* the mother? Do reassure me by return as I am most uncomfortable about it. In any case it is too late to do anything about it, but I hope it is all right?

What did we call Josephine ultimately? She is figuring in the next Herries very considerably. I am coming to town on Friday to share in the bombing and sign some *Bright Pavilions* when they are ready. I *do* hope we haven't made a blunder with *two* Sylvias!

Yours,
H. W.

He was duly reassured.

For the first time since the war began he was now able to enjoy the pleasures of Brackenburn without being dragged back to thoughts of death and destruction. He grew calmer each day, and his nightmares gave place to happier dreams:

I woke up in the middle of last night, saying aloud: "Love is the thing," as though I had made the most marvellous discovery ever. Then I turned over, was asleep at once, and dreamed of a wonderful pie made of blackberries, thrushes' eggs, honeycomb and watercress.

He found time also to potter in his library and rearrange his books as he had so often loved to do in the past. He dug out the works of his old friends Conrad and Henry James, and replaced them in new positions of honour. "I could stay here for ever," he wrote. "Meanwhile I must not funk London!" There were by now solid reasons for fear, since the London blitz had begun, but it was a refreshed and fortified Hugh who travelled south on September 6 to face the venom of the *Luftwaffe*.

CHAPTER TWENTY-SIX

THE CITY UNDER FIRE

I

THE final chapter of Hugh's life may well begin with his first experience of air-raids, since, whatever the immediate cause of his death, he was as surely killed by the Second World War as his old master Henry James had been killed by the First. James had been a much older man, and for him the final blow was the wanton destruction of European culture at the hands of war, rather than direct personal danger. Hugh was fated, or at any rate felt impelled, to endure the prolonged ordeal of the Battle of London, in which noise, terror, and lack of sleep gradually wore down the strongest physiques. His temperament, always a nervous one, was subjected to a series of ever-greater shocks, until his heart, weakened by years of erratically judged insulin injections, could stand no more.

Night after night as darkness came, the sirens wailed out their hideous warning and strained nerves listened for the crash of guns, the whistle and explosion of bombs, hour after hour until with the first light of dawn the All Clear was sounded. On September 11 Alan Dent came to dine at 90 Piccadilly. Soon after dinner a noisy raid began, and they went down and sat with the servants in the basement kitchen. After a while Hugh grew bored and declared that he was going to bed regardless. So upstairs they climbed once more, and Alan Dent was settled in the sitting-room with the opening chapters of *The Killer and the Slain*. The sequel shall be told in his words:

Hugh prepared for bed in spite of bangs louder and nearer, and I set about a tale of a passionate hatred between two men, more exciting than anything of the sort since *The Old Ladies*. I exclaimed aloud at the arresting quality of the opening pages. He was as pleased as a schoolboy at my praise, for he knew it was critical praise.

Some time afterwards I looked into his room to say good night, and was startled to find Hugh on his knees by his bedside at his prayers, like a little child. This was quite obviously a nightly custom, and it was wholly without self-consciousness that he climbed into his bed, saying: "I was just putting up a little prayer for your safety, Jock." Other men of the world, doubtless, if the truth were told, still submit themselves to the same spiritual exercise. But they would hate to be caught at it, whereas Hugh laughed aloud at my acute embarrassment on finding him out.[1]

That night a bomb fell in Bond Street, another in the grounds of Buckingham Palace just across the Park, but Hugh slept well. It was only gradually, through the following weeks and months, that the strain wore down his health and spirits. Early next morning he walked along Piccadilly, observing in the sky the crimson glow of still-burning fires, in the street the glittering greenish piles of broken glass, "like a scene from *Vathek*." He had now a definite engagement to broadcast twice a week to America and the Dominions, which gave him both a reason for staying in London and also the long-desired feeling that he had something useful to do.

On the night of the 12th a bomb fell opposite the flat on the near side of the Park. Hugh experienced "a most unpleasant suggestion as of this building holding itself together and wondering whether it would fall or no—a shudder as I should imagine an earthquake would be." But the house stood firm, windows and all. Next morning, as the sirens sounded for a daylight raid, Hugh took up *The Killer and the Slain* and was soon lost in it, just as in the earlier war he had written *The Dark Forest* in the confusion of the Great Retreat.

But Piccadilly was becoming uncomfortably noisy, and that same day he moved out to Hampstead. There, each night between eight and nine, the garden-shelter was occupied by Hugh, Ethel Cheevers, Nada the Cornish maid, and Leo the Cheevers's pekinese. Hugh always carried with him an armful of his most cherished possessions. Besides his teeth in a tooth-bath, these consisted of the manuscript of *The Killer*, the current volume of his journal, a blue box (successor to the one he had clutched in the cab from Seascale long ago) containing ivory figures and other small objects, photographs of Harold and Boleslawsky, a Cromwell letter bought at the Red Cross sale, and always a picture, usually a Matisse oil of which just now he was particularly fond. "We sleep beautifully," he wrote, "but in the middle of the night when

[1] Published in *John o'London's Weekly* (20 June 1941) and reprinted in *Nocturnes and Rhapsodies* (1950).

nature drives me out I slip into a world suddenly frantic with noise, huge tea-trays smashing all over the sky—lovely starlit sky with a vast full moon. There is always the sinister whirring of a plane. Then all suddenly stops and the peace is exquisite."

One night a policeman friend of Harold's arranged for Hugh to spend the night at Beak Street police station. He slept on a mattress alongside forty policemen, but not for long. Bombs fell all around them, and at three o'clock in the morning he was taken along Oxford Street to see the fire at John Lewis's department store. "The full moon was huge and golden, and all round it shrapnel was blazing and dancing. The fire leapt to heaven, the noise was like a thousand thunderstorms, and above one's head the swift thin clouds made the glittering stars [look] like fast-moving aeroplanes."

On September 27, in the midst of the inferno, *The Bright Pavilions* appeared. It was the last of his books that he was to see published, and he had dedicated it to Ronald Storrs. Reviews were favourable and sales excellent considering the times. It was not till later in the war that the sales of books soared to heights never known before, so that everything between covers was bought and read directly it appeared in the shops. By 1945 the whole of Macmillan's considerable stock of Hugh's fifty-odd books had been exhausted—by the demands of readers, not by enemy action.

Driving from Hampstead to Piccadilly grew daily more difficult. Craters and unexploded bombs caused many streets to be roped off and their traffic diverted. The flat took on more and more the air of a beleaguered outpost, but by walking the last part of the way Hugh managed to get there most days. He lunched with Michael Ayrton and decided that he was "a bit of a genius," attended a congratulatory luncheon to Charles Morgan on the publication of *The Voyage*, and carried on with his wireless talks. Owing to the bombing he had to speak and make recordings at many emergency branches of the B.B.C. To North America he spoke repeatedly in a series of talks called "Within the Fortress," but early in 1941 he was switched to a regular programme called "Hugh Walpole Talking."

Day by day he mourned the destruction of favourite buildings—St James's Piccadilly, Holland House, Pagani's restaurant, and the others.

On October 18 he travelled to Bristol and lectured there in the Central Library on "The Romantic Novel in England." An air-raid was in progress outside, but his gift of oratory did not fail him, and his audience of over seven hundred was held, despite the uproar overhead.

All this time he was using *The Killer and the Slain* as an outlet for his nervous emotions, reserving *Katherine Christian* for the blessed inter-ludes at Brackenburn. The theme of *The Killer* had been with him for years, but into its treatment he poured all the twisted agonies of his present state. "It may be awfully good," he wrote when it was half-finished. "I can't tell till I come to the hard part, which is the second half. Meanwhile what a lot of nastiness, and pity for my own nastiness, I have in me! It's all coming out in this work."

There may be some significance in the fact that this was the first of all his novels to be dedicated to the memory of Henry James. He had never forgotten his old benefactor, had re-read most of his books at intervals, and often upheld him in print as a neglected giant, but there was something about the pattern of the two wars, and James's death in the earlier one, which now brought him strongly into Hugh's mind. Psychologists may perceive a deeper connection, and Leon Edel has written a brilliantly ingenious "psychocritical" analysis of *The Killer* and its origins.[1]

But now Hampstead, like Piccadilly, became too hot to hold him. On October 15 a stick of four bombs fell in the road outside, and though the house itself was miraculously preserved, Hugh went through all the sensations of imminent dissolution—the swish of the bombs, explosions, cries, screams, and the noise of falling rubble. Four days later, at about eight in the evening, he was sitting in the dining-room reading *War and Peace* ("of course," as he put it to a friend) when without warning a bomb fell, "as it seemed right upon us. The window behind me blew in. I heard a rush of falling glass. Ethel was coming downstairs and I thought she was killed. However we met in the hall. Main damage to pantry, where part of the bomb had penetrated. Windows smashed, doors blown in." Harold and one of his sons had seen the bomb fall from a distance, and now ran up in great distress, fearing the worst. They agreed that since the house was barely

[1] "The Fantasy of *The Killer and the Slain*" (*American Imago*, December 1951).

habitable and they were all suffering from shock, it would be wise to seek an at any rate temporary refuge in Cumberland. Arranging for Harold and Ethel to follow him as soon as possible, Hugh took train for the north on the morning of October 22.

2

He was never wholly himself again after this last bomb-incident, though he lived for another six months. Harold and others close to him noticed that his nerves became more edgy than ever, and that his health played him tricks. The train, crammed with soldiers, was three hours late at Penrith, where Jack Elliot met him with the car. During the drive home they had to stop for Hugh to be sick by the roadside. Then, at last, "Oh how wonderful the cottage, smelling of mountain streams, chrysanthemums, Ranter!"

He had scarcely begun to absorb the undisturbed quiet before his conscience was pricking him for not staying in London. He salved it by deciding that he had earned a respite and could legitimately stay where he was until the middle of November. Indeed he was fit for little else, since the symptoms of delayed shock soon began to appear. Sickness, jumpiness, sleeplessness, nightmares, digestive trouble, attacked him severally and jointly. Only *Katherine Christian* had the power to hold and soothe him.

The Cheevers arrived a few days later, as did Athene Seyler, to settle her daughter and her infant granddaughter into Copperfield, the gardener's cottage in Grange, part of which Hugh lent them for the duration of the war. At the end of the month he went for two nights to Temple Newsam, Leeds, where he opened the new Art Gallery.

When he got back to Brackenburn he retired to bed with what he described as "a sort of gastric flu," and was compelled to stay there a whole week. In all his sixteen years at Brackenburn he had never so far spent a complete day in bed there, and he was sufficiently alarmed about himself to call in Doctor Cameron of Keswick. He made a thorough examination, decided that Hugh had narrowly escaped a diabetic coma, prescribed a return to his original dose of insulin, and advised him to consult his London specialist as soon as he could. Hugh pooh-poohed this diagnosis, but admitted in his journal that for two days he had "suffered the pains of hell. Harold says my face was absolutely grey." However, his recovery was rapid. The day he got up he wrote two articles and more than forty letters: next morning he delightedly began a new chapter of *Katherine Christian*. Unfortunately he was due to deliver two broadcast talks in London, and it was with the utmost reluctance that he travelled south on November 14.

3

Both Piccadilly and Hampstead were still out of the question, so for this stay Hugh had booked a room at the Dorchester Hotel in Park Lane. It was on the sixth floor, but the first night he was so tired by his train journey that he slept well. Next day he delivered his two broadcasts, one to America, the other on the Home Service, and came back to a "fearful night. Hotel simply rocked." The new anti-aircraft guns in Hyde Park were largely the cause of the rocking, but in the small hours Hugh could bear the noise and loneliness no longer. Clad in his dressing-gown he trailed down seven floors to the basement, where he found Lady Cunard "and the other smarties, smoking long cigarettes and chattering in hard shrill voices." He lay down but when, soon after, an old lady on the next bunk said: "I don't know what you think, but the hot-water system is all round this shelter. One bomb and we'll all be boiled alive," he decided that he preferred the hazards of the sixth floor. Up he climbed, only to discover that he had left his key behind, and by the time he had been down and up once more he was so exhausted that he fell asleep at once.

Next morning John the valet telephoned to say that all the ceilings and one wall of the Piccadilly flat had been blown in during the night. After lugubriously inspecting the ruins of his beloved rooms, Hugh felt he could face no more nights in central London. The Botts offered him refuge at Ham Common, and he gratefully accepted. For a week he enjoyed comparative quiet, and was able to start on *The Killer* once more. It should not be forgotten that, besides the scripts of his B.B.C. talks, he was all this time contributing his weekly book-page to the *Daily Sketch*.

In the early morning of November 23 his peace was shattered by a
heavy raid, in the course of which nine bombs were dropped in close
proximity to the Botts' house. Hugh had to see what was happening,
so he rushed out on to Ham Common in his dressing-gown, wearing
his spectacles and a French steel helmet several sizes too small for him
which he picked up in the hall. In his excitement he had forgotten his
teeth, so that when an elderly female admirer recognised him and
begged Josephine Bott to introduce them, he could neither handle his
headgear with decorum nor even acknowledge her compliments articulately. Thus grotesquely did Mr Pooter make his final appearance
in Hugh's story.

Later that day Hugh left to spend a couple of nights with Ronald
Storrs in Essex. Josephine Bott drove him there and back to Richmond. "Jo really is an angel," wrote Hugh, "and good to me beyond
all knowing."

Even his return to Brackenburn on the 30th was not without its
terrors. The big London railway stations were particularly nerve-
racking places at this time, with their huge glass roofs, their lack of
shelter, and their power of magnifying the sounds of guns and air-
craft. To catch the night train Hugh had to stand for half an hour
wedged with sailors and other passengers on what his porter told him
was the least dangerous part of the platform, then to sit for almost
another hour in the blacked-out train before it finally started.

But then, "Oh Joy! Oh Glory!" The next day "was like heaven.
A lovely frosty day with amber light and silver shadows everywhere.
I walked on the fell with Harold and Ethel, finished a chapter of
Katherine, and Athene came to tea. I felt as though a whole barrage was
lifted off my head."

4

The Botts came up to stay for a week in the first half of December,
and on the 18th Hugh travelled to Edinburgh, to spend what was
destined to be his last Christmas with his brother and sister. He confessed in his diary on Christmas Day that his head, neck, and legs hurt
him like toothache, and that there was now scarcely a day when he
felt really well. Nevertheless he wrote on at *The Killer*—"a very odd

402

4

Since my night at Belloc's and my last quarrel with Eve things have been moving faster and faster. I feel as though I were being hurried along towards some climax. I dream horrible dreams at night. One especially seems to recur although I may have dreamed it only once and thought about it afterwards. I am in a prison deep down in the bowels of the earth, naked chained to a wall sweating with damp. Rats fight their way over my bare flesh. Tunstall, grinning, looks down at me through a grating — "Jacko!" he says softly "Jacko!" — But

Page of manuscript of *The Killer and the Slain*

book that nobody will like . . . all these months of fear, uncertainty, restlessness are behind it." On New Year's Eve, after compiling in his diary the last list of his fifteen best friends, followed by five runners-up, he closed his journal for the year with "End of 1940. *Thank God.*"

Back at Brackenburn, he ruefully contemplated the falling due of his large life assurance policy. The cheque for £15,800, which would once have meant so much to him, now seemed useless. He learned that the serial and film rights of *The Blind Man's House* had been sold for £6,000, months before the book was due to be published. Twenty-eight thousand copies of *The Bright Pavilions* had been bought by the public in three months, but what use was all this money, this success, to him now? Most of the money would go to the Government in taxes, there was little he could buy with the remainder, and worldly success was worth nothing without peace of mind.

On January 7 he finished *The Killer and the Slain*.

This book I *had* to write. In all my long literary life I have never known anything so like automatic writing. I simply put down what I *had* to put down. This doesn't mean of course that it is good. But technically at least it is, I think, the best of my macabre. Very difficult, but the difficulties, I fancy, are not evident.

On the 21st the Cheevers, after three months of rest, returned to their patched-up Hampstead house. Hugh was sad to see them go. "We have, all three of us, a most wonderful friendship, with perfect understanding and a great sense of humour." Without them he lived "a hermit's life," working at *Katherine Christian* and feeling gradually stronger. He found time to record in his journal that "Stonier in this month's *Horizon* attacks me for deserting *Perrin* and my horror stories. Instead I am writing 'flimsy-flamsy' Herries! I might have been 'a serious artist' but am only 'a very good entertainer'! This is the old regular 'highbrow' attack. How sick I am though of this long-continued attempt to make the novel a solemn, priggish, intellectual affair, removed from the ordinary reader. Surely the novel should *entertain* first, and then let all else be added unto it!"

At the end of the month he received a "letter from Inland Revenue saying I've paid no taxes since 1936! Some error here." On February 9 he decided that the next two hundred days would be "the most important in the history of the world," and that he would tick them off in his diary. He was able to number only a hundred and one before his last illness set in. But now *Katherine Christian* claimed most of his time, and he had finished half of it before on the 20th he once more took train for London.

5

After a few days at Hampstead, Hugh returned to 90 Piccadilly. The flat was "like Lazarus raised from the dead." Walls, ceilings, and windows had all been repaired; the few remaining books had not been damaged; and when Hugh had hung on the walls a number of pictures, new and old, by Rowlandson, Cotman, Romney, Wyndham Lewis, Lord Methuen, Jack Yeats, and Graham Sutherland, he commented: "Nothing irreplaceable, all lovely."

The air-raids had mercifully slackened in intensity, but he found that he no longer enjoyed being alone in the flat from seven in the evening till eight next morning, "sitting there reading and listening for the guns," and then lying, as Alan Dent put it, "all Danaë to the bombs," so he spent most nights at Hampstead. Now that *The Killer* was finished he had nothing to write in London, but almost at once two books crept into his head. One, *Fragments of Delight*, "about my books, pictures, fun in general," he shelved in favour of *The City under Fire*, whose first story he now began—"just to keep my hand in." On March 6 he bought four pictures by Paul Klee for £50 apiece, and a week later his fifty-seventh birthday, for which Alan Dent sent him fifty-seven jonquils, called forth another statement of account:

I should say that, in spite of the war, this is the peak of my life. I have fame, more money than I shall ever have again, pretty good health, my working faculties are excellent, and more love around me than I deserve. That I, egoist, spoilt, selfish and a boss, a fusser and dogmatic, should have the love of such people as H. C., Dorothy, Robin, Ethel, Jim, Dick, Owen, George Blake, John, Alan, Jo, Ronald, is nothing short of a miracle. In fact it is *all* a miracle, for my talents are small (limited in scope) and my character very middling.

After a few more refreshing days with the Shirleys in Cornwall, Hugh returned to Hampstead. The nights were quieter now, or at any rate less consistently noisy, so that plans for future books began to assemble. One day, as he was walking down the hill to get his hair cut, the whole of the next Polchester novel, to follow *Katherine Christian*, "came into view." It was to be called *The Church of St Eustace*.

6

April was a cruel month. It opened with the shattering news of Virginia Woolf's suicide. She had occupied a very special place in Hugh's life, and though the war had accustomed everyone to the expectation of sudden death, this blow seemed unbearably wanton and unnecessary. Hugh broadcast about his dead friend and wrote at least two articles about her,[1] but her death haunted him, and his grief for her certainly hastened his own end.

Ironically enough, his bank balance continued to mount as the possibilities of his enjoying it declined. Macmillan's royalty cheque for £2700 now arrived to swell the total, but what was there left to buy? Three pictures by Old Crome came into the market—an oil painting and two water-colours, belonging to an old woman who had recently died in Crome's Norfolk village at the age of a hundred and one. Hugh snapped them up.

On the night of April 16–17 there was a particularly heavy raid on London. Hugh had taken Harold and Ethel to see his favourite Max Miller at the Palladium, and they were back in the Piccadilly flat listening to the news when the alarm sounded. Harold drove them up to Hampstead "through a chaos of noise and flashing lights." Hugh went to bed but not to sleep. It was the noisiest night he had known, except for that last one at the Dorchester. Hour after hour he lay there, feeling the house rock, listening to the uproar, thinking: "At any moment they may drop one just for fun—and that is the end! I thought of my Old Crome pictures I had just bought, and of finishing *Katherine C*—but mostly of Harold."

That night was too much for him. Its first results came three days later, on April 20. Here is his own account, written within the week:

---

[1] *John o'London's Weekly* (18 April 1941) and the *New Statesman & Nation* (14 June 1941).

I had a *crise de nerfs* on Sunday of which I am thoroughly ashamed. At tea I said something snappy to H. C, to which he replied snappily, upon which I left the room, head in air, carrying my Old Crome oil like a banner. I then sat looking at my unfinished article on Virginia Woolf. A wave of melancholy dashed over my head. I got my hat, waterproof, umbrella, and walked out of the house. I am vague then—I caught a bus, talked to a soldier from Bohemia in the tube, visited the Athenæum, went to a cinema (Fredric March was in something), caught a tube back, and re-entered the house at 9.30.

I knew I had behaved badly, and went to bed like a whipped child. All this time I was profoundly miserable. I slept like the dead from 9.30 to 7.30, but woke quite unrefreshed and more miserable than ever. The porridge was lumpy, and after a scene with Harold I threw on my clothes and rushed out of the house, swearing I would put an end to everything!

Of course I didn't, but wandered about the Suburb. Suddenly there was an Alert and, as though it were a call to arms, I rushed home, threw off my clothes and went to bed.

I felt then so frightened and miserable that I sent for Thompson.[1] He came, tested heart, blood-pressure, found all perfect, spoke soothing words but plainly thought me an ass. I felt perfectly well and even happy.

This ridiculous exhibition must not occur again. My brain-storms either of temper or hysteria are nothing but self-indulgence.

Here Hugh went too far in self-abasement. In the past his childish fits of temper might have been traced to self-indulgence, but now there was a graver cause. Nor was he correct in stating that the doctor "found all perfect." In fact Dr Thompson had his doubts concerning the condition of Hugh's heart, and urged the taking of an electro-cardiogram. But Hugh felt suddenly quite all right again and refused to listen to this sensible advice, preferring to "celebrate" his recovery by the purchase of a Cotman drawing and a Landseer oil painting of Coniston.

On the 2nd of May ("sinister month!" as Hugh so ominously headed it in his journal) he attended the Private View at the Royal Academy, where he encountered many old friends, including Gerald Kelly and Muirhead Bone. On the 3rd he gave his last broadcast talk, planning to begin another series in June. On the 5th he heard Beethoven's Pastoral Symphony played at Queen's Hall; and on the 6th, carrying

[1] It was in fact Harold who summoned the doctor, and incurred Hugh's displeasure thereby.

with him a new pair of cherry-coloured corduroy trousers and reading a life of Frederick the Great, he travelled for the last time to Brackenburn.

7

Hugh's journal for the last month of his life is largely occupied with news and prophecies of war. Why had Hess landed by what Hugh always spelt *parashoot*? What was Darlan up to? Would the Germans take Crete? But Brackenburn, in its remote and tranquil beauty, transformed the war into a far-distant, almost a chimerical, horror. The weather was lovely, the air full of mist and cuckoos, *Katherine Christian* waiting to be finished. Hugh read through *The Killer and the Slain*, decided that it was "certainly a nasty book," and turned with relief to the betrayal of Thomas Wentworth, Earl of Strafford.

On May 12 he realised that he was describing Strafford's execution on its exact anniversary, and his mind travelled back to his childhood's determination to write a novel about this unhappy man. He did not remember that he had in fact written one, or that it lay in one of his cupboards, bound in brown paper and dated 1900—the circle was completed.

On the 14th Arthur Ransome came to see him, bringing a present of trout, and the same day the last of the books and pictures arrived from London in a van. When they were all safely stowed away—and the congestion was by now immense—Hugh sat down and compiled a list of his twelve favourite pictures, beginning with the Utrillo. But it was a hopeless task: how could he choose a dozen from the hundreds and hundreds of pictures and drawings which filled every cranny of the cottage, the library, and Copperfield?

On the 17th he took part in the opening ceremonies of Keswick's War Weapons Week. The proceedings began with a long march through the streets of the town. Some of the older and wiser participants fell out soon after the start and rejoined the column just before the finish, but Hugh marched every step of the way, though he was in no condition to do so. At the end of the march he made a public speech from a platform in the Fitz Park, and then drove home utterly exhausted.

The mortal effects of this exertion were not immediately apparent. On the 18th he "had a day off the novel, but read gloriously Wordsworth, Browning, Tennyson, Shelley, Scott, Hazlitt." On the 19th he confessed to feeling "not at all well," but "got to work lustily on Cromwell," besides reading the *Memoirs of Colonel Hutchinson*. Next day, after more work on the novel, he wrote to Michael Ayrton:

I have been here quite alone for a fortnight now, and never has this place done me so much good. I have been working on a Civil War Herries, and Cromwell has made me forget Hitler. I've been reading obscure Civil War pamphlets, Clarendon, etc, until I *am* a fat red-faced seventeenth-century squire.

He had been alone because Harold had been obliged to go down to Cornwall to look after his old parents, who had suffered in the air attacks on Plymouth and Saltash. Now, on May 20, "H. C. arrived, God be praised." The Cromwell chapter of *Katherine Christian* was finished that day, and after one more short chapter the novelist laid aside his pen for ever.

On the 21st he complained of bad indigestion, but managed to fill a page or two of his journal. The pain grew no less, and on Saturday the 24th Harold sent for Doctor Cameron, who immediately put Hugh to bed. At two o'clock on the morning of the 26th Hugh called Harold into his room and complained of an agonising pain. Harold managed to give him some relief by means of massage, but as soon as it was day he summoned the doctor again.

By the time he arrived Hugh had relapsed into a diabetic coma, though after treatment this lasted only a short while. Doctor Cameron, taking a grave view of the condition of the patient's heart, sent for a specialist from Carlisle and for Hugh's brother and sister.

Dorothy arrived on the morrow, Wednesday the 28th, and Robin later. The specialist diagnosed a coronary thrombosis and told Hugh that he must lie absolutely still for six weeks. When he had gone, Hugh felt a little easier, insisted on a pile of Book Society proofs being put on his bed (though he was too ill to hold or read them), and even managed to scrawl a few lines to special friends. When his sister arrived, he told her that he had been very ill and had nearly died, that Harold and Doctor Cameron had been wonderful, and that he had not been frightened at all.

For three days he lingered on, only intermittently in pain, but unable either to sleep deeply or to make much movement. Dorothy, Harold, and a trained nurse sat in his room by turns, day and night.

On the evening of Saturday the 31st he had his first deep sleep, and waking much refreshed in the middle of the night, he asked Harold to put on the light and to sit close beside him. "Let's have a talk," he said. "It may be our last chance." This was the only reference he made to dying, but, as dying men are supposed to do, he retraced to Harold the pattern of his whole life. For almost an hour he talked with complete clarity, in a mood of happy, grateful resignation. Love and friendship were what mattered in life, he several times insisted. He himself had had a wonderful life, and the happiest thing in it had been his friendship with Harold. He recalled all the places they had visited together, all the fun they had had, all the sights they had seen. At last he grew weary, and the nurse took over the watch.

In the morning when Harold came into the room, he saw at once that Hugh was near his end. Dorothy and Doctor Cameron were with him. As Harold came up to the bed, Hugh held out his hand to him. Harold took it, and at that moment, as though he had been waiting for just that, Hugh died. It was about half-past eight on the morning of Whit Sunday, June 1, 1941.

He lies, as he wished to lie, in the churchyard of St John's, Keswick, under the shadow of Skiddaw, looking across the waters of the lake to Cat Bells and the mysterious deeps of Borrowdale.

THE   END

APPENDICES

THE WALPOLE FAMILY

Sir Robert Walpole, first Earl of Orford, First Minister for twenty-one years, had a younger brother named Horatio (1678–1757). This Horatio, a very able politician and diplomatist, was Ambassador to Paris for several years. He has been somewhat damaged in the eyes of posterity by the very rude things said of him by his nephew Horace, who could not bear him. He built a fine house at Wolterton in Norfolk, and ended his days as Lord Walpole of Wolterton.

The Earldom of Orford died with Horace in 1797; but in 1806 Horatio, second Lord Walpole of Wolterton, the eldest son of the above, was himself made an Earl in 1806 and took the title of Orford. This title continued with his descendants, who were both Earl of Orford and Lord Walpole, until it died with the late Earl of Orford in 1931.

The second son of the first Lord Walpole of Wolterton was Thomas (1727–1803), of whom the present Lord Walpole is the eldest living male descendant. Being descended from the first Lord Walpole of Wolterton, he inherited that title on the last Earl of Orford's death in 1931; but not being descended from the second Lord Walpole of Wolterton, he could not succeed to the Earldom.

The third son of the first Lord Walpole of Wolterton was Richard (1728–1798), none of whose male descendants is now living.

The fourth son of the first Lord Walpole of Wolterton was Robert (1736–1810), from whom Hugh was descended.

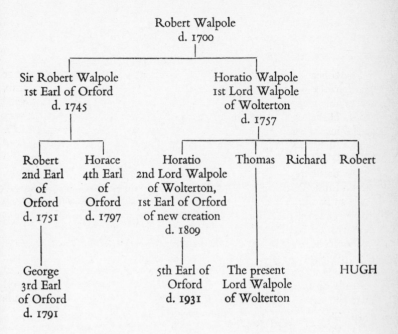

Robert Walpole
d. 1700

Sir Robert Walpole
1st Earl of Orford
d. 1745

Horatio Walpole
1st Lord Walpole
of Wolterton
d. 1757

Robert
2nd Earl
of
Orford
d. 1751

Horace
4th Earl
of
Orford
d. 1797

Horatio
2nd Lord Walpole
of Wolterton,
1st Earl of Orford
of new creation
d. 1809

Thomas   Richard   Robert

George
3rd Earl
of Orford
d. 1791

5th Earl of
Orford
d. 1931

The present
Lord Walpole
of Wolterton

HUGH

HUGH WALPOLE'S OFFICIAL ACCOUNT OF THE FIRST RUSSIAN REVOLUTION

DESPATCH FROM HIS MAJESTY'S AMBASSADOR AT PETROGRAD RESPECTING THE RUSSIAN REVOLUTION OF MARCH 1917

Sir G. Buchanan to Mr. Balfour (Received April 5th)

Petrograd, March 20, 1917.

Sir,

I have the honour to transmit to you herewith copy of a detailed account of the Russian revolution, with a short appreciation of its causes. This account has been drawn up, at my request, by Mr. Walpole, and I would draw your attention to its extremely interesting and picturesque character.

My thanks for this admirable document are also in a large measure due to Dr. Harold Williams, who, owing to the intimate relations in which he stands to many of the leading members of the present Government and to the fact that he was at the Duma day and night during the past week, was in a unique position to assist Mr. Walpole in compiling his narrative.

I myself provided Mr. Walpole with some of the points in the report, which will, I venture to think, prove to be an accurate account of the events of the past ten days.

I regret that it has been only possible to forward one copy of this report, and I would ask that, when it is printed, I may be sent a few dozen copies for the use of the Embassy.

I have, etc.

GEORGE W. BUCHANAN.

THE RUSSIAN REVOLUTION

I. *March 16, 1917.*

1. Whatever immediate causes led to the revolution in Russia, its success was only made possible by the change of public feeling towards the Throne and Government since 1905. The first four years of the so-called new Constitution destroyed all belief in the sincerity of the Emperor's promises, and it was felt that he was merely a representative of his bureaucratic entourage, so that he gradually fell into the background of the political situation, and his place was taken by the Government.

For a moment at the outbreak of war the country was actually united in a single ideal, and internal dissension was forgotten, but the sudden importance and uplift of the people, and the power that threatened to arise from their unity of purpose, created mistrust in the Government. However, as long as things went well the people were content, but the failure in Galicia aroused their first suspicions of the good faith of their Ministers. It then began to be felt that the Government was influenced by two motives, namely, open pro-Germanism and the self-interest of bureaucracy, and their fears were confirmed by the replacing of proved traitors by men of similar tendencies. The appointment of Stürmer as Premier and Minister for Foreign Affairs finally destroyed any lingering trust in the Government, and from this moment it was evident that the internal struggle was of paramount importance.

2. The feelings of the Empire found their first outlet when the Duma met in August 1915, on which occasion the Government was denounced with, up to then, unheard-of violence both in the Chamber and in the press. The next opportunity was in November 1916, at the opening of the Duma, which had been delayed as long as possible by the Government. The example of France and England in reforming their Cabinets at this time gave additional impulse, and, for the first time since 1905, the will of the people prevailed and Stürmer was removed. The exposures made by Miliukof and Pourishkevitch of the "dark influences" at work behind the Throne and Government brought not only the upper middle classes, but even the nobility and some of the clergy, into line with the people, so that the Government was henceforth deserted by all except the extreme reactionaries and the pro-Germans. For a while the situation improved under the premiership of Trepof, but when he was quickly succeeded by Golitzin it was clear the secession of every class to the popular party was either ignored or despised by the bureaucracy. This bureaucracy was a small but easily recognisable group of men, led in the Ministry by Protopopof; in the Council of the Empire by Scheglovitof, who was dismissed from Ministerial office at the same time as Sukhomlinof; in the Duma by Markof II; in the Church by Pitirim, the Metropolitan of Petrograd; and at the Court by the Empress and Rasputin. After the latter's death Protopopof became the rallying point of the reactionaries.

3. At the back of every responsible Russian's mind since 1905 there had been an ideal of Constitution. Since the first failures of the war this had become acutely intensified. It was felt that the Government was inefficient in its conduct of the war. The principal difficulty was one of transport, and the disorganisation arising from insufficient railroads was increased by the division of transport into civil and military spheres. In this way the civil population was inadequately served. This system, such as it was, completely

broke down when the export of supplies from one Government to another was prohibited, a measure which immediately caused great waste in some and scarcity of the same commodities in other districts, and everywhere a vast increase in prices. Even after this system had proved a disastrous failure it was also extended to Finland.

To combat this disorganisation the Unions of the Towns and of the Zemstvos and the War Industry Committee did invaluable service. Their importance and influence became daily greater, and so roused the alarm of the Government, which did all in its power to hinder their work. During his term of office Stürmer introduced a number of regulations placing obstacles in the way, and on his retirement Protopopof continued the same policy, and in December 1916 forbade the general congress of these unions in Moscow, on the ground of their infringing on work which should be done by the Government. Another measure directed against these organisations was a law passed under article 87 of the Constitution giving the police the right of being present at all private meetings of any organisation.

Increased irritation began to be felt against the police among all classes. By means of the same article Protopopof strengthened the police all over the Empire, providing them with arms and machine-guns intended for the army. At the beginning of February he handed over the entire administration of internal affairs to his two assistants, and devoted his whole energies to the departments of the police and the press censorship.

This censorship, always rigorous, had now become intolerable. Though not permitted by law, Duma speeches were continually censored, and in January the press was warned not to refer to the Government except in favourable terms. In short, the people as a whole felt that the Government were making the best use they could of the war, while it lasted, to strengthen their own hands at the expense of civil liberty.

4. In the army disaffection was no less keen. Its use as a fighting machine was daily handicapped by the inefficiency of the War Administration. No national effort was encouraged to provide them with shells, guns, and equipment, as was the case in France and England, while it was known that much of what was sent by her allies to Russia never reached the front, either through carelessness or deliberate misappropriation. The removal of the Grand Duke Nicholas had a depressing effect on the army, for he was implicitly trusted, and this complete trust was never quite given to the Emperor owing to the suspected German sympathies of his wife. It was believed that Petrograd held as many enemies as Berlin, and this belief was enormously strengthened by the liberation of Sukhomlinof. This state of affairs was accentuated by the huge unnecessary mobilisation of December 1916.

The country, however, had no idea of revolution, as such a course would only increase their disorganisation and play into the hands of the enemy.

Moreover, they had no confidence in the success of such a revolution. They could not be assured of the army's support, and were faced by the enormous reinforcements of the police at home. The Government's belief in the supineness of the people was strengthened by the calm way in which the postponement of the Duma was apparently received in January 1917. From this moment it is evident that the Government resorted to provocation, for they believed they could successfully deal with any disturbances, and be immensely strengthened by the people's failure.

On the 9th February the Labour Group of the War Industry Committee were arrested on a charge of conspiracy against the Throne, and imprisoned without trial. Social democratic agitators appeared in the factories urging the people to strike and express their dissatisfaction. In expectation of disturbances at the opening of the Duma on the 27th February machine-guns were concealed in commanding positions to sweep the streets, and although the Duma was successful in its efforts to ensure quiet, these guns were not removed. Provocations to revolt still continued, and when M. Miliukof in a letter to the press exposed the dangers of disturbances, this letter was at first forbidden to be published. A similar proclamation from the Labour Group, urging no cessation of work, met the same fate.

5. As an act both of provocation and as a precaution for their own safe-guarding, the Government removed Petrograd from the northern army area and constituted it a military district by itself. The people resented this menace, and when the new Governor, General Khabalof, issued his first proclamation warning them, for their own good, of the penalties of disorder, it was believed that this was intended merely as an additional provocation.

6. By this time the food and fuel crisis had become acute. All through an exceptionally severe winter the people had to wait in queues daily for several hours to obtain a ration of bread which was quite insufficient. By the beginning of March even this supply began to fail, and the people were faced with starvation. The supply of fuel was equally insufficient. The people bore with this state of affairs as long as they could. In the bread queues they continually urged each other to endure these hardships for the sake of the war, until at last they could bear it no longer, and began to march the streets demanding the wherewithal to live.

II. *Prelude* (*Thursday, March 8—Sunday, March 11*).

Thursday, March 8. Upon the afternoon of Thursday, 8th March, 1917, the crowds passing up and down the Nevski Prospect were startled for a moment by a small company of Cossacks who galloped down the street at full speed in the direction of the Admiralty Quay. Their passage caused a moment's gossip, people speculated as to whether there was trouble with the workmen on the other side of the river, and someone said that the bread crisis was serious, and someone else said that the present Government was abominable, and the little interruption was forgotten. At that moment there was very little news of importance; there had been no word from the Eastern front for a considerable time, and the recent successes on the Western front had been of too partial a kind for the average Russian to realise their significance. There was at that moment little or no talk about the Russian revolution; there had been some expectation that the opening of the Duma on the 27th February would have been a signal for trouble, but that date had passed quietly. The Duma itself at this moment was occupied with a dull and slow debate in which the Minister of Agriculture, Rittich, was elaborately defending his measures with regard to the food supplies.

One of the topics for discussion amongst the Petrograd "intelligentsia" on that Thursday afternoon was the recent *première* at the Alexander Theatre of a gorgeous revival of Lermontof's *Masquerade*, a performance that had been ten years in the preparing and was of a richness and extravagance that went oddly in company with a distressed and impoverished Russia. The weather was fine, the sight of rows of peasant women patiently waiting outside the bread shops was by now a commonplace, and it was argued that, as the people had shown such exemplary patience under exasperating conditions for so long, they would probably continue to show it a little longer.

Nevertheless, that little gallop of Cossacks marked the opening of the Russian revolution. Upon that Thursday afternoon and evening certain bread shops in the poorer parts of the town were looted, and a little procession of students and women passed up the Nevski very quietly, observing every rule of decency and order, but nevertheless a sign and a portent.

Friday, March 9. On the following morning it was very obvious that a spirit of unrest was abroad. A number of daily papers, the *Bourse Gazette*, *Russkaya Volya*, and *Den*, did not appear on this day, and the *Retch* had an article, in the course of which it said:

If the object is not to be overtaken by events, but to foresee and direct them, straightforward determination and openness are needed; the country must be organised and the population must be made to feel that everything will be done to relieve the critical position which has arisen. If only the population can be given this assurance we shall see a different picture at once. But without this all efforts will fail to cope with the feeling of uncertainty which at such a time grows like a snowball.

The general debate on the food question in the Duma was, meanwhile, curtailed in order to ask the Government as to what means had been taken to secure a supply of food for Petrograd. The answer to this was the announcement by the Government that the administration of the food supply of Petrograd had been transferred to the Petrograd City Department for Public Affairs.

On Friday morning the Nevski Prospect and some of the other larger streets of the town wore quite a holiday air. Crowds walked up and down, following, for the most part, some especial group of students or workmen, who seemed to have more deliberate purpose in their movements than the rest. An observer would at once have been struck with the fact that no one showed any anxiety; laughter and jokes were common everywhere, and the fresh colours of a brilliant winter's day added to this sense of gaiety and reassurance. At the same time the Cossacks now definitively patrolled the streets. When, however, they were given orders to clear some crowd it was noticeable that they advanced slowly and carefully; the crowd, on its side, always made way for them and cheered them as they passed. Groups of Cossacks could be seen with workmen, women, and students standing close to their horses' heads laughing and chatting. Cossacks could be heard on every side assuring the people that even though they were given orders by the officers they would not shoot.

This attitude of the soldiers on the morning and afternoon of Friday marks quite clearly a stage in the revolution. No revolt could hope for any success were the army not on its side; on the other hand, with the support of the army, everything was possible. From the moment that the soldiers appeared to be on the side of the people the Government had every reason for serious alarm.

Great hostility was, meanwhile, shown to the police. On this Friday morning stones and broken bottles were flung at them near the Kazan Cathedral, and a mounted police officer fired four times with his revolver. Moreover, in certain streets trams were broken and overturned, and there were some small collisions between the police and the crowd. During the afternoon a significant incident occurred: two workmen leaders were arrested by the police and concealed in a courtyard on the Kazanskaya. The crowd became very hostile, and appeared determined to rush the courtyard and secure their comrades' deliverance. A party of soldiers defending the yard already had their rifles to their shoulders, pointed at the people's feet, and the officer had raised his hand apparently to give the signal to fire, when a strong band of Cossacks rode up, dispersing the crowd, turned into the courtyard and bringing out the arrested leaders delivered them to the crowd.

It cannot, however, be said that anyone realised, as yet, that a revolution was in being. That spirit of curiosity, remaining, as it did, from the beginning of the revolution to the end, so that even on Monday and Tuesday women and children could be seen in the thick of the street-fighting, gazing with wide-open eyes as though they were watching some melodrama in one of their cinematographs, was the dominant note on this Friday afternoon. Everyone was waiting to see what would happen, and, except in the cases of contact with the police, everyone showed good humour and friendliness.

There was as yet very little mention of politics. Late on Friday afternoon, in the middle of the Nevski, a workman standing on an overturned tub addressed the crowd: "We must get rid of the Stürmers, Golitzins, and Protopopofs who govern us," he said. "The people need bread; they cannot work without bread." When someone in the crowd cried, "Down with the war!" he answered, "Remember that the blood of our brothers and sons must not be spilt for nothing. The first thing is to get rid of this Government; and peace, when it is concluded, must be an honourable peace." He urged the people not to cause any riots or do anything that would bring them into contact with the police:

"Not a window must be broken, not a stone thrown, for provocators appear in the workshops and urge the people to riot. These are Government agents; the Government wants an excuse to crush the people. Do not play into their hands by rioting, but keep cool; the one great thing is to force the Government to go."

He then urged the crowd to disperse to their homes "with songs." His speech, which lasted from fifteen to twenty minutes, was received with great applause, and, while he was speaking, a large body of Cossacks, a hundred or more strong, rode up to the outskirts of the crowd and listened, but made no attempt to interrupt the orator. This speech, although it was more political than a great deal that people were at that moment saying, was very typical of the tolerance and good policy that was everywhere abroad on Friday afternoon.

Saturday, March 10. On Saturday morning the town awoke to a new condition of things. It was patent to everyone that there had been meetings, processions, and speeches during the whole of Friday, and that these, instead of being checked, had been encouraged by the soldiers. The reactionaries must have realised on this Saturday morning that affairs looked very serious, and, indeed, on walking down the streets one could discern a new element in the atmosphere. Still there was curiosity, still there was a passive and even friendly attitude to the forces of law and order; but men said to one another that it would be a crime to allow the present opportunity for a determined and organised protest to pass. Everyone looked at his neighbour to see how far he was inclined to go.

The first sign of organisation appeared to come from the workmen. Saturday was their pay-day, and every man, after he had received his pay, went off to join his fellows and discuss the situation. The result of these discussions was an almost universal strike, and by Saturday afternoon it was noticeable that the mob, which now surged up and down the Nevski, contained a very prominent element of serious, resolute workmen, an element very different from the women and students who had made the greater part of the crowd on Thursday and Friday.

Still the attitude of the people was peaceful, although cheerfulness and laughter had disappeared. The crowds in the Nevski were now of enormous proportions, and a strange character was given to the scene by the enforced cessation of the tramways and sleighs. Some people tried to drive through in motor-cars, but these were generally stopped by the crowd; during the whole of that afternoon, however, no very definite event occurred. In the evening there was a little shooting, but the people refused to believe that it was soldiers who had fired the shots, considering that it was rather policemen who had disguised themselves in soldiers' uniforms.

In the evening the theatres were open, the cinematographs were crowded, the city scene, save for the absence of the trams, seemed to be wearing its accustomed colour. But everywhere groups were discussing the situation, workmen were holding meetings, and in the Duma there were acute expectation and apprehension.

"Tomorrow may be the greatest day in our history," a Russian said to an English friend. He spoke more truly than he knew.

III. *Incitement to Revolution.*

Sunday, March 11. It was immediately obvious early on Sunday morning that the Government had resolved on the very sternest measures. From one end of the city to the other notices, signed by Khabalof, the military governor of the town, stated that workmen who did not return on Monday morning back to work, would be immediately sent to the front, warning people also not to collect in crowds in the street, as the police and military would be authorised to disperse such crowds with all the force at their disposal.

It was evident, too, that the patrols had everywhere been very heavily strengthened, and that detachments of regiments had been called out to assist in enforcing order. The crowds were everywhere immense, although the police had warned everyone not to go out, as there might be shooting. The day was bright and fine, and as yet no one seemed to have any apprehension of danger; women could be seen everywhere with little children, running to any place where an especial crowd seemed to have collected, standing fearlessly near the horses and rifles of the Cossacks and mounted police. It was obvious enough that the warnings and orders of the authorities had no effect at all, and it was at this moment on the morning of Sunday, the 11th March, that the Government decided on immediate and, as they hoped, decisive action; but it cannot be too strongly emphasised that up to this moment the people had given no cause for complaint; they had, indeed, assembled in crowds, but their meetings and processions had been orderly, dignified, and restrained.

They had simply requested that some assurances might be given them that practical and immediate steps would be taken to deal with the terrible shortage of food, a shortage which, as every man, woman, and child in Petrograd knew, it was in the power of the Government to remedy.

During the course of the day a company of the Pavlovsk Regiment mutinied owing to its Instructional Detachment having fired on the crowd. The company, which was the first to mutiny openly, was disarmed by the Preobrazhenski Regiment. Firing also took place at about 4.20 p.m. near the Hôtel Europe and the Anichkof Palace. There was, so far as may at present be gathered, no case of wholesale massacre of the crowd, the deaths at the end of the day amounting to no more than some 200; nevertheless, these attacks were sufficient to give the revolution a definite basis of patriotism and even legality.

The attitude of the crowd was, even on Sunday morning, still one of tolerance to everything save the police. By the early evening the Nevski Prospect had been absolutely cleared and placed under an official and military guard. That guard, nevertheless, was too late. The movement had now definitely received a political motive: "We have stood everything from this Government. Now they shoot us down when we have done no harm. We will not cease now until that Government is removed."

At the same time numbers of Russians on that Sunday evening thought sadly that the revolution was already ended in the way that all Russian revolutions seemed doomed to end. "You see," said a Russian, looking at the bright shining expanse of the Nevski, guarded by patrols and empty of all civilians, "we've failed again. They're too strong for us."

Meanwhile, in the Duma great events had occurred, and in the afternoon Rodzianko, their President, sent the following telegram to the Czar:

Situation serious. Anarchy reigns in the capital. Government is paralysed. Transport, food and fuel supplies are utterly disorganised. General discontent is growing. Disorderly firing is going on in the streets. Various companies of the soldiers are shooting at each other. It is absolutely necessary to invest someone who enjoys the confidence of the people with powers to form a new Government. No time must be lost. Any delay may be fatal. I pray God that at this hour the responsibility may not fall on the bearer of the crown. RODZIANKO.

Rodzianko at the same time informed the commanders-in-chief of the various fronts of the first telegram, and added a request for their support in his action. Meanwhile the Government had been at a loss all day as to their best course. They finally, in the evening, decided to prorogue the Duma, Prince Golitzin, the Premier, having a blank form of prorogation which he was to use when occasion demanded. On hearing this, certain members of the Duma refused to be prorogued, continued to sit in a room by themselves, and elected a provisional committee of their own.

By Sunday evening, therefore, the revolution was constitutionally in being. No one knew as yet what form it would take, but no one doubted that a movement had begun that must be carried through to its final solution.

IV. *The Decisive Day* (*Monday, March 12*)

Monday, March 12. Throughout the night of Sunday there was violent agitation amongst the workmen and especially in the barracks. The soldiers saw quite clearly that their uncertain position of the preceding days could not possibly continue, and there were fierce disputes all ending in the same way. They were not to be compelled to shoot against their own fathers, mothers, and sisters; if tomorrow such orders were given to them they would know what to do.

The inevitable result followed. Early on Monday morning soldiers of the Preobrazhenski Regiment, the finest of the Guard regiments, and always the pride of Russian monarchy, being ordered to fire, turned and shot their officers. At once companies of the Volynski Regiment were sent down to coerce the Preobrazhenski, and they in their turn joined the mutiny. For the time there was chaos. Soldiers did not know where to go or what to do, and their officers knew that they themselves were powerless. At first the mutinous troops walked about aimlessly, not looting, but shouting, cheering, and arguing. Finally, in the middle of Monday morning, guided by work-men and revolutionaries, they stormed the arsenal. According to the account of eye-witnesses this was an affair very swiftly decided. Very little opposition was presented; a certain number of officers were killed and the military depôt of the arsenal, loaded with rifles and guns and ammunition, was in the hands of the people.

Events then moved with breathless rapidity. All regiments sent to quell the mutiny joined it, and now, by midday on Monday, the people could claim to have on their side the Volynski, Preobrazhenski, Litovsky, Kex-holmsky and Sapper regiments, in all about 25,000 troops.

During this Monday morning, it must, however, be remembered that, in the central part of the town, life seemed to be again almost normal. It is true that the trams were not running, many shops were still closed, and people crowded the Nevski Prospect, but men were busy over their normal affairs, children were with their nurses, and in the rinks on the Fontanka skaters appeared to have forgotten the very word revolution. The experiences of an Englishman whose house was at the corner of the Fontanka Canal and the Nevski Prospect may be given here, as they were typical of many Petrograd citizens on that day.

During the morning he had conducted some business on the farther side of the town. Returning to luncheon at his house on the Fontanka he heard rifle-shots at no great distance. He had been present at none of the scenes on the preceding day, and he was inclined to consider the whole affair as an abortive workmen's riot that had been easily quelled. Sitting in his office at about 4 in the afternoon he was surprised to hear a tremendous noise in the street next to his own—shouts, firing, cries, cheers, and the quick rattle of the machine-gun. He went to his balcony, and, standing there, was caught straight from his own world of reality into a world of incredible, almost ludicrous melodrama. Across the bridge and round the corner, down into his own street there tumbled an amazing medley of soldiers, civilians, women, and students. The soldiers were, some of them, packed into motor-lorries, their rifles pointing outward, a red piece of cloth tied to a bayonet and held high; students brandished naked swords, peasant women sang, and behind the lorries was a motley tumult of soldiers all shouting at once: "This way!" "No, that way!" "Down S. Street!" "To the Arsenal!" "To the Duma!"

It seemed impossible to the spectator that this could be a serious revolutionary army, or, if it were revolutionary, that it could attain any serious results. He stood there laughing. They looked up from below and shouted something to him that he did not understand. A moment later a bullet crashing through the windows behind him forced him to realise that he was a sharer in this melodrama, not merely a spectator of it. Realising then how serious it might be, he determined to go to the Astoria Hotel, where he had some friends for whose safety he was anxious. He stepped out of his house and was swept at once into a shouting, cheering mob. At every corner were scenes that, by their lurid colour and fantastic juxtaposition with the ordinary commonplaces of life, defeated his will to believe. At one corner a huge Cossack, standing in his stirrups, a red handkerchief in his cap, brandished his sword, shouting to the crowd: "Come, follow us. We must do as France did. Do not let the soldiers do all the work, citizens. Health to the glorious Revolution!" At another corner a group of soldiers had lighted a fire and were picketed, resting with their rifles piled in front of them. He saw no violence, no looting, no drunkenness. Turning a corner of a well-known street, he came suddenly upon a man stretched on his face against the snow, two women screaming, crouched against the wall; he heard a machine-gun crackling on the other side of the canal. Even as he hesitated a man in civilian clothes ran past him, then suddenly, without a cry, tumbled on to his face and lay still. The dusk had come on and every dark corner seemed to hide a gun. He suddenly ran for his life; he had no more doubts about the reality of the revolution.

It was as suddenly as this that the sharp realities of the new events came to many men and women on that Monday, but the actual revolutionaries had, during these hours, accomplished great things.

About 11 o'clock on Monday morning the Courts of Law were set on fire, and a barricade was put up outside them in the afternoon. Other detachments of soldiers, workmen, and students moved off to the various prisons

First, the Preventive prison was opened, and here a number of political, as well as a crowd of criminal, prisoners were set free. Secondly, the "Kresti" prison on the Viborg side of the town was opened and set on fire; here both political and criminal prisoners were freed. Thirdly, the Deportation prison was opened.

Afterwards, in the afternoon, the garrison of the fortress of SS. Peter and Paul mutinied, after very slight opposition by one of the few regiments who had hitherto remained loyal but now went over to the revolutionaries. There were also some burnings of local police stations, where many police records were destroyed.

Finally, and most important of all on this eventful day, the building of the political (secret) police, the chief seat of reaction, a nest of *agents provocateurs*, spies, and German emissaries, was raided, and the papers which it contained were taken out and burned in the street. The raiding of this place was of the first importance from many points of view. It had long stood in the public eye as the spider's web into which every honest patriot and upright politician was drawn. It had come to be regarded with an almost fanatical hatred, and the sight of the police papers burning was a signal to the whole of Russia, and even to the world beyond Russia, that the Russian people were again a free people, and that whatever mistakes they might make in the future, they were at least acting for themselves, their own rights, and their own liberties. What the taking of the Bastille was to France, the burning of the secret police dossiers was to Russia.

Unfortunately, a number of exceedingly interesting documents were lost in this fire, but enough were saved from destruction to prove amply and beyond any question the criminal indiscretions, dishonesties, and treasons of certain members of the late Government.

Meanwhile, in the Duma events had been moving very swiftly. The deputies who had remained the night before, instead of following the order of prorogation, now, in view of the supine inactivity of the Government, considered what steps should be taken. Rodzianko sent another telegram to the Czar, no answer to his first one having been as yet received.

His second telegram read as follows:

Matters becoming worse. Must take immediate steps, or tomorrow may be too late. The last hour has come in which to decide the fate of the country and dynasty.

Although no answer had been received directly from the Czar, the Duma learnt about midday that the Emperor had sent a telegram to General Belaief saying that he himself was coming up from the Stafka; that he had appointed Ivanof as commander of the army, and that his orders must be implicitly obeyed; and that he was coming very shortly to Petrograd with a large reserve of troops to quell the rioting. He added that had there been only civilian rioting it might have been possible to take other measures, but that the soldiers had broken their faithful oath to their Emperor, and must be dealt with by severer discipline.

This was the first sign that the Czar had given since the beginning of the revolution, and it was not calculated to reassure the offenders.

Meanwhile, early on Monday morning MM. Guchkof and Rodzianko consulted, and the executive committee began to sit. On the whole, it may be said that during the early part of Monday many of the members of the Duma were completely at a loss, and wandered about discussing exciting events, as completely taken by surprise as was the majority of the citizens of Petrograd.

There arrived before the Duma a delegation of the insurgent troops, enquiring as to the position taken by the representatives of the people. M. Rodzianko informed the delegation of the unanimous decision of the leaders of the Council. He said:

"The present critical moment is marked by the passing of the old authority and the coming of the new. In accomplishing this, the Duma is taking an active part, but, before everything, it is necessary to have order and quiet."

Simultaneously, the President of the Duma delivered to the delegates the text of the telegram sent to the Emperor at the Stafka, to the Chief of Staff, Alexeief, and to the three commanders on the front.

About 1.30 the first small detachment of troops arrived at the gates of the Duma, accompanied by working men. The deputies Kerensky (Labour) and Cheeidze (Socialist) went to meet them, and were applauded by the people. They made speeches, welcomed the troops, and asked them to maintain order, prevent excesses, and stand firm for the cause of freedom.

Kerensky, who was from this moment to stand forth as the strongest, ablest, and most far-seeing of them all in this crisis, asked the soldiers to stand guard over the Duma. The men accordingly took up their positions, and the regular Duma guard was removed by order of Rodzianko to avoid trouble.

At 2.30 a conference was held with closed doors, and it was decided that an Executive Committee should be formed, with full powers to maintain order and to arrange disciplinary measures during the crisis. Twelve men were elected members of this Committee, their names being M. V. Rodzianko, Nekrassof, Konovalof, Dmetrikof, Kerensky, Cheeidze, Shulgin, Schedlovski, Miliukof, Karaulof, Lvof, and Rjevski.

From this time, all through the afternoon, troops arrived at the Duma. The first company of the Preobrazhenski Regiment were brought there by a civilian Jew, presumably a revolutionary. The Duma gradually became crowded with soldiers, workmen, Jews, students, and girls. The soldiers also began to bring in police, reactionary officials, and many small bureaucrats.

Then in the evening came an arrest of great importance, namely, M. Scheglovitof, the President of the Council of Empire, formerly Minister of Justice, one of the best-hated men in the whole of Russia.

Finally, at 11.15 on that evening, a shabby-looking man, in a soiled fur coat, spoke to a student outside the Duma:

"Are you a student?"

"I am," was the answer.

"I would ask you to take me to the Committee of the Duma. I am the late Minister of the Interior, Protopopof. I desire the welfare of our country, and so I surrender myself voluntarily."

So ended the eventful Monday, the 12th March. During the day the question before all men had changed. It was no longer, as it had been yesterday, "Is this a revolution? Will the soldiers be with it enough to make a revolution?"

That question was answered. It *was* a revolution, and the army within the gates of Petrograd had made it one. But what of the army outside the gates? What of the rest of Russia? What forces were coming from the Czar? Upon that Monday evening it seemed to every man possible that the next day would show the world the bloodiest civil war in history.

V. *The Duma*

Tuesday, March 13. Contrary to expectations, however, it was the Duma that, during the whole of the next day, Tuesday, the 13th March, was the centre of events. None of the attacks, so greatly feared, from outside took place, for the very simple reason that there was no one to attack.

The troops that did arrive from neighbouring districts—from Oranienbaum, Strelna, and other places—went instantly over to the revolutionaries.

These troops put up at once the red flag and marched to the Duma.

In the Duma, meanwhile, the clearer it became that there was little opposition to be feared from outside, the sharper grew the division between the Duma Executive Committee and the Workmen's Social Democratic body. The former of these two bodies was determined on a Constitutional Government of some kind—the latter on a republic. The Democrats themselves were divided into the Moderates and the Extremists, but their own divisions did not at present appear very sharp. The Duma Committee had the weight and reputation of the Duma behind it, while the Social Democrats had on their side the revolutionary feeling of the masses and the power of democratic appeal to the soldiers.

It became more and more obvious that this struggle for a form of government was to become the ultimate struggle of the revolution—a struggle that would not be decided, perhaps, until many more years of Russian history had passed. But the majority of men already felt that, with the Germans on their frontiers and a Royalist party beyond the gates, this was no time for a yet further civil division—a division that might produce at any moment a Russian Commune—and that a compromise must be arrived at. Two Socialists, Cheeidze and Kerensky, formed the link between the two bodies. The Duma Committee called on its side Prince Lvof, the leader of the Zemstvos, a man universally respected, admired, and trusted throughout Russia. His name had been much in the people's mouths during these last days, and he now came up from Moscow to help the Duma. Gutchkof, Strube, and Prince Lvof now took the lead in the Duma Executive; M. Rodzianko still acted as rallying point for the outside world, but within the Duma he had fallen into a secondary place.

The Labour group at once put forward very democratic demands. The Duma group hoped to be able to establish a moderate system of Constitutional Government, but the power of Labour grew from hour to hour. Their position was continually strengthened by the arrival of new troops coming from the country, marching to the Duma and swearing allegiance. The Duma was the natural rallying point of these troops, but having got there, accompanied by cheering working men, they naturally very soon came under the control of the Social Democrats.

It is quite impossible to give any idea of the scene that the Duma presented on this Tuesday morning and afternoon. It was a complete babel of agitations, ambitions, disputes and alliances. In the first place, the floor was covered with Socialist agitators, by whom meetings for soldiers were held all day long. At first Rodzianko and other members of the Duma tried to counteract these efforts by their own speeches, but their voices gave out, whilst the Socialists' grew ever greater and greater in volume. Everyone made speeches— soldiers and workmen, Jews, speculators, merchants, and lawyers.

All this time regiments were pouring in and out, all cheering and shouting and waving red flags. The Duma courts themselves were now crowded with motors, armoured cars, machine-guns, provisions, papers, flour, bread, buffets for feeding the soldiers, and so on. Every kind of committee sprang up—committees for provisions, committees for passports, committees for journalists, committees for students, committees for women helpers. Everywhere soldiers could be seen electing deputies, and prisoners were being brought in, bells were ringing, men were singing songs.

A remarkable scene, that lasted practically from this Tuesday until Saturday, and out of which it seemed impossible that any real order could be restored.

Many officers appeared during the day in the Duma and offered their services. Colonel Englehart was made President of the Duma Military Committee, and he at once took the military movement in hand. Some important arrests were made during the day, especially those of MM. Stürmer, Kurlof, and the Metropolitan, Pitirim; late on Tuesday evening so many members of the old Government had been arrested that it may practically be said to have ceased to exist.

Outside the Duma during that day only two events of great importance occurred. One of these was the taking of the Admiralty. This building, in which the various departments of the Naval Ministry have premises, played the part of the last rallying point of the old régime. As soon as the revolutionary movement had broken out, General Khabalof, commanding the troops of the district, ordered a detachment of troops of all arms to take up their quarters in the building. In the court of the Admiralty were disposed fourteen guns and twelve machine-guns. Here also appeared detachments of Cossacks, mounted police, and others.

For the rest of that day the siege of the Admiralty was conducted by the revolutionary troops, the Government army keeping up an incessant rifle and machine-gun fire. The struggle was continued by night. On the morning of the 13th, however, the Naval Minister, General Admiral Grigorovitch, received a letter stating that if, in twenty minutes, the Admiralty was not surrendered it would be destroyed by heavy artillery fire from the Peter and Paul fortress, which had been occupied by the Kexholm Regiment a short time before. The Naval Minister informed Khabalof of this, and once more requested time to withdraw his forces from the Admiralty, as the destruction of the building would cause an irreparable loss to the active fleet. Khabalof agreed to this, and gave the order to cease fire. The troops under his command surrendered. General Khabalof was arrested with his staff, and on the gates and doors of the Admiralty appeared the notice: "Under the protection of the State Duma."

The other event that occurred in the town on the morning of the Tuesday was the attack on the Astoria Hotel. This hotel had been for a very considerable period allotted to officers for whom special terms were made. Officers of every kind stayed there, amongst them members of the Allied forces.

As a Russian remarked on Monday at dinner time: "I wonder they don't go for this place. A cabby goes to the public-house, and has to pay two roubles for an execrable meal. We have an admirable dinner for two roubles fifty, with wine if we want it." When the soldiers did attack the Astoria, however, it was for better reasons than a desire for pillage. At 8.45 on Tuesday morning a company of soldiers passed the hotel, the red flag flying, and a band playing. Shots were suddenly heard, quite unmistakably from the roof of the Astoria. The soldiers at once smashed the long windows that ran from ceiling to floor, and the hotel was at their mercy. A scene of great confusion followed. One lady was struck by a bullet in the neck; a general who had been caught shooting at the soldiers was killed. English officers coming downstairs protested. "I beg your pardon," said a soldier, politely, "but this is our affair." Too much stress cannot be laid here on the perfect politeness with which all Allied officers were treated. The English officers in especial were allowed to do what they pleased, and when the women and the servants in the hotel saw this, they put themselves under English protection.

There was practically no looting, and the greatest consideration was shown to everyone by soldiers, to whom the richness and extravagances of the Astoria must have been most inhumanly tempting. A lady, when a soldier went into her room, came to him with her hands full of money. "What's this for?" he asked. "We're on quite a different job here."

No Englishman who was an observer of the incidents at the Astoria Hotel on that Tuesday will forget the impression that the Russian soldiers made upon him. "To men who can behave on such a day in such a fashion," someone said, "the conquest of the world is possible."

The fighting in the town during Tuesday resolved itself into exchanges between the police and the soldiers. It now appears that machine-guns intended for the Russian army and appropriated by Protopopof for the use of the police had been placed on the roofs of the houses in Petrograd some weeks before. It is also stated that he offered the police 100 roubles a day for every day that they maintained their defence. Whether this be true or no, machine-guns were now in evidence on the roofs of innumerable houses in Petrograd, and during the whole of Tuesday and Wednesday firing continued.

On the whole, however, it may be truthfully said that, so far as Petrograd was concerned, by the Tuesday evening the revolution was over. The old Government had ceased to exist, and the whole army, so far as Petrograd and its environs went, had gone over.

Nevertheless, on Tuesday evening grave anxiety was felt as to the future. The Czar was expected on Wednesday morning. The struggle between the Social Democrats and the Duma was growing with every moment sharper. Royalist troops were expected from Finland. So successful, in fact, had everything been, so far beyond men's wildest hopes, that no one could believe that a sharp reverse was not in store. It was all too good to be true.

VI. *The End of the Revolution*

(*Wednesday, March 14 to Friday, March 16*)

Wednesday, March 14. The interest of the revolution had become now entirely political. Whatever troops had been supposed to be coming with General Ivanof would, it was now obvious, have a very serious organised opposition to face. News came that seemed to show that Moscow was turning over to the revolution without any signs of a struggle.

The whole drama was now centred in the fight between the Social

Democrats and the Executive Committee. Some idea may be formed of the aims and hopes of the Social Democrats by these extracts from the various proclamations that they issued at different times during the past three days:

To the People!

The time, long awaited, has at last arrived when the great cause of freedom is near to realisation. We have paid dearly for it. Many of our comrades have been killed and wounded, many have laid down their lives in the cause of the people—may their memories be held sacred!

All of us who are left alive should know and remember that the enemy is not yet put to flight, that there in the Winter Palace, that ancient nest of Czarism, evil enemies of the people have assembled around him a handful of soldiers who do not understand what they are doing, nor whom they oppose when they fire on the people . . .

Better to die for freedom than to remain in shameful slavery to the house of the Romanofs.

Long live great revolutionary Russia!

The following is a fine proclamation:

To the Soldiers!

Soldiers, the people of Russia thank you for your revolt in the cause of freedom. Eternal memory to those who have fallen!

Soldiers, some of you still hesitate to join the revolt of your and our comrades.

Soldiers, remember your weary lives in the villages, in the factories, in the work-shops, where the Government suffocated and oppressed you. Join the people, and the people will give you and your families a new and free life and happiness.

Soldiers, if you are driven from your barracks, go to the Duma; there you will find comrades whose joys and sorrows you will share.

Soldiers, do not shoot at random in the streets. On the roofs of the houses and in private flats the remainder of the police force is hidden, the "Black Hundred," and other vagabonds. Try and get them out by sharpshooting or correct attack.

Soldiers, keep order everywhere. Form companies and take charge of all military matters which concern the defeat of the enemy.

Soldiers, do not let hooligans molest peaceful citizens. Do not permit shops to be looted, nor private flats. That must not be done.

For all information and orders apply to the Duma, where there will always be found the Military Commission of the town of Petrograd.

Be firm and unbending in your decision to fight to death for freedom.

Better that than the enemy should triumph. Victims, your services and your honour will never be forgotten by Russia. Long live freedom!

But here are some sections of a proclamation of a more doubtful discretion:

(1) The orders of the War Committee must be obeyed, saving only on those occasions when they shall contravene the orders and regulations of the Council of Labour deputies and military delegates.

(2) In private life, standing to attention and compulsory saluting off duty is abolished.

(3) In like manner is abolished the address of officers as 'your Excellency,' 'your Honour,' etc, which shall be replaced by the address 'Gospodin General' (Mr. General), etc.

(4) Uncivil conduct towards soldiers of all military ranks and the addressing of them in private by the word 'thou' is forbidden. As also in all cases of misunderstanding between officers and soldiers, the latter shall report to the company committee.

It will be seen from these last extracts to what ambitious lengths the Social Democrats were now pushing. Throughout Wednesday they did everything in their power to extend their claims. Nevertheless, through the intelligent far-sightedness of such men as Kerensky, some common effort was made towards the formation of a Provisional Government, and the news that now arrived from outside strengthened that effort.

It had been expected that the Czar would arrive from the Staff at Tsarskoe Selo on this (Wednesday) morning. News, however, now came to hand that the Czar's train had been stopped at a small station, Bologoi; at first it was by soldiers, but afterwards it appeared by a workmen's committee, who pulled up the railway line in front of the royal train.

Rodzianko, on hearing this, at once sent the Grand Duke Michael a manifesto which he begged him that he would persuade the Emperor to sign. This manifesto set forth that the Emperor should grant a Constitution, leaving the executive the right to form a Ministry. There was in this first manifesto no mention of the Czar's abdication.

Later in the day, apparently, M. Gutchkof went to see the Czar, and proposed to him that he should abdicate in favour of his son. The Czar replied, "I will not part from my son," agreeing finally to abdicate on condition that his son also was removed from the succession. Gutchkof returned and announced this, proposing then with M. Miliukof that the throne should be offered to the Grand Duke Michael.

The whole of Wednesday evening was spent in lively and often acrimonious discussions with regard to this question of the deposition of the Czar.

Thursday, March 15. Thursday morning came to find the town in absolute quiet. Only the smaller shops were at present open, and the trams had not yet begun to run again. In many ways the town was a revolutionary town. The women and children wore red favours in their dress. Red flags waved everywhere. Already the artists and musicians were discussing eagerly the wonderful new era that was to transform the art world. The whole town was divided by this discussion as to the manner of government, whether it should be constitutional or democratic. On the whole, it was apparently the general feeling that the revolution had been achieved almost without bloodshed (it was thought that the deaths in all amounted to about 4,000), and that anything was better than new trouble. The soldiers themselves understood but little of the real aspect of the situation. One soldier was heard saying to another: "A republic! Of course we must have a republic, but we must have a good Czar to look after it." The Democrats clamoured for an immediate general election; the Duma pointed out that a general election would, at this moment, give the Germans a certain victory. The final word seemed to be: "Let us be content with so far as we have gone for the moment; our republic will come."

It was particularly to be noticed that there seemed to be very little bitterness about anyone. A Russian must at once sympathise with the "underdog," and there was no question as to who the "under-dog" now was. Even about Scheglovitof and Protopopof kind contempt was the attitude of the crowd.

Feeling was, however, quickly stirred on the afternoon of Thursday by the speech in the Duma of M. Miliukof. In this speech he announced the names of the new Ministers: Prince G. E. Lvof, Premier and Minister of the Interior (dramatic justice this, as his predecessor in this office had been his chief oppressor); A. F. Kerensky (he was only 32 years of age), Minister of Justice; Miliukof himself, Foreign Affairs; Gutchkof, Military and Naval Affairs; Shingaref, Minister of Agriculture. He then proceeded:

"I hear voices ask: 'Who chose you?' No one chose us, for if we had waited for election by the people we could not wrench the power from the hands of the enemy. While we quarrel about who shall be elected the foe would have time to reorganise and reconquer both you and us. We were elected by the Russian revolution. It so happened at the very moment when delay was impossible, a handful of people was found whose political past was well known to the people, and against whom not a shadow of those suspicions which brought the old Administration to its fall could be entertained; but we cannot forget that we ourselves quite recently defended the principle of responsibility of the Government to the electors.

"We shall not retain power for a single moment when we are told by the elected representatives of the people that they wish to see others, more deserving of their confidence, in our place. Believe me, gentlemen, the Government will fight in these coming days not for the sake of power. To be in power is neither a reward nor a pleasure, but a merit and a sacrifice. And as soon as we are told that this sacrifice is no longer needed by the people we shall give up our place with gratitude for the opportunity which has been accorded us. But we will not relinquish power now when it is needed to consolidate the people's triumph, and when, should the power fall from our hands, it would only be seized by the foe."

All this was received with immense applause. The debatable part of his speech was as follows:

"The despot who has brought Russia to the brink of ruin will either abdicate of his own free will or be deposed. The power will pass to a regent; the Grand Duke Michael Alexandrovitch Alexis will be the successor to the throne."

There was great disturbance after this, and Miliukof was compelled to admit that he was speaking here for only part of the Provisional Government.

It seemed on Thursday afternoon as though the consequences of this speech would be exceedingly serious. However, once more M. Kerensky saved the situation. News had come in that the Czar insisted on abdicating, for his son as well as for himself. The Empress, who was guarding her sick children at Tsarskoe Selo, had given herself up to the revolutionary troops, saying: "I am not an Empress now, but simply a sister of mercy over my sick children." It seemed by Thursday evening that the proposal of Miliukof could not possibly be entertained. Kerensky took advantage of this and, finding a council of workmen engaged in a very heated discussion, he jumped on to a table in their midst and shouted:

"Comrades, I have been appointed Minister of Justice. No one is a more ardent republican than I; but we must bide our time. Nothing can come to its full height at once. We shall have our republic, but we must win the war; then we can do what we will."

His influence turned the tide. The Democrats voted as to their support of this Provisional Government until the end of the war. The measure was carried by the vast majority of 1,000 to 15.

When on Friday morning it was known that the Czar had abdicated at Pskof, and that the Grand Duke Michael had printed a declaration stating that he would wait to succeed to the throne until the wish of the people was, once and for all, unanimous in his favour, it was clear that the Russian revolution was at an end.

Of the many vast and complicated issues to which such a crisis must give rise this is no place to speak. The consequences of the 8th–16th March will underlie the movement of centuries to come.

One comment only any observer of the affair is compelled to make. The reserve, restraint, and discipline shown by the Russian people during this week were far, far greater than their most optimistic supporter could have been encouraged to expect. That a people who had for months suffered from a severe and unmerited shortage of food, who had seen every civil liberty taken out of their hands, and had been forced to surrender every Minister who had their welfare at heart, and had then been fired on for the space of four days by police who numbered at least 28,000, should, when their hour of vengeance came, permit no violence, and control in themselves every impulse of greed and unlicensed possession, must always remain one of the great records of history.

CATALOGUE OF THE
HUGH WALPOLE COLLECTION
AT THE KING'S SCHOOL, CANTERBURY

I. MANUSCRIPTS

(Almost all bound in leather or enclosed in leather cases)

AGUILAR, GRACE. *The Days of Bruce.* 1156 pp. Quarto.[1] Also 272 pp. of corrected proofs. [Published 1852.]

ANSTEY, F. *Vice Versa.* 230 pp. Large quarto. [Published 1882.] Presentation inscription from James Payn to Horace Pym dated 1884.

AUSTIN, ALFRED. *England's Darling*, a play in verse. 82 pp. Folio. [Published 1896.]

BALLANTYNE, R. M. *The Black Giant.* 16 pp. in quarto exercise book. Children's story with coloured drawings.

BARRIE, J. M. *The Pockets of Alexander Pennycuick: a Story for Pressmen.* 22 pp. Octavo. Signed.

BATES, H. E. *The Poacher.* 374 pp. Quarto. Signed. Dated 1933–34. [Published 1935.]

BEERBOHM, MAX. *London Revisited*, a broadcast delivered 29 December 1933. 12 pp. Folio. [Published in *Mainly on the Air*, 1946.]

BELLOC, H. *De Fide* (six sonnets to Lady Diana Manners). Also *Lord Rumbo and Lord Jumbo*, a comic poem. Signed. 10 pp. in all. Quarto.

BENNETT, ARNOLD. *The Price of Love.* 486 pp. Small quarto. [Published 1914.]

—— Two small notebooks ($7'' \times 4\frac{1}{2}''$) containing pencilled synopsis, notes and ideas for *The Price of Love*.

BESANT, WALTER. *The Orange Girl.* Bound in two vols. Quarto. [Published 1899.]

BLACK, WILLIAM. *In Far Lochaber.* 275 pp. Octavo. [Published 1888.]

BLACKMORE, R. D. *The Maid of Sker.* 310 pp. Quarto. [Published 1872.]

BLAKE, GEORGE. *The Shipbuilders.* 259 pp. Folio. With letter from Blake to H. W. concerning the book and its writing. [Published 1935.]

BONINGTON, RICHARD PARKES. Letter to Mr J. Barnett with pen-and-ink drawing of flowers and cupids, franked 13 July 1827. 3 pp. Quarto.

---

[1] The terms "Quarto" etc. are here used not in the strict bibliographical sense, but as a rough indication of size.

BORROW, GEORGE. *The Romany Rye.* 6 pp. (three leaves) only. Quarto.

BRONTE, CHARLOTTE. Two pages (4" × 2½") of an early story, and two letters to Laetitia Wheelwright, dated 8 March 1854 and 15 February 1855, bound up with typed copies.

BRONTE, EMILY. Three fragments, in all 3½ pp. Duodecimo.

> (a) Sixty-six lines of translation and notes on the *Æneid*, Book I, signed "E. J. Bronti" and dated 13 March 1838.
>
> (b) Two fragments dealing with the drama.

BROWNING, ROBERT. An article on the acting of Macready. 3 pp. Folio.

BURNEY, SOPHIA. *The Juvenile Magazine* (January–June 1792). Octavo. Six parts bound in blue paper wrappers. A note to Sophia from her aunt Fanny concerning this production is attached to Part 1.

BYRON, LORD. Twelve lines of a translation of Dante on octavo sheet, with note at foot dated 23 March 1820.

—— Pocket book (3½" × 2¼") almost blank except for a few scribbles and Byron's signature dated August 1808.

CAINE, HALL. *The Eternal City,* a play. 47 pp. Octavo and quarto. [1901–02.]

CAMPBELL, THOMAS. *The British Grenadiers.* 3 pp. Quarto. Framed and glazed.

CARLYLE, THOMAS. Portion of an article. 4 pp. Folio.

CARROLL, LEWIS. *The Cats and Rats Again.* 5 pp. of prose, signed. 11" × 8½". A note on the manuscript reads "This is to be printed for the Monthly Packet. C. M. Yonge."

CHATHAM, WILLIAM PITT, EARL OF. Nineteen letters to his cousin John Pitt, 1747–57. 38 pp. Quarto.

COBBETT, WILLIAM. Letter to Henry Hunt. 26 pp. Folio. Bound up with the printed version as it appeared in *Cobbett's Weekly Political Register* for 25 April 1818.

COLLINS, WILKIE. *No Name.* 571 pp. Large quarto. Letter from Collins inserted. [Published 1862.]

CORELLI, MARIE. Letter, dated 11 January 1906, to "the new owners of *The Tatler.*" 5 pp. Quarto.

CRAWFORD, F. MARION. *Laura Arden.* 125 pp. Quarto. Signed and dated 11 May 1892.

—— Forty-five letters to W. Morris Colles, 1895–1909. 87 pp. Octavo.

DAVIES, W. H. Thirty-six letters to Edward Thomas, 1906–09. 48 pp. Octavo. Bound up with typed copies.

DE MORGAN, WILLIAM. *Bianca.* Bound up with typed copy. Several hundred unnumbered pp. Folio. [Published as *A Likely Story,* 1912.]

DE QUINCEY, THOMAS. *Memorial Chronology on a new and more Apprehensible System. In a series of letters to a lady.* 42 pp. Quarto. [Published in vol XVI of the *Collected Works* 1871.]

—— [*On the Political Parties of Modern England.*] 42 pp. Quarto. [Written in 1837, published in vol XV of *Works* 1863.] Bound up with above.

DISRAELI, BENJAMIN. *Ixion in Heaven.* Part I only. 38 pp. Folio. [Published in the *New Monthly Magazine,* 1832.]

DOUGLAS, NORMAN. *Paneros.* 92 pp. Folio. Index in Douglas's hand. [Published 1931.]

DOYLE, A. CONAN. *Bendy's Sermon,* a poem. 76 lines. 4 pp. Folio. Signed. [Published in *Songs of the Road,* 1911.]

DRINKWATER, JOHN. *A Lesson to my Ghost,* a poem. 3 pp. Quarto. Written in pencil. Inscription to H. W. dated 1921. [Published in *Seeds of Time,* 1921.]

ELIOT, GEORGE. (? part of) a short story. 10 pp. Quarto.

GARNETT, EDWARD. Sixteen letters to Arnold Bennett, with typewritten copies, and carbon copies of some of Bennett's replies. 39 pp. Octavo and quarto.

GOSSE, EDMUND. Review of *The Gurneys of Earlham* by Augustus J. C. Hare, 1895. 10 pp. Small quarto.

HAMLEY, COLONEL EDWARD B. Manuscript on the Crimean War in thirty chapters. Written in the Crimea, 1853–54. Quarto.

HOGG, JAMES. *The Adventures of Colonel Peter Aston.* 32 pp. Quarto. 1825. [Published in vol VI of *Tales and Sketches by the Ettrick Shepherd,* 1836.] Also an eighteen-line poem on the death of Aston.

JAMES, HENRY. *The Other House.* Book Third only. 154 pp. Small quarto. Note at top in James's hand: "Second half of eleventh instalment [for the *Illustrated London News*], September 12 [1896]." Clement Shorter's bookplate.

JAMES, M. R. "*Oh, Whistle, and I'll come to you.*" 20 pp. Folio. [Published in *Ghost-Stories of an Antiquary,* 1905.]

JEFFERIES, RICHARD. *Snowed Up: A Mistletoe Story.* 32 pp. Small quarto. Signed.

KAYE-SMITH, SHEILA. *Joanna Godden Married.* 109 pp. Quarto. Signed and dated February–March 1926. [Published 1926.]

KIPLING, RUDYARD. *Stalky and Co.* Part of the story called *The Last Term.* Two leaves. Folio. About 160 lines in tiny handwriting with corrections. [Published 1899.]

—— Nine pages of cut galley proofs of an interview with Jules Huret, a French journalist, heavily corrected by Kipling. Letter from Kipling to Huret dated 31 August 1905 inserted.

LAMB, CHARLES. Letter to Mr Serjeant Wilde. 4 lines. N.D. Framed and glazed.

LAWRENCE, D. H. *Movements in European History*. The epilogue only. 16 pp. Quarto. Signed. Bound up with typed copy. [Published 1921.]

LEAR, EDWARD. Twenty-seven landscape sketches in pencil and water-colour. Those dated are between 1835 and 1845. The subjects include Kendal, Lathom, Alderley, Iona, and possibly Switzerland.

LESLIE, SHANE. Letters and correspondence of Mrs Fitzherbert transcribed by Leslie from original sources. Letter of Mrs Fitzherbert's inserted. Quarto.

LINKLATER, ERIC. *Robert the Bruce*. 145 pp. Large quarto. Signed. [Published 1934.]

—— *The Prison of Cooch-Parwanee*. Signed and dated February 1932. 10 pp. Quarto. [Published in *God Likes them Plain*, 1935.]

MACKENZIE, COMPTON. *Sinister Street: Volume One*. 551 pp. Folio. Mostly in pencil. Bound in two vols. [Published 1913.]

MANHOOD, H. A. *Little Peter the Great*. 189 pp. Quarto. [Published 1931.]

MARRYAT, FREDERICK. *The Settlers in Canada*. Complete all but seven leaves. 290 pp. Folio. [Published 1844.]

MASON, A. E. W. *No Other Tiger*. 394 pp. Octavo. Dated October 1925–March 1926. Bound in two vols, together with some hundreds of odd sheets of manuscript. [Published 1927.]

—— *Hatteras* and *An Inconvenience of Habit*. Two short stories, in all 39 pp. Folio. [*Hatteras* published in *Ensign Knightley and other Stories*, 1901.]

MEREDITH, GEORGE. Three poems:
The Years had Worn their Season's Belt. Several versions and early drafts.
The Wild Rose.
On Como. Last three lines differ from published version.
In all 18 pp. $9\frac{1}{4}'' \times 7\frac{3}{4}''$. [All three published in *Last Poems*, 1909.]

MILL, J. S. $4\frac{1}{2}$ pp. on Ireland. Folio.

MONTAGUE, C. E. *Right off the Map*. 567 pp. Quarto. Bound in two vols. [Published 1927.]

MORRIS, WILLIAM. Two stout quarto notebooks containing pencilled pages of his translation of the *Æneid*. [Published 1875.]

—— *The Story of Magnus the Good*, by Eiríkr Magnússon, so heavily corrected by Morris in prose and verse as almost to be rewritten. 86 pp. Folio. [Published in *The Saga Library*, 1895.]

MUNRO, NEIL. *With the Scots in France*. An article, 9 pp. in pencil, dated 19 May 1917 by GHQ censor. Bound up with letter from George Blake who gave the manuscript to H. W.

NAPOLEON II. Grammatical exercises. 8 pp. Quarto. Dated 1827.

NELSON, LORD. Letter to Lady Hamilton. 2 pp. Quarto. Dated 17 May [1801].

NUSSEY, ELLEN. Seventy-six pp. concerning the Bronte family. Octavo.

O'FLAHERTY, LIAM. *The Return of the Brute*. 105 pp. Folio. [Published 1929.]

O'Shaughnessy, Arthur. *Songs of a Worker*. 110 pp. folio in the author's hand. 57 pp. in another's. Bound up with corrected proofs. [Published 1881.]

Ouida. *The Marriage Plate*. 53 pp. $10\frac{1}{2}'' \times 8\frac{3}{4}''$. [Published in *Pipistrello and other Stories*, 1880.]

Pater, Walter. *Diaphaneitè*. 9 pp. Octavo. Signed W. H. P. and dated July 1864. [Published in *Miscellaneous Studies*, 1895.]

Payn, James. An appreciation of Payn, and letters about him to Clement Shorter from Stanley Weyman, Walter Besant and Wemyss Reid. Bound up by Shorter with printed title page. Small quarto.

Pinero, Arthur W. *The Magistrate*. *An original farcical comedy in three acts*. Dated January 1885. Quarto. [Published 1892.]

—— *The Notorious Mrs Ebbsmith*. Dated 1895. Acts I and II typed with corrections. Acts III and IV in Pinero's hand. Quarto. [Published 1895.]

Plomer, William. *Cecil Rhodes*. 240 pp. Quarto. [Published 1933 and dedicated to H. W.]

—— *The Fivefold Screen* (limited edition, 1932) inscribed to H. W. and bound up with the manuscripts of seven of the poems.

Rossetti, Christina. 333 of her poems, written out by her as copy for her collected volume, *Verses* (1893). 389 pp. Quarto.

Scott, Walter. *The Fortunes of Nigel*. 216 pp. Quarto. Ruskin's book label. [Published 1822.]

—— *Count Robert of Paris*. 138 pp. only. Quarto. Partly in Scott's hand, partly in that of William Laidlaw. [Published 1832.]

—— *Tales of a Grandfather*. Part Two of second series of tales from French history. 176 pp. Quarto. Mostly in Laidlaw's hand, but with many corrections in Scott's. [Unpublished.]

—— Book of manuscript reviews, letters, notes, etc. Over 200 pp. Quarto.

—— Memoranda on book publication. 5 pp. Folio. Bound up with typed copies.

Sedgwick, Anne Douglas. *Philippa*. 316 pp. Folio. [Published 1930.]

Shiel, M. P. *The Spectre-Ship*. 64 pp. Small quarto. [Published in *The Pale Ape*, 1911.]

Sickert, Walter. *Le Convoi d'Opposition*. 7 pp. Folio and quarto.

Sitwell, Osbert. *Before the Bombardment*. 252 pp. Folio. Bound up in two vols. [Published 1926.] Included in vol II are four manuscript poems, *Mythology*, *Mrs Hague*, *Mary-Anne* and *Mr and Mrs Nutch*. [All published in *England Reclaimed*, 1927, where the first is renamed *Introduction*.]

Southey, Robert. Review of Sir John Barrow's *Life of Richard, Earl Howe*. 55 pp. [Published in the *Quarterly Review*, June 1838.] Bound up with a review of the Negro-English Bible (*Talkee-talkee Testament*). 12 pp. Small quarto. [Published in the *Quarterly Review*, October 1830.]

STEVENSON, ROBERT LOUIS. One quarto page (twenty lines) of an unidentified story.

SUTRO, ALFRED. *The Walls of Jericho: A play in four acts.* 59 pp. Small quarto. [Published 1906.] Presented by Sutro to Arthur Bourchier. Letters from Sutro to Bourchier and H. W. inserted.

SWINNERTON, FRANK. *Nocturne.* 112 pp. Quarto. [Published 1917.] Presented by Swinnerton to Martin Secker, July 1917. Note by H. W. saying he bought it from Secker, 26 April 1934.

SYMONS, ARTHUR. *The Sinister Guest.* 50 pp. of prose. Octavo. Signed and dated January 30–31, 1919. [Published in the *English Review*, August 1919.]

THACKERAY, W. M. *The Newcomes.* Four consecutive octavo pp. from vol 2 chap. 12, containing one paragraph never printed.

—— *Vanity Fair.* One octavo page (thirteen lines) from chap. 49.

—— Lecture on George IV. 4 pp. of first draft. Small quarto.

—— Lecture on Sterne. One page. Octavo.

—— Unpublished speech made at the Garrick Club. 3 pp. Octavo. N.D.

—— Letter from Paris to Mrs Elliot and her sister Kate Perry, dated 2 July 1855. 3¼ pp. Octavo.

—— Letter from Richmond, Virginia, to Albany Fonblanque, dated 4 March 1853, with pen drawing of negro waiter. 6 pp. Octavo.

—— Two letters to Mark Lemon about *Punch* payments, in all 3 pp. 16 mo. N.D. Bound separately.

—— Watercolour drawing for *Vanity Fair*, enclosed in a note to Lady Stanley of Alderley, dated April 1863. 4 pp. Octavo.

—— Four pen-and-ink sketches on one octavo sheet, with three letters from Anne Thackeray.

—— Note, signed J. Crawfurd, to Mrs F. Elliot, dated 26 January 1860, with pen drawing of himself. One page. Octavo.

—— Self-portrait as a German ("William Makepiece Quackery") and three smaller drawings. 2 pp. Folio.

—— Early sketchbook. 39 pp. (7½" × 4¾") with drawings on most pp. Note by Anne Thackeray reads: "Early drawing book, Paris."

—— Woodblock sketch for *Punch*. 4" × 3".

WALPOLE, HUGH. *The Abbey.* First three chapters only. 121 pp. Small quarto. [Unpublished.]

—— *Joseph Conrad.* 155 pp. Small quarto. [Published 1916.] Bound up with Acts II and III of *The Comfortable Chair: a Comedy.* [Unpublished.]

—— *The Crystal Box.* 222 pp. Octavo. [Published 1924.]

—— *The Crowning*, an article. 30 pp. Octavo. [Published in the *Daily Mail*, 13 May 1937.] Bound up with letter to H. W. from Archbishop Lang and other souvenirs of the Coronation of 1937.

WATTS-DUNTON, THEODORE. Two sets of corrected galley proofs of an introduction to *The Romany Rye* by George Borrow.

WAR POETS. Letters to Miss Jacqueline Trotter, concerning her anthology *Valour and Vision* (1920), from more than seventy poets of the first war, including Housman, Bridges, Kipling, Newbolt, Masefield, Binyon, Blunden, Sassoon, Graves, and Osbert Sitwell. Mostly dated 1919, but some (concerning a possible revised edition) 1923.

WELLS, H. G. *The World of our Grandchildren.* First and second drafts of a broadcast given on 2 November 1930, bound up with corrected type-script. 28 pp. Quarto. [Published, revised, in *After Democracy*, 1932.]

WEYMAN, STANLEY J. *The New Rector.* 299 pp. Quarto. [Published 1891.]

WHYTE-MELVILLE, G. J. *Holmby House.* 388 pp. Folio. [Published 1860.]

YEATS, W. B. *The Island of Statues: An Arcadian Fairy-tale in Two Acts.* 49 leaves. Folio and quarto. Signed. [Published in the *Dublin University Review*, April–July 1885.]

ZANGWILL, ISRAEL. *Uriel Acosta.* 109 pp. Octavo. [Published in *Dreamers of the Ghetto*, 1898.]

II. LIMITED EDITIONS
KELMSCOTT PRESS

The Poems of William Shakespeare. One of ten copies printed on vellum. Bound in vellum. 1893.

The Life of Thomas Wolsey, Cardinal Archbishop of York by George Cavendish. Bound in vellum. 1893.

Poems chosen out of the works of Robert Herrick. Bound in vellum. 1895.

Chaucer's Works. 1896.

The Shepheardes Calender. [By Edmund Spenser.] Canvas boards. 1896.

A note by William Morris on his aims in founding the Kelmscott Press, together with a short description of the Press by S. C. Cockerell and an annotated list of the books printed thereat. Canvas boards. 1898.

VALE PRESS

The Rubaiyat of Omar Khayyam. Canvas boards. 1901.

Bibliography of the Vale Press. Canvas boards. 1904.

ESSEX HOUSE PRESS

The Psalms of David. Bound in morocco. 1902.

DOVES PRESS

A Decade of Years. Poems by William Wordsworth 1798–1807. Inscribed "To my dear wife, the first copy bound. C[obden] S[anderson]." Bound in vellum. 1911.

ASHENDENE PRESS

Fioretti di San Francesco. One of twenty-five copies printed on vellum. Bound in limp vellum. 1904.

Don Quixote. 2 vols. 1927.

Ecclesiasticus. Printed on vellum. Bound in morocco. 1932.

GOLDEN COCKEREL PRESS

Troilus and Criseyde by Geoffrey Chaucer. Wood engravings by Eric Gill. One of six copies printed on vellum. Bound in morocco. 1927.

Canterbury Tales by Geoffrey Chaucer. Wood engravings by Eric Gill. One of fifteen copies on vellum. 4 vols. Bound in morocco. 1931.

The Four Gospels. One of twelve copies printed on vellum. Wood engravings by Eric Gill. 1931.

The Apple Trees by Hugh Walpole. 1932. Presentation copy from H. W.

The Glory of Life by Llewellyn Powys. Wood engravings by Robert Gibbings. 1934. Presentation copy to H. W. from Gibbings.

CRESSET PRESS

Gulliver's Travels by Jonathan Swift. Illustrated by Rex Whistler. 2 vols. 1930.

MISCELLANEOUS

The "Wanderer" of Liverpool by John Masefield. One of twenty copies. 1930. Two sonnets and watercolour drawings in Masefield's hand on blank leaves at the beginning. Bound in morocco.

Reynard the Fox by John Masefield. One of twenty-five copies. 1931. Twenty-three lines of the poem in Masefield's hand on blank leaves at the beginning. Bound in morocco.

Old Spain by Muirhead Bone. One of 265 copies. 2 vols. 1936. Inscribed to H. W. by Bone.

Coronation Service 1937. One of 350 copies. Oxford, 1937

Milton. A Poem in Two Books by William Blake. Facsimile edition. 1886. One of fifty copies. Quarto. Wrappers.

III. ASSOCIATION COPIES

BANDELLO, MATTEO. *XVIII Histoires Tragiques.* French translation. $4\frac{3}{4}'' \times 3''$. Contemporary calf. Lyon 1561. With the boyish signatures of Fulke Greville and Philip Sidney. A note by Dr Farmer, Master of Emmanuel College, Cambridge, reads: "This book formerly belonged to the great Sir Philip Sidney. It was probably made use of in teaching him French."

BURNS, ROBERT. *Poems chiefly in the Scottish dialect.* "2nd edition considerably enlarged." 2 vols. Small octavo. Contemporary calf. Edinburgh, 1793. William Wordsworth's copy with his signature on the title page of vol 1 and a note in his hand saying that the annotations throughout are by his sister Dorothy.

An Apology for the life of Mr Colley Cibber. 1st edition. Quarto. Contemporary calf. 1740. Horace Walpole's copy with many notes in his hand.

LYCOSTHENES, CONRADUS. *Prodigiorum ac Ostentorum Chronicon.* Quarto. Old calf. Basle, 1557. Arms of Duke of Newcastle on binding. Pencilled note on endpaper says: "From the library of William Beckford."

TENNYSON, ALFRED. *Tiresias.* 1st edition, cloth, 1885. Presentation inscription from Tennyson to Theodore Watts dated 15 January 1886. Two corrections to the text in Tennyson's hand.

WILDE, OSCAR. *Ravenna.* 1st edition, wrappers, 1878. Presentation copy from Wilde to Edward Burne-Jones.

WOOLF, VIRGINIA. *Orlando.* Tauchnitz edition (1929). Bound in half morocco with letter from Virginia Woolf to H.W., dated 14 May 1929, pasted in.

[YORKE, P. Second Earl of Hardwicke.] *Walpoliana.* Quarto. Contemporary half-calf. 1781. An interleaved copy which belonged to Horace Walpole and contains many long notes in his hand, correcting and supplementing the "anecdotes" of his father. Bookplates of Horace Walpole and Lord Rosebery.

IV. OTHER PRINTED BOOKS

BLAKE, WILLIAM. *The Grave*, a poem by Robert Blair, with twelve etchings by Blake (1808). Bound up with Blake's illustrations to the *Book of Job* (1825). Folio. Bound in leather.

MOORE, GEORGE. *The Passing of the Essenes.* Cut galley proofs, signed.

SHAKESPEARE, WILLIAM. Fourth Folio, 1685. Bound in leather of a later date.

—— *The Tragedy of Hamlet Prince of Denmark.* Small quarto. Modern calf. 1703.

SHAW, GEORGE BERNARD. *Cashel Byron's Profession.* 1st edition, wrappers, 1886.

[VORAGINE, JACQUES DE]. *La Légende Dorée.* Quarto. Black letter. Lyon, N.D. Bound in limp vellum at the Doves Bindery. Bookplate of Walter Crane.

V. MISCELLANEOUS

CAXTON. An original leaf from the first edition of *The Chronicles of England* (1480), enclosed with an essay on Caxton by Holbrook Jackson (1933).

QUEEN ELIZABETH. Great Seal, dated 2 September 1600, in morocco case.

KING JAMES I. Great Seal attached to a pardon of alienation from Sir Thomas Cave, Knight, to Sir Hugh Cholmeley, Knight. Dated Westminster, 1 April 1606.

QUEEN ANNE. Great Seal, 1709, in morocco case.

NAPOLEON I. Sale catalogues of furniture and effects from Longwood, St Helena, 1822, with prices and names of purchasers filled in.

WELLINGTON, DUKE OF. Coloured caricatures of the Duke of Wellington, 1825–48. 26″ × 19½″. Bound in leather.

KIPLING, RUDYARD. *The Absent-Minded Beggar*. 1899. 6 pp. on silk and paper. Folio.

CATALOGUE OF THE
HUGH WALPOLE COLLECTION
IN THE FITZ PARK MUSEUM, KESWICK

The manuscripts of *Rogue Herries, Judith Paris, The Fortress, Vanessa, The Bright Pavilions,* and *Katherine Christian.*

A morocco-bound notebook containing notes, scenarios, and lists of characters, for the first four Herries novels.

Letters addressed to Hugh, one each by Max Beerbohm, Arnold Bennett, Joseph Conrad, Walter de la Mare, Jacob Epstein, John Galsworthy, Henry James, T. E. Lawrence, John Masefield, W. Somerset Maugham, Charles Morgan, Osbert Sitwell, Virginia Woolf.

Bronze head of Hugh by Jacob Epstein.

Collotype reproduction of drawing of Harold Cheevers and Hugh by Stephen Bone.[1]

Drawing of Hugh by Mrs von Glehn.

Caricature of Hugh by E. X. Kapp.

Water-colour sketch of the top library at Brackenburn by D. B. Martin.

Twelve water-colours of Lake District scenes by Sir Charles Holmes. (These used to hang in the dining-room at Brackenburn.)[2]

Water-colour sketch of Brackenburn by W. Heaton Cooper.

Photograph of Hugh and his dog Ranter.

[1] The original is in the possession of Mr Harold Cheevers.
[2] Also in the museum, among other relics of the Lake poets, is the original manuscript of Southey's *Madoc*, which Hugh bequeathed to the museum.

LIST OF BOOKS BY HUGH WALPOLE

1909. *The Wooden Horse*
1910. *Maradick at Forty*
1911. *Mr Perrin and Mr Traill*
1912. *The Prelude to Adventure*
1913. *Fortitude*
1914. *The Duchess of Wrexe*
1915. *The Golden Scarecrow*
   Containing: *A Prologue: Hugh Seymour, Henry Fitzgeorge Strether, Ernest Henry, Angelina, Bim Rochester, Nancy Ross, 'Enery, Barbara Flint, Sarah Trefusis, Young John Scarlett, Epilogue: Hugh Seymour*
1916. *The Dark Forest*
[1916]. *Joseph Conrad*
1918. *The Green Mirror*
1919. *The Secret City*
1919. *Jeremy*
1920. *The Captives*
[1921]. *The Thirteen Travellers*
   Containing: *Absalom Jay, Fanny Close, The Hon Clive Torby, Miss Morganhurst, Peter Westcott, Lucy Moon, Mrs Porter and Miss Allen, Lois Drake, Mr Nix, Lizzie Rand, Nobody, Bombastes Furioso*
1921. *A Hugh Walpole Anthology*
1921. *The Young Enchanted*
1922. *The Cathedral*
1923. *Jeremy and Hamlet*
1924. *The Old Ladies*
1924. *The Crystal Box*
1925. *The English Novel* (The Rede Lecture)
1925. *Portrait of a Man with Red Hair*
1926. *Harmer John*
1926. *Reading: an Essay*
1927. *Jeremy at Crale*
1928. *Anthony Trollope*
1928. *Wintersmoon*
1928. *The Silver Thorn*
   Containing: *The Little Donkeys with the Crimson Saddles, The Enemy in Ambush, Chinese Horses, A Silly Old Fool, Ecstasy, The Tarn, No Unkindness Intended, The Etching, Major Wilbraham, The Enemy, Old Elizabeth, A Picture, The Dove, The Tiger, Bachelors*

1928. *My Religious Experience*
1929. *Farthing Hall* (with J. B. Priestley)
1929. *Hans Frost*
1930. *Rogue Herries*
1931. *Above the Dark Circus*
1931. *Judith Paris*
1932. *Four Fantastic Tales*
        Containing: *Maradick at Forty, The Prelude to Adventure, Portrait of a Man with Red Hair,* and *Above the Dark Circus,* with a new Preface
1932. *The Fortress*
1932. *A Letter to a Modern Novelist*
1932. *The Waverley Pageant*
1932. *The Apple Trees*
1933. *All Souls' Night*
        Containing: *The Whistle, The Silver Mask, The Staircase, A Carnation for an Old Man, Tarnhelm, Mr Oddy, Seashore Macabre, Lilac, The Oldest Talland, The Little Ghost, Mrs Lunt, Sentimental but True, Portrait in Shadow, The Snow, The Ruby Glass, Spanish Dusk*
1933. *Vanessa*
1934. *Captain Nicholas*
1934. *Extracts from a Diary*
1935. *The Inquisitor*
1936. *A Prayer for My Son*
1937. *John Cornelius*
1937. *The Cathedral* (A Play in Three Acts)
1938. *Head in Green Bronze*
        Containing: *Head in Green Bronze, The German, The Exile, The Train, The Haircut, Let the Bores Tremble* (*The Adventure of Mrs Farbman, The Garrulous Diplomatist, The Adventure of the Imaginative Child, The Happy Optimist, The Adventure of the Beautiful Things, The Man who Lost his Identity, The Dyspeptic Critic*), *The Honey-Box, The Fear of Death, Field with Five Trees, Having No Hearts, The Conjurer*
1938. *The Joyful Delaneys*
1939. *The Sea Tower*
1939. *The Herries Chronicle*
        Containing: *Rogue Herries, Judith Paris, The Fortress,* and *Vanessa,* with a new Foreword
1939. *The Haxtons* (A Play in Three Acts)
1940. *Roman Fountain*
1940. *The Bright Pavilions*

1941. *Open Letter of an Optimist*

1941. *The Blind Man's House*
1942. *The Killer and the Slain*
1944. *Katherine Christian*
1948. *Mr Huffam*
    Containing: *The White Cat, The Train to the Sea, The Perfect Close, Service for the Blind, The Faithful Servant, Miss Thom, Women are Motherly, The Beard, The Last Trump, Green Tie, The Church in the Snow, Mr Huffam*

BIBLIOGRAPHY

AGATE, JAMES: *Ego 4*, 1940
  Ego 5, 1942
BAIN, JAMES S.: *A Bookseller Looks Back*, 1940
BENNETT, ARNOLD: *Journals, 1896–1928*. Ed. Newman Flower (3 vols), 1932–33
BENSON, A. C.: *The Life of Edward White Benson* (2 vols), 1899
  The Trefoil, 1923
  Diary. Ed. Percy Lubbock, [1926]
  Arthur Christopher Benson as seen by some Friends. Ed. E. H. Ryle, 1925
BRUCE, H. J.: *Silken Dalliance*, 1947
BUCHANAN, SIR GEORGE: *My Mission to Russia* (2 vols), 1923
CRUTTWELL, C. R. M. F.: *A History of the Great War 1914–1918*, 1934
DANE, CLEMENCE: *Tradition and Hugh Walpole*, 1930
DENT, ALAN: *Nocturnes and Rhapsodies*, 1950
DONALDSON, A. B.: *The Bishopric of Truro*, 1902
DORAN, GEORGE H.: *Chronicles of Barabbas 1884–1934*, 1935
JAMES, HENRY: *Notes on Novelists*, 1914
  Letters. Ed. Percy Lubbock (2 vols), 1920
  Letters to A. C. Benson and Auguste Monod. Ed. E. F. Benson, 1930
JEAN-AUBRY, G.: *Joseph Conrad, Life and Letters* (2 vols), 1927
KARSAVINA, TAMARA: *Theatre Street*, 1930
KNOX, MAJ.-GEN. SIR ALFRED: *With the Russian Army 1914–17* (2 vols), 1921
LOCKHART, R. H. BRUCE: *Memoirs of a British Agent*, 1932
LOWNDES, MRS BELLOC: *The Merry Wives of Westminster*, 1946
  A Passing World, 1948
LUBBOCK, PERCY: *Portrait of Edith Wharton*, 1947
LUCAS, E. V.: *The Colvins and their Friends*, 1928
MACKENZIE, COMPTON: *Literature in my Time*, 1933
MANSFIELD, KATHERINE: *Letters*. Ed. J. Middleton Murry (2 vols), 1928
  Novels and Novelists, 1930
MARGETSON, W. J.: *G. H. S. Walpole: A Memoir*, [1930]
MARROT, H. V.: *The Life and Letters of John Galsworthy*, 1935
MAUGHAM, W. SOMERSET: *Cakes and Ale*, 1930
MAXWELL, W. B.: *Time Gathered*, 1938
[MORDAUNT, ELINOR] *Gin and Bitters*, by A. Riposte. New York, 1931
MORGAN, CHARLES: *The House of Macmillan*, 1943
PARES, BERNARD: *My Russian Memoirs*, 1931
  The Fall of the Russian Monarchy, 1939
STEEN, MARGUERITE: *Hugh Walpole: A Study*, 1933
SWINNERTON, FRANK: *The Georgian Literary Scene*, 1935
  Swinnerton: An Autobiography, 1937
TWEEDSMUIR, LADY: *John Buchan by his Wife and Friends*, 1947
TYRKOVA-WILLIAMS, ARIADNA: *Cheerful Giver: The Life of Harold Williams*, 1935
WAGNER, FRIEDELIND: *The Royal Family of Bayreuth*, 1948
WELLS, H. G.: *Boon*, 1915

INDEX

[This is selective and attempts to present only such salient subjects, persons and events as a reader is likely to want to look up. Passing references to even the most important characters are not included.]

Above the Dark Circus
conceived, 302; begun, 304; continued, 306; finished, 307; part rewritten, 319; published, 321; various titles of, 321 n.

Agate, James
H. lends money to, 274; his "ferocious attack" on H., 330–31; as intermittent "enemy," 331; praises *Apple Trees*, 338; H. softens towards, 347; H. at 60th birthday of, 386; H. attacks as book-reviewer, 394–95; on *Old Ladies*, 416; not a serious enemy, 419; on H.'s death, 420 n.

All Souls' Night
published, 339.

America and Americans
Conrad on, 179, 195, 203, 236; unchanged since *Martin Chuzzlewit*, 192; Kipling on, 274; H.'s visits to, 188–93, 226–32, 274–77, 311, 349–52, 359–69, 374–75; H. G. Wells on, 364.

Anderson, Percy
H. meets, 78; history of, 78–79; *Mr Perrin* dedicated to, 83; H. travels with, 85, 89; takes H. to see Elgar, 87; introduces H. to Colvin, 87; at Polperro, 98, 114, 117; H. stays with, 145; and *Chu Chin Chow*, 163; H. visits on deathbed, 298.

Annand, James
H. meets, 163; sees in London, 165, 186; H.'s affection for, 167; H. stays with, 175, 194; with H. in Liverpool, 177; goes to Canada, 186; H. in rage with, 188; at H.'s party, 217; high on list of friends, 251; H. visits in Toronto, 275, 311, 375; their last meeting, 404.

Anthony Trollope
MS. in N.Y. Public Library, 229 n.; written 281–84; published, 291.

Apple Trees, The
full of misspellings, 60; inaccurate on Hardy, 79; begun, 329; finished, 330; published, 337; Agate on, 338; V. Woolf on, 338; *quoted*, 39, 66–67, 72.

Arnim, Gräfin
see Elizabeth.

Awards
St. George's Cross, 139, 143; C.B.E., 165–66; James Tait Black Prize, 203; Knighthood, 380–81, 384.

Ayrton, Michael
encouraged and helped by H., 421; his gratitude, 421; "a bit of a genius," 432; H. writes to, 443.

Barker, H. Granville
H. sees act, 44; his position in 1909, 65; on Moscow, 110; H. eats with, 165, 298.

Barretts of Wimpole Street, The
H.'s share in, 213–15; H. sees acted, 319.

Bayreuth
H.'s first visit to, 85; Melchior engaged for, 231; H. visits with Melchior, 232–33; re-opening of Festival, 252; Elizabeth on, 252; tension at, 253; Melchior, success of, 253; H.'s last visit to, 263–64; H. meets Hitler at, 263–64.

Beaverbrook, Lord
appointed Minister of Information, 170; difficulty of working for, 170; a rumpus with, 170–71; apologises and proves sympathetic, 171; writes to H., 173–74; asks H. to write literary page, 177.

Bede College
Somerset Walpole appointed Principal of, 22; family life in, 23–26, 29; revisited, 403.

Beerbohm, Max
attends dinner to H., 73; H. buys twenty-three cartoons by, 211; H. bequeaths them to Tate, 391.

Beith, J. H. (Ian Hay)
attempts to teach H. at Durham, 28–29; at Ministry of Information, 170; at O.D. dinner, 403–04.

Belloc, Hilaire
in Rome, 401; on P. G. Wodehouse, 403.

Bennett, Arnold
his position in 1909, 65; H. meets, 76; Henry James on *Hilda Lessways* and *Milestones*, 88; on *Prelude*, 89; on *Forti-*

Bennett, Arnold (*cont.*)
tude, 96, 115; sends a useful present, 102–03; friendship with H. grows, 103; tells Doran to publish H., 104; Henry James on, 111–12; his article on H., 114–15; on *Mr Perrin*, 114–15; H.'s gratitude to, 115–16; driven by money-lust, 116; H. on *The Price of Love*, 129; H. writes to, from front, 141; H. stays with, 148, 186; on *Dark Forest*, 149–50; H. suggests *Books and Persons* to, 157–58; on life, 163; in Turkish bath, 167; on E. V. Lucas, 169; on clichés, 169; H.'s gratitude to, 169; joins Ministry of Information, 170; asks H. to write report on Ministry, 176; on *Secret City*, 178; on *Jeremy*, 187; *Captives* dedicated to, 195; on *Captives*, 198–99; compares H. with Trollope, 198; on Middleton Murry, 209; sends wise counsel, 211; on *Young Enchanted*, 216; H. replies to, 216–17; H. on *Mr Prohack*, 221; his reply, 221; exchange of letters with, 234–35; on tattle, 235; H. on *Riceyman Steps*, 237; on misers, 238; on the Lake District, 238; and James Tait Black Prize, 255–56; as companion, 282; sends H. a book on slimming, 282; kind and bored, 284; and the Book Society, 299; on abnormality, 301; and Virginia Woolf, 306; at Galsworthy's, 306–07; his death and memorial service, 321; H.'s estimate of, 321–22; H. unveils plaque to, 326; H. on his *Journals*, 329; rated second class, 378; *his letters quoted:* 102–03, 169, 178, 198–99, 209, 211, 216, 221, 234, 235, 238.

Benson, A. C.
on H.'s father, 5; on Dr. Barham, 6; H. meets, 32; described by Percy Lubbock and Henry James, 32; describes H. in his diary, 33; spots H.'s writing potentialities, 33; advises H. to be a clergyman, 37–38; H.'s devotion to, 39; H. visits in Sussex, 44–45, 60, 79; and at Cambridge, 47; on *Troy Hanneton*, 54; introduces H. to Henry James, 62; H. motors with, 68; Henry James's letters about H. to, 70; approves of *Mr Perrin*, 83; discusses H. with Henry James, 86; on H.'s Rede Lecture, 259; described in old age, 259–60; his death, 260; H.'s belated gratitude to, 260; as talker, 286–87.

Beresford, J. D.
H. meets, 90; compared with H., 92; consulted by H., 101; free from jealousy, 104; ignored by Henry James, 113; H. visits, 114, 162; collects for D. H.

Lawrence, 174; at York Terrace party, 217; reunion with, 393.

Besier, Rudolf
and *Robin's Father*, 94, 98, 101, 177, 287; and *The Barretts of Wimpole Street*, 213–15, 319.

Blake, George
H. meets on beach, 330; H.'s liking for, 332; comes to stay, 347, 358, 369, 378, 388, 397, 402; H. stays with, 378, 398, 428; at Coronation, 382.

Blind Man's House, The
roughed out, 412, 413, 415; begun, 417; continued, 418, 421, 422; finished, 424; serial and film rights sold, 438.

Blunden, Edmund
attends Hardy birthday meeting, 207; joins Book Society, 329.

Boleslawsky, Richard
H. meets in Hollywood, 350; reunion with, 360; gives Christmas party, 365; H. sad to part from, 369; a long-distance call to, 374; his sudden death, 377; H.'s sorrow for, 377; his photograph taken to shelter, 431.

Bone, Muirhead
H. meets, 236; H. stays with, 239; on short list of friends, 251; makes sketch of Brackenburn, 254; knighted with H., 384; lunch with, 403; H.'s last meeting with, 441.

Book Society, The
H.'s and Clemence Dane's work for, 292; unhappy result of *Red Ike* on, 295; foundation of, 298–99; Bennett and, 299; H. agrees to join, 299; meets at H.'s flat, 313, 326; H.'s power through, 318; burden of reading for, 327; Blunden replaces Priestley on, 329; gives farewell dinner to H., 358; H. rejoins, 370.

Bookshops
Hatchards, 177; H.'s love of all, 181; Bain's, 181; Maggs's, 181; in Guildford, 186; Gabriel Wells's, 193; at Mentone, 258; Bumpus's, 279; Bridger's, 326.

Bott, Alan
starts the Book Society, 299; takes H. to nursing home, 353; joins H. at Champneys, 358; H. stays with, 383, 386, 406, 413, 416, 421, 424, 435; at Brackenburn, 396, 436; houses H.'s pictures, 410; H. writes to, on affection, 417; defends H. in *The Times*, 420; H. quarrels with and apologises to, 427; *Open Letter of an Optimist* dedicated to, 427.

Bott, Josephine
H.'s fondness for, 383; at Brackenburn, 396; introduces an admirer to H. in the blitz, 436; drives H. to Essex, 436.

Brackenburn
discovery and purchase of, 236–37; H. moves into, 243; described, 247–48; satisfies only part of H., 249; outlook from, 250; bought by Stanley Long after H.'s death, 277 n.; H.'s daily routine at, 293–94; new rooms at, 313, 314–15; H.'s return to, described, 339; early morning departure from, 342; Copperfield an overflow from, 349; H.'s Hollywood longing for, 368; removal of trees in front of, 380; congestion of pictures at, 390–91, 442; described by Storrs, 396; typical day at, described in journal, 397–98; its peace in wartime, 409, 442; H.'s inability to stay at, 409; H. prophesies he will die at, 410; last journey to, 442; H. dies at, 444.

Brain-storms
H. liable to, 75; in Petrograd, 155; with the Annands, 188; self-admonishment about, 240; discussed in journal, 255; in London, 289; described in Roman Fountain, 289; in Sweden, 308; with Harold, 332, 353; with Bott, 427; at Hampstead, 441.

Brett Young, Francis
H.'s jealousy of, 103, 312; not jealous of H., 104; H.'s first meeting with, 148; too moral for Capri, 258; visits H., 295; gives H. room with a view, 309; H. visits, 340, 393.

Bright Pavilions, The
H.'s longing to begin, 388, 393; begun, 395; described to M. Steen, 395; continued, 397, 401, 402, 410, 412, 414; Father D'Arcy on, 402 n.; finished, 415; published, 432; dedicated to Storrs, 432; its success, 438.

Broadcasts
H.'s first, 301; his first solo, 306; in wartime, 425, 431, 432.

Broughton, Rhoda
H. lunches with, 74; her novels rediscovered, 414; her pet remark, 414.

Browning, Robert
read by H.'s parents 6; read by H. in Galicia, 138; his importance to H., 141; H. conceives play about, 213–15; Gosse on, 287; H. returns often to, 373; H.'s ast reading of, 443.

Bruce, H. J. (Benjie)
on Sir G. Buchanan, 135; H. meets, 152; brings news of Revolution, 159; effects a reconciliation, 163; a staunch friend, 319.

Buchan, John
H. meets, 75; a revelation to H., 92–93; H. sees at Foreign Office, 154, 162; H. stays with, 163; gets H. home, 164; encourages H. to enlist, 165; likes Green Mirror, 166; asks H. to be his private secretary, 170; winds up Ministry, 177; his advice remembered, 210; backs H. for Athenæum, 221; a talk with, 278; has high praise for Rogue Herries, 312; on Judith Paris, 327; H. mystifies, 353; H. stays with, 354; H. mourns, 418.

Buchanan, Sir George
described, 135–36; takes to H., 136; depressed by poison gas, 137; cables for H., 148; H. has long talk with, 157; his despatch on Revolution, 161 n., 449–69; calms H. down, 163; agrees to H.'s leaving Russia, 164; H. sees in London, 167.

Cabell, James Branch
H. meets, 192; H.'s admiration for and pamphlet on, 193; H. stays with, 274.

Cakes and Ale
see Maugham.

Cambridge
H. an undergraduate at, 31–39; his career there recalled, 259.

Canterbury
see King's School and Sellingegate.

Captain Nicholas
begun, 338; finished, 340; chosen by Literary Guild, 349; published, 351; dramatised, 404.

Captives, The (Maggie)
begun, 149; resumed, 170, 172; finished, 177; revised, 185; dedicated to Bennett, 195; published, 197; Conrad on, 197–98; Bennett on, 198; praised by Maugham, 218.

Cars
Harold taught to drive, 270, 277; H. buys Rolls-Royce, 274; a new Daimler, 278; damaged in smash, 280; Harold's skill with, 292; H.'s inability to drive, 292; a new Alvis, 307, 339; a surprise for Dorothy, 328; essential in Hollywood, 350, 360.

Cat Bells
Brackenburn built on, 236, 247; in *The Fortress*, 327; H.'s seat on, 341, 389.

Cathedral, The
partly based on *The Abbey*, 43; begun, 177; continued, 185, 186, 194, 195; laid aside, 202; resumed, 218; H.'s parents shocked by, 218; finished, 219; published, 227; H.'s father's anonymous defence of, 227–28; H.'s "best story," 372; MS. sold at auction, 426.

Cazalet, Victor
H. lunches with, at House of Commons, 278; takes H. to visit Winston Churchill, 297–98.

Cazalets, The
H.'s friendship with, 221; visits to, 234, 313, 400; introduce H. to P. G. Wodehouse, 268; H. takes to bad play, 287; Kipling and, 295–97, 366.

Chamberlain, Neville
and Munich, 396–97; H. lunches with, 403.

Chanter, Douglas
H. engages, 223; explores Lakes, 249; on short list of friends, 251; leaves H.'s service, 286.

Chaplin, Charlie
imitates H., 231; entertains H. in Hollywood, 350; gives dinner for Wells, 364.

Cheevers, Ethel
her great qualities, 285; seriously ill, 340; her Cornish pasties, 382; her sponge cake, 385; in the blitz, 431, 433.

Cheevers, Harold
history and description of, 268–69; his character, 269; H.'s plans for, 270; H.'s trust in, 273, 343; H.'s thought of, 275; fourth on list of friends, 275; enters H.'s service, 277; installed at Hampstead, 284; in sole charge, 286; fails to teach H. to drive, 292; as swimming instructor, 292–93; H.'s growing affection for, 293; *Rogue Herries* dedicated to, 307; refuses to obey H., 308; H. gives power of attorney to, 310; first on list of friends, 311; unsusceptible to ghosts, 320; becomes "hero of the islands," 326; and seat on Cat Bells, 341; arrives in Hollywood, 351; acts in a film, 352; and H.'s picture-buying, 354, 416; welcomes H. home, 356; H. lonely without, 366; returns to Hollywood, 368; portrait of, in *John Cornelius*, 371; on Giorgione, 385; his calm at Munich

crisis, 396; one of "only three friends," 404; *Roman Fountain* dedicated to, 418; H.'s love for, 424; H. clings to, 425; H.'s last talk with, 444; at H.'s death, 444.

Chess
supplants backgammon at Brackenburn, 332; S. Bone draws picture of, 340; H. on his play, 342; emotional stress caused by, 347–48; in Hollywood, 352; on Greek cruise, 356; H. irritable after losing at, 376; compared with blitz, 423.

Chesterton, G. K.
healthy and invigorating, 154; H. debates with, 202.

Childishness
in H.'s nature, 74–75, 320, 324; in his writing, 312–13; in the best authors, 321; H.'s and Bennett's, 329; H. on his own, 389.

Christmas
the Walpole tradition of, 177; H. moved by, 203; last full family one, 256; with Melchiors in N.Y., 275; a surprise present for Dorothy, 328; in nursing home, 353; in Hollywood, 364–65.

Churchill, Winston S.
H. taken to lunch with, 268; H. visits and describes, 297–98.

Cobbles, The
see Polperro.

Colefax, Sibyl
introduces H. to Frederick Macmillan, 110; tells H. to come home, 144; at York Terrace party, 218; gives highbrow lunch, 240; H. sees in London, 402.

Collier, John
H. helps towards Hollywood, 354; in Hollywood, 360; H. best man at wedding of, 365; wants to be damned, 369.

Colvin, Lady
H.'s tribute to, 87; on Galsworthy, 88; on Drinkwater, 88; not amused, 88; H. stays with, 176; on *Jeremy*, 187; at York Terrace party, 217; her death, 253.

Colvin, Sidney
H. meets, 87; introduces H. to Conrad, 168; H. stays with, 176; at York Terrace party, 217; seconds H. for Athenæum, 221; H. at memorial service for, 278.

Conrad, Joseph
H. reads at Cambridge, 31; his position in 1909, 65; H.'s book on, 116, 136; commiserates with H., 158 n.; H.'s first meeting with, 168; on H. G. Wells, 168; on *Dark Forest*, 168; on *Green Mirror*,

171; on *Secret City*, 179; on Americans, 179, 195, 203, 236; on journalists, 186; on F. M. Hueffer, 195; on Russians, 195; on *Captives*, 197–98; on his friendship with H., 203; writes foreword for H., 203–04; uncomfortable week-end with, 215; on *Young Enchanted*, 215–16; his distress at Pinker's death, 219; embraces H. publicly, 219; *Cathedral* dedicated to, 227; H.'s last visit to, 236; excited by Proust, 236; his death, 253; as companion, 282; as talker, 286; Sickert likened to, 300; Boleslawsky compared with, 377; his books rearranged, 429; *his letters quoted*, 158 n., 197, 203, 215–16; *his sayings reported*, 168, 171, 175, 176, 179, 186, 187, 194, 195.

Cooper, Duff
on first meeting H., 54–55; H. writes to, 56–57; at Admiralty House, 394.

Corelli, Marie
her house described, 426.

Coughlin, Father
H.'s meeting with, 386–87.

Courtney, W. L.
praises *Fortitude*, 96; to be spewed forth, 102; on *Dark Forest*, 149; "imbecile" on *Green Mirror*, 166.

Crawford, F. Marion
influences H.'s early writing, 26; his new novel condemned, 31; his perennial charm for H., 230, 373; described by Henry James, 230; H. walks in garden of, 401.

Cricket
H. watches, 252, 313, 349, 358, 370, 393, 402; Oval Test scene described, 273; H. listens to, in Spain, 303; H. "cracked on," 315.

Criterion, The
Two chapters of *Old Ladies* published in, 241.

Crystal Box, The
begun, 220; continued, 226; privately printed, 255; MS. at Canterbury, 475; *quoted*, 17–18, 18–19, 25, 42, 44, 69–70, 180.

Cukor, George
H. travels to Hollywood with, 349; H. stays with, 360; gives Christmas party, 365; H. sad to leave, 369.

Cumberland
H.'s absorption in, 12; first visits to, 26–28; H. plans to settle in, 225, 233; H.'s gratitude to, 247; lyrical impulse inspired by, 250; preferred to Cornwall, 254; H.'s longing to requite goodness of, 265; the beauty of, 279; H.'s debt to, paid, 333; H.'s ambition to be connected with, 334; H. taken for native of, 357.

Cunard, Lady
H. detests, 278; chatters in the blitz, 435.

Dalmahoy
H.'s mother buried at, 261; H.'s father buried at, 304; revisited, 388.

Dane, Clemence
"raves over" *Man with Red Hair*, 265; visits H. in his convalescence, 283; H.'s appreciation of, 292; joins Book Society, 299; as book selector, 313; and *Cakes and Ale*, 317; in Hollywood, 352; asked to pray for H., 358; in London, 376; likes *John Cornelius*, 386.

Dark Forest, The
compared with *Mr Perrin*, 93; conceived, 136; begun in Carpathians, 138; verisimilitude of, 141, 142; continued in Petrograd, 143; finished, 144; first edition destroyed, 149; published, 149; Arnold Bennett on, 149; Galsworthy on, 150; Conrad on, 168; Rebecca West on, 172; as work of art, 254; "my best book artistically," 372; *quoted*, 144–45.

David Copperfield
H. agrees to write film-scenario of, 348; difficulties with, 349, 350, 351; H. acts in film of, 351; H. sees film in London, 354.

Davidson, Jo
H. meets, 226; H. sits to, 310; visited in U.S., 311.

Davies, Hubert Henry
H.'s friendship with, 110–11, 117, 119, 261.

Death
H. reflects on, 261; H. not ready for, 346; H. forecasts his own in *John Cornelius*, 372; H. prophesies place of his own, 410; H. prepares for, 419.

Death and the Hunters
see *Dark Forest*.

Dent, Alan (Jock)
H. meets, 394; finds H. praying, 430–31; on bombing, 439; gives H. a birthday present, 439.

Denwood, J. M.
H.'s interest and disappointment in, 295.

Derwentwater
H.'s first impression of, 27; and Brackenburn, 247; frozen over, 417.

Diabetes
H.'s diagnosed, 266; neglected, 279; worse, 282, 292; insulin injections for, 302, 330, 430; Hollywood suits, 352; in H.'s last illness, 443.

Dogs
Jacob, 91, 146, 172; Grock, 197, 202; Mopsa, 207, 218; Bingo, 341, 342, 356; Ranter, 356, 368, 383, 385, 434.

Doran, George H.
Bennett approaches, 89; accuses H. of jealousy and meanness, 104; becomes H.'s publisher, 104; extremely effusive, 149; persuades H. to lecture in U.S., 178; fêtes H. in N.Y., 189; good offices of, 239; offers good advances, 270; "so kind and good," 274; H. attends party for, 284; his firm absorbed by Double-day, 309.

Dostoevsky
H.'s discovery of, 90; Henry James on, 91; H. reads in Moscow, 127; H. reads on way to front, 137; H. compares himself with, 141; H. constantly reads, 373; rated first class, 378.

Douglas, Lord Alfred
and Civil List Pension, 403; described in H.'s journal, 413.

Doyle, Arthur Conan
H. reads as serial, 26; H. attends séances at house of, 280; H. still loves books of, 373; and knighthood, 381.

Dreams
nightmares, 12–13, 18; in Russia, 142; at Conrad's, 175; a horrible one described, 340–41; of S. Lynd, 397; of royalty, 411; of a wonderful pie, 428.

Drinkwater, John
Lady Colvin on, 88; watches rugger with H., 202; at York Terrace party, 217; with H. at prize-giving, 289; at Bennett's memorial service, 321; his death, 379; H.'s sketch of, 379.

Duchess of Wrexe, The
begun, 95; H. sticks in, 101; H.'s mother sleeps through, 104–05; finished, 105; published, 109; Henry James on 112–13; MS. sold to American, 294; and Maurice Hewlett, 303.

Durham
H.'s hatred of, 21, 29; snobbery at, 23, 218; subscription library at, 24; and Polchester, 145; revisited, 237, 403–04.

Edinburgh
Walpole family move to, 79; H.'s habit of beginning books in, 80; H. dislikes climate of, 108, 378; house-hunting in, 307; Dorothy's new house in, 310; in blackout, 417.

Egypt
H.'s visit to, 257–58.

Elgar, Edward
H.'s visits to, 87.

Eliot, T. S.
likes *Old Ladies*, 241; H. a little afraid of, 254; defends H. in *The Times*, 420.

Elizabeth
H.'s first letter from, 46; his first meeting with, 47; H. wires to, 48; teases H., 49–50; annotates his diary, 51; H.'s later friendship with, 52–53; their mutual affection, 53; mellowed, 87; in fancy dress, 88; H. stays with, 108, 208, 233; Henry James on, 109; on James Annand, 163; H. sees in London, 167; "a gorgeous time with," 186; asks Murry to tea, 210; "something of the boss about her," 210; at York Terrace party, 217; on *Parsifal* and Bayreuth, 252; praises *Old Ladies*, 255; witchlike, 278; renames *Hans Frost*, 281; clutches her literary reputation, 281; H. copies working hours of, 293.

Enemies
essential to H.'s cosmos, 223; St John Ervine enrolled among, 223, 312; a dagger in hands of, 316; Agate intermittently among, 331, 386; H. naked without, 338; H. makes peace with, 419–20; one lurks in ambush, 420.

English Novel, The
see Rede Lecture.

Epsom College
reasons for H.'s choosing, 55; H. teaches at, 56–62; an ex-pupil's description, 59; *Mr Perrin* based on, 78, 83; H.'s breach with, 83; H. gives prizes at, 384.

Epstein
H. buys work by, 241, 298, 321, 339; H. sits to, 343; described at work, 343.

Ervine, St John
H. meets in N.Y., 192; invited to join dining club, 204; organises birthday present for Hardy, 206–07; at York Terrace party, 218; incident of the Brazil nuts, 222–23; H. considers an "enemy," 223; H. stimulated by, 278; his "atrocious" review of *Rogue Herries*,

312; re-enrolled as enemy, 312, 316; at Bennett's memorial service, 321; praises *Cathedral* play, 338; enmity with, wearing thin, 391; H. makes peace with, 419–20; his obituary of H., 420 n.

Eves, R. G.
H. sits to, 402, 416; H.'s portraits by, 418 and n.

Extracts from a Diary
origins and publication of, 346 and n.

Eyesight
H. short-sighted, 17; H.'s disability discovered, 28; prevents H. from enlisting, 117, 143, 166; a handicap at the front, 128; causes breakdown, 169, 171, 172; again troublesome, 292.

Farthing Hall
origins of, 279–80; begun, 282; finished, 285; published, 303.

Ferris, W. A. T. (Chug)
H.'s friendship with, 58; H. stays with, 60; *Wooden Horse* dedicated to, 69; heads first list of friends, 80; sends along Douglas Chanter, 223.

Films
H. weeps at *Beau Geste*, 276; difficulties of making, 350, 351; H. acts in, 351; of *Vanessa*, 351, 352, 354; Harold acts in, 352; of *Kim*, 361, 366, 368, 369; of *Little Lord Fauntleroy*, 361, 362; of *Jamaica Inn*, 380, 383; of *And So—Victoria*, 388, 389, 393, 394.

Food
H.'s love of high tea, 26; H.'s compared with Woodforde's, 250; H. homesick for English, 365; breakfast H.'s favourite, 365; at Brackenburn, 397–98.

Ford, Ford Madox
see Hueffer.

Foreign Office
H. works in, 165–70.

Forster, E. M.
H.'s predecessor at Nassenheide, 49; on *Wooden Horse*, 59; H.'s opinion of, 113; praises *Old Ladies*, 255; gives H. tea, 313.

Fortitude
portrait of Mrs. Lowndes in, 75; begun, 80; famous opening words of, 80; and Marlow, 81; diverted from Mills & Boon, 85; finished, 94; published, 96; Bennett on, 96, 115; H.'s mother on, 96; Galsworthy on, 96–97; Henry James on, 97; published by Doran in U.S.A., 104; among twelve most popular novels of

year, 106; H.'s later opinion of, 186; quoted in sermon, 411; *quoted*, 19.

Fortress, The
begun, 319; an original for, 320; continued, 321, 323, 326, 327; finished, 328; H.'s reflections on re-reading, 328–29; published, 331–32.

Fowler, Arthur
H. meets, 76; H. dines with in N.Y., 193; looks after H.'s U.S. income, 229; *Man with Red Hair* dedicated to, 229; fails to send Christmas letter, 256; welcomes H. to N.Y., 274; H. stays with, 275.

Franciscans
H.'s visits to, 416, 421.

Frere, A. S.
starts the Book Society, 299; H.'s friendship with, 299; H. meets future wife of, 309; watches cricket with H., 313; asks H. to intercede with Maugham, 323; H. stays with, 383, 402, 421.

Friendship
the quest for the ideal friend, 32; H.'s insistence on, 32; budding ones often broken, 32, 56; with Percy Anderson, 78; first list of friends, 80; H.'s need of, with families, 168; between men, 193; with Melchior, 197, 207–08; Melchior the ideal friend? 212, 215; Melchior heads list, 240; another attempt failed, 253; and Harold Cheevers, 268; does last, 309; exhausting, 344; and H.'s 50th birthday, 346–47; H. broods on, 357; "only three friends," 404; H. thirsty for affection, 417; H.'s dying insistence on, 444.

Frost, Robert
H. likes hugely, 277; dominates everything, 311.

Fyfe, Hamilton
H.'s host in Petrograd, 130, 131; H.'s description of, 135; helps H. to pack, 137; H. dines with, 143.

Galsworthy, John
his position in 1909, 65; promises to read *Fortitude*, 85; embarrassed by Henry James, 87; Lady Colvin on, 88; on *Prelude*, 89; on *Fortitude*, 96–97; H. stays with, 102, 301, 313; on *Dark Forest*, 150; H. talks with, 154; and E. V. Lucas's jokes, 165; and Society of Bookmen, 204; at York Terrace party, 217; H. discusses imagination with, 280; and

Galsworthy, John (*cont.*)
revision of MSS., 294; Whitsun holiday with, 306–07; with Bennett, 306–07; beaten at croquet, 307; his death, 338; and knighthood, 381.

Generosity
H.'s to other writers, 103–04, 325–26; Edith and Osbert Sitwell on H.'s, 325; Swinnerton on H.'s, 325; to friends and relations, 324–25; H.'s ignored in *Times* obituary, 420.

German Garden
H.'s stay in, 48–52.

Gilchrist, R. M.
H.'s friendship with, 84.

Gin and Bitters
H. accused of writing, 323; H. a character in, 323; and Somerset Maugham, 323–24, 326; Elinor Mordaunt author of, 326.

Gissing, George
Conrad speaks of, 176; Gosse on, 278, 287; H. compares himself with, 362; rated third class, 378.

Glasgow, Ellen
H. visits, 193, 228, 274; clutches her literary reputation, 281.

Golden Scarecrow, The
dedicated to Elizabeth, 53; arranged by Pinker, 105; finished in Russia, 131; published, 145.

Goncourts, The
H. reads, 54; H. plans to emulate, 424.

Gordon, George
H. much taken with, 285; joins Book Society, 299; as book selector, 313; H. stays with, 402.

Gosforth
see Sower Myre Farm.

Gosse, Edmund
takes fatherly interest in H., 76; and Henry James's 70th birthday, 99; and the Sargent portrait, 106–07; nostalgic evening with, 186; H. debates with, 202; on Gissing and Carlyle, 278; neglects Feuchtwanger, 284; a thrilling talker, 287.

Greece
H.'s first impressions of, 355–56; second cruise to, 392–93.

Green Mirror, The
conceived, 105; begun, 107; continued in wartime, 117, in Russia, 123, in Warsaw, 127; laid aside, 136; "my true style," 142; resumed, 146, 147; finished, 148; accepted by Macmillan, 155; published, 166; Conrad on, 171; Scott Moncrieff on, 414 n.

Hampstead (Garden Suburb)
Cheevers family installed in, 284; a refuge to H., 285; H. finds he can write in, 306; in wartime, 425; in the blitz, 431–32, 433, 440–41.

Hannen, Nicholas (Beau)
a welcome guest, 310; acts in Ervine play, 391; at Botts', 406.

Hans Frost
begun, 277; continued "in V. Woolf's manner," 279; Elizabeth's name for, 281; continued and finished, 281; possible influence of V. Woolf on, 303; published, 308; V. Woolf's opinion of, 309.

Hardy, Thomas
H.'s meeting with, 79, 286; 81st birthday present to, 206–07; denounced in Bloomsbury, 301; and *Cakes and Ale*, 316–17; H. constantly reads, 373; centenary celebrations of, 423–24.

Harmer John
begun, 223; abandoned, 232; continued, 239; laid aside, 239; continued, 242; difficulties with, at Bayreuth, 253; finished, 254; connection with Melchior, 254; serialised in U.S., 255; Frederick Macmillan on, 267–68; dedicated to Melchior, 270; H.'s special feeling for, 270, 358; Maugham charming about, 274; published, 274; sales disappoint H., 276.

Harold
see Cheevers.

Hawthorne, Nathaniel
H.'s early reading of, 24; his influence on H., 25, 166, 193; H.'s unpublished essay on, 25; example of his uniqueness, 363.

Head in Green Bronze
published, 391.

Hearst, William Randolph
H. at party given by, 362; his fantastic ranch, 364.

Hepburn, Katherine
H.'s devotion to, 350.

Hergesheimer, Joseph
H. meets, 189; his pamphlet on H., 189; *Thirteen Travellers* dedicated to, 190; happy days with, 193, 226; H.'s affection for, 229; revisited, 311.

Herries
     first outlines of, 247; conscious stirrings
     of, 264–65; begin to take shape, 279;
     possible origin of name, 279 n.; H.'s
     further plans for, 302, 346, 367, 415,
     428; fill H.'s mind, 328; their success
     brings admirers, 330; "one real romantic
     book," 331; M. Steen on, 333; "all in
     water-colour," 339; H.'s hunger for,
     388; *The Herries Chronicle*, suggested,
     402; discussed, 414; success of, 416;
     Mark disentangles family tree, 428.

Hersholt, Jean
     H. meets in Hollywood, 350; reunion
     with, 360; helps H. buy first editions,
     363; gives Christmas Eve party, 365; H.
     sad to part from, 369.

Hewlett, Maurice
     H. meets, 94; and the Henry James por-
     trait, 106–07; H.'s recollections of, 303;
     H. compares himself with, 362.

Hitler, Adolf
     and Winifred Wagner, 263–64; H. meets
     at Bayreuth, 263–64, 411; described in
     Roman Fountain, 263 n.; H. moved to tears
     by Melchior's singing, 264; Chamberlain
     and, 403.

Hollywood
     H.'s first glimpse of, 191; H. accepts job
     in, 348; his salary there, 348, 361–62;
     H.'s arrival at, 349; Harold's success in,
     351; H. leaves, 352; H. returns to, 359;
     described in journal, 360–61; H. takes
     house in, 360; Christmas in, 364–65;
     compared with prison camp, 366; H.
     finally leaves, 369.

Homosexuality
     unknown in Russia, 135; rare in male
     friendships, 193; Kipling on *Well of
     Loneliness*, 296; discussed in Blooms-
     bury, 301; Bennett on, 301; H.'s inten-
     tion to write about, 345.

Housman, A. E.
     H.'s impression of, 301.

Howells, W. D.
     with H. and Henry James at the theatre,
     72.

Hueffer, Ford Madox
     his position in 1909, 65; H. questions
     importance of, as poet, 144; Conrad on,
     195; P.E.N. Club Dinner to, 275; dedi-
     cates book to H., 326.

Income Tax
     H. perpetually worried by, 224; H.
     makes no allowance for, 367; shelved,

     369; struggles with, 377–78; arrears of,
     418; an error in, 438.

Inquisitor, The
     begun, 344; continued, 347, 351; pub-
     lished, 361; Priestley on, 361; its success,
     364.

James, Henry
     on A. C. Benson, 32; H. writes paper
     on, 36; charmed by H., 47, 290; first
     writes to H., 62; his position in 1909, 65;
     first meeting with H., 68; H. first stays
     with, 68; on Eustace Miles, 70; thanks
     A. C. Benson for H., 70; introduced to
     H.'s benefactors, 72; as playgoer, 72, 73;
     on publishers, 73–74; on *Maradick*, 77–
     78; original of Henry Galleon, 81; on
     Mr Perrin, 82–83; as dedicatee, 83;
     describes H. in *The Outcry*, 86; speaks
     of H. to A. C. Benson, 86; lectures
     Galsworthy, 87; on Pinero, 88; on *Hilda
     Lessways*, 88; on *Milestones*, 88; on *Pre-
     lude*, 90; on Dostoevsky and style, 91–
     92; recommends a literary agent, 93; at
     Ockham, 93; his one great passion, 94;
     consoles H., 95; on *Fortitude*, 97; on The
     Cobbles, 98; commotion over his 70th
     birthday, 99; sends H. furniture, 100–02;
     complains of brevity of H.'s letters, 101;
     H. baffled by *A Small Boy and Others*,
     102; on high jinks, 105; the Sargent por-
     trait, 106–07; his article in *Times Literary
     Supplement*, 111–13; on *Duchess of Wrexe*,
     112–13; H. writes to, from Russia, 125–
     27, 128–29, 130–31; defends H.'s reputa-
     tion, 132; advises him to come home,
     133; H.'s reply, 134–35; H. writes to,
     from front, 141; H. telephones to, 145;
     his last letter to H., 146–47; receives
     O.M., 148; his death, 153; his legacy to
     H., 155; H. influenced by, 166; his
     letters read aloud, 186; H. lectures on,
     189; H. reads *Letters* of, 193; on Marion
     Crawford, 230; *Mr Oddy* partly based
     on, 258; and death, 261; as companion,
     282; H. calls up spirit of, 285–86; as
     talker, 286; H. enjoys writing about,
     330 ; his books re-arranged, 429; *The
     Killer* dedicated to, 433; *his letters quoted:*
     32, 67, 68, 69, 70, 71, 73, 74, 77–78, 82,
     83, 86, 90, 91–92, 95, 98, 100, 101, 102,
     105, 108, 109, 113, 118, 129, 132, 133,
     146–47.

Jeremy
     publication fixed, 155; begun, 156–57;
     written during Russian Revolution,
     159, 161; finished, 162; published, 187;

Jeremy (cont.)
many boys named after, 187; Lady Colvin on, 187; Bennett on, 187; Katherine Mansfield on, 187; "sweeping America," 191; *quoted*, 20.

Jeremy and Hamlet
begun, 208; read aloud to family, 211; finished, 215; published, 234.

Jeremy at Crale
begun, 267; continued, 270; finished, 272; published, 283; William Roughead on, 283.

John, Augustus
his portrait of H. at Canterbury, 22; H.'s enthusiasm for work of, 271; Kelly introduces H. to, 271–72; H. sits to, and describes at work, 272.

John Cornelius
begun on shipboard, 358; H.'s special feeling for, 358–59; continued in Hollywood, 362, 363; set aside, 366; resumed, 369; finished at Brackenburn, 370–72; self-portrait in, 371; H. prostrated by end of, 372; dedicated to Boleslawsky, 377; Dorothy weeps over, 385–86; discussed in journal, 385; published, 385; *quoted*, 20, 167, 371.

Jones, Sir Roderick
as Director of Propaganda, 170; keeps H. busy, 170; proves sympathetic, 171; writes to H., 174.

Joyce, James
H. ignorant of, 144; H. on *Ulysses*, 220; V. Woolf tired of being caged with, 327; Alfred Noyes and *Ulysses*, 405.

Joyful Delaneys, The
origin of, 372–73; begun, 375; continued, 376, 378; finished, 387; published, 394.

Judith Paris
original title of, 302; fills H.'s brain, 307; begun, 308; continued, 309, 312, 313, 316, 318; finished, 319; published, 327; Buchan on, 327; V. Woolf on, 327; H.'s reflections on re-reading, 328–29.

Jung, C. G.
attends H.'s lecture, 314; on *Prelude to Adventure*, 314.

Karsavina
H. charmed by, 137; describes H. in Russia, 152–53; a staunch friend, 319.

Katherine Christian
begun, 427–28; soothing power of, 434; continued, 435, 436, 438, 439, 443.

Kelly, Gerald
H. sits to, 116; sittings resumed, 218; H.'s friendship with, 218; sittings resumed, 271; his portraits of H., 271 n.; H. outgrows work of, 271–72; his magnanimity, 272; blamed for spending hours on buttons, 300; H.'s last meeting with, 441.

Keppel, Mrs George
H.'s father objects to, 34; H. visits, 35–36; H.'s later opinion of, 36.

Keswick
H.'s first visit to, 27; house-hunting round, 236; H. stays at, 243; H. makes friends in, 250; H. buried at, 444; H. W. collection at, 480.

Killer and the Slain, The
origins of, 386, 433; begun, 425; continued, 427, 431, 433, 435, 436; MS. taken to shelter, 431; H.'s comments on, 433, 436–38; dedicated to Henry James, 433; finished, 438; H. re-reads, 442.

King's School, Canterbury, The
H. a pupil at, 21–23; his affection for, 21; his benefactions to, 21–22; shown to Melchior, 234; F. J. Shirley and, 21, 358, 370; H. addresses boys at, 383; manuscripts presented to, 389; evacuated to Cornwall, 425.

Kingston Deverill
the Moore family at, 15; H.'s childhood holidays at, 15–16.

Kipling, Rudyard
on Americans, 274; on false teeth, 283; H.'s description of, 296–97; on the abnormal, 296; on *Silver Thorn*, 296; on his Jane Austen mistake, 296; "so great a man," 303; absolutely good-hearted, 306; H. and film of *Kim*, 361, 366, 368, 369; death of, 365; on ending stories, 366; and knighthood, 381.

Knopf, Alfred
H. impressed by, 190; introduces H. to Willa Cather, 193.

Lake District, The
H. first visits, 26–28; H.'s essay on, 347, *quoted*, 27, 28; H.'s collection of books on, 180; H. rediscovers, 224; H. haunted by, 228; Bennett on, 238; H. explores with Chanter, 249; H. plans series of novels on, 264–65, 279; further exploration of, 385.

Lawrence, D. H.
H. brings to notice of Henry James, 105; Henry James dismisses, 111, 115; H.

joins protest at suppression of *The Rainbow*, 147; H. sends money for, 174; his sort of love not H.'s, 255; denounced in Bloomsbury, 301; V. Woolf on *Sons and Lovers*, 324; V. Woolf tired of being caged with, 327; H. meets widow of, 369.

Lawrence, T. E.
at Conrad's, 195; his letter to H., 278; H. sells *Seven Pillars*, 278–79.

Lecturing
H.'s first, in Liverpool, 45; H.'s enjoyment of, 75, 189; Doran suggests, 178; first U.S. tour, 188–93; second U.S. tour, 211, 226–32; third U.S. tour, 274–77; in the north, 286; Keedick's offer, 291; fourth U.S. tour, 311; in Germany and Switzerland, 313–14; in Hollywood, 352; on Greek tour, 356; fifth and last U.S. tour, 374–75; at *Sunday Times* Book Fair 398; at Eton, 416; in Bristol air-raid, 433.

Letter to a Modern Novelist, A
written in N. Africa, 329; Agate's attack on, 330–31.

Lewis, Sinclair
H.'s first impressions of, 193; H. stays with, 274; at Brackenburn, 291.

Library
first book in H.'s, 24; H.'s plans for his own, 180; eventual size of H.'s, 180; at Brackenburn, 248, 314–15; H.'s sold after his death, 351 n.; last rearrangement of, 429.

Liverpool
H.'s six months in, 40–46.

Lloyd George
H.'s impressions of, 310.

Lockhart, R. H. Bruce
entertains H. in Moscow, 123–24, 130, 153; H. writes to, 143.

London
H.'s arrival in, 65; H. takes house in, 194; H. takes flat in, 240, 241, 243; H.'s inability to manage, 249; impossible to write in, 257; more exhausting than any lecture tour, 278; H.'s prayer before, 342; exhaustion of, analysed, 348; the blackout described, 410; in the "phoney" war, 415–16; H. plans account of bombing of, 424; in the blitz, 430–33, 435–36, 440–41.

Long, Stanley
H.'s friendship with, 277; and Brackenburn, 277 n.

Love
H.'s lifelong need of, 10, 17; the Russians on, 131; H.'s sort not D. H. Lawrence's, 255; H.'s for A. C. Benson, 260; does last, 309; happiness based on, 329; H. thirsty for, 417; H.'s dying insistence on, 444.

Lovelace, Lady
H. stays with, 71, 79, 92, 93; her life at Ockham, 71; her usefulness to H. 74; H. drops, 75, 316.

Lowndes, Mrs Belloc
gets facts wrong, 49; H. meets, 75; introduces H. to Bennett, 76; and to the McKennas, 80; as literary strategist, 85; comes to tea, 87; H. writes to, from Moscow, 129; suggests H. returns home, 132; Henry James writes to, 132–33; H. prophesies to, 157; at York Terrace party, 217; H. revisits, 310.

Lubbock, Percy
on A. C. Benson, 32; at Cambridge, 38–39; on death of Henry James, 153; reads aloud James's letters, 186; fails to write to Benson, 259.

Lucas, E. V.
gives H. good advice, 93; dances the farandole, 95; his jokes puzzle Galsworthy, 165; discussion with, 168–69; introduces H. to Turley, 207; at York Terrace party, 217; backs H. for Athenæum, 221; H. mourns, 394.

Lynd, Robert
on *Green Mirror*, 166; Conrad annoyed with, 187; James Stephens *chez*, 310; dinner with, 402.

Lynd, Sylvia
joins Book Society, 299; as book selector, 313; H.'s dream of, 397; describes 90 Piccadilly, 405.

Macaulay, Rose
attends Hardy birthday meeting, 207; at York Terrace party, 217.

MacCarthy, Desmond
at highbrow lunch, 240; reviews *Roman Fountain*, 418–19.

Mackenzie, Compton
H. meets, 84; H.'s jealousy of, 103, 312; Henry James on, 108, 111, 113; H. on *Poor Relations*, 192; on H.'s knighthood, 381; H. sees in London, 402.

Macmillan, Frederick
H. meets, 110, 163; H.'s happy relations with, 166–67; described in *John Cornelius*, 167; invites H. to write book on

Macmillan, Frederick (*cont.*)
Trollope, 185; suggests limited edition, 211; at H.'s party, 217; proposes H. for Athenæum, 221; thinks *Harmer John* wonderful, 267–68.

Macmillan, Harold
H.'s friendship with, 167; suggests one-volume *Herries*, 402.

Macmillan, Messrs
accept *Green Mirror*, 155; plan uniform edition of H.'s works, 185; issue Cumberland edition of H.'s works, 342; H. at staff dinner of, 399.

McCullough, Carleton B.
H. meets, 190; H. stays with, 191, 228, 275; on H.'s first American tour, 193.

McKenna, Ethel
H. meets, 80; H. visits, 118, 234; sees H. off to U.S., 188; finds H. servants, 195; her affection for H., 196; continues to help, 202; in Venice with H., 210; at H.'s party, 217; H. stays with, 237, 242; *Old Ladies* dedicated to, 254; visits H., 293; H.'s grief at her death, 308; their last meeting recalled, 308.

McKenna, Theodore
H. meets, 80; becomes H.'s solicitor, 196; in Venice with H., 210; at H.'s party, 217; rebukes H., 237; H. stays with, 237, 242; visits H., 293.

Maggie
see *Captives*.

Mann, Thomas
H. on *Magic Mountain*, 280; H.'s impressions of, 314.

Mansfield, Katherine
and *Rhythm*, 98; mocks *Jeremy*, 187; on *Captives*, 200; answers H.'s letters, 200–201.

Maradick at Forty
its origin, 60; finished, 72; read aloud to Robert Ross, 73; published, 76; A. C. Benson on, 76–77; Robert Ross on, 77; Henry James on, 77–78; Thomas Hardy nice about, 79.

Mark, Thomas
H.'s debt to, 167; and Herries family tree, 428.

Marlow
H.'s sufferings at school at, 17–21; war favourably compared with, 139; worse than prisons and morgues, 277; legacies of, 347, 365.

Marquis, Don
H. meets, 226; on short list of friends, 251.

Marriage
H.'s one proposal of, 174–75; attempts to force H. into, 176; the finest relationship, 348.

Marriott, Charles
H.'s correspondence with, 45; H. writes to, 50, 52, 53; H. encouraged by, 57; H. stays with, 57–58; first impressions of H. 57; introduced to Henry James, 72; on H.'s social behaviour, 74; on *Mr Perrin*, 81; on *Prelude*, 88–89; H.'s literary debt to 390.

Masefield, John
H. stays with, 202; praises *Old Ladies*, 255; in Hollywood, 365; Drinkwater and, 379.

Mason, A. J.
at Truro, 4; H.'s godfather, 9; Canon of Canterbury, 22; later details of, 22 n.; his engagement, 27; H. writes to, 27–28.

Maugham, W. S.
H. meets, 84; H. dines with, 110; praises *Captives*, 218; H. meets in Florence, 220; H. reads *On a Chinese Screen*, 228; first night of *Our Betters*, 233–34; charming about *Harmer John*, 274; *Cakes and Ale*, 316; his letter of denial, 316–17; his later admission, 317 n.; H.'s reflections on, 318, 319, 320; and *Gin and Bitters*, 323–24, 326; character in *John Cornelius* based on, 371; rated third class, 378; and Drinkwater, 379; forgiven, 419.

Mayne, Ethel Colburn
H. meets, 36; visits H. at Cambridge, 38; criticises H.'s early writings, 42; H. sees in London, 44, 56; gives H. lesson in reviewing, 67; introduced to Henry James, 72; unable to stand the pace, 281.

Melchior, Kleinchen
H. distressed by arrival of, 253; H. begins to like, 253; "miraculously good," 275; third in list of friends, 275.

Melchior, Lauritz (David)
H. meets and invites to York Terrace, 197; turns H.'s life upside down, 202; H. visits in Denmark, 205; causes sensation at Polperro, 207; sings for Queen Alexandra, 208; sightsees with H. in Paris, 208; the ideal friend? 212, 215; *Young Enchanted* dedicated to, 215; guest of honour at York Terrace, 217; swings H. into sea of music, 218; sings in Edinburgh, 218; plans for his future, 218–19; takes lessons from Beigel, 218–19; with H. to Vienna and Munich, 220; takes German lessons, 220; H. visits in Den-

mark, 223; H. accompanies to Dublin, 224; engaged for Bayreuth, 231; H. allots money to, 232; rehearsing at Bayreuth, 232; H. takes to Canterbury, 234; heads list of friends, 240, 251; engaged for Covent Garden, 242; his début there, 243; in *Parsifal* at Bayreuth, 253; his second wife, 253; H.'s struggle for friendship with, 253; and *Harmer John*, 254; H. visits in Berlin, 256; his first visit to Brackenburn, 261; at Bayreuth in 1925, 263–64; "greatest *Heldentenor* in the world," 263; Hitler moved to tears by, 264; his successes in Berlin, 266; *Harmer John* dedicated to, 270; arrives during General Strike, 270; at Covent Garden and Brackenburn, 271; "sweeter than ever," 275; H. spends Christmas with, 275; in *Otello*, 291; in *Tristan*, 303; demoted on list of friends, 311; H. visits in Germany, 331; in London, 339; one of "only three friends," 404.

Melville, Herman
Conrad scoffs at *Typee*, 187; H. under enchantment of, 363–64.

Mencken, H. L.
H. meets, 190; on H.'s lecture tour, 228.

Mersey Mission
H. offered post on, 38; his work on, 40–41, 43–45; H. looks back to, 286.

Methods of work
H.'s described, 185; at Brackenburn, 248–49, 293; on *Wintersmoon*, 256; H. imitates Elizabeth's, 293; H.'s inability to revise, 294.

Ministry of Information
H.'s work in, 170, 171, 175, 176, 177, 181; his report on, 176.

Moore, George
on *Parsifal*, 252; at Elizabeth's, 278; as talker, 286; checked by impotence, 306; his death, 338.

Morley, Christopher
H. meets, 190.

Mr Perrin and Mr Traill
origin of, 78; finished, 79; published, 81; Charles Marriott on, 81; Robert Ross on, 81; Henry James on, 82–83; its success, 83; H.'s preface to Everyman edition, 78, 83; compared with *Dark Forest*, 93; Arnold Bennett on, 114–15; as work of art, 254; MS. of, given to Fitzwilliam, 294; H.'s "truest" book, 372.

Murry, J. Middleton
offers H. reviewing, 98; attacks *Thirteen Travellers*, 208; Bennett on, 209; Elizabeth asks to tea and defends, 210.

My Religious Experience
quoted, 12–13.

New York
the Walpoles there in 1890, 11; H. stays in, 189, 190, 192, 193, 226, 231–32, 275; H. revisits seminary in, 190; H.'s lectures "packed" in, 228; the Walpole collection in Public Library, 229 n.

New Zealand
H. born in, 3; the Walpole family in, 8–10; their difficulties there, 10.

Nicolson, Harold
attends dinner to H., 73; H. stays with, 195; on Greek cruise, 355.

Norwood, Cyril
H. nearly works under, 55; H. meets on Greek cruise, 355.

Novel-writing
essential to H., 185; H. discusses with Bennett, 198–99, 216–17, 235, 237, 238; and works of art, 254; H.'s pleasure in, 310, 421; H. on his own, 361; discussed in journal, 378; H.'s only whole-hearted work, 383.

Noyes, Alfred
at Keats's grave, 401; H.'s unfortunate visit to, 404–05, 427.

Obituary
The Times's venomous, 420; C. Morgan on, 421; Ervine's of H., 420 n.

Old Ladies, The
begun, 239; origins of, 239; finished, 240; two chapters published in *Criterion*, 241; published, 254; praised by writers, 255; MS. of, given to Bodleian, 294; dramatised, 354, 355, 416; Agate on, 416; quoted, 20.

Open Letter of an Optimist
H. agrees to write, 418; dedicated to Bott, 427.

Palmstierna, Baron Erik
H.'s friendship with, 301, 306; H. visits in Sweden and is peevish with, 308; taken to theatre, 319.

Piccadilly, No. 90
discovered, 240; described, 241; H. moves into, 243; Harold's first visit to, 269; H.'s thoughts on returning to, 329–30, 346; H. convalesces in, 353; H.

Piccadilly, No. 90 (cont.)
watches Jubilee from, 357; described by
S. Lynd, 405; in the blitz, 430–31; a beleaguered outpost, 432; damaged by
bombs, 435; repaired, 439.

Picture-buying [see also John and Sickert]
H. buys works by: "Bellini," 393;
Boudin, 423; Braque, 367, 376; Cézanne,
367, 404; Constable, 404; Cotman, 441;
Crome, 440; Degas, 411; Derain, 367;
Despiau, 411; Dufy, 390; Forain, 230,
280; Gauguin, 252, 367; Grant, 280,
326; Klee, 439; Landseer, 441; Manet,
402; Matisse, 423; Matsys, 399; Modigliani, 423; Picasso, 367; Piper, 418;
Pryde, 271, 411; Renoir, 283, 291, 354,
367, 391; Rossetti, 411; Rowlandson,
418; Matthew Smith, 418; Steer, 341;
Stevens, 271, 411; Tintoretto, 404;
Tissot, 390; Turner, 418; Ethel Walker,
418; Watts, 411.

Plays [see also Besier]
The Comfortable Chair, 172, 213; The
Limping Man, 308; The Cathedral, 320,
337, 338; The Haxtons, 388, 393, 398,
400.

Plomer, William
destroys a manuscript, 43; V. Woolf
introduces H. to, 324; H. sees, 326; and
swimming incident, 326 n.

Polchester
origins of, 145; H. confuses Truro with,
220.

Polperro
H.'s first glimpse of, 85; H. finds cottage
at, 94; H. moves into, 98; The Cobbles
described, 99; Henry James sends furniture to, 100–02; tranquillity of, 104,
114; war comes to, 116–17; H.'s return
to, 146; his mother stays at, 148; "the
pivot of all the earth," 154; sick leave
spent at, 170; Melchior causes a sensation
at, 207; H. decides to leave, 210; farewell
visit to, 212; Brackenburn preferred to,
250; revisited, 326.

Pooter, Mr
H.'s likeness to, 41; reappears in Lon-
don, 80; at Chelsea Arts Ball, 110; in
Liverpool docks, 158; sees H. off to
U.S., 188; at Hollywood wrestling, 362;
last appears in the blitz, 436.

Portrait of a Man with Red Hair
serial sold on synopsis, 232; begun, 232;
finished, 233; repudiated by Vance, 239;
H. dissatisfied with, 239; published, 265;
Clemence Dane "raves over," 265;

Benn Levy asks to dramatise, 266;
dramatic version produced, 287.

Portraits of H.
by Gerald Kelly, 271 n.; by Augustus
John, 272; by Sickert, 299 n.; by Jo
Davidson, 310; by Stephen Bone, 340,
480; by Epstein, 343, 480; by Rothenstein, 417; by R. G. Eves, 418 and n.

Prayer
and Julian Huxley, 342; H.'s theory of,
342; H.'s before London, 342; H.'s habit
of, 430–31.

Prayer for My Son, A
conceived, 351; first two chapters dictated, 353; continued, 356, 357; finished,
358; published, 370.

Prelude to Adventure, The
written in six weeks, 85; published, 88;
Charles Marriott on, 89; Galsworthy on,
89; Bennett on, 89; H.'s father on, 89;
Henry James on, 90; its success, 90;
C. G. Jung on, 314.

Priestley, J. B.
H.'s first impressions of, 265; evening in
London with, 274; plans for collaboration with, 279–80; dedicates Good Companions to H., 280; begins Farthing Hall
with H., 282; "an enchanting companion," 282; H. stays with, 285;
Farthing Hall finished, 285; the best
talker, 286; approves of Anthony Trollope, 291; H. rejoices in company of, 295;
joins Book Society, 299; H. never jealous
of, 312; as book selector, 313; stays at
Brackenburn, 315, 412; and Cakes and
Ale, 316, 317; and Arnold Bennett, 322;
Judith Paris dedicated to, 327; leaves
Book Society, 329; H. visits in I.O.W.,
340, 405; on shipboard, 353; dislikes
Inquisitor, 361; on H.'s enthusiasm, 399;
described in H.'s journal, 412, 416; at
start of Rogue Herries, 414; defends H. in
The Times, 420; "a changed creature,"
424; speaks against a tax on books, 425.

Proust
H. reads in Moscow, 123; Conrad
excited by, 236; H.'s sympathy with,
257; as train reading, 291; H. returns
often to, 373; rated first class, 378.

Queen Mary
described at Jubilee, 357; H. tells of Russian Revolution, 387; H. reads to, 387.

Quiller-Couch, A. T.
quoted, 3–4; H. reads as serial, 26; entertains H. at Cambridge, 259.

Ransome, Arthur
 H. takes his name in vain, 61–62; arrives in Moscow, 130; introduces H. to Harold Williams, 136; helps H. to pack, 137; responsible for Anglo-Russian Bureau, 148; H.'s quarrel with, 154–55, 419; brings trout, 442.

Reading: An Essay
 origins and writing of, 265; *quoted*, 59–60.

Rede Lecture
 H. asked to give, 255; begun, 258; finished, 259; delivered at Cambridge, 259; Quiller-Couch and A. C. Benson on, 259.

Reid, Forrest
 praises *Mr Prohack*, 221; H. meets, 313.

Religion
 H.'s doubts at Cambridge, 32, 37–38; at Liverpool, 40, 43–44; churchgoing, 92, 344, 397; H. analyses his, 218.

Richardson, Dorothy M.
 describes H. in youth, 90–91, 92.

Robin's Father
 see Besier.

Rogue Herries
 planned in H.'s mind, 279; H.'s longing to begin, 281, 282; first words written, 284; H. apprehensive about, 284; continued, 288, 291, 293, 294; finished, 302; H. believes influenced by V. Woolf, 303; dedicated to Harold, 307; published, 311; "atrocious" review by Ervine, 312; Buchan compares with *Jude*, 312; H. re-reads, 315; C. B. Purdom on, 320; its sales, 321; H.'s reflections on re-reading, 328–29; "my best book romantically," 372.

Roman Fountain
 H.'s first visit to Rome imaginary, 76; H.'s meeting with Hitler described in, 263 n.; brain-storms described in, 289; begun in Rome 401; continued, 402; finished, 406; published, 418; Mac-Carthy's review, 418–19; *quoted*, 21, 289.

Ross, Robert
 H. delighted by, 73; *Maradick* read aloud to, 73; reviews *Maradick*, 77; on *Mr Perrin*, 81; and Henry James, 93; Somoff's resemblance to, 132.

Roughead, William
 H.'s fondness for, 240, 284; at evensong in blackout, 417.

Royde-Smith, Naomi
 at York Terrace party, 217; on H. and his enjoyment, 222.

Rubinstein, Harold
 H. meets, 54; H. abandons, 55; on H. as potential novelist, 55.

Russell, Countess
 see Elizabeth.

Russia
 H.'s plans to visit, 107, 114, 116; H. sets off for, 117–19; his arrival, 123; his homesickness in, 125–27; on Russian character, 130–31; H. serves with Russian army, 137–43; propaganda in, 148, 151–64; H. treated as expert on, 162; H.'s farewell to, 164; H. lectures on, 189; Conrad on Russians, 195.

Russian Revolution
 described in H.'s diary, 159–61; H.'s prophecy concerning, 161; H.'s official account of, 161, 449–69; Bolshevik Revolution, 164; H. tells Queen Mary of, 387.

Sackville-West, Vita
 visits H. at Polperro, 174; her distinction, 195; her memory of H. in "Bloomsbury," 290 n.; H.'s affection for, 301; H. broadcasts with, 301; on Greek cruise, 355; H. beats at chess, 356; H. visits, 400.

Schooldays
 at Truro, 12–14; at Marlow, 17–21; at Canterbury, 21–23; at Durham, 23–26, 28–30.

Scott, Sir Walter
 H. discovers, 15; H. reads at Durham, 24; *The Talisman* first book bought, 24; as bagatelle champion, 25; H.'s early writings influenced by, 26; H.'s pilgrimage to Abbotsford, 79; H. weeps over *Heart of Midlothian*, 172; H. decides to collect library of, 180; H.'s lifelong devotion to, 180, 373; H. believes himself reincarnation of, 180; H. buys corrected proofs of *Redgauntlet*, 181; H. buys 57 letters of, 191; *Guy Mannering* part of traditional Sunday, 194; H. buys lock of W. S.'s hair and MS. of *Count Robert of Paris*, 194; H. buys Wilkie drawing of, 202; H. buys MS. of *Fortunes of Nigel*, 206; H. buys Abbotsford Correspondence, 206; H. speaks at S. dinner, 218; his *Journal* very nearly H.'s favourite book, 219; V. Woolf on, 240; H. plans anthology of, 291; H. cheered by fluency of, 294; Kipling defends his mistake over, 296; *The Waverley Pageant*, 327; centenary of his death, H.'s

Scott, Sir Walter (*cont.*)
part in, 329, 330, 332, 337; H. talks to
Queen Mary of, 387; his *Journal* a solace
in blackout, 410; H.'s last reading of,
443; MSS. at Canterbury, 474.

Sea Tower, The
origins of, 277, 372; begun, 388; continued, 391; finished, 393; ending re-
written, 399; dedicated to A. Seyler,
406; published, 411.

Secker, Martin
H. meets, 85; his taste, 85; becomes H.'s
publisher, 93; takes over *Rhythm*, 101;
encourages H., 145; and destruction of
Dark Forest, 149 n.

Secret City, The
begun, 162; finished, 170; published,
178; Bennett on, 178; Conrad on, 179;
de la Mare and, 179; wins James Tait
Black Prize, 203; *quoted*, 156.

Self-portraits
in *The Dark Forest*, 144; in journal, 251,
252, 255, 257, 272–73, 318–19, 328–29,
339–40, 342, 376, 398–99, 439; in letters
to Frere, 309, 345; in *John Cornelius*, 371.

Sellingegate, Prior
H.'s MS. collection housed in, 22, 43;
handed over to K.S.C., 389; MSS.
arranged in, 389.

Selznick, David
H. travels to Hollywood with, 349;
saves H. from operation, 349; tries to
dry H. up, 351; H. misses vitality of,
360; asks H. to write scenario, 361; and
English film-scenario, 367.

Seyler, Athene
H. affection for, 114; a welcome guest,
310; H.'s trust in, 343; acts in Ervine
play, 391; and *Sea Tower*, 406; defends
H. in *The Times*, 420; at Brackenburn,
434, 436.

Shaw, George Bernard
H. hears lecture, 39; H. sees *Doctor's
Dilemma*, 44; H. takes his mother to *St
Joan*, 242; absolutely good-hearted, 306;
H. sees at Malvern, 327; H. describes,
370.

Shirley, F. J.
at King's School, Canterbury, 21; H.'s
first meeting with, 358; his progress at
K.S.C., 370; H. stays with, 416, 418,
425–26, 439.

Short stories
Mr Oddy: partly based on Henry James,
258; reprinted in wartime, 411; *The*
Whistle: description of Harold in,
quoted, 269; *The Tiger*, 275; *The Little
Donkeys*, etc., 281; *The Tarn*, praised by
Kipling, 296; *The Last Trump*, 303; *A
Carnation for an Old Man*, 303; *Tarnhelm*,
308; *The Silver Mask*, dreamt by H.,
319, published, 339; *Mr Huffam*, 340;
The German, 344; *The White Cat*, 362;
Having no Hearts, 363; *The Train*, 366;
The Exile, 366; *The Haircut*, 370; *The
Faithful Servant*, quoted, 390; *The Perfect
Close*, 394; *Service for the Blind*, 398;
Miss Thom, 404.

Shorthouse, J. H.
H. discovers *John Inglesant*, 28; his influence on H., 166; his sense of evil,
284.

Sickert, W. R.
H.'s first enthusiasm for work of, 271;
H. exchanges picture for three drawings
by, 280; agrees by telegram, 298 n.;
paints H.'s portrait, 299; H.'s description
of 299–301; prefers *Freckles* to *Madame
Bovary*, 300; compared with Conrad,
300; H. buys works by, 330, 341.

Silver Thorn, The
stories collected for, 285; published, 295;
praised by Kipling, 296, 303.

Sinclair, May
likes *Prelude*, 88; likes *Fortitude*, 96; H.
reads in Russia, 127, 129; at Henry
James's funeral, 153; H.'s consideration
for, 207; praises *Old Ladies*, 255; unable
to stand the pace, 281.

Sitwell, Edith
attends Hardy birthday meeting, 207;
recalls H.'s consideration, 207; on H.'s
generosity to writers, 325.

Sitwell, Osbert
quoted, 139 n.; P.E.N. Club dinner to,
275; H. sees in London, 319; on H.'s
kindness to authors, 325.

Society of Bookmen
H. initiator of, 204; Galsworthy at early
meeting of, 204; its achievements, 204–
05.

Somoff, Konstantine Andreevich
H. meets, 132; H.'s affection for, 136,
143; sees H. off to front, 137; H. stays
with, 143; sad parting from, 145; *Dark
Forest* dedicated to, 149; H. living with,
152; H. reads aloud to, 157; as companion, 162; supplanted by Annand,
163; sees H. off during Bolshevik Revolution, 164.

Sower Myre Farm
  youthful holidays at, 26–28; revisited, 385; its importance to H., 390.

Spiritualism
  H. dabbles in, 280; H.'s most exciting venture into, 285–86.

Squire, J. C.
  H. ignores opinion of, 237; Bennett defends, 238; H.'s appreciation of, 283; and Virginia Woolf, 306.

Stanmore, Lord
  H. works for, 76 and n.; neglected for Perrin, 78; appoints H. secretary, 83; becomes tiresome, 85; telephones from Chelsea, 86; dies, 87.

Steen, Marguerite
  looks for a ghost, 320; comes to lunch, 328; visits Brackenburn, 332; H.'s affection for, 332; H. helps, 333; her book on H., 333, 339.

Stern, G. B.
  H.'s liking for, 319.

Stopes, Marie
  H.'s visit to, 412–13.

Storrs, Ronald
  H.'s friendship with, 392; on Brackenburn, 396; H. sees in London, 402; Bright Pavilions dedicated to, 432; H. stays with, 436.

Strong, L. A. G.
  and H.'s need for "enemies," 223; H.'s friendship with, 344; asks H. for suggestions, 374; likes John Cornelius, 386; his understanding article on H., 387.

Swinnerton, Frank
  and Rhythm, 101; H. meets, 148; and Green Mirror, 166; H. sees in London, 167; H. seeks consolation from, 173; his plans for retirement, 185; attends Hardy birthday meeting, 207; agrees with Bennett on H.'s narrative skill, 216, 217; H. enjoys his letters, 226; praises Old Ladies, 255; breach in H.'s friendship with, 274–75; as companion, 282; on H.'s generosity to writers, 325; H. sees in London, 402.

Tate Gallery
  H.'s bequests to, 211, 391 and n.

Thirteen Travellers, The
  origins of, 187; dedicated to Hergesheimer, 190; finished, 192; published, 208; Murry's attack on, 208, 209; Elizabeth on, 210.

Tolstoy
  H. reads Anna Karenina, 39; Henry James on, 91; and Proust, 291; and Judith Paris, 327; rated first class, 378; H. reads in blitz, 433.

Trollope
  H. reads as a boy, 24; and at Polperro, 104; H. asked to write book on, 185; H.'s attempt to get republished, 185; his style compared with H.'s, 187; H. claims derivation from, 193; Bennett compares H. with, 198; H. answers, 199; H. reads straight through, 281–83; H. writes most of his book on, 281–83; "how well the old boy lasts," 283; H. finishes book on, 284; H. buys his copy of Cloister and Hearth, 341.

Truro
  created cathedral city, 3; building of cathedral, 4; Bishop Benson at, 3–5; its isolation, 6; H. at school at, 12–14; Polchester originally based on, 145; revisited, 220; H. takes Harold to, 273.

Tunney, Gene
  H. meets, 277; receives H. with open arms, 311.

Turkish baths
  H.'s addiction to, 84; Arnold Bennett in, 167; dirty in N.Y., 193.

Turley Smith, Charles
  H.'s friendship with, 207; H. stays with, 220; finds rooms for H. and family, 273.

Turville, Owen
  H. meets at Prom, 332; H. stays with, in West Indies, 338, 344–45.

Tweedsmuir, Lord
  see Buchan.

Van Vechten, Carl
  H.'s friendship with, 229–30; fails to send Christmas letter, 256.

Vanessa
  begun, 328; continued, 330, 332; difficulties with, 333; finished, 333; published, 341; film of, 341, 351, 352, 354.

Wagner, Richard
  H. bowled over by, 53; Götterdämmerung unsettles H., 57; H. sings in bath, 90; George Moore on Parsifal, 252; H. glimpses widow of, 253; difficulties of staging, 263.

Wagner, Siegfried
  engages Melchior for Bayreuth, 231; H.'s description of, 232; and Hitler, 263.

Wagner, Winifred
H. takes to, 232; a trifle overpowering, 253; storm-centre at Bayreuth, 263; and Hitler, 263–64, 411.

Walpole, Dorothea (Dorothy)
born in New Zealand, 10; in New York, 11; contributes to H.'s prizes, 26; in theatricals at Durham, 29; visits Robin in hospital, 165; takes her mother to South of France, 258; her courage, 261–62; her final medical degree, 266; H. helps with money, 266–67; H.'s confidence in, justified, 267; visits her father with H., 279; at her father's death, 304; house-hunting in Edinburgh, 307; picnics with H. at Watendlath, 308; moves into Corstorphine house, 310; a surprise for, 328; H. stays with, 358; H. writes to weekly, 367; H.'s deep affection for, 378, 385–86; and John Cornelius, 385–86; visits parents' graves, 388; goes to concert with H., 428; at H.'s death, 443–44.

Walpole, G. H. S.
early life, 4; at Truro, 5; A. C. Benson on, 5; falls in love, 6; his engagement, 7; his forebears, 7; married, 8; in New Zealand, 8–10; his difficulties there, 10; offered chair of theology, 10; in New York, 11; his writings, 11; courteous to children, 16; moves to Durham, 22; discusses H.'s future, 25; appointed Rector of Lambeth, 31; objects to H. staying with Mrs Keppel, 34; withdraws objection, 35; his sympathetic treatment of H., 44; on school-mastering and the literary life, 60–61; elected Bishop of Edinburgh, 79; on Prelude, 89; and St Mary's Cathedral, 161; H. helps with money, 191; reassured about Captives, 199–200; reports on York Terrace, 205–06; shocked by Cathedral, 218; defends Cathedral anonymously, 227; pleased by Jeremy and Hamlet dedication, 234; at North Berwick, 279; recovers from heart attack, 284; his sudden death, 304; H.'s tribute to, 304–05; H. opens memorial to, 339.

Walpole, Mildred
childhood, 6; in love, 6; engagement, 7; marriage, 8; in New Zealand, 8–10; writes home, 9–10; shyness of, 8, 24; discusses H.'s future, 25; H. sends present to, 84–85; on Fortitude, 96; stays at The Cobbles, 148; H.'s heart bleeds for, 190; upset by Cathedral, 218; her health fail-

ing, 242; happy time with H. in Italy, enjoys St Joan, 242; ill in south of France, 258–59; back in Edinburgh, 259; H. writes to almost daily, 259; her last illness, 260–61; H.'s last talk with, 261; her death, 261; the family "only half-alive" without her, 264; her memorial in Linlithgow, 339 n.

Walpole, R. H. (Robin)
born in New York, 11; contributes to H.'s prizes, 26; in theatricals at Durham, 29; wounded and convalescent, 165; H. telephones for, 261; picnics with H. at Watendlath, 308; at Jubilee, 357; H.'s deep affection for, 378, 386; the King's resemblance to, 384; visits parents' graves, 388; H. visits at Stratford, 426; at H.'s death, 443.

Watendlath
H.'s discovery of, 250; Dorothy Wordsworth on, 250; to be used in Judith Paris, 308; H. settles a dispute at, 379.

Waverley Pageant, The
H.'s idea of, 291; preface written, 327; dedicated to V. Woolf, 327 n.

Wells, H. G.
his position in 1909, 65; attends dinner to H., 73; calls him Hughie, 76; likes Mr Perrin, 83; gives fancy-dress dance, 88; passage on H. from Boon quoted, 144; "degraded and decadent," 154; "most fascinating," 165; Conrad on, 168; "malevolence lurks" in, 306; H. sees in London, 319, 321; arrives in Hollywood, 364; on America, 364; "gleefully pessimistic," 404; hated by Lord A. Douglas, 413.

West, Rebecca
hits back, 172–73; H.'s fear of, 173; H. makes it up with, 284; and Arnold Bennett, 321, 322.

Weyman, Stanley
H. reads as serial, 26; H.'s praise of, 373.

Wharton, Edith
Henry James praises, 111; and Henry James's death, 153; Bennett and H. on, 238.

Wilder, Thornton
H. debates with and describes, 311.

Williams, Harold
H. meets, 136; H. dines with, 143; becomes H.'s colleague, 151; his knowledge of Russia, 151; in March Revolution, 160.

Wilson, J. G.
prince of booksellers, 181.

Wintersmoon
begun and discussed in journal, 256; continued, 258, 264; finished, 267; serial rights sold, 277; published, 287; William Temple on, 288; sales of, 288, 291; *quoted*, 266.

Wodehouse, P. G.
H. tries to emulate, 60; H.'s first meeting with, 268; describes H.'s blind spot, 287; and Kipling, 366; at Oxford, 402–03; Belloc on, 403.

Women
H.'s relations with, 32; qualities H. demanded in, 114, 332; H.'s one proposal of marriage, 174–75; H.'s dislike of most, 187; as book selectors, 313; Epstein on, 343.

Wooden Horse, The
begun, 54; read aloud to Mrs Darwin, 56; difficulty of writing at Epsom, 57; a colleague's opinion of, 57; finished, 58; criticised by Charles Marriott, 58, by Ethel Mayne, 58, by E. M. Forster, 59; submitted to Smith Elder, 60; accepted by them, 66; published, 69; dramatised, 94, 98, 101, 177, 287.

Woolf, Virginia
H.'s affection for, 98; on Walter Scott, 240; praises *Old Ladies*, 255; and H.'s style, 279; H. presents Femina Prize to, 289; asks H. to dinner, 289; H. on *Orlando*, 289–90; her friendship with H. analysed, 290; H. on her death, 290; H.

visits, 301, 313; H. believes himself influenced by, 302–03; worried by Bennett and Squire, 306; H. fails to write book for, 307; on *Hans Frost*, 309; proclaims herself unreal, 310; and Arnold Bennett, 321, 322; on *Sons and Lovers*, 324; on *Judith Paris*, 327; suggests changing cages with H., 327; *Waverley Pageant* dedicated to, 327 n.; H. longs to be counterpart of, 328; on *Apple Trees*, 338; H. dines with, 354, 418; tea with, 398, 401; H.'s last meeting with, 421–22; her suicide and H.'s grief, 440.

Yonge, Charlotte M.
H. reads in Galicia, 142; Lord Balfour shares H.'s love of, 222; H. boasts of his knowledge of, 229; H. has complete works of, 373; R. Broughton ends as, 414; H. likened to, 414 n.

York Terrace, No. 24
H. rents, 194; H. moves in, 196–97; Melchior comes to stay at, 197; contretemps at, 202; parties at, 203; Society of Bookmen first meets at, 204; H.'s father stays at, 205–06; Hardy birthday meeting held at, 207; ambitious party at, 217; incident of the Brazil nuts, 222–23; decision to sell, 225; H. reconsiders, 226; sold, 228.

Young Enchanted, The
begun, 202; continued, 205; laid aside, 205; finished, 208; limited edition arranged, 211; published, 215; dedicated to Melchior, 215; Conrad on, 215–16; Bennett on, 216.